A MILLION DROPS

ALSO BY VÍCTOR DEL ÁRBOL

THE SADNESS OF THE SAMURAI

A MILLION DROPS

VÍCTOR DEL ÁRBOL

TRANSLATED FROM THE SPANISH BY LISA DILLMAN

OTHER PRESS / NEW YORK

Production editor: Yvonne E. Cárdenas
Text designer: Jennifer Daddio / Bookmark Design & Media Inc.
*This book was set in Adobe Garamond and Helvetica by
Alpha Design & Composition of Pittsfield, NH*

1 3 5 7 9 10 8 6 4 2

LIBRARY OF CONGRESS CATALOGING-IN-PUBLICATION DATA

Names: Árbol, Víctor del, author. | Dillman, Lisa, translator.
Title: A million drops / Víctor del Árbol ; translated from the Spanish by Lisa Dillman.
Other titles: Millón de gotas. English
Description: New York : Other Press, [2018] | Description based on print version record and
CIP data provided by publisher; resource not viewed.
Identifiers: LCCN 2017043661 (print) | LCCN 2017048886 (ebook) | ISBN 9781590518458
(paperback) | ISBN 9781590518465 (ebook)
Subjects: LCSH: Suicide—Fiction. | Revenge—Fiction. | Spain—Fiction. | Psychological fiction.
Classification: LCC PQ6701.R364 (ebook) | LCC PQ6701.R364 M5513 2018 (print) |
DDC 863/.7—dc23
LC record available at https://lccn.loc.gov/2017043661

To my father, and to our walls of silence

She-wolves, too, are mothers.

ANTONIO REYES HUERTAS, *Cuentos extremeños*, 1945

"All truth is simple." Is this not doubly a lie?

FRIEDRICH NIETZSCHE, *Twilight of the Idols*, 1888

PROLOGUE

EARLY OCTOBER 2001

The landscape took on a certain density after the rain, the colors of the forest seeming deeper. The windshield wipers were still beating back and forth, though less desperately than an hour earlier, as they were leaving Barcelona. Ahead lay the mountains, which now, as night began to fall, were nothing but a dark mass off in the distance. The young man drove carefully, paying attention to the road, which narrowed as it wound higher, curve after curve. The cement mile markers along the edge of the road didn't seem like particularly good protection against the cliff that dropped off steeply to their right. From time to time he glanced in the rearview mirror and asked the boy if he was queasy. The kid, half asleep, shook his head, but his face was pale and he kept his forehead pressed to the window.

"Not long now," the young man said to make him feel better.

"I hope he doesn't puke; this upholstery is new."

Zinoviev's hoarse voice brought the driver's attention back to the road.

"He's only six years old."

Zinoviev shrugged, extended his enormous hand, tattooed with a spider much like the one covering half his face, and lit a cigarette with the dashboard lighter.

"Well, the upholstery's only three years old, and I'm still paying it off."

The young man's eyes darted quickly to the cell phone on the tray. He'd taken the precaution of silencing it, but it was too close to Zinoviev. If the screen lit up, he'd see.

The main road led to a dirt one, overlooking a valley surrounded by trees. People called it "the lake" although in fact it was a small dam, which supplied power to an electric plant built in the forties. In the summertime, the area filled with tourists eager to spend a day in nature. Over the years, they'd made it easier to get to, built a little slate-roofed hotel with stone façade, a playground with swings, and a café. But in October the forest ranger's cabin closed for the season, there were no day-trippers to serve at the prefab unit with the Coca-Cola ad, and the plastic chairs stacked at the cafeteria's barred doors were a snapshot of sadness.

The young man stopped the car so close to the shore that the front tires almost kissed the water. He turned off the engine. On the north side of the lake was a fenced-off area filled with heavy machinery and a few billboards put up by the Ministry of Public Works. They were going to drain the reservoir in order to build a luxury development. The drawings advertised semidetached homes with private swimming pools flanking a huge golf course. They'd already begun to clear the area and cone off the surrounding forest; tree trunks were piled chaotically around stacks of rebar, concrete, and mounds of sand. Nothing could be heard but the howling wind rocking the firs along the shore and the intermittent banging of one of the hotel's shutters, which hadn't been battened down properly. Rain fell on the lake, dissolving in gentle waves. It all seemed surreal.

Zinoviev opened the door. When the young man tried to do the same, he stopped him.

"You wait here."

"It's better if I go with you. The boy only trusts me."

"I said wait here."

Zinoviev opened the back door and asked the boy to get out. He tried to be nice, but this sort of thing didn't come naturally to the Russian, whose voice and tattooed face were already frightening enough. The boy began to cry.

"You'll be just fine. Go on," the young man said encouragingly, forcing a smile.

He watched Zinoviev take the boy's hand and begin walking toward the gray water of the lake. The boy turned back to the car, and the young man waved confidently. Through the flicking of the wipers he could discern the wooden boardwalk and gazebo. It was almost entirely dark. Disobeying Zinoviev's order, he got out and approached. Dry leaves crunched beneath his feet and soon the wet ground penetrated the soles of his shoes. When he reached the gazebo he saw Zinoviev's broad muscular back, his hands in his pockets and a spiral of bluish smoke swirling over his shoulder.

The Russian turned slowly and gave him a look. "I told you to wait in the car."

"We don't have to do this, there's got to be another way."

Zinoviev took the cigarette from his mouth and blew on the tip.

"It's already done," he said, starting back to the car.

The young man walked to the edge of the lake, its calm waters glimmering like brass. *Come,* the darkness beckoned, *Come, forget about it all.*

The boy was floating facedown like a starfish, and rain blurred his body, which slowly began to sink.

.   .   .

Eight months later, Zinoviev was concentrating on his breathing. He liked to go for a run in the mornings, eight or ten kilometers at a decent pace, listening to music on his headphones for motivation. This morning it was Tchaikovsky's *Nutcracker.* As he ran, jumbled thoughts cluttered his mind, things impossible to articulate in exact sentences. He was thinking of all the men he could have been, if he wasn't who he was.

Spiders were to blame for everything. Zinoviev's biggest fear had its roots in the basement of his childhood home—a cold cellar, full of spiderwebs. Small spiders, tiny really, colonized the darkness by the thousands. He could feel them crawling all over his legs, his arms, his neck, into his mouth. Attempting to wriggle away from them was useless; they were everywhere, touching his skin with legs like hairy fingers, trying to ensnare him in their sticky silk traps. Had it not been for that cellar, he'd probably be another man today. He'd learned to conquer his fear, to turn it into a strength. His spider tattoos were a declaration of intent: Whatever doesn't kill you makes you stronger.

The last stretch of his run was the hardest. As soon as he could see the house through the fog, he clenched his teeth and picked up the pace. Behind the fence he heard the familiar gruff bark of Lionel, his Doberman.

"Not bad, not bad at all," he said to himself, trying to catch his breath as he checked his GPS watch. His heart rate began to slow. Opening the front gate, he gave Lionel a friendly kick. The Doberman was still limping—an American Stafford had almost ripped off his hindquarters in the last fight. Zinoviev stroked the dog's square head, his powerful jaws. He should get rid of it. What the hell was the point of a fighting dog that could no longer fight? But he was fond of him.

"What do you say, warrior? Any visitors today?"

He walked to the porch and sat on the front step, rummaging in his belt pouch for his cigarettes. He loved smoking, even right after a run, before his heartbeat had fully recovered. The tobacco hit his lungs like an avalanche. Wiping his face on the sleeve of his sweatshirt, he exhaled a mouthful of smoke. Renting this house had been a good idea. Isolated, quiet, a portrait of bucolic countryside. Surrounded by dense pines, it was almost invisible, even from the top of the hill. If anyone got lost and approached the gate, Lionel dissuaded them from doing anything but carrying on their way. And if that wasn't enough, there was always the Glock he kept hidden behind the TV.

Zinoviev took off his muddy running shoes and walked across the creaky wood floors. The fireplace was lit and its heat quickly warmed his damp socks. He turned on the TV and smiled, seeing the cartoon channel. He was using Disney cartoons to learn English, but the truth was he really liked that big mouse. Every time he saw Mickey, he wondered at the fact that he had once been eight years old. That was a long time ago. Too long. He looked away from the plasma screen and went into the kitchen to make a protein shake, still listening to the television.

Suddenly, over the sound of the TV, he heard the dog growling. Retracing his steps, Zinoviev looked out. He'd forgotten to close the front door. The dog growled, hackles raised, paws pressed into the floor, staring at the fence. Zinoviev inhaled sharply.

"What's the matter, Lio...?"

The first shot shattered the dog's chest, and the animal jerked up into the air with a throaty whimper and then landed heavily on his side. A powerful shot, a sawed-off shotgun, almost point-blank. Zinoviev ran for the TV to grab his Glock. He didn't see Mickey hand Minnie a bouquet of roses. Snatching his gun, he turned. Had he not hesitated, Zinoviev would have had time to take aim. But for a fraction of a second he stood still, mouth open in shock.

"You?" he asked

All he received in exchange was a cold stare, a look that left no doubt as to the man's intentions. Before Zinoviev had time to react, the butt of the shotgun slammed into his forehead.

How many ways are there to end a man's life? As many as he can imagine. And the worst of them were passing through Zinoviev's mind when he opened his eyes to find himself with a wool hood pulled tight over his face. The fabric cut into his mouth, suffocating him. The hood stank of sweat. He was naked and had been handcuffed in an unnatural position, to some sort of post or beam. His arms and shoulders were killing him, supporting the weight of his entire body, his feet barely brushing the ground. Hanging there like a sausage, he felt his muscle fibers tearing, felt the metal handcuffs cutting through the flesh of his wrists.

"You shouldn't have killed him. He was a harmless little kid."

The voice, coming from behind Zinoviev's head, made him tense up, as though an invisible rod had been rammed through his spine. He began to sweat and tremble. The worst can always get worse. He shivered as something cold and sharp grazed his back. A knife.

"How many people have you injected with your poison? Do you paralyze them first so they can't move while you do horrible things to them?"

Control yourself. Get a grip. He's only trying to scare you. Zinoviev was clinging to this idea, but the first slash of the machete disabused him of such a thought. It was quick, between the ribs. He clenched his teeth. *Don't scream. It's only pain.*

"The innocent don't fear monsters, did you know that? Children aren't afraid of evil."

Zinoviev felt the machete's blade being drawn from his clavicle down to his nipple.

"I'd like this to last awhile. So do me a favor and don't die right away."

Zinoviev knew, now, that his death was going to be atrocious, like returning to the cellar of his childhood with all of those spiders waiting for him. Millions of them.

He withstood as much as possible. But in the end, he let out a shriek that no one heard.

Laura gazed at the pieces of wood washed up on the sand, the plastic bottles with seagulls pecking desperately, frenetically among them, like vultures on carrion. The previous night's swell had dragged all kinds of detritus onto the beach. It wasn't a very bucolic image, but she liked this barren landscape, preferred it to the hustle and bustle of summertime crowds with their umbrellas, and the little biplanes with ads on them that buzzed over her balcony like irritating dragonflies.

She turned back to the bedroom and saw that he was still sleeping, tangled up in the sheets. Going back in, she sat at the foot of the bed, watched him for a few minutes. Had he told her his name? Possibly, but if so she'd forgotten it immediately.

Things still weren't clear in her mind. She'd been out drinking until late the night before. He'd approached her directly, like one of those predators that can pick out its prey from the entire flock with nothing but a glance. The last thing she remembered was the two of them fucking in an ATM booth and then taking a taxi here. Traces of cocaine remained on her nightstand. Along with her wedding band. She always took it off when she slept with someone else. Not that she had any reason to; after all, Luis was the one who'd left her. But still, she hadn't gotten used to his absence.

She reached out a foot and jiggled sleeping beauty's shin. He hardly even registered it, letting out a gentle babyish whimper and slobbering on her sheets. He smelled of dried sperm. Judging by the scratch marks on his back, he must have been a good lay. Shame she couldn't remember a thing.

"Hey, Adonis. I'm sure you've got some other place to keep snoring, and I've got things to do." He gave a hint of a smile without opening his eyes and reached out a hand, trying to grab Laura's wrist and pull her back into bed, but she freed herself from his unsteady fingers. One mistake per night was enough. She decided to give him a little reprieve while she showered. After sequestering herself in the bathroom, she turned on the water and took off her T-shirt and panties before the mirror. She looked awful, and it wasn't just because, after a certain age, going overboard takes a crueler toll than it did when you were twenty. Her eyes stared back at her with a look of defeat far more devastating than anything caused by sex with strangers and too much booze and drugs.

"Can I come in? I really have to piss."

Laura opened the door and stood aside. She saw his erect penis and felt not one iota of desire, just a vague queasiness.

"Sit down to pee. I don't want you spraying the toilet with that hose."

How strange, to share the intimacy of hygiene, bathroom routines, the excretions of another man who wasn't Luis. When they first started living together, she had found it shocking, Luis's hang-up, the way he insisted on locking himself in the bathroom to defecate. She didn't care about seeing him sitting there with his boxers around his shins, but something about it upset him. It was as though this facet of himself was somehow incompatible with weekends on the ski slopes, dinners at fancy restaurants, evenings at the Liceo, and making love on a catamaran docked in the bay of Cadaqués. Luis never realized that he didn't have to be perfect in order for her to love him. In fact, she was sure now that it was actually his weaknesses, more than anything, that had kept her by his side all those years.

The man in the bathroom realized that it wasn't him Laura's gray eyes were gazing at. It was time to grab his clothes and get out of there, before the bitterness starting to show on her pretty lips turned into something much worse.

"I'll just get dressed and get out."

"That's the idea."

Laura got into the shower and pulled the flowered curtain closed. She could hardly fit in the little tile-floored stall and yet somehow the two of them had apparently found a way to do it together the night before. Four handprints were still visible on the tiles. Feeling a wave of nausea roil her stomach, she wiped them away and let the water stream over her.

Laura exited the bathroom in the hopes of finding herself alone. The guy had gotten dressed but he was still there. His evening attire—shiny tight black shirt, leather pants to emphasize his bulge—seemed out of place in the cold light of day. He was snooping around in the corner of the living room she used as an office.

"You didn't tell me last night that you were a cop." In among her books was a framed photo of Laura in her dress uniform: Deputy Inspector Laura Gil. In one corner of the frame hung a police decoration of merit.

"There are probably lots of things I didn't tell you," Laura responded, annoyed that the man was rummaging through her things.

"You also neglected to mention that you're married," he added, pointing to her wedding photo.

The verb tense pricked Laura's skin like a needle. She almost smiled, seeing herself with Luis, the two of them so young, him in a tux and velvet bow tie, her in a pretty tulle dress with no veil but a beautiful long train. Other times.

"You should go. Now."

The man nodded, slightly disappointed. He made a move as if to stroke Laura's damp neck, and she stopped him with a look that left no room for doubt. There was nothing he could do. The guy clucked his tongue, though it wasn't so much in disappointment as it was wounded pride. He flexed his biceps and puffed out his chest as though attempting to point out what she'd be missing, then headed for the door. Before walking out, he gave her a snide glance.

"You should get some help, Deputy Inspector. You fuck like a praying mantis. Plus, I don't think you're too stable, and in theory people like you are supposed to protect people like me. As a citizen, that concerns me."

Laura repressed the urge to make his muscular body double over with a well-aimed kick to the balls.

"If I fuck like a praying mantis, you should thank me for not biting your head off. And as for you, keep practicing. There are exercises you can do to help with premature ejaculation, you know."

Once she was alone, Laura opened the armoire in search of clean clothes. Luis's were gone, his polos and summer shirts, the Bermuda shorts he wore on weekends, his loafers and flip-flops. The empty plastic hangers were a metaphor for the spaces Laura didn't know how to fill. She put on a long-sleeve Nirvana T-shirt with a V-neck damask sweater on top, and slipped a CD into the player. The opening of the *Pathetique* filled the air like an infectious virus.

There came a knock at the door.

What does that idiot want now? She wondered.

She went to open the door, prepared to show the guy just how unpleasant she could be when pissed off, but the man before her was not the one she'd been expecting.

"I just bumped into some maniac going down the stairs, hurling insults that not even you would want to hear. I don't know what you did or didn't do to the guy, but he's really pissed off."

Alcázar was leaning against the wall, wearing his standard cynical smile. Laura frowned, annoyed.

"Just one more asshole. What are you doing here?"

She liked Alcázar. His huge gray military-style mustache hadn't changed in fifty years, and she found this comforting, despite his unpleasant habit of sucking it under his lower lip when he was pensive. If he twisted his mouth, the mustache moved like a curtain, left to right, so you could never actually see all of his teeth.

"Aren't you going to invite me in?" Alcázar asked, peeking over his top student's shoulder. Behind her he saw clothes strewn on the floor. He also saw the remains of coke on a mirror on the nightstand, and the empty bottles.

"This isn't a good time."

Alcázar nodded, taking out a toothpick and sticking it between his teeth.

"I'm not surprised, with that music. What's it called, 'Invitation to Suicide'?"

Laura shook her head. "You should try listening to something besides boleros and rancheras. Could you stop digging around in your gums with that thing? It's foul."

"Everything about me is bothersome and foul. That's why I'm being retired. That's all us old fogies are—black marks and dark clouds on the horizon of the young and their delusions."

"Don't be a cynic. That's not what I meant."

Alcázar put away his toothpick.

"I saw a little beach café on the other side of the cove. They have breakfast specials."

"I'm not hungry," Laura protested, but Alcázar stopped her with a raised index finger. He used to do the same thing at the station, when discussions had gone on so long that he lost patience and decided it was time to lay down the law. When Alcázar raised an index finger, that was the end of all democracy.

"A table has already been reserved, with tablecloth, candles, and flowers. I'll meet you on the beach in five minutes."

.   .   .

Wind buffeted the faded awning. Inside, the café smelled of tackle and fish that was none too fresh. There was no one there except the owner, a bored-looking man reading the paper, one elbow leaning against the bar. He didn't look very happy to see the two of them walk in. Alcázar ordered coffee. Laura ordered nothing; her head hurt and her guts were churning. Even though she'd brushed her teeth as if attempting to obliterate them, the taste of Cointreau was stuck stubbornly in the back of her throat. Alcázar ordered for her: a cheese sandwich and a Coke Light.

From their table they could see a stretch of beach and the rocks along the bluff. Seagulls hovered against the wind. Some floated lightly, others folded their wings and dove, skimming the crest of the gray waves.

"How did you find this place? It's depressing." That was Alcázar's opening gambit. He was a city man, a man who liked crowds, the smell of gas, and pollution.

Laura liked the sea because she could disappear into the horizon simply by looking at it.

"It's as good as any other place. Why did you come, to make sure I'm not doing anything stupid?"

The owner brought over their order and deposited it carelessly on the table before them. Alcázar laced his fingers on the tabletop, as though waiting to bless the cheese sandwich that Laura had no intention of even tasting.

"Zinoviev is dead. More than dead, I'd say. They really did a job on him before finishing him off."

Laura paled. She tore at the crust off her bread, oblivious of her own actions.

"What kind of job?"

"Unpleasant. Very unpleasant. Flayed him alive, strip by strip. Cut off his balls and stuffed them down his throat."

"I can't say I'm sorry. In fact, I almost feel the urge to jump for joy."

Alcázar's skeptical look made Laura uncomfortable, like when she was a rookie and he—her boss—would offer her a piece of candy from the glass jar on his desk. She hated those candies, they were always stale, gummy, and stuck to the wrapper, but if he gave a slight nod she had no choice but to smile, pop one in her mouth, and hide it under her tongue until she walked out of the office, where she could covertly spit it into her hand. It left a bad taste in her mouth for days. But the next time she was in his office she always accepted another.

"What do you expect me to say? The son of a bitch killed my son."

"We don't have proof of that. We never did."

She found his words pathetic, obscene.

Laura clenched her jaw and watched him for a few seconds, her expression inscrutable.

"But we both know he did it."

"It makes little difference what anyone knows if there's no evidence to prove it."

"You didn't seem to care too much about evidence a couple decades ago."

Alcázar kept his cool despite the low blow. He calmly finished his coffee, staining the tip of his mustache.

"Times have changed. We're not living in the seventies."

Laura began to tremble, as though she'd suddenly come down with malaria.

"Of course not. Scaring kids was your thing. Wasn't hard to get a confession out of the little ones, was it?"

Alcázar held her gaze. "In theory, democracy was invented so that guys like me couldn't keep doing what we used to do. You, better than anyone, should know that."

There came a tense silence; Alcázar was visibly uncomfortable.

"I'm sorry," Laura said, gazing absently out at the beach. She saw her six-year-old son running along the shore, Luis following. She saw another time, one that had existed until just eight months ago, and then disappeared as though it never was.

"Did you come out here to arrest me?"

Alcázar held his breath and then let it all out at once, like someone deciding to jump into a tub of freezing cold water. Determined.

"I want you to tell me if it was you. I can help, but I need to know."

Laura gently evaded her boss's gaze.

"I understand why you'd suspect me. I understand perfectly," she murmured.

"I don't think you do. Zinoviev's wrists were cuffed to a beam. With police-issue handcuffs. Yours. He also had a photograph of your son, Roberto, staple-gunned to his heart."

Laura shivered and sank her nails into the paper tablecloth, as though imagining it was Zinoviev's black eyes and she could rip them out and wrench them from her nightmares. She struggled to stand and had to hold on to the table.

"If you think it was me, you know what you have to do."

"Don't be stupid, Laura."

"Are you going to arrest me?"

"I'm not, but by now there's probably a patrol car at your front door."

She looked at Alcázar as though all the life had seeped out of her, as though the only thing holding up her empty body was air.

"I'm not planning on going to jail."

Alcázar sucked on his mustache.

"I think you're going to have to start considering it. But I'm not going to stop you from walking out that door. I wasn't here. Got it?"

Yes. Laura got it perfectly.

PART ONE

THE
LEAN
WOLF

1

"You don't understand. This bitch is trying to take everything I have, she actually wants alimony for life."

Gonzalo had never wanted to be a lawyer, despite what the sign hanging on his office door said: GONZALO GIL. SPECIALIZING IN CIVIL, MATRIMONIAL, AND TRADE LAW. He would have been just as happy to be standing behind a butcher's counter. He'd simply let fate decide for him, and given that he was now in his forties, there was no point in complaining.

"The law is on your wife's side. I think you should come to a settlement agreement. It would save you time and energy."

His client lifted his chin and gave Gonzalo a look that suggested he'd just had a finger rammed up his ass.

"What kind of a lawyer are you?"

Gonzalo understood the man's perplexity; the guy was expecting to be lied to. Everyone was, when they walked in the door. It was as though rather than legal counsel, people came in search of some sort of wizard, someone to solve their problems through sorcery. The thing is, Gonzalo didn't know how to lie. For a moment, he considered the possibility of handing his client one of the pretentious-looking business cards bearing the logo of his father-in-law's firm. All the man would have to do is walk out of Gonzalo's office and down the hall to the end. No need even to exit the building.

"You should have consulted with an expert before you put your wife's name on the deed to your house and property. I'm afraid I can't help you."

He could just imagine what his father-in-law would have said in response to such an admission, rolling his eyes: "When are you going to learn that in our profession a lie does not presuppose the absence of truth but a resource to disguise it with legal subterfuge to the point of being unrecognizable." Besides being one of the best lawyers in the city, his father-in-law, Agustín González, was a die-hard cynic. Gonzalo had seen him virtually hypnotize clients with a tangled web of words that left them spellbound, ready to sign whatever he placed before them even if only to avoid admitting that they didn't understand a word of his mumbo jumbo and were trying to escape the old man's look of reproach. He always bade them farewell with his best smile—the one that said, ever so politely, *You're fucked.*

Ten minutes later, Gonzalo's assistant, Luisa, walked through the door. She always came in without knocking, and after this many years, Gonzalo had given up trying to convince her otherwise. Luisa was a whiz at office software, cell phones, and every other device and program he had no idea how to operate, which in this day and age made him a functional illiterate. Besides, he liked the geraniums she'd planted on the balcony. "This place is so sad. It needs a little color, and I'm going to provide that," she'd said the first time she walked into the office, sure of the fact that this reasoning would lead Gonzalo to see he had no choice but to hire her. She was right, of course. Before this young woman walked into his life, his flowers always died, turning into desiccated clusters that disintegrated on touch. Naturally, he hired her, and he hadn't regretted it. He just hoped she'd be able to keep her position after his firm was folded into his father-in-law's.

"I see we've earned another devoted client for life." In addition to being efficient and dressing colorfully, Luisa possessed a sarcastic wit.

Gonzalo shrugged. "At least I didn't bleed him dry in exchange for empty promises."

"Honesty only honors the honorable, Solicitor. And we've got bills to pay, the rent on this gorgeous office is due to your father-in-law, and—oh, yes, small detail!—there's my paycheck."

"How old are you?"

"Too young for you. I could report you for child abuse."

"When you have your own firm, I'm going to be terrified."

Luisa flashed him a roguish smile. "As well you should. I'm not going to let clients slip away like fish through a net full of holes. By the way, your wife just called. She said not to forget to arrive home at six o'clock. On the dot."

Gonzalo leaned back against his faux-leather armchair. Ah, yes, the annual "surprise" party in honor of his birthday. He'd nearly forgotten about the ritual.

"Is Lola still on the line?"

"I told her you were *exceedingly* busy."

"Good girl. I don't know what I'd do without you."

Luisa's sharp look quickly replaced the tinge of sadness and disappointment in her expression.

"I hope you remember that when you have your meeting with the old man."

He started to say something, but she saved him the embarrassment by speeding out of the office. Gonzalo inhaled deeply and took off his tortoiseshell glasses, which were as heavy and as outdated as his suits and ties. He rubbed his eyes, and his gaze alighted on the portrait of Lola and the kids hanging on the wall. An oil painting, his wife had given it to him when he first opened the office and his dreams were still big. Things had really changed, and not in the ways he'd hoped.

He walked out onto the balcony to get some fresh air. The geraniums shared what little free space there was with an air-conditioning unit and a bicycle he'd never ridden. The firm's first advertising sign still hung on the railing. In all these years it had never occurred to him to change it. The sun and exposure to the elements had faded the letters, though if truth be told it had barely been visible from the street even when it was brand-new. The sign was symbolic, the absurd flag of a tiny island uselessly proclaiming its independence from the adjacent offices, all of which were prop-erty of AGUSTÍN GONZÁLEZ AND ASSOCIATES, SINCE 1895. Sometimes Gonzalo was convinced that the only clients who walked into his office actually did so by mistake, opening the wrong door. He also suspected that from time to time his father-in-law sent him a few losers—the crumbs, the lost causes he felt weren't worth his time. After all, Gonzalo was his daughter's husband, and that had to count for something, even if don Agustín considered him a com-plete idiot. A milquetoast, to be precise.

After fighting it for years, he'd finally had to succumb to the evidence: He was going to accept his father-in-law's proposal to associate, as soon as it came through. It hadn't yet been for-malized, but in practical terms it meant that Gonzalo would be working for don Agustín. His sign would disappear, maybe his geraniums, too. The mortgage, his daughter's English school fees, and the upcoming year's tuition for Javier at a private Jesuit uni-versity for blue bloods were to blame. That, and his lack of courage or ability to stand up to his father-in-law, had turned his life into a farce in which he was a bit player.

He lit a cigarette and gazed out over the city as he smoked. Soon the weather would change and the real heat would arrive, but on afternoons like this you could still go out onto the bal-cony without the AC blasting you in the face. Everyone assumed that he loved being right in the heart of the city, but the truth was he'd never liked Barcelona. He missed the mountain skies of his childhood, the way the sun tinged the lake red when his father took him fishing. Actually, he didn't have any real memories of that time, if in fact memories could ever be real; his father had disappeared when he was only five years old. But his mother had told him the stories of going fishing with him so many times that it was as if he remembered it exactly the way she described. It seemed strange to miss something invented—as strange as leaving flowers every June 23 on a grave where the only thing buried are the worms and ants that leave little cones of earth piled up in summer.

For years he tried to convince Lola that they should fix up the old lake house and move out there with the kids. They'd be only an hour from the city by car, and nowadays it was easy to live in the country with all of the comforts they might want. Patricia, their young daughter, could be raised in a healthy environment, and he could take her fishing so that when she grew up her father wouldn't be just a hazy ghostlike presence. Maybe if they were in a more peaceful atmosphere, his relationship with Javier would improve, too. But Lola had always flatly refused.

Taking his wife away from the wide avenues, boutiques, in-town neighborhoods, and hustle and bustle of the city would be tantamount to amputating her legs. In the end he'd let himself be talked into buying a place in the city's posh *zona alta*, a house with private swimming pool and views of the coast, four bathrooms, a large garden, and wealthy, discreet neighbors. He'd bought an SUV that guzzled more gas than a tank and had determined, despite the fact that he couldn't afford any of it, that this was the life he wanted.

People in love do things they don't want to, and then pretend they did them of their own free will, when in fact it was simple resignation.

Lost in pointless conjecture, Gonzalo turned toward the adjoining balcony, where a woman was smoking, absorbed in a book. She looked up absently, perhaps thinking about what she'd just read. She was tall, probably about thirty-five, and had red hair that looked like it had been cut by Edward Scissorhands—jagged shocks on both sides, long bangs that brushed her nose and that she kept pulling off her face. Two large butterfly wings were tattooed on her neck. Her eyes, brown-flecked gray, were friendly and challenging at the same time.

"What a coincidence, you're reading my favorite poet," Gonzalo said.

Judging by the woman's expression, he must have looked like a convalescent, someone you couldn't expect to muster much strength.

"Why is that a coincidence? Do you think we're the only two people in the world to have read Mayakovsky?"

Gonzalo set the wheels of his memory in motion, searching for long-forgotten words. His Russian was very rusty.

"You must be kidding. You could count on one hand the number of people in this city who can read Mayakovsky in Russian."

She gave him a surprised smile. "And I suppose you're one of them? Where did you learn my language?"

"My father learned Russian in the thirties. When I was a little boy he used to make my sister and me recite the epic poem, *Vladimir Ilyich Lenin.*"

She nodded, out of politeness perhaps, and closed her book. "Good for your father." She gave another half smile before retreating indoors.

Gonzalo felt stupid. He was just trying to be polite. Well . . . *just* polite? Perhaps his glance down at her cleavage had been too obvious. He was out of practice when it came to gallantry. Gonzalo stubbed out his cigarette and went into the bathroom next to his office. He washed his hands thoroughly and sniffed his fingers to make sure no tobacco smell lingered. Then he adjusted the knot of his tie and smoothed his jacket.

"You're in there somewhere, you little bastard, aren't you?" he said under his breath, staring into the mirror.

Each Sunday, when he went to visit, his mother reminded him what a handsome boy he'd once been. "You *used to* be just like your father," she'd say. Same inquisitive green eyes, broad forehead, defined brow, prominent cheekbones, and that classic Gil gap between the two front teeth, which he'd managed to correct with years of orthodontics. Dark bushy hair, a wide neck, and a way of sticking out his chin that, if you didn't know him, made him seem arrogant. Nobody mentioned the fact that his ears stuck out and he had a flat boxer's nose, nor did they comment on his mouth, which had a bitter expression. When you added it all up, he wasn't especially attractive. At any rate, even if young Gonzalo had promised to be a chip off the old block, a drop in his father's ocean, time had scuppered that possibility. In the pictures Gonzalo had saved, his father at forty was still irresistible, even with only one eye. Tall and strong, he gave off an air of unquestionable authority, of being ever surefooted. Gonzalo, by contrast, had become a pushover, a weakling, shorter and fleshier, with a soft belly that he never found the time or discipline to do anything about. His receding hairline was a sure sign of encroaching premature baldness, and his eyes were no longer inquisitive; in fact, they no longer even glimmered. Now they showed only a fragile-seeming kindness, the lack of confidence of a timid man who, at best, inspired indifferent condescension. The children of heroes never measure up. This wasn't a hurtful affirmation but an unquestionable statement of fact.

Before leaving, he stopped to speak to Luisa. "Do you know who rented the apartment next door?"

Luisa tapped her lips with the tip of her pencil.

"No, but I did notice when they were moving. Don't worry, I'll find out by Monday."

Gonzalo nodded and said goodbye with a fake smile. The woman on the balcony had intrigued him.

"By the way, happy birthday. One more year," his secretary said when he was already on his way out the door.

Gonzalo raised a hand without turning.

Twenty minutes later, he parked his SUV in front of the house. Someone had spray-painted the wall: a bull's-eye, with his name in the target. A few workers Lola had hired were trying to get rid of it with a pressure washer. This had become like a game of cat-and-mouse: Night fell, and the graffiti would reappear in the same place yet again. Gonzalo didn't have to be a handwriting expert to know who was doing it. From the other side of the wall, in his backyard, came murmuring and the sound of someone laughing stridently over the other voices. The guests had arrived and he could hear the background music: Chilean bolero singer Lucho Gatica. He and Lola had vastly different tastes in music. Generally, that meant that whatever his wife wanted to hear, won. Unlike him, Lola didn't mind arguing one bit.

He held his keys in his hand and wished all those people were anywhere but here. Although actually, it was he who wanted to disappear. He wasn't going to, of course. Something that shocking was unthinkable to someone as boring, predictable, and old as he was, in those people's view. So Gonzalo took a deep breath, straightened his shoulders, and slid the key into the lock, forcing himself to wear the most genuine expression of surprise he could, even though no one really cared. All they asked was that it look convincing, and it did.

He made his way through the living room, shaking hands, kissing cheeks, greeting. Several partners from his father-in-law's firm stood clustered in a circle, a few last-minute friends had been rounded up, and Lola had recruited some neighbors to bulk things up; everyone congratulated him effusively, phonily. He could see Patricia by the pool, playing with other children amid the flowerbeds. She turned and waved her muddy hands at him. Gonzalo waved back, feeling bittersweet. Patricia was growing up too fast. She hardly had to stand on tiptoe anymore to kiss him on the cheek. She was slipping though his fingers. Like all the good things in his life, his kids' childhood was vanishing before he'd had time to enjoy it.

Of all those present, Lola shone the brightest, in a beautiful off-the-shoulder mauve dress. His wife had taken entering her forties—an age often so troubling—far better than most women. She looked confident and happy, and others sought her out, touched her, hugged her, hoping that her vitality was somehow contagious. She was beautiful, more beautiful than he could ever have hoped. But beauty didn't mean much anymore, he thought, when she came over to wish him happy birthday with a quick kiss on the lips.

"Were you expecting this?"

Gonzalo gave a baffled look. Lying is easier when the person you're lying to is predisposed to believe it.

"Not at all."

"Everyone came," she said triumphantly.

This wasn't entirely true. There were absences that it was difficult to hide. Life went on, but it left cadavers in its wake. From a distance, Gonzalo caught sight of his father-in-law.

"What's your father doing here?"

Lola rested her manicured hand on his shoulder. She was trying to look casual, but it was clear she was nervous. Gonzalo could tell by the slight tremble of her fingers on his jacket.

"Try to make nice, okay? He came to talk to you about the merger."

Gonzalo nodded dully. *Merger* was a kind way to avoid saying *servitude*. He was about to become a lackey, and his wife was asking him to be polite about it. It was exhausting, this endless charade in which she seemed so comfortable.

Lola crinkled her nose and narrowed her eyes. Her long lashes were clumped with mascara.

"Have you been smoking?"

Gonzalo was totally unfazed, even managed to seem offended.

"I gave you my word, didn't I? I haven't had a cigarette in five months."

She gave him a dubious look. Before he lost the upper hand, Gonzalo changed the subject.

"I saw the workmen out there at the wall."

Lola tucked her hair back, exasperated.

"You should report that lunatic to the police, Gonzalo. This has been going on too long. I spoke to my father and—"

Gonzalo cut her off, annoyed. "Do you tell him every time I go to the bathroom, too?"

"Don't be so unpleasant. All I'm saying is that this has got to stop."

Gonzalo saw his father-in-law approaching. Lola gave him an affectionate kiss and managed to shuttle the two of them off to speak privately, by the pool.

"Marvelous party," his father-in-law said. Even when trying to be gracious, the man's voice was coarse and so was his countenance, always hovering on the verge of disdain. The color of his eyes had faded, but they still glinted with a mocking intelligence, and he possessed an enviable vim and vigor. The man was full of passion. *Just the opposite of you*, his expression said. Gonzalo could never get over how belittled he felt whenever the man was near. At almost seventy, Agustín González still hadn't reached the critical point when some men begin to feel sorry for themselves. In many ways he was detestable and deserved his bad reputation: a tough nut to crack, a litigant with endless notches on his belt, an unscrupulous pirate who was arrogant and at times offensive and had the cavalier air of a man who's been at the top of his game for far too long and believes himself invested with the divine right to remain there. But he was also a stand-up kind of guy, educated and very prudent. He weighed each word before speaking, taking care not to say anything he might later regret. There were many who hated him, but none—not even his enemies—were stupid enough to laugh about him behind his back.

"I'd like to have a little chat with you about our association. Stop by the office on Monday, about ten."

Gonzalo waited for his father-in-law to add something, but he was as sparing with his words as he was with his gestures and simply emitted grunts that might have been intended to be friendly. Then he ambled off toward a group of guests.

His father-in-law's girlfriend waved from a distance, wineglass held aloft. She was much younger than Agustín. Gonzalo had forgotten her name, if she'd ever told him, but it would take quite some time before he forgot the risqué dress hugging her every contour and revealing her frilly bra, which lifted her breasts so high they seemed to be struggling to break free of the lace. This was the kind of woman his father-in-law liked: excessively immodest yet obedient. Since becoming a widower, he'd gone through quite a collection of them. She swished her hips as though sashaying across her own pretend stage, all lights on her. Touching the corner of her mouth, she glanced with displeasure at a lipstick-stained fingertip.

Gonzalo saw Javier under the wooden pavilion that decked the far end of the garden. Isolated from the other guests, as always, his son stood out, a fish out of water. He was leaning against a pillar, taking refuge in the music on his personal stereo and staring blankly at his father. Visible beneath his Bermuda shorts was a long scar on his right leg. Though many years had passed, whenever Gonzalo caught sight of the scar he felt guilty.

The accident, if you could call it that, took place when Javier was nine years old. The two of them had been perched on top of a crag, Javier was staring down at the calm clear water below. It really wasn't very far, but to him it must have seemed an insurmountable distance. Lola shouted from below, encouraging him to jump, and Javier faltered, wavering between fear and the urge to close his eyes and jump. "We'll do it together. It'll be fine, you'll see," Gonzalo said to his son, grabbing the boy's hand tightly. Javier smiled up at him. If his father was there, nothing could go wrong. This was his first taste of eternity—the sensation of falling and yet feeling weightless, hearing the roar of his own voice screaming, and his father's. The world nothing but a circle of intense blue and then the sea, parting to swallow him in its bubbles and then shoot him back up to the surface. His father had laughed, proud of him, but then suddenly his expression had morphed. The water around Javier began to turn crimson, and Javier felt a searing pain in his leg.

That was the first time Gonzalo had failed him. The limp he'd never lost on his right side reminded him of it every day.

"I guess I'm supposed to say happy birthday." Javier's voice was sleepy, bored, gruff. A half effort.

"It's not obligatory, but I'd consider it a nice touch."

His son glanced around. The look of a teenager weighing up his possibilities.

"I bet half the people here don't give a shit about you. Though you all seem to do a good job faking it."

How much can a father truly know about his seventeen-year-old son's inner world? On the Internet, boys his age talked openly about themselves, their emotions, their feelings. They talked endlessly, but it was hard to form any clear conclusions about who they really were, or thought they were. Gonzalo had watched his son go through a painful transformation, seen the way Javier was burdened by his solitude, realized that he was entering increasingly introspective years, and knew he'd have to deal with them on his own.

"I guess you just can't resist hurting my feelings whenever the opportunity arises, huh?" Gonzalo couldn't shake the mild irritation he felt whenever his son was before him. It was as if they spoke different languages, with neither one making the slightest effort to learn the other's.

Javier looked up and observed his father with a mix of yearning and discomfort, as though he wanted to tell him something but couldn't. Lately he seemed older, and sadder; it was as though his first year at the university was going to put him in a no-man's-land, a place where he was no longer a boy but did not yet fully belong among adults.

"What do you expect me to say? It's another surprise party. The same one as every year."

Gonzalo glowered at his son. "Do you mind telling me what's the matter with you?"

"Nothing. I just want to be left alone for a minute."

"Let's not start, Javier. This isn't the time."

If only they could shout at each other, hurl insults, express all of the resentment they had stored up. But it wasn't going to happen. That's just the way things were.

"Fine, let's not."

Gonzalo remained pensive for a moment, watching Lola as she circulated among the guests. Javier was the spitting image of his mother—same eyes, same mouth—and yet there was something about his broad forehead and coarse frizzy black hair that Gonzalo found repulsive. He was trying to repress the desire to brush him off, and Javier somehow intuited that.

"Sometimes I think you're too much like your mother. You've got a special skill for pushing away the people who love you."

Javier rubbed his temples, wishing he was alone.

"You don't know Mamá. You live with us but you don't know us."

Gonzalo smiled sadly. Javier admired his mother as much as he hated Gonzalo, for no real reason unless it was instinct. The truth was, what he worshipped was a ghost—though wasn't that what Gonzalo himself did, too?

Someone at the gate caught his attention. An older, burly-looking man stood gazing fixedly at him, smoking a cigarette. The smoke seemed to get stuck in his bushy mustache. He looked vaguely familiar, although Gonzalo was sure he'd never seen him before. Perhaps it was his appearance, which aside from the mustache was totally anodyne. There were sweat stains at his armpits, and his beige trousers were creased. A big belly threatened to pop the buttons off his waistband, as if he'd had to stuff it in below his belt. But the huge grayish mustache really reminded Gonzalo of someone. A question began to take shape in his muddled mind.

Still staring at Gonzalo, the stranger mopped his shaved head with a handkerchief.

Gonzalo approached. "Excuse me. Have we met?"

The man took his credentials from his pocket, flashed them, and nodded heavily.

"So what are you doing here?"

Alcázar stared at him, unruffled. "It's about your sister, Laura."

The name rang a bell in Gonzalo's mind, like a mild irritation long forgotten. His sister had disappeared off the map more than ten years ago. He hadn't seen her since.

"What did the lunatic do now?"

Alcázar tossed his cigarette down and ground it out, rotating his heel back and forth. His hooded eyes, buried beneath tangled gray brows, bored into Gonzalo.

"Killed a man and then committed suicide. And by the way, the *lunatic* was my partner."

The powdery sand blowing in from the beach dusted the chairs and table on the balcony in a soft film, and the white walls gave off a suffocating heat.

Siaka studied the sea through the window, calm and indifferent. The woman snoozed, facedown, cheek smashed into the pillow, mouth slightly open and slobbering, sweaty burgundy-colored hair plastered to her forehead. She was solidly built and rosy-cheeked, with a nose piercing, one of those tiny diamonds that looked like a shard of glass. The white marks left by her bikini called attention to the redness of her skin, scorched by the sun. Tourists never learned; the second they hit the beach, they sprawled on their towels like lizards, as if the sun was going to run out. Siaka wriggled cautiously from under the arm over his pelvis and peeled himself from her skin, sticky as marmalade. She'd let out a horselike bray before she came and then flashed him an obscene, lascivious look. "How did you learn how to do all those things?" she'd asked. "I was born knowing." She smiled. Siaka was convinced she hadn't even understood, and then she'd fallen asleep like a baby with a pacifier.

He dressed silently, leaving his shoes for last, and rummaged through her purse until he found her wallet, which contained a thick wad of cash; she also had an expensive-looking watch and a cell phone. He took her passport, too—American passports brought in a lot of money—but then, after thinking about it for a moment, placed it back in her bag, along with her cell phone. No doubt Daddy could wire her money from some bank in New Jersey or wherever she was from, but losing a passport was more complicated. Dozens of women named Suzanne, Louise, and Marie came from the United States and wherever else in search of the vacation of their life, something to remember on long cold nights in Boston and Chicago. Russians, Chinese, Japanese, they weren't bad, but he preferred the Yanks. They had a certain naïveté he found almost endearing and were satisfied with little more than their boyfriends gave them back home. Plus they were generous. No cheap hostels or quickies in the back of a rental car for them. They brought him back to their hotels, and Siaka had a thing for five-stars: the cocktail shakers laid out and waiting, the expensive embroidered sheets, the thick robes and bath salts and clean carpet. But what he liked best were the flags. The flags flying at five-star hotels were always shiny and new.

You couldn't understand what the so-called first world really was without seeing those flags from the balcony of an oceanfront five-star hotel. When tourists asked him where he was from in their flustered, lascivious voices, he lied to them, and it made no difference. To most people, Africa was an ocher-colored stain in the middle of nowhere. Its borders were indistinguishable, its countries all the same. A place of misfortune, famine, and war. A few tearful stories, which they listened to with looks of pity, reaching their long fingers across the table of some expensive restaurant, made them feel superior, but also guilty. Siaka would change his tone, then; he liked to wow them with his knowledge of African music, to explain how to play the *mbira*'s metal tines, mounted on a hardwood soundboard—an instrument from Zimbabwe, like him. Or he'd tell them about Mukomberanwa, one of his country's most distinguished sculptors. And then their pity turned to admiration, and over the course of dinner, as the empty wine bottles accumulated, their hands or feet would slip under the table and onto his crotch, the age-old urge to possess a man surfacing once more. They would ask, with tipsy, unfocused eyes, if it was true what they said about black men, that they were huge—because of course to be black you had to be endowed with great masculinity. This was what they thought, and this was what Siaka offered. He was, in fact, well endowed, and at nineteen he had real stamina. And plans for the future.

Siaka walked out of the room and put his shoes on in the hall, slipping the cash inside. It didn't happen often, but sometimes hotel security would search him, especially if they remembered his face.

He had no trouble getting out onto the street and hailing a cab.

"Where to, sir?"

Siaka smiled in satisfaction. He liked being called *sir*; he might be black, and not have papers, but expensive clothes and designer sunglasses made you seem whiter. And as far as papers went, the only ones that people truly cared about were tucked into his shoe.

"Do you take U.S. dollars?" he asked, holding out a hundred. Money makes you less illegal.

Gonzalo Gil's house, in a luxury development on a hilltop overlooking the sea, was almost hidden by a high stone wall. Laughter could be heard over the wall, and the sound of splashing in the pool. From the window of his taxi, Siaka watched a catering van pull up. The tall, dark elegant woman who came out to meet it must have been his wife. Siaka tried to remember her name, but all that came to him was the phrase "conceited bitch." From what he knew, the lawyer had two kids: a son about Siaka's age and a little girl. On a couple of occasions he'd seen them getting onto a school bus nearby.

"Hey, the meter's running, and at this rate it's going to make me rich."

"If I call you in, say, half an hour, will you come pick me up? I'll give you a good tip."

Siaka walked the length of the wall, inhaling the scent of orchids. That and the smell of fresh-cut grass reminded him of a Fitzgerald novel and, in a way, of something far darker that had happened at his school when he was little. He stopped in front of a few workers who were getting rid of some graffiti, and smiled. This must have been a gold mine for them. Every three or four days they'd show up to remove insults aimed at Gonzalo and threats against his beautiful wife and cherubic kids. One of the men stood staring at him. Siaka waved casually and the guy went back to what he was doing. Just in case, he crossed the street and strolled by the neighboring properties. Some people sure knew how to live, that much was clear, and it had nothing to do with luck.

Siaka leaned against the wall and lit a cigarette. He adjusted his sunglasses and closed his eyes, allowing the smoke to float out from among his white teeth.

"Happy birthday, Solicitor."

2

Gonzalo looked up and compared the address on the building with the one on the paper he'd been given at court. Among his sister's belongings had been a key to the apartment where she'd been living for the past few months. On the building was a faded plaque with arrows radiating out like rays of sun, and the words PROPERTY OF THE MINISTRY OF HOUSING. You could guess when it had been built by a tangle of cables that would terrify even the most experienced electrician. The narrow lobby was full of mildew stains, the light wasn't working, half of the mailboxes had been ripped out, and those that remained either had their locks jimmied or their cheap sheet metal fronts bent back. Without much hope, Gonzalo glanced around for an elevator that didn't exist and then, resigned, eyed the steep spiral staircase.

By the time he reached the top floor, sweat ran down his back. He took a minute to catch his breath before pulling the key from his pocket and slipping it into the keyhole of the only door. It opened with the sound of bolts clicking. The stench of dry sweat and black tobacco welcomed him as he felt around the wall for the light switch and flipped it. A lamp with no shade turned on at the end of the long hallway.

The place had almost no natural light. The living room was small, its terrazzo floor sticky, the walls bare. There was hardly any furniture: a chest of drawers, a shabby armchair, an old TV. On a coat stand hung a robe with cigarette burns on the sleeve. Gonzalo tried to picture his sister smoking and drinking herself to oblivion, the blinds pulled, immersed in darkness.

To the left, he saw a small desk with papers, books, and magazines piled high. And empty beer cans and cigarette butts. A framed wedding photo lay on the floor, its glass broken. Gonzalo crouched to pick it up and wiped away a footprint to get a better look. The day Laura got married, her eyes had flicked side to side in fear, like a disoriented swallow fluttering wildly, searching for him among the guests gathered at the church. She wore the same look in this photo and seemed to be shrinking from Luis's arm, which encircled her waist. His ex-brother-in-law looked young. Gonzalo had always liked Luis, it was a shame things turned out the way they did, ten months earlier. He would have liked to keep in touch.

Gonzalo went into the kitchen. It smelled of rotting food. A calendar several years out of date hung from a hook beside a stopped clock. The furniture's wood joints were dark with gunk, and on the Formica table sat a dirty plate and cup. It was as though Laura had just stepped out for a moment and would be right back to finish her lunch. This was where she had shot herself in the stomach. The police found her with a gun in her hand. Not her police-issue weapon, which had been confiscated when her son was killed and Laura was forced to take medical leave for psychological counseling. No one had foreseen the possibility that she might have another gun at home.

The coroner insisted it had been a painless death; they'd found barbiturates and alcohol in her system, which Laura had no doubt ingested before shooting herself. Gonzalo had been allowed to see only his sister's face, but beneath the sheet he caught a glimpse of the sutures running from her belly button to her trachea. Without its organs, Laura's body had deflated like an empty wineskin.

It didn't strike Gonzalo as a very pleasant death. A trail of dry blood wound its way from the door to under the table, where she'd sought refuge like a dying dog. The large pool had left a dark stain on the old linoleum floor, along with the vestiges of the paramedics' futile attempts to bring her back to life: latex gloves, bandages, syringe caps, and an IV. When the police arrived, music had been blaring. They said they didn't know what it was, and even became angry when Gonzalo kept asking, as though it didn't matter. But it did, of course it did. Gonzalo saw the CD case on the stereo. Laura had chosen Shostakovich's Symphony Number 7, *Leningrad*, to silence the boom of the gun and the sound of her own agonized cries so the neighbors wouldn't hear. Their mother detested Shostakovich; perhaps that was why Laura had picked him.

He sat down on a chair and took in the surroundings, as strange and unfamiliar to him as the person he'd seen—or what was left of her—on a cold metal gurney in the morgue. His sister's death, no matter how much he wanted to feel it, had only had a vague effect on him, the kind of discomfort you feel at the death of an acquaintance or a distant relative you know nothing about and have no ties to. A distant cloud on a sunny day. But the longer he sat there, the more dust was raised, bringing back memories of a childhood in which Laura was the only touchstone Gonzalo had.

Walking into her bedroom, he felt embarrassed, which was silly given the circumstances. No one cared about Laura's bras and panties strewn all over the room, the unmade bed, or the smell of sex and booze. On the nightstand he could see traces of cocaine. Laura's finger marks were still visible in the crystal dust, as were those of another person—perhaps one of her lovers. He sat on the edge of the bed and stared out the window, which opened onto a balcony overlooking the beach. This was what she saw every morning when she woke up: one strip of sky, another of land, and the sea. Maybe the sight of it provided some sort of solace when she opened her eyes. Perhaps at night she looked out at the stars and breathed in the salty humid air, maybe with her beloved Bach playing in the background, or Wagner—another composer their mother hated and therefore Laura adored. In the mornings, when the sun rose, maybe she swam in the sea (she'd always been a better swimmer than him, he recalled), out to the buoy floating in the deep, and then turned, exhausted, and swam back. Or perhaps she just sat with her arms and chin resting on the rusty railing, smoking and drinking the hours away, thinking about her son.

What kind of brother had he been? The kind of brother who knew nothing about his sister. He remembered a conversation he once had with Laura. Gonzalo had been fourteen years old at the time and had a project to do for school. They were supposed to make a collage that told the story of a relative's life. Without thinking twice, Gonzalo chose his father and asked Laura to help him collect photos and objects that had belonged to him: a strip of cloth from his vest, a button, a box of the brand of matches he used to light his enormous cigars. The idea was for the picture of his father, dressed as a Soviet officer, to be surrounded by a saintlike aura composed of these objects. Gonzalo attended a school run by Claretian monks and knew that they'd see this as an unacceptable act of defiance, knew that he'd be suspended. But he didn't care.

"Did you love him?" he remembered his sister asking, as he worked on the collage. He was scribbling verses from Mayakovsky's poem to Lenin, some of the words unfinished, as though he was too impatient to complete them and needed only to copy them down in part to mark their presence, mixing Spanish phrases in with long paragraphs in Russian.

"Love who?" he asked, distracted.

"Our father."

Gonzalo looked up at his sister in surprise. How old was Laura back then? Twenty-one? Twenty-two, maybe? She was already a self-assured young woman who traveled all over and had friends her mother deemed undesirable but Gonzalo found interesting and fun. They read Jack Kerouac and listened to Bob Dylan and let him smoke when his mother wasn't around.

"Yes, of course I did."

"Why?"

"Why? He was our father."

"How do you love someone you don't know? Just because he's your father?" His sister flashed him a look that lasted only an instant, but it was a look he'd always remember: a combination of pain and incomprehension and sorrow.

Her question and her look were still here, in this apartment where there was no longer anything for Gonzalo to do. He'd come in the hopes of finding some sort of connection to the past, but it was pointless. He had nothing in common with the woman who had lived and died here.

Gonzalo was getting ready to leave when he noticed the armoire, its door ajar. On the left side hung Laura's shirts, dresses, and trousers; the right side was filled with empty plastic hangers, all lined up in a row. There was an industrial-size garbage bag on the bottom shelf. Vaguely curious, he opened it partway, and suddenly his eyes filled with the excited glimmer of a child on Christmas Eve. His mother's bomber jacket!

He opened the bag all the way and spread the jacket out on the bed. How long had it been since he'd seen it? At least thirty years. The leather had cracked and darkened, but it was clear that Laura had made an effort to preserve it. You could still make out the insignia—rotor blades over the hammer and sickle—of the Soviet Aviation School on the patch sewn onto the right side, the flag of the Spanish Republic below it. The sheepskin lining around the neck was filthy but still as springy as Gonzalo remembered from childhood. Slightly self-conscious, he tried it on. Back then the sleeves had been far too long and he'd almost tripped over the waistband at the bottom, which was also wool. Now it was impossible to fasten it; he feared the zipper would break. Gonzalo sniffed the wool—still redolent of the conditioning oil Laura had applied—and was transported back to 1968, 1969, even 1970, when he and Laura used to pretend they were fighter pilots. Gonzalo always asked to wear the jacket, and his mother always gave in on the condition that he'd be careful not to let it get scratched. He didn't always manage, and if ever he fell down a slope, defeated by Laura's enemy fire (she was always a German Messerschmitt, and Gonzalo an RAF Spitfire, so in theory she was the one who should have been defeated, but she obstinately refused to give up), and the bomber jacket got dirty or a bit scratched, Gonzalo would burst into tears, partly in anticipation of the spanking his mother would give him, but also because he loved that jacket more than anything else in the world. He'd given it up for lost a long time ago and never guessed that Laura had saved it.

Eyes still twinkling with excitement, he came upon something in one of the inside pockets: an envelope containing what appeared to be an antique—an old silver object with a cover and catch. Still wearing the jacket, Gonzalo sat down on the foot of the bed to examine it more carefully. It was crudely engraved on one side, as though it had been done with a knife or some other sharp object. The lettering was worn and Gonzalo had to hold it all the way up to his glasses to make out part of it. It seemed to be a woman's name: *I*, then maybe *M* or *N*—he wasn't sure—and an *A* at the end. The rest had completely worn away.

He fiddled with the cover and the latch gave, springing open to reveal the very faded sepia image of a young woman. You could hardly make out the right side of her face. Her deep, serious eyes contrasted with her partially visible mouth, which seemed to be smiling. It might have been a studio portrait: You could see part of a curtain behind the chair on which she sat with her legs modestly crossed. Though it was hard to be entirely sure, there seemed to be a little girl on her lap. All that could be seen was a small black shoe with a buckle and the frill of a skirt, and above that a braid with a bow.

Gonzalo didn't recall ever having seen this locket and had no idea what it was doing in the jacket pocket, but his mother might know. His mother. He didn't know how to tell her that Laura had died, couldn't imagine how she'd react to the news. At eighty-six, his mother was now frail and seemed to talk nonsense more and more often, to lose track of reality. She would be explaining something about the past and then suddenly look at her son as though she had no idea who he was. Her notion of time had become distorted, like a rubber band that stretched and shrank at will. The doctors swore it wasn't Alzheimer's. Esperanza still had an extraordinary memory and was as sharp as a tack. She read from her collection of Russian writers assiduously and had recently begun a series of charcoal sketches—landscapes from her childhood, still lifes, and portraits of Elías adorned the walls of her room. The problem, her caretakers said, was that his mother decided when and where she wanted to live without ever leaving the residence, imposing her will on memories, conjuring or dismissing them at whim. Despite her harsh character, she gave the caretakers no trouble and they were fond of her. She ventured out into the nearby pines with the help of a walker, sat on a bench by the sea to read, and was scrupulous about her hygiene. His mother detested having to ask for help to get into the shower or get dressed, and often, at night, she would drag herself to the bathroom to change her own diaper if she soiled it. More than once the nurses had found her the next morning on the bathroom floor, but despite their scolding, Esperanza refused to be humiliated by having them see her defecate on herself.

.   .   .

"Today's not Sunday," she said by way of greeting when he arrived.

Sundays at eight o'clock on the dot, she would sit waiting for Gonzalo to pick her up, always impeccable, as though awaiting inspection. They'd stop at the same florist each time, Esperanza would select the best roses with a fussiness that the clerk had grown accustomed to, and then they'd drive up to the lake house to lay them at a grave where the only things buried were memories. Gonzalo would leave his mother sitting beneath the fig tree that shaded the tombstone so she could be alone for a while, and he'd inspect the ruins of the old house until his mother decided it was time to leave. They always made the drive home in silence. Sometimes Esperanza cried. Gonzalo would squeeze her gnarled hand, but his mother hardly noticed. She was far, far away.

"No, it's not Sunday."

Through the cretonne curtains, the day seemed to wilt. The unvarying image of tall cypress trees, standing guard along the gravel path, was a sad sight in wintertime. Now, it was just tolerable. Esperanza's eyes were battling age and exhaustion, almost at war, and still she refused to wear the glasses Gonzalo had bought her. Today she was sitting at the little bureau in her room, gripping the pencil at its tip, her long nose pressed to the yellowed sheets of paper.

"I came sooner because something terrible happened."

"Has the world ended, is that it?" she asked, not lifting her eyes from the paper.

"Only for Laura, Mother. She's dead."

The old woman remained still. So fragile it was frightening to behold. Her shock seemed to siphon off what little flesh remained on her face. She tensed her neck, making prominent the corded veins struggling to course beneath her skin, which looked hollow. Esperanza let out a sort of hiccup, not even a whimper. Then she wrung her hands and went back to her drawing, though she could hardly control the pencil.

"Did you hear me?"

The old woman shook her head slowly. "She died a long time ago. All that's left now is to bury her. So do it."

Gonzalo turned red. "Don't talk like that; she was your daughter."

Esperanza closed her eyes. If she spoke that way about her daughter's death it was only because Gonzalo was too little to remember what had happened, and she was too old to forget. She put the pencil down and turned to the light filtering in through the window. It took her quite some time to speak, and when she did, her voice seemed to come from far away.

"On the kitchen table we used to have a fruit bowl, full of ceramic fruit: bananas, a bunch of grapes, avocados. They were so smooth, more perfect than real fruit, and they shone temptingly. But they were just painted clay. I remember a fly mistakenly landing on the fruit bowl one time. Your father was in an armchair, taking his siesta, and it flew over to his cheek and perched there for a good long while, right on his half-open lips. You were little, and you were captivated by the image, until your father closed his mouth and accidentally swallowed the fly and kept right on sleeping. You waited for it to come out but it never did. All summer, you felt guilty, convinced it would lay eggs in his stomach and that one day hundreds and thousands of flies would come out of his mouth, his ears, his nose. You had nightmares, thought he'd die a horrible death and you'd be to blame because you hadn't dared to swat it away for fear of waking him. One afternoon I heard you tell your sister about it. You were inconsolable, crying, convinced you'd done something terrible. And I heard what she said to you. *I hope you're right and he does die.* She was thirteen years old, she should have consoled you, told you not to worry, but she chose to make you believe you were a killer. That was your sister."

"She was just being mean, kids do those things. Like when we were playing and I'd ask her to go into a tailspin to be downed by my Spitfire and she'd refuse, or when she'd run to you to tell on me for getting the bomber jacket dirty."

Esperanza looked sidelong at her son. "Why are you bringing up this nonsense?"

"Look what I found at Laura's apartment." Gonzalo held out the bag he'd brought.

Esperanza came to life, moved away from the bureau and, for a few seconds, with that old aviator's jacket in her hands, she became sixty-eight years younger. She covered her mouth with her hands and gazed at her son, eyes glimmering with the sort of nostalgia that comes only at the end of a life.

"I found this inside the jacket." Gonzalo held out the engraved silver locket.

Esperanza's mouth turned down in a frown, drawing attention to the downy hair that had sprouted above her lip over the years. She put pencil to paper, attempting to write, but couldn't move. Then, abruptly, she pressed too hard and broke the lead. Her eyes began to water, tears streaming out. Gonzalo crouched before her and took her face in his cupped hands. His mother's fat tears rolled between his fingers; she obstinately refused to look at him.

"What's wrong, Mamá?"

"It was inevitable," she murmured.

Disconcerted, Gonzalo gazed at the sheets of paper on the floor, the books around her bed, the pink robe hanging on a hook behind the door. Something in the room had suddenly changed. The light. It was darker, though the same radiant sky shone outside.

"What was?"

"Death," she whispered.

Three days later Gonzalo received authorization to proceed with Laura's burial. The coroner had been searching for traces of blood or skin belonging to Zinoviev that would tie her to his murder. He didn't find anything, but the prosecutor thought there was sufficient evidence to prove her responsibility: He'd been chained to the post with Laura's handcuffs, and her son's photo was stapled over Zinoviev's heart. Experts had been able to prove that the staples came from a gun found in a tool drawer in her apartment, and the extreme savagery of the murder suggested a strong emotional component, plus they'd found a map in her desk indicating where Zinoviev was hiding out. The fact that Laura had committed suicide just a few hours after telling Alcázar she wasn't planning to go to jail was taken as proof of her guilt. As far as the police and prosecutor were concerned, the case was closed unless new evidence turned up.

Legally, responsibility for Laura's body fell to Esperanza, but she refused, leaving Gonzalo with the paperwork. He didn't know if his sister had a burial policy in her life insurance, and soon discovered that she did not, which meant he had to take care of all the preparations. There was no will, nor any last wishes, and Gonzalo wondered if his sister would prefer to be cremated rather than buried. Exasperated, he decided to contact Luis. After all, his ex-brother-in-law knew Laura better than anyone else.

Luis was surprised by the call. Gonzalo broke the news awkwardly, unable to find the right words. For one long minute, there was no sound on the line other than that of a photocopier.

"I'm not sure if you know, but we got divorced soon after Roberto died."

His voice betrayed no emotion whatsoever. And yet he agreed to meet, saying he'd be at the café across from Gonzalo's firm in an hour.

The only thing Gonzalo could say about Luis was that he liked him. He was discreet, came from a good family, and was exceedingly well educated. In short, someone whom Gonzalo had never seen as the kind of man his sister would marry. Luis had told him he lived in London now, and that he was with someone else. It had been sheer coincidence that Gonzalo had found him at the architecture firm he and two brothers ran in the upscale northern part of Barcelona. He was supervising a construction project and returning to London that night.

The man who walked into the café seemed totally different from the one Gonzalo had once known. At first Luis hardly spoke, it was as though they'd never met. His straight-cut stylish suit and impeccable hair—carefully coiffed back—gave him a supremely self-confident air. His watch, cuff links, and Italian shoes announced one of those men who aspire to own the world. He'd gained weight, not in the same way as Gonzalo but in a way that went with his naturally tan skin: outdoor sports, sailing, the kind of thing people in his world did for an adrenaline rush. But despite his wardrobe, Gonzalo intuited that somewhere in him lurked the veil of darkness: A patina of sadness peeked out of his dark eyes against his will, one he'd never be able to shake.

It was utterly absurd, but Gonzalo felt compassion for this man whom women eyed with barely concealed lust and men observed with suspicion. He was charming, any way you looked at it. The kind of person who makes you believe that it's you who shines bright as a star, when in fact it's only the residue of his own glimmer.

They exchanged a few platitudes, unable to shake the awkwardness of an encounter neither of them knew how to handle. Luis seemed more anxious, his unease notable in the exasperating lethargy of his movements, in the way he set his coffee cup down on the saucer, in the precise way he asked and answered questions without altering the mask he wore.

"I think she'd prefer cremation. Our son is in the El Bosque columbarium. That's where she'd want to be. Needless to say, I'll cover all the costs."

Gonzalo hadn't had enough time even to cry for his sister, to accept that she was gone, much less think about funeral expenses. For now, Laura's death was something that others spoke of with an air of remorse and that he accepted as though it were part of a performance in which he felt ill at ease. That very morning he'd stopped before a shop window that had a cookbook on display and remembered that Laura made fruit salad like no one else. It was something that seemed so simple, but it wasn't. You couldn't just peel fruit and let it sit in its juices, or add a pinch of sugar (Laura added cinnamon). She said the secret lay in the way you combined things—acidic with sweet, pulpy textures with softer ones, for instance banana with grapefruit. You had to select the best pieces and allow them to marinate for just the right amount of time, no more, no less.

He didn't understand why his ex-brother-in-law was talking about funeral costs.

"She never told me how you met; I was wondering what sort of chance occurrence drew your fates together."

For a few seconds Luis's face lit up with the warmth of near-forgotten joy.

He'd met Laura in Kabul. His father had business to conduct there and Luis had taken advantage of the fact to accompany him and tour the country on a dusty old Guzzi motorcycle laden with saddlebags. He looked like a brigand, with his filthy skin and huge biker glasses on his forehead. Luis liked to imitate the locals, so he wore billowy clothes and covered his head in a traditional Afghan *pakol*. His guide was a short man with weatherbeaten skin, two cartridge belts of high-caliber bullets strapped across his chest, and an old Kalashnikov on his back. Luis had forgotten the man's name but not the fact that he smiled with the openness of a person who's unafraid of life, half of his teeth missing. That guide was the one who'd told him about a little inn on the Khyber

Pass between Pakistan and Afghanistan where Europeans often stopped. *Women, too,* the guide had said, winking.

The first time he saw Laura, she was sitting out on a stone and adobe patio, contemplating the dusk as it spread over a rocky, ocher-colored desert. She seemed absorbed, so far removed from that physical space that she could have been a beautiful statue, sculpted a thousand years ago. "I heard there was a Spanish woman here." She gave him a classic look, annoyed at the interruption, and then turned back to continue gazing out at the desert. And then Luis got the urge to sit beside her, to be infused with whatever truth seemed to connect her to the landscape. An urge that maybe he should have checked.

"If I'd resisted the temptation to brush her arm with my elbow, my life would probably have followed the easy path awaiting me on my return home. Back then I was engaged to a childhood friend, the daughter of some of my father's associates. I'd go to the United States to do a master's in architecture and have precious twins who would one day inherit the family empire. Had I not inserted myself between Laura and her view of the desert, we'd each have gone on our way, in our own bubbles, without interfering in the other's life." Luis stroked the coffee cup as though thinking of something he'd reflected on before. "It all starts with something simple. The first drop to fall starts breaking down the stone, right?"

Gonzalo didn't know how to respond. Maybe it was true: change, disaster, revolution, resurrection—it all started some-where, at some seemingly trivial point.

Luis leaned back in his chair and stroked his palm, as though dusting off an old manuscript where his memories were written.

"The eighties were not a good time to be traveling there, espe-cially for women. The Soviets had occupied Afghanistan and the warlords weren't about to accept their rule. But Laura never worried about the future. She lived those early years with such intensity, traveling and writing for a historical magazine. And even though she supplemented her income by working as a Russian interpreter for the pro-Soviet government, she had no qualms about traveling to the other side of the country to interview the warlords fighting the invaders."

Gonzalo got a fleeting image of the games they'd played as kids, of his sister refusing to let herself be beaten in any fight, real or pretend, with other children.

"She was really special," he agreed, smiling with long-overdue pride. Luis nodded emphatically in agreement.

"Laura was the kind of woman you'd turn to look at on the street, no matter how old she was. She was beautiful. More than beautiful—extraordinary. I think what made her so different was her determination, it really changed the whole atmosphere of a place. She had this irrepressible urge to live that was infectious. Being alive wasn't enough; she wanted to turn everything she did into some sort of miracle."

They looked at each other in surprise, as though, after an affirmation like that, it made no sense that the two of them were sitting there talking about her funeral. Luis had married Laura just ten months after meeting her, and he didn't regret how hasty the wedding had been despite the arguments it had led to in his family. His parents and friends were so complacent, so satisfied with themselves and their lives; he could never make them see that having Laura by his side meant living life to the fullest, that the only thing that mattered was giving themselves to each other.

Luis raised his head, like a Roman senator worthy of Michelangelo, and his eyes glimmered; he seemed filled with a despairing sort of melancholy.

"She brought into the world the one thing I loved most: our son. He set the benchmark for total fulfillment. You have kids, you know what I'm talking about."

Gonzalo looked away. Luis's words forced him to confront his own limitations as a father. He thought of his daughter, Patricia. It was true that until he held her in his arms he'd never actually felt what it was to be alive. His little girl was his rock, the place where all his feelings, fears, and hopes resided. But when he thought about Javier, those feelings were hazy and complicated: Love and tenderness were tangled up in a ball of reproach and resentment.

"Laura and I put everything we had into to our little boy. Everything we did, everything we thought, our plans for the future—it all revolved around him. I worked my tail off in order to build something that would make his world a little more comfortable, and his arrival even succeeded in reuniting my family. My parents accepted Laura graciously, proud and happy to have a grandson to hold." Luis fell silent for a few seconds, searching for the words to express what he was about to say; he hesitated, tried to begin, faltered, and then looked at Gonzalo as though imploring him for help. "Laura always loved you so much, Gonzalo, she never stopped thinking about you. When Roberto was born, I suggested it might be a good time to make peace with you and your mother. I never understood—and she always refused to tell me—why you'd fallen out."

Gonzalo didn't know either, at least not exactly. He did know that if you once loved someone, your hatred and rancor for them were all the stronger, so when discord erupted in their family, it had been too much for all of them. Perhaps it was Laura's decision to leave her brilliant career as a historian and journalist in order to join the police, a move their mother found incomprehensible given what her husband had gone through over the course of sixty years of struggle. Or maybe it was the article Laura published about her father in 1992, destroying his legend. Their mother never forgave her, just as Gonzalo never accepted Laura's reproach when he married the daughter of a well-known Franco militant. Laura detested Lola's family as much as Lola came to hate Laura.

The whole explosion of rage and resentments had inevitably faded and, for the past several years, Gonzalo was able to experience the distance between himself and his sister without hatred, feeling only scorn and a sense of abandonment that had grown so large it was unsalvageable.

"None of that matters much anymore, does it?"

Gonzalo took off his heavy glasses and pinched the bridge of his nose, where the cushions on his frames had left little indents. Without his glasses, everything became blurry, like a painting splashed with turpentine. A world of shadows that ironically, he thought, was perhaps truer than the one he saw clearly when he put them back on again.

"But if you were happy, if you had the solid bond everyone aspires to, why get divorced?"

Luis jutted his neck out and flexed his shoulders. It was clear that his body was tense beneath his jacket. He didn't like talking about this. Little by little his stiffness seemed to give way to a sort of languor, as though physically submitting to the evidence, and he almost seemed to pour himself onto the table.

"I never forgave her for our son's death," he said flatly. But he no longer felt the rage of before. It had dissipated, having been chewed up and spat out every day for the eight months that had passed since Laura told him, crazed, that someone had taken their son from the school gate, in broad daylight, with all the teachers and parents standing there in shock and fear. "One day, soon after Laura and I met, I found her sitting in the dark in the bathroom. She was crying and trembling like a leaf. I'd never seen her like that, and I was scared. She was sobbing, her words tumbling out, tears and snot running down her face. She told me that it was impossible to love someone you didn't really know, that true love can develop only as the result of truth, and that silence is simply a deception. I couldn't get her to tell me what was going on, aside from those few incoherent sentences. The next day I saw her again—we weren't yet living together—and she gave me a big kiss and made me promise not to ask about it. I respected her wishes.

I should have realized that her desperate outpouring was a sign, that there was something lurking beneath her apparent happiness, something that had been hurting her, damaging her irreparably for God knows how long.

"Children living in poverty or being abused were her obsession. Every time there was a news item about it her ears pricked up, but she'd never talk about it. For me, having been brought up in a warm, loving home, the scenes of abuse described were inconceivable. They made me unbelievably sad, but at the same time, I felt like it was so far from our reality. Laura, on the other hand, took it personally. I watched her fall apart, as though she herself were experiencing it all. She started to write about it, conduct research, join different associations. We even took in foster children on several occasions, kids who didn't know how to play, kids who when you gave them a bath you saw they had damaged bodies, cigarette burns on their skin, little girls who told stories about sick fathers. Laura despised the parents who had done those things with such intensity, said they'd 'stolen childhood' from these kids. And she spent day after day trying to fight them, taking on so much that she wore herself out. I soon realized it was eating her up. I told her that she couldn't fight all the evil in the world by herself, that her efforts were a drop in the ocean. And you know what she said to me? 'What is the ocean, if not a million drops?'

"She felt the need to get truly involved rather than stand on the sidelines or even write about what was going on. I couldn't understand it: We had money, we had standing, we could do whatever we wanted. So I was stunned the day she told me she was giving it all up to join the police. We argued bitterly, for months, but there was no changing her mind. Laura had made her decision and that was all that mattered.

"I watched her slowly turn into a woman who no longer believed that life was a miracle, and it was as if once she'd seen that for a lie, it became unbearable. I tried to convince her to quit her job, because I saw that it was destroying her. But she swore she was fine, said she felt useful, that she could keep working. This lasted three or four years. Maybe in the end she realized that birds can't fly forever, that they have to stop and rest, and that they need a place to return to. When our son was born, I thought it would all change, that she'd focus on me, on our child, our lives. But I was wrong. Her job started to affect us, we argued all the time. Laura began drinking, and her character changed for the worse. I don't know exactly what she was investigating. She never wanted to talk about her work. All I know is that it was dangerous, and that it was consuming her completely. Sometimes she'd be gone for weeks and call only for five minutes, at night, to hear Roberto's voice. I imagined her staying at roadside motels, dingy places she had no business being. I spoke to her angrily, told her she was being selfish, that she was letting her son be raised in his grandparents' arms, that instead of saving all the children in the world she should worry a little more about that fact that her own son cried when she picked him up, because he no longer recognized her."

Luis stopped. He was having trouble speaking, swallowed hard, realized his coffee had gone cold and ordered another. Gonzalo told the waiter he didn't want anything and simply stared at Luis—so together on the outside, so broken on the inside. He suggested they forget about the coffee and go for a walk. Luis agreed: Some polluted city air would do them both good. He said he missed the Barcelona sun, the sea, and color of the Mediterranean. But really, Gonzalo realized, what he missed was Laura.

"Do you mind if I smoke?"

Gonzalo said no and forced himself to turn down a cigarette. He'd promised, sworn up and down to Lola that he hadn't smoked in five months. The truth was he'd broken that promise, but suddenly he felt an intense need to keep his word. Not one more, he told himself. Luis exhaled a long puff of smoke, not picking up on—or else not caring about—the admiring look a beautiful young woman shot him. She reminded Gonzalo of the woman on the balcony, the one with butterfly wings tattooed on her neck. The reader of Mayakovsky.

Calmer now, Luis returned to his tale of those final months.

"One morning, last September, someone rang the doorbell and Roberto went to open the door—I used to joke that he had a calling to be a bellhop, because every time the doorbell or phone rang, he'd run to open it or pick it up. When I went to see who it was, I found my son standing there, staring, eyes wide open, not saying a word. A dead cat lay on the landing with its throat slit and a picture of Roberto tacked to its chest. The picture had been taken in the park, with a telephoto lens. I asked Laura to stop her investigation, whatever it was. And she promised to request a transfer, said she would ask to be put on desk duty, but she lied. I found out a few days later, when a guy with a Russian accent called my office and told me they were going to kill Roberto. They knew what school he went to, knew our daily timetable, everything. I was so scared I hired private security, and also got Roberto out of Barcelona, took him to the farm my family has by a village in Empordà. I gave Laura an ultimatum: Either she quit, or I'd leave her and take Roberto with me. Two weeks later, everything went back to normal. Or at least that's what I believed. Roberto went back to school, Laura kept her word—or so I thought—and was working regular office hours, spending more time with Roberto... We even planned a vacation to Orlando over Christmas. We loved the idea of Roberto getting to see Mickey Mouse."

Here Luis paused. Perhaps he was hoping that Gonzalo would say something to encourage him, or maybe to stop him. But Gonzalo lacked the courage to bear the burden for Luis's desperate need.

"One afternoon, Laura called me at work, completely beside herself. Someone had taken our son from the school gate. Two days later he turned up on the bottom of that lake not far from where you grew up. The police knew he was there because there'd been an anonymous tip. I lost my mind; Laura did, too. But whereas I sank into a bottomless pit of grief and sadness, not understanding how this could have happened, she threw all of her rage into finding whoever had done it. She didn't sleep, didn't eat, almost stopped coming home, and when she did was often drunk or high and smelled of other men. Honestly, by then it didn't matter, I really didn't care anymore; I couldn't save myself from my wreck much less pull her from hers. I realized I was starting to hate her, and one night I said terrible things. I told her that it was her fault that Roberto had been killed. She scratched my face, we fought, and...I punched her—as hard as I could, ended up busting her lip. I was horrified at the blood in bed, and yet I had no desire to calm her, in fact I wanted to keep hitting her, to let out everything I'd been holding in. It was all I could do not to, and that's when I realized it was over. I packed my things the next day while she was out, and I left. A week later I had a law firm send her divorce papers, and she sent them back, signed. And that was it. I moved to London, met someone else, let that someone love me, and pretended I was coping. I'm still pretending, and maybe one day it will really be true."

For a few seconds Gonzalo thought about all the people trying to apply the same axiom: Accept defeat, because no matter how hard you try, things don't always turn out how you'd dreamed, and all you can do is hope and dream and pretend something else will work out.

He realized Luis was staring at him.

"That Russian with the tattoos, Zinoviev—he's the one who killed my son, isn't he?"

"According to Alcázar, the inspector in charge of the case, there's no proof of that."

"But Laura thought so, I'm sure. Do you think she did it? Do you think she killed him?"

"The proof is pretty overwhelming. Alcázar is convinced it was her."

Luis shook his head slowly, finishing his cigarette. He'd put on his sunglasses, and the dark lenses made it impossible to read his expression.

"I'm not asking for proof, or what that inspector thinks. She was your sister, my wife. Do you really think Laura could do something like that?"

Gonzalo thought back to their aerial dogfights, the two of them, arms extended, chasing one another, *ta-ta-ta-ta-ta-ta-ta*, imitating the sound of gunfire. There was the day Laura finally agreed to go into a tailspin, windmilling her arms and eventually collapsing in the barn. *Why did you let me win?* Gonzalo asked. *Because today you fought so well you deserved it,* she said, hair covered in hay, snuggling him in her arms. Gonzalo had turned and seen his mother through the barn window, smiling. She'd heard, too. But maybe she didn't remember.

"No, I don't," he said with absolute conviction. He didn't know where it had come from, but it was genuine.

"I don't, either," Luis replied, flicking his cigarette butt into the man-made lake.

3

The railway police officer, his expression impenetrable, cast his glance back and forth between Elías and his passport. The glee reigning in the train compartment five minutes earlier had vanished. When the four students heard the call for "Documents!" they fell silent, obeying like automatons. After five long minutes, the officer handed Elías back his passport without altering his severe expression, and then repeated the operation with the other three. Finally, when all was in order and the officer left, they exhaled in relief, and Martin—the red-haired Englishman who had boarded when the train reached Warsaw—allowed himself to make a few jokes that the others acknowledged with halfhearted laughter. Suddenly, the young scholarship recipients got the sense that Moscow wasn't going to be all fun and games. Bolsheviks took the proletariat revolution very seriously, and this officer's icy stare had been a warning. The train slowed noticeably a couple of miles before arriving at Moscow's impressive station. Elías hunkered down in his coat and peered out the window, not caring how bitterly cold the wind, or how ugly his first glimpse of the paradise his father had spoken of so often.

Despite its three million inhabitants and being renamed capital in 1918, Moscow resembled an immense village full of narrow roads, chaos spreading outward like a stain at an alarming pace. Legions of workers labored day and night, building the Metro. Everywhere, old buildings were being torn down and grand palaces from the time of the czars were literally being moved, stone by stone, so as not to impede the design of enormous new avenues. Classic and modern were being juxtaposed, and soon it would be a beautiful city. But for now it was a mess: construction, demolition, scaffolding, and traffic. Still, not even the enormous columns of blue-black smoke rising beyond Stalin's iron-and-steel metropolis put a damper on the excitement of the engineer from Asturias, Spain.

"Being a non-Soviet Communist is seen as suspicious, even in the Union of Soviet Socialist Republics," said Claude sarcastically. He was a young Marseilles architect and had won a Lenin scholarship to continue his studies at the Moscow Institute of Architecture. Claude motioned to the others to take note of the group waiting for them on the platform, clustered at the bottom of an enormous mural of Stalin in military cap, beneath what seemed a slogan of the Five-Year Plan: *In ten years we will make up the hundred we lag behind industrialized nations.* Despite their smiling faces and civilian attire, it was obvious that they were police.

"They're not going to take their eyes off us, even though we're the ones who came to help."

"We didn't just come to build bridges and canals. We came to learn, to be apostles and preach throughout the West what's happening here. As Stalin says, you can't create something new without profound knowledge of the old. And this is a nation full of knowledge," declared Michael, the short bowlegged Scotsman who hadn't left Martin's side. He knew what he was talking about. This was his second trip to Moscow. He'd been sent by the Party cell in Edinburgh, and his father had worked as a fur trader in

Siberia. Michael was here to work on the huge Dnieper Hydro-electric Station and put his book knowledge of generating cheap energy into practice. Of the four, he spoke Russian the best and knew the most about the USSR's technical and industrial progress. Elías smiled, thinking of his father at their shack in Mieres a week ago, giving him an effusive bear hug and saying goodbye. His heart filled with tenderness when he recalled his father's hands, the hands of a miner, holding a copy of Chekhov's *The Seagull*, one of his favorite books. Elías was aware of the fact that he'd received a rare privilege, being able to finish his engineering degree in the land of Gorky and Dostoyevsky. He was hoping to stay long enough to learn the language of these gods his father worshipped, so that he could recite Pushkin like a real Soviet upon his return to Spain. He knew nothing would make his father happier.

"Do you think, as part of our welcome, Stalin might receive us in audience at the Kremlin? I've heard his library is amazing."

His three friends gave him a perplexed look and then burst out laughing. And in their laughter, especially Claude's, Elías detected an almost sinister sense of humor.

"Careful what you wish for, *amigo*; you might get it."

The guide they'd been assigned introduced himself as Nikolai Ozhegov and shook their hands enthusiastically before insisting on taking their cases. He spoke perfect English, and his Spanish, when he addressed Elías, was more than acceptable. Elías felt an immediate fondness for the ungainly, talkative sandy-haired man, though he also understood the significance of his presence: As Claude had intimated moments earlier, Nikolai was a *rabkor*—in theory a "people's correspondent," in reality a police informant. They were everywhere, in factories, schools. Nikolai would be their shadow, give regular reports on their behavior, their activities, even their ideas. But this didn't concern Elías—he had nothing to hide, he was a Communist through and through, there to learn as much as possible before returning home.

The four friends were picked up by a black Ministry of the Interior car (later, Elías learned that Muscovites referred to these police vehicles ominously as "crows") and driven the length of Frunze Avenue and along Tverskaya Street, now renamed Gorky Avenue at its widest point. Their guide proudly pointed out the eye hospital—housed in an eighteenth-century building—the Museum of History and Iversky Gate, which led to Red Square and the Kremlin. Awestruck, Elías watched the construction being undertaken on the great Lenin Library, a splendid neo-classical building destined to house forty million books and documents and located between the Kremlin and the Manège, the czars' imperial riding academy and stables. Heading north on Leningradsky Avenue, they continued their tour, passing the telegraph office and central bank. Elías took it all in, eyes wide open, and got the strange feeling that everything he saw possessed a sort of tragic grandeur. He had to force himself to blink when, off in the distance, he caught sight of the eighth wonder of the world—Saint Basil's Cathedral.

"What do you think?" Nikolai asked in passable Spanish.

Elías nodded, amazed. He'd heard so many charges against Stalin—that he was the destroyer of a thousand churches, an uncultured Georgian, a savage peasant—that the sight of the church left him gape mouthed.

Nikolai smiled derisively. "When you go home, you'll be able to tell people that we barbarians are becoming civilized."

The car pulled up before the gates of the Government Building, also known as the House on the Embankment. It was an immense complex occupying seven acres and quite imposing—sinister-looking, even—in style, on the banks of Moskva River. Construction had begun five years earlier and still wasn't finished, but its five hundred apartments housed a good part of the regime's intelligentsia: artists of all sorts, top government officials, and technicians. The well-appointed modern facilities, central heating, and furnishings were the envy of all Moscow. This was to be the young students' lodging.

Martin, the red-haired Englishman, whistled in admiration. He was hoping to work with Boris Iofan, the building's designer and one of the architects responsible for the city's modernization plan.

"Don't get too excited," Claude advised quietly. "It's a brilliant move: They put all the country's best minds in the same place, lavish them with privileges, and it's far simpler to keep tabs on them this way. I bet there are peepholes in all the walls and OGPU microphones hidden everywhere."

Michael, a Scotsman who'd already spent time in Russia, touched his arm amicably. "Please, Claude. We come as friends. We're not counterrevolutionary spies; in fact, just the opposite. Don't upset our Spanish friend with paranoid gossip about the Political Directorate."

Claude smiled patiently. "Did you know that the leader the great Stalin admires most is Ivan the Terrible? I'm just saying: Be careful what you do and say in there."

Elías's apartment was bigger than any other place he'd ever lived, certainly much larger than his humble room in Madrid's Student Residence or the dismal bedroom at his house in Mieres. The furniture was austere: a table and lamp, a single bed, a small armoire, stove, and bathroom. It had a sad air, but rather than a dungeon, it resembled a monk's cell, a place that fostered sobriety and hard work. A curtainless window looked out over the immense cement forecourt, crisscrossed with paths leading to other buildings. The people down below looked like ants, rushing haphazardly from place to place. The sun shone cold but bright. The temperature was bearable, at least inside his apartment. Nikolai showed him the room like a solicitous bellhop and then said goodbye, shaking Elías's hand once more.

"I'll come for you tomorrow at six. You'll go straight to work. For now, rest. Welcome to the Union of Soviet Socialist Republics."

Elías fumbled, searching his mind for the right words with which to thank him in Russian, and Nikolai gave him a pat on the shoulder, bemused.

"Let's hope you build bridges better than you speak Russian."

That same evening, Elías wrote a letter home, giving his father his first impressions. He described the cities they'd traveled through on their way to Moscow, the desolate beauty of the landscapes he'd seen, and the people he'd met on the train, including his three new friends. Elías was surprised by how much seemingly unsophisticated people—workers and peasants—knew about literature and music, both classical and popular. It wasn't uncommon to overhear heated arguments about who was the better composer, Verdi or Bizet, or to hear Bach and Prokofiev being played on pianos in any old café.

> *Outsiders seem to believe that people here are on their knees,*
> *and I'm not yet in any position to affirm or deny this. It's true*
> *that the police are everywhere, and that when people mention*
> *Stalin they call him "vozhd" and lower their voices if they're*
> *not sure who might be listening. The Soviets have a proverbially*
> *wry sense of humor, it seems, and often use the word "sidit,"*
> *which means both to be sitting down and to be incarcerated.*
> *But how many of our compatriots do you know who can play a*
> *Bach fugue? Or recite Spanish poets the way, here, a fisherman*
> *recites Mayakovsky? They say Stalin is a great music lover; well,*
> *I can say that at least he shares his love with the people. Classical*
> *music is a required subject starting in elementary school. What*
> *they're building here, Father, is incomparable to anything*
> *humanity has ever built before, there's no doubt about it. I am*
> *very excited and can't wait to start work.*
>
> *Take care, and give Mother a hug.*

The following days were intense. First thing in the morning, well before dawn, Nikolai would come to pick Elías up at the gates of the residence, and then together they'd take the tram to the outskirts of town. Elías traveled alongside port and railroad workers, breathing in the potent smell of their clothes, rolling tobacco, strong coffee, and alcohol. He scrutinized their tired faces as they nodded off against the tram's windows, listened to the women's conversations, and grilled his "shadow," asking him questions about anything that drew his attention and begging Nikolai to speak to him only in Russian. Elías was curious about everything: the architecture of the buildings they passed; Moscow's history, literature, and music; and, of course, politics. He wanted to know it all: who was who, how things had gone since the civil war. And he was drawn like a magnet to the omnipresent figure of Stalin. The man's image was everywhere—there were portraits along the large avenues, signs with his proclamations inside the tram cars, images on the sides of public buildings and even on the walls of the most secluded alleys. Stalin was like an omniscient god, watching everything with his deep eyes and enormous mustache.

Nikolai would answer some questions frankly, obviously proud of his people's culture. He was from a city in the Urals whose name Elías found unpronounceable, and swore that without the Great Leader's literacy project, he would never have had the opportunity to read Tolstoy or Dostoyevsky, much less move to Moscow. And yet Nikolai gave vague replies to any slightly indiscreet questions, when he didn't evade them completely. After spending a few days with him, Elías realized that even in the USSR, openhearted sincerity was a rare virtue. Nikolai weighed his words carefully, and it was clear that survival instincts took precedence over his principles. Elías could never tell what Nikolai truly thought about certain subjects. And his own instincts soon told him that he himself needed to be discreet with comments and opinions. After all, he was just a Spanish student who couldn't understand the context surrounding what was happening in his host country. Nonetheless, his enthusiasm and sincerity made keeping his mouth shut quite a struggle.

The job site he'd been assigned to was, at the time, the greatest feat of engineering ever undertaken by man: an enormous canal that would connect the Moskva and Volga rivers to supply the city's water and connect Moscow with the great White Sea Canal. Using sluiceways and lateral canals, thousands of miles of river would be rechanneled, altering the natural course of waterways that had until now defiantly refused to be tamed. Hundreds of thousands of men and women, children and old people toiled night and day with picks and shovels on this massive undertaking.

"Moscow will be the Port of Five Seas," Nikolai proclaimed with obvious pride. Its Great Canal would connect to the Volga-Don and flow into the White Sea, the Baltic, the Caspian, the Sea of Azov, and the Black Sea. "The most celebrated leaders, from Alexander the Great to Peter the Great, dreamed of something like this. But we, the Bolsheviks, are the ones creating canals in the steppe to make it possible."

It was impressive indeed, Elías admitted, examining the plans for this titanic endeavor. But he was also confronted by the harsh reality of the inhuman means by which it was carried out. The canal's construction was overwhelmingly supplied by forced labor, prisoners sometimes convicted on ridiculous charges. Stealing a loaf of bread could carry a five-year sentence. Prisoners condemned to death for felonies had their sentences commuted in exchange for working like slaves, constantly watched over by armed units from the OGPU and the GULAG administration—the police that ran the forced labor camps headed by Matvei Berman and Genrikh Yagoda. Just the mention of their names was enough to harden Nikolai's expression.

"You don't understand," he charged one morning, when Elías kept going on about it. Nikolai praised the educative labor being carried out by prisoners, but as he spoke, Elías saw a prisoner being savagely beaten with clubs by a couple of guards, and no one batted an eye or dared to intervene. Where was the education in that? Where, in the deaths caused by scurvy, malaria, overexposure, and beatings, Elías wanted to know. He was horrified.

"There is education in silence and in death. A lesson for the living that they will not forget," Nikolai responded, his caustic Soviet irony on full display.

"What about the people?"

"The masses are simple, they are brute force, fickle and easily manipulated. Any faith in their love is misguided. The only guarantee of their loyalty is through fear."

"But these are the same people who need a better quality of life. Otherwise, what's the point of all this?"

Nikolai shrugged. "The peasants want to live in palaces. There can't be palaces for everyone."

Reality, and the constant shock of its contrasts, smacked Elías in the face again and again; it was all so disconcerting. No sooner would he get his bearings in one setting than he'd be whisked off to another where things couldn't be any more different, with no time to process. From the swamps on the canal—thigh-deep in mud, surrounded by unspeakable hardship and suffering—he'd be taken straight to visit Lenin's astonishing mausoleum, or to a performance by the Bolshoi Ballet or a reception with local authorities who for hours subjected him to hot air he could only partially understand. He hardly had time to rest or write about his day in letters to his father, which he gave to Nikolai to take to the post office. His letters were contradictory, as were his emotions and the reactions he had to all that was unfolding before his eyes. The enthusiasm he'd felt at the beginning had not abated in the three weeks Elías had been in Moscow, but there were now shades of gray that made him question the means by which Stalin had decided, at any cost, to bring the Soviet Union into modernity. He wondered, in his letters, what would happen if Spain's new Republic were to adopt the same methods: army purges, forced labor, intense fervor. His conclusion was clear: We Spaniards couldn't endure this. We lack the Soviets' stoicism and self-sacrifice.

Nikolai never eased up. As though instructed to give Elías no downtime, no space to reflect, he'd turn up at his apartment at night, dragging him out to the bars on Frunze Avenue, where everyone sang and drank to excess. The Russians' spirit was as beautiful and melancholic as their culture. When drinking, they recited poetry with such tragedy that Elías, though he didn't fully understand, ended up with a knot in his throat. Works by condemned poets and writers repudiated by the State were recited only when people were very drunk. That was when they told astonishing stories: that of Mayakovsky's suicide, or the time Osip Mandelstam slapped Alexei Tolstoy, the "Red Count," in the face. And the wee hours, in the haze of alcohol, was when the *yurodivy*, or holy fools, appeared. Prophets of God, they conferred with czars and yet were still greatly respected. Only they could tell the truth, could openly criticize members of the Politburo or even Stalin himself, with a biting wit that was always met with laughter. Listening to them, Elías thought they were like the court jesters so brilliantly portrayed in Velázquez's paintings. Only the jesters had dared to tell the kings that they were nothing but idols with feet of clay. On nights like these, Elías once again felt he was living in the Russia of Gogol, Gorky, and Dostoyevsky; he wondered which of the men and women present might have inspired fictional characters like Anna Karenina and the brothers Karamazov.

One night, the four friends all met up at Nikolai's suggestion. This was the first time they'd seen each other since their arrival in Moscow, three weeks earlier. They embraced merrily, interrupting one another with stories about the experiences they'd had, laughing. They had dinner together and drank themselves silly under the supervision of their guide, who observed from the sidelines, wearing an expression both empathetic and disdainful. He was like a father giving his children free rein for the first time and then watching them let loose in amused curiosity. Yet something in the four young men's souls had evolved. Each, to different degrees, realized and expressed the fact that they were undoubtedly living a historic moment, both beautiful and terrible. Comparisons between what was happening in their respective countries and the Soviet Union were inevitable, and in one way or another they all came to the same conclusion, drunk on youth and vodka: Europe, old and frail, was dying, and a daunting and brutal new force was fighting to take its place. And they were privileged eyewitnesses.

Claude was perhaps the most taciturn of the four. Unlike the others, he'd managed to shake his guide on more than one occasion and roam the streets, chatting with people more freely. That night he took long pulls from glass after glass of vodka and kept quiet.

"Come on, Claude, don't look so unhappy," Martin blurted out. He was exceedingly drunk, keeping his balance by holding fast to a chair back, but his body still swayed side to side, like a ship about to founder. Michael and Elías, on his left and right, helped keep him on his feet when the rocking became too perilous.

Claude shot a sidelong glance at Nikolai, sitting one table over. He looked relaxed, talking to his comrades and drinking, though no doubt he hadn't taken his eyes off them.

"I don't understand your enthusiasm," he replied quietly, his voice almost inaudible amid the noise of the packed bar. "I remember the first time I saw Lenin. It was in Vienna, before he'd had his first stroke. This was at the height of the war with the White Army, and European powers like England and France were on the verge of intervening to tip the balance in favor of the czar. Lenin was a force of nature, touring Europe to convince the world that the Bolsheviks didn't pose a threat. But they did, and the old European dynasties trembled in the face of this little man who'd decided to turn Marx's dream into his reality. Behind him, silent, brooding, was Stalin. We called him 'the Bear' because he was so big and had those bushy eyebrows and penetrating eyes. He wasn't Party secretary then; at the time he was just one more leader, not even the most brilliant one. But I remember, watching him, that I couldn't help thinking that this man would do anything to further his aspirations. And that what mattered was figuring out what it was he aspired to."

"What are you trying to get at?" Michael asked impatiently, intuiting that the conversation was drifting into dangerous territory. "I don't know what Stalin wanted then, but I've seen what he's doing now and it's unbelievable. He's turning the Soviet Union inside out like a sock! It's astonishing."

Claude nodded and then gave a little chuckle that irked the others; it was as though he knew something they did not. He pointed at Elías with his glass.

"You've worked with the convict brigades on the Great Canal. You've seen the conditions these poor wretches live in."

Elías shot a quick look over at Nikolai, who seemed not to be paying attention, and was disturbed to realize something that he became conscious of only at that moment: fear of expressing oneself openly was contagious; he too now felt reluctant to speak.

"The majority of those people are criminals. They have a debt to society and they're paying it off with their labor." Immediately, he felt an instinctive horror at what he'd just said. He imagined the profound disappointment his father would feel on hearing those words. "It's true that conditions are deplorable," he added, trying to make amends, "but what can we do about it?"

Claude banged his hand down on the table. Luckily, the noise level was so high that no one paid any attention.

"Are you bloody kidding me? We've got eyes to see, ears to hear, and brains to think. You say most of those working on the canal are convicts, ergo they deserve whatever happens to them because they've done something wrong. I beg to differ, but even if it were true, what about those who haven't done anything wrong, what about those who actually do not—as you say—'have a debt to society'?"

Martin stared at his friend's drooping eyelids, his heavy tongue poking out between his teeth. His head lolled back and then jerked forward, which seemed to clear a bit of the booze-induced haze from his mind.

"I've heard things," Claude went on. "They say Yagoda and Berman have proposed to Stalin a deportation plan. They want to cleanse Moscow of what they call the lower classes—beggars, drunks, and pickpockets—but also of peasants fleeing the collectivizations. Apparently the bastards have proposed a massive emigration, to repopulate the northernmost part of the country. Nobody wants to be sent off to freeze to death in Siberia. So the police make up any damn excuse to send them there, no trial, nothing. All it takes is not having an internal passport."

"That's bullshit!" Michael exclaimed. "Defeatist propaganda from the damned Mensheviks still hiding out with kolkhoz farmers."

The three friends became embroiled in an argument that Elías observed, dumbstruck and inebriated, but not so drunk that he didn't pick up on the fact that their vehemence had aroused the attention of Nikolai and his friends. Nikolai held his gaze with a mocking smile, as though inviting Elías to join in the discussion. *Cat got your tongue?* his eyes seemed to ask. Elías felt his guts churn.

"I'm going to be sick," he murmured, bringing a hand to his mouth.

Curiously, this gesture stopped their conversation short.

"Don't even think about throwing up in here. What are our Soviet comrades going to think of us? A man who can't hold his drink is not to be trusted," Claude warned, laughing.

Elías struggled to his feet. He'd had too much to drink. Maybe not compared to his friends, but way too much for his tolerance.

The bar was in a cellar and Elías dragged himself up the stairs, hands pressed to the wall so as not to lose his point of reference. The others let him go, laughing and teasing. Except for Nikolai. He wasn't laughing.

It was freezing outside, far colder than anything Elías had ever felt in his life, and despite wearing a heavy jacket he trembled like he had malaria. The dark sky was heavy with clouds, an icy slush raining down, but the moon above looked beautiful, bathed in a luminous aura that made Elías feel very far from home. The concern he felt over his friends' conversation and Nikolai's penetrating eyes eased a bit. There was nothing to fear. Yes, they were young, impetuous idealists, but they were honest and prepared to work hard. When it came down to it, what difference did a few critical words spoken in the heat of vodka make? He unzipped his trousers and, as he urinated, softly sang an old nursery rhyme in Asturian dialect, amusing himself by drawing circles in the snow.

He didn't see them coming.

There were two of them. One was smoking, leaning on the running board of a car. The other stood watching Elías, legs wide, hands inside his military coat. Elías didn't realize they were police until the one smoking flicked his cigarette at him. Elías started to protest and then saw the cartridge belts and holsters. At that point he tried clumsily to apologize, but all of the damned Russian he knew had vanished from his mind. One of the men barked at him, sounding like a rabid dog as he demanded identification. Elías didn't have it on him and tried to tell them that Nikolai and the others were in the cellar below and could vouch for him, but when he made a move to return to the bar, one of the officers tripped him. Elías fell flat on his face. The freezing snow filled his mouth and one of them stomped a boot on his head, crushing him to the ground as both men laughed. They were drunker than he was, drunk in the terrifying and aggressive way of police who hate their jobs. He recalled similar experiences in Spain, humiliations at the hands of guards in his town who frisked men for no reason, or purposely frisked women in the presence of their husbands. It was the same all over: Men whose power was illegitimate couldn't help abusing it.

Elías thrashed with rage passed down from generations and grabbed the leg holding him captive, jerking it violently. The guard fell and Elías managed to sit up. The other man pulled his gun, or tried to. Instinctively, Elías punched him in the face and ran. To run in the wrong direction can mark one's fate. It's that simple. Had he gone back down the stairs to the bar, Elías might have had some problems, but Nikolai could have intervened in his favor. But Elías ran without thinking, in the opposite direction, toward the train tracks, distancing himself from the police and the faint light that was his only hope. He could hear the men shouting, hear their heavy breathing, their footsteps in the snow. And then a bang almost like a firecracker shrank the distance between them.

The first drops of blood stained the snow. Elías was surprised to see that it was coming from his hand. He stopped to contemplate the thick droplets hanging from his fingertips before he fell, the sound muffled by the snow. He didn't feel the impact. Elías was so astounded that he didn't realize that one of the police officers had fired his gun. The realization sank in and filled him with shock. He'd been shot! They were trying to kill him, for no reason, over an absurd misunderstanding.

He had no chance to react. They caught up and pounced like rabid dogs, kicking him savagely. Elías tried to protect his face with his hands and curled into a ball to protect his genitals. And then he felt a crack on his side and an exceedingly sharp pain. They'd broken a rib. He couldn't stop thinking that this was all a terrible mistake. He shouted Nikolai's name, mumbled the few Russian words he could bring to mind, but the police weren't listening. Enraged, they continued to beat him viciously. Until Elías felt a heavy blow to the head and everything went dark. The same dark, disguised as white, that he'd been trying to escape.

The water stain was shaped like a dragon with its wings spread, talons poised to attack its prey. It changed form with the light filtering in from a high barred window, giving the impression that it was moving across the ceiling, growing and shrinking. Sometimes Elías reached out a hand as though the brownish stain might come to life and land in his palm, like a little sparrow. It had been four long days and nights, and everything that had happened outside of that enclosed space had become hazy and surreal. His trip to Moscow, his friends' faces, the experiences he'd had in his time there—all came crashing up against the reality of this cement cellblock whose walls were covered in graffiti he couldn't understand, phrases and names scratched into the damp plaster with a fingernail or pin. Elías passed the time huddled in a corner by the straw mattress, eyes darting between the sealed door separating him from the sounds outside and the filthy hole where he moved his bowels. At set times, as though following a routine, a rat would poke its nose out of the hole and then scurry along the cell walls, ignoring him; the rat would eat the black bread Elias hadn't touched and then disappear again. Elías almost missed him. His only contact with other human beings was through the sliding hatch in the door. It opened twice a day, morning and night, and a hand—not always the same hand—passed him a tray with a scrap of bread and some exceedingly salty vegetable soup. No water.

Fear and impatience were driving him crazy. Luckily, the bullet had barely grazed his hand, and after recovering from the beating he'd received, Elías had convinced himself that Nikolai would appear at any moment to clear up this terrible mistake. Naturally, Elías was planning to lodge a formal complaint and probably ask for the officers to be arrested or punished. He imagined his guide apologizing and took delight in picturing his attackers' panicked faces. He wasn't some peasant or drunkard they could beat the daylights out of without facing any consequences. He'd been invited by the Party, was a brilliant, promising young engineer who had willingly offered his talent to the Soviet people's cause and didn't deserve to be treated like a dog. But the hours dragged on and Nikolai did not appear; no one gave him any explanation, and when he demanded one—banging on the door in rage the third day, and it finally opened—what he got was a blow to the neck with a club. Now he cowered uneasily each time he heard the hatch slide open.

There must have been others like him. He heard cries and footsteps outside his door, the sound of gates slamming. The voices of men and women. And yowls that made his nerves stand on end, especially during the long nights. The crying and whimpering had him on permanent alert and kept him from sleeping. If he did manage to shut his eyes, wrapped in his blanket, his nightmares were no better than the reality awaiting him when he opened them back up. Somewhere far away, out the high window that barely let in any daylight, bells were ringing. He assumed they must be the chimes of a church or monastery. There must also be some sort of chemical industrial complex nearby, judging by the columns of smoke in the distance and the horrible rotten-egg smell that filled his cell when the wind changed direction. Religious bells, industry, prison cells, and a rat emerging from his own feces—this was certainly not the picture of the Soviet Union that his father had painted since the time Elías was a boy. He'd always pictured Russia like Leonid Pasternak's *Charge of the Light Brigade*: Bolshevik horsemen attacking an invisible enemy, floating above the clouds; or like the barren beauty of the steppe, where the selfless and unpretentious hero was pitted against Dostoyevsky's haughty, stupid aristocrats.

Finally, the door opened with a long, slow creak that put Elías on edge. A guard signaled for him to stand. Oddly, the clean smell of his leather belt and just-shaved beard filled Elías with an absurd flurry of hope. After all, outside this cell lived reasonable, civilized human beings. It was all going to be put right. They took a service elevator to an upper floor, and when the grate opened they walked down a wide corridor with large picture windows overlooking an inner courtyard. It was raining, leaves whipped back and forth in the wind. In the distance he could make out the winding path of the Moskva River, the cupolas of a Russian Orthodox monastery. That must have been where the bells were coming from. The officer stopped at a wooden door, rapping on it with his knuckles. A deep voice responded. Elías was sent in and told to sit in a chair facing the wall. He obeyed, frightened, and stunned by the change in atmosphere.

He'd imagined being led to some sort of interrogation room, a dreary, sordid place, but this was an enormous gallery with high ceilings painted with classic frescoes portraying the greatest events in Soviet history almost biblically—except that here it was the generals of the Red Army and peasants with chests like buffalo clutching sickles, workers with their fists held high against a background of cranes and brick chimneys. On either side were wide granite columns with gold-leaf vines winding around their capitals; the baroque furniture was equally ornate—claw-foot armchairs and an enormous mahogany desk. From the center of the ceiling hung an intricate crystal chandelier casting light in all directions, and everywhere hung classic portraits: Peter the Great, Ivan the Terrible, even Catherine the Great.

"Surprised?" the official sitting at the desk asked. He was a tiny man with a childlike face. Perhaps it was to compensate for this that he sported a thin mustache, blond as his short hair, which complemented his blue eyes. "This is one of Nicholas the Second's recreational palaces," he explained unnecessarily while gesturing curtly for the guard to take his leave, which the man did, robot-like. "It's in the outskirts of Moscow; he used it to meditate at the nearby monastery you no doubt saw on your way up. Nicholas was a very pious czar, did you know that?"

Elías could barely understand what the little man was saying as he circled the desk, coming to stand before him. Instinctively, he shook his head in response. All he wanted to do was explain himself and clear this whole mess up.

The officer spread his arms wide, taking in the room.

"Yes, indeed. He would come here to pray after ordering his adversaries to be executed. He was tortured by guilt, and that made him weak," the little man declared with a cruel snicker.

"I don't know what I'm doing here. I'm a Spanish engineer who came as an apprentice. Nikolai can vouch for me. This has all been a horrible mistake."

The officer looked on, unmoved.

"Spain is a great country," he announced with surprising glee. "We adore Cervantes. You probably don't know this, but *Don Quixote* is very popular among children here. Personally, I'm an admirer of Calderón de la Barca. So many metaphors and literary devices one can make use of! I love his dark romanticism, the desperate force of his vitriol. But if memory serves, it was Napoleon who said that the Spaniards were hot-blooded and stubborn, a superstitious, murderous people controlled by traitorous untrustworthy clergy. What do you think? Are Cervantes and Calderón right about your people, or is Napoleon's conclusion more accurate?"

It was clear that the man was toying with him, a cat with a mouse that has no chance of escape. Yet he wouldn't kill him with a single swipe; it would be too boring. He approached a little side table, picked up a pitcher, and poured himself a glass of water. He drank slowly, gazing at Elías with undisguised satisfaction. All he had to do was look at the prisoner's blackened lips in order to see that he was dying of thirst. And yet he didn't offer him a drink. Not yet. He placed the glass down within Elías's reach and let him contemplate the droplets sliding down its surface, forming a wet spot on the table. Elías's eyes watered at the sight of it.

"May I have a drink, please?"

The officer sighed. "Potable water is a limited resource here in Moscow. We are building the Great Canal in order to have a sufficient supply, and that is why you're here. To help us. Or is that not why you're here?"

Elías focused his attention on the liquid, which turned the dust in his mouth to cement. His throat was rough as straw.

"Are you a Judas, Elías?"

The question, posed with no animosity, more like the affirmation of something obvious than an honest query, rattled Elías's brain.

"No! Of course not! What happened with those police officers was a tragedy. They shot me!" he exclaimed, holding up his bandaged hand.

The official's silence and expression were charged with particular intensity.

"You can tell me the truth and then have a drink," he said amiably, after a few seconds.

The truth? What did that mean? Why didn't this man believe him? He *was* telling the truth!

"Admit that you are a Trotskyist agent come to infiltrate the workers' ranks and sabotage our work. This is the truth, is it not?"

"What? What on earth are you talking about? My father adores Stalin. I've been a Communist since I was fifteen years old! I came here of my own free will to work and continue my studies."

Elías discerned rage boiling up in the officer's eyes as the man slowly nodded his head. He turned on his heels and strode to the table. Picking up the phone, the official gave a curt order. When he hung up and returned to Elías, his expression was ruthless.

Nikolai was washing his hands in the stone basin. Drops of blood quickly disappeared into the soap bubbles slipping off his fingertips. He examined his hands in wonder before drying them. He was a peaceful man, as a boy he'd wanted to be a baker like his father, kneading dough, touching soft, pliable things. He never imagined that these strong hands would end up being used on something no less pliable—the human spirit. He dried them with a towel, gazing into the mirror at the reflection of Claude's unmoving body in the chair. He had lost consciousness momentarily, but the guards would revive him quickly. It's always the same, he thought, slightly disappointed. The tough guys, the ones who act the strongest, are the first to cave. He rolled his shirtsleeves back down and put on his jacket. The knuckles on his right hand stung; he'd have a hard time explaining the swelling at home tomorrow.

"Wake him up and have him sign the declaration," he ordered the guards, scornfully surveying the Frenchman's bruised face and the bloody stumps where two of his fingers had been. The fingers were now scattered across the floor. Claude was the last one. Only the Spaniard remained.

Nikolai rode up in the freight elevator, his face a picture of concentration. The guard at the door opened it without question and Nikolai marched in. He didn't bother to return Elías's shocked and—poor fool—hopeful look. Instead he strode directly to the table and handed the officer a stack of declarations. The two of them chatted quietly for a moment, and the officer approached Elías with an unmistakably satisfied air. In one hand he held the declarations given by Elías's friends. In the other, something horrifying: all of the letters Elías had written to his father, which Nikolai had obviously never posted. One by one, the officer placed them into Elías's trembling hands: There were things underlined in red all over, and comments in Russian in the margins.

Utterly bewildered and with a heavy heart, Elías raised his head to look at Nikolai, desperate to understand what sort of trick this might be. Nikolai held his gaze, unperturbed, as though he'd never laid eyes on him before.

"It seems you consider our methods to be cruel and barbarian. You don't hesitate to reveal our plans for the canal, the people working on it, the difficulties we have encountered; you even venture to call the project overambitious, demented, unachievable. Not to mention what you make of those in charge of it: inept bureaucrats simply using the people like oxen."

Elías felt woozy. Never by any means would he have imagined that his correspondence might be violated, his words taken out of context in order to paint a completely distorted picture of who he was. Why? To what end? He looked to Nikolai for an explanation. And then, staggered, he recalled conversations at his apartment in the House on the Embankment, the seemingly innocent way that his guide had coaxed out of him sentences that now sounded venomous, dissenting, or critical of what he was seeing and hearing. And he recalled Claude's warning to be careful of what they said inside that building, his prediction that there were holes in the walls and microphones all over. How many random statements had this savage copied down in order to build a case against him?

"Those police officers were not drunk, nor did they simply stumble upon you. They were sent to arrest you, and you resisted violently," the official spat, visibly satisfied by the devastating effect of Nikolai's arrival. "As if this were not enough, we have more against you. Your three comrades have all signed declarations naming you the leader of a cell of Trotskyist spies. Those poor dupes were attempting to sabotage the Great Canal, at your orders."

It made no sense whatsoever; this was ridiculous, absurd. Had it not been for his thirst, for the pain he was in, for his wounds, for Nikolai's stony gaze, Elías would have laughed at the utter madness of it. But this was all deadly serious.

"Confess and you may drink. The water is cool and fresh. Your friends did. They all swear you were the ringleader."

"Of *what*?"

Faced with total absurdity, the mind becomes foggy. When confronted with basic needs, people are dumbstruck, flummoxed. He was thirsty, tired, stunned. He wanted to close his eyes, go to sleep, and wake up on a train headed back to Spain. Wanted to forget this nightmare. He set his gaze on the crystal-clear water. He thought of the rat rooting through his shit, of the lice in his blanket, the dragon on the ceiling above his head. He shuddered, recalling the screaming he heard in the night, on the other side of the door. Had it been them, his friends? Claude, Martin, Michael, being tortured, denouncing him? Why? Why him?

The official offered him the glass, softening his gaze, altering the expression on his strange childlike face so much that he looked friendly.

"Drink," he said encouragingly.

In the end, Elías picked up the glass, brought it to his lips, and with one sip sealed his fate.

4

In the dream, Gonzalo can see a man's back, his shirtless torso hunched over a typewriter (a Densmore with an ivory keyboard) in the lamplight, pecking at keys with two fingers, amassing one cigarette butt after another in the saucer beside him. The woman with the butterfly wings tattoo—a younger version of her, just a girl, really—stands straight as a rod behind his chair, heels together, patent-leather shoes touching, bony knees peeking out a few inches from beneath her plaid skirt. Her right sock is down at her ankles, the left one pulled high. The girl's voice is trembling as she recites something, which in the dream is inaudible. It's like watching TV with the sound turned down. Her voice is drowned out by the clackety-clack of typewriter keys and the sound of the carriage return. The man is ripping out sheet after sheet of paper with increasing fury. At one point, the girl with the butterfly wings glances to the right and tries to smile at a boy who is crouched down, watching her from the corner of the room. The boy is him. She can't see him but knows that he is there. Listening. She is trying to soothe him, but her eyes are full of terror.

You have to concentrate, her expression says; he can hear her and knows that he has to search for the right words, find them in his mind and say them aloud. He knows they are there, in his brain somewhere, but he can't find them. Then the man grabs the girl by the wrists. His face has been transfigured, as though flames burning inside him had scorched half of it while leaving the other half cold—glacial, really—and when the two sides met they morphed into some unreadable inkblot. He becomes furious, lifts her into the air by the shoulders like a rag doll and hurls her violently to the floor. The girl lies there, facedown with her nose bleeding, blood forming a small pool and staining the floor. Then she reaches her fingers out toward the darkness where the boy who is Gonzalo is hiding, touches the tips of his shoes and thinks she must teach him to tie his own laces. *You have to remember; say the words*, her eyes implore. But the boy's feet step back, disappearing into the darkness. And then the boy remembers the words and tries to say them. But nothing will come out of his mouth, no matter how hard he tries to shout.

Gonzalo opened his eyes and thought he was going to die. Not at some vague point in the distant future, not a long time from now, but right at that moment. He put a hand to his chest, trying to calm the panic of the little boy who appeared in dreams each night to the adult he had become. He looked at the digital alarm clock: 3:20 A.M. Lola was asleep in a fetal position at the far side of the bed, in voluntary exile on the edge of the mattress, as was her custom every time they argued. She was breathing steadily, lips slightly parted, right elbow beneath the pillow and the left one tucked between her knees and stomach. Gonzalo stroked the curve of her back through her nightgown. He could count her vertebrae. She stirred, and he took his hand away.

Gonzalo went downstairs to the kitchen without turning on the light, feeling his way around the furniture. He still wasn't used to the new layout. The storage room was full of moving boxes yet to be opened, things that weren't strictly necessary for day-to-day living and that Gonzalo had promised to sort through as soon as he found the time. Lola often accused him of being a hoarder, and it was true that many of those things he no longer used, but he couldn't bear to part with them.

On one of the boxes he'd written in marker: LAURA'S THINGS. Lola was pestering him to get rid of her clothes and personal belongings. He turned on a lamp and sat on the floor to sort through the books, her baroque music collection, some stationery and office supplies that Luis hadn't wanted. A few of those things still smelled like his sister, there was a slight trace of her perfume.

The cremation had been a sorrowful affair, almost pathetic. It was hard to understand how some people lived to a hundred without even trying, while for others each minute is an epic struggle, Luis had said, and Gonzalo agreed. Cremation wasn't what he'd expected. Nothing like the funeral pyre of Hindu rituals, and certainly no Viking ship set ablaze with the hero sent out to sea. It was all so clinical: a sort of chamber that looked no different from a bakery oven or a butcher's storeroom. They explained that the coffin, sans crucifix, was completely degradable, as though being eco-friendly was a top concern at a time like that, as though it mattered that the dead produced no pollution. One button raised the coffin to the oven door; another button ushered it inside, where the crackling of a furnace could be heard, although no flames were visible. A worker closed the door and handed him an oval-shaped nugget. It was made of some indestructible material and had an ID number etched into it to avoid possible mix-ups. When he received the ashes, this number would prove that they belonged to Laura. In ten thousand years, when there are no more ashes or remains, he thought, people will wonder where their ancestors' bones are. And on archaeological digs they'll find thousands, millions, of stones like this.

There had been a downpour during the service, one of those furious summer storms, and it destroyed the beautiful wreaths that

Luis had bought for the hearse. Gonzalo's contribution had been one made of tulips—he knew his sister loved them—with a gold sash that read: *From your brother and mother who love you.* But his mother had obstinately refused to even approach the open casket in the funeral parlor to say goodbye. In her black mourning dress she stood, stoic and absent throughout the ceremony, and when Luis approached, she hardly deigned to look at him. Despite Gonzalo having held an umbrella over his mother's head to protect her from the rain, she'd caught a cold and had a slight fever, which at her age could be serious. Her only reaction to anything was when she caught sight of Chief Inspector Alcázar, standing alone, off at a distance.

"Who's that?" she asked, squinting.

"Laura's partner and boss."

Later, when Alcázar came over to give his condolences, his mother refused to speak to him.

"It's been a long time, Esperanza."

"Not long enough, as far as I'm concerned," she retorted, turning her back.

Gonzalo was shocked. "You know each other?"

Alcázar looked at him like he was an idiot. "Like wolf and sheep."

On the drive back to the residence, he asked his mother what the inspector had meant by that, but she refused to answer. At no point on the way home did she mention Laura's death or funeral. She did, however, note that it was a shame her dress had gotten ruined in the rain.

Alcázar's words were still swirling in Gonzalo's head, like food that won't go down.

"Aren't you coming to bed?"

Gonzalo could see Lola's body silhouetted through her nightgown in the light. She wasn't wearing any underwear. It was an erotic vision, yet somehow vague and distant. He got a nostalgic pang, but Lola's impenetrable expression made clear the distance between them.

"I couldn't sleep and didn't want to wake you by tossing and turning."

Lola picked up on her husband's despondent look, and then saw what was in his hands. She'd sensed an undercurrent of resentment between them for some time now, something slowly eating away at the foundations of their relationship. And she knew it wasn't just the imminent merger meeting with her father.

"Nightmares again?"

Gonzalo nodded, although he didn't tell her that this time his sister's face had been replaced by that of the tattooed redhead.

Lola gave the open box a look of appraisal. She'd never liked her sister-in-law, and that wasn't going to change now that Laura was dead. It was unnecessary and would have been hypocritical, and although she hadn't said anything to Gonzalo in order not to hurt him, she had trouble understanding his overnight devotion to Laura. They'd never spoken about her in the past and she didn't see why he was suddenly so affected. She knew it was cruel of her to think like this, but the truth was that Lola detested everything about Gonzalo's family: all the stories about his father, his mother's arrogant disdain when, on rare occasions, she came to visit. The woman acted as though by virtue of her father, Lola and all those of her class were to blame for her misfortunes, real and invented. But what irked her the most, and scared her as well, was the way Gonzalo seemed to change when surrounded by his family, to become someone who made her uneasy.

"She was a great collector of words," Gonzalo said, stroking the binding of an old Russian-Spanish dictionary.

"Excuse me?"

"Laura. She'd catch them midflight and write them all down in a little cloth-bound notebook she kept in her purse. Then she'd repeat the words over and over, like she was chewing them up, or trying to tame them."

"What kind of words?"

"Wild ones. She'd look up the meaning of a word in the dictionary and underline it in fluorescent highlighter. And then, if she ever looked it up again and saw that she'd already highlighted it, she got mad, like a little kid."

"I didn't know that," Lola said, touching his head lightly, as though she'd already done all she could to console him. Gonzalo blinked hard, as if he'd just had a terrible realization. For a few seconds he gazed at his wife's face, sounding her out.

"The truth is I didn't know much about her either. Ten years of not speaking is a long time."

"It wasn't your fault. She was the one who pulled away."

Gonzalo nodded mechanically, not actually feeling the truth of those words. He gazed at Lola's profile, as if attempting to make sure she wasn't lying. The lamplight reflected on her face made it look hazy, like a profile you see through the window on a rainy day.

Lola smoothed her hair and pressed her hands to her cheeks.

"I think I need some coffee."

She made it in silence; it had been years since she'd made Gonzalo coffee or fresh-squeezed orange juice, stirring in a spoonful of sugar. Gonzalo sat, his mind blank, watching her bustle about the kitchen. Then she came and sat down next to him with a steaming, invigorating cup.

"Have you spoken to Javier lately?"

"I've at least tried," Gonzalo replied, looking at his wife, waiting for her to go on.

"I'm not sure, but recently I've found money missing—not much, just small amounts, but it's been happening regularly. I asked him about it and he got furious."

"Not surprising, if you accused him of being a thief."

Lola looked at her husband like he was impossible. It was so difficult to get Gonzalo involved in anything, especially if it had to do with his son.

"I didn't accuse him of anything, I just asked him about it, and not because of the money but because I'm worried. He's been acting strange these days, sad and absent. I went through his things."

Gonzalo gave her a disapproving look. "What were you expecting to find?"

"I don't know—drugs maybe, anything. Do you know what he said to me after dinner? That as soon as he turns eighteen he's leaving home forever."

"Everyone feels the urge to go somewhere at eighteen. He'll get over it."

"You shouldn't talk like that about your own son. It doesn't make you sound like a very good father."

Gonzalo glanced at his wife. Sometimes he had the urge to tell her what he'd seen that morning eighteen years ago. But mentally he always tiptoed back down the stairs without a sound, as he had that day, as though nothing had happened. As though that door had remained closed.

"What kind of mother does it make you sound like?"

Lola picked up the empty cups and dumped them in the sink.

"The kind who will do what's necessary to keep her family together. You should get some sleep. Tomorrow's your meeting with my father, and the old man will take full advantage if he sees you off your game."

Siaka's black skin turned miraculously yellow in the glow cast from each streetlight as he walked beneath it. Dogs barked as he passed the vine-covered walls. He could see almost no house lights through the windows, just illuminated gardens and swimming pools. What Siaka liked about the night, what he'd always liked, was the feeling that the city belonged to him, had been built just for him. Especially in the wee hours before dawn, when the dim light just began to peek over the hill against the horizon. At night the lawyer's house looked different, as though buildings, too, needed to close their eyes and rest lazily. He sat on the ground and leaned his back against the low wall across the street. A pleasant breeze carried the scent of jasmine and pine. Maybe I'll have a house like this one day, he thought, though in truth Siaka preferred hotels. Nothing compared to the feeling of not being tied down to anything, the feeling that whatever you want is yours at the push of a button. The rich, in general, were not very attractive. Perhaps that was why they bought big cars and big houses. So that rather than look at them you looked at what they possessed.

He was tired of this life and determined to change it, to take charge. The time had come. He was planning to return to Zimbabwe. Siaka had saved up some money and his aunt had written, telling him of an old building complex in Chizarira National Park that for a reasonable price could be turned into a tourist hotel. A hotel with pristine flags. Laura had promised to help with his papers, help him change his identity, give him a past he wouldn't have to feel ashamed of when he returned home, maybe a university degree. Why not? Something no one would bother to check. His father would have been proud of that: the first in the family with a degree, and from a European university at that. But Laura was dead. Like Zinoviev, like the boy. All of them dead, except him.

The deputy inspector had been right when she said there were many ways to kill a childhood. He was familiar with several of them: a father who beats the crap out of you for no reason; an older sister who gives you to her boyfriend to rape you; a militiaman who hands you a Russian assault rifle and makes you fire on villagers; a few drunk soldiers who force you to rape a dying woman. And none of these was really any worse than sitting in a

Mercedes on the lap of an obese old man who wants a blow job, or being forced to fuck a girl at a luxurious mansion while party guests—men and women in elegant suits and expensive jewels—gather around the bed and ogle in sickening titillation. Day after day, hour after hour, childhood flees from these horrors, taking refuge in a memory, in games played by Lake Kariba, in nursery rhymes and cartoons. Only by keeping the memories alive can you continue believing that you're still human.

Siaka let the breeze flow across his open legs and for a moment wondered what it would be like to have dreams come true. Not to borrow them for a few hours or days but to own them, take possession of them, reclaim them from the world. It would be better, he thought. A better world.

The lights went out in the lawyer's kitchen and Siaka contemplated the fresh graffiti on the wall. *Everything we do has consequences, Gil. And you're going to pay them.*

"A nice desideratum," he murmured. Siaka liked that word; the deputy inspector had taught him how to pronounce it.

Luisa knocked on the door and entered without waiting to be called in, exuding an air of efficiency. It was Monday, another life. Gonzalo appreciated the fact that she didn't look at him like a cripple. She'd offered her condolences for Laura's death, brought him a strong coffee and a painkiller, and begun working as usual.

"Don Agustín is waiting for you in the boardroom."

"You're calling him 'don' Agustín now? He was 'stupid old jerk' until Friday."

Luisa didn't bat an eye.

"It's quite likely that when you emerge from that meeting it will be as part of Agustín and Associates. I'd like to keep working with you, and if I have to get down on my knees in order to do it, as long as it's nowhere near that man's crotch, then so be it."

Gonzalo smiled at Luisa's impudence. He liked people who didn't beat around the bush.

"I might put up a fight. Maybe I'll manage to keep us independent."

Luisa shot him a dubious look but had the good taste to keep her mouth shut.

"One more thing. You asked me to find out who rented the apartment on the right. The hottie with the butterfly wings is named Tania something-or-other, her last name is unpronounceable."

"Akhmatova, like the poet," Gonzalo said, reading off the card Luisa held out.

"She's a photographer, and despite looking like a Slavic model and having tits to die for, she's an incredibly nice young woman. She told me if I ever needed her services, she's got a little studio at this address. I'd say she's not married, or at least she doesn't wear a ring, and that she's foreign, though that much you could guess by her name. It's funny, she asked me about you, too, and I didn't even mention you."

Gonzalo blushed slightly. "What did you tell her?"

"What *could* I tell her? The truth: that you're a lawyer of no means, boring, in terrible shape, half blind, you work too much, and are a little stingy when it comes to your assistant's wages."

Gonzalo smiled. Luisa's impertinence, if nothing else, served to ease the tension in his shoulders before he confronted his father-in-law. He took the business card without really knowing what he was going to do with it and adjusted his tie and jacket perfunctorily.

"Here we go."

The boardroom had been designed to intimidate visitors. This was one strategic advantage that Agustín knew how to make the most of. When he had important business to conduct, he'd summon the other party to his office and await him in his presidential armchair, pretending to be preoccupied by some document he held before him. On this occasion, however, as he awaited his son-in-law, his preoccupation was not feigned. He'd spent a good deal of his weekend studying the documents relating to ACASA, one of his biggest clients. The project they had in mind would yield several million in profit if he could play his cards right. The problem was that, in an ironic twist of fate, the foundation on which the entire project hinged was about to walk in the door.

Agustín set his glasses down on top of the documents and took a sip of whiskey, contemplating the portrait of his daughter and grandchildren. He'd never liked Gonzalo. The very first time Lola brought him home, Agustín knew that this timid-looking boy would never have the strength of character to give his daughter what she deserved or even form part of the family. He had the kid checked out and learned that he was the son of a Communist who'd disappeared in 1967, when Gonzalo was a boy. The mother was of Belorussian descent and half crazy, and his sister had been in Afghanistan during the Soviet conflict, writing articles of dubious intent. That fact that Gonzalo had gone to a Claretian boarding school until he was sixteen was a point in his favor—not quite a Jesuit university like the one he himself had attended, the one that Javier had already been admitted to for next year, thanks to his patronage—but he'd been expelled for discipline problems. When they first met, Gonzalo was in his last year of law school at the Universidad a Distancia, working part-time jobs as a waiter and warehouse assistant.

He didn't have his father's political affiliations, but Gonzalo was a far-left sympathizer and often attended the meetings of splinter groups. Obviously, although Agustín never showed Lola the report, the boy was not an especially qualified candidate for family membership. At first it wasn't too unpleasant. If his daughter wanted to fall in love and have a little fun with some low-class

kid, he couldn't stop her. He knew Lola; she was like the strong
north wind—tempestuous for a few days but then dying out. He
trusted that she would settle down one day, finish her econom-
ics degree, and tire of deadbeat boyfriends and traveling around
the world. But he was wrong. The Communist's son had slipped
quietly into the family like a wolf in sheep's clothing, refusing to
accept Agustín's help (and thus his control). Before he had time to
realize how wrong he'd been, the old man found himself planning
a lavish wedding.

Searching for a silver lining, he decided to do something with
the wastrel, maybe give Gonzalo an internship and slowly bend
him to his will. Again he was wrong: Right after the wedding,
Gonzalo set up his own firm and refused any help or counsel
until a few years ago, when he agreed to occupy the office Agustín
offered him in his building, right next door, at a reduced rent.
Twenty years had gone by and he had two wonderful grandchildren, and Lola seemed moderately satisfied. He had to admit that
Gonzalo was intelligent, accepted only lawsuits he had a chance
of winning, played along when Agustín reached out to him, and
would pretend to go along with things, but in the end the bastard
always managed to slip out of his grasp and carry on his way.

Well, that was all going to end, right here, right now.

At exactly ten o'clock his secretary informed him that Gonzalo was waiting.

"Make him wait ten minutes." Enough to let him stew. "Then
send him in."

Gonzalo had to admit, he'd never understood Cubist art, but
he had no doubt this painting was incredibly valuable—his father-
in-law never bought anything that wasn't. Still, the only thing
this jumble of geometric shapes inspired in him was confusion; it
looked like broken glass. He tried to concentrate on the painting

in order to keep his back turned to the secretary. Once the allotted time had passed, she informed him he could now enter through the imposing solid-wood door. She said it as though granting permission for his entry into the Sancta Sanctorum, and Gonzalo adopted the doleful expression he assumed was expected of him. His father-in-law sat at the far end of the immense office, reading something, a tray with whiskey and water placed strategically to his right. The gray porcelain-tile floor glimmered in the light that streamed in through immense picture windows. *So this is what success looks like,* Gonzalo thought, cowed by the minimalist elegance of the room.

Agustín raised his head and motioned for him to approach but did not stand to shake his hand, nor did he wear a friendly expression. It would have been counterproductive. He'd taken off his jacket, which now hung over the back of his chair, and loosened the knot of his tie. This was his way of saying he had no intention of observing niceties. Gonzalo sat down to his right. He didn't take off his jacket or loosen his tie. He simply took out his pen and a small notebook. Agustín leaned back in his chair and the leather creaked.

"First, I want to say I'm sorry about what happened with your sister."

Liar, Gonzalo thought. *You can't even be bothered to fake it.*

"At any rate, from what I understand, you weren't in contact. Better that way—this whole murder-suicide thing is quite gruesome. We might objectively conclude that your sister was a... *complicated* woman."

What an odd way to say "troublesome," Gonzalo thought. He stared at his father-in-law and felt the urge to ask him what on earth he was talking about. Gonzalo hated this old man as much as the old man despised him, and they both knew it. But they had to stick to the script.

"Can we just concentrate on what we're here for?"

A crease of irritation formed on his father-in-law's brow.

"You've already guessed what my proposition is: that you join my firm as an associate. You could still have a brilliant career."

Gonzalo knew that any colleague in his place would be levitating at the opportunity. Working with Agustín would unquestionably put him on the road to jurisprudential heaven. But none of his colleagues was the man's son-in-law. The sight of his father-in-law sitting across from him, legs splayed, summed up exactly where his life was inexorably headed. All his hard work, the dreams he'd had as a kid at that Claretian boarding school for the underprivileged... He had dreamed of being like his father. And since he never really knew what his father was like, it all came down to the vague ambition of living free, like the lean wolf in Aesop's fable, which they'd had to memorize in Latin at the age of sixteen. He knew better than to interrupt Agustín before the man had finished, and knew that once finished the only answer his father-in-law was prepared to hear was a resounding, unqualified yes. An unconditional surrender. He'd come mentally prepared for this. For twenty seemingly interminable minutes they looked over paperwork. Gonzalo leafed through the dossier vaguely, not really paying attention. He made only a few trivial requests.

"I'd like to keep working with Luisa."

Agustín raised no objections. Things were all rolling smoothly toward their logical conclusion—until Agustín stood, walked around a bit, and returned to the table with the ACASA file.

"What do you think of this? A luxury development: five-star hotel, golf courses, highway access via new roads, private sewage system and electricity grid, its own phone network. Lots of contracts and subcontracts to be negotiated. This will be your first assignment with me. We're talking about millions of euros."

Gonzalo felt a flush rise through his body. He'd never dealt with anything close to this scale of negotiation. Litigating with expropriated landowners, bringing proceedings before the appropriate authorities, providing legal counsel for concessionaires.

"Why me? I'm not up on the documentation; I'd have to study it all in quite some detail."

Agustín nodded impatiently. He'd already foreseen this.

"Did you know that when I was younger I used to run marathons? That's right. I'd spend months training, eating right, studying the course and potential rivals. I never left anything to chance. And yet my most important race was a disaster, because of one stupid detail: The day before the race I went for an easy jog along the boardwalk to loosen up my muscles. I didn't realize that a little sand got into my shoe, and a tiny pebble got stuck in the insole. The day of the race, when I started running, I could feel it but didn't give it much thought; I assumed it would pass, eventually disappear. But it didn't. Mile after mile that tiny pebble in my shoe grew larger and larger, torturing me; it felt like a shard of glass. In the end I had to stop and take off my shoe and sock. I lost my stride and precious time. It was a failure I've never forgotten."

"I'm not sure I follow you."

Agustín González showed him the blueprints for the development and pointed out a spot in the center. Gonzalo looked at his father-in-law. Suddenly he understood why he'd been so conciliatory with the merger.

"My family's property is in the affected area. That's the stone in your shoe."

"Precisely. And it could bring the whole project down."

"But that property doesn't belong to me. It's my mother's."

"Only fifty percent of it. The other fifty is split between you and your sister. Now that she's dead, since she had no will, her twenty-five goes to your mother. That's seventy-five for her and twenty-five for you."

"I can see you've studied this."

"Never leave anything to chance. That piece of property is holding up the entire deal. But now we can concentrate on your mother. Try to convince her, we can offer her a good price on a house that's worth nothing. Enough for you to be able to afford a luxury nursing home for her in Marbella, if that's what she wants."

Get as indignant as you want—won't change a thing. This is what his father-in-law's expression said. Gonzalo squirmed anxiously; he took off his glasses and his green eyes became small dots buried in folds of flesh, like marbles in a hole in the ground.

"That still leaves my twenty-five percent."

Agustín waved a hand, as though shooing away a tiresome fly.

"Associate your firm with mine and you take on the ACASA case. The two go hand in hand. If I don't get one hundred percent of this property, there's no deal. We've got a lot at stake, and you more than I. Take the file home, study the documents, think about it, and give me a call. I'll expect your answer tonight."

"Even if you do get my share, my mother will never sell; there's no way. That land means everything to her."

Agustín González gave a caustic little laugh.

"Oh, she will, I assure you."

A large pastel seascape took up one entire wall of the nursing home lobby. It was of a ship with three beautiful masts, attacking the rough waves, its keel rising above the choppy foam. Alcázar smiled. His wife, Cecilia, would have gotten queasy just looking at it; she'd have thrown up on a little rowboat in the Ciutadella Park lagoon. Thinking of her, Alcázar was moved. He could picture Cecilia, bent over double and clutching her stomach, white as a sheet, saying with characteristic Andalusian wit that water was for frogs and fish.

Through the large shuttered window, he caught sight of Esperanza's stooped silhouette. Or should he say Caterina Orlovska's silhouette? He was surprised at her seeming vitality, given her age. Cecilia would never have had that much energy at the end. Esperanza was made of sterner stuff. He went out through a side door and approached, coming close to her face to give her time to recognize him. The old woman raised her head like a mole, almost sniffing him before he was close enough to identify. It wasn't easy: In addition to the fact that Esperanza was now almost blind, thirty-five years had passed and they'd both changed a lot.

"Hello, Caterina."

Esperanza hadn't heard anyone use her real name for ages, and the sound of it now made her start.

"Who are you?"

"A long time ago, when we were both a little younger, I wore a toupee. Maybe that's why you don't recognize me. I'm Alberto Alcázar. We met in 1967: I was in charge of the investigation into Elías's disappearance. I saw you at Laura's funeral."

Alcázar let his words sink slowly into Esperanza's brain. This was the key he needed to open the door to her memory and slip in through the crack. Instinctively, the old lady covered her spit-covered lips with a tattered handkerchief she clutched in one hand, no doubt to dab at the constant streaming from her right eye.

"You probably know that your daughter and I worked together these past few years."

Esperanza shook her head, in a gesture that looked more like an involuntary muscle spasm than a conscious response.

"I have nothing to say to you. Leave."

Alcázar brought his lower lip over his mustache. There were only twenty years between them: Esperanza was nearing the end of the road, and he'd begun the final descent. Maybe that was why he felt sorrow, sitting down beside this old lady and recalling a woman who'd been so full of fire at fifty in 1967 that she'd spat in his face and called him a murderer in front of his subordinates. Alcázar was another man then, only thirty years old, and felt the need to prove so many things that he'd slapped her and had her taken to jail. Neither of them had forgotten the slap, or what happened the night of San Juan, the night Elías Gil disappeared.

"It would be absurd for me to ask forgiveness at this stage, don't you think? Newer sins, graver sins, have buried the old ones. But I see you're still a woman to be reckoned with, as you were back then."

Esperanza persisted in her stubborn silence. She tried to use her walker to get away, heading for the front of the garden, but she moved so slowly that Alcázar could keep up without even trying, walking beside her, hands in his pockets, staring at her all the while.

"I didn't see you shed a single tear at your daughter's funeral. Sort of makes you a heartless mother, don't you think?"

She whipped around to face him in fury, a fury that could have broken her feeble wrinkled neck. A lock of hair split her face in two.

"A daughter who vilifies her father's memory and betrays her own flesh and blood by working with the officer who killed him doesn't deserve to be called a daughter. The murderer of her own father!" Esperanza's face contorted in rage and hatred so deep that it seemed impossible for her tiny ailing body to contain it. But Alcázar was not moved, nor did he lose his cool.

"We're alone here, no one can hear us, so no need for you to keep playing mother courage or the wronged wife in pursuit of justice. Not with me, Caterina. Laura knew the truth, that was why she came to me after so long, and that's why she asked me to accept her into my unit. And I did, for the same reasons you decided that she was dead to you. You were never fair, or brave, no matter what those in search of a hero or a godless saint might say. The truth, the only truth, is that he disappeared. And we both know why."

"No! You murdered him! You shot him in the back and threw his body in the lake that night!"

Alcázar took out a newspaper clipping dated a few weeks earlier.

"Can you read this yourself, or shall I read it to you? 'The Ministry of Development has resolved to shut down what was once Cal Guardia substation. Built in the forties, the station is

powered by a dam which, according to reports compiled by specialists, has sustained serious structural damage, requiring that
it be drained before demolition. Known informally as "the lake,"
the reservoir is a threat to both adjacent agricultural areas and the
area's own ecosystems. Environmental groups are opposed to the
project, arguing that technical pronouncements are simply excuses
to cover up the real reason for the station's closure: the development plans of a major business consortium that has set its sights
on rezoning the area.' That's why you're refusing so stubbornly to
sell your land to Agustín González, isn't it? It's got nothing to do
with the old house or family memories or that ridiculous empty
grave where your gullible son takes you every Sunday to lay flowers. You don't want the lake to be drained because you know
there's nothing at the bottom of it. And when that's proved, how
will you keep feeding the lie you've lived with all these years?
You'd rather remain in the dark than be proved wrong. Gonzalo
doesn't know a thing, does he? He doesn't have a clue what happened that night. He was just a five-year-old boy and believed
everything you told him."

Esperanza rocked back and was on the verge of losing her balance. Alcázar helped steady her; she tried to shake him off, but the
inspector wouldn't let go until she was sitting on a bench among
the cypress trees. Behind them, the sea purred like a sleepy cat.
Soon night would fall, but you could still hear children laughing
on the beach and the cry of seagulls flying up in the cloudless sky.
Alcázar took an envelope from his pocket bearing the Agustín and
Associates logo and placed it carefully in her hands.

"Sign this bill of sale, Esperanza. Sign it and you can keep being
what you've wanted to be all these years: the hero's widow, guardian
of dreams in a world you invented to keep from losing your mind.
Or don't sign, and become Caterina Orlovska again, but in that
case, your son will discover the truth, I give you my word."

When Alcázar walked off he didn't dare turn to look back. He felt despicable and vile, and thought that wherever Cecilia was watching him from, she'd be doing it full of sadness and disappointment. He could hear her rebuke, through the crashing waves of the motionless seascape in the lobby: How can you live with yourself, Alberto? And he replied that he had no choice but to behave like what he was. Being faithful to himself was all he could do, now that she'd left him and he was alone.

5

Patricia sat at the edge of the pool, her legs dangling in the water, feet swishing to create gentle waves that rippled out in expanding circles. She stared at the tile bottom, transfixed by the sun's sparkling reflection. Javier watched for a moment from the kitchen window without Patricia realizing. He adored his kid sister, her tiny freckled nose and hair that changed color—from golden blond to brown—depending on the light. She was a know-it-all and a daddy's girl, spoiled and sometimes capricious, but also completely without guile. He knew she missed him, that she admired him and was hurt when he blew her off, and sometimes Javier felt bad for not giving her more attention.

But he wasn't always willing to deal with her endless questions. Patricia's insatiable and often absurd curiosity was enough to drive anyone crazy. A few days earlier he'd caught her smearing his shaving cream all over her face, razor in hand. Rather than get upset, Javier burst out laughing and then, delighted, spent twenty long minutes explaining to her the intricacies of shaving. He couldn't remember having laughed so hard in months. But in general he tried to avoid her.

Though he would never admit it, Javier was jealous of his sister, of the ease with which she basked in her father's affections, of the long and dogged conversations she and Gonzalo had and the patience and pampering he lavished on her. He could have tried to console himself, thinking that as Patricia grew, their bond would break—his sister would enter a very different world and their father would sink into perplexity and isolation without knowing how to handle the change. But this didn't make him feel any better. He'd never had the sort of closeness with his father that she did, never seemed to merit anything more than cold distance, and at times he glimpsed in his father's expression a look of surprise. It was as if rather than consider Javier his son, Gonzalo saw him as a strange creature who had furtively slipped into his life. He was convinced that his father didn't love him, had never loved him, and he couldn't understand why. It was as though Gonzalo felt uneasy whenever Javier was around and found little ways of letting him know. He never scolded him but made his displeasure clear in his silences. That was what Javier hated the most, his father's constant silence.

He'd always tried to live up to Gonzalo's expectations, but it was exhausting, knowing that every step he took was being scrutinized, put to some sort of never-ending test: the way he examined his grades with arched brow, asked stupid questions about friends and girls, surreptitiously sniffed Javier's clothes and breath when he got home Saturday nights. Javier even suspected that his father had been rummaging through his stuff, though he'd taken care not to leave any tracks. Things were in slightly the wrong place— some clothes moved, a book on the wrong shelf. Javier smiled maliciously: maybe he was expecting to find notebooks full of porn, women with huge silicone tits, contortionists in some hard-core circus, a baggie full of drugs and syringes, or wads of cash from dubious sources. It would all be so much simpler if his father simply sat down and talked to him, but he never said a word. He preferred to keep quiet, avoid facing up to the truth.

Javier glanced up and saw his sister standing in the doorway. She hadn't dried her feet and left a trail of water on the floor behind her.

"What's up?"

"There's a black man outside, looking into the backyard."

Javier went out to see. From the gate he saw the "black man"—a young guy, more or less his age, walking down the street, a linen jacket over his shoulder, one hand in his pocket. There was nothing remotely suspicious about him.

"Just someone going for a walk, looking around," he said, and went back inside. And then, in horror, he saw what Patricia was holding.

"Give me that! Right now!"

For several seconds Patricia gripped the .38. It was old and rusty but still worked. Javier had tested it, firing the revolver out in the country. Luckily, he'd emptied the drum. He snatched it out of her hands.

"How did you find this?"

"I saw you hide it in the garage."

Evidently he hadn't hidden it very well. If Patricia had found it, anyone could.

"Personally, I don't care, but Papá will be really mad if he finds out you have that," his sister said, staring at him with an intensity atypical of a ten-year-old girl. Javier got a sudden glimpse of something, a shrewdness peeking through the cracks in her childhood.

"There's no reason for him to find out if you don't tell him and promise me you'll never touch it again."

Patricia now sat in the swivel chair in the living room. She was pushing off and spinning in circles, feet held up in the air. Javier stopped the chair midspin, so brusquely that Patricia's body was hurled forward. Her cheeks were flushed and she looked a little dizzy.

"Promise me!"

"You don't have to shout at me."

"I'm not shouting at you."

"Yes you are, and I know why you're mad all the time, too."

Javier felt his cheeks burn. "What is it you think you know?"

"What you do. And how you always cry after. It doesn't bother me. You should tell Papá."

Javier gave his sister a defiant stare. "You don't know shit."

Patricia was unfazed. "I know what I know."

He became furious, grabbing her tightly by the shoulders.

"You're hurting me."

"You think this hurts? Do you know what happens when you grow up?"

His sister shook her head, her face frightened.

"You learn about real pain."

"I'm telling Papá when he gets home."

Javier raised his hand, but before letting it come down across his sister's face, he contained his rage.

"No, you're not. Promise me. Because if you do, I'm going to leave and you'll never see me again."

Patricia noted with relief that her brother's hand had relaxed once more.

"If you promise you'll take me with you, I promise I won't say anything. Please don't leave me alone here ever, ever, ever."

Javier accepted his sister's embrace, disconcerted. She'd thrown her arms so tightly around his waist that it was like she was trying to weld herself to him. He swallowed hard, touched, sad, and frightened. Javier stroked his sister's wet hair and kissed the top of her head.

"I promise; we'll always be together."

He'd arranged to have lunch with his mother. Lola's travel agency was in the Gracia district, on a street with hardly any direct sunlight, even in the summer. The place wasn't big, but she didn't have to pay rent on it, and his mother, ever the pragmatist, had valued this above all else. The street got very little traffic and the agency was on the first floor, with no front window, just a metal plaque on the front that was barely noticeable to passersby. Javier knew his mother didn't need the business, and that it wasn't particularly successful. His grandfather Agustín made sure they had everything they needed, but the agency was a way for her to stay busy and to believe she was still an independent woman.

Two enormous sculptures stood guard on either side of the door—expressionless ebony nudes, a man and woman. The man's erect phallus brushed against Javier's knee; the woman's vulva had been sculpted in such painstaking detail that customers were sometimes offended by the sight of her. Javier stroked her vagina with his middle finger, pretending to see her shudder in pleasure as the big-dick male cursed him from stony immortality, burning with jealousy.

He heard his mother's voice through the stairwell; she was upstairs. There must have been someone with her—she laughed in that fake, drawn-out way only in the presence of people she didn't know very well. Javier climbed the narrow spiral staircase and negotiated a path through the piles of travel brochures. His mother stood leaning against the wall with her arms crossed, clearly amused by something. Javier followed her gaze to a guy wearing a sorcerer's mask, clowning around. Suddenly aware of Javier's presence, the clown stopped and took off his mask. Lola froze and turned to the stairs.

"Javier! What are you doing here? We weren't supposed to meet until later."

Lola touched a hand to her hair, voice trembling a bit, as though caught in a compromising position. The awkwardness in the air intensified as she did up a button on her blouse, which had been revealing more cleavage than necessary. Javier didn't shift his gaze from the pretend sorcerer. Instead, with his eyes, he asked: *What should I make of this?*

"You know Carlos, don't you? He's going to be leading our August tour of Burkina Faso." His mother walked over to the young man and took the mask from him without knowing, suddenly, what to do with it.

Javier nodded. Of course he knew Carlos. His mother had clearly forgotten he'd been the one to introduce them. Five or six years older than Javier, Carlos was studying humanities at the university and repeating his senior year. They'd met a few months earlier at a bar and struck up a friendship. He was looking for a summer job and had worked as a guide in the past, leading tours through Africa, so Javier thought it would be a good idea to introduce him to his mother; she hired him on the spot. Carlos's résumé was better than a NASA candidate's. No doubt half of the information on it was fake, but it hadn't mattered to his mother. Carlos was a natural Don Juan: long blond Nordic hair with messy curls, a razor-sharp goatee with hints of red in it, Crocodile Dundee–style necklace with fake sharks' teeth, and macramé bracelets that gave him a sort of retro air. He dressed with calculated carelessness: stone-washed jeans showed off his attributes—a great ass and a dick that could compete with the statue downstairs—scuffed-up hiking boots, and a Greenpeace T-shirt. A professional beefcake, fully aware of his allure and only too happy to exploit it.

"Teaching my mother a few shamanic rituals?"

"We were just fooling around, chilling out." His voice was deep but friendly; he could have been a radio announcer or soap-opera star. To top it all off, he had perfect teeth. Though his mouth smiled at Javier, his almond-shaped eyes did not. He acted friendly because Lola was present, but the concessions he was willing to make to a wary son had their limits, those eyes said. They weighed each other up in silence for a few seconds and the atmosphere grew tense, until Carlos relaxed his shoulders. Javier picked up on the mockery in the way Carlos shook his hand when they said goodbye.

"See you around."

Lola walked him out, and Javier followed them downstairs in time to see the friendly kiss on the cheek they exchanged.

"Is it me, or were you a bit hostile just now?" his mother asked once they were alone in the shop. She was nervous and upset.

"Are you into that guy?"

She glanced at her son with undisguised alarm. "What kind of a question is that?"

"The kind it sounds like."

His mother planted herself firmly before him, hands on hips, conjuring up all the authority she could muster, but it still wasn't very convincing.

"What kind of nonsense is that? I'm offended."

"Listen to me, Mamá. This guy's no good for you. I know what I'm talking about."

Lola barked out a sharp laugh much different from the one Javier had heard a few minutes earlier. It sounded like a dry stick being snapped in two.

"Well, I see Mr. Expert has spoken. In the first place, I don't even know why we're having this conversation; Carlos is going to work for us, and that's all. And in the second place, what is it you think you know? You have a very excitable imagination. I don't need him to be 'good for me,' I just need him to do his job, and I assure you he can do it well."

Javier shrugged. "All I'm saying is be careful with him."

Lola slung her purse over her shoulder and jingled the shop keys in her hand.

"I dislike the tone of this conversation with my seventeen-year-old son, so let's go to lunch and forget about it. Agreed?"

"I'm almost eighteen." *And I have a gun*, he added silently.

"I don't care if you're forty, Javier," Lola retorted impatiently.

They walked down to Plaza del Reloj, a square with a clock tower at the center, and found a spot at a restaurant there. Lola sat with her back rigid and focused her attention on a flock of pigeons fighting over crumbs at one of the tables outside. She was uncomfortable at the erroneous impression her son had formed of what he'd seen. But now she wondered how she herself should interpret it.

What did she think she was doing with Carlos, a boy hardly older than her son? Maybe it was a childish urge to prove she was up to snuff, that she wasn't just an attractive older woman or Carlos's boss but a woman who deserved his attentions. An innocent slip-up on her part, trivial. She had no intention of sleeping with her son's friend. It would have been too predictable—cliché, and pathetic at that. Forty-something woman with young stud. She'd never do that. Would she?

It wasn't the first time something like this had happened. Lola looked at her son. She loved Gonzalo, there was no doubt about it. But she'd loved him eighteen years ago, too, perhaps more than she did now, or at least more passionately. And yet she'd crossed the red line she herself had drawn: You can fantasize about the life you want, but this is the one you've got, the one you chose and the one you have to fight for. She broke the rule and had an affair that lasted several months, with an old friend from the university, one of those men who reappear in your life to convince you that you lost out on something in the past but are still in time to get it back. He didn't mean much to her really, but he did get her pregnant. This was her secret and she was the one weighed down by the burden of it. She could have left Gonzalo at the time, could have taken another path, but she didn't dare to, or perhaps want to. It didn't make much difference either way. All these years she'd tried to convince herself that she'd made the right decision. Then Patricia came along. Her birth was like a huge rock blocking Lola's escape route. There was no turning back, but she couldn't help feeling that she'd lived a bottled-up life since her marriage. Without realizing it, she'd slowly given up more and more parts of herself in the name of her family, and little cracks were appearing once more, barely noticeable fissures in her sense of security. Who was this other woman inside her, always trying to undermine her?

"Why did you ask me to lunch?" Javier asked, saving her from her swirling contradictory thoughts.

"We need to talk about your father. He's going to need your help, Javier. Not just because of what he's been through, it's more complicated than that: his sister's death, his firm's merger, the new house... and quite honestly, you don't make it easy on him."

Javier held his mother's look, his face blank. He didn't want her to see anything but indifference.

"What about you? Do you make it easy on him?"

Lola was shocked. She moved her lips, uncrossed and recrossed her legs under the table, and tried to focus her gaze on the little bouquet of violets in a vase on their table. The flowers were wilting, as were those on other tables: No one watered them or changed the dirty water in which floated blue and white petals that would soon be thrown in the trash.

"Your father and I share a life together. It's a road, and sometimes it's easy to keep moving forward and other times you feel stuck. But we work out our differences because we love each other."

"By pretending, keeping quiet. That's what I see at home. Is that what loving someone means? That you lie? Is that the way to nourish love?"

Lola's face tightened the way it did after she applied firming creams each night, becoming a solid mask. Her son had no idea what he was talking about. Ignorance is always outspoken, and he believed in the arrogant power of words. He put too much stock in them, not realizing that words can be like broken glass—you can't force someone to walk over them in bare feet.

"You have no right to speak to me that way."

Javier simply moved his spaghetti around on the plate in front of him and took small sips of mineral water. His mother stared insistently at him. She'd hardly even tasted her tortellini but was on her second glass of white wine.

"Don't you have anything to say?" she probed, awaiting an apology.

Javier saw himself like the punching bag hanging from a chain in the garage, something there for other people's frustrations to be taken out on, something to be kicked and punched while it remains silent, doing nothing but lightly sway. He'd seen his father punch that bag furiously after work or an argument with his mother. When he was done, the surface of the green bag was smooth and tight, no trace of his knuckles, as though nothing had happened. His father would go take a shower, dress as meticulously as ever, and sit down at the table with the grave demeanor of a Lutheran pastor. This was what his family was like. He'd grown up amid strangers who struggled to give the impression that everything was under control yet couldn't help giving themselves away by their gestures. It was sick, to have let himself fall into their trap, to become one of them, full of secrets and lies and uncomfortable silences.

He leaned back in his seat and slowly shook his head, imagining what would happen at home if he told them what he'd done, or worse: what he was. His father would strut around, heavy on the heels, shoes squeaking, then stare at him for a few minutes and perhaps say something awful, but he'd do it in such a civilized way that the abject cruelty of his proclamation would be almost imperceptible. And his mother would be speechless, eyes flitting desperately from one side to the other. She might cry but would quickly recover, hold him in her arms, kiss his hair, and call him all the baby names she still liked to use because it scared her to think that her little boy now had pubic hair, and for a few days she'd bring him breakfast in bed. And then at night Javier would have to cover Patricia's ears so she couldn't hear the terrible things their parents said to each other—the never-ending reproaches, the refusal to accept responsibility, blaming each other for everything. What could he possibly gain? Some sort of absolution that was no longer possible and that perhaps he no longer even wanted? Who were they to judge him?

"You're right, Mamá. I'm sorry. I shouldn't have spoken like that. I'll make things right, I'll be nice to Papá."

Lola observed her son mistrustfully. "Promise?"

Javier watched a few gray pigeons fighting over crumbs under a table. They pecked furiously at one another, fluttering their wings and leaving in the air a cloud of broken feathers. He gave his mother a beatific smile, the best one he could manage. In their family, everyone made promises they didn't keep. What difference did one more make?

"Of course. I promise."

A buzz notified him of an incoming text on his phone: *See you tonight, same place? I need your help.*

Javier remained pensive. He typed a quick reply: *I don't want to see you again. I thought I made that clear.*

His finger froze before hitting Send. He thought better of it and rewrote the message, in a swirl of emotions that included both desire and defeat: *I hope you're not going to stand me up this time.*

He hit Send and then erased the message from his in-box before he had time to regret it.

His mother looked on curiously. "Girlfriend?"

Javier clenched his fists beneath the table. What's the point of having eyes? People were so blind it would make no difference if they had buttons sewn on instead, covering the holes left by their empty expressions.

"Something like that, yeah. Can you lend me some cash?"

Lola opened her wallet and handed him three folded bills.

"I don't think we need to mention this to your father."

Javier glanced down at the crisp notes before tucking them into his wallet.

"Are you referring to the money, this conversation, or what happened at the agency?"

Lola bore the weight of her son's caustic expression. Gonzalo might not be his real father, but Javier had sure inherited his character.

From the top of the road you could see, in the distance, an enormous crater being excavated by diggers. Close to the dam, trucks moved back and forth along the edge of the lake, enveloped in a thick cloud of dirt and lime dust. Gonzalo got out of his car and made his way down the stony slope, the blueprint his father-in-law had given him in hand. He'd been surprised at his mother's sudden change of heart. When he went to see her, to lay out Agustín's proposal, Gonzalo had been prepared for a long and fruitless argument, but astonishingly she'd hardly put up a fight and actually seemed eager to close the deal quickly. He got the impression she was expecting what he was going to say and had already made her decision.

The wooden bridge over the creek was still there. He wondered if its old planks would still take his weight but decided not to test it. It would have pained him to see how much heavier adults are than children, for reasons that had nothing to do with their girth. Perhaps his and Laura's names were still carved in the wooden handrail; it would be good, he thought, to see that some things don't change despite neglect. The house looked trapped between the rugged mountain and a ravine, a couple of steep paths being the only way down. Gonzalo hesitated, as though trying to convince himself not to stop and simply to return to his car, but at the last minute he took the key from his pocket and unlocked the gate.

There was hardly a trace of the old stone road leading to the main entrance, and the flowerbeds his mother once doted on were out of control, nothing manicured about them. The climbing rosebushes were like escapees that had made a break for it, no stakes to hold them back and hopelessly covered in aphids. The roses themselves looked drawn and haggard, giving the place the joyless air of an abandoned cemetery. The façade of the house itself showed perilous cracks, though it still emanated a sort of dignity alien to the atmosphere of abandonment surrounding it. This house had always been destined to be a monument to oblivion.

The inside was demolished. There was broken furniture throughout the living room; someone had kicked down the doors and splinters still clung to the hinges. In one corner stood a chest of drawers, miraculously intact, enshrouded in thick spiderwebs. A field mouse darted in and out among fossilized flowers, gnawing on a stalk. Its glassy little eyes observed Gonzalo, seeming to ask what he was doing there. On a cement shelf sat an old radio, its innards smashed. He pushed a button that made a click, which rang out in the silence like echoes of the old songs he and his mother sometimes sang while gazing out the window, when she was doing well. *"And I searched your faded letters, for an I-love-you, my sweet..."* Songs from other times. He opened a drawer and a lizard scurried to the back. Among the disintegrating rags that had once been table linens, he found an old green school notebook, multiplication tables printed on the back. Gonzalo wiped the dust and shook it out. *Five times one is five, five times two is ten, five times three is fifteen...* He smiled, recalling the students' singsong voices as they chanted in unison, their teacher directing them, ruler in hand like a conductor. Two-seater desks with an inkwell in the middle, maps of all the rivers in Spain, the alphabet—written in gothic letters—hanging on the wall. Days and years of tedium, watching the rain through a window as priests spoke of Saint Paul, the Scholastics, and the theories of Copernicus, and Gonzalo dreamed of going home for the summer and spending time at the lake, swimming with Laura in its murky waters. And each June, when he returned with his old bedroll, came the realization that they'd grown a little more distant. He still blushed, recalling his shock at discovering that his sister had grown breasts. Firm white breasts with pink nipples. And her look of shame at feeling herself observed. After that she no longer swam naked with him. That's what becoming an adult meant: hiding from others.

He walked outside and circled the house. Rotting leaves had piled up along the edges of the path. Out back, part of the old shed was still standing. Peeking through its barnlike door, which no longer closed properly, he felt his father's presence carried in on the wind and envisioned him working on the old Renault, leaning over the open hood with his sleeves rolled up, checking spark plugs or pistons or whatever it was he checked with a rag and metal rod, Gonzalo behind him, pint-sized and eagerly awaiting instructions, excited to hand him a monkey wrench or a hammer he could barely even hold.

He pushed the door and it gave way with no resistance, as though it had been awaiting his return. The roof was full of holes and the air inside had a stale, closed-in smell. Gonzalo was confronted by disarray impossible to put right. He slid a hand along the walls as though trying to conjure faded memories by touch: hours spent chatting quietly with his father so as not to awaken his mother during siesta time, the smell of the cheap cigars he smoked, afternoons when his father sat in a chair typing feverishly on the old Densmore. Memory is a strange thing: You forget crucial incidents and remember insignificant details. He recalled the old typewriter perfectly, the same one as in his dream: it was an 1896 model but still worked perfectly, black and gold with round ivory keys whose letters had faded. The carriage return still worked, and when you got to the end of a line it would ding like a bicycle bell. The rods that stamped the letters fanned out in a semicircle, and there was no way to change case or font. You needed strong fingers to press hard enough to move them. Slowly, one after the other, the letters formed words, and the words, sentences. Gonzalo wondered where all of those words had gone, what their fate had been. What stories they told.

"What do you want to be when you grow up, Gonzalo?" his father once asked.

"I don't want to grow up. I want to be your son forever," he'd replied, as though it were a matter of remaining five for the rest of his life.

He walked out of the shed and circled around the back. An old plot now covered in dense brush overlooked the valley. From among the weeds emerged a crooked grave—no cross, no marker—identifiable only by the raised mound of compact earth with poppies growing out of it and hornets buzzing all around. Gonzalo had agreed to dig it because his mother had asked him to, agreed also to bury a gray suit in place of the body that never surfaced. It was the suit his father had worn the day his parents were married. For a long time, his mother had thought he'd return, that one day he would again put on the suit she'd so carefully saved all those years, that everything would be the same as before. She dreamed of a *before* belonging solely to the two of them—not to the world, or to their children, or to legend. Their private world. And yet now she was willing to surrender that hope to the teeth of an excavator. Why?

Near the grave stood a fig tree. He'd once hung an old tire on a rope from one of the branches. Gonzalo remembered swinging on it, gazing out at the valley while on vacation from school, shortly before being expelled at age sixteen. The priest who taught religion had been telling them about Judas Iscariot and his tragic end. Gonzalo paid almost no attention to the traitor's tale, he was interested only in finding out if Judas was hanged from an olive tree or a fig, cared only about discovering what type of tree had borne the weight of his cowardice. Suicide was for cowards, he thought, that summer long ago. Now he wasn't so sure. Love proves how futile our preconceptions are.

The sky was clear, but dotted with clouds at the horizon, as it always had been. Gonzalo sat with his back against the tree trunk and contemplated a landscape that had once belonged to both him and his sister. It felt strange to be sitting there, as he often had, after so long. Even in those days he was the quiet one and Laura talked nonstop, about anything and everything. His sister actually wondered at one point if he might be a bit slow, and although it didn't make her love him any less, she did worry about his silences, about the way he was always so lost in his own world. When he was back from boarding school, she would watch him as though fearing that if he kept holding everything in, he might explode.

When they were kids, it often snowed in wintertime. Laura would jump out of their bedroom window and dive headfirst into mounds of fluffy snow, while he chose to pack it tight, making animals and other things. From early in the morning he'd pack the snow that had fallen in the night, sculpting amazing ephemeral shapes. By that time, they were already very different, and their love for each other was no longer enough to conceal their differences. Gonzalo was the patient one, the keen one; Laura would destroy his snow shapes just to watch him turn red in fury. Thinking back to those cruel games made him smile. Laura could never sit still and thought he was too serious, too concerned about the lives of others and not concerned enough about his own. She was right: Gonzalo was always too prudent for his age, a withdrawn boy with big protruding ears who scolded his sister for going out with the older boys in town.

He missed her. Not the woman she later became but his big sister, the one who held his hand and took him on outings to the lake when he was five years old and scared as a sparrow. Their distance had eventually destroyed them, and often when he visited his mother at the nursing home, he would sit with her and ask why she was so bitter, why she never made her peace. But his mother only stared at him, and in her look he saw no remorse, no guilt. Only profound hatred. And now it was too late. There was no point settling a score with someone who was no longer alive to keep tally, but Esperanza was still vehement in her hatred for Laura. All because of the damned article his sister had written about their father.

He wished Laura had never written it. Words are nothing but rough sketches that never truly convey reality, but his sister couldn't see that. She accumulated them, jotted them down, looked them up, and memorized their meanings; she was moved by the power of expressions but didn't realize that, often, they die of insignificance. Her words were too lofty, she expected too much of them, was blinded by their sound yet didn't hear the booming silence they left in their wake. Things that truly matter don't need to be spoken to be true, and sometimes silence is the only truth possible. He and his mother could have forgotten the words she wrote, overlooked the way she slandered Elías; they could have erased her words from memory or burned them. But how to quench the fire seething inside? What to do with the ashes if, despite all attempts to scatter them, the wind kept bringing them back and piling them up at the door?

"I shouldn't have come back," he murmured. Perhaps his father-in-law was right and it was best to let the bulldozers raze the place. Memories are always flawed when held up to the cold light of reality. It made no sense to insist on returning to places from the past, even when they were still standing. It was always disappointing. What's gone can never return. He'd like to believe that opening the doors and plugging the leaks would be all it took for everything to return to the way it was: remodel the house, move back as he'd dreamed of doing years ago, before he surrendered to the life that Lola and her father demanded. But how to rebuild the memories of people—his father, his mother, his sister, even himself? How did that all fit in? Still, Gonzalo was chained to this place forever, like the house dog in the fable he'd been forced to memorize as a boy. Aesop was right: It doesn't matter how long the chain is, there comes a time when you feel its restraint.

He closed his eyes, as he had when Laura made him play hide-and-seek and then hid close enough to be easily found, because being alone scared him. *Where am I?* Far away, Laura, he thought, you're so far away. Nothing is wholly true, nothing is wholly false. Beneath the surface lies the evidence, and beneath one piece of evidence lies another. Gonzalo wondered what role his sister played in reality, what part he himself did, what part the house and the past. Together they formed a whole; split into disparate particles they were nothing but broken dreams.

He made his way slowly up to the road. Before climbing back into the car, he took one last look at the grounds surrounding his old home. From where Gonzalo stood he could not see the grave behind the shed, or what its ruins contained. A cloud of construction dust at the lake rose up from the valley like an erupting volcano.

6

The noise of the propeller engine was deafening. Half a dozen men on either side of the plane's wings pushed while the pilot executed a 180-degree turn on the frozen runway. Snow whirled all around. It must be a 1918 French SPAD XIII, Elías deduced. He would have recognized it just by the sound of the turbine. An old model, not very efficient compared to English Sopwith Camels or German Fokkers, but a beautiful machine nonetheless. One day he'd seen a biplane like that flying low over the gray skies of Mieres. The mining company's postal service had bought a few of them after the Great War, and once a month a plane came into view amid the mine shaft towers, bringing packages and large sacks, landing at the small airfield behind the mining complex.

His father and the others would stop what they were doing for a few minutes and wave their caps in the air, cheering the low-flying pilot, who dipped his wings in response. Little kids began running after the plane the moment it touched down, as if it was a magical dragon that had landed on the soot-blackened roofs of their shacks. Everyone admired the pilot Elías never got to meet, not because he brought their wages but because what a miner admires most is someone who spends his time so far above ground. Elías, too, had dreamed of being one of those men exploring the clouds, had dreamed of seeing the world from up high, soaring through columns of smoke and hearing the buzz of the blast holes being drilled in the mountain as nothing but a sound in the distance. That was why he'd decided to study engineering. Not to build bridges—which is what he ended up doing—but to be suspended in the air.

"Move!"

A rifle butt to the kidneys made him stumble against the truck's running board. Elías climbed into the back—no canvas over the top—and sat down in an empty spot. He turned his head to look at the airfield. The SPAD took off hesitantly, like a bird forced from the nest for the first time, and then evened out and gained elevation, disappearing above the airfield's powerful reflective lights. Elías's dreams and his childhood seemed as far off as this plane disappearing into the Moscow night.

"Where are they taking us?" he said nervously to the woman who'd been made to sit next to him. Elías looked sideways at her, making room on the bench even though the truck bed was already packed and guards continued to force on more and more men, women, and even a few children. The woman was clenching her hands so tightly her knuckles were white. She had a schoolteacher air about her, and he imagined her being strict with the unruly children, sweet to the more diligent ones. Here, however, her composure had vanished.

It was pointless to wonder what he was doing there, what any of them was doing there. Most of those in the military truck wore the same uncertain expression: a mix of fear and incredulity. No one said a word. After Elías had signed his declaration, he'd been told they were sending him straight to the border, for "counterrevolutionary and anti-Bolshevik activities."

He wondered what had happened to Michael and his sidekick Martin. And Claude. As strange as it might seem, he bore them no ill will. He was simply overcome by profound sadness. After all, Elías had signed his name to a string of lies in exchange for a glass of water, but he didn't have to bear the guilt of having betrayed or slandered anyone but himself. They, on the other hand, had been beaten perhaps for days, had been forced to denounce him, and would have to bear the weight of that for the rest of their lives. How could they ever believe in a cause again? He'd have liked to see them one last time, to look them in the eye, say goodbye with a hug—perhaps not a warm or healing embrace, but enough to let them live their lives out in peace.

The idea of being deported almost cheered him. And yet Elías realized that something didn't add up, as he observed the stricken faces of the despairing folks all around him and saw the way mothers embraced their children to protect them from the lacerating cold that whipped through the open truck bed. The vehicle started off with a jerk that sent its occupants flying and headed full speed down a road parallel to the Moskva River and into the darkness.

"They're taking us for a nice moonlight ride," an old man with a sarcastic tone announced. "Courtesy of the OGPU."

Igor Stern had no fear. He'd become immune to it at the age of nine, when a unit of Cossacks flayed his father alive, in Sebastopol. For hours he listened to his father's cries as skin was detached from muscle and left hanging in tatters around his legs like an old shirt. One of the Cossacks had poured gasoline over him and then forced Igor to set fire to his own father. He did it unflinchingly and for several minutes stared in fascination as the human torch his father became writhed in the snow, lighting up the night.

After that, everything in life had become much simpler.

The fact that they were going to execute him was nothing out of the ordinary. Stalin himself had quoted Alexander Nevsky as saying, "Whoever comes to us with the sword, will die by the sword. On that Russia stands." Igor had lived his twenty years like a wolf: free and wild, taking by force what fate had denied him. Murder, death, revelry, suffering, love, and hate were all you could hope for. He was no coward, wasn't about to beg for his life the way he'd seen those before him in the firing line do. Some had shat in their pants, their feces leaving a trail in the trampled snow. Had his hands not been tied, Igor himself would have stabbed them with a bayonet. He detested the weak. Sentenced to death—wasn't this simply the human condition?

While awaiting his turn (they shot prisoners in pairs), Igor hummed a song made popular by the great Lyubov Orlova, muse of film and dance. If there was one thing he lamented, it was not having been able to enjoy more of these refined sorts of pleasures. Although, like Lenin, he openly declared that he understood nothing about art, Igor got a special feeling when watching a play or listening to an orchestra. Like a wild animal, he sensed a kind of power that could never be tamed by the expressions of the human soul. Sometimes he mocked his fate, wondering whether he too could have been a leader like Stalin, had he fallen into the hands of the right people rather than a band of mercenaries. What would have happened if he'd had a chance to train the beautiful voice people swore he had? Could he have sung in the Grand Opera of Moscow? Could he perhaps have become Orlova's lover? He could have. But it was easier to think that his singing sounded better in the dead of night, alone like a wolf howling at the beautiful moon whose light now fell on a wall spattered with brains. When it was his turn, he stepped forward. He didn't need to be coaxed with a bayonet, as his companion—a damned Georgian crybaby—had been. Had the scumbag sobbed while raping and killing little girls and women? Igor bet that he had not. He bet he'd acted fierce as a rabid dog then.

"Conduct yourself, faggot, or I'll tear your jugular out myself before these shitbags have time to fire a bullet into your chest," he growled.

How many men had Igor killed? And why? Did it even matter now? Robbery, rape, murder. The scars all over his body were testament to his hundreds of fights, years of prison and correctional facilities that had left his skin covered in tattoos, one for each year he spent there. Igor had never expected a long life, but he did expect a satisfied life. Fuck piety and mercy, fuck God and angels. The present moment was all there was. And his was coming to an end. Why didn't they shoot already? He was tired of listening to this fucking Georgian whimper. It was cold and about to snow again. The squad leader had yet to give the order for his men to aim. Six rifles for two chests: easy odds as long as they had steady hands and didn't close their eyes when they pulled the trigger. Igor glared at them, full of hate. Kids, he thought, rookies who are scared to death.

"My ass is getting cold, comrade!"

The squad leader, a veteran sergeant, fired a scathing look his way and then turned his back, focusing instead on a man in a black raincoat who was showing him a piece of paper. Igor sensed that something strange was going on. He knew what the GULAG officers were like, the deportation police. You had to be very careful with these bastards. They were capable of beating the everloving life out of a reptile like him just to prove they could make him howl in pain. After a few minutes' deliberation, the sergeant in charge ordered the men at ease. A Chechen jailer approached, getting just inches from Igor's face.

"You're one lucky Jew pig. But I'm afraid those you meet from now on will not be."

Igor flashed his rotting teeth. "If I could, I'd rip your tongue out; you know that, don't you?"

The sergeant barked out a maniacal laugh and gave him a ruthless head butt, opening a gash in Igor's brow.

"Get this scum out of here and onto the trucks. Now!"

. . .

Shortly before dawn, after three hours on the road, the truck stopped without warning. They were in the middle of nowhere, surrounded by the dense fog rising up from the riverbanks. On either side rose huge birch forests. Elías thought they had been taken there to be shot, as did many others, who began to stir uneasily and murmur. When the door was thrust open and the guards forced them out, their murmurs turned to screams and fits of hysteria. At one point there came a tremendous uproar. Guards were struggling to make everyone climb down, but people were refusing, clinging to one another and screaming. It was absurd, Elías thought suddenly.

"Maybe we've only been banished from the city," someone whispered. It was illogical reasoning, completely improvised, but it gave them hope. And the most fragile hopes seem ironclad when there's nothing else to cling to. Everyone was forced to line up single file. Other trucks had arrived before them, and more and more headlights appeared from the edges of the forest. Elías noted in shock that there were hundreds of people there. This was a large-scale operation. Slowly the human column grew to several hundred yards long, and then after a signal they began to move like a disciplined army, flanked by armed guards. Soon, railroad tracks came into view, and the lights of a freight car. Steam rose from the locomotive at the front like a snorting thoroughbred. Ironically, people cried out in relief: This sinister train meant that, regardless of what was to come, their journey had not reached the end. It was just beginning.

"To the east," murmured a young man walking with Elías. His arm was in a sling and his face horrifically disfigured from a recent beating.

"Excuse me?"

The man pointed first to the river, then the train tracks and the direction the locomotive was facing. His name was Anatoli and he was a geographer. From Leningrad. The resignation on his face was clear.

"Siberia, maybe Kazakhstan. But we're headed for the steppe."

Through swollen eyelids, Anatoli glanced meaningfully at Elías's heavy coat.

"You'll do well to take good care of that. Believe me, you're going to need it."

Slowly the horizon took on a steely gray tone offset by the long convoy of wooden train cars. Guards filled with a sudden sense of urgency, as though everything had to be done before the day dawned, tried to direct the crowds to the trains. It was a night of different accents, lamentations, excuses, supplications, insults, and threats. But one after another, people fell silent as they were forced through the dark doors assigned them.

Inside the cars, the air was stifling. The floor was covered in rotting straw. Dozens of people crowded against the cars' narrow wooden slats, hungrily ensuring their own access to the cold outside air. Shoved farther in by those entering behind him, Elías was forced toward the back. He wondered how many more were going to be put in this car; there was hardly enough space to move as it was, and it was impossible to avoid the breath of those around him, inches from his face. To the degree possible, he turned his body sideways so that at least his arms could move. Something strange was happening: Though they had less and less room, those at the back of the car had stopped moving, leaving a full third of the space unoccupied.

"Move back or we'll suffocate," he shouted in his tentative Russian.

No one listened. In fits and starts, Elías elbowed his way as best he could to the front of this human wall to see what was going on. Those around him turned away or stared at the floor, frightened; some even chose to back up and be crushed in the crowd.

"What's going on? Why won't you move into this empty space?"

Half a dozen men leaned calmly against the car's wooden walls, some even stood smoking with their legs apart. One had

lain down, stretching out the full length of his body and using a
sack for a pillow.

"Don't go near them. They're common prisoners, murderers, rapists, bad people," an old woman said, seeing the rage on
Elías's face.

One of the men's faces was covered in scars and multiple tattoos. He sat in a squat, toying with a sharp piece of wood he'd
pulled from the carriage wall, sharpening it with a rusty nail. Elías
caught a look of merriment in his eyes; it was as though he found
everyone's fear amusing.

"You need to squeeze together," Elías said firmly. "We have to
share this space."

Igor Stern set his penetrating gaze on Elías. His expression
was one of tremendous viciousness and utter assurance.

"You have to earn your rights here, we don't give them away.
You want more space? Come fight for it," he challenged, as the
other prisoners snickered.

Elías was strong, probably stronger than this threatening man.
But he knew that brute force had nothing to do with reputation in
the world he'd been hurled into. His pride told him that he should
cross the invisible line in the rotten straw, that once he entered the
fantasy kingdom of this small band of prisoners the others would
follow. There were more of them, and what could a few thugs do in
the face of a desperate horde? And yet he didn't move, fearing that
perhaps they would not, in fact, follow. Fear was the only kind of
strength that mattered here. Those who inspired it ruled the world,
always had and always would. A small number of men endowed
with uncommon cruelty controlled the subservient masses.

Through narrowed eyes, Igor weighed up this kid who could
hardly speak Russian. He was good at gauging people. It was
how he'd managed to survive—by picking his battles wisely and
not underestimating his rivals. Others, many others, in fact, had
underestimated their rivals, and this turned out to be a deadly

mistake, even with him. They were dead and Igor was alive. He decided to put the kid's determination to the test.

"I like your coat."

Elías was paralyzed by fear, which only increased as he watched those around him shrink back, crowding together like sheep who sensed wolves about to attack. They turned their faces away in the absurd belief that if they couldn't see the danger, danger couldn't see them. He who was outside the compact mass was a sacrificial lamb. And Elías was alone there.

"Come get it," he said, unaware of his words and lacking the determination to back them up. They had simply spilled forth, from a time in his childhood at the mines when the foreman gave the orders of the day and other boys tried to take Elías's job aboveground pulling trolleys to avoid being sent down the ventilation shafts, which were dangerous and disgusting. Often the foremen and older miners would gather around to cheer as boys fought to stay above the pit; they placed bets and formed a circle to fence Elías in, jeering and encouraging him to fight. He always felt the burden of his fear, and his hatred for violence made him tremble in rage and terror. But he never let anyone take his job.

Igor scratched a gaunt cheek with the sharp end of his improvised awl. He sank his head into his shoulders and let out a giggle that made Elías's whole body shiver. Slowly his laughter grew, until he was bellowing. Igor liked acting, liked the tragedy of life, liked playing roles. Not only did he have a good voice, he'd always been a good actor, donning one mask or another according to the circumstances or his frame of mind. Mother Russia had lost a great actor, he often thought; he was quite a player. He straightened back up, stretching tall like a giant emerging from the depths, and leaned back against the wall, feigning appeasement as he watched Elías. Elías, for his part, realized that he'd misgauged the prisoner. Once erect, Igor was nearly as tall as he was, and judging by the way he maneuvered his sharpened stick, the man knew how to use a knife far better than Elías ever would.

"The little puppy dog wants to cut his teeth. He thinks he's ready for a fight."

Igor's entourage of laughing hyenas feted his joke. They were waiting for him to take the first swing before pouncing, still thankful for their fate. A few hours ago they'd been praying to their mothers—those who had met them—in their jail cells and listening to the terrifying monotony of the firing squad's executions in the prison yard. Those who believed in God prayed; those who did not prayed as well. They spent what they thought were their last moments on earth reflecting on life, some thinking it hadn't been too bad, most simply envisioning a grave enveloping them before the ground froze. And now, a miracle had been worked. They'd been set free like a pack of restless wolves among a flock of sheep. All for them. This was a dream.

Was his opponent brave or stupid? Igor wondered, weighing his chances of victory. He'd met all sorts of men and hadn't learned much from most of them. He liked the brave ones, as long as their bravery came not from insanity or suicidal stupidity but from a force that kept them from acting like anyone but who they truly were, even at their own peril. How many beatings and scars had his body received for not having obeyed a guard or not backing off a fight that he was bound to lose? He detested men who were easily influenced, scum that bent in the wind and never broke entirely. Ass kissers, stool pigeons, snitches, men who were weak against the strong but cruel against the weak. Souls of jailers. All that mattered, the one thing that merited his respect, was the will to be true to oneself. He didn't care if that truth was an angel or a devil; what counted was loyalty to one's nature, regardless of consequences. Was that this kid? Or was he just a bully caught in the vanity of his ill-timed pride. He could have given Igor his coat without complaint, but it wouldn't have saved him. Next Igor would have demanded his boots, and so on, until the boy was left naked, and even then he'd likely have stabbed him with his awl just to set an example for the cowering masses.

Igor refused to let anyone usurp his position, not when he was surrounded by wolves still wondering if they could be the leaders of the pack. The thing was, he liked this kid. The way he stared at Igor without hatred and also without concealing his fear, but with his legs apart, knees slightly flexed, ready to fight for his coat— which at this moment was a metaphor for everything he had—and unwilling to let it be taken from him if he could help it. Igor could have let things be. There would be plenty of opportunities, battles more easily won. He considered the possibility of taking him into the flock but sensed that it would never happen, he could see it in Elías's eyes. He was a decent kid, and the thought almost made him burst out laughing: decency. Thousands of decent men were rowing the boats of hell, lamenting their lost decency.

His mind didn't stop to think. He didn't order his hand to move and acted with no hesitation or doubt. When his instinct kicked in, reasoning was overpowered. In a fraction of a second, Igor Stern—son of a Jewish cartwright skinned alive by a band of Cossacks—bridged the distance between himself and Elías Gil—son of a union miner, engineer, the great promise for a better tomorrow—and stabbed his right eye with the tip of his awl. He could have gone deeper, pushed the sharpened wood in with force, severed the kid's optic nerve and bored into his shocked brain, but he didn't. Instead he let him stagger around, shouting in pain with the awl in his eye as his body convulsed, reeling and then falling backward where there wasn't even space enough to hit the ground.

"I said, I like your coat," Igor repeated drily. Take what you want until someone stops you. That was his motto. He leaned over Elías's bloody face and yanked the coat violently, and no one stopped him. He tugged on one sleeve and then the other.

"No!" Elías roared, clutching it with astonishing rage.

Igor stopped, perplexed. And before his surprise turned to rage, he felt the tip of Elías's boot against his nose and knew immediately, by the crack, that this maniac had just broken his septum. Dazed, he straightened up, touched his face with both hands and contemplated his bloody fingertips in astonishment. Worked into a frenzy by the fight, Igor's entourage pounced on the fallen prey. Elías whimpered, pierced by the searing pain in his eye, yet with everything he had, arms and legs flailing, he managed to hold on to his coat.

Like a miracle conceivable only among humans, the mass of anonymous faces parted, this time not to run away but to surround the poor young man and his coat. Hands and arms hid him from the ferocious wolves, protecting him at the center of the flock. How paradoxical for the sheep suddenly to close ranks and stand up to the wolves, who in turn backed up, disconcerted, returning to the safety of their circle. Growling, hackles raised, but slowly edging back.

In the days and nights that followed, Elías lived in the bleary haze of fever and delirium, unaware of almost everything. Sometimes he'd awaken to see a woman's face, watching him with a concerned expression, her voice murmuring like the ocean, speaking words that didn't reach him. Then he'd sink back into troubling darkness, a place fraught with jumbled images and thoughts impossible to string together. His body surrendered and his mind sizzled like lava before turning to stone. When he regained consciousness, he could feel the prickle of infection in his eye beneath the filthy bandage, could smell the wound's foul stench—the smell of his own rotting flesh—and hear the shouting of guards beating people, beating him.

The woman remained steadfastly by his side and forced him to drink, holding a bowl of soup—boiled water, really—to his lips.

Then she made him swallow crumbs of frozen bread that she had softened in her own mouth, patiently feeding him, like a child with a wounded sparrow. Meanwhile, their journey continued, the vastness swallowing up human beings, turning them into tiny insignificant particles much like the snowflakes falling impassively onto the trees.

Elías woke up on a night when the sky was full of stars so close it was as though he could reach out a trembling hand to touch them, as though they were painted onto a cupola. His head was heavy and his body like jelly; he'd lost weight and a scratchy beard had sprouted beneath his eye socket.

"Welcome to the world."

It was the voice of the woman who'd been caring for him. Her shirt was partially open and the scent of her warm breasts reached Elías as she bent over him to lift the bandage, sliding an index finger into the gap where his eye had been as though to return it to its place.

"The infection is getting better, but you're not going to get that pretty green eye back. Try to think that from now on you'll see things as if you were winking."

"Where are we?"

"In the middle of nowhere, somewhere between Moscow and Tomsk."

Elías touched the bandage and gave an involuntary shiver. The image of Igor piercing his right eye with that awl, the fight for his overcoat—which he still had—seemed something out of another life, and yet it had all been just ten days ago. Standing by the woman was a man wrapped in a blanket, hands reaching out to seek the fire's heat. His right hand was bandaged in a dirty rag and missing two fingers. Elías struggled to sit up, resting on one elbow, and focused on the young man's profile.

"Don't stare at me; you should see what *you* look like."

"Claude? Is that you?"

The young man uncovered his head and for a few seconds the pair of them weighed each other up in silence.

"I'll leave the two of you alone." The woman stood and walked off toward a group of people hunched over another fire. They were everywhere, dotting the landscape, hundreds of little bonfires, sources of heat surrounded by clusters of moving shadows. The train had stopped in the middle of the plains.

Claude offered Elías a tiny roast potato, all of his unspoken excuses implicit in this gesture.

"This is a treat—half my rations, so don't waste it."

Elías accepted the food. For a few minutes Claude watched him bite into it with patience.

"It was Michael. He was the first to sign a statement against you, then Martin," he said finally, contemplating the fire's bluish flames that seemed no longer to give off warmth, speaking so quietly it was as though he was talking to himself.

"What happened to your hand?"

Claude raised his amputated fist like a trophy he was no longer proud of.

"I was the last to sign," he replied simply.

Elías looked away, gazing out to see what was going on beyond the firelight. Despite all the people camped there, the silence was deafening. It was as though they were all alone.

"And what happened to them?"

"Our friends turned out to be born survivors. It took them no time to join Igor's gang—Igor is the prisoner who did this to you. They're his little toadies; he whistles and they come running, like little lapdogs."

Elías shook his head. He found it hard to believe that his old companions could be so fickle—especially Michael.

"This is the land of prodigies," Claude said bitterly. "Peasants can be czars. They're bringing in more prisoners. I don't know where the hell they're getting them all from: the 'land of socialism' seems to be a never-ending breeding ground for offenders," he added, driving his point home as he squinted to look out into the darkness.

Elías said nothing in reply. He still wasn't ready for Claude's diatribes. His glance darted from bonfire to bonfire, searching for the woman until he found her. She was holding a little girl, perhaps two years old, in her arms.

"Who's she?"

"Her name is Irina. They say she was a surgeon at a hospital in Kiel. She's the only reason I didn't lose my whole hand. You owe her your life, too; she hasn't left your side for a minute these past days."

Elías observed her in the distance. She was ragged, like all of them, dressed in tatters and men's clothes that were far too big. Filthy and humbled, her skin had the telltale pastiness of tuberculosis. Yet she shone with her own light and dignity, like a sun whose sphere was untouched by its surroundings.

"And the girl?"

"Anna. Her daughter."

"What happened to the father?"

Claude shrugged. "She doesn't talk about him."

Elías and Irina exchanged glances for an instant. The determination in her expression was as fierce as it was sorrowful.

Before dawn, the guards, aided by a horde of prisoners, set upon the people, attempting to force them back onto the train cars. Lying facedown on the ground, Elías awoke with snow piled heavily on the back of his coat. The wet had soaked through his boots and socks and an icy wind lashed his face. He was still very weak and felt dizzy when he tried to sit up. People were breaking camp, and there was no sign of Irina. Claude, too, had disappeared. Guards were recruiting men to haul bundles from an outbuilding to the train. One of them gave him a kick.

"Get to work!"

The sack Elías was told to lug was too heavy; he had to drag it between the railroad ties like a dead body. He was weak and feverish with infection, and the sack seemed to weigh a ton. He dragged it two or three yards and collapsed into the snow-covered tracks. Then he stood, tugged on it once more and stumbled yet again. After fifteen seemingly endless minutes, Elías gave up. He was so exhausted that despite being kicked and screamed at by the guards, he didn't move, deciding it would be better to wait for the snow to bury him alive, as it had others.

Lying there, Elías began to reminisce about the warmth of his old life, which seemed so far away it was as though it had never existed. He missed things he'd thought long forgotten: his father sitting in a wing-backed armchair reading Chekhov aloud, his mother's silhouette flickering intermittently in the firelight. Just a few weeks ago he was still a young man ready to take life by storm, walking the streets of Madrid, going to cafeterias, party meetings, movies; he had friends who loved him, plans for the future. Everyone was convinced he was going to overcome fate, break out of the cycle of poverty in which his family had been trapped for generations. Everyone—parents, cousins, aunts, and uncles—had put their entire savings toward his studies, and he promised himself that he would live up to their sacrifice, to make it worth it.

But Lady Luck had stopped smiling on him. He was going to die an absurd, unexpected death in a land he hadn't had time to become familiar with. And even if he had learned about the country before his arrival, he could never have grasped what the enormity of the distances and the vastness meant. What he thought of as immense was nothing but the gateway to infinite space.

Despite all of that, he didn't feel upset. What he saw around him was so beautiful it was unreal. Incorruptible Mother Nature did as she saw fit with humans, and the only thing for him to do was to stop fighting. Day was breaking in the vast expanse, bare trees and crows on the building's roof becoming visible in the mist. To his right, a river flowed gently, parallel to the train tracks; beyond that, endless forest.

Then he saw it: an enormous elk. Beautiful and aloof, the animal emerged from the mist and stopped a few meters away, casting a sidelong glance at Elías with one giant dark glassy eye—king of its world, master of its time—as though attempting to predict the fallen man's intentions. An apparition! Elías wished he had the strength to approach it slowly, to reach out and touch it.

Suddenly a loud *boom* shattered the air, then another, and another. Elías pressed his face to the snow, covering his head with his hands to protect himself. Looking up, he saw the animal rock backward, eyes wild, then its front legs buckled and it fell, dead. Guards continued to shoot it with their rifles, giggling with insane delight, firing long after the animal lay felled and motionless. When silence resumed, everything had died. The crows flew off, cawing; the wind stopped blowing; even the river seemed to stop in its course. All that moved were the rivers of blood streaming from the elk's nose and mouth, pooling in the soft snow.

Elías sobbed like a baby.

The shrill train whistle signaled that it was time to resume their journey. A guard ordered Elías to get up, but he didn't budge. The man prodded him with the tip of his boot, gauging how much life was left in him, and shrugged, prepared to leave him there like carrion. Elías wouldn't have minded staying there, staring into the elk's motionless muddy eyes as the snow soaked up its blood. That would be better than carrying on, suffering this intensely only to die alone a day later, a few meters on.

"Don't give them the satisfaction. That's what they want—for us to die without them having to get their hands dirty. What kind of executioner shirks his own job?"

A pair of holey old boots with no laces stood inches from his nose. Elías saw a pair of legs bend down in the mist, saw a hand with exceedingly clean, delicate fingers reach out and touch his stiff, frozen hair. It was her: Irina.

"If they want to finish you off, they'll have to do better than that."

Elías looked up doubtfully into the big gray eyes giving him an urgent, penetrating look. *Up*, the eyes said. He accepted Irina's hand, knowing that the woman who held it out was a castaway, too, and that all he could offer her was the promise that they would sink together.

7

The animal was old, but even in captivity it gave off the ferocious air that must have made it leader of the pack when it roamed the miles and miles of its hunting grounds. A transparent partition less than two meters high separated beast from visitors, though at that hour there were very few visitors around. Despite signs in multiple languages prohibiting the throwing of objects and the feeding of animals, the moat around the wolf's artificial island was overflowing with trash: soda cans, pieces of fruit, ice cream wrappers. Gonzalo even saw a worn-out running shoe. To the right of the enclosure hung an informational plaque: The Great Gray Wolf weighed up to 85 kilos and was found in many parts of Europe, Eurasia, and North America; its teeth were powerful enough to rip apart its prey; primarily cold regions were its natural environment, which explained why the animal's coat was gray on the back and very white at the paws. King of the Steppe, where nothing could thrive without true survival instincts.

All of that notwithstanding, this particular wolf's glory days seemed a thing of the past. It lay in front of a man-made den, muzzle between its front paws. The animal's gray and white fur was dirty and shedding by the handful. This was molting season, and despite the thermostat in the enclosure being set to a low temperature, a Siberian wolf could never adapt to the muggy heat of a Mediterranean city. The wolf raised its head, ears pressed back, and let out a prolonged yawn. In another time, Gonzalo thought, the yawn would have been accompanied by a long, deep howl that caused half of the animals in the forest to tremble in fear. But years of captivity had eroded the pride in the beast's almost-white eyes, which now observed him indifferently. Nothing remained of its instincts; there was only sadness and submission.

Gonzalo observed the wolf, waiting for something. He'd have liked the animal to regain its strength, to see—at least once—its body stand erect on the manufactured cardboard-and-stone rockery, howling, reclaiming the legacy of its ancestors. Defiant, free, despite it all. But all the wolf did was lie tamely, licking at its paws. After a few minutes, the animal struggled onto its front legs, shook out like an old stray in the rain, and dragged itself to the darkest corner of the den.

That's me, Gonzalo thought. A tame wolf. Since returning from the lake house, he couldn't stop thinking about the crazy, senseless plan he'd hatched. It was so unlike him, and yet he couldn't get it out of his head.

"Excuse me, sir. We're about to close."

Gonzalo cast a sidelong glance at the zookeeper and nodded.

He didn't feel like going home and facing the routine of it all. He felt strange, as if something was struggling to surface and he wasn't sure he could control it. No one knew that he was paying for a little studio in the Barceloneta quarter; he'd rented it a year ago, when on the verge of separating from Lola. She had no idea how close they'd been to splitting up. Gonzalo had gotten over it but decided to hold on to the studio, to have a space that was his exclusively. Sometimes, not very often, he went there when he needed solitude.

The building had a doorman, a short bald guy whose name Gonzalo didn't even know. Every time he went to the studio, he'd shrug the man off with a curt greeting. Gonzalo took the elevator up, leaning against a wood-paneled wall in serious need of a layer of varnish. A small mirror returned his reflection: disheveled hair, bags under his eyes, drooping mouth, skin sagging, the knot of his tie too loose.

Gonzalo was greeted by the desolate image of empty space, the only furniture on the dark parquet floor a wooden table, two chairs, a stereo and VCR, some books, and a mattress and box spring, still wrapped in plastic. There was a pile of CDs, an ashtray, and in the fridge a bottle of mineral water, a couple of pieces of fruit, and some juice. Three incandescent lightbulbs hung from the ceiling where there should have been halogens. The windows had no curtains, and the nineteenth-century Palau de Mar building was visible from the sliding-glass door leading to the balcony. The sounds of the city were a distant buzz. Lights flashed like a heart beating slowly, at rest. Gonzalo dropped a bag containing his dinner onto the marble counter in the kitchen and drank straight from the tap. The water stank of chlorine. Inserting a CD into the player, he turned the volume down low. Aretha Franklin's throaty voice told him that it wasn't a good time to be alone. But loneliness didn't bother him, he'd never minded being on his own.

Gonzalo went out onto the balcony. There was no breeze and the humid air coming in from the sea felt sticky. The solitude, background music, and being in a space he shared with no one allowed him to pretend he was still twenty years old, his future before him. This was why he was furnishing the place slowly, picturing what it would look like when he was done. Gonzalo was in no rush, felt no need to fuel this fantasy of lost independence. This space was simply his, the last bastion, the only one that he hadn't given up. For a few hours here, he could be whoever he wanted. It didn't matter whether it was real; just believing it was possible was enough.

Gonzalo's house, his real home, wasn't far: a ten-minute drive, but symbolically a world away. Lola would have had dinner by now, perhaps be half asleep on the sofa, reading one of those novels featuring a woman who travels to the other side of the world—she loved those. Perhaps waiting for him to call and say that he'd had the meeting with her father, that the merger between their firms was a done deal. Patricia would be in her room, sleeping with one eye open, waiting for the sound of his keys in the door and his fingers typing the code into the alarm so that she could jump out of her bed and run to his arms. Javier would be at his computer, lost in one of the endless conversations he had in chat rooms.

Someone knocked softly at the door, twice. Gonzalo wasn't expecting any visitors, no one had ever come here; that was the whole point. The knuckles rapped again, more insistently this time. The light in the hallway was on, and Gonzalo could see a shadow moving in the crack under the door. When he opened it, there stood the doorman, a cardboard box in his arms.

"Just bringing you a delivery. Someone dropped this off downstairs."

Gonzalo shot the doorman a skeptical look. These were not normal delivery hours. The doorman read his surprise correctly.

"A black kid brought it, insisted that I deliver it in person, directly to your hands." He neglected to add that the kid was good-looking and well dressed, and that he'd given him a generous tip—in dollars—to ensure that he actually did it.

Gonzalo looked at the box. "There must be some mistake."

The doorman pointed to a name, written on the box, in marker. His name.

Gonzalo thanked the doorman, took the box, and closed the door on his expectant face. He took it to the kitchen, set it on the countertop, and opened the refrigerator. After pouring himself a large glass of pineapple juice, he sat down and stared at the package. Finally, he resolved to open it. Inside was a laptop. The most-used keys had sticky fingerprints. His eyes went to a photograph at the bottom of the box. It was partially burned, as if whoever had set fire to the photo quickly had a change of heart and extinguished the flame before it was destroyed.

"Oh, my God," he murmured, recognizing the image.

In it were two large fir trees, a frozen lake and, a short distance beyond it, the house. *His* house. Laura was smiling, wrapped in a fleece, wild hair covering her forehead. Large eyes peeked out from beneath her bangs as though she was spying from behind the curtains. The burned part of the photo was beyond recognition—all he could discern was an arm and a hand, holding a boy's. A hand with clean nails and fingers that looked strong, like the arm. A black hand.

He turned the photo over. One word was written on the back, in capital letters: MATRYOSHKA. Gonzalo turned on the computer, and when the screen asked for a password, instinctively typed in the word. The computer unlocked, showing a series of icons over a background photo of Laura, Luis, and their son Roberto on a beach with a sign at the roadside: ARGELÈS DE LA MARENDA. A vacation photo from the south of France, they looked happy. Was this Laura's computer?

He clicked on the first icon and an Excel spreadsheet opened, revealing a sea of codes and numbers. Gonzalo didn't completely understand it but got the impression it was an exhaustive list of bank transfers, account numbers, and initials that might refer to names. Of what? People? Companies? In several places he saw the initials ZV, with black ticks next to them. Zinoviev? The other icons were similar: They contained lists of ports all over Europe and what might have been the names of German, British, French, Dutch, and Spanish container ships. Dates of arrival were listed, along with the ports of exit, many in Africa and Central America, but also some in Canada and Russia. Beside each entry was a list of names, and a number: Assam, Miriam, Bodski, Remedios, Matthew, Jérôme, Louise, Siaka, Pedro, Paula, Nicole, and on and on, there must have been a hundred. The accompanying numbers were almost all single digit, although a few were double. The highest number was 15, the lowest, 2.

One folder was labeled *Confidential.* Gonzalo clicked, but it was password-protected. He guessed a password at random: *Laura.* A window popped up informing him that he had two more tries before the folder would be automatically blocked. He gave up and instead tried opening a folder containing photos. Zinoviev appeared in almost every one. They'd been taken from a distance with a zoom lens. In some the man was alone, in others accompanied, often by a tall young man—a good-looking, well-dressed black man. Gonzalo returned his gaze to the burned photo. Was it his hand there, holding Roberto's? Was this the man who'd just delivered the laptop?

For a long time, he observed Zinoviev's tattooed face. According to Inspector Alcázar, Laura had killed this man, but how could she have done it the way the police had claimed? Not by shooting him but by hanging him from a beam, using her handcuffs, after savagely torturing him, probably for hours. The man's fierce appearance and his height—at least six feet tall—and girth made it seem highly unlikely that his sister could have done anything of the sort. It would have required a tremendous amount of physical strength to overpower this man and then toss him around like a rag doll, and no doubt he'd have put up a violent struggle. The medical examiner had said there were no traces of skin or blood on Laura not belonging to her. When Luis asked if Gonzalo thought Laura had killed and tortured this man, he'd instinctively said no. Now he was almost convinced.

It suddenly seemed more than obvious what all the information on the computer was: Laura's investigation, the reason she'd lost her son and husband, the thing she'd been obsessed with all that time. So these names and numbers...

Gonzalo opened the next folder of photographs.

He gagged and almost vomited pineapple juice onto the keyboard. There were hundreds of images of children, some very young—almost babies—who'd been horrifically abused. Many of the photos were hard-core porn so explicit they'd make anyone want to jump out a window.

"Good God, Laura, how could you cope with all of this alone?"

He closed the folder, feeling sick, and went to the window. His fingers trembled as he lit a cigarette. He had promised Lola he wouldn't smoke, but what the fuck did it matter now? Inhaling deeply, he felt a sob rising up in his throat. How was this even possible? How could such depravity exist in the world? Gonzalo wasn't naïve, he was a lawyer, knew the ins and outs of human misery, how nasty people could behave, but this...It was beyond all conception. Again he inhaled deeply, looking out at the night. Peaceful, calm, serene. A couple leaned against the hood of a car, kissing, laughing, kissing again. Gonzalo felt the urge to tell them to run, to get as far away as they could, as fast as possible, before the depravity caught up. How could Laura have kept seeing the world after descending to these pits of hell?

It took more than an hour before he could return to the laptop. He delved in with no idea what he was after, opening files and folders, and then once more tried the one labeled *Confidential*. This time he tried *Roberto* as a password, but the window popped up again, now warning him he had only one more try. He decided not to waste it.

What should he do with all this? Go to the police, of course. He thought about calling Inspector Alcázar immediately; he'd know what to do. The case on Laura and Zinoviev was closed, but it would have to be reopened in light of this new evidence. They would order a thorough investigation. He picked up the phone, but something stopped him, a question that had been buzzing in the back of his mind from the start: Why had someone sent him his sister's computer?

The answer was there, he was certain, in the folder he couldn't open. The password had to be somewhere. It was absurd for whoever had sent it to him to give him access to the laptop, the photos of child pornography, all of this information, and yet deny him entry to that one folder. He went back to the box. Tucked into the flaps he caught sight of the corner of a gray business card bearing the logo of a five-star hotel. His heart began to pound as he picked it up; perhaps it contained the password to the confidential file.

Instead, he found a laconic warning: *If you tell anyone about this, we'll both be dead. Believe me.*

There was an address, too, where the person instructed him to be three days later, at a specific time, along with a threat: If Gonzalo didn't show up, or went to the police, the unidentified person would disappear forever.

When he got home an hour later—home to the house he shared with Lola and the kids—Gonzalo sat down in his daughter's room to watch her sleep. She smelled so good and her face was so trusting; she was so happy, so fragile. He thought of the nights that Laura, too, must have spent at the foot of her little one's bed, watching him sleep, trusting, safe, protected. He imagined the anguish she must have felt stroking his face after having seen all those other children. And then, when her son was no longer there, she must have kept sitting on his empty bed, stroking the pillow, the sheets, his pajamas.

Gonzalo wept. He wept silently like he'd never wept in his life.

That night he crossed the invisible border separating him from Lola and spooned with her, shaping himself against her bent legs, draping an arm over her waist and telling her he loved her. Lola didn't hear him, but her body did and responded to Gonzalo's touch, surprised and pleased.

In the morning he was another man, he wanted to be another man. Lola and Patricia, each in her own way, realized that something was different, and the change—or the will to change, at least—surprised them both; they were hesitant in their joy. Gonzalo had gotten up before them and made a continental breakfast that, for lack of experience, was excessive: juice, toast, coffee, cereal; he'd even tried to replicate Laura's fruit salad, a valiant but fraught attempt that ended up wasting half of the fruit. The kitchen curtains were open, as if he'd wanted the sunlight to bear witness to this declaration of intent. The vase of flowers he had placed on the table was in the way and took up too much room, but Lola appreciated the gesture and wasn't upset at Gonzalo for not knowing that her routine breakfast was nothing but a large coffee, or that Patricia was allergic to grapefruit juice.

When Gonzalo said good morning, kissing Lola on the lips, he felt a little shudder of both joy and guilt. There was nothing new in the way Patricia launched herself into his arms as though she were still four years old, but what was different was his renewed devotion to her that morning. They sat at the table with fresh excitement. Gonzalo was chatty and witty in his own spare, awkward way; what counted was the clear determination to emerge from his recent stagnation. Lola observed without daring to participate in the forced joy, fearing that his song and dance would be short-lived. She also wondered why he felt the need to stage all of this, to stroke her hand under the table, gaze into her eyes, sweet-talk Patricia. She mistook the reason.

"What are we celebrating? The merger?"

Gonzalo's expression contorted for a fraction of a second, which translated into too much butter on the tip of his knife.

"Not yet. I don't want to rush into such an important decision."

Given his outpouring of effort, Lola was willing to overlook Gonzalo's shortcomings that morning, but this response disconcerted her.

"There's no alternative, I thought it was all set."

He picked up on the arrogant presumptuousness in her tone, but today he was able to endure it.

"I can't renounce eight years of struggling to survive as an independent attorney just like that, Lola." He made sure to restrain the damper in his tone, and this prompted her not to continue and thereby ruin what had started off so well.

But the black cloud was back between them already. It wasn't yet evident, but things remained festive only because of Patricia's incessant chatter. At that moment she intuited something special, realized that in some way it was her turn to keep it alive. Her parents tacitly acquiesced, compensating her effort by laughing, chatting about things both serious and frivolous, trying to end breakfast pleasantly.

"Where's the family hermit? I didn't see him in his bed last night," Gonzalo said finally. He couldn't conceal the slightly mocking tone that annoyed Lola, always on the lookout for signs of the subdued battle Gonzalo waged with his offspring. Each time her husband attacked Javier, she took it personally.

"I told him he could sleep at a friend's house."

"What friend? He's seventeen years old, it would make sense for him to sleep at home. I bet they spent all night studying," he said ironically. He was trying to be lighthearted, but Lola picked up on the paternal contempt. Words seduce, they create moods, and Gonzalo specialized in destroying those moods. By the time they cleared the dishes, the charm offensive he had so hopefully launched in the attempt to win Lola back had failed abysmally, leaving in its place a sad, disheartening emptiness.

"Last night there was more graffiti on the wall. The neighbors are starting to get upset; no one wants a psychopath wandering the neighborhood, and I'm started to get worried, too," Lola said flatly, as though Gonzalo himself were the perpetrator.

He understood immediately her look of warning. Until now he hadn't paid much attention to the threats. He'd been too busy dealing with Laura's death, as well as trying to project a restrained response by making light of the matter so as not to scare his family. But the fact was that after the first time it had happened, Gonzalo bought an old gun, which he kept hidden in the garage, out of the kids' reach. Not even Lola knew he had it, she'd never have allowed it. Gonzalo had no intention of using the thing, in fact he didn't even know how to aim. It was a preventative measure. But it wasn't enough. He had to do something.

Miranda Acebedo must have been a real looker in her day. A copper-haired beauty who no doubt captivated the many tourists traveling to Cuba in search of women like her. The walls of her modest hair salon were covered in mementos from her time as a showgirl in the dance halls of luxury hotels. She danced moderately well, especially *cumbia*—which wasn't even Cuban but the tourists didn't care, as long as she shook her curvy hips and wore flouncy skirts as skimpy as her sequined bras. The pianist Bebo Valdés once heard her sing and told her she had talent. But talent counts for nothing if it doesn't also come with luck.

"I'd rather be a hooker than a beggar," Miranda told Gonzalo the first time she came to his office, a year and a half ago. She'd walked in with a black eye and one arm in a plaster cast. Friends had signed the cast and drawn cartoons on it, but they'd also left her alone with the man who swore before God to love and protect her when she married him in Havana and began abusing her before they'd even landed in Barcelona.

Miranda wanted to get divorced and take her husband, Floren Atxaga, for everything he had. *I want him to pay for every day of hell he's put me through,* was the way she'd put it. Gonzalo had bent over backward to get her to file domestic abuse charges. It was the only way she'd be able to lose the husband but keep the apartment where—for better or for worse—she'd raised her two kids, the "mestizo bastards," as Atxaga called them. Gonzalo himself had accompanied her to the police station, advised her throughout the trial and, after endless litigation, managed to get her a divorce and the house, and him four years prison on charges of rape, battery, and psychological abuse. Miranda was so thankful that she'd made him an amazing caramelized banana-and-yam dessert, and at the end of the meal offered to dance for him. Gonzalo had taken her up on the dessert but chosen to leave before being trapped by the dance.

There was nothing left of that Miranda in the woman now standing at the door in a washed-out quilted bathrobe.

"They shouldn't have given him that furlough; they had to know he'd run," she lamented, pained by the obvious.

Gonzalo said nothing. Life always stopped living up to expectations the moment you began to expect too much from it. And Miranda had hit the jackpot when it came to assholes.

"Has he come around?"

She shook her head, terrified at the possibility.

"The police have stopped by a couple of times, and they gave me a phone number. As if I could protect myself from the pig with that," she said, pointing to an Office of Victim Assistance card magneted to the refrigerator.

"Do you have any idea where he might be?"

"Out looking for some other gullible fool to fall into his trap."

"Brothels, bingo parlors?"

Miranda smiled as though ready to bark.

"No, no. Floren's a Sunday Mass kind of man. Doesn't smoke, drink, or gamble—even on checkers—and he definitely doesn't go whoring. Even hookers would laugh at his pathetic little dick. He's all smiles and good manners, with a stray-dog look to break your heart. He kept it up until we got married and moved here. Then he started in on me about my Cuban friends, began criticizing me for reading books—he called it an obsession, said I was trying to act like an intellectual. He said I read all the time just to make him look bad for being uneducated, like I was some nuclear engineer, even though all I ever read were dime-store novels. Then he started in on me for singing all the time, as if I did it to make fun of him. The first time he hit me was because he couldn't get it up. The second time it was because he couldn't get it all the way up. The third, because I got pregnant. By the fourth time he stopped bothering with excuses. But I'll tell you this, we never missed Sunday Mass and then roast chicken lunch at the in-laws', me wearing my best face even if sometimes the bruises on it were so dark that not even makeup could hide them."

"Which church did he go to?"

"One in the neighborhood, close to here, Our Lady of Lourdes."

Gonzalo craned his neck into the living room. Sprawled on the sofa, a honey-skinned teenager watched TV with a bored air. He must have been about fifteen, Miranda's older son. If Floren Atxaga turned up, this kid didn't exactly look set to defend her.

"I don't think he'll show his face; he knows the police are looking for him. But if he does come around, don't hesitate to call me, any time of day."

Gonzalo noticed a scratch behind Miranda's ear, deep and recent. And when her robe fell open as she moved forward, he caught sight of a bluish shadow on one shoulder.

"Are you seeing anyone now, Miranda?"

Quickly, she pulled the robe tight around her, covering her shoulder.

"A nice man. If that monster Floren shows up, he'll show him what's what. A woman needs protection, right?"

Gonzalo felt heavy with resignation. Bad luck was like a vocation for some people. Some mistakes last a lifetime. That's what he

saw in her look—that, and fear, sadness, and pity. No pride and
no love.

"Will you call me if your ex-husband makes any attempt to
contact you?"

She said yes, but Gonzalo knew she wouldn't do it. Just as
he knew that one day Miranda's body would be flung from the
balcony and land on the shiny hood of a car parked below. By any
one of the countless Atxagas prowling the planet in search of their
next prey.

He thought of Laura's laptop and once more debated taking
it to Alcázar. There were too many wolves in the world, and he,
despite his desire to be the opposite, was nothing but a sheep. It
was all too much for him, a simple civil attorney. His only foray
into criminal territory had ended up forcing him to buy a rusty
revolver because he felt threatened by an altar boy who tortured
his wife. If he couldn't deal with that, how was he possibly going
to confront the tidal wave that had swept his sister away? He was
tempted to call the inspector, but the warning that the stranger
had placed in the box dissuaded him. With the phone still in his
hand, Gonzalo decided he would give it three days, meet whoever
had left him the laptop, and then make up his mind. Meanwhile,
he'd inform the police of Atxaga's threats and call a security company to come install cameras on his property. Lola would rest easier, and he would regain at least some of the feeling that he was
capable of handling this threat.

Rather than call Alcázar, he dialed Lola. He wanted to tell
her that breakfast hadn't been a fluke. He was going to take care
of the graffiti issue; he would keep them safe, never let anything
happen to them.

"Is Javier back?" he asked. Lola said no, and Gonzalo sensed
concern in her voice.

.   .   .

It was an adequate room, that was about as much as you could say for it. There was hardly enough space for the creaky double bed, its faded magenta-colored mattress covered in bleach stains. Folded-down sheets were tucked beneath the pillows. The only window was misaligned in the sash and there was a TV hanging immediately above it, which made opening the window problematic. There was nothing to see anyway, just a heap of cement cylinders covered in bird shit. He turned on the bathroom light and the fluorescent bulb buzzed like a trapped dragonfly. The sink's brass faucet was leaking and had left a rust stain trailing down to the drain. A bar of soap, with no sanitary seal, had been placed in one corner of the shower. The toilet tank had no cover, and when water ran through the pipes on the floors above his, the floater bobbed.

He went back to the bed, took off his shoes without untying the laces, and lay down, interlacing his fingers behind his head and staring up at the ceiling. The smell of deodorant wafted into his nostrils. Javier wondered how many people had been in this bed before him, perhaps just hours ago, hiding from the world, furtive as criminals. He'd certainly seen nicer places.

"Kind of a strange place for us to meet."

"You don't like the view? It's spectacular."

Carlos had taken off his shirt and draped it over the back of a chair. He was counting the money Javier had given him.

"This isn't enough, I need more than this."

"It's all I could get. I'm not your personal ATM."

Carlos frowned, disappointed. He was about to say something but then thought better of it. Instead he lay down next to Javier and kissed him full on the lips. Javier flinched, a look of repulsion on his face. Carlos watched, calm and scornful. It was as if he could read Javier's thoughts and was mocking them.

"What's with the face?"

His eyes hurt Javier, physically hurt him, as if they were making incisions on his skin. Suddenly he saw Carlos for the crass hustler he was, and everything about him seemed petty and unsettling. He'd seemed like an interesting guy when they first met, five months ago. Carlos had sat down next to him one night at a gay bar. At first he didn't say anything, didn't even look at him. He ordered a soft drink and sat watching the dance floor. "My name is Carlos," he'd eventually said, turning to Javier, shaking peanuts like dice in his hand and flashing a smile full of promises. A worldly guy, no ties, no moral qualms, a free spirit who took what he wanted when he wanted it and went on his merry way. That's what he'd seemed like. Javier had seen too late the error of his judgment.

It was, of course, no coincidence that Carlos had sat down beside him. He'd targeted him the second he walked into the bar. It was a matter of laying eyes on him and knowing that Javier would be his next victim. "First time?" he'd asked, placing a warm palm near Javier's crotch. The combination of that hand and Carlos's empty expression should have set off warning bells, but he was burning with desire. An hour later Javier was crammed into the backseat of Carlos's gray Ford, giving his first blow job as Depeche Mode played in the background. He'd never guessed that the taste of a hard penis could be so sweet, despite having fantasized about it a thousand times. And when he felt Carlos's breath on his own crotch, felt the explosion of pleasure and guilt at ejaculating into his mouth, he was hooked. Since then, Carlos had him eating out of the palm of his hand like a helpless little sparrow. Whenever he called, Javier came running, no matter what time it was or what he was doing, if it meant he could spend a few minutes with him. Sometimes Carlos didn't show up, and the next time they saw each other he wouldn't even bother giving an explanation.

Little by little, Javier had dropped everything that wasn't his obsession for Carlos. It was sick, he knew, but he couldn't help himself. Carlos drove him to distraction, and he couldn't make himself stop despite knowing that he was being used. It didn't take long for Carlos to start asking for increasing sums of money. Sometimes he begged, others he simply demanded it with a semi-veiled threat, saying he'd leave Javier. This was the reason Javier had helped him get a job at his mother's travel agency. But now he realized that the job was the real reason Carlos had tried to get close to him in the first place—to gain access to Javier's family.

"I'm not an idiot, you know. I might be younger than you, and in love, and blind to certain things. But I'm not a complete fool."

"I have no idea what you're talking about."

"You know exactly what I'm talking about. What are you playing at with my mother?"

"I'm not playing at anything. You wouldn't understand."

"What is there to understand? That you want to fuck her? I know what I saw at the agency—your little masquerade game, my mother's ridiculous smile. And I know what both of you are like."

Carlos gave him a blank look, then adopted a bemused expression and burst out laughing.

"Are you actually jealous of your own mother? That's kind of sick, don't you think? I want nothing to do with her. I might act like a tease—after all, the woman is my boss and she's attractive. But I have no intention whatsoever of seducing her."

"Is that what you think you did with me? Seduce me?"

Carlos shook his head back and forth. Sometimes it was hard to believe people like Javier still existed at all—so naïve, so convinced that the world revolved around them and their existential anguish, their complexes, and the stupid shit troubling their little heads. Sometimes when they were together he'd gaze at Javier's flawless skin and feel like he was making love to a marble statue. Other times it was like sinking his hands into a trough of soft, malleable butter.

"Nobody forced you to walk into that bar; you went in because you knew what you'd find. You got into my car of your own free will, and you weren't exactly raped, were you? If I recall correctly, I told you not to get your hopes up with me. Look, I don't care if you believe me or not, but I have no desire to sleep with your mother. I need the money and the job, end of story—though you should see her when she's with me. She laughs, becomes young again, it's like she lets loose the real Lola hiding inside her."

"I don't need you to tell me what my mother is like. You've known her for three months; I've been with her all my life."

"You're wrong. You have no idea what she's like."

Carlos forced himself to quash his urge to teach Javier a lesson, the kind of lesson he himself had been taught since he was a little boy. But that wasn't why he was there. He took out a bindle of coke and tapped it out onto a small mirror he kept in his pocket. After setting up two lines, he took one.

"Look, we haven't seen much of each other lately, let's not waste time bickering like some old couple. If you don't want to see me anymore, just say it. I'll be out of your life and you'll never hear another word about me, I swear."

Javier's silence made him smile. This kid would stick around, follow Carlos like a puppy until he hung him out to dry. He knew his targets, knew how to pick them. Carlos held the mirror out to Javier so he could do his line. Afterward, Javier fell back onto the bed, eyes glassy and absent. People can tell when they're headed down the road to perdition but rarely have the strength to stop it. Carlos undid Javier's fly and kissed his belly button, tickling him with his stubble.

"We're here now. The past is over and the future doesn't exist. This moment is all there is. And it's ours."

When Javier snorted a second line, his eyes turned watery again. He knew what Carlos was like, knew he should keep the guy from getting close to his mother, knew that he'd destroy the family, hurt them all. He already was hurting Javier, the man was like woodworm—visible only when it's too late. If only he could speak to his father, tell him everything. If he could just find a way to do it. He had to let his father know that he didn't blame him for the injury he'd gotten when they jumped off that cliff together when he was a boy, didn't blame him for the fact that he still limped. What mattered was that they did it, they jumped together. He wanted to tell him that he needed his father to jump with him again, wherever that might be. The two of them, together, again.

But the words, and his thoughts, got stuck in his throat when he felt Carlos's warm breath on his crotch.

8

The room was unbearably hot, so hot it was physically oppressive. The windowpanes rattled each time a heavy truck passed on the national highway, which was every five minutes. On the far side of the motel was a gas station, where a couple of prostitutes sat in folding canvas chairs. One wasn't wearing any panties and spread her legs whenever a car pulled in to refuel. The other sat talking on a cell phone and fanning herself with a magazine. Her dress was so tight it was hard to believe she could breathe. *Black people don't get hot, do they, Snowflake?* Zinoviev had once asked. "Snowflake" was the name he'd given Siaka the first time he saw him. Back then Siaka had no idea there was such a thing as an albino gorilla. Years later, when he saw one behind the glass at the Barcelona zoo, he felt total empathy for the animal. He, too, earned his living as a circus attraction.

Siaka opened his mouth as if attempting to swallow what little air was being circulated by the fan blades. He lay on the floor in flip-flops and denim shorts, his naked torso shimmering with sweat. Several old scars covered the right side of his body—knife and bullet wounds. He took a sip from his bottle of cold water and let a little of it dribble down his chin.

The first time Siaka was sold, it was for less than three thousand dollars. He was six years old at the time, and the man who sold him was his father, who delivered him to filthy slave quarters where some local warlord, a thirty-year-old Angolan, was rounding up a militia. The man kept him locked in a cardboard-and-sheet-metal shack for a week. Each time the door opened and Siaka saw his mud-stained boots walk in, he cowered like an abused puppy. Beatings, beatings, and more beatings. For no apparent reason. Just to tenderize the meat. Then came the drugs and rapes, the fights he was forced to have against a boy from the other side of the lake, a boy as scared as he was, the two of them facing off in a pen like cocks with deadly spurs. And he fought—oh, did he fight—becoming unhinged when his opponent tried to run from the pen, one arm broken in three places. Siaka crushed his head with a rock that weighed more than he did; he had no idea where the viciousness had come from, the animalistic howl he let out. And then it was over, and the man picked him up and rocked him in his arms, held his bloody hands up to the frenzied horde, and called him "my son."

Siaka looked at his watch. The train to Paris was departing in three hours. From there he'd fly to Frankfurt. And from there to Africa, where he planned to disappear forever. If Laura's brother didn't turn up. He'd made a bet with himself and was sure he was going to win. The lawyer would be a no-show.

The second time he was sold, Siaka was eleven. But by then he was no longer a boy. The boy had died—or that's what he thought during the years he spent in the jungle and desert, training in camps before the long weeks of transporting arms, ammunition, and drugs like a slave. Killing was easier than dying. But dying was easier than living. He quickly realized that his heart no longer truly beat, and that his fear disappeared if he transferred it to others, to those in the crosshairs of his rifle or under the blade of his machete. Zinoviev had bought him for two boxes of Kalashnikovs, three of ammo, and one of Russian-manufactured hand grenades. He said he liked Siaka's ferocity and compared him to the fighting dogs he was so fond of. But more than his ferocity, Zinoviev liked his face—so innocent looking, despite it all—and wiry man-child body. He was going to introduce him to another war, to a place where they used other arms, he said. To Europe. There he'd teach him other skills, talents that his clientele— demanding in their perversions—would appreciate in such a good-looking eleven-year-old boy. Siaka shrugged: One hell is as bad as another. Makes no difference where you burn, he thought. But he was wrong. There's always a deeper ring that you can sink into. Siaka discovered that.

He approached the window and looked through the dirty glass. Only the hooker with the cell phone was at the gas station now. Still talking on the phone and fanning herself with the magazine. The one with no panties had disappeared, and her chair had become a footrest for her friend, who had taken off her high heels. It made for a sad sight: the woman's bare feet, shoes cast off in the gravel. And that's when Siaka saw Gonzalo climb out of his SUV by a gas pump and stand there, like a bewildered little boy, glancing uncertainly from one side of the road to the other, mopping sweat with his handkerchief. The hooker must have said something obscene to him, and he trudged across the street with pitiful footsteps. Maybe Laura had been right after all when she told him that her brother was by far the bravest man she'd ever met.

Five minutes later the two of them stood face-to-face in the room, weighing each other up mistrustfully. Gonzalo cast a furtive glance at the half-packed bag on the bed. He had a laptop case over his shoulder. Siaka's head moved slowly, examining Gonzalo. He'd been watching him for weeks, but now that the guy was so close he seemed the antithesis of his sister. Everything about him oozed formality. It was like he was walking on tiptoes, wearing a suit that must have been incredibly uncomfortable in this heat, the knot of his tie so tight that not even the top button was visible. His thick glasses gave him a perplexed look. He was orderly, the kind of man who needed things to be taken care of properly, the kind who placed each book back on its shelf, each record in its sleeve, each shirt on its hanger. Each corpse and person in its place. Siaka bet Gonzalo was the sort who organized canned goods by color and label in the pantry, the kind of man who had no vices. He'd never liked people who had no vices, didn't trust them. Despite Laura's opinion, Siaka was not impressed.

"Did you look at what's on the laptop?"

"Some of it... Who are you?"

That's a hard question to answer, Siaka thought.

"Didn't you see my name and photo in the files?"

"There are lots of names and photos in the files."

Too many, Siaka thought. How many like him in the world? Hundreds of thousands? Millions? He was just one more. *You're alive, and you're young—very young despite everything you've been through. You'll get past this.* That was how Laura had convinced him to strap on a microphone and record Zinoviev's conversations. All it took was a few kind words, a Coke at a seaside café in a small coastal town, and the promise that his life, regardless of the past, was just beginning. That was all he'd needed, one clean look from someone who didn't classify him as a monster. *Never forget one thing, Siaka: You are not defined by what others made you do. They are the aberrations, not you.*

"I was cooperating with your sister in her investigation. I was her informant."

Was that all he'd been? No, he was more than that. Laura had liked him, and Roberto had liked him even more, from the day they first met at a park. What a sight they must have been for the old folks feeding pigeons: a young black man and a little white boy, strolling hand in hand while an attractive white woman watched attentively from the distance. At first Siaka had trouble understanding Roberto when he spoke, but he had no problem interpreting his actions: running after a soccer ball and taking a clumsy shot, having a fit when his mother refused to buy him an ice cream, falling asleep in Siaka's arms as if it were the most natural thing in the world. He came to love that boy like a brother—just two regular kids, one a scared young boy-soldier, the other a quiet, slightly odd-looking kid. Two angels roaming a world neither could understand, a world of dangers that were clearly discernible in Laura's fierce eyes. She was there to protect them, to grant them a fictional normality.

"Her informant?"

"The Matryoshka. I was one of them."

After an enjoyable afternoon with Laura and her son—the three of them pretending to be a normal family—Siaka found going back to the den where Zinoviev hosted his parties a punch in the stomach. It got harder and harder to calm the young Nigerian girls whimpering as he dressed them up like Western whores before handing them over to depraved clients. The girls were little kids, like he had once been, like Roberto still was. Zinoviev no longer had Siaka sleep with clients for the most part. Since he'd turned sixteen, Zinoviev considered him too old for his clientele's taste. So he became one of his pets, like the dogs that Persian satraps kept in order to appear exotic and sophisticated. Siaka was in charge of moving the girls, making sure everything about them was perfect before they were put on display, sometimes in magnificent salons, others in stinking hovels or factory cellars. Siaka was there for dramatic effect. Spaniards were as enthralled with his kinky hair and flat nose as they were with his height and muscles. A eunuch, guardian of the harem.

"I was there the day Zinoviev killed Roberto. I drove the car to the lake and saw him drown. I was Zinoviev's right-hand man. His second lieutenant."

Laura had been patient with him, she'd known how to wait without pressuring him, without making threats that would have sent him into hiding, made him run off with all he knew—and he knew a lot. Everything, in fact: Monsters grow weak once they've eaten all of their enemies; they become sloppy and overconfident. A piece of paper full of names gets left on the table, a bankbook full of account numbers and itineraries is found in the sheets after an orgy. Sometimes ogres reveal secrets in the wee hours of the night, when even monsters dream of being kind.

Siaka had hoarded information for years, biding his time, day after day. No one knew more about the Matryoshka than he did, not even the head of the Matryoshka—if indeed the enigmatic leader Zinoviev was so afraid of actually existed. He'd done it unintentionally, acting out of instinct, just as he had the day he was sent—at age eleven—to massacre a village, drugged up to his eyeballs. He made sure everyone saw him butcher corpses, pretending to be the cruelest of them all. *I'll do it*, he told Laura one day, out of the blue, while Roberto ran around chasing pigeons that seemed about to be caught, only to fly off at the last minute. *I'll help you catch these fuckers, all of them, starting with Zinoviev*. A few weeks later, the boy was dead. Siaka didn't understand why his death affected him so deeply. Plenty of people had died all around him, he'd seen it happen countless times in his short life and never felt touched. But the kid was different.

"That boy was the closest I had to a real family." And he'd let Zinoviev kill him. The Russian was dead, and that made the world a little better, made it slightly easier to breathe. But it was poor consolation.

Gonzalo heard voices swirling in his head: his sister, the voice of his childhood, calling to him when he got lost in the forest; his mother, singing in Russian; his father, whose voice he no longer recalled and only invented, telling him that what matters is for children to be proud of their parents. He was terrified, and confused.

"Why are you telling me these things? Why did you send me the laptop? The police are the ones who should be dealing with this."

Siaka let out a sad, malicious laugh. "I suppose you tried opening the confidential folder."

Gonzalo nodded. He'd tried twice and had just one more chance.

"That's the file where your sister kept the Matryoshka's organizational chart, the names of their leaders all over the world, their sources for laundering the money they earned from illegal activities, the tax havens, banks, companies, as well as a long list of officers, many of them attorneys, prosecutors, judges, and police. Zinoviev was just a henchman. In theory he was in the import-export business: sporting equipment. But in reality he was a hit man for the organization. They have a headquarters in Russia and branches all over Europe that Laura had been investigating for years. They're into all sorts of illegal dealings, but most of their income is from child prostitution. Boys and girls from all over the world, the younger the better—as you know if you've seen the files. The police don't care about closed cases. And with both Laura and Zinoviev dead, their accounts are all squared. You're a lawyer, you know how it goes."

Gonzalo shifted uneasily. A lawyer, yes, but an unexceptional one who dealt with civil proceedings and was too squeamish for some things, a lawyer who refused to get involved in these sorts of issues and never understood why his sister had given up everything she had to sink into the depths of such filth.

"What do you want from me?"

"It's not what I want. It's what your sister would have wanted."

Siaka had promised her he'd find out where Roberto was and rescue him. He told her to trust him, said they couldn't risk sabotaging all their years of work. When Zinoviev showed up with the kid and told him to get in the car, Siaka had tried to let her know by texting a single word: *lake.* But she got there too late. Siaka had never forgotten what she said to him, completely beside herself, had never forgotten the hatred in her eyes. When he found out she'd committed suicide, he went to her apartment. He was afraid, scared that the police would find something that might connect him to Laura. It wasn't the police he feared, though; it was the Matryoshka. He found her laptop hidden behind a dresser with the picture of the three of them from the day she took him to see the house where she'd grown up, so he took it all.

He was convinced that the Matryoshka were the ones who'd killed Zinoviev. He'd gone off the rails, become too unrestrained, and was attracting too much attention with his dog fights, brawls, and ranting and raving. No one had ordered him to kidnap— much less kill—Roberto. They must have set it up to make it look like Laura had done it: the handcuffs, the photo nailed to his chest with a nail gun police later found at her place. Nobody had foreseen the possibility of her suicide, but it did save them a hassle. Two birds with one stone.

Siaka knew the Matryoshka's methods and he knew Laura. She'd never have been capable of killing Zinoviev like that, no matter how much she hated him. It had to have been professionals. He was convinced: the way the body had been flayed, the severed testicles. And if they found Siaka, they'd do the same to him. He knew the names of police informers, could provide the names of clients, show them videos so graphic that the public would be sickened beyond belief and have to stop pretending to be oblivious. Plus, he'd promised Laura that he would see it through to the end—for Roberto, and for himself—provided she stuck by him. Laura had promised that she would. But then she'd committed suicide, and now he was all alone.

Rather than make a run for it and start a new life someplace far away, he'd given Gonzalo her laptop and now here he was, wondering whether or not to get on the train to Paris. Why? Because of a conversation he'd had with her that day at the lake.

He'd known Laura for three years, been working with her all that time. He'd watched Roberto grow, gone to her house and even met her husband, Luis. But until that day at the lake, Laura had never talked about her life, her father, the memories contained in her childhood house. Good memories, although Laura seemed sad recalling them.

That was the first time he had heard about Gonzalo. Laura had shown Siaka their names carved into the handrail on the bridge over the creek, shown him the places where they played at being pilots, told him about the snow sculptures she and her brother used to make in wintertime. She was proud of him, and saddened by the distance between them. *If anything ever happens to me, look him up. Gonzalo always knows how to take care of things. He'll help you.*

Siaka was no longer concerned about what might happen to him. The worst had already been done; they'd taken everything he had. But he wanted a final triumphal entry, and for that he had to make sure arrests were made, with courtrooms, cameras, and stenographers. Snowflake's last stand, before disappearing into the mist forever. And Gonzalo, whose bravery he saw no evidence of whatsoever—despite Laura's claims—was his last chance for redemption.

"I'll give you everything I have: proof, recordings, ledgers, names...and the password to that confidential file. But only if I'm sure you'll go through with this regardless of the consequences. That's what Laura would have wanted."

Gonzalo moved with difficulty, touching his side. "I'm not going to lie; this is overwhelming."

Siaka wiped a drop of sweat from the back of his neck. At the moment, his future was not looking bright.

"My train leaves in thirty minutes. And I'm not missing it. I need an answer now. And I want to warn you: You might feel tempted to get involved because you think you owe it to your sister; if that's the case, forget it. Brotherly love is sweet and all, but you have no idea who you're dealing with. They won't just go after you and me. They'll go after your family, your kids, the way Zinoviev did with Roberto. If you say yes, you have to do it for you. Do you understand?"

"I can't handle this on my own. We have to go to the police."

Siaka flat out refused. The only reason he was still alive was that Laura had kept her word and not revealed his identity to anyone.

"No cops. Your sister had a prosecutor she trusted, and I'll give you his name, but that's it until I see you're serious about this."

Gonzalo remained pensive for a moment.

"I know someone who can help us. Chief Inspector Alcázar. He worked with my sister."

Siaka's face tensed on hearing the name. "I don't know what kind of cop he is now, but I know what he was like thirty-five years ago."

"What are you talking about?"

Siaka frowned disbelievingly. "You seriously don't know?"

"Know what?"

"Your sister told me that your father disappeared in 1967 . . ."

"What does that have to do with anything?"

"The guy she worked with, her boss Alcázar, was the man in charge of the investigation."

Gonzalo couldn't remember. He was just a boy back then, but the first time he saw Alcázar was in 1967. Alberto Alcázar was a deputy inspector at the time, dressed in a light-colored summer shirt. A drop of sweat ran out from beneath his brown toupee and down the middle of his forehead. He was leaning against the counter, having a soft drink and smoking a filtered Rex cigarette. Gonzalo's father came to town on the first Monday of every month to stock up on provisions. Rita's supply store was the only place in the village that sold wholesale back then. You could find anything from farm tools, quicklime, and bulk oil to fuses for a meter box or candles to light the long nights when the power went out, which was often. Elías Gil would cram the old Renault full and Gonzalo would be forced to sit straddling sacks of onions between his legs. The memory had faded but not the smell. To this day he still hated the smell of onions and didn't know why.

It was hot that morning, and the store's fan was broken. Alcázar kept looking at Elías, who stood negotiating the price of sparkplugs with the shopkeeper. They exchanged glances once and Alcázar's mustache quivered, as if he'd just smelled something rotten. It wasn't long until the night of San Juan, and Elías wanted his wife and daughter to look nice at the dance that was held at the lake each year. He went to the counter to choose a few silk ribbons from a glass jar by Alcázar's elbow. The deputy inspector hardly moved, adjusting his body only enough for Gonzalo's father to have to look up and ask him to kindly move for just a moment so that he could open the jar. Alcázar stood staring at Elías for several seconds, wearing something that resembled a smile but was in fact simply a way of showing his teeth.

Elías prudently averted his one eye, although by the way he tensed his neck it was clear that he'd had to force himself to do so. He was fifty-six years old, gray and balding, and his good eye was almost buried beneath a bushy brow and the fleshy fold of his eyelid. Alcázar couldn't have been over thirty; he was nearly as tall as Elías, and well built, too, though not as stocky despite the additional bulk of a holster in his waistband. Elías would have been more than capable of breaking his windpipe with one hand in the time it would take the officer to reach for his gun. There were stories about just that—things that had happened in the forties and fifties, when Elías was smuggling political prisoners and those fleeing Franco's regime out of Spain, running people through the Pyrenees.

"My father sends his regards, Gil."

Elías selected a purple ribbon for his wife and a scalloped gold one for Laura. He handed them to Gonzalo and motioned for him to go and wait in the car. Before leaving the grocer's, Gonzalo had heard his father's voice, the gruff tone that threatened a coming storm. But of course he had no recollection of this.

"I don't know who you are or who your father is, but I don't like your tone of voice."

Alcázar let out a grating laugh, it sounded like the chains on a suspension bridge, rattling. An ominous jangle. The few customers prowling nearby shelves hurried to disappear.

"My father is Inspector Ramón Alcázar Suñer. I think the two of you have had your ups and downs in the past."

"Your father was a good man. I think he still is."

Alcázar shrugged. "Ask the Reds like you that he locked up and got out of the way if he's good or not."

"He always treated me well. That's what counts."

"Maybe, but he's retired now, and even though I never understood why he protected someone like you, those days are over. I'm not my father, and you're never going to get chummy with me. To you, I'm Deputy Inspector Alcázar. Got it?"

Elías wanted to laugh out loud. Alcázar's attempt at playing the tough guy was pathetic, as awful as his Floïd cologne. He wondered for a moment what opinion Alcázar Senior must have of his offspring. Not very high, he imagined. Times had changed, and kids were getting soft.

"Of course. I apologize."

"Deputy Inspector."

Elías Gil let Alcázar see the flash of amusement in his eye.

"I apologize, *Deputy Inspector.*"

Exactly twenty days after this first encounter, as the last few firecrackers echoed on the night of San Juan, Elías Gil disappeared without a trace.

Like wolf and sheep. That was what his mother had said at Laura's funeral when Gonzalo asked if she knew Alcázar. Now he understood what she meant, understood why his mother had refused ever to speak to Laura again after she joined the police. It wasn't just about the article she'd written discrediting their father's legend, claiming he'd left them when they were kids and not been murdered by Franco's police, as his mother had always claimed. What Esperanza had never forgiven her daughter for was having chosen to work for the man who, she swore, obstructed the investigation in order to cover up his own crime.

Alcázar had agreed to let Gonzalo come meet him at his little office on the top floor of the building where the judicial police's regional services division was housed. It wasn't exactly your standard police station, instead resembling a command center where various brigades and central services were coordinated and conducted. Gonzalo saw a few uniforms, but not many. Had it not been for the holstered guns and handcuffs hanging from belts, most of the officers there could easily have passed for efficient company workers. Many were young, and the whole place buzzed with energy. The chief inspector's office was bright: A large window looked out over the street and light was filtering in through the blinds. Although the furniture was less than luxurious—gray metal, preassembled—the black armchair, photos, and the diplomas on the walls made the place feel warm. Sitting across from Alcázar, Gonzalo had time to look at the frames while the inspector poured coffee into little plastic cups. Alcázar had had a long, prosperous, and eminent career. A career that was coming to an end in just a few weeks, as the two packing boxes in the corner attested to.

"It was too much for me. Your sister's death was the last straw, the push I needed to decide. I'm retiring; there's nothing left for me here." Alcázar slid a steaming cup toward Gonzalo and lit a cigarette. "Who told you I was in charge of your father's investigation? Was it Esperanza?"

Gonzalo hesitated. He'd come to the inspector in order to ask questions, not answer them.

"Why didn't you tell me yourself when you came to my house?"

"Your sister and I had an agreement. When she came to see me and sat in the same chair you're sitting in right now, I asked her if she knew who I was. Obviously, I had read her article. She told me she knew exactly who I was and said that was why she'd come. If she'd believed the story your mother told all those years was true—that I killed Elías Gil and then covered up the evidence— she would never have asked to join my squad, don't you think? I've done a lot of things I'm not particularly proud of, but I've never killed a man. Did I hate your father? Not especially. Of course, I had him watched. He was the top dog, the dissident, the trade unionist, and I was an ambitious young man, but every time I got close to him, someone would stop me."

"Are you insinuating that my father was under police protection? That he was a collaborator?"

Alcázar disabused him of any such notion. "I assure you that your father was a man of strong convictions, and when it comes down to it, I admit that that was admirable. I know that in the fifties and early sixties he was detained several times and got pretty roughed up. But they never broke him; I'd have found out if they did. The list of collaborators was pretty extensive—you'd be surprised by some of the names on it—but your father's name never appeared. No, he was no snitch. By the late sixties things were different, the Communists were no longer our top priority. The government was teeming with technocrats; U.S. assistance and the economic upturn had shifted our priorities. Let's just say that

pragmatism trumped ideology. Obviously we were still persecuting
dissidents, but our targets began to center more on universities and
Basque separatists. ETA terrorists were causing a lot of headaches
and there weren't enough of us. Besides, your father was a model
worker at the valley sawmill. The reports we got from his foreman
were nothing to be concerned about—no labor disputes, no protests or uprisings. If he was up to anything—smuggling young
people into France, storing leaflets for the UGT workers' union or
student unions—we never found out about it. I could never catch
him; he was smarter than me and that's the truth. What I can tell
you, Gonzalo, is what your mother always refused to accept: that
your father left you. One day, just like that, he decided he couldn't
go on living his dreary life and took off. We never found out for
sure where he went, or what sparked his decision. He just disappeared, like so many others. And God only knows where he ended
up. That's the truth."

No, it wasn't the truth. But it was what the lawyer wanted to
hear, and after all these years a few more lies weren't going to do
any more damage than had already been done.

"Laura and I made a deal. If we couldn't forget the past, we
could at least ignore it when it got in the way. And if occasionally
we tripped over it, we'd just stand back up and walk around it in
order to keep moving forward."

It wasn't that simple for Gonzalo. And he was convinced that
it hadn't been for his sister, either. Their father's memory loomed
too large, it was omnipresent. He felt confused and didn't know
what to think. His mother swore that the police had killed her
husband; Alcázar was supporting the assertion Laura had made in
her article, but perhaps out of self-interest. He was right, though:
His sister would never have worked with the man who murdered
their father; she must have had reliable proof. So why, when Gonzalo read the article, did he side firmly with his mother? Perhaps
because he couldn't accept the alternative that his father—or the

image Gonzalo had constructed of him, the man he so admired—
had selfishly abandoned him.

Regardless, this wasn't why he'd come to see the inspector. He
was there to feel him out.

"Do you still think my sister killed Zinoviev?"

Alcázar's mustache twitched slightly as he wrinkled his nose
in alarm. He intuited some unconnected form of coercion in the
attorney's expression, which was magnified by his thick glasses.
Alcázar knew all the tricks that crafty lawyers used, and if they
were good, they never asked or insinuated anything without being
certain of the answer beforehand. The question was whether or
not Gonzalo was the crafty kind.

"It's not that I think it; the evidence proves it."

Gonzalo steepled his fingers, elbows on the table, head leaning forward as though the credible explanation for something the
inspector had yet to discover were contained in the hollow space
between his hands. Gonzalo worried that his inability to lie was
now more dangerous than ever. With Siaka's warning in mind, he
ventured into speculative territory, which was his father-in-law's
terrain, a place where he felt himself at a distinct disadvantage.

"What if I were to tell you that I have proof Laura didn't kill
that man?"

Of course this wasn't true, not entirely. It was a hunch that he
hadn't substantiated, one that he had no practical support for, at
least not yet. But he managed to make it come off like the truth,
judging by the inspector's disconcerted expression. Gonzalo congratulated himself on how quickly he was learning.

"I'd say, tell me what that proof is and I'll reopen the
investigation."

"But you're retiring in two weeks. You said you were done
with all of this."

Until then Alcázar had been slouching comfortably in his
armchair. Now he adopted a more austere posture, straightening

his spine, the leather creaking as if it were the cogs of his mind being set in motion.

"Why don't you tell me exactly what you have in mind?"

What did he have in mind? Gonzalo didn't know—maybe to unburden himself of a little of the weight Siaka had placed on his shoulders. He'd started blindly down a path that seemed to border the edge of a cliff, and the only thing keeping him from tumbling over it was his instinct.

"I think I can prove that this whole thing was set up by the Matryoshka to frame Laura for that murder."

The inspector's modest excitement came to a screeching halt. He face clouded over.

"Where did you hear that name?"

"My sister had an informant, someone inside the organization who passed her information. You didn't know?"

Alcázar stared fixedly at Gonzalo. His eyes had stopped flitting around and were now frozen in their sockets, like those of a statue.

"That's insider information. How did you find out?"

Gonzalo hated cards, hated having a hand in the games his father-in-law sometimes brought him along to as an extra when he was playing with his buddies at the club. There was no logic to the face-offs between card sharks, the men won or lost based not on their cards but their cunning. Who knew what? Who was bluffing? Who had the best hand?

Before seeing the images on Laura's computer, Gonzalo didn't understand why she'd decided to become a cop. He understood the reasons Luis gave him for why she got involved in that sad and sordid world. Laura was never one to stand on the sidelines and watch her life go by, that much was certain; she always had to be in the thick of things, the one holding the reins. But she could have found other ways to fight evil, even without quitting her job. Gonzalo was as shocked as Luis was when she chose to join the police; she didn't have what it took for that kind of work, they all thought, forgetting that the habit doesn't make the nun. But when he saw the word *Matryoshka*—the password he'd used to log on to Laura's computer—on the back of the singed photo, he suddenly got it. Matryoshka are Russian nesting dolls, a game of illusions where there is only one truth, and when it finally appears, the truth and all of its reflections look identical—but that doesn't mean that they're the same thing. Our eyes believe what they see: the first doll. If we're patient, we get to the second one, a little smaller and yet identical, and so on. Three dolls appear, then four. The smaller they are, the more concealed and true. Until finally we discover the last one, almost as small as an index finger. The painstakingly painted miniature, as detailed as the largest doll, is the baby, the whole reason for the game. This embryo is the starting point of everything, it's where the artisan puts the most thought and effort. And only after all of the dolls have been opened, lined up by size, do we realize that what is identical is in fact different—simply the road we had to travel in order to reach this ultimate secret.

Complicated. Simple. Gonzalo bet that Laura was the one who named the child pornography operation the Matryoshka. A nod to her past, to her real reason for entering the game—and now he was being asked to play. *Where am I, Gonzalo?* Far away, he'd thought when reminiscing about their childhood games back at the lake house. Now he saw that this wasn't the case. Laura never hid far; she stayed close so that he could find her easily when he was alone and afraid. All he had to do was to look and see, open each successive doll in order to find the baby. All the same, all different. A game, that's all it was, a game with its own rules.

He doesn't know, Gonzalo thought, noting the inspector's grave expression. He doesn't know Siaka exists. Laura never told him.

"I'm going to formally request a reopening of the investigation."

Alcázar ran his hands across the top of his head. A deep fold appeared on his neck, above his collar. He was trying to keep calm, and it was precisely the restraint of his movements that proved how nervous he was. For a moment, Gonzalo felt a déjà vu that brought him back to the conversation he'd had with Laura's husband the day he told him that she was dead.

"Don't do this, Gonzalo. Don't get involved, it's not worth it. Give me the proof, tell me who the informer is and I'll take care of it. You have a family and future to think of. You shouldn't even be here; it's only chance that brought you. But I owe it to Laura, she was my partner."

Gonzalo took off his glasses. Sometimes he preferred the hazy world of indistinct shapes. Contrary to what people thought, he could see better this way because there was no point looking. That was how he felt about Alcázar's blurry face: It was simply a thick fuzzy outline, a smell of coffee and cigarettes. And heavy breathing.

"I owe her, too, Inspector. She may have been your partner, but Laura was my sister."

Gonzalo put his glasses on again and it all melted away, the appearance of normality rushing furtively back. But it was too late. He stood, preparing to leave, and then remembered that he had one more question for the inspector—who in two weeks would no longer be an inspector.

"After the funeral, you went to see my mother, didn't you? You were the one who convinced her to sell my father-in-law the lake property."

Alcázar, too, stood. He'd recovered his habitual aplomb, but Gonzalo picked up on a slightly odd vibe. Not a threat, more like a sense of resignation, the sort someone feels when they've done all they can to avoid tragedy and finally throw up their hands.

"From what I understand, she didn't sell it only to your father-in-law. You're his partner now, so you benefit as well."

This was not, in fact, true. Not yet. Gonzalo still hadn't signed the agreement.

"Why did you intervene on Agustín's behalf?"

Alcázar's heavy eyelids moved slowly. His retirement benefits were a joke, so he had to find ways to make ends meet. From time to time, he'd stop by at law firms, poke around, leave a business card here and there. There was always some job that needed to be done, if you knew the game.

"Your father-in-law and I have had our dealings in the past, he in his role as attorney and me in mine as officer of the law. We weren't always after the same thing, but we've always had a good relationship. He filled me in on the situation and I offered my services."

"Does he know you were my sister's boss?"

Alcázar smiled, wondering if Gonzalo was really this oblivious or just pretending.

"Is there anything in this city that Agustín González doesn't know?"

Gonzalo intuited something in the man's eyes, a deep wound, and suddenly was seized by the idea that Alcázar was many men. And that not all of them were nice.

"How did you convince my mother? What did you say? She hates you; she'd never do anything you said without a pretty compelling reason."

Alcázar bit his mustache. Was the past a compelling reason for an eighty-six-year-old woman? No doubt it was, as were the fear of losing her only remaining child's love and the thought of dying alone.

"That's something you need to ask her."

As soon as he was back outside, Gonzalo called Siaka. It took two rings for him to answer.

"I see you missed your train to Paris."

"There are others, I can wait a little longer. I've made my decision. Have you made yours?"

"I'll do it."

"Are you absolutely sure? There'll be no turning back, Lawyer Man."

Gonzalo realized that his palms were sweaty. No, of course he wasn't sure. He thought of Javier, that day up on the cliff before he jumped. He thought of his son's fear and the way his anxiety vanished when Gonzalo took his hand. Who would be there to help Gonzalo?

"Yes. I'm sure."

"All right, then. Do you have a piece of paper? I'm going to give you the password to the confidential file."

Gonzalo took a piece of paper and pen from his briefcase and leaned on the hood of a parked car, cell phone lodged between his shoulder and ear.

Rather than take down what Siaka said, though, he held the pen motionless; the phone fell to the ground. Gonzalo didn't need to write the password—he knew it. Five capital letters: *IRINA*. He automatically reached into his pocket for the locket he'd found in his mother's bomber jacket, fingers stroking the letters engraved so long ago. Though they were partially illegible, their impact on Esperanza had been enormous the day he showed her the faded photo of a woman and girl.

He could hear Siaka's voice coming from his phone on the ground. "Lawyer? You still there?"

Gonzalo picked up his cell. "I'll call you later."

Twenty minutes later he strode into Agustín González's office, ignoring the secretary's furious protestations. His father-in-law was on the phone and gave him a look of surprise before motioning his secretary to leave. For a full minute, Gonzalo stood there, refusing Agustín's silent invitation to take a seat. When the man hung up, he pressed his spread fingers down on the desk.

"I hope you have a good reason for storming into my office like this."

"I'm not selling."

"Excuse me?"

"You heard me. I'm not selling the land and I'm going to appeal my mother's sale of her seventy-five percent. I have reasons to believe she signed under duress."

Agustín was staggered. He looked at his son-in-law as though he'd lost his mind.

"So you're going to report yourself? Because as far as I'm aware, you're the one who convinced her."

"Don't toy with me, Agustín. I know you sent the inspector who does your dirty work to convince her. I don't know how he did it, but I'm going to prove he took advantage of his authority. And if necessary, I'll use my mother's fragile mental health."

"Do you mind telling me what on earth is the matter with you? We had an agreement."

"You wouldn't understand. I could sit here all day and explain it to you and you still wouldn't understand."

"I presume you know what this means."

"I know exactly what it means. The merger is off, and I can't say I'm sorry about it. I'll speak to Lola; we'll have to rethink our options, but we'll manage."

Agustín banged a fist on the table. "Who do you think you're talking to? This project is going forward with or without you, do you understand? You'll sell that piece of shit property or I'll destroy you!"

Gonzalo blinked as though he had an eyelash in his eye. His self-assurance was wavering.

"Like it or not, I'm your daughter's husband. If you come after me, you come after her and your grandchildren as well."

"Don't be a fool. They are my family. You are not."

Gonzalo swallowed and stood tall. "Do as you see fit. The lake property is not for sale."

He walked out of the office with a lightness in his shoulders that he hadn't felt for ages. Glancing sidelong at Agustín's secretary, what he saw was a dinosaur at a wooden desk, a lifeless insect with a bitter expression and sagging flesh. He'd been so close, he thought, walking nimbly down the hall and into his own office with a spring in his step. Luisa was typing up a memo.

"The sign from the balcony—where is it?"

"In the storeroom, why?"

"Put it back out and have it repainted. I want it in big letters."

"What's going on?"

"There's no merger."

"Dear God! And in my mind I'd just kissed the unemployment line goodbye."

Gonzalo glanced at the stack of files on his assistant's desk, resigned.

"We might both end up in that line, but we're going to put up a fight. Oh, and the geraniums, put them back out, too. I like them there."

"The way you like the Russian in the apartment next door?"

Gonzalo blushed. "Don't be impertinent. I'm a married man."

"Of course you are, and I planned to be a virgin when I got married."

Luisa was radiant with unexpected satisfaction. Gonzalo himself, despite his decision, was not so optimistic. Acts of bravery are often leaps of faith that have unforeseeable consequences. But he couldn't deny that at that moment, he, too, felt what some people might describe as happiness.

He phoned Lola. She'd already heard the news—Agustín had been quick. Gonzalo let her vent, listening to a string of objections regularly punctuated by tears, which seemed more of indignation than sadness. Her father had given her all the details and for ten long minutes she emotionally blackmailed Gonzalo, talking of the children's futures, the house, and anything else that occurred to her. He let her talk.

"We'll speak tonight, Lola."

He hung up feeling bittersweet. Nobody said the lean wolf had an easy life. Checking his watch, Gonzalo picked up his briefcase: There was still time to make it to visiting hours at the retirement home. His mother was going to tell him everything, starting with what it was that Alcázar knew and how he'd broken her determination not to sell the lake property, and then who Irina—the woman in the locket—was. And this time he wasn't going to let her tangle herself in a web of silence or run off to her desert island of memories.

Walking out of the office, Gonzalo headed for the elevator. The underground parking garage was only half lit since one of the large fluorescents had burned out. Gonzalo clicked the remote on his SUV to guide himself by its flashing taillights and the beep the vehicle made before automatically unlocking its doors. His spot was at the back, between two thick cement pillars, which necessitated endless maneuvering in order to fit between them each morning. If he'd sold the lake property, he would have gotten a larger spot on the upper level, where Agustín and his associates parked at no risk of scratching their paint on columns. Tough luck.

He opened the back door to put down his briefcase.

"Remember me, asshole?"

Gonzalo barely had time to turn. A look of shock flashed in his eyes and he opened his mouth to shout, but he didn't have a chance.

Something heavy struck the base of his skull. He became intensely dizzy and felt everything lose texture. The second blow caused him to fall flat on his face. And then came something sharp that pierced all the way to his lung—once, twice, three times, in rage.

9

They were exhausted after a long journey through soft snow, which in some places was up to their knees. It had been several arduous days of crossing ghostly forests and traversing grubby hills and swamps, constantly set upon by the guards and their minions. Elías carried little Anna in his arms. She was very pale and shivered the entire time; although her mother tried her best to warm her body, a tattered shawl was simply insufficient. Bundled inside Elías's coat she could breathe slightly better. Irina was too tired to carry her anyway, although she refused to admit it. Still, she sang to her, cooed in her ear, made up stories about mythical animals, and pointed out anything she could in an attempt to turn their journey to hell into some sort of adventure her daughter could bear.

But even Irina paled at the sight of the immense complex extending along the frozen river's banks, where finally they were ordered to stop. They'd arrived at Tomsk, where all of the deportees had been sent for distribution to the camps of Siberia. Makeshift wooden barracks and watchtowers were visible from the right bank of the Tom. On the river's other side lay the city, and beyond that, the mining areas. There were thousands of deportees, and more and more kept arriving. Mounted patrols continuously drove them on, guiding humans like a river toward the camp's entry, a gap in the barbed-wire fencing.

Elías observed the macabre spectacle before him with his one eye.

"What kind of insanity is this?" Enormous cargo barges were arriving at improvised docks, and hundreds of people were being forced to climb onto them through portholes and beneath canopies. Claude, stricken, said he wouldn't go.

"It's important that we stick together. From what I overheard from the guards, the authorities were totally unprepared for this. There are too many of us, no administration, and there has already been major turmoil. Last night, from what they said, there was a massacre. They're sending us upriver, to other camps beyond where the Tom joins the Ob."

Irina stared at him in alarm. They looked otherworldly, but their cold and fear were totally real.

"That can't be. There's nothing there, out beyond the Ob."

Claude shrugged, gazing at her with bulging eyes, his face so gaunt they looked like huge black bubbles.

"Well, that's where we're being sent—into the nothing."

Elías refused to accept it. Like many, he still believed that his ending up there had been some terrible mistake and that somebody in some office of the Kremlin would be sorting it out right now. Like him, others clung to absurd hopes to keep from succumbing to despair. Some had children or brothers in the Red Army, even in the police; they were the most arrogant, and the guards showed more restraint with them, just in case. Others took refuge in their ignorance, refusing to doubt—mothers with young children, housewives or factory workers with only minor offenses such as missing work, writing something snide on a bathroom wall, or simply leaving home without their internal passport. There were also a vast number of peasants who'd entered

Moscow or Leningrad illegally, attempting to escape the famine of the countryside. They seemed resigned to their fate, trusting that it couldn't be too bad. Their hope was to be sent back to where they'd come from, wait there for a time, and then try once more to reach a big city, perhaps with better luck.

By moving farther back into the Tomsk camp, they managed to stay together. The barrack they took refuge in was shockingly overcrowded—so much so that it was hard to breathe—but the guards wouldn't let them leave, much less get anywhere near the bridges leading to the city.

During their days there, Elías saw Igor Stern prowling the camp several times. He seemed to grow stronger by the day, and his band of henchmen crueler. Igor often strolled the barges and barracks with a thick birchwood club, its tip round and hard. He'd beat stragglers like an impatient shepherd trying to keep his flock together. Elías felt strangled by rage so deep that he often fantasized about creeping through the snow one night, sneaking into Igor's tent—a luxury that the monster had wangled from the guards—and slitting his throat as he slept.

He knew this was impossible, of course: Igor was untouchable. But the mere idea of it afforded him a few moments of calm. What upset Elías most, however, was seeing Michael and Martin, his old comrades, trail after him like lapdogs. They'd become lackeys, running from one place to another as the column's rear guard, robbing anyone who lagged behind and then rushing to hand over the booty to Igor or one of his lieutenants. It revolted Elías.

One morning he decided to talk to them, to make them see reason, but Claude convinced him that it was pointless.

"I've already tried. Michael, in particular, is the worst. You know what happens to converts: They mask their guilt and remorse with excessive cruelty. He's convinced that sticking with Igor is the only way he'll survive, and honestly, it may be true. He's got a better chance of getting out of here alive than any of us do."

"But at what cost?"

Claude looked at him like he was a child unable to comprehend the most simple reality.

"The one that has to be paid, Elías. The only way to repent the things you've done is to be alive after doing them and look back. Which means surviving."

Elías gazed at an old woman so weak she could hardly stand. She struggled unsteadily to a makeshift latrine, a simple hole that prisoners had dug in the hard snow with their bare hands. Privacy was unthinkable in the circumstances, and yet a group of women surrounded her, shielding the old woman with their bodies so that she could heed nature's call free from the eyes of other prisoners. Claude was wrong, and his cynicism was simply a different kind of shield, something used for protection. Dignity was important, the only thing that would allow them to sleep in peace for the rest of their days, if they managed to make it out alive.

If you only looked, small gestures of kindness were visible amid the desperation, things that made Elías believe that compassion and humanity were not lost. People still assembled, old friends and new, to discuss common interests. They warmed one another with coats or tattered blankets, shared petrol, firewood, and food despite never having enough. They were still human, united in their misery; they drowned their anguish by singing old songs beneath the stars, around bonfires—fires that Elías, a young foreigner, found mysterious and magical. The mere act of survival was heroic, carrying on without sinking into the depths of despair despite the obvious justification for it, fostering hopes and offering small gestures, slivers of decency to which they clung.

"What about Martin?" he asked, pointing to the young man trailing after Michael, looking lost and guilty.

Claude coughed cavernously and spat blood. His fever had returned and seemed to be getting worse. He stared disbelievingly at Elías, a flicker of scorn in his eyes.

"Martin is in love with Michael. Come on, don't look so surprised. You honestly couldn't tell? They were caught with their pants down back at the Government House. Sodomy is a deadly sin even in a proletarian dictatorship. Freedom is only for men, my friend, not women and effeminates. That's why they were sent here. Besides, our redheaded friend is weak; his soul is effete, he's nothing but a shadow. He'd go to the pits of hell if Michael asked him to."

Elías had never allowed himself to consider whether he was attracted to men.

"What are you smiling at?" Claude asked.

Elías clapped his friend's shoulder. "Even in the worst places on earth, you can find relief in beauty. That's what my father used to say."

"What do you find beautiful about a country that hates you?"

"It sounds like this is where Martin found the love of his life."

It began snowing again, but people made no move to run for shelter. There was no place to run to. Most simply stood, like clay statues, dissolving slowly.

Food distribution was the worst time of day at Tomsk. Driven by hunger and thirst, people forgot their humanity and became a frenzied mob in their attempts to make off with a crust of bread hurled from a distance by the guards. They bit, kicked, hit, and stomped on one another. The weakest had no chance: Old people and small children were dependent upon family members or the charity of anyone who might take pity on them. Elías and Claude made a good team and had developed a technique: Whenever they sensed that there was about to be a distribution, they remained unmoved by the nervous hysteria rushing over prisoners like a wave. Calmly, they positioned themselves like a single being, as close to the guards as possible. And when the time came, they launched a coordinated, combined attack.

Elías was a big man. He'd regained his strength quickly, and his reputation—after the Igor episode—had earned him the fear of other prisoners, and he exploited this by removing his eye patch. The sight of his dark, empty socket made even the most fearless recoil. What's more, he had no problem using his arms and legs to clear a path. Once their rivals were blocked, Claude, who was much nimbler, would race forward, literally tackling and climbing over bodies like a rugby player, attempting to catch the food being thrown. If they were lucky, some days they made off with provisions for themselves, Irina, and her daughter. If they were not, they shared their hunger together. Food distribution was not an equitable affair, and no one expected it to be. The few women who were there—a distinct minority among the prisoners—offered guards or other prisoners their bodies for it if they had to. There were rapes and other abuses as well, but no one had time to worry about that.

Igor—and others of his ilk—stole whatever they wanted from the prisoners, and felt no remorse. He even set up a profitable black market for purloined goods, which the weakest prisoners were forced to use in order to survive. Anything could be bartered for and everything had a price, be it one's body, labor, or personal belongings. Elías had watched in horror as an old man literally wrenched the gold teeth from his mouth to buy bread he would then be unable to eat, but that would feed his grandchildren. Others sold now-useless identification papers, books, family jewels, blankets, clothes…anything. And sometimes for nothing. There was no way to lodge a complaint if Igor randomly decided to keep payment without giving in exchange what he'd promised.

Amid this chaos, Michael had risen, becoming an efficient accounts administrator for his new master. Soon the sight of his stocky legs running all over the camp became infamous. Ledger under one arm, he'd make note of deposits, bribes to be paid the guards, debts to be collected in the form of beatings or stabbings behind the barracks—generally after nightfall—and the names of people who for one reason or another might be of interest to Igor: possible informers, those willing to serve him, as well as potential enemies to be eliminated before their power or reputations posed a threat. Martin—in effect, his shadow, just as Claude had said— simply accompanied him, increasingly gaunt and drawn. Michael, on the other hand, riotous and enraged, seemed to thrive, always ready to turn violent, especially if he sensed that Igor or one of his lieutenants was watching.

That morning, Elías was preparing for battle with Claude when he saw Igor approach. The man strode around like a field marshal inspecting enemy lines before sending his soldiers into the fray, wearing the serene smile of one who knows he holds the strings of destiny in his hands. Not far behind trailed Michael and Martin.

Igor Stern was a happy man. All men are when they feel they occupy their place in the world, and this was his: chaos, where the brute force of instinct, not the constraints of civilization, was what mattered most. For the first time in his life he felt free, free to be what he truly was with no fear or restraint. But this had nothing to do with the other prisoners, or with Martin and Michael, who had jumped on like fleas the very first day. Igor was not happy simply to survive and unleash his instincts. Instead he thought, biding his time, wondering how best to use this unique opportunity. He'd never been a czarist boyar, that much was clear, nor would he make officer in the Red Guard, or marry a princess in exile. His blood was tainted: Rather than blue, it was red and purple. Still, why couldn't he dream of a dacha on Lake Balaton? Why not picture himself in one of the motor cars that were now starting to be seen on the streets of large cities?

Perhaps, if he played his cards right, he would one day wear a frock coat, grow old by the fire, surrounded by grandchildren and well-trained dogs in an old czar's palace, reading all the books ever written, dictating his life to a scribe, hobnobbing with top officials or even Stalin himself, going to the opera and having a private audience with Lyubov Orlova, while his empire grew by spontaneous generation. In war, most men suffer and die. But a few know how to create opportunities amid the suffering; and this was war, was it not? To have it all—wealth, power, and time to enjoy them both—that was what he wanted. To forget his past as a Jewish cartwright. He had always been sure he'd be pushing up daisies by the time he was thirty, that he'd die in some cold ditch in a random town, stabbed in the back. But suddenly, growing old and prospering seemed possible.

Igor observed the surge of bodies, advancing and receding like waves, crashing into the bluff of officers distributing food. You could see the soldiers' unease, their fear of being overwhelmed by a hungry mob. These soldiers were too young. They were scared, and armed. A bad combination.

And then, amid the gray mass, he discerned the green coat of the Spaniard whose eye he'd taken out on the train. He smiled with an electric sort of excitement. Challenges gave him a thrill. Igor hadn't seen Elías since they left Moscow and he'd assumed the kid had died of hunger. Something inside him was pleased. He turned and instructed Michael to approach him.

"Isn't that your friend, the Spanish engineer?"

Michael saw Elías with Claude, both glaring at him from the distance. Michael nodded.

"What's he here for?"

Michael looked around. Why were any of them there? For the uranium mines, the prospecting. To provide the overwhelming amount of slave labor required to colonize Siberia, a plan hatched by a few bureaucrats who'd lost their minds. The excuses for having imprisoned them in this wretched land were almost immaterial.

"Criticizing Stalin and the Communist system in letters to his father."

Igor shook his head back and forth mockingly. This was a marvelous country, a place where you could rape, kill, and steal—

provided it wasn't in the name of politics. And writing a critical word could turn out to be worse than any of that. A joke about Stalin's mother was punished as severely as rape: a ten-year sentence. Words, in those strange times, were like a sea of broken glass on which some men were forced to walk barefoot. It was safest to remain silent. And yet still, a few naïve or foolish men spoke out, assuming the risk.

"Go tell him I want to talk to him tonight."

Michael nodded, bowing his head in embarrassment. Like a scared dog, he approached his old comrades. Igor delighted in the heavy morning air, knowing he was king of the world.

Elías watched Michael approach.

Claude grabbed him by the elbow. "Keep calm, Elías," he whispered.

The three, once friends, stood face-to-face. Not more than a few weeks had passed since they'd been laughing in a train compartment, on their way to the Soviet Union, full of plans. Now they stared at one another in mistrust and hatred. All of their bonhomie was gone.

"How could you do something like this?" Elías spat, unprompted.

Michael held his gaze unflinchingly. "It was easy," he said cynically. "A simple matter of calculation: This is what yields the greatest probability of success. A formula to resolve the unknown, that's what we mathematicians do. Once the decision is made, there's no point contemplating alternatives."

"You swine," muttered Claude.

Michael let out a heartfelt laugh and then arched his brow, gazing at the Frenchman in amusement.

"Very Shakespearean of you. A bona fide villain, so the hero can really shine at the end of the show. Who am I, Othello?" His face suddenly hardened. "This isn't some fucking play. This is real life, you know? So hold your reproach until the holy men write your posthumous biographies. 'I knew Michael, the traitor.' Eventually, time will be the judge. For now, it's the living who judge us."

With that, he turned to Elías. "Stern wants to see you in his tent, tonight."

Elías clenched his fists. He'd removed his eye patch and the bulging socket gave him a terrifying air.

"Run and tell your master that this dog isn't on a leash."

Michael was undaunted. "You still don't get it. There's no choice in this matter. If you don't go on your own, he'll come find you. And he won't be nice to you ... or to them."

Michael pointed to Irina, Anna in her arms, making her way toward a wooden stable where a soldier watched a pack of horses paw and stamp at the ground, steaming up the air. Irina said something that Elías couldn't make out from the distance. The guard laughed, raised the latch on the fence, and let her through to the animals, where she held her daughter's face to the horses' nostrils, trying to warm her with their breath. Then the guard shouted something. Irina placed Anna on the ground, and he slipped his filthy hands inside her blouse, pulling out one of her breasts before forcing her behind the fence. Elías looked away in shame.

"This could all get so much worse, Elías. Don't forget: tonight." And with that warning, Michael walked off.

Igor stood motionless at the entrance to his tent, looking out into the night. He observed the darkness in silence—eyes stony, nose sniffing the air—alert to distant groaning that suddenly turned into an agonizing, hair-raising shriek. He, however, was unmoved. Perhaps it was the endlessness of the dark expanse that sedated him. For a moment he seemed sad, emanating the sort of sorrow that derives from utter loneliness, but suddenly the play of light and shadow from an oil lamp created a pantomime of expressions that changed each second, from anger to calm and back again.

After a minute he turned and fixed Elías with a disturbing gaze. Elías tried to keep his composure but knew that this lunatic might slit his throat at any moment. They weren't alone in the tent: Two of Igor's toadies were huddled together under blankets at the back. One of them gnawed on a piece of salted meat, unable to bite off a hunk. Michael and Martin had accompanied Elías to the tent but had not entered. They hadn't earned that right.

"How's the eye?" Igor inquired in a kindly tone, as though it had nothing to do with him.

Elías was seething inside, but fear and survival instincts overpowered his rage. "Not bad."

Igor nodded. He turned, suspicious, like a buzzard fearing a trap as it approaches carrion in the snow.

"An eye is expendable. You've got another one, at least for now." He placed a hand on Elías's shoulder and then let it run down the length of his overcoat. "I still want this. It's a good deal: an eye for a coat, which you can steal off anyone."

The tent was like a small warehouse of stolen goods: suitcases, clothing, food, cigarettes. Igor was wearing an old gray wool sweater and a woman's soft fur coat. He didn't need Elías's.

"It's a matter of principle, you know?" Igor declared, reading Elías's thoughts. He walked to a corner of the tent and rummaged through some odds and ends until he came upon what he was looking for: a book, its cover broken.

"I took this little book off some kid. He was so absorbed, reading in the middle of a wind storm as if nothing mattered but the words on the page, not even freezing to death. So I thought, this must be really important to him. When I asked him for it, he said no, fought the way you did for your ratty coat. Absurd, don't you think? Clinging to things that aren't ours to begin with. Not even our lives belong to us, though we should at least try to hold on to them." Igor shook his head, as though truly unable to comprehend that kind of attachment. He held out his arm and, like a trained monkey, one of his men handed him a canteen that reeked of vodka. Igor took a long pull and wiped his mouth on the sleeve of his coat.

"It was only a damn book; that idiot got himself killed over a few words!" scoffed the prisoner with the salted meat. The other one apparently agreed, swearing and saying something Elías couldn't understand. Igor eyed the book and laughed derisively.

"Who knows, maybe happiness lies somewhere between truth and desire. What do you think?" he asked Elías, and then smiled quickly, as though it didn't matter at all. "Do you understand why I want your coat? A Siberian wolf takes what he wants, no explanations."

There came a silence so tense that the only sound heard was that of the canvas tent, flapping in the night wind.

"I've never seen a Siberian wolf. From what I hear, they're the kind of predators who avoid confrontation if they're not sure they're going to win. But goats and mules can break backs, too, you know."

Igor's lieutenants stood menacingly, but he stopped them with a look of surprise and admiration. He'd have given a lot to have this Spaniard in his ranks instead of those other foreign sissies, the bowlegged kid and the redheaded mincer. He'd always detested bootlickers and cowards and admired those like Elías, who acted like he had nothing to lose despite fighting to control the fear coursing through his body right now. But he knew Elías would never submit to him—he had what it took, had the fire in him that so few men manage to keep alive. And that was a shame.

"What do you think's going to happen when we're moved upriver, with no guards, no food, and no refuge? In fact, there will be nothing at all there—except me. You'll have nowhere to hide, nothing to save you, no hope and no chance. Just the island, the river, the steppe, and me."

With a quick move, Igor grabbed Elias's face in his stubby hands and wrenched off the patch protecting his empty eye socket. He brought his mouth so close Elías thought he was going to bite his nose off.

"Hold on to this eye, my friend. I want you to see your world crumble around you. I know your kind. You think you're better, think you won't succumb to the horror; you cling to little things like that stupid kid whose hands I cut off so I could take his book. Empty gestures, believe me. There are no heroes in hell, and that's where we're headed."

Igor slowly released Elías's stricken face and then held the book to the oil lamp, its flame growing as it licked the pages.

"I'm not going to take your coat. I'm going to sit here and wait for you to come back and beg me to accept it. When you do, I'll use it to bury you. And you'll thank me."

Before going back inside the shack that served as his refuge, Elías vomited. He'd broken out in a cold sweat and had to clench his hands tightly to keep them from trembling.

Irina emerged from the shack. In the full moon, her face had a ghostly air, almost blending in with the snow. Elías straightened, ashamed, but she pretended not to notice the brownish pool of vomit on the ground or the damp stain that had formed on the front of his pants. Instead she smiled at him, and her smile was like a fire by which to warm and protect himself.

"It's not that easy to get rid of me," he said. He needed to fill his lungs with cold air, get away from the filth.

She paid no attention to this outburst of childish bravery. Elías had nothing to prove to her, but sometimes men needed to convince themselves that they were more than scared little boys.

"I know you saw me this morning, at the stable with the guard. I could tell by the way you looked at me."

Elías gazed at her in silence.

"I am not a whore," she said angrily, unnecessary cruel to herself.

Elías reddened. "You mustn't speak like that, Irina. Not even here."

She stared into his eyes. "Don't worry. They're my words, not yours. You're just the echo."

Something about him reminded her of her husband, a fact that scared and attracted her in equal measure. Silly idealists, capable of sacrificing everything over a question of pride. Men who seemed dry and brittle on the outside but were coursing rivers on the inside—edgy and rugged but also stubborn and hard to tame. His name was Viktor. On his detention file he was listed as a piano teacher at the state conservatory. The man was pure passion, which meant that he was free, because he feared nothing in life. Irina couldn't forget the way he'd smiled in incredulity when they came for him, like he thought his detention was a joke. He was naïve like that, wore bright happy colors and gazed at everything in boyish wonder. A believer in the great utopias that never came to be but were always just around the corner. A Russian Jew who read Schopenhauer, recited Maupassant, Rimbaud, and Verlaine, and spent hours studying Barbusse and the French symbolists and German expressionists.

Like all dreamers, he, too, was convinced that Russia was a great land of theater, music, and literature. It would never have occurred to him to think that its men and women could be as foolish, hateful, and cruel as people anywhere. He loved the Andalusian sensitivity of García Lorca's language, in fact preferred it to Mayakovsky, who was always so blunt and unromantic. *Wine from another's vineyard always tastes sweeter*, he liked to say, only half joking. He said García Lorca suffered the disease of life, so long drawn out, with great dignity. That was why Viktor was shot: He wanted to be cured of the pain and, like Don Quixote, refused to believe that the windmills would always be stronger than those who tilted at them. Her husband died like all visionaries, convinced that the only thing that would save Man was brotherhood and not some epic destiny. But expressing that—writing and disseminating it—amounted to intolerable treason.

She had been sentenced to three years as a collaborator. How could she not have collaborated with her husband? At the bottom of Irina's detention order, it stated that her daughter had an "unknown father." One more humiliation, a denial of the truth that robbed her past of dignity. Anna had just started to speak when Viktor was taken away. She was a shy girl, beginning to feel her way in the world with unsure arms; sometimes her voice was like that of a baby chick, teeth chattering in the cold, and her father was the only one who could calm her. He loved his daughter with utter devotion, but when she grew up and Irina was no longer there, those who'd killed him would tell her that her father was a nobody, convince her that her mother was a whore who'd lain in a cot with a stranger—as she had with that guard, opening her legs in exchange for a bit of warmth for her daughter. When the soldier flipped Irina over, she'd been met by her daughter's tiny eyes, which she could see through the horses' legs, wide and incredulous. And as he grunted, thrusting, Irina smiled and told her not to cry, saying it was just a game. That was a condemnation she could not bear.

"In theory, they should have taken her from me, put her in an orphanage. But it didn't happen. And that irregularity was the only thing the official who signed my deportation order seemed to care about. That's the problem with bureaucrats: They refuse to see people—their faces, their hair, their skin. They never stop searching for them in absurd paperwork but can't see that they aren't there, that the people are right in front of them. It's not what they do that makes them despicable but the way that they do it, dressing everything up in ridiculous language and concepts to justify themselves and clear their consciences. And this is what allows them to become killers, hiding behind their desks and reports."

She gazed at Elías and then went to him. It was incredible, but beneath the thick layer of rot and filth on him, she felt signs of another life. She perceived, through his pores, his hair, the faint smell of soap, the lingering scent of rosemary on his neck. He had the same voice as Viktor, steady as a road with no forking paths, and asked for nothing, not even reassurance or certainty. Just as a bird doesn't ask what its wings are for and simply spreads them to fly, Elías's voice conveyed his unquestioning character. She could see in his good eye the same recklessness that Viktor once displayed, convinced that despite it all, standing firm and dignified was worth it. He had faith in his ideals and would surrender to them; he'd end up sacrificing his life over something as stupid as a coat.

"You look after my daughter and me. You worry about us and comfort her. I've seen the way you look at me. I know what you're starting to feel."

Elías blushed but Irina forced him to meet her gaze, lifting his chin.

"You make me feel alive, but you'll get yourself killed by a guard, or some prisoner like Igor, over a coat, a loaf of bread, or some offense you won't be able to tolerate. You'll take your honor and your valor and your useless pride to the grave, but I will be left alone, and I'll have to stay alive to take care of my daughter. I'll have to let a guard paw me, let eyes like yours judge me, drag myself through the mud and feel dirty."

She was crying. Elías moved closer, touched her tears and felt them burn. There was no regret or self-pity in those tears. Just life, slowly seeping out, as though asking forgiveness for having been there at all.

"I am not a whore."

Elías smothered her words in kisses. "No, you're not."

"Say my name," she begged. "Help me to exist."

And Elías whispered into the night. "Irina."

They made love standing up, desperate with desire. Outside their own private world, that night civilization and barbarism were one, but Elías and Irina forced the horror to retreat, like an imaginary shadow.

PART TWO

YELLOW LETTERS

10

Walking into Bar Flight was like entering a time capsule, like stepping back through the years to a place where everything was frozen in the past. A cavernous bar, Flight was filled with blue smoke on nights when they held readings. Part-time poets stood on a small carpeted stage at the back to recite their verses. There was only one condition, and Uncle Velichko was adamant about it: All of the bards had to recite in Russian.

"How's your mother?"

Uncle Velichko wasn't actually Tania's uncle, but his forty-plus-year friendship with her mother had earned him the title. He'd been in Tania's life for as long as she could remember, an old man, very old—frozen in time, like his bar. Each night, when she took a seat at the bar facing the stage, he poured her a shot of vodka and asked the same question. And each time, she gave him the same answer.

"Why not cross the street and ask her yourself?" Her mother's bookstore was less than three hundred feet away, and yet her uncle bridged the distance separating their businesses no more than two or three times a year. Her mother made the reverse trek even less often. She detested bars and couldn't stand Velichko's wistful desire to live in the past.

But Tania loved the place. The exposed brick walls were plastered with photos, most of which formed part of her uncle's memory. There were pictures he'd cut from encyclopedias, old newspaper clippings, portraits and posters painstakingly collected and maintained over the decades. Each of them related to "his" country, not "this Russia"—which he claimed bitterly not to understand—but the heroic Russia of the war against the Nazis. Sometimes Velichko let her use the bar for her own exhibitions, and he stubbornly imposed the same condition as he did on the poets: The subject had to be Russia. But Tania fought to convince the half-deaf old man that, after all these years in Spain, it was time to show a little interest in the country that had taken them in. So, finally, he grudgingly agreed to let her "denigrate" his walls (that was the word he'd used when she hung the photos) with a couple dozen black-and-white scenes from everyday life.

"Personally, I don't like them," he said, scrutinizing the photos with a look that said he'd made up his mind a priori. "But other people seem to; you've already sold several. I don't understand why people buy photographs rather than take them."

That was typical of his reasoning. After all, he was still an obstinate old Siberian, tough as salt fish.

"For the same reason they buy books and paintings, Uncle Vasili. Because everyone appreciates art, but not everyone is inspired to create it."

The old man shrugged his drooping shoulders, uncomprehending, as though this were a mystery never to be resolved, and then tossed a dish towel over his shoulder and concentrated on the glass he was polishing.

"You should find a husband, a good man to take care of you," he declared, as though this were the only logical conclusion. "Someday you're going to have to get married. It's fine to be a rolling stone, passing through other people's beds, but everything gets old."

Tania smiled, recalling the last conversation they'd had about her single status and her sex life, which was too promiscuous for her uncle's liking. At least on this, he was in total agreement with her mother. Often it seemed to be a two-pronged nagging attack, as if they'd rehearsed it.

"I'm waiting for my white knight," she replied teasingly.

"And I'm waiting for my Soviet hero's medal, but it's never going to come, no matter how long I give it," Velichko grumbled.

Tania had never seriously contemplated getting married or living with someone. Maybe it had to do with the fact that she and her mother had always been on their own and things had gone all right for them without a man. She couldn't recall the last time her mother had brought someone home. It wasn't that she hadn't had lovers; she was and always had been her own woman, mistress of her destiny, and very attractive, but she tried to be discreet and keep all of that separate from her personal life. And as for Tania's private life, she didn't really know what to think. The closest she'd come to a proper relationship was when she was twenty years old, and that hadn't been with a man. She'd never spoken to her mother or uncle about Ruth, the fine arts professor. Anna's liberal streak had its limits, and Uncle Vasili's was nonexistent.

Ruth was half West Indian and half European, with stunningly beautiful copper skin. She was also ten years older than Tania and had seduced her—or perhaps Tania had let herself be seduced—with breathtaking ease. They toyed with the idea of moving to Holland together, but things never progressed after a stormy, torrid vacation in the land of canals. Ruth was passionate and quick to anger, and Tania was as proud and stubborn as her mother, so it didn't last. What remained of that trip were memories of their amazing sex and blazing arguments, and the butterfly tattooed on her neck. There had been other women and men after that, but nothing serious. Tania was strangely impervious to people's emotions. She never thought it was the right time to commit, never felt the need to take things to a deeper level.

Until she met Gonzalo.

Furtively, she pulled from her pocket the photo she'd snapped of him sitting on a bench, staring into space, and studied it for some time. What did she see in him? He wasn't handsome or even attractive, at least not by the standards she'd adhered to until then. Remorseful, withdrawn, he looked like the kind of man who views life as an accident and has nothing significant to show for it. And yet, behind those glasses and that veneer of restraint, something shone, a distant glimmer in the depths of his faded green eyes. Gonzalo Gil was an enigma, like a photograph whose mystery is revealed only once it's been developed. She'd seen something in him, one of those little things that go unnoticed by most people but that she'd felt compelled to immortalize in a picture. He was one of those men whose potential had not been realized, and yet there was something real, pulsating beneath his anodyne gray façade. She wanted to find out what lay behind the apparent fragility, to discover what he kept locked beneath the surface.

The room was dark, the only light a bare red bulb above the door. The blinds were drawn, but through the crack beneath the door, pale light filtered in from the hallway. He felt an intense pressure on his chest, as though a boulder had been deposited on his rib cage. It was Lola's head, resting there. She was listening to his heartbeat. Her eyes were open, staring at him like a cat in search of attention. It had been years since she'd looked at him like that. Although half asleep, he felt her stroke his messy hair, awkwardly tucking it out of his eyes, her fingers unaccustomed to demonstrations of affection. She sat up and chastely kissed his dry lips, barely brushing against them.

"Sleep, my love. I'm here."

Where were his glasses?

He sank back down into a fetal, liquid darkness.

"He should be dead."

"But he's not."

"It's a miracle."

The word *miracle* gouged his consciousness like a spike. *Wake up.*

Harsh light penetrated his eyelids. He blinked and opened his eyes, then immediately wanted to close them again. Reality, sharp and sudden, in his parched mouth. He tried to move his neck and felt the orthopedic brace restrain him, forcing him to keep his eyes on a blue recessed light fixture on the ceiling. A low ceiling. He heard voices murmuring quietly, whispering.

"Nobody can believe it. It's a miracle."

That word again. Shock, suddenly penetrating the fog of his brain. Laura was dead. He, apparently, was not. Gonzalo stirred beneath the coarse sheets. He wanted them to go, to leave him alone. Too late. A nurse noticed him wake up and was now by his side, taking his pulse or maybe just holding his lifeless wrist, an IV sticking out of it.

"How are you feeling?"

She smelled like... What did she smell like? Starched uniform, antiseptic soap, disease, and a faint trace of life outside the hospital: beer, tapas, cigarettes. *Like the resurrected,* he thought sardonically. He wasn't at death's door, but her almost lashless eyes, ringed by dark circles, watched him as though he was.

"What happened?"

The nurse shot a glance toward the foot of the bed. A stranger sat observing him, arms crossed over a short-sleeved shirt whose buttons were straining at the man's paunch, threatening to pop off. Alcázar.

"They got you good. You'll be pissing the color of a good Bordeaux for a while, but you were lucky," he said, mustache waggling side to side.

The nurse concurred. Eight stitches at the base of his skull, cervical sprain, four broken ribs, bruising all over his body, and three stab wounds so deep that he had internal hemorrhaging. They'd already operated on him twice, and for a time things had been touch-and-go in the ICU. But now he was out of danger.

Gonzalo felt around beneath the sheet. They'd inserted a catheter.

He asked for water. The nurse brought a plastic cup to his swollen lips. He took a short sip, observing Alcázar over the top of the cup.

"What are you doing here, Inspector?"

"Worrying about you." He sounded sincere.

Gonzalo had to go back to sleep. Rest. It was so nice, that state of unconsciousness.

"I'll be back tomorrow."

He barely heard the inspector's voice, melting. Gonzalo nodded. Or thought he did.

His sleep was becoming less deep and dense, the darkness less safe and comforting. Pain was becoming a constant presence, like the images of what had happened: the attack in the garage, Atxaga's face disfigured by rage. He was regaining feeling.

"That's a good sign," said the doctor, who came by each morning. "You're coming back to life."

Well, life hurt—a lot—and the painkillers were no longer killing his pain.

And then one morning as the nurse helped him sit up, placing a pillow behind him so that he could eat his first breakfast (juice and a greenish puree that he vomited up), his mind suddenly cleared and he shouted in alarm.

"The laptop!"

"Excuse me?"

Siaka, the Matryoshka, the merger with his father-in-law... The computer. He'd had it on him when Atxaga attacked him.

"The stuff I had on me the day I was attacked—where is it?"

"I don't know. I imagine that's a question for the police."

A question for Alcázar.

That very afternoon the inspector came again, at the same time. He'd become a discreet yet familiar presence over the course of those days. He sat in an armchair at the foot of the bed for fifteen minutes but didn't give the impression that his visits were an obligation, more like a field study, Gonzalo being the subject of his detailed investigation. Most of the time Gonzalo was either exhausted or asleep, but this didn't seem to bother the inspector. To the contrary, he'd relax in the chair, cross his legs, and simply watch him. Sometimes Gonzalo pretended to be asleep so as not to face the scrutiny. There was something disconcerting about Alcázar and he couldn't put his finger on it; he was like a crossroads with no signs indicating what lay down each path. But that afternoon Gonzalo's desperation to find out what had happened to the laptop forced him to communicate.

"I don't need a babysitter. You don't have to come every afternoon and sit watching over me. The nurse and doctor say I'm out of danger."

Alcázar brought his face right up to the headboard.

"That's not the way I see it." He pulled out a photo taken from the security camera and held it a foot from Gonzalo's face. "The parking garage camera recorded everything. This is the guy who beat the crap out of you. Recognize him? Is this Floren Atxaga?"

Gonzalo nodded.

"I'd say that as long as this guy is on the loose, you're not out of danger."

"Miranda Acebedo, his ex-wife..."

"Relax. I gave her police surveillance."

Gonzalo sighed painfully. He felt air wheeze through his lungs like a broken bellows.

"Weren't you supposed to be retiring?"

Alcázar's mustache rose like a curtain, his way of smiling.

"Officially, I'm just another civilian. I handed in my badge two weeks ago, just like I said."

"Then what are you doing here?"

"Just because I left the police doesn't mean I don't have bills to pay. Us old folks have the annoying habit of not wanting to die when we retire. So for the past few months I've been laying the groundwork, and now I'm a free agent. Your father-in-law hired me to protect you and your family."

"How considerate of him..."

"Don't fool yourself. You're nothing but an investment as far as the old man is concerned. But your family, they're top priority. I talked to your wife."

"You've spoken to Lola?"

"You were in a coma. I had to act fast and that's what I did. There are two men stationed at the door of your house, watching your family, ensuring their safety. They're good guys."

Gonzalo hadn't taken the graffiti seriously, hadn't truly seen it as a threat. He'd thought of Atxaga like a Pekingese, the typical little shit that yaps a lot but only bites the hand that feeds it.

He'd put Lola and the kids in danger. The mere thought of it made him gag.

"I thought I could handle it..."

"And clearly, you were wrong." Alcázar brought him up to speed: Atxaga had been staked out, waiting for him in the garage, behind a column. When he saw Gonzalo approach, he came out from his hiding place and struck him in the head with a crowbar. Gonzalo lost consciousness almost immediately, but the guy kept furiously kicking and beating him. "He stabbed you three times. He was trying to kill you, there's no doubt about it. Luckily, someone showed up and scared him off, a woman. She was the one who called the police."

"A woman? I didn't remember there being anyone else in the garage."

"Well, you didn't see Atxaga, either. Anyway, she left before the patrol car got there, but we don't need her testimony. We have the video."

Gonzalo locked eyes with the inspector, who was scrutinizing him as though he were a lost cause.

"The things I had with me…there were documents in my briefcase"—he tested out his lie; it sounded fairly plausible—"and my laptop, with all my clients' personal data…"

Alcázar tried to calm him. "The police gave everything to Lola. I don't think anything's missing. Atxaga wasn't trying to rob you."

Was he lying? Or was what Gonzalo sensed not a lie but ill-concealed superiority, like that of a caretaker with a patient, like the nurse who helped him eat or the doctor encouraging him to start physical therapy as soon as possible? In truth, the inspector's patronizing tone derived from a conviction that Gonzalo was naïve and probably weak, a man who knew nothing about the real world, the danger that others can inflict, a man who had suddenly taken a crash course in reality. *And you think you can take on the Matryoshka? Now you see what can go wrong, how a perforated lung feels. Welcome to my world.*

"When I was lying there, right before I lost consciousness, I thought I was going to die. Really die."

Alcázar scratched his chin with the knuckle of his index finger. He inhaled and held his breath for a moment before releasing it slowly, with an almost inaudible purr, the result of chronic bronchitis, the result of smoking two and a half packs a day. It was just a matter of time before he died of emphysema, if he kept up at this rate. But the inspector wasn't listening to any purring cats, even if they came from his throat.

"It's awful, isn't it? The certainty that you're going to die. It's an idea that's with us from the day we're born, yet the second it goes from theoretical to being an indisputable experience, it becomes unbearable. You can't think about anything else, fear paralyzes all other things: the love for your family, the interior monologues people supposedly have. That stuff about your life flashing by in a second? Bullshit. Your sphincter unclenches, end of story. Don't feel bad about it. Nobody wants to die, Gonzalo."

The idea of death made Alcázar think of Cecilia, the agony she went through, him watching her those last few weeks as the cancer devoured her, minute by minute, and there was nothing he could do for her but be there, witnessing her panic and suffering. Alcázar stood, ready to leave.

"But you dodged a bullet this time. You'll never forget; it'll be there, lying in wait, stalking you. From time to time it'll come bite you, laugh at you, scare the crap out of you, but life makes you take sides, and you'll side with life and get on with it."

Gonzalo sensed no moralizing or counsel on the inspector's part. He was simply describing his own experience, with a complete lack of emotion.

"Don't let that monster get close to me or my family again."

"Relax. He won't come anywhere near. And if he does, I'll be waiting for him."

Alcázar made as if to leave but then stopped short and held a finger to his lips.

"Oh. One more thing. Your kids mentioned seeing a young black man prowling around the house. A well-dressed guy, good-looking."

Gonzalo was sure the inspector saw his face change expression. He tried to cover, but his lies and evasions were vague; it
was like someone trying to hide behind a curtain that's too short,
leaving his feet poking out.

"I remember Lola mentioning it, but I don't see how that
ties in."

Alcázar cocked his head, as though exposing the absurdity.

"No, of course not. But if he shows up again, let me know."

Lola arrived two hours later. Before she'd even had time to
put her purse down, Gonzalo asked anxiously if the police had
given her the laptop that had been in the back of his car. Lola
thought about it for a moment but was almost certain there was no
computer among the things the police had delivered.

"I thought you hated those things, anyway. You're always
saying that if it weren't for Luisa, you'd be lost in the world of
computers."

Gonzalo improvised, a bit less carefully than he had with
Alcázar.

"I'd just started trying to learn. You're *almost* sure the
police didn't find it, or you're absolutely sure? Think, please, it's
important."

Lola found his excessive concern over a laptop odd.

"I'm absolutely sure. It can't be that big a deal; surely you
made backups."

Had Siaka? He hoped the young man was better at this than
he was. The possibility calmed him slightly, but he couldn't stop
fretting about whose hands the information Laura had collected
had fallen into, and what they planned to do with it.

Lola came to the hospital alone. The first time she visited,
she'd brought Patricia, but his daughter had been so frightened
that she couldn't stop crying when she saw the mass of flesh that

sounded like her father but looked nothing like him. Since then, Lola hadn't brought her back. As for Javier, he hadn't so much as stopped by. As usual, Lola tried to defend him.

"You know what he's like. He asks about you, sends his regards, but he doesn't want to come…Anyway, I think he's got his head in the clouds these days."

"What do you mean?"

"I could swear he's met a girl."

Gonzalo detected a note of joy in his wife's eyes, something almost akin to envy, the rekindling of emotions long ago lost or forgotten in the pages of their history. They, too, had once been young and in love, rash and fearless; they, too, used to blow off the rest of the world to see each other for five minutes and make out, returning home with their clothes disheveled and a telltale flush to their cheeks. He reached out a bandaged hand, IVs of saline attached to his wrist, and touched Lola's painted fingernails, her hands resting on the sheets.

"I'm so sorry about all of this," he murmured. His voice was still thick, his intonation not yet his own.

Lola smiled faintly and tried to look understanding, but the truth was she simply looked exhausted.

He was alive, and there was a gruff-looking man at the door—a guard Alcázar had posted there in case Atxaga was tempted to come back and try to finish Gonzalo off. Lola was fine, and so were the kids. That was what mattered.

"I should have taken the graffiti thing more seriously."

"That doesn't matter anymore."

They looked at each other in silence, so many unsaid things swimming in their eyes. Rebukes, pleas, excuses. Why was it all so hard to say?

"I love you. You know that, right?" Lola's eyes glimmered.

Gonzalo swallowed. His right eye was full of blood, his left so swollen it was hard to keep open. The bloody one inspected her.

Five minutes, tops. That was as long as he'd spent, frozen, at the half-open bedroom door that day eighteen years ago. All eyes, all shock. He could see part of the bed, tangled sheets and their feet entwined, swishing back and forth like the tentacles of a jellyfish, bunching and separating in time to the groans. Hers, his. He'd never wanted to know the man's name. He'd seen part of his back—tanned and muscular—and one white buttock, boyish in contrast to the rest of his dark, toned, sweaty body pressing into her. Lola, buried in his arms, his body. Moaning. And the sound of it was still between them. Gonzalo wished he could wrench it all from his brain, the moaning and the sight of their feet stirring in the sheets. He wished he could erase the image he saw every time he looked at his wife. But he couldn't.

"We haven't talked about what's going to happen, now that the merger is off."

The door that Lola had opened hopefully now suddenly slammed shut in displeasure. She leaned back, withdrew her hand, and placed it on a shapely knee, still sensual, peeking out from beneath her pencil skirt.

"It's nothing that can't be fixed. I spoke to my father, he understands the situation and is willing to wait for you to convalesce. I promised him you'd reconsider your decision, that you'd think about us, about your children and their future, about our well-being."

Lola's hard expression, lips painted with subtle flesh-colored lipstick, left no room for speculation. Gonzalo brought his hand to his chest, the IV trailing behind. This slow movement was the only sign that he was still breathing.

"I can't do it, Lola."

"Yes, you can."

She didn't understand what was going on inside him, didn't realize that what had begun as tiny cracks in the wall now threatened to bring down the whole edifice, a complete and total collapse.

"I need to hold on to the lake house, and I need my firm to remain independent. It's important to me."

"Memories are worthless, Gonzalo. Aren't you the one who used to say we take them with us when we move, that it's like putting them in a backpack? There's no reason to tie your memories to that house."

"It's not about memories, and it's probably not even about the house—which, you're right, is worth nothing. But I still dream of being the man I once was, or the one I hoped I'd be. It's not too late, not yet. We don't need a big house with a pool, we don't have to send the kids to such expensive schools, we can get by. Let me take care of you and the kids without your father's help. I can do it. I want to do it."

Lola wasn't even listening, had already dug her heels in. She didn't understand what had happened to Gonzalo since his sister died, what sort of torment it had set off inside him. But she sensed that the results would be disastrous.

"How are you planning to take care of us, Gonzalo? The same way you took care of that man who almost killed you and filled our lives with fear? Two armed men, paid for by my father, staked out at the door! That inspector prowling around like a prophet of doom!"

Cruelty was her desperate, last-ditch effort. She refused to accept the situation without putting up a fight. She knew her father, knew what he was capable of if anything got in his way, and right now Gonzalo was the obstacle. He was refusing to give up whatever it was he had in his head—rash romanticized notions of freedom and dignity, nonsense that Esperanza, the old witch, and his crazy sister had filled his head with ever since he was a kid. And yet in his selfishness he dared to demand that she and the children give up precisely the same thing that he would not. Lola had already given up so much by marrying against her father's wishes, against her class. The son of a Communist, an atheist, a lowlife who didn't have two cents to rub together when she met him. And she'd suffered endless humiliation, belittled by her friends and family; she burned in shame when they argued about politics, stood in the crossfire without losing her composure, feeling alone when Gonzalo looked at her with scorn: The poor always saw poverty as a virtue, and he looked down on her as though she, his wife, were despicable and corrupt just for being rich. And she'd suffered through all of that because she loved him, and because with infinite patience and dignity she'd built a world around them, to protect them, and to keep Gonzalo from the bad influence wrought by his invented memories of a father he'd concocted.

She thought she'd won, but now it was clear that she had not. People don't change who they are, they simply dress up as something else. Eighteen years of guilt was a long time to repent, every day and every night suppressing the urge to tell him the truth—a truth that, had Javier not been born, would have been insignificant. She had been young, and those of her class reminded her that she still was. It had stopped being so fun to be married to *the son of the Red*, she had her doubts, wondered if she'd been too rash in marrying him, maybe they were right and she was wrong. So she succumbed and had an affair, which time and the realization that she truly loved Gonzalo should have rendered meaningless, anecdotal. But Javier was born, and it was as though Gonzalo could sense that the boy was not his son, and she knew that was the real reason for their constant battles, for the war that wounded them both equally. Every night she had the urge to tell him, to make him see that mistakes are things we learn from if we don't make them again, but she kept quiet, again and again, and now there was no way to speak those words. This was why they were still together, and why she'd renounced so many things, renounced herself. But she wasn't going to let Gonzalo's stupid adolescent defiance drag her family down. They weren't twenty years old anymore; they had two children to worry about, and whether he liked it or not, this was the world they lived in.

"I'm not going to change my mind, Lola. I won't sell the property and I'm not going to sign the merger with your father."

"Even if it means losing me? Even if you lose your children and everything we've built together?"

Gonzalo thought of the story his mother had told him about how his father had lost his right eye trying to hold on to a stupid coat that someone wanted to steal when he was young. Sometimes we lose things that matter by defending things that others find insignificant.

He gazed at Lola in sadness.

I lost you eighteen years ago, said the silence in his eyes.

His time in the hospital was like a break from reality—Gonzalo was in his own world. Luisa visited in the mornings and insisted on bringing him chocolates (Gonzalo didn't even like chocolate but he used the bonbons to bribe the medical staff). She'd sit by his bed and tell him how things were going at the office since his decision not to sell the lake property or join Agustín's firm.

"For now, I'm keeping the wolves at bay, but I don't know how long I'll be able to hold out without backup."

"They're saying I'll be discharged in a few days, but it will take time before I'm back in shape. Broken ribs take months to heal completely."

Luisa giggled in amusement. "When have you ever been in shape?"

This was her way of hiding her concern. Despite the glittering new sign hanging outside, clients were barely trickling in, and she suspected it was due in large part to the recruitment campaign Agustín's secretary had launched. More than once Luisa had come upon the woman chatting with someone in the hall who would later, coincidentally, decide to end their business relationship with Gonzalo's firm. Luisa didn't want to worry him too much, so she didn't mention the letter that had arrived from the building administrator that morning, informing them that their lease was up in three months' time and was not being renewed. Things were looking as black as the bruises on Gonzalo's face.

"I need you to do me a favor. I want you to get the tape from the parking garage's security camera."

Luisa gave him a surprised look.

"The police have it and are examining it thoroughly. What do you need it for? You really want to watch that guy almost kick you to death?"

"It's personal." He couldn't tell her that he needed to see what had happened to the laptop. "Do you think you could get your hands on it, discreetly? I don't want anyone to find out."

"I've got a friend down at the command center. I'll see what I can do..."

Coming from Luisa, this meant: Consider it done.

"Oh, and another thing. Try to get some information on Inspector Alberto Alcázar, anything you can find."

For once, Luisa didn't joke. The inspector's name was enough to make her serious.

"Are you in some kind of trouble?"

Gonzalo smiled. *Trouble* was a generous term for the situation he had gotten himself embroiled in, with its many fronts.

"I don't like that guy, Gonzalo. Lately he's been coming around your father-in-law's office a lot, and I don't know how to explain it, but he scares me."

"Would it bother you less if I told you he's officially no longer a cop?"

Luisa didn't seem comforted. Still, she said she'd do what she could to comply with her boss's wishes.

.   .   .

When did he stop caring about his job? Alcázar couldn't remember. From among his inventory of excuses and justifications, he'd selected the date of Cecilia's death as the beginning of the end. But that wasn't true, and at this stage in the game, who did he think he was fooling? The fact of the matter was that he'd never liked his job, although that didn't mean that for a few years, while his father was still active on the force, he didn't enjoy it. He did, but always in a seemingly surreal, disjointed way. It had been like a game, and then the game became too real. Was he going to miss his old routines? Not a chance.

"What have you found out about Atxaga?"

Agustín González was dressed for a formal dinner. He looked good in his black tux and bow tie. You have to be born with a kind of poise in order to make sophistication seem natural, and the old man had been. On walking into the office at Agustín's house, Alcázar had seen a girl who couldn't have been more than nineteen or twenty. She wasn't your typical floozy; this one was refined: Persian-looking features, slim waist, and inconspicuous bust. Agustín—*don* Agustín—was getting soft; he went for the wild outrageous girls less and less these days. They were all getting old.

"Out of the picture. But as soon as he shows his face, I'll break it."

Agustín adjusted his cuff links, which perfectly matched his platinum watch. A watch like that would have been enough to send Cecilia to a private clinic in the U.S. for cancer treatments; that was what all terminally ill rich folks did. It wouldn't have saved her life, but she'd have gotten a few more months and a less agonizing death. This was what made Alcázar so sick, when it came down to it—not her pain, but his, and the knowledge that if you have money, not even death is the great equalizer. Forget what poor wretches said—the illusory hopes for some sort of final justice, the bullshit about every pig going to slaughter on the Feast of San Martín. It just wasn't true. Here was the old man in all his splendor, making pacts with the devil. How many people had he fucked over? Too many to count, a fair few of them with Alcázar's help.

"I admit that if the bastard had finished off my son-in-law, he would have done me a favor."

"What about your daughter and grandkids? Would he have done them a favor, too?"

"They don't need him. They've got me. I take care of everything, that's what I do. And now I have to take care of this piece-of-shit property that's gone from being a headache to a migraine."

Alcázar stared at a photo on a small side table. In it were Agustín González and the inspector's father. The image of his own father, so young, shocked him, as it always did. The fifties had been their Golden Age, a time when they were free to make and break all the rules in the book. The lawyer was a minister's son; the commissioner, a man with no scruples. It was easy to see who'd taken the bigger slice of the pie. But it was also true that this photo was the reason Alcázar was able to rub elbows with the old man, call him *tú* rather than *usted*. He recalled afternoons when his father used to take him along to the dog track to take care of business. Like it or not, his dad had paved the way.

"You did a good job on Gonzalo's crazy mother. How did you convince her to sell?"

Alcázar was evasive. Luckily, there were things even the old man didn't know about.

"If he starts incompetency proceedings for his mother, the contract won't be worth the paper it's written on. And even if he doesn't, you can't begin work orders without his twenty-five percent."

Agustín González inspected his nose, teeth, and cheeks in the dresser mirror. He wasn't stupid enough to be fooled by his own mesmerizing appearance but did feel satisfied at what he saw. A world where everything was always coming up daisies, that was what was expected of him and that was what he, the consummate actor, was going to present. Still, maybe tonight his self-assurance—even with a girl as gorgeous as the one waiting in the living room for his arm—wouldn't be enough to convince his clients that the lakeside project was running along smoothly, full steam ahead. People like that didn't care about fireworks. They had no interest in bells and whistles. What they wanted were facts, data. And until now this was what he'd offered them. But Alcázar was right: He had a problem on his hands. And to powerful people—infinitely more powerful than he was—problems were like wrinkles in the red carpet: Someone had to smooth them out before they walked by, and that was his job.

"I don't know what kind of trick you played on Esperanza, but pull another one out of your hat and convince her idiot son to sell."

"I'm all out of rabbits."

Agustín González adjusted his bow tie and frowned, noticing how low his jowls hung.

"Well, hunt one down wherever you can. Time's running out, Alberto. I bet your father would have known what to do."

He'd seen the old man give that look before, the empty glimmer in his eyes that said to hell with scruples, morals, good and evil. He was made of sterner stuff, he lived in that limbo where gods live, impatiently watching the strife of mere men. He didn't want to be troubled with details, unseemly or otherwise. He wanted the contract on his table. That was what he was saying when he brought up Alcázar's father. But Agustín didn't understand that times had changed. Gods no longer raised their arms in Fascist salute, went hunting with "El Caudillo" Franco, or whoring with his son-in-law, the Marquis of Villaverde. You couldn't toss dead bodies in a ditch or throw them out the police station window these days. But the old man didn't realize that. Or he did but didn't give a shit.

"You do know we're in a bind here, right?"

Agustín González examined his own face, now transformed, in the mirror. "What do you mean?"

Alcázar stroked his mustache. Even the gods had pimples on their asses. He pointed to the hand-painted Russian dolls Laura had given him. They were beautiful, inexpressive but brightly colored, dressed as peasants, with floral handkerchiefs tied around their heads. The old man had insisted on buying them when he saw them in Alcázar's office. He wanted them as a trophy, like the deer, boar, and wolf heads he displayed in the library, from a time when all of Spain was a private hunting preserve for those of his class.

"If it's true that your son-in-law has grounds to reopen the case—"

Agustín González was irritated but didn't raise his voice. He never lost his sense of decorum, never came out of character. "He's got nothing."

"What if he does?"

Agustín smiled, consulted his platinum watch. The young lady with Persian features would be getting impatient.

"Then you do whatever it takes to get it from him."

"Whatever it takes?"

The old man shifted his gaze from the inspector with scorn.

"You know, I really miss your father. You never had to repeat things with him."

11

Things were slipping away. Nothing seemed real, and at the same time everything seemed all too real. Confronted by this impossibility, Elías clung to Irina each night. Slowly, after Anna had fallen asleep, she would take off her clothes and lie beside him, like a leaf falling into his arms. A leaf that sometimes trembled and others seemed not to know he was there. Making love in silence, surrounded by strangers—stretched out at the back of the barge, pretending to sleep or turning away to give them a modicum of privacy—was not easy. At daybreak, as the sun began to peek out hesitantly, she would dress in the same silence, a silence that hurt Elías. Except at night, Irina refused his touch. Any sign of affection only heightened her fear and panic, as if she sensed what everyone feared and no one said aloud. The closer they got to Nazino, the less willing she was to harbor any illusions of hope. The ship charted its maddeningly slow path through the waters of the River Tom, nothing to see but the endless sterile landscape of sandy banks and small islets. No possible life.

Irina had a small book of poems that she kept hidden. Elías sometimes saw her reading it. Occasionally, she'd look up and fix her stony gaze on the riverbank, lost in the distance, and no one could bring her back. She'd recite a poem in her contralto voice, always the same poem. And when she got to the end, she'd stop and blink, as though the final verses had been erased from her memory. Then she'd cover her mouth with her hands and begin to cry. Elías had tried to console her, but she only looked at him— coldly, hurtfully—from the corner of her eye, refusing to share the pain that was hers alone. A night or two later, she'd come back to him, lie by his side on the rotting wood of the barge's floor, curl up in his arms and kiss his wrists, the palms of his hands, his chest. Elías had learned that it was pointless to ask her anything and took comfort in that moment, breathing in her body not through his nose but with his fingers, his mouth, his skin. He'd hold her until he felt, once again, that spark of life being rekindled, the warmth that he so needed.

For several weeks the barge made its way glacially forward, until they reached the confluence of the Tom and the Ob, chunks of ice melting in the coming spring. At this point the currents became powerful, the river filled with gorges, and large islands appeared, barren but for sparse clusters of black spruce and fetid swamps. The barge was forced to reduce speed to keep from running aground in the muddy sand. It cleaved its way through the water, churning up frothy white crests ahead, its wake disappearing almost instantly behind. And then finally, one morning, the boat's engine stopped whirring, and they turned right, toward the shore, coming to a stop at an old abandoned dock. Someone with a macabre sense of humor had posted a wooden sign: WELCOME TO THE ISLAND OF NAZINO. ENJOY THE SCENERY. IT WILL BE YOUR GRAVE.

There was nothing to see. Nazino was a remote island some three kilometers long and over one kilometer wide, at the confluence of the Ob and Nazino rivers, an uninhabited territory with a few clusters of pines and huge expanses of murky swamp, which in the summer became a breeding ground for all manner of insects. Out beyond the southern shore lay the vast expanse of the steppe, inaccessible.

"They can't leave us here," Elías murmured, when the prisoners were forced to disembark.

In total there were more than two thousand people, guarded by some fifty poorly equipped soldiers and a handful of exceedingly young officers. The only structures were a very few makeshift barracks for the guards, which had been thrown together from the remnants of old fishing shacks abandoned long ago. No living quarters, no administration, no medical unit, no latrines. Nothing but a few old canvas tents, surrounded by bolts of barbed wire that hadn't even been unrolled. The authorities hadn't bothered to put up more than a few watchtowers, close to the shore and wooded areas; no one in their right mind would attempt to escape. There was simply nowhere to go. Tomsk was more than 800 kilometers away; Moscow might have been around the corner and still no one could possibly reach it.

Prisoner brigades were organized. They were ordered to erect their own prison, to build with their own hands the very structures that would incarcerate them, and yet there were almost no tools, wood, or nails. Each brigade was led by an auxiliary police officer of sorts, whom the guards had recruited from among the common prisoners. When it was Elías's turn to be assigned a brigade, the officer pointed to Igor Stern, who was to be his leader. This was not a coincidence. Igor gave a sardonic salute from the tent he'd already appropriated. Claude, Irina, and Anna were sent to another brigade. At least Claude would be nearby. Elías knew the Frenchman would do anything within his ability to protect them, though this was slim comfort. Nothing could be done without the consent of men like Igor and his ilk, and from the first moment they made it clear to Elías that his life was going to become a nightmare far worse than it had been thus far.

. . .

Elías often bumped into Michael—with his shadow, Martin, always trailing close behind. They tried to avoid each other, but when an encounter was inevitable, Michael would fix him with a furious gaze, as though somehow Elías were to blame for what he had become. Martin would offer a guilty, timid smile and even sneak him food or clothing when no one was looking. His excuses and justifications were pathetic and infuriated Elías, especially when he then went on to rob or beat someone mercilessly, simply to please Michael. For the time being, Igor Stern was too busy organizing his thieving operation and imposing a reign of terror to worry about Elías. But when they crossed paths, he'd smile callously to remind him that they had unfinished business.

"I still want your coat."

Typhus and dysentery soon ravaged the camp. The only rations were woefully insufficient sacks of flour, which many people cooked after mixing it with the filthy, toxic water. People were starting to die of dehydration, high fever, and hunger—the hunger was appalling. What few rabbits and squirrels there had been soon disappeared, and even the rats that had been on the barge with them were highly coveted. There were almost no birds flying overhead on their way to warmer, less rainy climes. The brigades led by prisoners worked piecemeal, clearing scrub, raising columns, and moving tons and tons of sandy ground, sometimes with their bare hands. None of it seemed at all logical, unless the aim was to exhaust what little energy the deportees had left.

Soon an air of madness and disease hovered over the island, the silence was unbearable; it was like an insane asylum where empty shells of people wandered from place to place, absent, hollow, hopeless.

Although the brigades were kept separate during the day, at night they all congregated on the barges moored at the dock. This was the only shelter they had. Elías would find Irina and Claude, and they would comfort one another by telling stories, trying to remind one another they were still human, that they had a past and maybe a future. But their hopes and memories soon became a sickness almost as debilitating as typhus, for by evoking the past or thinking about the future they lost the will to face the present. And in the end, even those attachments dissolved. Day-to-day survival became their only topic of conversation: where you could get a potato, where to steal a cape, which guard might be kinder, how to avoid being clubbed by Igor's lieutenants.

Only Elías still clung to the belief that the whole nightmare would end, refusing to admit that this mayhem could possibly be the result of a premeditated plan on the part of the authorities. There was no logic to it, no conceivable reason they would decimate people this way. After all, he repeated obsessively, he was a Communist, he'd committed no crime. And his constant mantra was that Stalin could not possibly know what was going on; the Great Father would never allow these atrocities. The first few days, Claude retorted with caustic rejoinders and the two of them would become embroiled in political and ideological arguments. Though they never came to blows, they did sometimes spend a couple of days angry with each other. And Elías couldn't help seeing that his friend was even more vehement when Irina was around, just as he could not help noticing that on at least a couple of occasions, Claude had pretended to be asleep, eyes half closed, while actually spying on Irina and him as they made love in silence.

In the last week of April, Claude's condition grew markedly worse. His fever rose higher and higher, and the stump where his fingers had once been became reinfected. Like a sick dog, he crawled off to be alone, avoiding company, including theirs. He would find out-of-the-way corners and hunker down, his back to

the world. Irina could do little for him with no medicine, no qui-
nine, and no clean bandages, yet still she refused to leave his side.

"You have to eat something," Elías insisted when his friend
refused even a small ladleful of the viscous soup given out once
a day.

"Why?"

"Because I need you by my side. Without you, I'll never be
able to keep going."

Claude smiled for a moment, looking at him out of the corner
of his eye, and almost made a teasing face but then stopped himself. He drank a little but vomited it up almost immediately.

"And what makes you think you'll be able to keep going if I'm
alive?" he asked, eyes glassy, wiping his mouth on the back of his
festering hand. "Have you seen what things are like in this god-
forsaken place? Yesterday I saw a group of prisoners drag a woman
into the forest. Guess who was among them?"

Elías could imagine. Michael's savagery was becoming noto-
rious. Elías and Claude had argued about their former friend's
horrific transformation. Elías could not conceive of an educated, hardworking idealist—*a civilized man*—undergoing such
a metamorphosis. Claude's view was that Michael had always
been a psychopath just as dangerous as Igor, but up until the
moment they met, their circumstances had been different.
Michael had concealed his contempt beneath a patina of sophistication and restraint, but in the current environment of absolute
impunity, where the law of the jungle reigned supreme, his criminal potential had been exposed. In his opinion, Michael would
have behaved with similar cruelty—subtler, perhaps, but cruel
nonetheless—as a commissar or even a father. His was a somber
but categorical conclusion.

"Men like Michael cannot be redeemed. They have to be
eliminated, like vermin. I watched him drag that woman off by
the hair to the tents where Igor and his lieutenants stay, and the

guards did nothing to stand in his way. I thought they were going to rape her, and then realized that's not the worst thing they can do to you here. I listened to her screaming for hours. Hours. I tried to cover my ears, but her cries slipped through, ringing out in my brain. They didn't just rape her, Elías. They cut her up. Do you understand what I'm saying? They cut her up and ate her."

Elías stared at Claude, sickened. It was the fever, he thought. His friend was delirious. And yet a few days later there were new episodes of cannibalism. Bodies found tied to pines who had had parts of their thighs torn off, their stomachs ripped out, horrific stories being told by the deportees, who tried to stick together like a frightened flock of sheep growing smaller by the day as new bodies turned up at dawn, eviscerated. The two garrison commanders had already hanged several prisoners suspected of being the guilty parties, but they were young and felt overwhelmed by the situation.

A terrifying thought began to torment Elías. He couldn't get out of his head the idea that Irina and Anna were at the mercy of these animals.

"For now they're safe," Claude said, trying to calm him. "Irina is a surgeon and the medical officers protect her because she's useful to them. But I don't know for how long. You've got to get them out of here, Elías. This is insane, and it's going to get truly demented, barbaric."

"If we could just go back and start again, go back to before it began..." he murmured.

"Don't be naïve, Elías. She'd never have glanced your way—or mine. We both know that. We should thank Stalin, in the end, don't you think? It's because of him that we got to meet her. Neither of us could ever have competed with her husband...The book of poems that upsets you so much? It belonged to Irina's husband. He knew Mayakovsky personally, they were friends. When the poet blew his brains out—goaded by Stalin—and fell into disgrace, Irina's husband sent a piece to *Pravda* with his last unfinished poems. He knew his actions amounted to signing his own death sentence."

Elías observed his friend, disconcerted. Claude seemed to cough half his guts out and then spat green phlegm.

"What did you expect?" he asked, flushed and panting. He was struggling to breathe, wheezing like a broken bellows. "I'm a man, too, you know."

Elías nodded with an indulgent smile. He might have only one eye, but it had been enough for him to see that his friend was in love with Irina, too.

The guards had improvised a makeshift table using two barrels and a board, which they placed on the shore by the dock to distribute the flour rations. Irina stood in line beneath the watchful gaze of the guards, who stood with their fingers on the trigger. They were nervous and tired, there had already been altercations at previous distribution times, and they wouldn't hesitate to fire into the throng of prisoners if they felt threatened. Still, a swarm of arms groped at them wildly, pushing and shoving. Elías watched the scene in alarm. People surged back and forth like a wave, and Irina pressed Anna to her legs to keep her as close as humanly possible. A very young soldier grew nervous when a gang of deportees burst forth like an avalanche, landing atop the improvised table and sending sacks of flour to the ground. Instantly, the hungry mob fell upon them, scrabbling for crumbs.

The soldier fired on the first man to land on him, and this created a concertina effect: Other soldiers copied him, despite the order to cease fire shouted by the officer in charge. None of the men, stricken by panic, listened or was able to obey. In no time, it was complete pandemonium. Some ran pell-mell for a nearby wooded area, others dove into the river and attempted to make it to the far shore—a suicide mission given the freezing temperatures and distance. Fearing a mass escape, the soldiers opened fire indiscriminately, shooting those who tried to flee and spearing them with bayonets. Some of the deportees counterattacked, in a wildly unfair fight, trying to grab the soldiers' weapons, striking them with sticks, stones, anything they could find, including their bare hands and teeth.

Elías ran toward Irina. Amid the chaos, she stood turning in circles, disconcerted, clasping her daughter to her chest. Anna was shrieking, terrified. Everywhere, bodies fell and gunfire rang out. Elías punched and kicked his way through the mob in order to reach them. Leaping, he pulled Irina and Anna to the ground, protecting them with his body.

"Don't move!" he shouted.

When the last gunshots stopped echoing, the island was littered with bodies. The air reeked of gunpowder. Even the soldiers, whose violence only minutes earlier had been brutal, contemplated the horrific scene in silence, shocked and horrified at the results of their rage. Some vomited, others sobbed disconsolately. More than two hundred men, women, and children died that day. Barely half a dozen soldiers fell.

And suddenly, in the distance, penetrating the mist rolling in off the river, came the sound of music. Surrounded by corpses, an old man sat on a fallen trunk, playing harmonica. Sorrow engulfed his tune. The scene before them was atrocious, hallucinatory, and somehow incredible. But the old man was real, the sound of his harmonica rising above that of the moaning of the injured. The man's belly, his ruddy peasant face, greasy hair, and bloody hands holding the harmonica were as true as the sound coming from his lips.

The commander who had ordered his soldiers to hold their fire approached the old man, revolver in hand, advancing like a robot. Everyone thought he was going to shoot him. For one seemingly endless minute, he stood observing the old man. Then he removed his coat and gently covered the man's shoulders as if it were his father or grandfather. The officer sat beside the old man, absorbed, as he listened to him play; he pushed the brim of his cap back with the tip of his gun, his gaze lost among the fallen bodies, some in grotesque positions, on their knees with eyes and mouths open, gazing up at the sky. With trembling fingers, he found a cigarette in his combat jacket, lit it, and took a long drag. Then he aimed the gun at his own temple and blew his brains out.

The officer's body fell sideways over the old man, who finally stopped playing the harmonica, his face now covered in blood. For a moment, his stubby kulak fingers hesitated at the officer's skull, but then he pulled the young man's head to his belly, as though it was a broken toy.

After an instant of bewilderment, arms and hands swarmed the pair, stripping them of clothes, boots, and anything else that might be of value. From among the whirl of bodies, Elías saw Michael take the officer's revolver and hide it in his clothes. And then the horde moved on, taking part in a ritual as old as human folly: Like bands of desperate buzzards, they set to stripping every dead body of anything they could.

"I've got to get you out of here," Elías murmured, holding Irina and Anna to his chest.

Claude passed away two weeks later. He'd been nearing death all morning, as he lay with his head over Irina's shoulder, nestled between her breasts. His lungs whistled and wheezed at irregular intervals, in what approximated breathing. Irina rocked him in her arms, whispering a nursery rhyme into his ear and kissing his burning forehead, as Elías had seen her do with Anna so many times before. For a few seconds, Claude opened his eyes and looked out at the world, cooking up one final witticism. For that brief moment, in the fluttering of his eyelids, he once more became the dashing, rangy young man he'd been, the confident cynic whose razor-sharp irony always left a trace of bitterness.

"You should have picked me," he murmured. "I'm better looking than that Spaniard, and less melodramatic."

Irina looked down at him with a timid smile, caressed his cheek fondly, and nodded, as though confessing that, indeed, she'd wasted her time and kisses on the wrong man. It wasn't true, and all three of them knew it, but that didn't matter. Sometimes lies are the only consolation there is.

Elías left the barge and headed for the far end of the dock. He sat by the river's edge, disconsolate, and for a long time observed the reddish rays of sun marbling the water, the mist that never burned off all the way, the barges with their prows submerged in the muddy sand. It struck him that men were like the stunted trees on the opposite shore. They would never be able to take root in ground this muddy, but they'd fight to the end to survive, trying desperately to reach up toward the sun, only to inexorably rot and molder and die in the attempt. He was filled with sorrow, thinking of Claude's laugh, the vim and vigor he'd shown the day the four of them met on the train to Moscow, which seemed like a thousand years ago.

In the end, his friend's life had been nothing but pyrotechnics, fireworks in the sky that turned out to be useless illusions in the face of death. Everything that mattered to Claude—the buildings he wanted to build, the women he could have loved, books, music, impassioned conversations about politics, success and failure, joys and disappointments—all of it died right there. Right then. Death was beyond comprehension; his friend was crossing the great divide alone, as they all would. And nothing had been gained by Irina's white lies, or Elías's embrace, or any of the theories and religious rhetoric about the existence of some kind of God, some great beyond. He was alone.

Elías noticed a perch or bass of some sort floating in the water and grabbed a stick to try to pull it closer. The fish's scales had fallen off and its eye sockets were empty. The rotten stench it gave off was almost unbearable, but it would do for dinner. Hiding it between his legs, he was suddenly seized with the fear that someone might try to steal the putrid fish from him. And in that precise moment, he knew that if he managed to survive, his suffering would serve to rob him forever of any future joy or pleasure. Nothing, save pain, would seem real from this point onward.

Irina approached Elías with something in her hand, and he realized Claude had died. He placed a hesitant hand on her cheek and tucked back a lock of her hair. Irina made to shrug him off, but then clung to his fingers and kissed his knuckles instead.

"He wrote this, for you."

Elías read the words, made with a blackened branch scratched onto paper: *They can't take everything. My death is mine alone.*

Elías observed the fingernail marks Claude had left on Irina's skin, the imprint like a claw. He'd clung fiercely to her until the end.

"I don't want to die here—not like this, not without a fight," Irina murmured.

The smell of damp wood, kindling the bonfires, came in thick gusts. Beneath the blanket of mist, they could see swollen bodies floating by, adrift. Others had become trapped in the river's bends, entangled in the branches of fallen trees. Elías studied the thick gray expanse to the north. The steppe was what lay beyond their prison with no walls. Thousands upon thousands of kilometers of absolute silence, nothing between them and the Urals to the west and the Arctic Ocean to the north. Looking east was almost worse: Eastern Siberia and the taiga.

But Elías had already made up his mind. They were going to escape, so they could die far from here. At least that way they would be on the move, heading someplace.

.   .   .

Martin let out a stifled cry, a mournful-sounding groan. For a few seconds, Michael felt his lover's rapid heartbeat beneath his hand. They shouldn't be using up their energy this way, he thought, pulling away, his penis still erect. Plus, it was dangerous. If Igor caught them, he didn't even want to imagine what would happen. Michael had seen him sodomize other men, but rape as a display of dominance and ownership was one thing, and what he and Martin did each night something else entirely. They made love.

"Do you think he'll take us with him?"

Michael stroked Martin's red hair. "He needs us," he replied to calm him, though he didn't actually believe it.

Igor's plan was to head northwest. He'd found a map showing routes intended to link the mining areas of the Urals with the lowlands of Western Siberia and Yenisei River, crossing the Kyrgyzstan steppe. The grandiose plan had been abandoned at the turn of the century—too unrealistic—but several kilometers-long sections of it still existed, and there were some abandoned wagons a few hundred kilometers away, somewhere between Nizhnevartovsk and Vampugol. Following that route would be a long detour, weeks at least, but it would finally enable them to wade across the Ob and then circle down to Tomsk.

Thousands of kilometers of empty expanse, nothing in sight, no food, surrounded by wolves, at risk of dying in a swamp, or of hunger, thirst, or cold. Even contemplating the idea was absurd. And yet they were going to do it. Igor had been studying the map for weeks, stockpiling essentials, anything that might prove useful—clothing, shoes, what little provisions they could find, as well as a few firearms stolen off the bodies of murdered guards. He claimed that in less than a week they'd come to a small village or at least some Siberian farm. And after that, everything would get easier.

In addition to this, Michael had an ace up his sleeve. He had the commander's pistol, and no one but Martin knew about it. Every night he crawled out to the hiding place where he'd stashed it, opened the chamber and counted the five remaining bullets. The sixth was lodged in the officer's brains. How much could be accomplished with five bullets? Plenty, if they were used wisely. One had Igor's name on it. Michael was planning to blow the monster's brains out the moment he was sure they were free and clear. He detested Igor with every fiber in his body. The second and third were for him and Martin, if the plan failed. Igor was recruiting young men with the promise of taking them along on the trip. The fools didn't realize what he was actually intending to do. Igor planned to use them as pack mules for the exhausting journey and then, when hunger became unbearable, treat them as livestock. Michael had no intention of allowing those parasites to use him or Martin for food, if it came to that. Igor had already forced them to carve up one poor woman and then made them eat some of her flesh. No matter how many times he vomited or filled his mouth with sand, he couldn't get the sickening taste out of his mouth.

"We should ask Elías to come with us," Martin said. He was absently strumming the three strings of a Russian balalaika. He'd traded a girl a pair of holey boots in exchange for it and fantasized about learning to play one day, even though he knew that sooner or later it would end up as firewood.

Michael stroked Martin's neck, still red from where he'd bitten it a few minutes earlier as they made desperate love. Suddenly his heart skipped a beat and he got a funny feeling: Martin wasn't going to make it. He was too weak, thought too much, and couldn't seem to shake off his scruples, which weighed him down like stones in the pockets of a man tossed into the river. He chased the premonition away, ran his fingers through his lover's hair, and then kissed his shoulder lightly. Michael couldn't recall the first time he'd seen Martin nude, the first time they'd kissed. Six months ago? A year? It didn't matter; the days there were like centuries.

"Elías would never come with us, Martin. We informed on him to the OGPU, and he detests us for serving Igor. You've seen the way he looks at us. He'd rip our throats out with his teeth at the first chance, if he could. Besides, he'll never leave that woman and her daughter."

The truth was, he hadn't even attempted to get Elías on his side. Claude's death had brought about a change so marked in the Spaniard's character that it was almost inconceivable. Far from sinking into depression or desperation, Elías had taken on a cold, calculating resolve. He'd clashed with the guards several times and savagely beat anyone who bothered Irina or her daughter. Michael had seen him crush a man's skull with a tree trunk, smashing the branch against his head again and again long after the poor prisoner's face was nothing but a pulpy mass of flesh. He stopped only when Irina approached cautiously, placing a hand on his arm. For a second Elías had looked at her as though he had no idea who she was, as though he'd crush her, too, if she seemed to pose a threat. But then he'd hurled the bloody branch like a dead cat and walked off to the beach, his good eye fixed on the misty haze.

Igor, too, had noticed the change and no longer provoked Elías with insinuation—"I'm still waiting for your coat"—when the brigade went to work. Now he threatened him openly, and knew exactly how to get to him. One morning he approached, flanked by two of his men. Elías was digging a ditch that could have been intended only as a mass grave. Up to his knees in mud, his muscles tensed with each shovelful of dirt; insects hovered, buzzing around his sweaty head. Using a friendly tone of voice, Igor asked him to stop digging for a moment and listen: He had a proposition.

"I've seen that woman you're with all the time. She's Siberian, right? I want you to sell her to me."

Elías glared back, his only eye full of calm, compact hatred. He no longer feared Igor, and this meant there was nothing Igor could take from him.

"I can't sell what doesn't belong to me."

"I want the girl, too. She's still too young, but I hear children's flesh is tastier. Maybe I'll fuck her first, and then let these hyenas rip her to shreds."

Without no hesitation, Elías picked up the shovel he'd been using and raised it above his head, as though to crack his skull. He barely touched Igor, but his intentions were clear, and that was enough. Before he could strike a blow, the two men with Igor leapt and began to beat him. Rather than merely defend himself, Elías fought back like a rabid dog backed into a corner.

"A true Siberian wolf, at last," Igor said with absurd pride, as though he himself were responsible for creating this new Elías.

Igor stopped the men before they killed him, and then bent over his victim and placed a foot on Elías's head as he lay in the dirt, whispering words that cut like a knife.

"In two nights' time you will come to my tent. You will bring the woman and the girl, clean and well groomed. Irina will wear your coat. You will hand them over to me, and you'll thank me for letting you live."

That night, Elías took off toward the woods. Nobody in their right mind went there, not even the guards, unless it was in the light of day and with plenty of company. Packs of deranged deportees congregated there, wandering among the trees and the high brush, committing atrocities like a band of lunatics who've escaped the asylum to sow a reign of terror. Venturing into the forest was an act of suicide. But Elías had no choice. He'd been building a raft since the day of the massacre, and it was hidden in the scrub there. Besides, there was something he had to get back.

He found the man he wanted in a clearing. The full moon illuminated his squatting figure as he pushed and strained, guts gurgling in the darkness like a wild beast in the forest. The man was defecating, and using Irina's book as toilet paper. He would read a page, tear it out and then wipe his ass. The man's name was Evgueni and he was thirty years old, though he looked far older. In a previous life he'd been a member of the Academy of Writers and hailed from Inner Mongolia. His crime? Claiming that Gorky was a damned stooge and that Stalin knew as much about literature as he himself did about astrophysics. Evgueni's braggadocio came to a swift halt the day Yagoda's men burst into his tiny apartment and carted him off. Raving mad and friendless, he now rambled through the woods half naked at all hours, reciting poems from the *Shin Konkinshu*, an anthology of imperial Japanese poetry edited by Fujiwara Teika, who Evgueni claimed was the only poet worthy of that title. Irina had traded him her Mayakovsky for a few pieces of bluish meat of dubious origin, and the only reason Evgueni wanted it was that he missed the feel of toilet paper. The yellow pages struck him as the most sublime of pleasures.

Elías gave the man a swift kick in the head before he had time to shout and draw the attention of the other forest psychopaths. Evgueni fell flat on his face and then turned sideways; the last thing he saw was an enormous rock coming down on his head and one enraged eye sending him to hell where he could meet his beloved Teika.

Returning immediately to the barge, Elías woke Irina.

"Wake Anna, we're leaving. Now."

They took off before dawn. The rickety raft was barely solid enough to keep Anna—bundled in Elías's coat—above the water's surface. He and Irina would have to stay in the river, clinging to branches for stability. Elías had made a careful study of the currents and although it was impossible to swim through the whirlpools to the opposite shore, they could drift downriver. If they managed to stay afloat for a hundred meters, avoid the fallen trees and vortexes that sucked every passing thing into their swirling eddies, they'd come to a bend where the river turned sharply to the left with a deafening racket as the water rushed over rocks and small shoals. At that point, there was a meander where the current became gentler, and from there they'd have to swim, staying afloat by holding on to remnants of the raft, which would have shattered, and praying they had strength enough to reach a cluster of trees whose thick roots were submerged in the slimy mud on the other side of the river.

What came after that didn't bear contemplating. Chances were, they'd never even make it to the other side of the river.

Before plunging into the water, Elías had presented Irina the book of poems. He'd wrapped it as carefully as he could to protect it. Irina looked at the book; pages had been torn out at random, thanks to Evgueni and his bowels. She gazed at him, sorrow pooling in her eyes.

Irina, too, took out a small carefully wrapped package she'd hidden in her tattered clothing. She handed it to Elías before stepping into the water, asking him to hold it for her until they reached the other side.

"If anything happens to me, give this to Anna, and tell her that her mother loves her very much, and that she did everything she could to give her a future."

Elías didn't argue. There was no point lying, claiming that everything would be fine, that Irina could keep whatever was in the package and give it to Anna herself, later. He tucked it away, frowned, and then tied a rope tightly around Anna, who was kicking and sobbing, terrified.

"Make her shut up or we'll be discovered," Elías said coldly. Irina kissed her daughter's hands repeatedly, stepping fearfully into the frigid water.

"I'm right here, Annushka, Mamma's not going to let you go."

Slowly their raft drifted toward the middle of the river and then, as Elías had predicted, began heeling to the right, requiring him to tug down forcefully to keep it from capsizing on top of Irina. As they drifted from shore, he saw a silhouette among the barges. It was Michael—Elías recognized his wide bowlegs and broad shoulders. He observed them calmly, hands in his pockets, looking almost amused. After a moment, he raised an arm as though to say *Bon voyage*, or perhaps *See you soon*. Then he turned and ambled off.

Elías knew they had a chance as soon as they'd made it a third of the way across. The current was not as strong as he'd foreseen, and though the water was painfully cold—it felt like teeth biting his extremities—he could take the pain of freezing. He tried to reassure Irina but could see her only when Anna, who was tied at the waist to the raft, was rocked to the side. Elías saw Irina's purple fingers, desperately clinging to a tree trunk. When the current got stronger, her head would disappear under the water, and Elías would wait anxiously for her to pop back up—gasping for air, mouth open, hair plastered to her forehead. At one point she smiled at him. For the first time in weeks.

Yes, he thought, they could make it. It was too early, however, to be carried away by euphoria. By struggling continuously to stay afloat and keep the raft from flipping over—crushing Irina and drowning Anna—they had a chance. The river's bend was in sight, muddy tree roots visible in the spume, and the rocks were like Good Samaritans ready to throw them a lifeline as soon as they were within reach. But the raft began drifting away from the meander, caught in a current that spun them like a top, faster and faster.

Elías cried out, desperate. They were so close! If they didn't reach those trees, the river would toss them out like trash farther down, swollen like the rotten fish they'd eaten the day Claude died. He had to be fast and decisive; no way was he going to drown now. So he dove into the swirling water and hugged the bottom of the raft, crossing underneath until he made it to Irina's side.

"We've got to turn!" he shouted. They would need to climb on top and push down as hard as possible. There was a chance they'd flip, but it was their only choice. Elías pulled Anna toward them for additional weight, and the raft tilted perilously.

"No! She's going to fall off!" Irina shouted, seeing her daughter flung into the air like a rag doll. The raft's rope had come loose, its branches were beginning to split apart. But Elías kept pushing, frenzied. They had to get out of the current, had to turn. Desperate, Irina began to hit and scratch him, convinced that her daughter was going to sink, that Elías was going to kill her. He didn't feel her blows or hear her screams. All he cared about was reaching the shore.

And then the raft flew up into the air, shattering with a clean snap, as though the river had grown tired of playing with a paper boat. Elías was pulled toward the bottom as Irina tried franticly to climb over his body to the surface, where Anna was clinging to a trunk. Neither of them had enough air, neither could get to the surface. Irina was in a complete state of panic and Elías had no way to soothe her, to tell her to calm down or she'd end up drowning them both. She grasped his neck, scratching in desperation.

Elías felt like his lungs were going to explode and he couldn't see; everything was dark, and he felt things colliding into him: branches, algae, rope, and Irina's desperate hands. He rammed an elbow back, hard, and felt it make contact with her soft body. Again he swung his hands wildly, until he felt her letting up. Just before she let go entirely, he reached out a hand and managed to grab her hair as it swished like a jellyfish. Closing a fist around it, he attempted to pull her toward him, but instead Irina sank toward the bottom of the river.

Desperate, Elías swam up for air.

He surfaced and was forced under, again and again, the current tossing him like a rag, until finally his body crashed into something solid. It was a broken tree root, sticking out from the bend like a muddy bridge leading to the shore. He'd made it to the trees; or, rather, the river had hurled him in their direction.

Holding tight to the trunk, he searched everywhere for a sign of Irina or Anna. A few arm's lengths away, lodged between two rocks emerging from the water like burial mounds, Anna clung to the remains of the raft. Elías swam toward her and pulled the rope that was still tied to her waist. After twenty long minutes in which he was forced under again and again, and nearly drowned, he managed to pull her to shore.

For an hour he waited anxiously. *The river gives back what it takes*, his father used to say. A man who liked fishing, he said that was why they had to release the small fry: One day they would come back as big fish.

But Irina never came back from the dark depths of those waters. The only sign of her that Elías saw were a few yellow pages of her book, floating gently on the surface, as though the verses of her poems were searching for her. Accusing him.

12

He'd been waiting patiently for an hour on the other side of the street, smoking one cigarette after another in the negligible shade of the only tree. This neighborhood was quiet in August—most of the businesses were shuttered, so it was relatively easy to find parking, and an aura of calm pervaded the air. Too peaceful for Alcázar's taste. It had changed a lot since the last time he'd been here. The streets were paved now, and the Metro came all the way out. You still found spaced-out kids hanging around in concrete plazas, killing time in the midday sun, but they were no longer the hopped-up car thieves of his day. Now they were immigrants, a mix of Muslims, South Americans, and Africans who tacitly demarcated the boundaries of their spheres of influence without causing trouble. The Majestic had closed long ago, and when he asked around, wondering where the prostitutes had gone, a few kids looked at him like he was an alien.

"That was like a million years ago, man. The only prostitutes here now are Eastern European, and they make house calls," a pimp told him, giggling and holding out a card for Paradise Massage

Club. At least the names were still as pompous and absurd as ever, Alcázar thought wryly.

Cecilia had never been happy until she met him, in the mid-seventies. That's what she always said, and not just to make him feel better. It really was true. She was a good girl, always had been, too good to make it in a whorehouse as sleazy as that one, despite being named the Majestic—which was clearly a joke when the lights came on revealing a stained carpet covered in burn marks, cheap curtains, molding glued to the furniture, and a row of doors where the women collected their fee. Cecilia was naïve enough to believe that men had a need to be listened to, that if shown love they fell in love, that justice transcended people's actions and tended to be served sooner or later. It's not that she was stupid, or even idealistic; she saw the world around her but decided to look at it through rose-tinted glasses. Maybe that was what had attracted him to her the first time, her optimism, her faith in *mankind* despite the fact that *man* screwed her every night and *kind* rarely came into the picture.

You have to open your eyes if you want to see, and what I see is the sadness behind the rage, the fear behind the violence. You'd be surprised to know how much a hug and a kind word can do. Try it sometime.

It was astonishing that she could say things like that, in a world where hookers kept condoms tucked into the elastic of their panties, where pimps hid extendable billy clubs in their socks, where winos vomited between the legs of women they were too drunk to go down on. It wasn't love that had taken him to that filthy brothel the first time; it wasn't mercy that placed Cecilia in his path. It was the urge to have a good time and get laid after a long day of work and regret, his knuckles still red and the prisoner's screams still ringing in his ears. He'd wanted to get so drunk he passed out while a woman pinched his nipples, her head between his legs. And that woman turned out to be Cecilia, and dammit, it was a fucking miracle, something that pierced his soul: the certainty that her sad yet strong eyes had been waiting for him.

He didn't rescue her. It was Cecilia who pulled *him* from the pits of hell. Who promised that they'd grow old together, that they'd have a slew of kids to take care of them when the time came, that they'd all get together every Christmas and see their grandchildren be born. But then she got cancer, the greatest con in the world, that fucker. A hustler, calling: Where's the little ball, ladies and gentleman? Keep your eyes on the ball. And the ball is your happiness, and it's never still, always mocking you, slipping from one shell to another, hidden by the con man's hand. Ten years, that was how long he got to be with her. And the rest of his life to miss her.

More and more, memories were not something he evoked voluntarily; they just appeared, playing like a movie in which his past was enviable and ideal (he never remembered their terrible fights, when Cecilia would get furious and break anything she could get her hands on), untouchable and alien. That, he thought, could mean only one thing: He was getting old, and he felt terribly lonely. He pulled the travel brochure from his pocket and read it for the hundredth time. The Florida Keys—tropical climate, beaches, mangroves, raging storms, and humidity so intense it melted even your brain. Palm trees and old cars, men wearing Panama hats and women in bikinis so skimpy the only thing they covered up was a date of birth. Cecilia always wanted to buy a little house there, with a motorboat so they could go fishing in the late afternoon when the sky was blazing hot, a little porch—with a green swing, in her dream—to sit on, drinking low-alcohol beer.

Who knew why a girl from Valdepeñas de Jaén, in southern Spain, a girl who'd crossed not a single body of water aside from Besòs River when she moved to the stinking shores of Barcelona, was so obsessed with Florida. Perhaps it was the 1950s American movies she liked to watch at the Saturday matinee, or an overdose of *Miami Vice*, with that loudmouth Don Johnson. Alcázar swore he'd take her there on vacation at least once, but he didn't keep his promise. And now he was the one skulking around all day, fantasizing about giving it all up and buying a little house and a fishing rod, learning to speak English with a Cuban accent. Yes, he felt the need to adopt Cecilia's dreams in order to face his old age with a little presence of mind. Why not? It all started with the spark of possibility; the rest would come naturally, and all he'd have to do was let himself be whisked away. But first he had to tie up a few loose ends. He didn't want to spend the rest of his life in paradise looking over his shoulder in fear.

His wait paid off. Alcázar looked up and saw the old lady emerge. Was it fair to think of her as an old lady? Only if he thought of himself as an old man, recently retired. He put the brochure away and began to tail her, keeping to his side of the street. Alcázar had to admit she looked good—one of those women who accepted the passage of time with dignity, no resentment or drama, and time seemed to repay them by granting a very gradual, regal descent. She was quite the lady, and in that neighborhood stood out in stark contrast to her surroundings. Just as Cecilia had. Once he was sure, he crossed the street and caught up to her. She glanced at him out of the corner of her eye but didn't behave like your standard old lady, clutching her purse in fear whenever a stranger got close. Instead she stopped in the middle of the sidewalk, squinting against the sun or perhaps just examining him in curiosity.

"Hello, Anna," said the ex–chief inspector. "It's been a long time." And in fact, it had.

It took everything Gonzalo had to get out of bed, but the nurse refused to help him. He had to do it on his own, she said gently, like a mother watching her offspring's first steps, arms at the ready in case of a tumble. Gonzalo felt the compression bandage squeezing his chest, sighed deeply, and took a step toward the window, dragging one slipper and then the other, back and forth across what seemed an impossible distance, grabbing onto the door handle.

The bodyguard Alcázar had hired to protect him was leaning on a counter down the hall, chatting amiably with a nurse, not seeming overly concerned about his job. If Atxaga put in an appearance at the hospital, he'd have no trouble slipping into the room and smothering him with a pillow before anyone realized. The burly guy, who looked more like a bouncer than a retired cop, straightened up when he saw Gonzalo appear, followed closely by the nurse. He made as if to assist him, but Gonzalo waved him off.

At the end of the hall was a small waiting room with vending machines and a sliding glass door that opened out onto an enclosed patio. It was a rectangle hardly more than ten square meters and offered a panoramic view of the hospital wing. The transparent domed ceiling allowed sunlight to filter in between the ferns and palm fronds planted in the middle. It was nice and cool there, and the damp greenhouse air was pleasant. The nurse helped Gonzalo sit down on the only stone bench.

"That was pretty good. Now you rest here and catch your breath, and I'll be back in ten minutes."

Gonzalo touched his side and nodded. Ten minutes outside of his room felt like an amazing privilege, the sort granted to a prisoner in solitary who's finally allowed into the high-walled prison yard.

He thought about what Javier had said the day before. He'd shown up unannounced, without Lola. Gonzalo was in the bathroom, clenching his teeth in order to heed nature's call without screaming in pain. When he opened the door, sweaty and out of sorts, he found his son staring out the window looking worried. He'd left a bag with clean pajamas on the bed and brought a few magazines.

"I didn't know what you'd want so I brought a little of everything."

Gonzalo quickly glanced at them: copies of *National Geographic*, a few of *History* magazine, and a couple of books from his library.

Javier asked him how he felt, because it seemed an inevitable question. Gonzalo gave an equally clichéd response and then made a joke about the bruises having deformed his face; his son gave a pity-laugh. Gonzalo could never have made it as a comic. After that, the conversation died painfully and they both sank into the awkward silence that always made them so uncomfortable until finally they parted, feeling relieved and guilty. But this time Javier stayed, pondering something he left floating in the air, unstated. Gonzalo waited in silence for his son to speak, assuming that, like always, he'd finally trail off, abandoning his attempts at communication. But Javier leaned forward, as though making an effort not to hide this time. And suddenly he asked a question. Far from being formulaic, it dropped like a bomb, something that had been waiting in his mouth to explode.

"Papá, why do you hate me?"

Gonzalo suddenly felt himself flush, felt a knot in his throat, which he forced down by swallowing. He thought how unfair it was for his son to bear the blame for something that was entirely not his fault, and felt wretched and petty. He wanted to hug his son, to hold him to his broken ribs without so much as wincing in pain. But habit and shame—so stupid, with someone you love— kept him from doing it. Instead, he simply squeezed Javier's slim forearm tightly.

"I don't hate you, Javier, don't say that."

"But you don't love me either, do you?"

Now, contemplating the sunlight and shadows dappling the ferns, breathing in the smell of wet grass by the palm tree, he regretted his inadequate and evasive response, which Javier had greeted with a look of incomprehension. Gonzalo didn't hate him; he'd never hated him. Javier was his son—*he was*, Gonzalo insisted, to convince himself. It didn't matter if the boy's biological father was some stranger who'd spent the night in his bed, Javier belonged to him just as much as Patricia did. He'd held him in his arms since he was a baby, had put him to sleep, soothed him when he cried, tended his fevers; he'd watched him grow up, at first clinging to Gonzalo's legs and then slowly letting go, getting farther and farther as the years passed and he approached adolescence. And now, on the verge of manhood, Javier was ready to fly solo and yet afraid of the void, despite his seeming arrogance. Gonzalo should have told him the truth. Should have said *I love you*, and that the years of silence between them didn't matter, that he'd always be there for him, no matter what he did, come what may. He should have told him that he was his son, and nothing in the world mattered more.

"Do you think Grandpa Elías would be proud of you?"

The question, which Javier asked just before leaving, had thrown Gonzalo for a loop. It was clear that his son was on edge, going through something. The loneliness of his transformation was tearing him up and he didn't know what to do about it.

"I don't know," Gonzalo replied honestly. He'd spent his whole life in the shadow of a ghost he called his father—a myth, a legend. The son of a hero, whose faint light couldn't compete with a blazing sun whose rays burned all they touched. He was like the ferns in the courtyard, struggling pitifully to reach the sunlight blocked out by the giant palm.

Gonzalo thought about his son's question again. And the thoughtless response he'd given.

"A father's pride is important until you have your own children. Then you realize that the past isn't what matters. I don't know whether or not my father would be proud of me, Javier. But I do know that I'd like you to be."

Javier had bowed his head, searching for the words, trying to find his way through the door that he himself had opened. Then he gazed at his father in sorrow, as though trapped at the bottom of a well, his arms raised as he cried for help.

"There's something you should know...something I want to tell you, but I don't know how to start."

"At the beginning. Start at the beginning."

But Javier immediately backpedaled, regretting his outburst of sincerity. What was the beginning? he wondered. It was too confusing, he didn't even know how or when he'd started becoming something he didn't want to be.

"Forget it, it's nothing."

"Javier..."

"Really, it's nothing. I hope the pajamas are the right size. I picked them out myself."

The truth was, the pajamas were enormous and, frankly, hideous—dark brown with white piping. But he wouldn't have taken them off for anything in the world. The two of them had been so close to true communication that Gonzalo felt exasperated at the way Javier had suddenly backed off. Something had frightened him, maybe the possibility of them finally having the courage to be honest with each other. His son had darted up like a little fish curiously approaching a scuba diver's fingers, and then at the last minute swished back off into the dark waters from which he'd come.

But Javier would be back. Now that the door was open, he'd be back.

Gonzalo wondered if his ten minutes were up and looked down at his watch; it had only been five. Time seemed to shrink and expand in his mind, unconnected to the real world. He wanted a coffee and could either wait for the nurse or try to make it on his own, first to the sliding glass door and from there to the waiting room where the vending machines were. He took a deep breath and held it, and then forced his aching body to stand. This must be what getting old is like, he thought, shuffling toward the door: Your body turns against you, puts up a fight, breaks down, undependable.

He had no money. The realization struck him as he stared at the coin slot. It reminded him of being a kid, at the weekly market, standing at the churro stand, gazing enviously at the greasy paper cones people were walking away with. And then Laura would appear and give him a sad face that said, *You can't always have what you want. Even if it's just a paper cone full of churros.* Or a crappy vending-machine coffee.

"Let me treat you. Black?" Without awaiting a reply, the young man slipped some coins into the slot and handed him the small plastic cup. Then he repeated the operation. Gonzalo noticed that he ordered tea for himself, no milk.

"What are you doing here, Siaka? I thought you'd have gotten on that train to Paris when you didn't hear from me."

Gonzalo sensed veiled joy in the young man's smile.

"Don't think I wasn't tempted, several times. But when I found out what happened to you, I decided to wait a little longer. So, how big was the truck than ran you over?"

Gonzalo glanced at the clock on the wall above the vending machine. The nurse had said she'd be back in ten minutes. It had already been eight.

"The laptop is gone, with all the files. When Atxaga attacked me, I lost consciousness, and when I came to, the computer was gone. I have no idea who took it, or what they'll do with the information."

Siaka held his gaze, unblinking. "Did you open the confidential file?"

"I didn't have time."

Siaka took a folded-up piece of paper from his pocket and handed it to Gonzalo.

"This is the prosecutor your sister trusted. You need to go see him and tell him what's going on."

"Did you have a backup?"

Siaka shook his head resolutely.

"So what are we going to do?"

To Siaka the answer was obvious. "What you're going to do is get out of here and start looking for that laptop. And as for me, I'm going to hide out until the prosecutor calls me to testify."

"You must be kidding me."

No, he was not.

"We made a deal, Gonzalo. When I make a deal, I follow through to the end. So try not to let that guy kill you, at least until after the trial." Siaka smiled faintly, as though the situation were mildly amusing. "And I'll try to keep the Matryoshka from hunting me down... By the way, you need some serious help with fashion sense. Those pajamas are awful."

The doctor flat out refused to discharge him, insisting that Gonzalo needed one more week in the hospital under observation. Coming out of a coma was not the same as getting over a cold. But Gonzalo had made up his mind and nothing was going to change it. So they had him sign a voluntary discharge and gave him a brusque warning that the hospital would not be held responsible if any complications arose. After sitting patiently through the sermon, he packed his things, without informing Lola. He was sure that the preoccupied watchdog supposedly guarding the door would tell Alcázar, who would in turn immediately inform his father-in-law.

After walking out of the hospital, Gonzalo raised his arm and hailed a taxi, his body feeling like a punching bag. The pain was

so deep it hurt down to his very soul, but he managed to climb
into the taxi.

"You can't be serious."

But Gonzalo's expression made clear that this was no joke.
He was leaving home, at least until the whole Atxaga business was
taken care of. He didn't want that maniac coming anywhere near
Lola or the kids.

"It won't be for long. The police are looking for him, Alcázar,
too. One of them will find him."

It was a flimsy excuse. The house was as secure as a bun-
ker, cameras and motion detectors all over the place. And if
that wasn't enough, the two men chatting amiably with Patricia
down by the pool looked more than capable of protecting them.
The inspector had been right: His father-in-law took his family's
safety very seriously. The truth was, he needed to be alone so
he could concentrate on the Matryoshka. He'd learned his lesson with Atxaga and wasn't going to let his investigation put his
family at risk. The bodyguards might be able to stop a small fry
like Atxaga, but Gonzalo might have to deal with guys as bad as
Zinoviev, or worse. And as soon as word got out that the prosecutor had filed to reopen his sister's investigation, there would
be no stopping it.

But...was that really the reason? It was important, yes, even
vital. But it was not his only motive for wanting to get away from
Lola for a little while. His aborted conversation with Javier had
made him reflect: He was losing his family, and not because of
external circumstances he was caught up in but because of eighteen years of silent recrimination. He couldn't forgive or forget,
but he didn't have what it took to ask for a divorce or turn the page
either. And having sat on the fence for so long was taking its toll.
He had to make up his mind and not keep avoiding a decision.

He had to get away so he could think, get some distance, feel the weight of his own loneliness.

That night he packed a small overnight bag, just a few essentials. No need to pass the point of no return, not yet. Lola sat on the bed the whole time as he folded a few shirts and some underwear. She made no move to stop him; there were no tears, no scenes. Gonzalo's final image of Lola was of painted toenails, her feet together, knees pulled in to her chest, and a penetrating, accusatory look. When he went to give her a kiss, she turned her face away coldly.

"A month ago you told me you were a new man, that you were going to take care of us. You begged me to let you prove you could do it. And now you're just taking off. I don't understand."

"That's exactly what I'm doing, Lola. Taking care of you."

He told Patricia and Javier that he was taking a trip for a few days. Patricia asked endless questions, as usual, and he invented a string of lies on the fly; finally she was moderately appeased when he promised to bring her something back. Javier walked him out to the car, carrying his bag. Since their conversation at the hospital he'd seemed more somber, more restrained.

"You're not really going on a trip, are you?"

"In a way I am. But not the kind of work trip I told your sister."

Javier nodded, grateful that his father had at least not lied to him. Tacitly acknowledging this, he reciprocated by not demanding an explanation that his father wasn't going to give him anyway.

"How's this all going to end?"

Gonzalo couldn't answer a question like that with a cliché, couldn't fire off some lighthearted response. His son's troubled face deserved better than that. He would have liked to sit down with him on the porch, have a few beers and secretly share a cigarette, bonding over the way they were breaking Lola's rules. He'd have liked to explain everything, even though Gonzalo himself didn't know what to explain. What was everything? When and where had it all begun? At the lake? With his father's memory? With Laura? Or his discovery of Lola's infidelity, which had brought his son into the world?

"I don't know, Javier." That was as sincere as he could afford to be. "But one way or another, it will end."

Javier felt strange in Gonzalo's embrace, slightly uncomfortable, maybe because he sensed how awkward his father felt. They were out of practice. His father wanted to hug him like a man, an equal. But Javier still longed for the warmth and affection Gonzalo showered on Patricia. He stood at the garage door, staring after the red taillights until his father's car disappeared around a curve at the end of the street. For a few seconds he could still hear the engine, and then came silence, broken by a dog's frenzied barking. His father was right. Everything comes to an end, one way or another.

The prosecutor's office had a sort of sad yet dignified air, somehow bleak yet industrious, like the man himself, who sat listening with polite concentration, mimicking Gonzalo's expressions to demonstrate his solidarity. His favorite composer—Rossini—was on in the background: an aria. Once Gonzalo had finished explaining what had brought him there, the prosecutor turned down the volume.

"The information you've just given me is of capital importance," he whispered, with the air of a cloistered monk who had little access to the outside world. His gaze was fixed on a small calendar propped up on one corner of the desk; each month had a different illustration. The one the prosecutor was staring at featured an elaborate stone balustrade overlooking a lush garden, its colors standing out against the yellowish-blue sky visible above the rooftops. It made you want to be there, contemplating the sunset, carefree, floating motionless like a specimen in a jar of formaldehyde. Maybe that was why the prosecutor hadn't changed the month and the calendar was still on June.

"Laura detested those people as much as I do," he added.

Gonzalo studied the man carefully. His face looked sharp, like a knife. He probably didn't get enough sleep or eat well. Gonzalo wondered if he was on some kind of anti-anxiety medication. Or perhaps, like Gonzalo, he simply worked all hours of the day and night to keep from thinking.

"So what are you going to do about it?" Gonzalo asked, perhaps too vehemently, causing the prosecutor to raise an eyebrow and shoot him a look that hovered between compassion and displeasure. Something in his manner told Gonzalo that the man was conflicted. The Rossini in the background gave him the aura of one of the saints depicted in tapestries and paintings on the walls of his boarding school, when he was a kid. Troubled-looking saints who wrestled with their faith, unable to live holy lives while surrounded by so much evil. Broken martyrs, frail of flesh, whose mystic sacrifices did nothing but inspire fear and revulsion and the desire to run away.

"What exactly do you expect me to do, counselor?" he asked, his eyes calm and striking but full of sorrow.

"This means Laura didn't murder Zinoviev," Gonzalo pointed out.

The prosecutor spread his hands in a gesture demonstrating that rather than consolation, this news was somehow unsettling.

"And your sister's witness contacted you, and he's willing to testify against the Matryoshka... Is that correct?"

Gonzalo nodded. Though he didn't say so openly, the prosecutor's question seemed to indicate that he'd made some sort of decision.

"Why do I get the terrible feeling that I'm being used in a way I don't understand and for a purpose I can't divine?"

"What do you mean? You serve the Ministry of Justice, it's your responsibility to intervene."

The prosecutor suddenly stiffened and gave Gonzalo a look of slight disapproval, but he remained unruffled. And Gonzalo saw then his graciousness and restraint, his humble melancholic nature, and the pride that allowed him to evaluate Gonzalo's words to the best of his ability.

"My obligation, Counselor, is to find the most legitimate path between truth and appearance. Setting the wheels of justice in motion to trap these people will not be an easy task. You've already intuited as much, and as I told your sister—whom I was very fond of, I might add—the truth is not enough when it comes to the law. It must be proved, beyond any reasonable doubt, despite others doing everything in their power to distort it. They will use every trick in the book, and there are plenty of them. You can think me weak if you like, think that I'm afraid of the challenge, but the fact is that I play this game because I believe in its rules. You want me to bite off more than I can chew, and I'm willing to do so... provided you've got conclusive proof. Bring me those dossiers, back up your claims with solid legal grounds, and I'll listen. I'm not going to let them destroy my career and harass my family if I'm not convinced that this will be worth it. When you show me I've got grounds to take on the scores of lawyers who will be waiting to pounce on me—and the examining magistrate—then you can rest assured that I'll take this on. In the meantime, good day."

Gonzalo walked out of the office feeling as though he'd behaved like an idiot, insulting and doubting a good man. Everyone was expecting things from him, and he wasn't sure he was up to the task, but he had no choice. This had all been dumped on his shoulders.

He had to find that laptop, or none of Laura's work could be used as evidence.

Two hours later, when he walked into his own office, exhausted, Luisa leapt up as if she'd seen a ghost. She rushed from her desk to take the crutches Gonzalo was using and gave him a hug that made him grit his teeth to keep from screaming in pain.

"Look at you! Like one of the musicians on the *Titanic*."

"Excuse me?"

Luisa spread her arms wide, looking around the office. Not one piece of paper on the desk, not one phone ringing. Total silence and meticulous order made it clear that his assistant had too much time on her hands and had used it to organize the chaos of the past eight years. *It's all over*, her arms seemed to say.

"You've come back to go down with the ship. What's our last tune?"

"Fuck 'em," Gonzalo said absurdly.

"I don't know that one, but it sounds good."

He dropped into a chair and gazed warily at the immaculate office, a clear sign that going out of business was imminent. Gonzalo was struck by the thought that he'd already lost, before he'd really even started to fight. All it had taken was a few rash words spoken off-the-cuff to his father-in-law, a reckless challenge, and the old man had set the wheels in motion to end his career. No one in the city would hire him now. And the strange thing was that he didn't really care. In spite of his confusion and anxiety about the present, Gonzalo was convinced that he'd get by. He wasn't sure how, or when, or what he'd have to give up, but he was going to make it.

"Make what? What are you, the prince of tides?"

Gonzalo blushed, realizing he'd been voicing his concerns aloud.

Luisa dropped two envelopes onto his desk. "The one on the right is the Alcázar file you asked for. Everything about him, it's in there. Career, promotions, charges of brutality...After joining the Armed Police in 1965, his career skyrocketed, in part due to his father, Ramón Alcázar Suñer. Name ring a bell?"

"Should it?"

"He's from Mieres. Isn't that the name of your father's village? They're more or less the same age, and given that Mieres isn't exactly Calcutta, they probably knew each other."

Gonzalo had never heard the name in his life. According to Luisa's file, Alcázar's father had been a bigwig in the BPS—Franco's secret police—until 1966, when he retired as superintendent. He was known for his brutality and a lack of scruples, which yielded very positive results and therefore made him popular with the higher-ups.

"Hold on to your seat; that's not all. It seems that our Ramón was very well connected to one of Franco's ministers—the minister of justice—in '63. And do you know who that was? Fulgencio Arras—"

"Holy shit, Lola's grandfather."

"That's right, your father-in-law's father. Agustín and Ramón were tight. So the relationship between the Alcázar family and your father-in-law's family dates back at least that long. And the inspector has been doing all sorts of jobs under the table for Agustín, getting paid for them."

"A crooked cop?"

"That depends on whether you think of your father-in-law as a crooked attorney," Luisa said with a wry smile. "Everything in this file is legal."

Gonzalo guessed what came next. "And what about what's not in the file?"

"Gossip, stories, hearsay. Loved by some and hated by others. When the inspector was young he was known to be as tough as his father; I suppose he wanted to live up to Daddy's expectations. Abuse of detainees, torture, tampering with evidence, and forcing confessions to 'solve' cases. Some people say that was no different from what all cops did back then and that he even got himself in trouble, disciplinary action, for trying to put an end to that kind of thing. Anyway, something changed in 1972. He met a prostitute, Cecilia something-or-other, married her, and seemed to undergo a change of character. But in 1983 she died of cancer. Since then, rumor has it Alcázar's been taking bribes in exchange for looking the other way... Some officers claim he's saved up a nice little nest egg and now that he's retired he's going to live it up. But others told me that the work he did in the special unit that your sister was part of was exemplary. Dozens of arrests, lots of successful operations, well-deserved respect. Among his most notable investigations is the one he carried out in 1968, looking into your father's disappearance. You should take a look, it's detailed, nothing superficial about it, very professional. I don't know what kind of officer he was, but he took that investigation very seriously. Definitely a man who's got his bright spots and his dark corners."

Who doesn't? Gonzalo thought, studying an ID photo of the inspector as a young man, balding prematurely and sporting an earlier version of that mustache. He had an intelligent but smart-aleck look about him, as though he didn't take himself too seriously.

"Anything else?"

"He lives in a small apartment right in the Barrio Chino, has a blind dog named Lukas, rents videos a couple times a week—boring stuff, no porn, all westerns—and likes fishing on the breakwater. His neighbors say he plays music too loud; apparently he's big on boleros. The guy at the supermarket below his apartment says he doesn't buy much to drink, and he has no known vices—which of course doesn't mean that he doesn't have any. Maybe he secretly collects bottle caps," Luisa said with a laugh.

Maybe, but Gonzalo had a hunch that wasn't the kind of hobby that would interest somebody like Alcázar. He closed the file and contemplated the envelope on the left, then glanced up at Luisa, who nodded.

"The security camera recording from the day you were attacked. I'm not going to tell you what I had to do to get it, but let's say you owe me one."

"Have you seen it?"

Luisa shook her head, arms crossed. "Gory movies aren't my thing."

Gonzalo wasn't exactly looking forward to reliving the event either. But the recording had to show what had happened to the laptop.

VCRs were a complete mystery to him—it would have been easier to decipher the Rosetta stone than to figure out how the player worked—so he was forced to ask Luisa for help. With the patience generally reserved for teaching simple things to old people, his assistant explained how to play, stop, and fast-forward the recording, as well as how to show it in slow motion and capture print images.

It all happened so fast. Atxaga had shown up ten minutes before Gonzalo, walked down the parking garage ramp, and started checking out car models and license plates until he found the right SUV. Gonzalo calculated that he had already left Agustín's office by that time and must have been speaking to Luisa about the woman in the apartment next door. Then he'd taken the elevator down.

After that, Gonzalo himself came into the frame. He observed himself with a sense of pity; it was like watching a movie you've seen before and knowing that the protagonist is about to get walloped. A sad little man, he looked like a weary office worker, lost in thought, overwhelmed by the realities of everyday life. He dragged his feet, shoulders slumped, as if there were an anvil and not a laptop in the computer bag banging against his thigh.

Atxaga suddenly appeared behind him and said something. Gonzalo turned, and the guy delivered a quick blow with whatever was in his right hand. After rewinding and studying the sequence again, carefully, Gonzalo counted no fewer than twelve kicks, punches, and blows in under a minute, not including the repeated knife jabs. Gonzalo's stomach lurched as he relived the attack. Watching it without sound made the whole thing even more violent and horrific. There he was on the ground, by the SUV's tires, and Atxaga just kept beating him maniacally, as though he'd spent his whole time in jail patiently stockpiling hatred and was now unleashing every ounce of it in one go. How long can it take to kill a big-boned man, to beat him to death? One second. Hours. Time doesn't pass; it freezes. The most distressing thing about it was his utter defenselessness against the savagery. He felt sick. It was like watching one of those documentaries where the hyenas pounce on their wounded prey and mercilessly tear it apart.

Violence of any sort made Gonzalo panic, almost paralyzed him. Alcázar had told him at the hospital that Atxaga was trying to kill him and, judging by what he saw, it was clearly true. And he might have succeeded had it not been for the headlights of the car parked right in front of Gonzalo's suddenly starting to flash wildly on and off. Though he couldn't hear the sound, Gonzalo deduced that the driver was also honking the horn to call attention. Luckily, it worked, and Atxaga fled.

Then a woman stepped out of the car and rushed to his aid. Luisa and Gonzalo looked at each other incredulously.

"Isn't that the redhead from next door, the photographer?"

It was. Tania. The face in the image on-screen was frozen, a stone wall, totally impenetrable, and Gonzalo's eyes swept over it like the shadow of the setting sun. That didn't change anything, just made him see it in a new light.

The red lightbulb in the darkroom blinked on and off a few times. That meant someone was at the door. Tania washed her hands in the sink and glanced quickly at the last set of photos she'd placed in the developer. It would take a few minutes before she could see them clearly. She walked out, and there stood her mother.

"We have to talk." Anna Akhmatova spoke Russian only when she was seriously upset about something. Tania listened, surprised; it took her a second to adjust to the language of her youth.

"What's the matter?" she asked, her syntax awkward and rusty.

Anna calmly smoothed the folds of her skirt, looking around at the mess in her daughter's small room. She asked herself what she'd done wrong for Tania never to consider emptying even one of the many ashtrays strewn around.

"Gonzalo Gil."

Tania felt a pang in her stomach but managed to cover.

"I don't know what you're talking about," she replied, not batting an eye.

Anna didn't fall for it. Words carried weight in the moment they were spoken and became lighter as time passed, trailing off. She sighed, exasperated.

"What do you think you're doing, going anywhere near him? We had an agreement. You promised me."

Tania felt her neck tingling. It was her butterfly wings—they wanted to fly away.

"I'm telling you, Mamá, I don't know what you're talking about."

The old woman glared at her daughter, who was smoking beside the selected works of Gorky. She'd long ago given up trying to convince Tania that if she couldn't give up the filthy habit, she should at least not do it anywhere near Anna's beloved books. She often wondered what Martin would think of Tania. He'd always been such a skittish Brit, flitting around like a bird in a cage. Neither of them would ever have guessed that the one time they slept together would produce a girl as beautiful and full of life as Tania.

"I begged you to stay away from him. Why are you so hardheaded?"

Tania realized it was pointless to keep lying. "If I hadn't been there, that man would have beaten him to death."

Anna took off her tortoiseshell glasses and began polishing them with a cloth. She kept staring at them, even after the lenses were spotless, not sure whether to put them back on and hide her deeply wrinkled eyes.

"That man has a life, and it's his alone. Neither you nor I has the right to get involved in it."

"But he's being deceived."

"No, he's not. He made the decision to forget, and he's got every right to do so. I wish Laura had done the same."

Tania exhaled heavily, blowing smoke and looking around for an empty ashtray. Not finding one, she tapped ash into the palm of her hand and thought fleetingly about the photos she had left in the darkroom. They must have fully developed by now, must have revealed their secrets.

"How did you know I saw him?"

The old woman made no reply, ruminating as she looked at her daughter. She made a face, puckering her lipstick-caked lips as she thought of Alcázar, who had approached her in the middle of the street just an hour earlier. He'd greeted her naturally, as if they were close friends, as if it hadn't been thirty-five years since they'd last seen each other. Going for a walk around the neighborhood, he told her stories about its streets as if the two of them were out sightseeing, and then he suddenly stopped and looked at her with those eyes that Anna had almost managed to forget. That was when he'd told her about the security recording and what it meant that her daughter appeared in it. Did Anna understand? he wanted to know. Did she understand how reckless Tania had been?

Yes, Anna understood perfectly, but her naïve daughter did not.

"You have no idea what you've just unleashed, Tania."

13

Vasili Arsenievich Velichko nodded his head, as if anyone could see him, and slowly hung up the phone. For a few seconds he sat there, cradling the handset, pensive. From the window of his tiny office in hangar twenty-two each morning, he could follow the construction on the Great Canal, the progress being made to join the Volga and Moskva rivers. The project fascinated him as an engineer, but more than that, as a Muscovite and Party member, it thrilled him. The ingenious plan, intended to supply the city with water and provide access to five seas, was gargantuan. *It is both awesome and unbelievable, what man is capable of,* he thought, as he prepared to write his daily column for *On Guard*, the newspaper of the Osoaviakhim, the paramilitary organization that created reserves for the armed forces.

Vasili had trouble concentrating enough to carry out the task expected of him. His concerns of the past few days had left him sleepless, and he still hadn't gotten used to this new post in Tushino. He knew that he should be grateful: Forming part of the instructors' corps at the Osoaviakhim School of Aviation and providing the political and intellectual training for future pilots was a job many would never have dared dream of at the age of twenty. But he missed his apartment by the Kremlin. Despite his attempt to brighten up his office with books and a few pictures that he'd brought from his last posting, he still found the airfield hangar depressing, especially when the sun wasn't out and fog blanketed the river.

If it was raining as well, like today, the railroad cars on the opposite shore had a ghostly look, the noise from factories and sawmills bored into his head, and the barges' whistles brought to mind images of ships sailing to the underworld. In this state of mind, it was impossible to convincingly enumerate the virtues of the Five-Year Plan, or to sing the praises of the Central Committee that had launched it.

Velichko smiled tiredly, imagining what his mother would say if she could hear what he was thinking: *You must be the only fool who still believes what he writes.* Maybe he was, he thought with a touch of pride. He believed in Stalin, trusted him, although he'd seen the man only once, giving the closing remarks on Workers' Day the year before. To be sure, Stalin hadn't been a brilliant speaker, and he was rather a coarse man, compact. Yet he'd managed to rouse all those present with his single-minded determination. Not everyone, however, agreed. There were plenty of unfavorable rumors about Party members, purges, and power struggles, an all-out dirty war in which the line between friend and enemy was blurry. You had to have eyes in the back of your head to keep from making a false step.

He tried to stop thinking like this; it verged on insanity. What he needed to do was to convince himself of the worthiness of what the Party was doing: changing their massive country forever. But the phone call he'd just received weighed on him and he didn't know how to react; he was vacillating between his convictions and the need to be prudent, between the courage of a young idealist and the self-censure of a civil servant aspiring to progress in his career, which showed every indication of taking off provided that he didn't do anything stupid.

Finally, knowing there was no turning back, he wrote two words: *Óstrov Smerti.* Immediately, he was tempted to crumple up the paper or, better yet, burn it so that no one would ever find out he'd written such a thing. But what he did instead was put it in a drawer beside his pack of cigarettes, the ink pad and stamps he used to accept or reject recruits, and his revolver. Next he solemnly donned his combat jacket, ensuring that the Voroshilov Paratroopers and first-class marksman badges on his chest were properly shined. Before walking out of the office, he made sure to remove his round glasses and slip them into a pocket. His mother said they made him look boyish, and an ambitious instructor at Osoaviakhim flight-training school could not afford to give that impression. He wanted to instill the same predatory fear he'd experienced in the halls of the Central Committee, and for a time he'd even tried growing a mustache, but he lacked the gravitas and gray hair required to pull it off successfully. All in good time.

It had stopped raining, but that wasn't necessarily good news. The sky was clearing quickly, which meant that soon the temperature would drop several degrees. No doubt it would snow before nightfall, leaving the roads impassable. Then the snow would turn into a compact layer of dirty ice that would put everything on hold. Velichko detested the motionlessness of the landscape when everything was frozen, hated seeing his breath, hearing the crunch of snow beneath his feet or tires, seeing icicles hanging from the bridges and quivering trees. He pulled up the collar of his tabard and strode confidently across the airfield's runway, leaving behind the hangars that were used as classrooms for various subjects.

A few recruits were doing a simulation, jumping off of a wooden turret to practice landing position as if having dived from their planes. Behind the perimeter fence where the gliders were kept, a couple of instructors explained how to disassemble a rotor to a large group of students. It was not uncommon for women to be in the ranks of hopeful mechanics and technicians, pilots, and paratroopers. Yes, this is what we want, Velichko thought, lighting his hundredth cigarette of the morning: a more just and equal society. This is why we made the revolution.

He could almost hear his mother laughing under her breath. *People are starving to death because of the Five-Year Plan, and here you are smoking English cigarettes. Now that's what I call a revolutionary.* Velichko loved his mother, he truly did, but she didn't understand the work he was doing, the need to identify and exterminate enemies of the people. Cancer came in many forms: Trotskyist saboteurs, large landowners, wealthy anti-Stalinist peasants known as kulaks, comrades old and new attempting to sabotage the committee's plans, straying from orthodoxy for their own personal gain. It was exhausting work, and sometimes Velichko had his doubts, wondering if the repression and terror ravaging the country were necessary. The purification of society was turning into something of an orgy. But there was no doubt they were changing the face of history, and generations to come would be the ones to judge them for it. After all, he was but a simple ideology instructor.

On the sentry box at the aircraft-manufacturing complex was a large cement plaque bearing the Osoaviakhim insignia: the red star, with propeller wings and a rifle crossed over it. The place was enormous, divided into manufacturing and storage bays, and the level of activity was frenetic. He headed for the glider division and had no trouble finding the loading docks, lined up on an alley where large trucks maneuvered, unloading thick steel beams. To his right, a stairway led down to an old training school and a series of offices that had gone unused for some time. The door opened with a gentle push.

At the end of a long corridor, disused furniture had been piled up—tables, chairs, filing cabinets—barely visible in the dim light. The windows were too high and narrow, essentially serving as skylights so that it wasn't totally impossible to see. It smelled of old urine and excrement, and rats darted with alarming speed among the remains of rotting garbage and wooden planks strewn across the cracked tile floor. It was ridiculous, and he'd never have admitted this in public, but Velichko had been afraid of rats since the night he awoke to a sharp pain in his ear, only to find that it was literally being eaten by one of those sickening rodents.

As if to magically ward them off, he shined a torch in that direction.

"This way, Instructor Velichko."

The familiar voice of subaltern Srolov calmed him. Srolov was a good man, had been on a kolkhoz, and kept both a little book filled with pictures of saints and a well-worn portrait of Stalin tucked into its pages—which was something of a contradiction. Srolov was as loyal as a stray dog who'd been shown a bit of affection. Velichko wasn't hard on him, didn't insult him, and from time to time would chat with the man over a cup of coffee, sharing one of his English cigarettes. That was why the stocky old man had called him first; he realized how serious the matter at hand might be.

"Where is he?"

The subaltern shined the torch at a small iron storm door that led to a lower floor.

"I thought it would be safest to hide him in the sewage tunnels."

Velichko nodded; it was a good idea. They climbed down a metal staircase and found themselves in a vaulted tunnel where it was impossible to stand up straight without banging your head into the network of pipes. The mildewed brick floor trembled beneath their feet; they were directly below the loading bays. Every ten yards, the tunnel bifurcated, creating a maze of narrow corridors. Without the torch, if you didn't know your way around, it would be very easy to get lost. Clearly it had been years since anyone had been down there.

Finally, the subaltern stopped where two paths branched, hesitated for a moment, and then turned right.

"Where the hell are you taking me?" Velichko asked Srolov's backside.

"Almost there."

The narrow passageway led to a sort of cave that seemed only half dug. Its walls and ceiling were minimally supported with beams that looked none too stable, and the ground was like damp clay, covered in droplets of moisture. Velichko took the torch from Srolov and turned in a circle, illuminating the space around him until he came to a lump against the wall. It resembled a pile of rags so filthy that it had solidified. Were it not for the subtle rise and fall of breathing and a coughing fit, he'd never have guessed this was a human.

"That's him?" he asked in shock and disgust.

Srolov nodded, and then, as though to prove it, pulled back a frayed blanket on top of him.

A man—if this pile of skin and bones could be called such a thing—recoiled, trembling and murmuring something unintelligible.

"What's he saying?"

Srolov shrugged. "I don't know. He just babbles. Probably delirious. I searched him, but he doesn't have any documentation on him. All I found was this. He tried to bite me when I took it off him; I had to hit him."

He held a small locket out to Velichko. It looked to be of poor quality, worthless. Opening it, he saw the picture of a young woman and a little girl. The woman had the aristocratic bearing of the kulaks Velichko detested. Arrogant and intractable, they were difficult to win over. Some people might consider her attractive—gray eyes, straight dark hair pulled into a high bun, unadorned ears, and a symmetrical face that was framed by a lace collar. The girl was her daughter, there was no doubt about that. A miniature of the woman, with the same steady, watchful eyes.

"Maybe it's his family."

Srolov seemed unconvinced. "He probably stole it."

Velichko turned the locket over. A name had been coarsely carved into the back, with a jackknife from what he could guess: *Irina*. Perplexed, he gazed at the man, who whimpered in the darkness and then made as if to scuttle away like a rat. An enormous gray pestilent rat. Velichko held on to the locket.

"How did you find him?" he asked.

Srolov glanced toward the doorway, which was completely dark. Suddenly he seemed hesitant, as though regretting having brought his superior here, or as though he hadn't counted on being asked such an obvious question.

"Years ago, I worked in the glider division, so I knew there were unused offices down here, a lot of wood and old furniture. Nobody wants it, so I thought I could cut up the wood, bit by bit, and take it home. Coal is so expensive now, and you have to keep the fire burning..."

"You've been stealing from the State, but that's not what concerns me at the moment. Get to the point."

Srolov was shaken by Velichko's frosty tone.

"I saw someone hide. I thought it was a dog, but I threw a rock and heard him cry out. That's when I realized it was a person. At first I thought it must be one of those beggars that doesn't have a passport. I tried to trap him, but he got away, and I followed him here."

"What makes you so sure that he's an escaped deportee?"

Srolov glimpsed the possibility of redemption. He bent over the man, who groaned weakly, and tore off the remains of his tattered shirt. Then he asked his superior to shine the light. On the man's chest were two tattooed words: *Óstrov Smerti*.

Velichko's eyes widened as he studied this human waste.

Seek and ye shall find, said the Gospels. Well, he'd found without having to seek. But far from being pleased about it, he agonized. If what he suspected was true, if this man had come from the island of Nazino, from *Óstrov Smerti*, and he could keep him alive long enough to talk, then Velichko's future was about to change forever, in one way or another. Since late May of the previous year, he'd been collecting partial testimonies, baseless comments, and military gossip about what had happened deep in Western Siberia, near the confluence of the Ob and Nazina rivers. A sickening holocaust, more than four thousand dead in three months. Until now he'd had no proof, no way to corroborate his suspicions that what people were saying was true.

"What are we going to do with him?" Srolov asked. "According to procedure, we're supposed to hand him over to the OGPU; he's a fugitive."

Velichko held up a hand, demanding time to think. He knew the protocol, dammit, he didn't need to be reminded. But was he prepared to confront Genrikh Yagoda, the powerful chief of the OGPU, and Matvei Berman, head of the GULAG? They were the pair responsible for the so-called special settlements, which led to an ambitious deportation plan aimed at transferring more than two million people to uninhabited regions of Siberia and Kazakhstan. As they'd told Stalin, the idea was to make over two million acres of barren land productive in a period of no more than two years. The plan was too grandiose to be feasible using only peasant labor and enemies of the people for the work.

First they'd emptied the prisons, but this proved insufficient as well. The Five-Year Plan was causing famines in the countryside, and peasants were immigrating en masse to large cities. To stop them, Yagoda and Berman had come up with the idea for internal passports. Anyone not registered in a city was ineligible for a passport, and without one they had no right to be there and could be detained and deported immediately. This had unleashed a veritable nightmare. Pressured by their superiors, the police conducted indiscriminate roundups, mindlessly casting their nets like fishermen who trawled for anything they could catch.

There was talk of monumental blunders. Velichko had already managed to document a few. For instance, an old woman named Guseva, from Murom, whose husband was an old-guard Communist and had been station chief for twenty-three years, had gone to Moscow to buy some bread. The police had arrested her for not having papers on her, and she'd disappeared. Despite her husband's demands, he had received only excuses and conflicting information from the authorities. In another case that had been brought to Velichko's attention, a young man named Novozhilov, a stoker in a compressor factory who'd received multiple awards for his productivity and was a member of the labor committee, had been deported for no reason at all. According to what his wife told Velichko, the only thing he'd done was go outside to smoke while waiting for her to go to the movies. A couple of guards happened by, and they wouldn't even let him go upstairs to his apartment for his papers. The list went on and on, and every one of these horrific tales ended at the same place, which the relevant authorities swore did not exist: the island of Nazino.

Perhaps this man just barely clinging to life, this man whose flesh hung from his bones, could be of some use. Provided that he hadn't completely lost his mind.

"Find a safe place to hide him, and have a doctor you trust take a look at him. I don't want anyone to know he exists for now, at least not until he's able to speak."

The subaltern swung his heavy head like an ox.

"I'm not sure that's right. We should turn him in."

Velichko raised the torch and glowered. His eyes, green and flashing, left no room for doubt.

"Do as I say or it will be you climbing aboard one of those barges headed for Siberia. Stealing from Osoaviakhim is a very grave offense."

Srolov grew pale, made a face, and nodded. "As you wish."

Velichko crouched down before the man, who recoiled from the light, curling up like a snail. He smelled like death itself, and his entire body was covered in filth and blood, both scabs and open wounds. He was emaciated and his scaly skin hung loose, looking as though it might come off in your hands if you touched him. The man covered his face with his forearms; Velichko couldn't get a look at it.

"Can you understand me? No one is going to hurt you. You don't need to be afraid. We just want to help you."

Speaking quietly, he managed pull the man's forearm down and had to make a concerted effort not to scream at what he saw: the right eye socket empty; cheekbones jutting out violently, pulling taut the skin around his jaws, which were missing half their teeth. The escapee had been beaten savagely, judging by the lacerations and bruises still visible, and his swollen nose had been broken, perhaps some time ago. His left eye, dark as a button, watched the instructor, frightened as a cornered animal. He was moving his cracked lips but saying nothing comprehensible, repeating some sort of litany under his breath.

When Velichko stood back up, the man suddenly reacted. A gnarled hand shot out from the dirty rags, quickly grabbing hold of the instructor's forearm. Velichko felt the man's fingernails digging into his combat jacket and instinctively recoiled in horror. Srolov made as if to strike him, but Velichko stopped him. The man's other hand emerged, palm open, as though begging. It took a few seconds for Velichko to realize what the hand and eye were asking.

"The locket? You want me to give back your locket?" He pulled the medallion from his pocket and put it in the man's hand. "All right, I will. On one condition. Tell me your name."

The man clamped his fingers shut and recoiled once more. Shrinking back in the darkness, he said: "My name is Elías Gil Villa."

.   .   .

She was alive; she had to be, he said to himself, stroking the locket's photo. It was the only consolation he had. Anything else was too awful to contemplate. Sitting in a chair, hands on his knees, Elías gazed out the window. On the table was a bowl of broth with a few vegetables, which he hadn't touched, and a carafe of wine, which was almost empty. He blinked nervously and stretched his neck, uncramping his muscles.

"I know more about the internment camps than any of you. I know what the camps are like, what the barges used to transport deportees smell like. I know what the snow tastes like, what it feels like to be bitten by guard dogs. I know the sound it makes when a rifle butt breaks a tibia or an elbow. Yes, I know all about you."

Instructor Velichko was surprised at how much the prisoner had changed in a few short weeks. Despite Srolov's reservations and his desire to get rid of the problem this man posed as quickly as possible, he'd done his job well. First he had made Elías bathe. Without the layer of blood and filth caked on him, in a used but clean cotton shirt, he looked a bit more human. He was much younger than Velichko initially thought. His one eye flickered like a candle, and a beard, coarsely trimmed but clean, had begun to grow on his cheeks and around his swollen lips. His nose was oddly shaped, the bridge sunken; it would never regain its natural shape.

"You don't find our methods to your liking? What a pity. Do keep in mind that you are a deportee, not a guest here to visit the Bolshoi. You were arrested for a reason, that much is clear."

Elías clamped his hands in his armpits. Suddenly he had a chill, the sort of chill that lived within him, came and went in waves. Raw.

"So, what is a Spanish student of engineering doing with these words tattooed on his chest? How did you get to Nazino? And more important, how did you escape and make it to Moscow?"

Elías looked at him suspiciously. He no longer had the terrified expression he'd had upon arrival. The empty eye socket had been covered with a crude patch. He didn't reply and again looked out the window. Rocking softly in his chair, Elías moved his lips silently. Velichko called over the girl who had been coming in the afternoons to change his clothes and bandages and look after him. Until then, she hadn't said a word. The instructor ordered her to repeat the question in Spanish.

"He says they're not going to hurt you, and that you have to cooperate. Otherwise, you will be handed over to the OGPU."

Elías glanced at her in surprise. She gave a faint smile, barely perceptible. He must have liked hearing his own language, albeit the tortuous unnatural version of it she spoke. He looked up at Instructor Velichko and then suspiciously at Srolov, who remained at one side. Slowly, like the wheels of a train just pulling out, he began to speak.

People who don't know the steppe tend to think of vast expanses of snow, a wide-open landscape where temperatures plummet as soon as the sun goes down. But that's only in the winter. In the summer, after the thaw, the steppe is a hot, steamy hell where the sweat sticks oppressively to your body and attracts flies and mosquitoes by the thousands. It drives you crazy, there's no way to get away from them. They hound you day and night, attacking your body, crawl into every orifice they can find. It's like you're a rotting carcass, except they don't have the patience to wait for you to die; instead they eat you alive. And for hundreds of miles, there's nothing but stinking swamps and marshland, endless shrubs, and not even a single berry to eat.

From time to time you see a hare or a bird, completely unfazed by the presence of a human. All they do is hop off or move to another branch, dodging the poorly aimed stone tossed weakly at them. It's torture, watching prey mock your attempts to hunt as you starve. The horizon is enough to drive you insane, blending in with the cloudless sky at some indistinguishable point in the distance—nothing, no sound, no houses, no roads. It must be the same loneliness the first men on earth felt. Agonizing. The earth is simply a grave, patiently awaiting its tribute.

Elías walked for hours, like a zombie, shifting Anna from his arms to his shoulders until his body was numb, and then dropping to his knees or falling and pulling the girl along with him. Sometimes he was delirious for minutes at a time—which seemed like hours—gazing at the sky and not caring about anything, until Anna moaned or her grubby little fingers touched his face. Then, somehow, he would find the strength he didn't know he still had and set off again. Moving onward, it didn't matter where. To chase away the hunger he would think. And his only thought was of Irina, and the river where he'd let her drown to keep from being pulled under himself.

He conjured up the hazy scene that seemed so long ago: Irina sinking in the turbulent waters, him swimming to the surface, his lungs about to explode, the pages of her little book of poems floating in the water. One night he carved her name into the locket with a stone. He cried for a long time, contemplating the photo, contemplating Anna's tiny trembling body. The girl was so weak she hardly moved or made a sound, as if some primitive instinct urged her to reduce all activity to a minimum in order to survive. And still they weren't going to make it, Elías was fully aware of that. The girl would die before him, in a matter of days, if not hours. And then...then he could eat.

He gagged just thinking about it. But still, he thought about it. And he knew. Knew that when the time came, he'd do it. She seemed to sense this and pulled away, determined to live.

The afternoon was scorching hot, the landscape turning scarlet. And when, miraculously, a breeze came along and scared off the cloud of mosquitoes buzzing all around him, Elías felt a slight ray of hope. One night he managed to catch a rat in his bare hands. He crushed its head under a rock and skinned it with a piece of flint. After dismembering it with his teeth, he softened it in his mouth until he'd formed a pinkish paste, which he forced Anna to swallow. Then, desperate in his thirst, he drank a bit of water from a natural well and spent the following two days shitting in his pants. Elías didn't even bother to stop, simply letting the liquid run down his legs and behind him like a watery trail of death.

The worst night came after countless others on his endless march; time loses all meaning when there is nothing to mark it. It had been raining for hours, and Elías wrung out every drop of water from his clothing, drinking it himself or giving it to Anna. The little girl began to shiver, her eyes feverish, teeth chattering so hard it was as if they might shatter; the sound of it drove him to distraction. He hugged her to his body, trying to warm her. Anna's face had become almost transparent, veins snaking beneath her skin. The girl's lips were horrifically swollen and purple, the same color as the bags under her eyes and the spots that had appeared on her neck. She would die that night. Elías sensed it when he rested a palm on her chest and felt her heartbeat growing weaker.

He didn't want her to die, and yet at the same time he wanted nothing more. For her sake, for his. For both of them. He kissed her forehead and brushed her filthy hair out of her face, stroking her gently. A hand placed over her mouth and nose, that was all it would take. No need to press hard; he'd simply leave them there until she gave a little shudder and stopped breathing. It would be over so fast she wouldn't even realize... He wanted to, but then couldn't, not yet. Elías wasn't going to be the one to make that call. So he resolved to wait, not moving from the small crag he'd found by a hill. He would stay there with her, waiting motionless, for as long as it took.

At some point Elías drifted off and had horrific, twisted nightmares. It was impossible to tell if he was awake or asleep in this perverted jumble of things real and invented: Irina and his father; Claude, pointing at him with amputated fingers; Igor holding his skewered eyeball on a stick, laughing; the detention center and that guard, offering him a huge glass of water with worms floating on the surface. And Irina, reading her poem, eyes full of seaweed. In his dream Elías killed, died, came back to life, gnawed on Anna's bones, vomited them up, and ate them again.

He opened his eye and blinked at the sky, filled with stars that changed position every night. For a few seconds he wasn't sure whether he was still dreaming, but he heard an animal snarl, a throaty sound and then teeth, snapping. He reached out a hand and touched the space where Anna's body—perhaps already dead, cold—should have been. But all he felt was a paw, slipping from his fingers. He turned his head slowly and saw a small gray wolf, straggly and sick looking, attempting to drag the girl's body off, its fangs clamped on one arm as it backed furtively away, like a fox in a chicken coop.

Elías felt around without taking his eyes from the wolf, which had raised its hackles upon being discovered, separating its front paws, ears pressed back. Elías grabbed a stone the size of a hand grenade. Not big enough to do any good, but he stood up regardless, prepared to fight for Anna. For her life, or his dinner? It didn't matter. He wasn't going to let that wolf carry her off. He'd never seen a wolf before, and this one looked like it was in bad shape, didn't even seem to be in its natural habitat. The animal was as disconcerted as he was, but Elías realized that one stone against that wolf's yellow teeth would do nothing. He was going to lose, and he knew it.

He raised his arms and shouted, as though this was the way to scare off all wild animals, but the wolf stepped forward, lip raised in a snarl, growling angrily. Had it been a dog, it would have barked, but wolves don't bark. They give no warning. They attack. Suddenly. The animal pounced on Elías, downing him. Immediately it went for the jugular, but Elías whipped to the side and instead its teeth sank into his forearm. The animal's legs tangled around his own in a frenzied dance; with his left hand, he punched its side with the rock but the animal hardly even registered the blow.

Then came the sound of a shot. The wolf flew into the air with a plaintive yelp and landed on Elías, body facing the direction the shot had come from. It had been hit and was bleeding, a trail of red coming from its hindquarters. Undaunted, the animal backed up and then turned and slunk away, limping into the darkness.

Elías sat up—clutching his wounded forearm, still in shock—and saw two silhouettes at his feet. One unsteadily gripped the revolver that had been fired. The other was bent over Anna.

"She's alive."

"Give her some water."

Elías recognized the voices before he saw their faces. Michael and Martin.

Michael approached Elías and held his gaze, not saying a word. Still gripping the pistol. He didn't look like himself, but then, none of them looked like themselves. He wore no expression, like a ghost that had come out of nowhere and with a snap of the fingers might disappear once more. He tucked the revolver into his trousers and looked at Elías's forearm.

"Those teeth cut like a saw. We've been following that wolf for a week, and it keeps getting away. At least this time I hit it. Maybe tonight we'll have a good dinner; it can't have gotten far. Look at us—house dogs gone feral, chasing a wolf. The world's gone crazy." Michael's eyes were like a river, almost frozen. He took out a cigarette—Elías's jaw dropped in awe—and lit it. After a long puff, he smiled, a magician who's astounded his audience with a trick.

"Aren't you going to say anything? We just saved your life."

Elías watched Martin with Anna. He was rocking the unconscious girl in his arms and holding the canteen to her lips. Clean
fresh water dribbled down her chin. Elías's throat gurgled like a
clogged pipe.

"Where did you come from?" he asked, as though they were
demons from hell.

"The same place as you," Michael replied. Elías's eyes searched
for signs of Igor Stern and his gang. No doubt they were hiding,
watching the scene unfold in amusement.

"He's not here," Michael said, "but he can't be far and I bet
he's pretty mad. We stole half his provisions. I have the pistol I
took off that commander, but there are only three bullets left and
at least five of them—provided they haven't eaten anyone else.
When we left the island, we were eight. A young kid from Kursk
was with us. Poor guy, the only thing he did to get sent here was
sleep with the daughter of a tank commander. He was the first one
Igor and his pack of wolves devoured. They're voracious, so when
they started giving Martin strange looks we decided it was time to
strike out on our own." There wasn't the slightest hint of sarcasm
or humor in his words, no trace of emotion. "We'll probably all
end up dead, but not like that."

Elías looked away in shame. Michael noticed, glanced over at
the girl in Martin's arms and understood, but made no comment.
He passed Elías the cigarette and let him smoke. Each of them had
to survive as best he could.

Two days later they came upon the wolf. It was limping, some
two hundred yards ahead of them. Seen from the distance it looked
like a drunk, lurching around unable to keep its balance. Michael
shouted with joy, but none of them wasted energy running after
it. All they had to do was wait. On the fourth night, the animal

collapsed. Michael pulled out a knife and plunged it deep into the wolf's neck.

"They say dog meat is salty, but it's not bad if you roast it long enough. Besides, we've all eaten worse things than this by now."

The three men laughed—hysterical laughter, a dark malicious humor that made Anna blink, wide-eyed in shock and bafflement. Still, it was thanks to Martin's care and ministrations that she seemed to have come back to life.

Maybe it wasn't so bad, after all. From the sky above, anyone looking down would have seen a weak fire in the middle of an immense expanse of nothing, a group of humans gathered around it as if the flames would keep them safe. And a few miles back, advancing in the night, a pack of two-footed wolves, human wolves sniffing the air and tracking the scent of burned meat. Life, from a distance, must have looked fragile and volatile, a series of flukes and misfortunes over which men had no control. Erratic figures, like shooting stars, flames that burned bright and then a second later disappeared, without a trace of the light that had shone in the dark.

But men were not stars. They had beating hearts. The three of them said nothing of what troubled them, knowing that their words were clumsy and insufficient, and hid their differences behind silence because their lives were at stake. If the glances they exchanged contained resentment or accusation, they pushed it aside and focused instead on the hypnotic flames of the fire. And at dawn they set off once more, knowing that although destiny was not in their hands, they wouldn't give up without a fight. Because fight was all they had left. They had no cause. They'd fight God and Mother Nature and themselves. Until they fell, exhausted or starving. And then, finally, it would all make sense.

They'd left the wolf's remains behind, its guts must have desiccated weeks ago. Martin walked ahead, with Elías. The three men took turns carrying Anna, and it was Michael's turn. With his short, stocky legs he looked like a midget in the mines. He ambled behind them, the girl hoisted over his shoulders.

"Michael has really taken to the girl," Martin said. He was looking out at nothing in particular. Anything to avoid Elías's eyes. This was the first time they'd spoken alone together since they'd met up. "I think he's determined to get her out of here alive because he feels guilty about all the things he's done since our deportation—and before it. For having signed that false confession against you. Saving her is like his form of redemption. Do you think it's possible? Redemption? Do good deeds erase the bad?"

Elías gave a wry smile, as though laughing at a private joke or something he'd just remembered.

"What I think, Martin, is that everything we do is branded into us forever. It doesn't matter how we behave in the future; what we've done here will be with us for the rest of our lives. But I'm no priest. Maybe, when we get out of here, if we bathe in the baptismal font we'll see the light."

He thought of Claude and his dismal gray death on a filthy barge beached on a hellacious island. He thought of his friends, who'd done nothing to help him. And he knew that none of those thoughts were of any use at the moment.

And then a miracle occurred. It wasn't a burning bush or the parting of the waters beneath their feet. Their miracle came in the form of a post in the ground, a crow perched on top of it, observing them from twenty-five feet up. Then it flew to the next post, a hundred yards away, and the next one after that. Posts, every hundred yards, for as far as the eye could see. Posts that had been put there by men and would one day bring electricity or telegraph or telephone lines to a place where people lived.

How long had it been? None of them knew. But they'd reached the fringes of the world, like shipwrecked sailors heaved onto a beach. They had no idea where they were, but they were somewhere. Even the swarms of mosquitoes stopped attacking and buzzed off in a black cloud when they crossed this invisible border, the first explorers there to settle an uncharted territory.

But Igor Stern crossed the border, too, and he was less than a day behind.

For a second, Elías stopped speaking. He spread his hands on the table, as though expecting someone to rescue him. But the only ones there were the girl who looked after him, Instructor Velichko, and his assistant Srolov. Aware of the cold, aware of the present moment, he pulled his reddened fingers back. Then Elías stood and walked around the room a few times. He stopped before a small portrait of Stalin in dress uniform, embracing a young Georgian girl. The Father of the Soviet Socialist Republics. The great *khoziain*, loving father of the people.

He closed his eye and thought of the last night he'd seen Anna. In his mind, he brushed the hair from her forehead, stroked her face. Elías asked her to put on the locket; he wanted to see it glimmering on her little chest, which had so many times almost stopped breathing. The girl tilted her head over his shoulder, and for the first time he saw something that looked close to a smile. The locket gleamed, clean and beautiful on her dirty skin. She looked like a princess out of the kind of novel his father used to read. A real Russian princess.

"So have you seen many princesses around here?" Irina had once asked when, after making love, he compared her to a Gorky character.

"Yes. Every time I see you."

"With your one eye?"

Elías took off his patch. He not only let her see the empty socket but placed her fingers on the amorphous flesh. She felt blood coursing through the cavity despite his blindness.

"Sometimes I dream that this is all going to end," she said, taking her hand away.

"There's nothing wrong with that."

"Yes, there is."

"Why do you say that?"

"Because then I wake up and I'm still here."

"But I'm going to get you out. Some French postal service pilot is going to appear in his little biplane and fly us out."

"If that dream ever turns into a reality, take my daughter with you. Promise me."

And he promised.

He turned back to Velichko with the locket in his hand.

"We came from someplace, we have a past, a place where we were happy. That's what counts. With that, we can make new lives for ourselves... That's what Irina used to say. Do you believe it?"

14

Gonzalo checked the address on the business card Luisa had given him one more time:

Tania Akhmatova, Photographer
Calle Molino Nuevo 12, ground floor

What he saw before him, however, was not a photography studio but a little bookshop: KARAMAZOV BOOKSTORE was painted on the faded awning. Despite its unexceptional appearance, the shop was bright and spacious inside. There was a center table stacked with new releases, a few—not many—sporting little blue cards on the cover reading "Store recommendation." To the right was the cash register, and behind that a small area selling stationery. The rest of the space, essentially a long hall with a wider area in the back and a wooden staircase leading up to a second floor, was lined with white shelves, all full of books. The largest section was dedicated entirely to nineteenth- and twentieth-century Russian literature, with volumes carefully organized by size, edition, author, and subject. On one wall hung an enormous lithograph of Dostoyevsky. Strategically placed around the room were several small wicker armchairs and low tables with flowers and literary journals. The place smelled clean and orderly. Mussorgsky's *Night on Bald Mountain* played softly in the background, a strident mix of chamber virtuosity and folk music.

A pair of red shoes appeared on the staircase at the end of the hall. These were followed by two very white ankles covered in tiny blue veins and a flouncy skirt in multiple shades of orange. A hand, encircled by bright chunky bracelets, slid along the banister. It was a pianist's hand, though the nails were too long to play.

"Can I help you?"

Gonzalo stared in surprise at the old woman on the top step, her head slightly bowed so as not to hit the suspended ceiling. She wasn't exactly small but was somehow slight, as if her body had withdrawn inside a gauzy white blouse that matched her skin. She wore a touch of makeup and had liquid blue eyes that looked almost gray and were hidden behind stylish glasses attached to a little leather cord. Her hair—very white, short, elegantly cut with frizzy bangs—shone like a bright smile. She could have been a hundred years old, but Gonzalo got the sense she'd just been born into the world. He got a warm, familiar feeling, reminiscent of afternoons spent by the fire, eyes closed listening to Mussorgsky, or reading Chekhov with a cup of tea.

"I was looking for Tania Akhmatova's photography studio, but I must have made a mistake."

The old woman approached nimbly, shoulders curved forward as though she had a permanent chill, and she eyed the new arrival inquisitively, with a vague sense of recognition, almost inviting him to have a seat in one of the armchairs and tell her about his life. She was the sort of person who makes you sure nothing bad can happen when she's around.

The sense that he knew her, that the whole atmosphere was vaguely familiar, grew stronger when he got a faint whiff of her jasmine perfume and heard the gentle swish of her skirt.

"What makes you think you made a mistake? Isn't that what her card says?"

The woman's comment disconcerted Gonzalo, as did her rapid-fire laugh. It was as if she were teasing him, or perhaps just laughing at some inside joke.

"Is she expecting you?"

Gonzalo told her that she wasn't. Again the mischievous little laugh, which made her face crinkle delightfully. She must once have been breathtakingly beautiful, and in a way, she still was.

"Tania's studio is upstairs. Go on up, and if the red light above the door is on, then knock first, and wait. Tania doesn't like surprise visits."

The red light was on. Gonzalo knocked and waited. After a few minutes he heard footsteps and the door opened. Tania blinked as though emerging from the dark into a bright sunny day, momentarily blinded.

"The Mayakovsky reader," she said, recovering.

Gonzalo nodded. And suddenly he was hit by the amazing resemblance between Tania and the old woman. All it took was a little imagination to see that in thirty or forty years' time, Tania would look identical. The woman's daughter, maybe? Granddaughter?

"My secretary gave me your card," he said awkwardly, by way of greeting.

After seeing the parking garage security tape, Gonzalo had wondered how to broach this meeting, what to say, what to do. He'd gone over it meticulously in his mind, but one thing that had not occurred to him was that he'd feel like a nervous teenager, swallowing repeatedly, nor did he picture himself standing there stupidly, her business card in his trembling fingers.

"I can see that," Tania said, glancing down at it with a bored look. She'd been smoking; the smell of tobacco lingered. Maybe she'd had a drink as well, not a big one, but something strong. Her eyes were a bit red. Or perhaps she was just exhausted, or sleepy, or something had made her cry not long ago. She stroked her butterfly tattoo and flexed her neck gently, as though to loosen tight muscles. The elegant way she moved her ring-covered fingers only increased the similarities he now saw with the old woman downstairs.

"Did you want a photo shoot?" Her tone presumed the opposite. *Not even I could do much to improve that suit and haircut*, she seemed to imply.

"Actually," Gonzalo fumbled, "I was hoping we could talk about what happened in the garage the day I was attacked. First of all, I suppose I should thank you."

Tania frowned, creasing her perfectly shaped brows and grimacing as though she'd pricked herself with a pin.

"And then I'd like to ask why you left before the police arrived."

Tania's eyes remained fixed on the floor. She didn't look surprised. It was as if she'd taken for granted that his visit was inevitable, or as though she'd wanted him to come but not quite yet, before she was ready. She clucked her tongue and then looked up expectantly at Gonzalo.

"I could do with a beer, couldn't you?"

There were almost no customers in Bar Flight. It was a small place, below street level, its redbrick walls the same as those of the Roman wall in the Casco Antiguo. Overhead spotlights illuminated some sections and left other areas of darkness behind the historic columns, which the bar's designer had been obliged not to touch. Gonzalo was struck by the framed Russian newspaper clippings dating from the Second World War and the photos of heroes and soldiers hanging all over. Some were anonymous battlefield scenes, airfields, pieces of artillery with smiling gunners, pilots with their arms around smiling girls; others were famous colonels and generals from the Red Army. There was also a large oil painting of Stalin in his marshal's uniform. The contrast between that, the modern furniture, and the small stage at the back created a contradictory but agreeable effect.

Tania didn't have to order. The owner walked over with two beers and a little saucer of potato chips. He was an old man, in his eighties, but he still had a sort of youthful rosy-cheeked expression and lively blue eyes that twinkled kindly. He kissed Tania warmly on both cheeks and stared at Gonzalo for a moment before flashing him a brief smile.

"Having a bad day?" he asked, pointing to the faded bruises on his face. His accent was thick, the words rolling in his mouth before fighting their way out in guttural Spanish.

"No worse than others," Gonzalo replied curtly.

Tania and the old man exchanged glances. She shrugged, and the man walked off with a rag over his shoulder.

"He was just trying to be nice," she scolded.

The man's skin gave off a sour smell, like rancid lard, though it was nothing to do with his hygiene.

"I apologize . . . Why does he smell like that?"

Tania smiled. In time she'd learned to put up with the smell without turning her face away.

"Fear."

Gonzalo gave her a blank look.

"He spent years in prison camps. He fought against Hitler's troops when they invaded Belarus, and fell prisoner in the first war offensive; they deported him to a camp near Warsaw, and when the Red Army liberated the camp in 1945 he was found guilty of treason and sent to a gulag in Siberia. According to the Russian authorities, he hadn't fought hard enough. The fact that he was alive was irrefutable proof of his cowardice. He spent eleven years in Siberia, and he's smelled like that ever since. Like fear. Terror. It got into his skin and he's still sweating it out."

"So what's with all the Red Army décor? And the portrait of Stalin? Shouldn't he detest all that?"

Tania glanced affectionately at the old man serving a couple of men at the bar. Maybe life had dealt him a few bad hands, but he made up for it with a good-natured, ear-to-ear smile and immaculate dress. He had the instinctive kindliness of those who chose to see the bright side almost as a defense mechanism.

"He needs to believe that everything that happened made sense. He was a political commissar, you know? Even when he was in Siberia he refused to deny his past. It would have been like negating his whole existence. You won't find a more fervent Communist than Vasili Velichko, I can assure you of that."

"How do you know him?"

"He's an old friend of my mother's. The man's like an uncle to me."

"Was the old lady at the bookstore your mother?"

Tania gave him a long stare before nodding. Her eyes went straight to his heart, which fluttered and then pounded until she decided to let go.

"I'd be careful about calling her an old lady. She can still smack you around, you know."

Gonzalo smiled. "I like her bookstore."

"She'll be happy to hear that. Especially since you like Mayakovsky. That's her favorite poet; she taught me to read him," she added, pointing to a picture above his shoulder.

Gonzalo fixed his gaze on the glassy light illuminating the poet's photo. It was a half-body shot of Mayakovsky shortly before he shot himself in the head, leaving his last poem unfinished. Gonzalo was moved, a shiver ran down his spine. He pictured Laura sitting on the kitchen floor with an open book, reciting the man's verses in Russian as their mother looked on, ready to jump in if she made a mistake.

The memory brought him back to his reason for being there.

"Why did you leave without waiting for the police to arrive?" he asked, returning to the subject of the tape.

Tania clucked her tongue. Gonzalo watched her fidget, peeling the label off her beer bottle.

"So you're the type who always looks for some ulterior motive in people's actions," she concluded. Her eyes, however, looked hopeful.

"I've seen the tape. All the way through. The entire sequence."

"You're lucky I just happened to be picking up my car right at that moment," she claimed.

Gonzalo continued to gaze at her, wondering what it was that made some people more attractive than others. Maybe it was their skin, maybe it was chemistry—and yet Tania hadn't touched him, hadn't even brushed against him, and his body was charged with electricity. In the past he'd occasionally fantasized about a client, or a waitress, an actress, there was even a neighbor he often used to bump into at the newsstand in the mornings—but those were all passing fancies and he'd never seriously considered cheating on Lola. None of those women had awakened anything real in him, a concrete desire to make something happen. Maybe he'd been waiting to find one who wouldn't fill him with doubt and regret. And here she was right in front of him, feeding him lies without batting an eyelid.

"You'd been there for some time. I rewound the tape and saw you arrive."

Tania processed this information calmly, unruffled. She should have foreseen the fact that the garage would have a security camera, but she hadn't. In part, Gonzalo felt relieved at that.

"I don't know if it's in your best interest to pursue this conversation," she said, recalling her mother's warning.

"Let me be the one to decide that."

Tania shrugged. "I'd been curious about you since the day we met on the balcony. I liked your comment about Mayakovsky and the faraway look you had, gazing out at the street. When I went down to the garage I recognized your SUV and suddenly had the urge to see your stuff. People's cars say things about them, they leave things inside them: books, CDs, spare change in the ashtray, a pack of cigarettes under the driver's seat."

Gonzalo wondered what kind of message his things were sending about him, how Tania saw him. She wasn't planning to tell him, clearly, and for now, he decided not to ask how she'd even known he drove an SUV.

"When Atxaga attacked me, I had a computer bag with a laptop on me, or maybe I'd just left it in the car, I can't remember. Either way, that computer is really important and now it's gone. When the police arrived it had already disappeared."

Tania finished her beer and debated whether to order another or bring the conversation to a close. The butterfly wings on her neck seemed primed for a leisurely takeoff. Gonzalo got the feeling she was watching him with the same bemusement as her mother, as if she were somehow laughing at him.

"You know, some people might say I saved your life, and here you are accusing me of being a thief. Nice display of gratitude. If you've seen the tape, you already have your answer."

Gonzalo had, of course, studied every frame, searching obsessively for the laptop. After Atxaga had taken off, she'd tried to help him, covering his wound with one hand and using the other to make a phone call. She'd stayed by his side until the flashing lights of the ambulance came into view. And then she'd quietly slipped off. But most of the images were blurry, and from the angle at which they were taken, some of the attack was either partially obscured or off camera.

"No, no. I'm not accusing you of anything, definitely not. I was just wondering if you saw anyone else there."

Tania half closed her eyes, and Gonzalo thought it was like the sun setting on the horizon. Then, out of the blue, she stood. "It's late and I've got things to do."

Gonzalo got up, too. "I didn't mean to offend you."

She gave him an almost apologetic smile. Tania had a theory: Some people found themselves in places they didn't belong, as if they'd accidentally ended up in lives that weren't theirs. Gonzalo struck her as one of those people. He tried to walk her out, but she told him she didn't really go in for chivalrous gestures.

"Stay and finish your beer."

Gonzalo watched her leave, hair tousled, head held high, body swaying naturally beneath her clothes as though it was not in her nature to be constricted. He was certain that Tania was lying to him, or at least not telling him the whole truth. And what's more, he didn't care. He just wanted to see her again.

It took Gonzalo a minute to realize that the owner of the bar was staring at him.

Everything was in order—visas, local guide, hotels, tours. Taking a group of twelve tourists on a twenty-five-day trip through three countries in Africa required painstaking organization, but Carlos had done a good job. He felt satisfied and Lola eyed him discreetly as he pointed out possible itineraries on a map he'd spread on a table at the travel agency. His chiseled face lit up as he described possible tourist attractions in great detail. With a touch of malice, Lola thought that he himself would be one of those attractions for some female on the tour. It wasn't hard to picture.

"You've done a magnificent job," she said, touching his shoulder and leaving her hand there a second longer than necessary, aroused by the scene she'd just envisioned. Carlos gave her a penetrating look. So much so that she took her hand away, slightly embarrassed.

What are you playing at? she asked herself. Her life was a mess, and here she was flirting with some kid just to distract herself from her troubles. And Carlos had already made it quite clear, in more ways than one—meaningful looks, double entendres, undue solicitude—that he was ready to take things farther if she just said the word.

"How are things going at home?" he asked, voice full of concern he didn't feel.

Lola, stupidly, had unburdened herself to him and now felt uncomfortable with him asking about it. She'd fallen into the well of self-pity and felt victimized, something she hated in other women. Sleeping with a new man the moment yours walks out the door was a game for younger women, unbecoming of someone her age, and besides, she wasn't like that, she told herself angrily. Lola didn't need some kid to console her, didn't need his sympathy. Sure, she had problems, but she'd solve them, end of story. And yet Carlos had asked her to lunch to finalize details on the trip, and without even realizing it, over dessert she cried and complained bitterly about her life, enumerating the real and invented affronts she'd been forced to endure during the course of her marriage. And Carlos held her hand, willing and attentive.

"They're fine, thanks for asking."

Her clipped tone sent a message so at odds with the hand she'd left on his shoulder that Carlos was disconcerted, didn't know where he stood in the tug-of-war going on inside Lola. He opted for a prudent retreat. He could be patient.

"If you need anything, you know you can count on me."

Lola barely acknowledged the offer. She had been wavering, but she had to put an end to this right now. The last thing she needed was to get between this kid's sheets.

"How are things with Javier?" she asked. It was a desperate shot. Mentioning her son was a way of bringing things back down to an appropriate realm, and of reminding them both who was who.

Carlos's expression darkened, taking the hint. He began carefully folding the map.

"We haven't seen much of each other lately."

"Do you know if he has a girlfriend?"

He scoffed inwardly. "Not as far as I know. Why do you ask?"

"He's been very distracted lately, head in the clouds. And he keeps asking me for lots of money. I thought maybe it was for dinners, drinks, hotels..."

Javier had become something of an obstacle for Carlos. His little scenes and jealousy were getting old. It was no longer worth the hassle. Carlos had another target in mind now.

"We're friends; I hope you're not trying to turn me into your confidant. I don't think it would be fair of me to tell my friend's mother what he's up to."

Lola tucked her hair behind her ear, slightly embarrassed, and realized that her tone had wounded Carlos's pride.

"No, of course not. It's just that Javier is very quiet, and I'm sure he'd turn to you before coming to me if he had a problem."

"If that were the case, I'd let you know, don't worry."

Lola nodded. The charged atmosphere of a few minutes earlier had vanished, and although part of her was relieved, another part felt let down.

That morning she'd arranged to meet Gonzalo for lunch. She'd called him at the office and spoken to Luisa, his assistant. Lola had never liked the woman, whom she found slightly foul-mouthed and verging on the disrespectful.

"I'll give him the message. He's meeting with a client right now."

That wasn't true. Despite the newly painted sign and fresh geraniums on the balcony, day after day things were looking grimmer. The hours passed in silence, and though Gonzalo seemed very busy with his own investigation, Louisa herself had started looking for other jobs and sending out résumés.

Gonzalo couldn't blame her. In a few weeks he would run out of savings, and then they'd have to close the firm. Over the past few days his father-in-law had made a few attempts at reconciliation, tried to get him to change his mind. The old man was willing to loosen the noose with which he was strangling Gonzalo; all he had to do was step back, reconsider. There was no need to see it as defeat; it would be a smart move: Wise men reconsider. But wisdom wasn't one of Gonzalo Gil's fortes.

It was in this hostile, contradictory frame of mind that Gonzalo sat down for lunch with Lola. They'd been apart only a few days but the distance between them was huge. They struggled to look each other in the face, or to find anything to talk about beyond the kids, and therefore exchanged rote questions and pat answers. Too many things were swirling around in each of their heads, and although it was woefully apparent to both of them, neither brought them up, which served only to hinder any honest attempt to resolve their issues.

"This weekend my father wants to take Javier and Patricia to the house in Cáceres. I thought I might take advantage of it, take a little break. We could go away someplace, get a room at that little hotel in S'Agaró."

Gonzalo wasn't even listening. His attention was focused on the man sitting at one of the tables in the back. He'd come in with Lola and then discreetly withdrawn, but hadn't taken his eyes off the door. It was one of Alcázar's men that Agustín had hired to protect his family. It made Gonzalo feel a bit better to know that at least his family was safe. Gonzalo's own protection had been removed the moment he left the hospital. From time to time, Alcázar stopped by to see him, updated him on the search for Atxaga (zero progress), and asked about him, though not too much. The truth was, the inspector came around only to feel him out about the Matryoshka business, to try to wheedle information from him. Ever since their last conversation, when Gonzalo had said he had cause to reopen

Laura's case, the inspector had been uneasy. Gonzalo suspected that the man's attempts to find Atxaga would be stepped up considerably the moment he agreed to cooperate.

"How has it come to this?" he murmured with a sideways glance at the bodyguard.

An hour later, Gonzalo was back at his rental still wondering the same thing, unable to make sense of what had happened after he'd sent those words into space like a probe in search of life. Lola had grasped his hand tightly, repeating what she'd said a few weeks earlier: They could start over; they had two incredible kids; they still loved each other. She *loved* him, she stressed desperately. And it was that precise moment—the way she'd squeezed his fingers as he contemplated her bright-red nails—that Gonzalo knew he simply couldn't carry on with the charade anymore. He pulled a pack of cigarettes from his pocket and lit one. For a few seconds he watched the match burn between his fingers. Then he looked up and saw Lola's face crumble, saw her increasing distress.

"What are you doing? You promised me you'd quit."

A declaration of intent, a childish act of rebellion that meant no turning back. That was what his first puff of smoke equated to. And then he told her. Described in excruciating detail what he'd seen that day eighteen years ago, recounted one by one each of the particulars that he'd replayed endlessly in his mind since that time.

"I know I'm not Javier's father. That it was that guy who got you pregnant. I don't know how long it went on, or if it was just that one time, but it doesn't really matter. I waited for ages for you to tell me about it, just as I waited to gather the courage to tell you that I knew. I saw it all, Lola. And I realized the moment I laid eyes on Javier in the incubator."

Lola sat perfectly still, as if she was dead, observing the cigarette smoke waft up. And then she did something surprising:

She plucked the cigarette from Gonzalo's fingers and took a long, deep, expert drag, closing her eyes.

"So, what are we going to do with what we know?" she asked.

He was hurt by her directness. Stripped for the first time of all masks, her open expression was bare and merciless. No secrets. She didn't ask forgiveness or offer excuses. She simply took the cigarette and accepted that the time for lying was now past. *All right, then,* her expression and wave of the hand seemed to say, *you cut the deck, not me. What now?*

Gonzalo had gotten up from the table as if the person staring at him were an impostor.

"I don't know, Lola."

The evidence of their words was there, but it felt like none of it was really happening. Now, in his little half-furnished living room, listening to Charlie Parker's sax on "Perdido," freed of his obligation, he'd smoked half a pack of cigarettes. In the shop downstairs he'd bought a bottle of gin and several miniature bottles of tonic. The Chinese man who ran the place thought he'd misunderstood at first. This was attorney Gonzalo Gil. He didn't drink, didn't smoke. This was a man who always behaved as was expected of him, who acted surprised every year at his surprise party. The shopkeeper handed him the bottle with the gloom of a man who had a front-row seat for the collapse of civilization.

"You look like hell and smell like cheap liquor."

Gonzalo was driving slowly and hiding behind his dark glasses. He hadn't shaved and for the first time in years had shown up at his mother's residence without a tie.

"You, on the other hand, look wonderful, Mamá."

As he did each Sunday, Gonzalo parked in front of the flower shop and let his mother go in to do battle with the florist over which flowers to take to the grave by the lake. He had an unbelievable hangover; the last thing he remembered from the previous night was vomiting everywhere on his way to the bathroom. He had the hazy impression that he'd spent a long time on the floor, crying and holding the locket with the photo of Irina as Parker's sax urged him to feel like shit. When the alarm clock went off at dawn, he was lying on the floor, his neck was killing him, and the stench coming from his clothes was horrific. Pathetic.

"Do you mind telling me what's the matter with you?"

His mother had chosen different flowers this time: African impatiens with bright leaves, vivid colors, and a sweet scent. The name made him think of Siaka. Gonzalo had gone to visit him at the hotel where he was hiding out, and Siaka had told him stories about where he was from. Against all odds, he hadn't run off after the laptop disappeared, and despite rarely venturing outside of the hotel, he seemed bizarrely optimistic. Gonzalo had told him about his meeting with the prosecutor, how the man had warned him that without evidence there was no case. And the evidence was on the laptop.

"You'll find it, I know you will," he'd said.

Gonzalo himself was less optimistic.

"Gonzalo...?"

He glanced over at his mother. She'd worn her black dress and pulled her hair back with bobby pins. She smelled of hand soap and light cologne. The only irrefutable sign Gonzalo saw of her age were the wrinkles behind her earlobes, onto which she'd clasped a pair of fake pearls.

"I met a girl named Tania. She's Russian. When I saw her mother, for a second I got the feeling I knew her. Something about you just now reminded me of her."

"Old people all blur together, lose their contours. We all end up looking alike, acting alike. You should see the people at the residence. Same ailments, same expressions, same conversations. We show each other our pills and prescriptions like they were trading cards."

Esperanza was in a good mood. The presence of death earlier that morning had made her feel sprightly; it was a reminder that she too was on the waiting list. While others found this idea terrifying, to Esperanza it was simply evidence of what was clearly logical. A rest. Early that morning, the attendants had gone into the room next door. Esperanza had been writing when she first heard the wailing on the other side of the wall. She recognized the specific type of moan, yet still went out into the hall to corroborate. The doctor on call stood consoling a man, patting his shoulder. Seconds later the attendants emerged with a stretcher, her neighbor's silhouette visible beneath the sheet.

She hadn't spoken to the woman much; Esperanza preferred not to strike up friendships that might not last. Everyone there was going the same place, and they knew and accepted it. This was their last stop. They told each other their names, spoke of their kids and the past, and no one worried too much about whether what they said was true or not. It was like an open bar, and no one was going to demand a certificate of authenticity to validate the version of events anyone else presented. They read their last books, listened to their last songs, took their last walks, and played their last games. The common denominator in relationships between the residents was a sense of impermanence. That was why, after a time, family visits started to be upsetting. They brought false hope, evidence of the fact that outside those walls and grounds, life carried on.

Esperanza hadn't been able to resist the temptation to enter her neighbor's newly unoccupied room a few hours later. She'd sat down in a chair facing the bedframe, which now had no mattress. Every time someone died, they changed it. As if death were somehow contagious. Then she'd gone back to her room and the letters she'd written Elías. Esperanza spent a long time rereading them and was surprised to see that the last one was dated 1938. Too many years of silence. Without thinking about it, she began writing to him again, not with the passion of her youth but in the calm knowledge that there was only one thing left to say.

Dearest, we both know that this is my last letter...

Mother and son repeated the ritual every Sunday. The family house and property were slowly being engulfed by a sort of no-man's-land, surrounded by pylons, bollards, spotlights, and heavy machinery. Fascinated by the absurdity of destroying natural beauty in order to replace it with a simulacrum of itself, Esperanza watched the trucks coming and going on the roads around the lake, following the trails of dust they raised. Her little corner was still holding out, but it would end up being claimed by that pastiche of golf courses, townhomes with private yards, and luxurious facilities.

"When we moved here in the fifties there wasn't even a highway yet. Your father had to go down the mountain to get to the valley mill and then come back up the path after dark."

Gonzalo had heard these stories before, but this time he got the feeling that his mother wasn't speaking with nostalgia but simple acknowledgment. She was glad to have lived through those times but accepted that they were all in the past. And this seemed to free her.

Esperanza had slowly approached the mound beneath the fig tree, and Gonzalo was helping her pull out the weeds that had grown and to replace the old flowers on the grave with the fresh ones. He thought this was the right moment to tell her that he wasn't going to sell his part of the property and that she should refuse to sell, too. He'd been hoping she would be pleased at the news, but Esperanza only shook her head slowly, fingers stroking the burial mound's dried earth.

"He's not here. He never was, and he's certainly not coming back now. All this," she said, her eyes taking in the house, the valley, the lake, "is just a dream, something to cling to. I won't be coming back. I'm done waiting. I'm tired."

That was what she'd told Elías in her last letter. She was simply saying goodbye, with no bitterness and no tenderness.

Esperanza looked at her son and thought of all the things that could have gone differently but actually seemed fitting, all things considered. She was proud of him, despite knowing that his life had been built on false ideas. She understood what he was trying to do with this foolish act of rebellion, taking on the world over a piece of worthless land. After all, he was like Laura. And they had both inherited their father's combative character. She wasn't going to stop him. If he needed to stand up for himself against his despicable father-in-law, she would certainly applaud. But that was his fight, not hers.

"If you don't really love your wife, leave her now. It's not too late. It's not worth giving up your life for someone who will never be right for you."

Esperanza's skin was like fiberglass when he stroked her cheek. And underneath, her words were open and frank, the wisdom of a mother who has seen and heard too much. For years she'd watched her son sink into unhappiness as he contorted this way and that in order to be accepted by people who would always see him as an outsider, no matter what. He'd paid too high a price, gone against his very nature, hidden his true self so well that it seemed actually to have disappeared and left behind some inoffensive, characterless soul. And yet he'd still never been given a place at their table. Esperanza had been hurt beyond belief by Laura's betrayal. First the article she wrote, destroying her father's name, and then going to work for Alcázar, the man Esperanza hated most in the world. Those actions had irrevocably alienated her from her daughter, but she admitted that behind the cruel actions lay Laura's determination to be her own woman, not to be swept along by the myths or buckle under the weight of Elías's reputation.

Fearless, determined, and irresponsible, Laura hadn't hesitated to break all ties with the past. She'd lived her life the way she wanted, even though she occasionally got lost because her direction was as changeable as her character. And she'd paid the price. But Gonzalo? No. Her son, the boy who had been packed off to Catholic boarding school because at the time it was the only way to get him a decent education and three hot meals a day, had given up all forms of rebellion the day he met his wife. And the only refuge he'd had since that time came in the form of believing his father was a god, a deity to pray to at night and to venerate as he sank into mediocrity.

Now he wanted to live his father's life as a means of reclaiming his own. Esperanza knew he was making a mistake but didn't have the strength or the willpower to tell him the whole truth. And what was truth, anyway? Facts? Events, exactly as they occurred? Or the reasons behind them? Which part of that hypothetical truth—the one that Alcázar had threatened her with so she'd sell her property—could she possibly tell him without destroying the shaky foundations on which his determination lay? Was that fair to do now, just when her son had finally decided to take a decisive step?

No, it wasn't. And besides, she told herself, truth was nothing but the other side of the lie, just as harmful and unreal. No more flowers, no more graves, no more yellow letters. If time was marching on, devouring everything in its path like those excavators down at the lake, so be it.

"I know what it's like to live with someone who never truly loved you. And if I could turn the clock back, I don't think I'd follow your father's footsteps again."

"Why do you say that?"

"Because it's true. Your father was fond of me, I don't doubt that. And in the end I think he was genuine. But love and affection are not the same. It's easy to confuse tenderness with empathy, passion with solace, need with habit... I was never the woman of your father's dreams. That private world of his—locked inside the shed, banging away on the old typewriter—belonged to Irina. The locket you found in my jacket...I'd forgotten about it. It was hers. She was the woman your father fell in love with before he met me. They were together for a very short time and she died in circumstances I'd rather not have to tell you about, but their time together marked him forever and filled him with remorse and guilt and sadness that affected all of our lives. She was a presence that never left him, and I spent all those years fighting her tooth and nail, fighting a ghost that would reappear out of the blue and steal my husband, take him from my bed, snatch him from my hands, and there was nothing I could do but wait quietly for him to return."

Esperanza spread the African impatiens on the empty grave like a fan, placing stones on the stems to keep the wind from carrying them off. She grabbed her son's hand for support to stand up and then looked out at the shimmering lake in the distance, just a stain between the mountains.

"I don't want you to make the sacrifices I made for something that isn't worth it. Blind love is not true love, it's just one more lie."

Was Elías really down there, as she'd always suspected? When the lake was drained, she would finally find out. But perhaps that hateful inspector was right and she was wrong. Perhaps Elías did run off after all, abandoning her because he simply couldn't carry on with the charade. Maybe that was why she didn't want them to drain the lake. And maybe that was also why her son shouldn't let them. It was up to him. All she wanted to do was go back to the residence to sit and wait for it to be her turn for the attendants to take the mattress from her room.

The doorman was waiting for Gonzalo. Someone had left another delivery for him at the porter's lodge downstairs. This time it had come certified mail, but there was no return address.

Gonzalo opened the large envelope, enduring the eager curiosity of the doorman, who peeked over his shoulder as though he too were involved in the mystery.

"Certified mail is always bad news," he said ominously, as though this absurd proclamation were borne out by experience. "Traffic tickets, repossessions, court summonses."

It was none of those things. Instead the envelope contained a long list of VAT numbers and private limited companies, with a handwritten note at the bottom of the page: "Money laundering." Two of the companies were highlighted in fluorescent marker. Their names sounded familiar. Gonzalo went up to the apartment and phoned Luisa.

"Do you have access to the company database?"

She did. He was referring to a tax database used in the legal industry that gave attorneys access to data on hundreds of companies with operations in Spain: their finance capital, known activity, tax address, board of directors, workforce, etc.

"Look up these two: Alfadac and Enpistrenm."

"Right now? It could take a little time."

Gonzalo was holding the paper in his hand, racking his brains trying to remember where he'd seen those names.

"I'll be here."

Five minutes later, Luisa called back.

"Alfadac and Enpistrenm are holding and investment firms. They're both headquartered in London but have offices all over the world. Their backing is Russian, and the boards and shareholders are, too. I'd say they have the same parent company. I can fax you the names if you want; they're unpronounceable."

"Send them over."

"Will do. One more thing: In the last three years, both companies have shown special interest in property development here in Spain. Together they add up to forty percent of the backing behind the ACASA consortium."

Gonzalo froze.

"You still there?"

"I'm here."

"Isn't your father-in-law the one representing them as consul-tant for the lake development?"

Indeed he was. And Gonzalo's refusal to sell had put the brakes on the project. Acted as a "pebble in his shoe," as Agustín had said. He gazed at the note at the bottom of the page: "Money laundering." The envelope contained a dozen or so documents detailing all sorts of operations—diversion of funds and other forms of whitewashing. What Gonzalo had before him was the Matryoshka's legal structure, their Achilles' heel. And at least two of their companies had ties to his father-in-law.

It wasn't the old man Gonzalo was holding up, he realized. It was the Matryoshka's shoe he'd slipped into.

He called Siaka. "How did you do it?"

"Do what?"

"Open the confidential folder and send me the list of Matry-oshka companies."

"I have no idea what you're talking about. I didn't send you anything."

Then who had? Gonzalo went back to the envelope and emp-tied it onto the table, searched through the papers until he found a photograph. It was an old picture of Laura, with her son Roberto. They were at what looked like a water park, waving at the camera and smiling identical smiles. Gonzalo turned it over and read what was written on the back: "Now you can convince that prosecutor to finish your sister's job."

15

You couldn't exactly call the yellow sheets of paper she wrote
on a diary. Esperanza had started writing them more like letters
to some vague, hypothetical person she hadn't quite identified.
Sometimes she thought she was writing to herself, to that other
girl she felt beneath her skin, like a twin sister who was very different from her, someone reserved whom she could communicate
with only by letter. Occasionally, they were simple observations
on everyday things, other times they were reflections that seemed
almost to be dictated to her by that other Esperanza, and often
they were full of doubts and unanswered questions.

But her tone had changed in recent weeks, as had the imaginary recipient of her correspondence. Now she knew whom she
was writing to, and knew that *she* was the one producing the words.

*I'm so happy you're slowly regaining your interest in food, drink,
and even laughter. It is a pity that all of the progress you've
made seems to disappear when you gaze at that locket, although
I understand. She was beautiful and you loved her. I have no
experience of that kind of love, I've only read about it, but I can*

see it in your one good eye and bet that I could even find it if I dove into your empty socket and swam all the way to your heart. What foolish things occur to me! You would think me mad if you read these things. Would you be afraid? I don't think so. You would give me your faraway smile and then cast me aside, as you do when you catch me spying on you as you sleep, or eat, or gaze out the window at the snow, lost in thought.

    Yes, you would laugh if I told you that I'm jealous of Irina, that pretty woman who stole your joy. Did you know that I don't tell Velichko everything you say? I don't translate your insults, or your rage against those who sent you to the gulag. I'm prudent for you, because you can't be. I also don't tell him about your feelings for that woman and her daughter, the lovely things you come out with that sound as if a poet had written them for you. And the reason I don't is that I choke on my own envy and sorrow, and it's very confusing because at night I spend hours weeping and don't know why. Is this love? I cannot know, for I have never been in love, although many my age are already mothers. But there is one thing I know for certain: I will erase the memory of Irina. She is dead and I am alive and I will bring you back to shore.

Caterina read those letters each night. Sometimes they made her laugh; other times she drifted off to sleep feeling melancholic and overcome by a sense of futility. Day after day, as she returned to the flight academy to take care of Elías, her feelings grew, taking shape in her mind and her heart. She loved that young man, and the feeling couldn't be expressed in words that only novelists or poets could write. She felt it in her breath when he was close, in the way she let a hand brush against him and pretended it had been accidental, in the dreams she had when she thought of him at night. There was no doubt, she knew it now. And she had to let him know, unconditionally.

. . .

Elías was allowed to take a walk each morning, out to an old loading bay. He was not, however, allowed to go beyond the crumbling wall, and Srolov kept an eye on him from a distance. You couldn't say the two of them had become friends over the course of those weeks, but Velichko's assistant had proved himself to be a discreet and patient guardian, as well as efficient. Under his care, and that of the girl who came each morning, Elías's health had improved quickly. He had clean clothes to wear, cigarettes, a little vodka, and hot food. For the time being he was not permitted pen and paper, or anything to read that was not the official press.

The girl would walk behind him, jumping into the depressions his feet made in the snow. Her own small feet swam in Elías's footprints, and this seemed to amuse her. She'd leap from one to the next, giggling. The truth was, despite almost all of her time being devoted to solemn matters, she was simply a girl who didn't want to have to grow up quite yet. Elías knew that she was sixteen and an orphan, the only child of an Osoaviakhim test pilot who'd crashed a prototype into the Volga and a tractor factory worker who had hanged herself from a crane shortly after her husband's death. The girl's name was Caterina and she spoke a smattering of Spanish because for several months her father had been flight instructor to a group of Spanish pilots sent by the Republic to learn to fly Russian fighter planes. She liked Spaniards, she said. They were carefree, slightly mischievous, and willing to take chances. They never took anything too seriously, not even their own lives: Two of the pilots on the course had died while trying to execute overly risky maneuvers. With the change of government in Spain, the students had been forced to return home immediately, but before leaving they had given her the sheepskin-lined bomber jacket she was wearing that morning, as well as a new name: Esperanza, which meant "hope."

"Why Esperanza?"

She shrugged and crinkled her freckled nose impishly.

"They said they'd be back one day, and by then I would be old enough to marry one of them. I was their *esperanza*, their hope."

"Any one of them in particular?"

"No. Any of them would do. I'd like to go to Spain."

"Well, then, Esperanza it is."

She smiled and turned her head to look back at Srolov in his gray coat, pacing back and forth like a dog on a chain, not letting them out of his sight.

"They still haven't decided what they're going to do with you, have they?"

Elías took a long drag on the cigarette he was smoking and raised his head to look over the wall surrounding the esplanade. For the first time in three days it had stopped snowing, but the sun was nowhere to be seen. On the other side of the wall were the brick façades of more industrial warehouses, and from time to time a barge horn pierced the air.

"I guess not."

It had been three days since Velichko finished his declaration. They had gone over it together dozens of times, edited it, added as many names as possible—those of any deportees, guards, or officers Elías could remember. In addition, the instructor had contacted the Spanish embassy to verify Elías's membership in the Spanish Communist Party and family history. Finally, when he had all of the necessary documentation, including proof of Elías's stay at the Government Building and the false declaration he'd signed before being deported, Velichko set off with a laconic proclamation: "Time to see how much weight the truth carries."

Elías was no longer worried about the future. At first he'd thought that the wait would kill him, but all he felt now was calm indifference. It was something he'd begun to experience out on the steppe, or even earlier—perhaps it had started with Claude's tragic death. It wasn't resignation but it wasn't the cruel, homicidal coldness of Igor Stern either. It was more like a hole inside him, like he'd been shot in the soul and was bleeding, and the hole had become a deep, dark, solid void. The parts of Elías that could still feel pain or fear or even love had been severed and hung in the silence like useless appendages. There was no longer any bitterness or reproach. He had come to understand that the immensity of what he'd been through had happened to thousands of others, not just in the Soviet Union but all over the world, everywhere humans beings lived. And he knew that it would continue to happen to thousands more, maybe millions. People would die for no reason, or for absurd reasons; they would cling to flags, to hymns, to trenches. They would kill, bite, destroy anything in their path in order to stay alive. And that was neither good nor bad.

He glanced over at Esperanza. The pilot's jacket was too big for her, and so were her eyes, trying to take everything in at once, before she'd grown enough to do so. Maybe she and those like her had a chance; maybe those who were still innocent would manage to find a point of balance. The Spanish pilots who had named her Esperanza were smart. It was always easier to fight for a pretty face and warm heart than for an ethereal concept like glory or homeland.

Elías thought back warmly to the day when Ramón, a childhood friend from Mieres, had accidentally killed a chicken in his father's yard. They'd been playing cowboys and Indians; Ramón was always the Indian, Elías the cowboy. He ran around as Ramón tried to shoot him with arrows made of reeds and bottle caps that had been flattened with a rock. Without meaning to, Ramón hit a chicken with one, impaling its neck. The two boys had frozen, dumbfounded at the trail of blood flowing from the animal. They looked at each other in panic. It hadn't even occurred to them that the arrow could have hurt them. Without a word they buried the chicken and kept their stubborn silence days later when Ramón's father realized the animal was missing. Out of solidarity, neither of them said a word, remaining stoic despite the beatings they received from their fathers. Years later, Elías bumped into Ramón at the Student Residence in Madrid. His childhood friend had joined CEDA, the Spanish Confederation of the Autonomous Right, which meant they should have been at each other's throats. But they remembered the chicken incident and reminisced about their heroic resistance, neither one ratting out the other.

"You could have said it was me, saved yourself a thrashing."

Elías nodded. "But you were my friend, which means we both killed the chicken. We did it together." They laughed and, to the great consternation of their opposing factions, resumed an old friendship. It would last, provided they avoided politics.

Srolov's voice made Elías turn on his heels. Esperanza gazed down in distress at the swirl of snow at her feet, as though it was a fork in the path that left her unsure which way to turn. Standing beside Velichko's assistant were two men in thick brown coats, civilian clothes. There was no need for them to identify themselves as police; it was patently obvious from their demeanor. They'd come for him. Elías shuddered briefly. Then he looked up and saw something spectacular: a blade of glass, and then another, and another, the three of them swirling up in the air in formation, making a triangle, pirouetting in the air as though dangling from invisible threads. He reached out a hand, not to catch it but as if to fly off with it, to be carried outside those walls.

"You'll be back."

Elías looked at the girl. She calmly smoothed her hair, her expression unbefitting a girl her age.

"Or maybe not," he said.

Esperanza nodded. "You have to take me with you. I decided to pick you over those pilots. I'm going to marry you; although, of course, I'm not giving up the jacket."

Elías was about to laugh and then stopped, mouth half open.
She was absolutely serious.

Without a word, one of the officers opened the back door of
the car—one of the OGPU's infamous "black crows." He hardly
glanced at Elías, showing not the slightest curiosity as he simply
jutted out his chin and slammed the door as soon as Elías had gotten
in and placed his feet firmly on the floor, hands on the fabric seat.

He didn't ask where they were going. He knew there was no
point. The driver quickly turned onto a road running parallel to
the docks along the river. Elías recognized some of the sites he'd
worked at only a few months prior. It was as though ten years had
gone by: Progress on the Great Canal continued at a frenetic pace,
a swarm of thousands of industrious hands toiling away. There was
nothing and no one they would stop for. Nothing.

The road led to one of Moscow's eastern thoroughfares, and
from there they took a bypass that took them to Gorky Avenue,
Red Square, and the Kremlin. The car, however, turned off at a
fork leading east. A few miles later they turned onto yet another
road, where Elías saw a sign indicating that they were headed to
Barvikha Sanatorium, some fifteen miles from Moscow.

"Why are you taking me there?"

One of the officers sensed his uneasiness and gave a twisted
smile in the rearview mirror. Elías recovered quickly and held the
thug's gaze until the man wiped the stupid grin from his face.

The sanatorium comprised several buildings, all of which
formed part of the Kremlin medical center. Some were redbrick
and had hundreds of windows, others were gray and semiconcealed
among clusters of leafy trees. There was a large snow-covered esplanade in front of the administration building, with a decorative foun-
tain in the middle, now dry. In general the place had a rather sad air
about it, and this was only heightened by the cawing crows up on

the highest window ledges. Elías didn't move until the police opened
his door. They quickly boxed him in between their burly shoulders
but used no restraints, as if they were more escorts than guards.

Inside, the main building was attractive and inviting, with
wood-paneled walls and a heated floor that warmed the soles of
one's shoes. Elías was astonished at the opulence of the foyer, its
contrast with the building's somber exterior. The high ceilings had
enormous chandeliers that threw off crisp, sparkling light, increasing the sense of spaciousness and complementing the polished,
impossibly white marble floors. A grandiose staircase led to the
upper floors, but the police took him to an elevator on the right.
They went directly to the tenth floor, and on the way up Elías
recalled that he'd once had a similar tour of opulence, on the lower
floors of an elegant palace where he was led to a majestic chamber
to sign his own confession in exchange for a glass of water.

Perhaps this trip was going to be the same, he thought. But
his attitude certainly would not be. And he was no longer thirsty.

The elevator shuddered slightly and came to a halt, its doors
opening from the outside. The first officer got out, followed by Elías,
and the other officer went back downstairs. A sign told him that this
was the Oral Medicine wing. The officer pointed to a group of three
people who stood chatting off to the right, at the end of a long hall.

"Go to those men."

Without understanding what this was all about, Elías obeyed.
His pulse quickened slightly and his palms started to sweat, despite
his supposed indifference.

On recognizing one of the men as Instructor Velichko, his
heart began to race. Velichko was with a stocky woman who
looked to be about seventy years old and wore a rather manly gray
suit, and a man whose back was to Elías.

Velichko was the first to see him and beckoned Elías over with
a hand.

"This is Elías Gil."

The man, who wore a tight-fitting jacket, greeted Elías somewhat defiantly.

"You have caused me more than one headache, comrade. Do
you know who I am?" he asked in crisp Spanish, with a slightly
Andalusian accent.

For once, Elías opened his only eye in boyish wonder, which
was both moving and comical at the same time. Any Spanish
Communist knew who José Díaz was—general secretary of the
Spanish Communist Party since 1932. They exchanged a brief,
firm handshake.

Velichko stiffened, visibly nervous as he reverently introduced
the woman: "Comrade Nadezhda Krupskaya."

She gave him a wise look from behind round glasses. Her white
hair was very short and her lips had the disenchanted look of all
those who remain in contact with power for too long. The woman
was Lenin's widow, and despite her differences with Stalin—these
were an open secret—in the end she was still one of the most
important women in the Soviet Union.

"Is everything you say in this report true?"

Her voice was neither gentle nor patient. More like the bark of
someone making plain that they will not tolerate a single false step
on a matter of such grave importance. Elías's boyish expression
disappeared, stifled by that tone.

"To the best of my knowledge, everything it says is entirely
accurate."

Nadezhda Krupskaya stared at him until he felt the full weight
of history she carried on her shoulders. Deportations, exile, war,
conspiracies to seize power, conspiracies to hold on to it, at the
behest of a man who was not always up to the task. And still she
remained faithful, loyal to the dream to the end.

"This is not the way we behave," she murmured slowly.

She wasn't asking forgiveness. She wanted Elías to accept it.
It wasn't the Union of Soviet Socialist Republics that had done

this to Elías, it wasn't the Bolsheviks who'd sent him to the gulag, wasn't the Party that had made him lose an eye. It wasn't the revolution that had taken Irina from him. It was a few specific men. The idea had to be preserved at all costs. She was demanding that he understand this.

Elías nodded. The old woman relaxed her cheek muscles, which could have been seen as a historic smile, though it was not. This was the closest Elías was going to get to any expression of sympathy.

"Arsenievich Velichko's uncle served my husband loyally and helped me on the education plan. He has given me the report and I have read it carefully." She showed no sign of the devastating effect it had had on her. "And I have come to a conclusion: It must not be made public, under any circumstances."

Elías stared in disillusioned shock, but she took no pity.

"If this were to become known, the most immediate consequence would be your execution."

The old woman turned to José Díaz and shook his hand with slightly more warmth. "You will explain to him."

Díaz crinkled his eyes, laughing as he brought one hand to his belly. "If this ulcer doesn't kill me, Spain will."

The woman gave him a teasing look. "Or one of the husbands of the many women you bed."

Díaz gave a roguish look and walked Lenin's widow to the elevator. Three police officers who had been standing unobtrusively in the background—her security—stepped forward.

Díaz motioned Elías over. "I need a smoke and it's a pleasant morning. Let's take a walk through the grounds."

José Díaz was a passionate, headstrong man, and in his eyes—dark as his rakishly disheveled hair—you could still see signs of the boy from Seville who'd started off as a baker. But he was also coldly analytical and had rare organizational skills. All of these qualities combined had led to his becoming general secretary of the Spanish Communist Party, after successfully orchestrating the strikes that followed José Sanjurjo's attempted coup in 1932. He walked slowly, bent slightly forward, and Elías thought he caught a grimace of pain as the man brought a hand to his stomach. When they came to a clearing in the pines, Díaz stopped at a bronze sculpture of Stalin, giving it a matter-of-fact glance.

"He's not that tall, and a little heavier."

"You know Stalin?"

Díaz puffed on his cigarette, holding it between the fingers of a black-gloved hand. Then he dropped it and crushed it with his heel.

"No one really knows Stalin. Great men are veiled in mist, and Stalin is a great man." He gave the statue a friendly pat and they walked on.

After a brief silence, Díaz stopped short at a dirt path leading to the respiratory wing of the sanatorium. This was where those with consumption, tuberculosis, and cancer were treated. People with money or influence. No worker could ever afford to come here, and Díaz gazed at the building with infinite sadness, as though the existence of this exclusive facility heralded the failure of what they were attempting to build.

"Have you heard the news from Spain?"

Elías shook his head. "I've been busy trying to stay alive."

Díaz was an uncommon leader, but he was a common man, and not ashamed of it.

"What you've been through, I can't even imagine. I wouldn't have lasted a week." He cast a quick glance at the eye patch Elías wore. "I know you were surprised by what Lenin's widow said. Let's just say that empathy and social niceties are not comrade Nadezhda's fortes. But she is right. Velichko's report must not be made public."

He waited for Elías to protest or show some sign of disapproval, but the young man simply turned his head to focus on the entrance to the infectious diseases building, where patients and white-coated staff came and went. His empty gaze, lost forever, filled Díaz with sorrow. And yet it was still his job to make the young man see that it was better to bury the whole affair.

"Spain is preparing for war. No one wants to believe it—despite the evidence all being right there—but it's inevitable. It started the very day the Republic was declared. King Alfonso XIII himself predicted as much before going into exile. 'I will go to avoid the spilling of Spanish blood,' he said. The truth is, he went because we kicked him out, but in a way he was right. Sanjurjo's coup was just a warm-up, a trial run. We responded, but now the government is in their hands, CEDA has the backing of the Church, the landowners, the Falangists, and the Sunday school teachers. The only reason they agreed to give women the vote is that the priests at the pulpits invoke women's duty as mothers and fuel their long-standing fears. Order, God, and Country...the old die-hard Spain."

"We'll throw them out, we did it before."

"It's not that easy. Gil-Robles wasn't named minister of war because they're planning to democratize the army. It's so that they can position their pawns—men like Mola and Sanjurjo and Franco—on the front lines. Their generals are making ready."

"If you know that, why don't you do something to avoid it before it's too late?"

Diaz's expression clouded over, his thoughts at odds. He pointed to a snow-covered bench.

"Every winter in Moscow it snows. Pipes burst, boilers explode, streets are shut down. Winter after winter, the same thing happens, over and over. Hundreds of crews are sent out to toil away, clearing roads, salting sidewalks, repairing pipes, and distributing food. But that doesn't keep it from snowing." He held out a hand and made a fist, the leather of his glove squeaking. "Power is in the hands of a reactionary, pro-Fascist government.

They are the snow, falling ceaselessly down on us; they control the forces of repression, the press, and the Parliament. Their power is legitimate, but their aim is now to destroy the system that brought them in. Why? Because democracy entails a rotation of power, and they don't want to share what they see as theirs by right. Do you think enthusiasm is enough to fight an organized, implacable enemy? We have to regroup, form a popular front, be pragmatic in our efforts, or we will surely fail. We are now the selfless workers toiling away, and all we're doing is damage control. But the Spanish Communist Party has only fifteen thousand in its ranks. Meanwhile, the Socialists are determined to go it alone, as are the other truly Republican forces. None of us, on our own, can defeat this threat. But still we don't prepare. Still, we gaze up at the sky and hope for a miracle, thinking maybe next year it won't snow."

Díaz exhaled deeply. As if the terrible certainty of the panorama he'd just described were right around the corner.

"Your father is a Communist."

Elías nodded.

"And so are you. That's why you came here, with our support. To train, to gain the knowledge that would one day allow you to contribute your grain of sand to the construction of a new country, a better country."

"That was what I thought..."

Díaz gave him a questioning look.

"What you thought? Nothing has changed, Elías. The reason you came to the Soviet Union was that your father set an example for you at the mines. What you saw persuaded you that we have a responsibility to the men of our times, and more than that, to those who come after us. Your father, like mine, like those of thousands of others, simply decided to change the world."

"The world doesn't change."

"You're wrong, son. The world never stops changing, it moves on and nothing can stop it, and we—you and I—are the tiny invisible cogs in the wheel. And if it means we have to bear what seems unbearable, then we do it. We have no choice. We can't do anything but move forward."

Elías looked out past Díaz. He thought of his fights with other boys at the mine, his father, getting up every morning before dawn. He thought of the moment he resolved to show the foreman that he wouldn't take any more abuse, how good it felt to punch him in the face, and then be beaten by the police and thrown out of the mine. He thought of the black smokestacks, the exhausted soot-covered faces of the miners, the laughter and songs he heard at the wells. Happiness was one weapon the powerful could not take away. The songs that women sang as they brought their husbands lunch after a hard day's work rang out in the valley louder than shotgun fire. That was what he thought when he was a boy, and he still believed it when he met up with his friend Ramón in a Lavapíes café, in Madrid, where they argued bitterly until dawn. "I'll take Federico García Lorca over José Antonio Primo de Rivera," he declared proudly, challenging Ramón's insistence on the need for order. Words over violence. That was the spirit that had brought him to the Soviet Union a year earlier, the same one that had brought his young friends Michael, Martin, and Claude.

But now he was not so sure.

"We are but the first drop, Elías. A sign of the coming storm that will wash away the old."

A few months earlier, Díaz's words would have moved Elías to the core. But now he felt nothing but the cold wind penetrating his borrowed clothes. He pictured Irina's body, trapped at the bottom of the river—perhaps it would stay there, beneath a layer of ice, and one day someone would find it floating in the ocean, a freakish sight. This storm that the general secretary spoke of so fervently would carry off men and women, leave parents without children, husbands without wives. Everything would be swept away, it would all disappear, and in time there would be nothing—no houses, no streets, no bones. They would never have existed; not even their memories would remain.

"Do you have a family?"

The question took Díaz by surprise. "A wife and three children. Why?"

"They must be a good reason for you to keep believing in your words."

"Indeed. None better."

"Do you really think there's going to be a war?"

"I'm afraid so."

"And what will happen?"

Díaz remained pensive, the pain in his stomach intensifying. "We'll fight. Perhaps we'll die."

"Can we win?"

At this Díaz smiled. "One day, we can. I have no doubt."

Elías understood. "But not today. And yet still, you're asking me to accept everything that happened to me and carry on as though nothing had changed."

"That's right. That's exactly what I'm asking."

Esperanza was sitting on the curb at the entrance to the industrial complex, trying to draw animals in the snow although none of them was remotely identifiable. She certainly wasn't going to earn a living as an artist, she thought, wiping away the dirty snow. But that didn't matter; at sixteen, not many people knew what would become of them, and she had already made up her mind about the only thing that mattered in her future.

"Does that jacket keep you warm?"

Her doelike eyes looked up at Elías. For a second, he thought of the elk that the guards had taken down and felt something inside him break. He was full of holes, like an old bulkhead, and sometimes he thought he'd never be able to stay afloat.

Esperanza nodded, and in her eyes he glimpsed something very different from his darkness—a distant promise that things might turn out all right, the improbable belief that somehow, miraculously, there could be a type of justice that had to do not with laws but with kindness. *Kindness*, a word he could hardly even say aloud. And yet there it was, in Esperanza's conviction that those pilots were heroes—with whom he'd soon have to compete—in the eyes of that elk, in the hand Irina had held out to him when he thought he couldn't carry on and collapsed on the tracks on the way to Siberia. There was kindness in his father, in Claude's caustic jokes, in the way he died, even in that commander who blew his brains out beside the old man playing harmonica. All of that was there, along with all the evil, engaged in a merciless war. And he couldn't simply watch it without stepping in.

"Well, I'd say it's a bit excessive for the Mediterranean climate."

"What's the Mediterranean?"

Elías didn't really know either. He'd never seen it. And he still couldn't understand how he'd let José Díaz convince him to accept a posting to Barcelona to join the Party's cell.

The truth was that the general secretary had given him no option. After his moral plea and ideological discourse, Díaz had become the pragmatist once more. With a bitter smile he'd made himself crystal clear: "Either you accept the posting or I leave you to your fate with the OGPU."

Elías had accepted, on one strange condition: The girl who'd been caring for him all that time could go, too.

16

Gonzalo leaned on his crutches and looked out the window at the garden below. As far as he could recall, he hadn't been in this house more than a dozen times in twenty years. In ordinary circumstances, he would have considered it a luxury to be invited by his father-in-law, but he was perfectly aware of the fact that this was no friendly visit. The living room they were in was supposed to look fashionably modern but came off as horrendously cold. The furniture was intended not to be comfortable or inviting, but to arouse guests' admiration, though in Gonzalo all it aroused was scorn. Each piece was arranged just so. It was like living in a home-furnishings magazine, and Gonzalo himself was the one thing that didn't match.

He observed the two glasses of whiskey on the desk. His own remained untouched; his father-in-law's, empty. It was only eleven o'clock in the morning, but Gonzalo was sure that the man had started far earlier.

"Have you read *The History of Rome* by Livy, or Shakespeare's *King Lear*?"

Gonzalo gave him a bewildered look. Agustín pointed to the volumes in question, on a high shelf.

"You should. Those books make it clear: Anyone who aspires to hold on to power must never show weakness, especially to those closest to them."

"Where are you going with this?"

His father-in-law gave him an offhand look, as though he were being blasé, but the abrupt way he refilled his glass and brought it to his lips told a different story.

"Do you know why I've been in the legal profession for forty years and no one has ever caught me out?" He spread his hands toward the bookshelves, the library. "It's not because I know the law better than anyone else, or because I'm a better speaker, or even smarter or cleverer than anyone else. Of course, I know how to pull the strings of power and move them to my advantage, but that's not how I made my name. It's because I can predict the hand. I know when I'm going to win and when I might lose, because I've got the cards before anyone else. You'll never trip me up, not you or anyone. Having all the information, calling in favors, turning weaknesses into strengths—that's power. And I know how to conduct it. As I said, you should read Livy and Shakespeare and forget about those romantic tortured Russians."

Was he drunk? Probably, but in that affable way that those of his class deemed acceptable.

"A good friend down at the public prosecutor's office told me that a few days ago you filed to have your sister's case reopened, to look into Zinoviev's death. According to the report, you claim to have overwhelming proof of her innocence. I'd like to know what that proof is."

"That's classified information. Nothing in the file is to be made known until the judge makes his pronouncement."

"Oh, come off it, Gonzalo. Did you really think I wouldn't find out?" Agustín snapped. "This isn't some crappy little divorce case. This is the big league. The firms you've asked to have investigated are majority shareholders that I represent. Respectable, foreign investors who are very interested in getting this case dropped. Otherwise, both investors will back out of the ACASA project and I'll lose a fortune."

Gonzalo considered the documents he'd given the prosecutor, the way the man had reacted. The vast quantities of information made perfectly clear what the Matryoshka was involved in.

This was much more than a matter of his father-in-law losing a big-money investment. The consortium was a network of aboveboard companies engaged in laundering money earned from child prostitution, drugs, and all manner of illegal activity. Banks, property developers, construction companies with headquarters in London, Lichtenstein, Monaco, Mauritius. Millions in currencies that would have to be offloaded quickly, since Spain was now adopting the euro, so as not to lose value against the dollar.

"This isn't just about an investment you stand to lose, you don't even need those millions. This goes much deeper, doesn't it?"

"I see you understand."

Gonzalo was vehement. "What exactly is it that I should understand? That you handle the legalities that enable a bunch of criminals to launder dirty money?"

Agustín continued to take sip after sip of his drink, and through a crack in his façade, Gonzalo saw the truth: The man was terrified. The great white shark had taken too big a bite. This was no longer about Gonzalo's refusal to sell the family property holding up the construction project. This was far more serious. His father-in-law was trapped in the Matryoshka's net. God only knew how long he had been doing business for them, either without realizing it or—worse—without admitting it. Hadn't he said that knowledge was power? He knew what they were like, knew what they were capable of. Gonzalo could sense all of this in the imploring look concealed beneath Agustín's bogus rage and bluster. Now he saw the full extent of it: The poor man was quaking in his boots, afraid of what they could do to him. They could take down not only his reputation and the empire he'd spent forty years building but also, and more important—and this awakened fear and compassion in Gonzalo, too—his daughter and grandchildren.

"You have to withdraw the lawsuit and forget about those people. You have no option, Gonzalo. I'm not negotiating."

"I'm not withdrawing the petition, Agustín."

"You've already put my daughter and grandchildren in danger once. There is absolutely no way I'm letting you do it again—do you understand me? I'll do whatever it takes to ensure their safety. Whatever it takes."

His eyes told Gonzalo that he meant what he said.

Old Lukas dozed in a patch of sunlight on the tile floor. Dogs were like people, or vice versa—always trying to warm their bones when it was too late to do any good. Alcázar went to the pantry and opened a can of dog food, mixed it with weight-control kibble, and held the bowl close to Lukas's snout. The animal had been born blind, his eyes pools of milky white; he would have been put down at the pound had Alcázar not taken a shine to him. After twelve years together, neither of them needed to be able to see in order to recognize each other in the dark. Not even all couples could say that.

The dog—part husky, part mutt—lifted his snout, sniffed his master's hand, and chewed, his old teeth all yellow. He didn't growl when Alcázar scratched and petted his big grizzled head. Alcázar had a way with dogs; his father had been a hunter and they always kept hounds at home. He knew how to treat them and in general found dogs far easier to get along with than people. A person might be faithful, but a dog was loyal, and not everyone understood the difference. Cecilia had.

Maybe that was the reason it was just the two of them, old Lukas and old Alcázar, in a five-hundred-square-foot apartment, scenically overlooking a brick wall covered in filthy graffiti where every drunk in the neighborhood came to piss and shit. Every man forges his own future, his father used to say. Alcázar had forged his, so he wasn't complaining. He was simply taking stock of the undeniable fact that for some time now, he'd been finding the bed too big for just him, and the ghost of Cecilia—who for so many years had slept on the right-hand side—was visiting a little too often.

He needed a change. It was time to live out the last few years of his life in peace, slowly sinking into nostalgia, a beer in one hand as he sat in the Florida Keys like a real golden oldie, watching the sun shining down on the ocean and turning it purple.

Alcázar made some coffee and spread a little soft cheese on a piece of toast. He was trying to make sure he had breakfast before his first cigarette. He'd been fooling himself, thinking he would actually quit one day. Nobody gives up the bad habits of a lifetime; it's the bad habits that put an end to your life. The TV in the kitchen was on. The commissioner was reading a press release. Alcázar turned up the volume.

Laura's case was still making headlines. Alcázar noticed the white whiskers poking out of the commissioner's nostrils. The man's jacket was too heavy, and he was sweating. It was clear he was uneasy.

"That bastard!" Alcázar said. So he'd done it: Gonzalo had found the same wasps' nest that his sister had and was now poking it with a stick like a dumb kid. And the wasps were buzzing furiously. The commissioner announced that the Financial Crimes Unit had just launched a far-reaching investigation to bring to light possible ties several companies might have with the Russian mafia. For now, at least, they hadn't officially named ACASA. But that didn't mean serious problems were not on the horizon, problems that he'd thought were behind him after Laura and Zinoviev's deaths. It was just a matter of time until Agustín González's name came to the fore, and then would come a few others...and then it would be his turn. Alcázar was under no illusions; he was the weakest link in the chain. The dream of living out his golden years in the Keys was slipping away by the minute.

Alcázar waited to see if the commissioner would say any more to the journalists during the question-and-answer session, but he adhered stubbornly to his official statement, so Alcázar lost interest and changed the channel. Just at that moment, the doorbell rang, a strident buzz that caused Lukas to give a croaky, halfhearted bark that wouldn't have scared a fly.

Anna Akhmatova was at the door.

"Have you seen the news?" the old woman fired point-blank.

Alcázar licked his mustache. "Well. Certainly didn't take you long. What's that you've got there?"

She handed him a package. "A book. In my country when you visit an old friend you haven't seen for some time, you bring a gift."

"So now we're friends? That makes me feel better."

Anna shot him a harsh look, and he glimpsed the enormous gulf between her expression and her soul, one concealing many things. It was like staring into a well.

"It shouldn't," she replied with a half smile.

The whole of Combray and its surroundings, taking shape and solidity, sprang into being, town and gardens alike, from my cup of tea.

Alcázar gave her a mistrustful look.

"What do people see in strings of convoluted words? Why don't they just say what they mean?"

"From time to time it's good to remember that people can be civilized and sophisticated."

And how far did that get you? he wondered. Those who were supposedly civilized could be terrifyingly heartless. Words and language were easily perverted, always found a way to get twisted. Alcázar eyed the woman as he put the book on a shelf. She looked fragile, small, but also strong, as though all the years amassed in her bones had hardened her. Her face still had a certain beauty, no longer that of youth but something subtler, more natural, a sort of calm that seemed to stave off the ravages of time, which was always in such a hurry to put an end to life. For most people, years go by and they become no more lucid or wise, just older. But she was not most people.

"From what I recall, when you were younger you were neither civilized nor sophisticated."

"Back then I hadn't read Proust." She smiled.

"I don't understand a word that man writes," Alcázar grumbled.

Anna shot him a disapproving look, as though he were an ignorant little boy. And suddenly, the inspector thought he caught a glimpse of something familiar in her look, something that reminded him of his own father, Ramón Alcázar Suñer—don Ramón, as he was known in the courts, on the street, at the station.

"Proust shows us that, in time, everything returns to its proper place."

"What are you talking about?"

The old woman tilted her head and licked her top lip with the tip of her tongue, as though struggling to find the words, but in the end she gave up.

"If you don't understand it, I can't explain it to you," she replied, glancing at the bookshelf. She'd seen a photo of Alcázar with his father, both in uniform, the day he graduated from the police academy.

Lukas came over to sniff under Anna's skirt. Over the years, she'd learned to control the uneasiness she felt whenever she was near a dog, particularly one resembling a wolf. She made sure to appear calm but didn't pet the animal, who ambled back to his patch of sun on the floor. Alcázar poured them both coffee and they sat on the sofa, each at one end, separated by a few embroidered pillows. Alcázar watched Anna stir her coffee, pensive, until suddenly she let go of the little spoon and looked up, gave a deep sigh, and gazed at the photo of Alcázar and his father once more.

"Memory is a prodigious thing. It orders one's life however it wants, using what it sees fit and forgetting things that get in the way as though they never existed. I'd say that's what Proust writes about..."

Alcázar wasn't fooled by her measured gestures, carefully chosen words, neutral pronouncements. He'd known Anna since the summer of 1967 and knew that when she wanted to, she could be impenetrable. Her eyes bored into the inspector like pile drivers into cement.

"Ever since Laura died, I've wondered what role you had in her death, and in Zinoviev's."

Alcázar reacted coldly, shaking his head but not emphatically.

"We should end this conversation. It's getting a little dangerous."

"A bit late for that, Inspector. We had a deal, and I've kept my side of it all these years. I wasn't the one who came to find you on the street the other day, in case you've forgotten; it was you who stopped me. I'm not the one stirring up shit with a stick."

Alcázar raised a hand to his mustache.

"If this is an interrogation, you should have warned me. I would have called my lawyer."

Anna smiled indulgently.

"Agustín González? After what's just come out on TV, that man is finished. It's just a matter of time. And you'll be next, I imagine you realize that."

"I've never been threatened so politely."

"I'm not threatening you. I am simply trying to understand how it is that you let Elías's son get involved in this. I warned you about Laura, and you refused to listen. And now you're letting her brother step into quicksand that he won't be able to get out of."

"May I remind you that Tania is your daughter and she was the one who approached him. If I hadn't recognized her with Gonzalo in the security tape, I would never have come to you, I can assure you of that."

"Tania won't be interfering anymore. I've made sure of that. But you have not answered my question."

"What question?"

"Laura, and Zinoviev's death. When the brother really starts nosing around, what is he going to find?"

"I don't like the way this sounds, Anna. I would never hurt Laura, never. After what happened at the lake in 1967, you should know that."

Anna carried their empty cups to the sink. For a few seconds she pressed her fingers against the cold marble, and then eyed Lukas. The old dog lay dozing in the slanted light streaming in through the blinds. He, at least, had managed to warm up. She turned back to face Alcázar and gazed calmly at him at length, light flickering in her eyes. She didn't want to hurt him. But sometimes hurting people is inevitable. Even necessary. And that was a shame.

"That prosecutor certainly seems sure of himself."

"Gonzalo has proof. I don't know how he got it, but I've got a guess. When he was in the hospital, he was all worked up about a certain computer that was missing. I'm willing to bet it was Laura's personal laptop, and that her Matryoshka informer gave it to him."

The old woman dried her hands on a dish towel. Matryoshka. Ridiculous name for an organization.

Alcázar had caught the change in her dark eyes. She was now wearing the same look he'd seen that night at the lake, when he found her beside Elías's unconscious body, her shirt bloody. It looked like thin ice cracking just before it gives way under your feet.

"I know what you're thinking, Anna. And you're wrong."

"And what am I thinking, Alcázar? That you murdered Zinoviev and then drove Laura to suicide to make it seem as if she was guilty?"

Alcázar held her gaze. "You should get back to your bookstore, Anna. Who knows, maybe someone's waiting for you to explain why Proust wasted all those years in search of his lost time."

She nodded. Alcázar walked her to the door.

"What's she like?" Anna asked, stopping abruptly, one hand on the doorknob.

Alcázar pretended not to understand.

"Caterina, his wife. What's she like now?"

"Old, like us. And her name isn't Caterina anymore. It's Esperanza."

"I always thought my mother would have made Elías a better wife..."

She leaned in and gave Alcázar a butterfly kiss, swift and gentle, on the cheek. It was an affectionate gesture that seemed out of place, and it disconcerted him.

"What was that for?"

"Nothing wrong with a little tenderness between two lonely old souls, is there?"

Old Lukas lifted his head on hearing the door close. He sniffed the air, recognized the acrid sweat of his master, and then, reassured, dozed off once more, muzzle between his paws.

Somehow, Gonzalo's feet led him to the waterfront. He often went there when he needed to think. Ever since he was a teenager, Gonzalo had enjoyed walking out to the breakwater and sitting on a rock to contemplate the sea and watch the fishermen cast their lines in the late afternoon. There was one girl on the shore, a scarf over her shoulders. It was starting to cool off at night. The wind ruffled her hair as she stared out to sea, perhaps dreaming of being a mermaid. For a while he watched a buoy bobbing near the mouth of the estuary. The cargo ships sailing along the horizon advanced so slowly they looked stationary, the lapping of the waves was hypnotic, and the faint dark outline of Montjuïc at the far end of the coast looked almost fake. He hadn't realized it was getting dark and the lights on the boardwalk behind him had already come on.

A beach sweeper raked the sand, its bright lights scanning the beach as it neared a couple making out, oblivious, lost in each other. On the next bench over sat a beer vendor with his cooler, drinking the warm cans he hadn't been able to sell during the day and softly singing drunken songs from his homeland. Two young pickpockets scouted for unsuspecting tourists until the blue flash of a police car in the distance sent them packing.

All this was going on around him, but Gonzalo remained entirely unaffected. The world seemed unbearably ugly if he didn't turn his back to it and gaze instead at the darkening water. What is it about the sea, he wondered, that makes everyone come to it in search of answers? Immensity, perhaps, the idea that you might become one with that vastness and disappear.

Behind Gonzalo, leaning against a lamppost with his hands in his pockets, ex–Chief Inspector Alcázar gazed out at the same horizon, his expression gruff and jaded. He looked awful: his cheap jacket wrinkled, the knot of his tie loose, an itchy three-day beard sprouting up unevenly around his bushy gray mustache. A rough-looking homeless man approached him with an emphatic sign around his neck: *I'm hungry!!* As though demanding tribute. *What do I care? Fuck off,* thought Alcázar, though he reached into a pocket and gave the man some loose change.

"You've got everyone pretty worried."

"How did you find me?"

Alcázar sat down beside Gonzalo, mopping his shaved head with a handkerchief, sweat stains peeking out from under his arms. He tucked the handkerchief away and interlaced his fingers, resting his elbows on his knees.

"Let's just say your doorman isn't the most discreet guy on the planet. You're a predictable guy, Gonzalo. I hope Atxaga hasn't realized that, or you're in trouble."

"I don't need a babysitter."

"That's what you told me at the hospital. And I thought I made it clear: I'm just doing my job."

"Trying to find Atxaga and protecting me and my family," Gonzalo retorted mockingly.

"That's right."

"And what else?"

"What do you mean?"

"What else do you do for my father-in-law? Why you and no one else?"

Alcázar had been studying Gonzalo since the beginning. It had been thirty-five years, and back then he was a quiet five-year-old kid, introverted and too serious for his age. Sitting between his mother and older sister on a bench at the station, he looked like he wanted to disappear. When Alcázar saw him in the hospital, he realized Gonzalo was still the kind of person who preferred to be invisible. The opposite of Laura. It was amazing to think that the two of them had the same mother and father.

"Coincidence is an illusion, it's just something people take comfort in. And it keeps them from digging deeper, finding the real reasons. You should try it. Make your life a little easier."

"It's a bit late for that," Gonzalo snapped.

Alcázar stroked his mustache, eyes focused on the violet dusk as its light played on the sea. He wondered what Cecilia would think if she could see him now. If his wife was waiting for him in heaven, she'd have to use all her powers of persuasion to convince Saint Paul—her favorite—to let him in when the time came.

"I suppose you're right. There always comes a time when it's too late to turn back."

When Cecilia was diagnosed with cancer, she accepted it—resigned but not bitter—with the quiet fatalism of her faith. She threw herself into Catholicism, attending Mass two or three times a week, surrounding herself with Bible verses, prayers, and Communion. For her sake, Alcázar pretended to feel the same devotion, putting on a performance in order to make her happy. He attended services with her at the Iglesia del Pi, waited patiently while she confessed, and when they got home he would sit down and read her Saint Paul's letters to the Corinthians. Her favorite was the one about the power of love. As he recited, "Love is patient, love is kind," she'd squeeze his hand and he would hide the anguish and rage he felt for a God who, as the disease progressed, had a greater and greater presence in their lives, a God to whom Cecilia showed utter devotion although He did not hear her pleas. What Alcázar hated most was watching her writhe in pain those last few weeks in bed, dying, too weak to get up, invoking His name as she cried and moaned. And He remained silent.

There were days when Cecilia was determined to live a normal-seeming life, pretending not to notice the disease was spreading day by day, rotting her from the inside out. Occasionally they still made love, and sex took on a sort of placid quality, a slow tenderness that bore no resemblance to the excitement and excess of the early days. Before she died, Cecilia told him that death appeared to her at night and was not frightening or dramatic or violent. This vision helped her remain calm as she awaited its arrival. She asked him to pray for her and not to turn his back on God. And he promised.

And soon after, Laura walked into his life, stepping out of a time he thought he'd left behind. Alcázar had gone back to work without mentioning that his wife had passed away, but he thought of Cecilia all the time and her death was a constant torment. He fulfilled his duties, going through the motions, stony and distant. Other people and their problems seemed a reflection of his own pain and loss. He became cynical and suspicious, taciturn and cruel. At night he'd go to the same church and sit in the last pew in the dim light of votive candles, railing against God, scrutinizing Christ's face on the altar cross, the symbol of eternity, of the everlasting, and it tortured him—an allusion to his misfortune, his own death, his loneliness. He would stare at the cross and feel convinced that they were both damned, he and Christ, destined to stare at each other in silence for the rest of time.

On the night before Christmas Eve, a chorus of altar boys stood practicing carols at the altar of Iglesia del Pi, accompanied by a young seminarian on guitar. A young woman came in and sat beside the inspector, rousing him from his thoughts. It was Laura. She smiled nervously when she told him who she was. Alcázar froze and then sat there holding his breath for so long she got scared. They left the church and went to have coffee in Plaza del Pi, the square outside, which was often filled with painters at their easels. Everything was bright and festive, bustling with people carrying Christmas trees and nativity scenes they'd bought at Feria de Santa Lucía by the cathedral. They were oblivious of the wintry joy that filled the air. The two of them spoke at length about what happened that summer of 1967. One thing that surprised them—and made them laugh, despite the seriousness of it all—was how different their memories of the same events were.

What had stuck in Laura's mind were the impressions of a frightened girl arriving at the police station with her mother and younger brother to report that their father had not returned after the night of San Juan. Etched in her mind were Alcázar's lopsided toupee and a drop of sweat that ran down the middle of his forehead and then fell onto his nose—which at the time had seemed enormous, although now she could see otherwise. She remembered the two of them speaking alone in his office, the inspector's sleeves rolled up, one leg leaning on the corner of his wooden desk, foot jiggling anxiously.

"Your shoelace was undone and I wanted to reach down and tie it for you, but I was so scared I didn't dare move."

And, Laura continued, the inspector offered her a glass of water, but what she really wanted was one of the cigarettes he smoked non-stop. She recalled his mustache—blond at the time, now almost white—bobbing up and down as he spoke, and the way he leaned so close that their noses almost touched, like Eskimos. And the way he'd said, very quietly, "I don't believe you. You're lying to me, and now you're going to tell me the truth." She panicked, got so scared that she dug her fingernails into her palms till it hurt. Laura told him she had no idea how long they were locked in that room together, or how many times she told him the same story—that her father had gotten angry and, in one of his fits of rage, smashed up all the furniture in the shed because she'd forgotten the words of an old poem; that he'd been drunk and hit her (she showed Alcázar the scratches and bruises on her arm, knee, and neck, which, while visible, were not excessive), and then, as he did every time, he'd hugged and kissed her and asked for her forgiveness.

After that, she'd heard the old Renault drive off down the lake road and, hours later, they'd found the empty car by the shore, its doors open. On the dashboard was a brief goodbye note, in his handwriting: *I need to escape. Please forgive me.* How many times did she repeat this story? A dozen, maybe more. In her memory it went on for hours, her retelling the same events like a constant refrain and the inspector jiggling his shoe, reading the note and shaking his head, repeating, "I don't believe you." Until finally she confessed the truth, told him about Anna Akhmatova, the Russian woman who had rented the house next door at the start of summer and had a daughter younger than Gonzalo.

"Actually, it was less than fifteen minutes," Alcázar said. He still smoked Ducados, as he had in 1967, but this time he offered one to Laura with a tired smile.

Fifteen minutes was how long it had taken her to tell him what really happened. She had wanted to, needed to get it off her chest. It was too much for a young girl to be burdened with. Alcázar hadn't even needed to scare her or be cruel. All he'd had to do was give her a little nudge and then wait. Once she stopped sobbing, he sent her back out to the hall where her mother and brother were waiting and ordered her not to say a word. Alcázar remembered feeling every fiber of his body tingle, excitement and doubt coursing through him like electricity. He was a young inspector who until that night hadn't had a single important case of his own, a man who lived in the shadow of his father, commissioner of the BPS—Franco's secret police, in Barcelona.

The disappearance of Elías Gil was so clearly too big for him that he did the only thing he could. Sensing that this could be the most important case of his entire career, Alcázar had called his father. He needed to be told how to proceed. And that was when his father made the decision that changed their lives forever. The decision involved only Alcázar, Laura, Anna Akhmatova, and Elías Gil himself.

For a few long minutes, ex–Chief Inspector Alcázar stood gazing blankly at the waves lapping gently against the breakwater. Time, in his head, was a jumble of events that—unlike for most people—were not ordered and successive but circular and simultaneous, a constant feedback loop that brought the past into the present and vice versa. Like right now. What was he? A nostalgic old man watching darkness fall by the seashore, standing beside a younger man who thought he knew the truth, as Alcázar himself had once thought.

"I've done a lot of things in my life that I'm not very proud of. But I've never killed anyone, I assure you. Your sister Laura knew that."

When he thought again about Laura, Alcázar remembered a determined woman, full of life. This was in the months leading up to the World's Fair in Seville and the Barcelona Olympics. Spain was on fire, effervescent, unstoppable; money flowed like a never-ending river; pirates, speculators, and mercenaries the world over disembarked, ready to take a slice of the pie via procurement contracts, construction gigs to build pavilions and offices, transportation services, you name it. Right when the country was about to leap into the world spotlight with no safety net in place, several cases of child prostitution and exploitation came to light, damaging the country's image; the politicians wanted the news buried—deep—on the double. They tasked Alcázar with creating a special brigade to fight child trafficking and sexual exploitation, but did so with the imbecilic frivolity of those who don't understand the issues and assume that the whole thing can be shut down with a cavalier wave of the hand, rather than real funding and the provision of material support to the agencies involved.

But Laura had come on board, and she was full of good intentions without being naïve, knew a lot about the world, had traveled widely, and was already in contact with associations fighting the scum involved in child prostitution. And Alcázar noticed something else, something more important. From the start, there was a personal side to her fervor; she had her own demons and was trying to exorcize them. Was that the reason he took her on? Maybe he thought he needed someone with her drive, someone who could convince him that what he was doing—no matter now trivial— was better than nothing and that despite having his hands tied, he had to carry on. But the real reason—which they'd never brought up after their first encounter years earlier—was that Alcázar felt he owed it to her. He had a debt to pay, they both knew this, and he was trying to make good on it.

Ten years later, they'd evolved in opposite directions. There were too many factors at play—all of which, truth be told, came down to the same thing: money. And it hadn't taken Alcázar long to confirm what he'd suspected from the start—that once he started stepping on toes and preparing to pull the rabbit out of his hat, he'd be left out in the cold. His superiors were looking for dramatic headlines, not actual scandal. That was when he'd first met Agustín González—amazing to think he'd been dealing with the old man that long. Back then Agustín was a lawyer who'd quickly read the situation at hand and adapted to the times, riding the wave, defending anyone with enough money to pay his exorbitant fees. He was smart and saw that Alcázar would never be able to defeat the men under his counsel; he also knew that the shit would keep flowing and all the city wanted to do was hide the stench. And it wasn't hard for him to convince Alcázar that he, too, could benefit from the scenario by playing his cards right.

So Alcázar became crooked, without intending to but without putting up a fight, simply accepting what seemed inevitable. He arrested those he could arrest, accepted congratulations and decorations when he shut down a brothel or broke up a minor child-trafficking ring, and also accepted—with rather less distaste—the generous handouts Agustín gave him in exchange for privileged information relating to his clients. He openly rubbed elbows with powerful people who kindly saw fit to invite him for a weekend of hunting in Cáceres or sailing in Ibiza—Russians, Azerbaijanis, and Georgians who'd begun spreading their tentacles along the Spanish coast, displacing the traditional Italian, French, and British mafias.

That was how he'd met Zinoviev, the arrogant, pumped-up thug and deranged pederast in charge of child prostitution. Until then Alcázar had never heard of the Matryoshka. It was Laura who'd found the name of a complicated tree diagram with multiple offshoots hanging in her office, and one of the branches led to Zinoviev, a known assassin. They weren't sure if the Matryoshka was a fabrication, a single person who ran the whole network, a consortium, or an abstract idea that Zinoviev and others used as a sort of umbrella.

When Alcázar had asked him directly, Zinoviev simply gave an evil laugh. "You just make sure that bitch on your team doesn't fuck with us too much."

Alcázar tried to help her; God and Cecilia were witness to the fact that he'd tried. When she went too far, he'd attempt to convince her to think of her family, weigh the risks, and if that didn't work, then he was forced to step in personally and make sure her raids were botched and her investigations led to dead ends, or to beg Zinoviev to ask his bosses to throw her a few scraps to keep her satisfied. Although Laura never knew it, Alcázar had more than once saved her life. But then she went too far. She managed to find an informer inside the organization.

Despite Alcázar's best efforts, she refused to tell him who it was. Her source assured her that there were cops and other authorities on the Matryoshka's payroll and, naïvely, Laura thought she was protecting Alcázar by not telling him her guy's name. She gained the support of a young prosecutor and an old-school judge, the kind who hated corruption above all else. Laura started getting search warrants, and then came the arrests and raids, and Alcázar didn't know how to stop it. He started to see that Laura was after Zinoviev but knew she wouldn't stop there. One by one she'd cross off the names on the diagram in her office. And at some point... she would come to his.

Laura was in a frenzy, like a hunter who can smell the prey and knows it's almost in her sights, wounded. Did she suspect him in the end? Probably. Of course, she already knew Agustín González. Not because he was her brother's father-in-law (a fateful coincidence) but because during Laura's time on the brigade the man's performances in court had become epic. Time after time, Agustín González's firm derailed her investigations, found violations of procedure and inconsistencies in her proof. Laura's detainees would be set free. She detested him. Agustín knew it, and also knew there was no way he could buy her off, so when the ACASA project took off, he suggested Alcázar feel her out. This was a terrible mistake. From that moment on, Laura avoided him like the plague. She never actually accused him of anything, but she also refused to let him in on anything. And shortly before it all went down, Alcázar found out she'd started investigating him. It was all just a matter of time.

And that was when the tragedy occurred. Zinoviev decided to act on his own, kidnapping Laura's son, Roberto. Alcázar remembered him—a lively little boy with unusual features, small eyes sharp as slits in his tiny, round face; he was slightly rebellious and totally enamored of his mother. Alcázar didn't find out about it until it was too late. Laura was the one who told him; she showed him the crass, anonymous handwritten note warning her to stop fucking with them. She was terrified, completely beside herself, as though she'd only just realized the full impact of what she'd done, as though until that moment she'd had no idea whom she was messing with. The boy was supposed to have been returned after two days. Zinoviev swore those were the instructions he'd received from the Matryoshka. And for the first time ever, Alcázar threatened him: If anything happened to that little boy, he was going to wish he'd never been born. Zinoviev calmed him down, assured him there was no reason to get worked up. It was just a warning, and the deputy inspector would see it that way. So why did they kill him? Was it a mistake, a misunderstanding? Firing point-blank can hardly be construed as an error. Maybe the kid saw their faces, maybe Zinoviev felt threatened and decided to take it upon himself to get rid of the evidence.

After that, Laura died inside. She was put on leave and forced to undergo psychological counseling, but by that point she wouldn't listen to anyone, not even that rich architect husband of hers. Their marriage had been on the rocks even before Roberto died. You can't be surrounded by horror every day of your life and not have it affect you. Laura had needed sleeping pills for years, and even with those she hardly got any rest. Then she moved on to amphetamines, booze. Alcázar had seen it happen to others, had even gone through it himself. The evil gets into your expression, melts into everything like wax.

A few months later, her husband left home and Laura was swept into a vortex of self-destruction. She started snorting too much coke, taking too many pills, drinking too much. She'd turn up at Alcázar's place in the middle of the night completely shit-faced, sob on the couch until she was spent, and when he woke up she'd be gone. She started going out with unsavory characters, anyone who would keep her company. She hardly ate, didn't sleep. And then one night there was a serious altercation at a pub: Laura had been very high and the bouncers refused to let her in. She'd taken out her service weapon and unintentionally fired a shot; it was a miracle that no one was killed.

She fled the scene and was found in her car the following morning, covered in blood. Laura had cut herself, was incoherent, in a state of shock, and had to be admitted to the psych ward at Valle de Hebrón hospital. When she was released, internal affairs was there waiting; they confiscated her gun and informed her that charges were being pressed over the bar incident. After everything she'd been through, she was being fired. Zinoviev's death was like her death knell. For Laura to commit suicide was simply a melodramatic way out, in a sense unworthy of her.

Unworthy? Alcázar shook his head, observing Gonzalo. The man was holding his head as if it might fall off his shoulders. He had purple bags under his eyes and a nervous twitch in his lip.

More than anything, Alcázar felt sorry for him. It was patently obvious that this was all pushing him to the limit, the man was about to collapse. And yet, by committing suicide, Laura had dropped him in the middle of it, forcing him to finish what she hadn't been able to. And judging by the headaches the man was causing Alcázar, she'd known what she was doing. If anyone knew Gonzalo Gil, it was his sister, that much was clear.

It was never going to end, Alcázar thought. Elías, Laura, and now Gonzalo. As long as one of the Gils was alive, the past would keep haunting him at night, coming back to bite him.

"It's time to forget about all this, Gonzalo. Now."

"The old man sent you to scare me, is that it?"

Alcázar scratched his mustache, pensive, and continued as though he hadn't heard him.

"The old man is right. You'll never be able to take them down, and you'll just end up destroying yourself and your family, like Laura. This isn't your war, it never was. You're a good family man, an unassuming but honest lawyer. Be happy with that, hold on to it, it's worth more than you think. If it makes you feel better, cling to the idea that your father was a martyr and assholes like me killed him. Bring your mother flowers, write a book...but forget all this. The old man will pay you handsomely for the land. Sell it. Join his firm, watch your kids grow up, and grow old with your wife without having to look over your shoulder every day. Carry on with your life, there's no reason to feel indebted to your sister's memory. I mean, you barely even knew her anymore. It wasn't your fault and you have no business finishing a story that's not yours to write."

"What if I say no? What if I never wanted to be a father or an unassuming but honest lawyer to begin with? What if I decide to be loyal to my sister and get to the bottom of this?"

"I already told you—they'll tear your life apart."

"I don't care," he fired back too rashly.

Alcázar patted Gonzalo's knee and stood. It was almost dark. The fishermen on the breakwater had lit their lanterns and the water was completely dark. His back hurt. He'd been hunched over too long. Alcázar pulled a photo from his pocket and placed it in Gonzalo's hand. He would have preferred not to do this and hoped it would be enough to convince him.

It was a picture of Patricia, Gonzalo's daughter.

"What does this mean?"

"Only the beginning, Gonzalo. Only the beginning."

17

On January 16, 1936, Elías Gil and Caterina Esperanza Orlovska were married in a civil ceremony at a Barcelona City Hall annex. He was twenty-four years old and she had yet to turn eighteen. It was a somber occasion, overshadowed by those who were absent. Elías's father had been killed after the October '34 miners' strike, summarily executed near Mieres along with several other labor leaders. Elías had returned to Spain just in time to attend the funeral and experience firsthand the fierce repression people were living under at the hands of African auxiliary troops outside Oviedo. His mother died a few months later, in the Zaragoza women's prison.

Now, back in the country, the truth of José Díaz's words was hitting him full force. He hardly even had time to mourn his parents' deaths. Terms like *war effort, revolution, committee order,* and *Party reorganization* were replacing terms like *mourning, sorrow, emotion,* and *love.* Elías was convinced, after seeing the havoc that Asturias had been plunged into, that Gil-Robles and his crony government had to be stopped by any means necessary and the CEDA sent back to the catacombs. So he threw everything he had into work, meetings, and plotting, burying his feelings, shoveling more and more dirt on to cover the now-enormous hole inside him—although anyone who got close enough could see the loss in his stony, lifeless expression. In late 1935 and early 1936, encounters with Party figures like Dolores Ibárruri and the promising young Santiago Carrillo became more heated: There were an increasing number of rallies, strikes, and boycotts but also increasing street violence.

He saw his old childhood friend Ramón once, in Madrid, shortly before the 1936 elections. They embraced affectionately and had dinner at a secluded restaurant in Aranjuez, far from prying eyes. Together they made a realistic—and thus quite negative—assessment of the current climate. Things could only get worse. Ramón had risen through the ranks of the CEDA, and Elías had become more entrenched in Communist agitation after the Asturias uprising, so they exchanged harsh words. For a moment it seemed as if the distance between them had become insurmountable. This was happening all over the country—neighbors, friends, and brothers hating one another—but somehow they managed to bring the situation under control.

"I'm really sorry about what happened to your parents."

He was being sincere, and Elías knew it.

"But you're on their side, Ramón."

Would the two of them start ascribing personal responsibility to each other for everything that happened? Elías recalled what Lenin's wife had said: *It's not the ideas that betray us but the individuals who carry them out.* Were they being swept up in a current impossible to escape, like the one on Nazino?

Despite the precautions they'd taken, two days later Elías got a visit from Santiago Carrillo. He had a resolved, intellectual air and gave Elías a clear warning: No consorting with the enemy.

"Ramón is not the enemy; he's a schoolmate, a childhood friend."

Carrillo eyed him with the officious, slightly hostile detachment he was becoming known for.

"No such thing as an innocent friendship, Elías. There's a line between the two worlds, and in case you haven't realized it, some people are on one side and we're on the other."

Elías and Esperanza—who had gotten rid of her birth name, openly embracing the person she'd decided to become—rented a small apartment in Carmelo, a poor hillside neighborhood filled with modest homes and unpaved streets. They furnished it as best they could, sometimes with things Elías found in the trash or was given by friends. Esperanza would see him carrying a mattress or a couple of chairs up the hill and feel lucky. They were building a life together, something new, a home, and little by little Elías seemed to be forgetting the past. Occasionally she'd find him with a far-away look, stroking that locket with the photo of Irina and Anna, but they never again spoke about what happened on Nazino.

"Do you love me?"

"That's what the ring says."

"Yes, but do you say it? Do you love me?"

"Why would I marry you if I didn't?"

People needed to love. Even if they had to force themselves to do it. That was what Esperanza thought when Elías gave her a quick kiss and avoided telling her his feelings. She was going to make a virtue of that, turn it to her advantage. She didn't care how long it took, Esperanza was willing to spend the rest of her life filling the hole in her husband's heart. Because she did love him, and had from the start, from the moment she saw him, looking like death itself, in the airplane hangar where Velichko had hidden him. Not once since her arrival in Spain had she questioned whether coming to this foreign country was the right thing to do. The decision was made, and she had love enough for both of them.

That September morning a torrential rain was falling on Barcelona, a city seemingly unaware that it was at war. In July, General

Francisco Franco had crossed the Strait of Gibraltar, entering Spain
with a rebel army that had been stationed in Africa. Other military units had also revolted, in Castile and in the north. But the
uprisings in Madrid and Barcelona had failed. And a strange sort
of euphoria had set in after the violence and killings of the first few
days. Everywhere you looked, members of the various militias—
the Catalan Socialist PSUC, the workers' CNT, the anarchist FAI,
and the Marxist POUM—were out patrolling, as were security
forces that had remained loyal to the Republic. Huge propaganda
posters roused the people's spirits, and at all hours of the day and
night, the radio broadcast patriotic dispatches and protest songs
exalting the Catalan people's fighting nature.

Caught up in this mystique, Barcelona's citizens felt like
heroes, one and all. It mattered little that occasionally there were
shots fired on the streets, scores settled for no apparent reason,
and that the hospital morgues were filling up. Those were simply
things they had to live with, one-off events that didn't alter everyday life. People still went to work, kids went to school, cinemas
kept showing *Modern Times* and *Mutiny on the Bounty*; the the-
aters on Paralelo still put on shows every night, stores still offered
clearance sales. No one wanted to accept the inevitable. People
said it would all be over in a matter of days, some even rejoiced,
seeing the situation as a historic opportunity. Now that the reactionary military had shown its true colors, there was no reason
to keep putting off a comprehensive purge of the right's political
forces—the church and the army. The time had come to do away
with them all, definitively eradicate the pro-coup cancer spreading
throughout Spain.

Elías Gil observed the excitement in the air, wary and alert.

"Whether we like it or not, none of us will be the same as we
were before the July 18 uprising," he said, glancing at an armored
vehicle parked in Cathedral Plaza with FAI painted on the side. The
anarchists, at the time, were the most organized of the militias.

They'd already sent columns of volunteers to the front and had
the most impressive arsenal, including armored cars like this one.

In order to get there, Elías had crossed several barricades and
checkpoints set up along the Ramblas, manned by civilians who
belonged to different parties and unions. At each one he'd shown
his credentials: He was cultural attaché to the Russian consulate, with offices on Tibidabo Avenue. Elías's papers stated that
he worked for Consul Antonov-Ovseyenko and that his job was
essentially to coordinate cultural exchanges between local organizations and the USSR, although this was obviously a euphemistic way of expressing what he did. The truth was that Elías—like
almost everyone at the consulate—worked under the orders of the
man accompanying him that morning: Ernö Gerö, alias Pedro,
alias Gere, alias Pierre.

Gerö was shorter than Elías, about forty years old—no one
knew his exact age—and had a penchant for expensive suits, especially bespoke suits made by a tailor on Ancha Street. He had Slavic
features, sharp and enigmatic, with the exception of his soft fleshy
lips. His eyes were slanted, giving him a somewhat reserved and
somber air. Gerö's Spanish was good albeit slightly choppy, and
only when he was truly enraged—which he never was in public—
did he fly off the handle in his native Hungarian.

The man, who looked rather like a tax inspector, was theoretically there to manage Soviet relations with the PSUC—the
party most aligned with Stalin—and its leader, Joan Comorera,
and to supervise the Party bulletin, *Work*. But the truth was, he
was the right-hand man of Colonel Aleksandr Orlov, who was the
top brass (at least in Spain) of the NKVD, the newly formed Soviet
secret police that replaced the OGPU. Gerö, meanwhile, headed
the NKVD in Catalonia. His mission was to root out spies, defeat-
ists, and anyone suspected of counterrevolutionary activities. But
more important, he was to ensure that the air of change ushered in
by the military uprising in no way ran counter to Soviet interests.

"The people are always right, are they not? If they believe we shall be victorious, then we shall. That's what they all want to hear." Gerö pointed scornfully to a POUM squad standing at a sandbag barrier by the Telefónica building, between Puerta del Ángel and Plaza Cataluña. "The truth is, they are almost never right, because they do not have access to all of the elements by which to judge the situation at their disposal."

Elías rarely contradicted his boss. But Gerö had not been in Asturias after the 1934 massacre. To the Hungarian, this was simply another posting, provisional at best. After completing his mission, he'd be sent back to the French Communist Party where he had come from, or anyplace else. He didn't grasp the reality on the ground, didn't understand the people's visceral hatred.

"The people are eager to exercise their right to justice directly. No one's forgotten what happened two years ago." Elias thought of his father, shot by a Moroccan volunteer firing squad, and his mother, who'd died of tuberculosis in an overcrowded prison. "People react violently against the abuse of power when it becomes unbearable."

Gerö shot him a grave look.

"The people, Gil, are a euphemism. The people do not exist. They are people when they're in our interest and stop being people when they're not. Demagoguery, my friend, is not something to be scorned. So they want to settle a few scores, play at war, plunder a little? Fine, let them. Soldiers have claimed their right to spoils since ancient times. I am a great fan of historical corollaries, but this is not Imperial Rome. The law does not belong to the people; it belongs to those who govern. And that is as it should be: The first important victory of a revolution is to make it systematic, never forget that. We are not in the service of a moment; we're in the service of history. And that means we cannot abide orgies and random acts of retaliation. The first thing we must do is win the war. And all of these militias, trade

unionists, and local leaders need to understand that. Freedom is a luxury that cannot be conceded to the masses, at least not at this moment in history. Wars are won and lost in the rear guard; they require discipline, effective control. And that's why we're here, you and I. This is not a game and we're not going to let it become one. Understood?"

They had passed Puerta del Ángel, and with it the remains of the old Roman wall that was destroyed in the nineteenth century to open up the city center to connect Barcelona to Gracia and the Eixample. It hadn't stopped raining, but Gerö didn't let up the pace. He seemed to enjoy having the rain soak his elegant dark blue suit. Finally, he pointed to a canopy awning at the intersection of Cortes Street.

"Let's have coffee."

The Coliseum Café was nearly empty. On the walls hung posters calling for people to rise up in arms, child education campaigns, appeals for productivity. And alongside these exhortations, the baroque mirrors and pink marble floor survived, as did the tables covered in fine linen cloths and the waiters in vest, apron, and bow tie. At a table in the back, three men constantly scanned the perimeter. It was obvious that each had a gun beneath his suit. At the next table over, a heavyset man sat eating poached eggs, serving himself coffee from a silver pot as he pored over several documents with a concerned look.

The man was Colonel Orlov, Gerö's direct boss and therefore Elías's boss as well.

"Comrade Colonel."

Orlov looked tired. Though probably not yet fifty, his hair was silver and his cheeks hung loose beneath his eyes, the flesh sagging. Breathing through his nose, he kept his mouth stubbornly shut. After nodding to Gerö, he turned to focus on Elías. For a few seconds Orlov remained inexpressive as he examined him, concentrating on the patch over Elías's eye.

"I have heard that your eye is not the only thing you left in Siberia."

Elías sensed not a trace of irony in the man's words. He could think of no way to respond. Almost three years had passed, and despite dreaming of Nazino every night, he'd never again spoken about it. What happened there was private, his alone.

"Did you also leave behind your Party loyalty?"

"I'm right here, Comrade Colonel."

Orlov cast a sidelong glance at Gerö, who gave a slight nod. Orlov was mulling something over, a thought turning between his bushy eyebrows, and he spat out the skin in the form of a snort.

"Sit, comrade."

Elías sat perfectly erect, not touching the seat back. Gerö remained standing to his right. Colonel Orlov showed Elías part of the contents of the documents he was studying.

"Yagoda and Berman have been removed from power and executed for high treason, I imagine you already know that. It would seem that Velichko's report reached those he wanted it to reach. Of course that doesn't mean that the testimony of a few Siberian deportees was in any way decisive, but when the time came, it all added up. I imagine you'll find this news satisfying."

"I simply recounted the events as I experienced them, Comrade Colonel."

"And managed to involve the instructor and his uncle—a direct associate of Stalin—not to mention Lenin's wife and the general secretary of the Party in Spain. They could have had you shot as a traitor, a deserter, but as it happens you are here and I've been asked to use your knowledge of the country. As it also happens, however, I don't like people who don't do what they should do. And you should have died on Nazino."

Elías made no reply to this. There was a price to pay for staying alive, sometimes very high, and judging by Orlov's expression, the man already knew how dearly Elías had paid.

Some people claimed that the colonel had an innate ability to read men in a single glance. This was a misconception; he had no natural talent. What he had was power, emanating from every pore. But inside, Orlov was just a man like any other. Like Yagoda, like Berman, he too was racked by fears, he too lived in terror of the purges taking place in the USSR. The only thing that Stalin—who was safely ensconced in the Kremlin—had to do was snap his fingers and Orlov would be whisked off as well. The higher a man's rank, the greater his fear.

Elías's advantage lay in the fact that he had no fear. Unlike them, he had no aspirations for power whatsoever, cared nothing for its privileges and showed reckless disregard for his own life. There was nothing they could do to him. Nothing.

Orlov quickly sensed this and relaxed his neck slightly.

"She's alive. The girl. She's alive."

Seeing Elías's face crumble, he gave a nasty smile, noting that all men have an Achilles' heel, after all.

"We know you gave her to that prisoner, Igor Stern."

Elías blinked slowly, as if the snowflakes falling that night in 1933 were caught in his eyelashes. He pictured Igor's silhouette walking in front of a stone fireplace, half of his body in light, half in shadow. Igor stroked Anna's hair like a loving father would do. But he was no loving father; he was a sick monster whose hands were still covered in blood. Michael lay off to the side, his throat slit. Martin was almost dead, hanging from a ceiling beam inside the cabin, feces sliding down his skinny white legs and forming a foul pool of shit and blood beneath his bare feet. Elías had been beaten savagely but that was all. His good eye gazed on the scene through a blood-filled retina. They'd been ambushed in their sleep. Exhausted after their arduous journey and believing themselves safe, they'd let their guard down. Michael was the first to see the men enter the cabin; he pulled out the revolver he'd taken from the officer on Nazino and fired, killing one, but the others leapt immediately and ripped him to shreds.

"I hear they made things pretty painful for that little pansy friend of yours. After forcing you to watch them torture him, they left him for dead. But he's not dead. He was the one who told the patrol that found him two days later about the deal you made with Igor Stern."

So Martin had survived!

"What your young friend could not explain was why they let you live."

Elías shuddered, recalling Igor's sickening breath as he crouched down to stroke Elías's coat. Through clenched teeth, Igor reminded him that he still wanted the coat. Had Elías given it to him on Nazino, Igor would have killed him on the spot. But he refused to give it up, and his pigheadedness—not pride but insanity—had taken Igor by surprise. In a sense, he was showing his respect. Elías had more balls than most men he'd met, Igor told him, but the time had come to make a decision.

"He offered you a deal, and you took it: You went free, in exchange for the girl."

"If I hadn't accepted, he would have killed us both."

"Perhaps. And who knows if that wouldn't have been more honorable. He told you what he was planning to do to the girl if you accepted. He wasn't going to kill her right away, first he wanted to have his fun and then let his men have a go. He warned you that it would take a long time—days, weeks. And you took the deal."

Colonel Orlov held him in his icy gaze. "No one is judging you. Your own judgment is enough. A man does what has to be done, that's my motto."

Ridiculous motto, completely untrue, Elías thought. No one else had to see Anna's imploring eyes as he walked away, leaving her in the hands of those animals. He did.

He gave Igor the coat. Took it off right there and handed it to him. Igor put it on and remarked upon how well it fit, then made a face and hurled it onto the fire. The two of them watched it go up in flames, crinkling into a black ball that gave off a sickly sweet smell as it burned.

"We arrested Igor Stern eight days later as he tried to attack a shipping line. We killed all of his men, but not him. He had the girl in his arms. She was"—Gerö searched for the words but, unable to find them, opted to omit what he'd been planning to say—"alive. And now she is in official custody."

"What happened to Martin?"

"Through the Red Cross he was sent back home. We don't want any problems with the British Crown. Prior to his departure, he collaborated with our investigation into the Nazino affair, declaring without coercion that the statements he, Michael, and Claude had signed against you were totally false."

"Igor Stern—"

"That does not concern you," Colonel Orlov interrupted, as though he'd already said too much about a topic that, frankly, was of little interest. "What you need to know is that the Party understands that you suffered an injustice and will not attempt to assess whether what you did in order to survive was honorable or not. You are here now, and that's what matters. You're being promoted to lieutenant."

"I'm not in the military."

"You are now. You will be given a Soviet Party card and access to classified material. You will have a stipend, and we will ensure that your young wife has everything she needs."

And in exchange, you will say not a word, or your story will come out in the papers and all of the prestige you earned in Asturias as the Spanish Communist who escaped Siberia alive will be destroyed. And then one fine day, someone will shoot you in the back of the head in an alleyway. Orlov didn't need to say that part, his expression made it perfectly clear.

Gerö gave his shoulder an affectionate squeeze; he was one of the gang now, the man's gesture said.

"I've looked into you, Gil, and I think I can trust you. You're currently assigned to the office of Consul Antonov and have personal access to him, is that correct?"

Elías nodded.

"Good. I have my suspicions about that Menshevik. I think he's betraying us, siding with Andreu Nin, that Trotskyist from the POUM. And this is making it very difficult for me to cut deals with Secretary Comorera of the PSUC."

"What we want is for you to gather information proving his disloyalty," Orlov broke in testily.

"What if he's innocent?"

"No one is innocent without my say-so."

The meeting was promptly terminated when one of Orlov's security guards handed the colonel a telegram. It was news from the Aragon Front, and not very promising judging by the man's furrowed brow.

Gerö signaled to Elías to stand, and he stood. But on his way out, Elías stopped for a moment, looked at the colonel, and asked, "Will I see her again?"

"Who?"

"Anna Akhmatova."

"I have no idea what you're talking about. Your job is to take care of Antonov."

Consul Antonov-Ovseyenko was summoned to Moscow in early 1937. A few months later he was executed for high treason. Much of the evidence used against him was provided by Elías Gil, his personal secretary and lieutenant in the newly formed Military Intelligence Service of the Republican Army. None of the evidence was ever proved true.

18

Gonzalo charged into the house, propelled by a terrible premonition. He'd forgotten that Alcázar had installed an alarm system, and its ear-piercing shriek startled everyone. Within seconds, Lola stood before him, fear and confusion reflected on her face. She looked at him as if he was a ghost, then keyed in the code to turn off the alarm; finally, the deafening sound stopped.

"What are you doing here? It's three o'clock in the morning."

"Patricia! Where's Patricia?"

"In her room. What's going on?"

Not stopping to explain, Gonzalo raced up the stairs. Standing in the hall were Javier and Patricia, both looking afraid. Seeing him, she became immediately gleeful, broke free of Javier's protective embrace, and sprang into her father's arms. Gonzalo held her tight, so tight in fact that Patricia whined delightedly as he pressed her to his chest. But he let go only when Lola asked curtly what all the commotion was about. Gonzalo patted his daughter, as though needing to prove to himself that she was really there. He realized he was scaring them and smiled nervously at Javier, who gazed on in silent condemnation. Gonzalo felt compelled to make something up on the spot.

"I got a bad feeling and wanted to make sure everyone was okay."

It sounded ridiculous. Everything at the house was perfectly normal, with the exception of his freak-out. And suddenly Gonzalo felt like a stranger in his own home, with his own family. Nothing had happened, and there was no reason anything should, but when Alcázar had shown him the photo of Patricia and made that veiled threat, he realized how precarious it all was. Their safety was at risk. Neither the children nor Lola sensed the danger in the air, but he did.

Javier was moving his head slowly up and down, not in agreement but a sort of condescending accusation.

"And you couldn't wait until morning? You scared us to death," he said, pulling his sister to him, reclaiming her. Gonzalo realized that his son had taken on the role of man of the house, and that his own presence was evoking hostility. *I can take care of them*, Javier's defiant expression said.

"I'm sorry," Gonzalo replied, and this seemed to satisfy his son.

Twenty minutes later, Alcázar turned up.

"Is everyone okay?"

He wore an expression of genuine concern. Overly solicitous, he avoided looking Gonzalo in the eye and focused instead on Lola and the kids. When Lola told him it was a false alarm, the ex-inspector shot Gonzalo a quick but meaningful glance: *This is just the beginning, and it's in your power to stop it*, his eyes said. Then he made a point of stroking Patricia's cheek.

"Your father worries so much about you."

Gonzalo trembled with rage but managed to contain himself. Lola walked Alcázar to the door, thanking him for coming and apologizing for the trouble, and Alcázar said good night with a smile so frank and open that it made Gonzalo's blood boil.

When Lola asked Javier to take Patricia back to bed, she protested vociferously and clung to her father, crying. Gonzalo had to use all of his powers of persuasion to convince her to go up with her brother.

"You have no right to turn up like this!" Lola fired reproachfully, the second the two of them were alone.

Gonzalo considered his words carefully, weighing how much he could say and what he'd have to keep quiet. He had an undeniable urge to tell Lola what was going on, but he didn't know how the events linked together or how to separate the parts that concerned both of them. In the end, he opted for a prudent approach; it was better to protect them, keep them in the dark about what was going on. Alcázar had given him a clear warning: no cops, no leaving town. Everything had to carry on as normal.

"I suddenly had this gut feeling that Atxaga was at the house," he lied.

Lola sighed and tilted her head back, as though searching with her gaze for someplace to escape to.

"My father is taking care of it," she snapped cruelly, and was instantly sorry for her words, for giving in to the childish urge to hurt him. But it was already done, and her condemnation echoed in the living room.

"Your father. What do you know about your father and his ambitions?"

Gonzalo, too, should have kept quiet and not let himself start down the slippery slope of tit for tat, knowing even as he did that his thoughts would go unspoken, leaving a question in the air for Lola to pounce on.

"What about my father? What's that supposed to mean?"

She waited for Gonzalo to say more, but he didn't, and she'd had enough of her husband's perpetual silence. Silence that, she now knew, could go on for years and then suddenly be broken, just like that. It was strange, but Gonzalo's revelation—that he knew she'd had an affair and that Javier was not his son—had shamed her for only a second. What she felt now was resentment: He'd forced her to feel guilty, to pretend for eighteen years, and he'd known all along…

"What kind of a man are you?"

Gonzalo made no reply. From his expression it was clear that he was no longer even there. Lola stared challengingly a few seconds more before giving up. It was all over, she thought. Their relationship, their marriage—it was done. And the certainty of that brought with it a sense of freedom that overpowered her sorrow.

"You can sleep on the couch if you like… But don't even think about smoking in my house."

Harsh comments, stupid petty outbursts concealing untold grievances from the past, a tangled web of contradictory feelings and recriminations they vented by acting out. This was what it had come to.

Gonzalo slept on the sofa, fully clothed. In the different shades of darkness he could make out the contours of the furniture. For a long time, he lay there listening to silence echo with all of the things—arguments, good times, laughter, and tears—that were contained in that house and no longer belonged to him. Lola's question pounded in his head. What kind of a man was he? A man who loved his family, despite it all. One who'd do anything to protect them.

He got up and went to the garage. His mother's things were stored up in the loft, but that wasn't what he was looking for. He put up a ladder, got a flashlight, and pushed aside piles of stuff at the front, feeling around for the metal box hidden among some plastic tarps. When he opened it, he grew pale.

It was gone. The rusty old pistol was gone.

A sound made him turn to the garage door. He shined the flashlight and saw a shadow skulking off.

"Javier? Is that you?"

.   .   .

"Señora Márquez called to cancel her appointment. That makes"—Luisa consulted the date book, running a fingernail down the page—"four cancellations. Isn't it great? Now you get the whole day off and I'm out of a job."

Gonzalo hunched lower in his desk chair. "There will be others, don't worry. You're not going to lose your job."

Luisa tried to come up with a snappy retort, but for once her acerbic wit failed her and it was her stomach that felt acidic. In her desk drawer was the note that Agustín's secretary had personally delivered that morning. They wanted her to work for them and would pay a much better salary than Gonzalo did, certainly far higher than what she'd get in the unemployment line if things kept going down this path. She'd walked into Gonzalo's office determined to quit, but on seeing his devastated look couldn't make herself do it.

"The old man is really turning the screws. He takes my clients, kicks me out of the office, and now he wants to steal the best assistant in all of Barcelona."

Luisa blushed.

"I saw the note on your desk before you had time to hide it. You should accept; it's a good offer."

"I should accept? Maybe, and you should have a shave and change your shirt. If by chance a client were to walk in, we wouldn't need your father-in-law to scare them off; you'd do it all by yourself." Luisa opened the door to leave and then stood with her hand on the doorknob.

"Is it really worth it? Putting everything you have on the line for an old house? I'm not doubting you, I'm just asking."

It wasn't the house, or the fact that his father-in-law was trying to impose his will through threats and intimidation. It was far more than that, but Gonzalo couldn't explain.

"Yes, it's worth it." He would have liked to be more forceful in his avowal, but not even he felt sure. And yet, for Luisa, it was enough.

"Well, maybe serving coffee in some mall wouldn't be so bad. People need to expand their horizons."

Once he was alone again, Gonzalo pulled open his desk drawer to study the locket, gazing at the faded image of Irina. He thought about the conversation he'd had with his mother. His father had loved this mysterious woman, had perhaps done what Gonzalo was doing right now—caressing the locket's worn surface, running a fingertip over her blurry name—thousands of times. Maybe Alcázar was right. Maybe his father simply hadn't wanted to live out the rest of his days a slave to his own reputation.

His head felt like it was going to explode and his body like two horses were pulling him in opposite directions, shredding his muscles and breaking his bones. What Alcázar was asking him to do was to betray not only Siaka and Laura but also himself, to admit that despite his ideals and illusions he was no hero, nor was he called upon to be one. He was nothing but a two-bit lawyer with no clients and no ambition, the father of a boy who couldn't stand him, a man whose marriage had collapsed due to his own stubborn silence. A father incapable of protecting his children, who'd already unnecessarily put them in harm's way. *Why, Gonzalo? Is it pride? What are you trying to prove? And to whom?* He didn't know what to do, whom to turn to. Putting the locket back in the drawer, he walked out to the reception area.

"Is the old man in today?"

"I don't spend my days spying on the competition, you know."

Gonzalo wasn't in the mood for Luisa's sarcasm, and she could tell.

"I think he's out of town. Asia."

How convenient, Gonzalo thought: The ACASA project blows up, Alcázar threatens to harm Patricia, and the old man disappears. The bastard goes on about his grandkids nonstop but doesn't think twice about using them as blackmail. And in the meantime, he skips town.

Gonzalo needed some fresh air. At least that was what he told himself. But he wasn't fooling anyone. In recent weeks he'd started frequenting Flight. He'd stop by late, in the hopes of seeing Tania again. Lately, the thought of that girl and her red hair was the only bright spot in his days. He wasn't harboring any illusions, but he couldn't help fantasizing about her.

That afternoon, Vasili greeted him with his customary faint smile and treated him to coffee. The two of them had tentatively begun having conversations that Gonzalo awkwardly tried to steer in the direction of Tania, though what the old man liked talking about were the photos of the Great Patriotic War adorning the walls. Vasili turned out to be an easy conversationalist with a quick tongue. Until 1941, he had been an instructor at Osoaviakhim, the Soviet military flight school. After that he was sent to the border with Belarus, where the German offensive took him by surprise after Hitler broke the 1939 pact by invading the Soviet Union. Assigned to a fighter squad, he battled the Nazis until he was shot down near the Polish border, only a few days after the start of the war. He was taken prisoner and sent to a military camp in Poland. While other comrades proudly displayed the Order of Lenin medals they'd received at the time, Velichko, when the war ended, was accused of treason. They claimed that he wasn't actually taken down by enemy fire, that he'd been trying to desert the army and had run out of fuel, which was why he didn't make it. He was sentenced to twelve long years in a gulag on the border with Kazakhstan and served each and every day of it. When he got out, in 1957, he had no family awaiting him, couldn't find work, and people kept their distance. Everyone was afraid to be associated with him. Everyone but Anna Akhmatova, Tania's mother.

Gonzalo caught sight of a faint number tattooed on Velichko's forearm, peeking out from beneath his rolled-up sleeve. Though the ink had faded over the years, the number was still there, branded into his flesh. Gonzalo wondered if it had been put there by the Germans, while he was in the camp in Poland, or by his own countrymen in Siberia.

"Why do you still revere them? They betrayed you."

Velichko gazed at him sadly. It was so hard to talk about the camaraderie of the front, the way fear not only tore men apart but also brought them together, the bonds it created, the way acts of abject cowardice were forgiven in a fleeting burst of heroism.

It was also hard to hold his tongue, to keep from talking about Elías Gil. But Anna had made him swear. In fact, if she'd known Gonzalo had so much as set foot in the bar, she would be furious. And yet Vasili risked her anger because Gonzalo reminded him so much of Elías, though of course he had no idea. Words are nothing without experience, nothing but smoke and mirrors, easily forgotten.

"People need something to believe in, and the war was our common cause. What happened before and after was tragic, and absurd. And I will never forgive the men who betrayed our ideals. But during the war years, we were free. I can't explain it." Those days—the days of Vasili and Anna and Elías—were gone, and now all he cared about was an idealized past, the dust-covered photos that no one asked about or wondered who they were and what they meant.

The old man glanced at the entrance and grunted.

"Well, it looks like the person you're actually here to see has arrived. No need to keep humoring me. The real reason for your visit just walked in." He pointed to the door.

Heaven had smiled on Tania Akhmatova. She was a radiant beauty in her loose-fitting blouse—the same dark blue as her eyes and long necklace—wide belt and tight jeans. Her open-toed espa-drilles had a slight heel that made her far taller than Gonzalo, who felt awkward and ridiculous as he stood to greet her. Tania took a seat beside him. Though there was plenty of room, she made a point of sitting so close that her elbow almost brushed against him.

"You look good. Those bruises will be gone soon."

Instinctively, Elías touched his side. Maybe the bruises would disappear, but his ribs were still killing him.

"That's a pretty tattoo on your neck," he declared idiotically, in an attempt to be glib. Tania looked amused and then leaned over and stuck her neck out so he could see it better.

"Tattoos aren't just there to look pretty, you know. They have a meaning, they're a declaration of intent. I like butterflies. There are more, you know, on other parts of my body," she remarked flirtatiously.

"So what intent are you declaring? That you want to fly? Have wings? Be free?"

She said it wasn't that obvious, that it was more to do with transformation.

"When I was little, I lived in really remote place out in the country in a 1970s building that had once been an isolation hos-pital for soldiers with mental problems. It was a horrible building, all cement with hardly any windows. But the surrounding area was beautiful, especially in the springtime. There were meadows all around and a pine forest nearby. When the cold finally ended and the rains stopped, all of the caterpillars that had gone into their little cocoons seemed to emerge at once, and thousands of butterflies would appear on the same day, fluttering in the pines. It only lasted a few hours but it was a breathtaking sight. If you lay in the grass and stayed very still, within seconds hundreds of them would land all over you—on your lips, your eyelashes, your fingertips, your nose. They'd all flutter their wings in unison, and it felt like they might lift you up off the ground, envelop you in a swirl of color and joy and carry you off, away from that awful building. But if you resisted the temptation to go with them, if you lay completely motionless and stopped breathing, then something even better happened: It felt like you were slowly turning into one of them, transforming, metamorphosing, like your body was their cocoon and not really a human body."

Velichko had sauntered over and was listening, eyes half closed in pleasure. It wasn't the first time he'd heard Tania tell this story, but she was so passionate that it seemed like the first time he'd truly listened. That, however, did not keep him from crabbily disagreeing.

"What I remember about that place are the insufferable swarms of mosquitoes and insects. There was no way to get away from them, no matter what you did. I saw mules go insane from the bites and hurl themselves into ravines, men so enraged they opened fire at the black clouds. I don't remember the butterfly stuff."

Tania stroked his arm. "I remember that, too, and my mother told me that people had to wear handkerchiefs over their faces just to go outside and thick rubber gloves to swing an ax, steam rising as they chopped. But I couldn't get a tattoo of a horsefly, could I?"

Velichko gazed affectionately at her. Memory, he thought, is a country, and each of us chooses to reminisce wistfully or look back on it with hatred.

"You'll never be a true Siberian."

Tania's expression changed. She downed her beer and stood.

"It's late, we should go." And with that she kissed the old man on the cheek, after whispering a few words to him in Russian.

"What did you tell him?" Gonzalo asked once they were out on the street.

"Something my mother often says, an old Russian proverb: *Yearning for the past is like chasing the wind.*"

Gonzalo slipped his hands into his pants pockets and turned to her, though she couldn't see his somber expression.

"Is that really what you think? That yearning for the past is like chasing the wind?

"Yes."

"I hardly even remember my own father. I know he used to take me to the lake to go fishing when the weather was nice, but only because my mother has told me about it so many times, in great detail, and I tell myself that I remember him staring into the bottom of the lake, telling me stories, teaching me to hold a fishing pole and cast a line. I talk about it like it was true, but it's just a borrowed memory." The image of Javier, when Gonzalo asked if he'd taken the gun, clouded his face. "I wonder if that's the way all children remember their parents, if Javier will simply think of me as something invented."

Tania gazed fondly at him. "The way children see their parents is never fair, Gonzalo. Until they become parents themselves."

I have no idea what you're talking about, Javier had said, but it was so obvious that he was lying.

"What about the way parents see their kids?"

Tania took his arm and pressed against him. "That, I couldn't tell you; I don't have kids. But I bet that no matter what it is that's troubling you, you'll find the answer. Sometimes all you have to do is tackle things head-on."

That was so easy to say, Gonzalo thought. And cliché. And yet often so true.

Somehow, unknowingly, they'd crossed an invisible border and found themselves in new territory. Realizing this, they were slowly finding their footing. Gonzalo didn't want to think about anything; he wanted only to experience these new feelings, to let them consume him before he had to come back down to reality. Just for a few minutes.

They reached Karamazov Bookstore. Tania dug out her keys and jiggled them in her hand. She was trying to act lighthearted, but it came off as unconvincing. Gonzalo both feared and prayed she would ask him to come up, but Tania slid the key into the lock and pushed the door open, switched on the hall light, and turned as though to say goodbye. He was gripped by the sense that the present was the only thing that mattered, that the past and the future—anything outside of that precise instant—didn't exist at all. His pulse was racing.

Tania smiled, as though reading him like a book. "Do you want to come up?"

Gonzalo couldn't control his pounding heart. *Boom, boom, boom.* One foot wanted to walk in, the other to make a run for it.

"It's probably not the right time," he said in a last-ditch attempt to avoid crossing that threshold, which was beckoning to him like an open mouth. *When is the right time, Gonzalo? If you wait for it, it might never arrive.*

It really didn't matter who kissed whom. What mattered was that they both wanted to.

Barcelona was dim and hazy in the predawn light. He could have been anywhere, and he didn't care. Geography was only a state of mind. Gonzalo walked down streets that belonged entirely to him at that hour. He lit a cigarette and rested his elbows on the handrail of a bridge crossing over a deserted avenue. The traffic lights flashed, changing color like a silly children's game. A cat crossed the street like a lone frontiersman, a blissful couple walked arm in arm, exhausted, no doubt making promises that they truly believed they'd be able to keep. Tania's skin was still on him, he could feel her on his fingertips, under his nails. The remnants of her perfume were trapped in his shirt; if he inhaled deeply enough he could smell her. Would he see her again? Absolutely. Whenever she wanted.

No matter what the old woman said.

He'd bumped into her on his way down the stairs, trying to be quiet. She was sitting in an armchair facing the counter, and

her silhouette, in the dark, had startled him. At first Gonzalo
had thought she was asleep, reading glasses and an open book
in her lap.

He passed by on tiptoe, but when he reached the door, her
sharp voice hit him like a hammer. "Are you like your father,
Gonzalo?"

He turned and saw that her eyes were empty, like those of a
statue. The look she was giving him was stark, inescapable.

"I'm sorry, I don't understand."

The old woman calmly closed her book and folded her glasses
before getting up. The weak dawn light outside reflected her profile in the glass.

"Are you like Elías? The kind of man who takes control of
people, robs them of everything, and then abandons them to their
fate? Is that what you're going to do to my daughter?"

Tania grew up knowing nothing of Elías's existence. And then
one day, when she was ten or twelve years old, she found a bunch of
newspaper clippings her mother kept hidden in the back of a dresser
drawer. A strapping man in an NKVD uniform whose Cyclops eye
looked all-seeing. Right away, she was both enthralled by and afraid
of that eye. When she asked her mother who he was, Anna became
furious, snatching the papers out of Tania's hands and slapping her
across the face (the one and only time she'd ever laid a hand on
her). For a long time, her mother refused to say a word about him,
wouldn't tell her who he was or why he was so important. But clearly
he was. Spying on her mother, she would see her go into her bedroom, gather up those clippings, and stare at them for ages, lost in
thought, a distant look in her eyes, as though she'd gone to another
time and place that Tania knew nothing about.

And as is always the case with forbidden places, Tania spent
her teenage years lurking around their edges, inventing what she

didn't know. Anna had photos of both of her parents on her night-stand. But Tania imagined that her mother's father—a teacher executed in the thirties for being a Trotskyist—was not her real father, that this one-eyed giant had been Irina's lover and the two of them had had an endless tormented, secret, passionate affair. Sometimes, if she voiced one of her crazy theories, Anna would look at her and shake her head in resignation.

"Did we come to Spain so you could find him?" she'd ask.

"We came to Spain to build a future, not to live in the past."

Vasili Velichko—Uncle Vasili as Tania had always called him, though he wasn't actually family—was no help. He denied knowing anything about Elías Gil, and when she interrogated him about the past he'd cling to the same story she had already heard: In 1934, Tania's grandfather and grandmother Irina were killed by the OGPU, leaving Anna alone in the world at the age of three, a ward of the state. Velichko met her when she was six, at an orphanage near Kursk that he'd gone to inspect in his role as commissar. He'd felt sorry for her, and for as long as he could he made sure to send money so that Anna would have everything she needed. Then came the war and his long imprisonment in Siberia, and for the entire twelve years he was there, Anna was the only person he corresponded with. She sent him clothes and food when she could. And when Velichko got out of the gulag, Anna took him in. There followed many hard years—very hard years—but in 1965 came an opportunity to start over, in Spain. Uncle Vasili had come alone first, to get set up, and years later was able to send for Tania and her mother. Those broad brush-strokes were all the detail her uncle and mother ever gave to account for twenty long years of their lives.

Though she never forgot about the mysterious one-eyed man, over the years Tania buried her thoughts of him in the shallow grave of things her mother was trying to forget. She grew up, and Uncle Velichko and Anna grew old, without any of them realizing it. When democracy returned to Spain in the mid-seventies, Vasili opened his bar, and Tania—then sixteen years old—joined the youth brigades of the PSUC, the Catalan Communist Party. She'd bring her friends to the bar, trying to impress them with the Stalin-era photos on the walls and the stories told by an actual people's commissar, and when she really wanted to astound them, she'd speak to him in Russian and get mad when he insisted on answering in Spanish in front of her comrades. Her mother opened Karamazov Bookstore in the late seventies, and it soon became a hub for Russian literature aficionados. But she never let Tania use the space for her meetings. Anna had no interest in politics and had become fearful, warning her daughter to be cautious. After the attempted coup in 1981, she got even worse and actually wanted to close the bookstore, but fortunately, Velichko talked her out of it.

The eighties were a difficult time for Tania and her mother. They argued a lot, unable to see that they were in fact as identical as two drops of water: same temper, same pride, same hardheadedness. Tania traveled around Spain and then went to France in late 1989. It was there, close to Le Boulou, that she happened upon an exhibit on the Republican internment camps set up for Spanish Civil War refugees in Argelès and Saint-Cyprien between 1939 and 1942. The exhibit marked the fiftieth anniversary of their opening, and associations to honor the memory of the dead had organized a reception for survivors, many of whom came with their children or grandchildren. It was held in a municipal sports arena, and Tania remembered the long aisles of objects on display: wooden suitcases, personal belongings, mementos, a few pieces of crudely built furniture, replicas of the shacks prisoners had been housed in, and more than a hundred black-and-white photos, many on loan from the Robert Capa Foundation.

There was a speaker, an expressive old man in a black International Brigades beret who recounted the tragedy that had brought more than four hundred thousand to French shores, a tragedy

Tania knew nothing about. Many of those in attendance, especially the older people, wept openly and nodded as they listened,
while their children—most of whom were French—consoled
them. Tania, who by that time had already decided she wanted to
be a professional photographer, began snapping away, capturing
everything she could.

And that was when she saw a slight-looking woman and
young man point to a large-format photo taken by the great
Robert Capa himself. The woman's gray hair was up in a bun,
with several strands falling loose, and she looked physically shattered. The young man wrapped his arms around her and lovingly
kissed the top of her head. Tania thought this would make a
beautiful photo and approached surreptitiously to try for a better
angle. And that was when she saw the image that had moved
them: a shirtless man, working outside the walls of the castle
at Colliure as a gendarme looked on. His emaciated torso, with
tattered trousers held up only by a cord tied around his waist and
his rope-soled sandals, was the portrait of dignified misery. Sensing the photographer's presence, the man had stopped chipping
at a huge rock and struck an arrogant pose, resting a hand on top
of the sledgehammer, his right foot on the boulder as though it
were a prized animal he'd just shot. He wasn't smiling, but his
face, toasted by the sun, had an almost jovial look, as though
proclaiming: *Look at me; I am not defeated.*

What made the biggest impact, however, was no doubt the
man's one eye. His right eye was covered by a filthy patch, while
the left one stared straight out from beneath a bushy brow.

Tania recognized him instantly. It was the man in her mother's clippings who was dressed in a Soviet uniform and wearing the
same expression on the Leningrad Front.

The old woman and young man had by this time joined
other visitors and were talking excitedly. Tania waited for the
right moment to approach, though she had no idea what she

could possibly say. *Hi, my mother has been collecting everything she can about this man for years.* Finally, she saw an opportunity when the young man—Gonzalo, she now knew—went outside for a smoke.

"Excuse me, I couldn't help noticing how moved you were by that photo."

The woman stared at Tania for some time, looking disconcerted.

"It's my husband. Lieutenant Elías Gil. We were here together in 1939."

"Did he die?"

The woman focused, as though absorbing all the light around her in order to brighten her own darkness, and then faltered. For a second, Tania caught a glimpse of the secret torment that lay beneath her ordinary appearance.

Just at that moment, the young man came back inside. Her son, Tania thought. They looked alike and had the same expression. The woman quickly said goodbye and went to meet him. Tania saw them speak quietly, and for a moment Gonzalo looked searchingly at her. She smiled and walked away.

That very night, sitting at an outdoor café in Perpignan, she wrote to her mother, telling her what had happened. Anna never replied, and when Tania returned to Barcelona months later, her mother refused to shed any light on the situation. That was when solving the mystery became an obsession for Tania.

She began spending time at Flight, trying to wheedle information out of Velichko without asking anything directly, until one day an opportunity presented itself. Her uncle had hung a Robert Capa photo bearing the slogan *¡No pasarán!*—They shall not pass!—behind the bar. It was the perfect excuse to bring up the exhibit at Colliure and the photo of that one-eyed militiaman. Vasili saw it coming and, although he was tempted, tried once more to avoid the topic. But Tania wouldn't give up. And finally, after all those years, old Velichko pulled up a chair and told her.

This was the first time Tania had ever heard of Nazino, and she was horrified. Vasili showed her the original report he had personally compiled and managed to have delivered to Stalin by way of Lenin's wife and José Diaz. It was like something out of a novel, something dreamed up by a writer's sick mind, and yet there were names, dates, statements, and documents proving that all of it was true. Tania's mother and grandmother had lived through that nightmare. And so had Elías Gil. Vasili showed her his testimony, and Tania read it very slowly, taking deep breaths because with each new sentence she felt like she was going to suffocate. She had to stop, take a break, go have a cigarette, and come back. The report was stark and laid everything bare, no beating around the bush.

"So that man killed my grandmother and abandoned my mother in order to survive?"

Velichko didn't correct her but also made her see that, in a way, he had been the one who kept them alive on Nazino. And for years Elías had made sure Anna had everything she needed, searching all over the USSR to find her.

"He was the only reason we got out of the Soviet Union."

Tania insisted she wanted to meet the man, but her uncle set her straight. "He's dead. He died in the summer of 1967."

So Vasili told her, then, about what had happened at the lake on the night of San Juan. He explained why her mother was a friend of Alcázar, the police officer, and why from that day on the three of them swore they would never again speak of Elías Gil. Her uncle had broken his promise now, he said, only because he owed it to Elías, and because as the oldest of the three he'd be dead soon (although ten years later, he was still running Bar Flight as best he could). Still, he made Tania swear that until the day he died, she would breathe not a word of it. After he was gone, she could do as she liked.

Tania promised, and although she kept her word, she never abandoned her investigation, never stopped trying to find out what she could about that man and his story.

The realities of her everyday existence—constant travel, photo exhibits, and her complicated love life—kept her from getting too close to the past Anna wanted to keep hidden. And Tania didn't tell her mother that in 1994 she traveled to the miserable island of Nazino, where all that survived as a reminder of what had occurred there was a simple rusted metal cross bearing an enigmatic inscription: AS PROOF OF THE HORROR, FOR THOSE WHO DISBELIEVE.

The town of Nazino was on the opposite shore, and Tania got someone to take her over on a small boat. The beach was swampy, inhabited only by black clouds of insects. There was almost no vegetation. When she asked the ferryman about what had happened there, he simply shrugged. "Things from the past."

Tania shot two rolls of film on that trip and kept them under lock and key. Though it was hard to keep her promise, she couldn't betray Uncle Velichko. Until he died, she would show the photos to no one.

But in October 2001, everything changed. More than ten years had passed since Velichko's confession. Tania was sitting watching TV when the news came on. They were talking about the murder of a suspected Russian mafia boss. The theory was that it had been payback, carried out by a female deputy inspector whose son had been killed by the crime boss. A gruesome story, too complicated for its thirty-second slot, and Tania would have paid no more attention had it not been for the fact that the next thing to fill her screen was Alcázar, her mother's friend, the one who had been put in charge of the investigation. This caught her attention and she turned up the volume to hear him explain. The deputy inspector's name was Laura Gil, daughter of a well-known Communist who became famous in the fifties among those exiled in France and then disappeared under strange circumstances in 1967.

Tania raced downstairs as fast as she could and found her mother behind the counter, watching the same channel on a small

TV. Visibly distressed, she lifted her chin and looked up at her daughter.

"I suppose it's time for us to talk," she whispered.

Why hadn't she listened to her mother? Why had she risked approaching Gonzalo, spying on him, following him and finding out everything she could about the man? What was she hoping to accomplish? What was she thinking? Maybe at first she'd simply been trying to come to grips with the demons her mother had been fighting since childhood. That man, Elías, was responsible for Anna having fallen into the hands of Igor Stern. In the end, Anna had told her that Velichko's story was true, but incomplete. He'd left out the hell that her mother had lived through after Elías exchanged her life for his own. Tania was furious, recalling the sad yet heroic portrait of him she'd formed that day in Colliure, before she knew that the old woman and her son were worshipping a monster. But as the months passed, something changed, not just for Gonzalo but also for her. There was something she was attracted to that had nothing to do with memory or grievances or the past.

Lying in bed now, alone, she stroked the wrinkled sheets where they'd made love. He'd stared into her eyes the whole time, a dim light glimmering somewhere in the depths of his expression. It was as though he was trying to see right through her, asking her to help him become the man he'd been once more, the man whose flame had not gone out.

Tania curled up and hugged her pillow. It smelled of him, and she thought of the scars and bruises on his body that she'd slowly kissed, one by one. And then, anguished, she remembered Atxaga, beating him in that garage, and the sense of loss she'd felt, the rage in her gut and the urge she'd felt to protect him.

Was it possible? Could she be falling in love with Gonzalo Gil? Or was she just trying to get close to the ghost of his father?

19

Elías Gil hoisted himself up onto a heap of smoking wreckage, to survey the devastation wrought by that bomb that hit the intersection of Balmes and Las Cortes at midday.

It was a nightmarish scene: The projectile dropped by an Italian Savoia had left a blackened crater several yards long, taking out a water main that now shot like a geyser up into the air. Several yards on, a military truck loaded with explosives had caught fire and blown up, leaving only a twisted mass of steel. Grenades were going off and weapons were still being fired, making it impossible to get to the bodies strewn all around. The blast had been colossal, taking out the windows of buildings for several blocks, leaving a sea of broken shards, streetlights had melted as though made of plastic, and trees were either entirely uprooted or stood burning like oversized candles. A bus crowded with passengers had been blown up and caught fire. It was impossible to count the dead, and the wounded moaned and screamed, their cries blending in with the useless blaring of the air raid sirens. Everywhere lay human remains so disfigured they would never be identified.

Air raids of this magnitude had been going on for three days and were no longer confined to the port and industrial areas. Mussolini had given the order for the Savoia SM.79 bomber squads based in Mallorca to concentrate on the civilian population, and Franco had put up no opposition. They were attacking both the center—streets like Entenza, Córcega, and Marina—and heavily populated neighborhoods such as Sagrera, San Gervasio, and San Andrés. Thirteen indiscriminate attacks had now been recorded, at regular intervals. The sight of massacred children at the church of San Felipe Neri, of overturned streetcars full of dead workers, of ships sinking at the docks all had the objective of ramming home the reality of war, to make it palpable to housewives, students, merchants, kids playing outside, people in line at the cinema or walking hand in hand through the gardens of Horta: Defeat was imminent. No one was safe, absolutely no one. And there was nothing that Prime Minister Negrín and his government, currently taking refuge in the city, could do; nothing the International Brigades on the verge of pulling out and abandoning Spain to its fate could do; nothing the columns of the Republican Army, now retreating on all fronts, could do.

The war was lost. All that remained was to see how long the suffering would go on.

There was no longer any point to the official propaganda, to the press releases with their inanely lofty language condemning the attacks and begging for international aid, which in the best of cases went little beyond feeble condemnations on the part of embassies already prepared to negotiate with the rebel government in Burgos.

"The defense service reports that they've taken down two Italian bombers. One fell in Campo de la Bota and the other exploded over the sea."

"Have they recovered the pilots' bodies?"

Elías's assistant was a fiery young man, a member of the workers' CNT who, after the bombing of Guernica in 1937, hadn't hesitated to join the Socialist PSUC and betray his ex-comrades. A baker by profession, he'd found his true calling in the Military Intelligence Service. He specialized in dealing with detainees at the secret prison known as Preventorio D, on Muntaner Street, where the MIS had their command. They called him the Chain, because he had a fondness for using shock collars during interrogations. And he was quite proud of the nickname.

"No. But we took one of the collaborators alive. Found him in a room at Hotel Colón with a portable transmitter and maps of the city, the targets already marked. He's been transferred to La Tamarita."

The man's rabid-dog smile made Elías's skin crawl.

La Tamarita was one of the MIS enclaves in Barcelona. It was located at the intersection of Doctor Andreu Avenue and Císter Street, far from prying eyes. Almost all of the staff there were Soviets, trusted men whom Orlov and Gerö had put in charge before returning to Moscow. The building resembled one of the bourgeois mansions that had sprung up around the city in the early nineteenth century, thanks to the Cuban slave trade and profits brought in from coffee and sugar. The grounds were well kept, with roses, carnations, and jasmine giving an impression of bonhomie that was contradicted on approaching the entrance, where sandbags were piled up around the doors and windows. Despite the fact that he was officially a lieutenant, Elías had never worn a military uniform; his job didn't require it. Nor did he have to show his ID at the checkpoint. Everyone in the MIS had heard about the silent Asturian, tough and efficient, and he was easily enough identified by the black patch over his right eye and the empty look in the left.

The captured fifth columnist had already been put through what they referred to as the Bell. It was a cement box no bigger than a coffin where detainees were often left for hours, obligatorily hunched over in an excruciating position. They were forced to listen to blaring, strident music, shouting, and a constant clanging of bells, which eventually drove them mad. Plenty of other horrors could be found at La Tamarita as well, including an electric chair (the Chain's personal favorite), which emitted shocks to a prisoner's feet, eyelids, anus, and testicles; and the icebox, where prisoners endured repeated freezing showers. Anyone who was taken down into the basement—originally living quarters for the servants—had little chance of making it back out alive, and if they did, there was no doubt they'd left their mental health behind.

The detainee was a young man. He had a wound on one arm and was bleeding from a gash that no one had bothered to treat. They brought him to Elías naked, trembling from cold and fear. Mostly fear. He'd been savagely beaten with a rubber tube and had several of his teeth kicked out. The man could hardly stand, and when the guards holding him up by the armpits let go, he collapsed heavily to the floor.

Elías felt sick at the sight of him, but he focused on the aftermath of the bombing—the mutilated bodies, the cries of the innocents—and his blood boiled. He also fueled the flames of his rage by thinking back to his own detention in Moscow, calling to mind the face of that officer who had gotten him to sign his own confession for a miserable glass of water.

"What do you have to say for yourself?"

The man refused to look him in the face, or perhaps simply didn't have the strength to lift his head. Elías grabbed his greasy hair and jerked the man's head back. Suddenly, from within the mass of pulverized flesh and blood, he caught a glimpse of the man's sheer terror, a light slowly dimming that would soon be extinguished. And in that faint light came recognition.

Elías ordered the man transferred to a cell not used for torture and gave clear instructions that he was not to be harmed.

"Have a doctor look at him and give him some food. When he's recovered, I want to interrogate him myself."

For several minutes after the prisoner was hauled off, Elías Gil stood lost in thought, gazing absently at the trail of blood the man's body had left on the floor.

An SIM car dropped him off at home with orders that he be ready at six the following morning. It was already eleven o'clock at night, and he still had several hours' work to do in his tiny office where People's Tribunal Against Acts of Treason files were piling up. Most of them had no judicial guarantee, and Elías knew it. Still, he sent them off promptly, so that the ministry could approve the sentence of prison or, often, death. It was simply a formality that had to be followed—by the time the ministry's blessing arrived, the executions had frequently already been carried out. How long would this bloodletting go on? It had been only a year since Gerö and Orlov forced him to denounce Consul Antonov, but it seemed another century. That act began an open war on the anarchists, the POUM, and anyone else in Barcelona whom Gerö deemed to be against the "war effort to counter fascism." This provided the excuse they needed to begin eliminating all those opposed to Negrín's Stalinist line.

They'd won. The Communist Party now held every key position in the army and government, but they were ruling over a battlefield of death and charred remains. Given how close Franco's troops were, and in light of the evidence that Barcelona was about to fall, Falangists and their collaborators in the rear guard were springing up everywhere and becoming more audacious. Elías's job was to root them out and exterminate them, but it was impossible to keep up. How much longer would the killing and suffering have to go on before they gave in to the evidence? Where would it end? With the last drop of blood. That was the order from Moscow. With the last drop of blood, which of course came not from the Soviets but from those who day after day were forced to watch the sky turn to flames over their heads.

Esperanza was in bed, lying on her side, head to the wall. She was still recovering from a miscarriage. Elías's eyes rested for a moment on her young body, the blanket silhouetting her hips and thighs.

"Are you asleep?"

Esperanza turned her head and gazed at him with a sort of placid indifference that had set in when she began to hemorrhage. The baby didn't *take hold*, was how the attending physician had put it. And the expression hit them both like a thunderbolt splitting a tree in two. The baby didn't take hold, hadn't wanted to attach to a womb offering the promise of life and preferred instead to let go before growing into anything more than an unfulfilled promise. Elías had seen the five-month-old fetus, which was almost formed, almost a baby. There was a heart, there were lungs, and a tiny purple mouth. Better that way, he thought now. Why be born into a world like this? To end up like the children massacred at San Felipe Neri? All of that effort simply to have a shrieking bomb shatter their illusions and those of their parents?

He'd never said that to Esperanza, nor had he told her that he felt relieved when the midwife wrapped the fetus in a cloth and took it off to who knows where. She'd have scratched out his one good eye with her fingernails, would never have forgiven him. Justifiably. The doctor consoled her, telling her that she was strong and it was the child who had not shown the determination to thrive, that she could have as many children as she wanted or could handle. It was simply a matter of time. But time was ticking away and his little Russian was not recovering. She chose to remain bedridden, holding her belly, which seemed to promise nothing but a barren future.

Elías decided to send her to Moscow. Things in Barcelona were getting worse, and it wouldn't be long before there was a mass exodus and then everything would become more complicated. But there was another reason why he sometimes wanted to send her away. He wasn't convinced that he loved her, nor was he sure he'd done the right thing by marrying her and bringing her to Spain. Elías had believed that her love would be enough for both of them and that in time—always a vague notion that never arrived— Esperanza could make him forget about Nazino, about Irina and Anna, about what he'd done to stay alive. When she laughed and made him laugh, he really thought it could work. Sometimes when they made love, she was so desperate to be his everything, to fill him with the present and leave no room for the past, that it seemed possible. It had worked for the first few months, when the past seemed so far away despite being just around the corner.

When they found out she was pregnant, Elías was afraid. And it had been a new kind of fear, nothing like what he'd felt in Siberia, a fear that pulsed beneath his hand whenever he rested it on Esperanza's growing belly. He became afraid of the future, of the possibility of happiness; he felt like a fraud, someone who had no right to be happy. Esperanza's miscarriage put an end to that fear and confirmed what he already suspected, that he would never be rewarded with peace and tranquility.

So he threw himself into his work, going at it hammer and tongs. His diligence was nothing like the untamed instincts of his bloodthirsty assistants, nor did it at all resemble the robotic incivility of the officials in his service. His fervor was detached, systematic, exhaustive, and implacable. And that was what was so frightening. The interrogations led by Lieutenant Elías Gil—the Cyclops, as people were starting to call him—were infamous in all the clandestine prisons in Madrid and Barcelona. He would pace back and forth, rhythmically flicking open and snapping shut the locket he kept in his pocket. No one knew exactly who the woman and little girl in the photo were, but after staring at them vacantly, he would turn his one vitriolic eye to the detainee. Some said they were his mother and sister, and that they'd been killed in the 1934 Asturias uprising. Others speculated that the woman was a lover, the girl an illegitimate child, but no one knew the truth. Elías never spoke about his past or his life. In fact, he spoke of nothing but the task at hand.

It was at about this time that he began having terrible migraines. The pain bored into his skull like a drill and made his body feel like it was melting. Army specialists confirmed that the optic nerve of the eye he'd lost had never healed properly, despite Irina's poultices and ministrations, and that the agony— intermittent but devastating—would be with him for the rest of his life. When he had one of his attacks, the pain shot up like a ball of fire into his empty socket, as though the missing eye were trying to grow back, desperate to see again. At those moments his hatred for Igor Stern—and in his absence, for whoever was around, including Esperanza—would explode.

She was the preferred target of his rage during those episodes; he'd shout and forbid her from making the slightest noise, force her to remain silent for hours on end, in the dark. He insulted her in Russian, and sometimes violently forced himself on her, as though the wolf in Siberia that had tried to run off with Anna were back. He would rant and rave, smashing everything in his path— furniture, bottles, books…and men and women. And aside from opiates, alcohol—in ever-increasing quantities—was the only thing that could temporarily calm him. It then left him in a state of deep depression, which in wartime was something he could not afford.

After each episode, he would take stock of how much damage he'd done and feel devastated. He'd beg Esperanza to forgive him, and she, downcast yet firmly clinging to her love for him, would promise that she would never leave him or fear him, no matter what.

"It's not you; it's *them*. They're destroying you," she would say, pointing resentfully to the photo of Irina and Anna.

Sometimes Elías would go weeks without coming home, especially after one of his episodes. He felt ashamed, hid in his office at the MIS command center on Muntaner Street, worked himself to death in an attempt to stop thinking. And the dirtier and emptier he felt, the more he avoided Esperanza and the deeper he sank into a pit of self-loathing, which was the one place he felt he deserved to be.

Like many of the men under his command, hardened by the violence and brutality of the job, he sought solace at one of the dives in the Barceloneta quarter, where a blind eye was still turned to prostitution. Elías frequented a place called the Gat Negre, the Black Cat, a clandestine hole-in-the-wall on Sal Street run by a woman Rubens would have adored. She was a Catalan from Lérida getting on in both years and girth but more resembled a Cordoban: long hair, dark skin, and a sharp tongue. A tough lady, she was stern and high-handed when it came to the half dozen girls working for her. Because of the nearby bombings earlier that year, a good part of the neighborhood had been evacuated, but the listless concubines of the Gat Negre refused to budge. They prowled the streets after dark, propositioning potential johns behind sandbags, mounds of rubble, and bombed-out buildings. Like queens of destruction in dusty dresses that had been torn and mended, they flashed dull-skinned thighs and cleavage, refusing to accept the end of days.

Elías didn't go for the sex, or for the booze. The madam of the Gat Negre had something much more valuable for him: information. She was a committed but shrewd old Communist, a woman he himself had recruited for the clandestine information service.

"Men are more likely to confess to a woman in bed than a priest in church," he'd said, doing his best to fake a low-class, streetwise accent. And it was true. After sex, even the toughest men cried like babies in the comfort of sweaty thighs; they'd sell the Republic for a promise of pleasure. Men could not be trusted when between the legs of a woman who knew how to love them, regardless of affiliation, guns, or flags. A man has no allegiance before a naked woman.

This was precisely the reason many of them ended up being hauled straight from the cots at the Gat Negre to prison ships like the *Villa de Madrid* and the *Uruguay*, sometimes literally without enough time to cover their asses.

"Everyone comes *here* for a drink," the matron said, pointing lewdly between her legs. "Italian Fascists, Nazis, Falangists, monarchists, priests, and even anarchists, Communists, and Socialists. They all need to quench their thirst and someone to talk to."

Elías was prepared to tolerate certain things in exchange for the services the madam provided him. Trafficking in morphine and passports, black market ration tickets. He knew she was building up a nest egg that she'd use to head to France if things got worse, which seemed more than likely. He wouldn't stop her, wouldn't accuse her of being a deserter. Everyone did what they had to in order to survive.

"Word on the street is that Uribarri ran off to France with all the cash, and plenty of compromising documentation."

Elías didn't deny it. Until the previous month, Manuel Uribarri had been in charge of the MIS. An old Socialist militia leader, he'd been on the job only three months before making off with a fortune in jewels and cash. The new boss was just a kid, a twenty-two-year-old greenhorn who'd had something to do with Calvo Sotelo's assassination in '36. The politician's death had triggered the Franco uprising. It was an excuse, of course, but the Socialists in La Motorizada, the militia unit, really stuck it to the nationalists.

"What about you? Are you and that precious Russki wife of yours going to jump ship? I bet they've got a stack of medals waiting for you in Moscow."

"Did anyone tell you that defeatism is punishable by firing squad?"

The grand dame was clearly in a touchy-feely mood, perhaps because she'd overdone it on the morphine that night. Her glassy eyes shone wickedly and she'd reached for Elías's crotch a couple of times, which was unlike her; generally the madam did not sleep around.

"What I wouldn't give to lick that black hole," she added, laughing obscenely, one hand reaching for the lieutenant's leather eye patch. Elías gently pulled away her fingers; they must once have pleasured countless men but now all they inspired was a hint of disgust.

"Do you still have those safe-conducts for the rebel zone?"

She flashed him a suspicious look, dubious. On the one hand, she feared a trap. Had she gone too far with the lieutenant? Maybe it was true what they said, that he had no heart because a wolf had ripped it out in Siberia. On the other, she sensed a risky—very risky—opportunity.

"Complete with official seals and stamps. Passports, too: Portuguese, French, British, and American. As you know, the keys I hold can open any door. Why do you ask?"

People like her sprang up all over the world in times of trouble, like poisonous mushrooms after an autumn rain. Scavengers, hyenas, vultures, survivors. People who under normal circumstances would never have excelled (what on earth had she done before the war?) but when chaos hit managed to rig things in their favor. On Nazino, Elías had been one of them, as had Michael and Martin in a way, and Stern.

"They're not for me."

"I never said they were."

"You may not have, but your expression did."

"So are you going to rip my eyes out?"

"Don't tempt me."

He wasn't kidding, that much was clear. So she moved back a little and, although her movements had the telltale languor of drugs, her face paled.

"Tell me what you need."

"Safe-conducts and papers for two adults and a one-year-old child. I'll give you the names and photos to put on the documents."

"When do you need them?"

"Now."

The house on Muntaner Street was better than La Tamarita, but that wasn't saying much. The ground floor, cellar, and garage had all been converted into cells. They were narrow cubicles painted in garish colors, their floors built on a twenty to thirty percent incline—as was the cement bench that doubled as a bed—making it literally impossible to remain standing. In addition, the floors had shards of brick sticking out, and prisoners were forced to remain barefoot. The only place they could stand was right beside the door hatch, where every five minutes a guard's penetrating eye appeared. The cells reeked of filth and excrement; you risked infection simply by breathing there.

For some reason, the fifth columnist arrested at the Hotel Colón was in his cell only thirty minutes before being dragged out and having his hands cuffed behind his back. The guards treated him roughly, but—following orders from the MIS commanding officer—no one laid a hand on him. He'd been given clothes, nothing new but they were reasonably clean. The clothes of a dead man, no doubt, he thought as he buckled a belt far too big for him. A doctor disinfected his wound and stitched him up, efficiently if not courteously. As he did so, the doctor kept musing that this was a pathetic waste of time. After all, he thought blithely, what was the point if the man would simply be thrown into a ditch along the road to Arrabassada that night, a bullet to the head?

Claiming to be prepared to die for the cause was a lie he'd been willing to believe. He knew perfectly well what he risked by joining the rear guard of the Falange cell, sending information to Italian bombers via transmitters they'd obtained in the most roundabout way. Certainly, death was always there, it was a presence. But until now it hadn't seemed like a reality. Death was what happened when a pedestrian was run over by a carriage, a motorcar, or the wheels of a tram. It was always, miraculously, something that happened to someone else. Colleagues of his had been captured by the MIS, but he put that down to the inexperience or stupidity of men who—unlike him—didn't know how to protect themselves.

He was exceedingly cautious, had military training, and his brief experience in the Guardia Civil—which he'd joined in '35, after the Asturias uprising—put him at a distinct advantage. So he'd convinced himself that the inevitable would not occur. Not to him. Until the door of his room at Hotel Colón was kicked down and a furious concierge stood pointing accusatorily. He hadn't even had time to get rid of the transmitter or send a coded message to alert the others. And there were plenty of others, like him, all over—in schools, in neighborhoods, even in the police force. Not much longer, the rebel officers in Burgos told them. Just hold on a little longer.

And now, as he was being led up the stairs, sweating, he couldn't stop thinking about what they might do to him. How long would he be able to withstand the pain and torture before informing on the others? He just hoped it was long enough for them to find safety. But he was going to talk, there was no doubt about it. He simply prayed that the MIS hadn't discovered the farmhouse near Sant Celoni where his wife and son were hiding. He'd taken them there, more than forty kilometers from Barcelona, to keep them from the chaos as well as to keep himself from having to hear his wife's constant accusations. She didn't understand how he could put their lives at risk for an ideal, just as she had never understood why he accepted a post as officer in the Guardia Civil—he, who'd gone to university, who'd studied engineering and could devote his life to building roads and bridges.

Approaching the top step, a spotlight blinding him, and the prisoner wondered if it had really been worth it, but he couldn't find it in himself to insist that it was, not even to himself. He wished he'd never met José Antonio Primo de Rivera at that 1931 rally at Madrid's Royal Palace, wished he hadn't let his friends at university—bourgeois Catholics who had nothing in common with his mining background—seduce him with their smiles, their fancy suits, their ideas about fascism, which they claimed only aspired to make men happy. Men like him. *Country* and *order* were hollow-sounding words now, as hollow as the sound of his own hesitant footsteps, which were taking him to be tortured. He felt his guts clench and prayed to God that he would have the fortitude not to shit his pants and be ridiculed by the guards in addition to everything else they were going to do to him.

Head bent over the file as he stared in horror at the man's real name—Ramón Alcázar Suñer—Elías Gil sat smoking a cigarette, one thumb pressed to his temple, as bluish smoke wafted up to the chipped ceiling. When it seemed the right moment, he looked up and gazed at the man without a word. Finally, he crushed out his cigarette in a green glass ashtray and ordered the guards to leave them alone.

"I didn't know you were married."

The comment, delivered almost cordially, surprised Ramón.

"It says here you have a son."

He made no reply, determined to sit straight although his chin was at his chest and his eyes were glued to the floor.

"Ramón, look at me. Don't you know who I am? It's me, Elías."

Ramón Alcázar, jaw hanging open, searched the man's face, trying to make a connection that struck him as impossible. He turned his head like an owl, unable to believe the evidence before him, which fear and panic had not allowed him see. Ramón's initial shock was followed by a glimmer of hope, the preposterous idea that maybe their childhood friendship could somehow be his lifeline. But immediately he picked up on Elías's cold manner, the way he looked at him with a total lack of curiosity, placid and indifferent, no glimmer of warmth.

"Sit down."

Ramón obeyed, his back slightly hunched, unable to stop staring at his childhood friend. Could this encounter save his life? Ramón doubted it. Maybe Elías would take pity, allow him to avoid torture in exchange for a quick confession that would undoubtedly lead to the scaffold.

"You've changed," he dared to say.

"Haven't we all?"

Slowly Ramón nodded. He could never have imagined this situation in a million years, and yet here he was in the middle of it, unable to close his eyes and wish it away.

"Please don't draw this out longer than necessary, Elías, I'm begging you. I'm not going to talk, just have me shot right away, for old times' sake."

"I heard you joined the Guardia Civil and that your father was with General Fanjul in Madrid."

"That's correct."

Elías frowned. "You should have stayed on your side, Ramón."

"This is where I was needed."

Elías held out a stack of photographs and spread them on the table. The faces of the Balmes bombing victims. All numbered. Men, women, and children who looked in no way human.

"For this?"

Ramón turned his head away, sickened. "It was not my intention to cause those deaths. My battle is with the military."

"What did you think was going to happen when you started dropping five-hundred-kilogram bombs in the middle of a city?"

"That wasn't what I was told. My job was to identify where the anti-aircraft artillery was located, and that's what I did."

"So you bear no responsibility for any of these deaths? Is that what you're trying to tell me?"

"What about *you*? What do you have to say about all the people being executed in your clandestine prisons? Or the nuns murdered in Vallvidrera, the dead bodies piling up every night in the outskirts of Barcelona?"

"I'm not here to compare my conscience with yours. Not every death carries the same weight; some are more justified than others."

"To those who are dead, none of them are justified."

"You have your blame and I have mine. But right now you're the one in that chair and I'm the one behind the desk. Which makes you guilty and me innocent. Tomorrow, or a year from now, it might be the other way around. But that doesn't change what we've done, Ramón."

"I don't remember you being this cynical."

"I'm trying to make sense of how it came to this. We were supposed to live out our lives, build roads and bridges, have families, and grow old surrounded by grandchildren."

"Ideals outrank personal interests; these are the times we live in. We've made our beds. It doesn't really matter whether the choices we made were conscious or we were simply swept away by circumstances."

"Ideals? Tell me this: If you could save your life right now, if I told you I could protect you and your family in exchange for your ideals, would you give them up? Alter them? Think about it before you answer, Ramón. Your death will not be quick, remember; you've seen all the toys we have in the basement, imagine the suffering. And if that's not enough, count the years you'll have lost, the future that won't exist, the things you'll never do with your wife and son. Can your ideals give you that? And whose ideals are they anyway? Those of a few parasitic army officers, dismissive egotistical men lashing out against some perceived affront; those of a few incompetent politicians, demagogues toying with our lives like giants kicking a few tiny insignificant balls, which is all we are to them. Ideals can make you a martyr. But there are already too many of those. No one will remember you. No one."

"Without ideals we're nothing but mercenaries, bodies without a soul, garbage blowing in the wind."

"You haven't answered my question, Ramón."

Ramón Alcázar Suñer thought of his wife and child, huddling terrified in a farmhouse, hidden from sight, not even speaking to the local peasants for fear of being denounced. They would be waiting for him, out of their wits, their nerves shattered. His wife would shout at him, call him reckless, crazy, foolish, would accuse him of being selfish for putting their lives in danger. Ramón would be furious, refuse to acknowledge that his son's whimpering drove him to distraction, that he felt as though the walls were closing in on him; his blood would boil, as he listened to radio dispatches from the front while he sat there doing nothing but hiding. Ideals were simply an excuse; that's all they'd ever been.

He knew enough about the world to realize that if men changed, it was for the worse, that the road to hell was paved with good intentions, and that heroic times were made for cowards looking for a way out of their pathetic lives. God, country, family, and order—they were big ideas, impassioned ideas that weren't worth a bullet to the head. It was all a charade, smoke and mirrors, an obscenity that had swept people into a state of insanity. He knew all of this, and as his wife—nothing stoic about her—said, the only ones he ought to show loyalty to were himself and his family. And yet...ideals were all he had.

"It's too late for us, don't you think? We've come too far, given up too much to admit that we're both wrong. If I have to die, let it be quick. But I will not cooperate."

Elías observed his old friend serenely. Despite his bluster, Ramón was as fragile and defenseless as a little bird. He'd made a bold claim in an attempt to summon the courage he wished for but didn't possess. Elías knew Ramón wouldn't withstand even a single day of torture: The mere mention of where his wife and son were hiding—which Elías had obviously verified—would be enough to make him collapse. Martyrs didn't actually choose to be burned at the stake. They prayed for a miracle, an epiphany, some form of divine intervention that might save them at the last moment. But they all went up in flames, shrieking in pain and shitting themselves. It was only later that their weakness was buried and they were reinvented as shining examples. Very few men faced death with any honor, and even those who did died with a flicker of doubt in their dilated pupils. He thought of Martin and Michael, of Claude, and of the officer on Nazino who'd blown his brains out. Each one of them had made his decision. And the world was not a better place for it. The world didn't even notice.

The ground shook for a moment, causing a few books to fall from their shelves and onto the floor. The windowpanes rattled threateningly but did not shatter. Elías walked over to the window and parted the curtain. A huge column of smoke was rising up from the middle of Entenza Street. Small bursts of flame dotted the sky with little pink clouds, spaced out like defective fireworks. It was anti-aircraft artillery fire, which had no chance of hitting the bomb squads dropping shrapnel nonstop from over fifteen thousand feet. Like a macabre orchestra came the crescendo of helicopter wings, fire truck sirens, and explosions.

From the distance, from that altitude, murder was a simple question of aim. It was like playing a game: Hit a courtyard, blow up a tower flying the Republican flag, target the cages at the zoo. Once, many years ago, Elías had dreamed of being a bomber pilot. Now, seeing the glare of explosions turning Barcelona into a plaything that pilots toyed with, he was glad that he was not. He preferred to see death up close, where he could touch it and smell it, and never forget it.

From the east came two Republican Mosca fighter planes: Polikarpov I-16s. They'd taken off from El Prat Airport. Perhaps the pilots had been trained at the Moscow flight academy; maybe one of them was the man who'd given Caterina his jacket and named her Esperanza. If so, Elías hoped it wasn't the man in the plane that had gone into a tailspin, crashing into the breakwater with a trail of black smoke. He thought, then, that from the roof of their apartment building they had a privileged view over the seafront. Esperanza might have watched the plane fall, seen it spinning out of control. He pictured her hugging her bomber jacket and weeping in silence.

"You're right," he said, turning back to Ramón. "We have to fight for something, and to believe that what we fight for is just, even if so-called justice serves only to cover up our acts. Even if our action is pointless, we still have to do it."

Elías gave Ramón a look that made him shudder, then strode to the door and ordered the guards in.

"Take him down and lock him in solitary. Erase his name from the arrest log."

Ramón knew what this meant. He wasn't going to be tried. They would simply execute him.

Darkness fell, and with it came the horrors of the night. People were rarely killed in the light of day, as though even murderers and executioners were racked by guilt and wanted to hide. Night was the land of the dead, of those who "fell" from rooftops, of agonizing cries in the cellar, shots fired in the alley, and stabbings in a doorway. It was the time for drives along the road to Rovira or Las Aguas, headlights illuminating the embankment where foreheads were pressed to the rock, hands cuffed behind the back.

Night littered the ground with corpses that got picked up the following morning by a truck that took them to the morgue to be tagged and numbered and put on display, a gruesome exhibit viewed by mothers and fathers, sons and daughters who came to find out if they'd won this sickening raffle, clenching their teeth in hopes they had not. And the world filled with disillusionment and revolutionary songs on one side and quiet prayers on the other. But most men simply waited in silence, like Ramón, their brains atrophied as they clung to a ludicrous platitude, believing that it couldn't happen to them. Eyes hooded, sunken, ringed in blue, they were excruciatingly alert to the sound of a floor tile, footsteps, a shadow on the other side of the door, barking an order.

"Out!"

That was when it became imperative to summon all of his strength, to force his legs to move, to clench his sphincter, to keep from sobbing. This was the closest thing to dignity he could hope for—not to embarrass himself at the last minute. To calm the maelstrom of his mind just long enough to formulate a thought for his wife and child. To quickly say *I love you*, murmur *Forgive me*, to whom he did not know; to smile faintly in search of comfort, knowing that he was utterly alone as he crossed the stone court-yard and men turned their gazes away. Guilty, all guilty. Why at night? Why like this, with the guard behaving in a cowardly man-ner despite loud-mouth antics as he shoved Ramón into the wait-ing car? *Give my best regards to Jesus-fucking-Christ your goddamned savior.* The guard, too, was afraid of himself, of his own brutality; Ramón could see it in the way his cigarette trembled between his lips, in the senseless hatred reflected in his eyes. *Soon it will be my turn.* This was what his eyes said.

The car, driven by a young man—judging by the back of his neck—set off down a road Ramón could not identify. Two aides along for the ride had put a hood on him and made him lie facedown on the backseat. So this, too, would be denied him—the sight of one last starry night, the chance to envision a magical place, something that would await him after the trench, up there in the sky above. For him, only the sour-smelling hood and the reek of the cloth seat. And then at some point, one of the guards lit a cigarette and rolled down the window, and there came the smell of pine, of forests far from the city, resin fermenting until spring, night whipping through the fields. It seemed to take forever for the car to stop, although men in such circumstances lose all notion of time. He clung to each minute, aware of each breath he took, each pain in his body, the hood's rough flannel touching his cheeks. This is it, he thought, when they pulled him from the car and ordered him to walk. A shot in the back, his head still covered and hands still tied behind him.

But nothing happened. He heard tires on gravel and was sure that the headlights' glare had been replaced by the milky moon. He listened. Night, silence, a woman's panicked cries nearby. His wife. He felt her frantic hands stroke the hood as though molding his features in clay as she whimpered, kissing him through the cloth. A firm hand removed his handcuffs and Ramón wrenched off his hood and inhaled deeply, desperately, as though surfacing from the bottom of the sea. But there was nothing but a star-filled sky, the silhouette of Montseny mountain in the distance, and the sprinkling of lights that was Sant Celoni village, close to the rail-road tracks. He embraced his wife, who wailed as though unable to believe it was him. Ramón saw his son, standing beside a car whose lights were out though the engine was on. The man holding his hand let go and the boy tottered awkwardly to his father's legs.

Elías Gil lit a cigarette and leaned against the car's hood. The men who would take Ramón to the front line and help him and his family cross were trustworthy—mercenaries, black marketers, bootleggers employed by the Gat Negre's madam. Elías handed him the papers without a word, without even looking at him.

"I'd be quick if I were you," he said then. "You've got a long road ahead of you. And Ramón, one more thing. Don't come back until it's all over. You've done your hero's duty."

He looked at the woman, at the boy who would never know that his father had been willing to sacrifice them both for nothing. They would remember that night as heroic, would recount it to their grandchildren and feel proud of Ramón Alcázar Suñer.

"Why, Elías?"

Elías Gil shrugged, crushed his cigarette beneath his heel, and walked back to the car. All men are forced to make decisions. And every decision has consequences. He knew that only too well.

The memory of Irina and Anna was a reminder of that, each and every day.

20

Leaving the hotel was risky and Siaka knew it, but summer had come to an end and the cruise ship flying the Union Jack would likely be the last one to dock in Barcelona for months. The stream of tourists was too tempting to pass up.

Sitting at an outdoor café across from the dockyard, he watched them file off the ship like rash little ants, marching toward the statue of Columbus and then up the Ramblas. They were comical, almost adorable, with their ridiculous out-of-season hats, their cameras and pale skin, trailing obediently after the guide, who held a closed umbrella aloft in order to be seen. It was kind of funny, the fact that he saw them as foreigners. This was his city, after all, Siaka thought, standing up.

He'd picked an attractive middle-aged blonde who was lagging behind, gazing at buildings. What initially attracted him was the fact that she wasn't snapping photos every five seconds. She chose to actually look at things rather than mindlessly try to capture them.

Good for you, Siaka thought. He liked getting a read on people, seeing things about them that they were unable to see in themselves. This woman, for instance: intelligent but overly sentimental;

easily swayed by appearances and vague promises, by the grandiosity of places she was just passing through; liberal profession, a lawyer maybe, recently divorced; the trip was an effort to get over the trauma of it all, an attempt to expand her horizons and ease the pain that had not fully healed; sexually active, fake smile, obvious effort put into seeming carefree and laid-back.

Perfect.

They parted ways a few hours later, she with a slightly mocking look in her eye. No doubt she knew that Siaka had tried to lift her wallet as she was getting dressed. The woman imagined his face on seeing what was in her purse, the shock he must have gotten. A Scotland Yard badge and a small semiautomatic .22-caliber handgun.

"Relax, I'm on holiday," she said, giving him a kiss on the lips and slipping a bill into his pocket.

He was losing his touch, Siaka thought, watching her head off in a taxi. He hadn't even been able to enjoy the sex, despite the fact that the hotel had been up to his standards. Satin sheets, fine robes, liqueurs and engraved glasses waiting on a silver tray, chintz curtains that matched the baroque furniture. His brain and his dick were at odds, going in opposite directions. Gonzalo's call hung in the air like a bad omen. The lawyer had insisted on meeting him at a bar not far from the hotel. Siaka asked what was going on, but Gonzalo refused to say anything except that he'd discovered that Alcázar worked for the Matryoshka.

Why wasn't he surprised? Inspector Alcázar—ex-inspector, actually—had never struck him as squeaky clean. He'd had his suspicions for a long time, and though Laura never said anything, Siaka had sensed that she no longer trusted him. But he was worried about getting trapped. Lately he was getting paranoid, couldn't shake the feeling that he was being followed and watched, and fear made it impossible to do anything.

Still smarting from his experience with the tourist, Siaka walked into the café-bar where he'd arranged to meet Gonzalo and ordered coffee. He was early.

It was time to rethink his options. He couldn't go on like this, worked up and stressed out all the time, or he'd lose his mind.

I should take off, get out of here, just go.

That was what his instincts kept telling him. *Run, Siaka, run.*

He thought about the attractive Scotland Yard officer. She could have turned him in to hotel security or, worse, taken out that pretty little pistol and shot him. Instead she'd treated him like a naughty little boy she'd chosen to indulge. Yes, he was definitely losing his touch.

Five minutes past the time Gonzalo should have arrived, Siaka began to suspect he wasn't going to show. Had he blown the meeting off or maybe just gotten stuck in traffic? Impatiently, he glanced up at the clock on the wall, still attentive to the customers coming and going. He checked the time again two minutes later, then three, then four; it seemed to stand still. The alarm bells going off in his head rang louder with every second that ticked by; it was unbearable.

From the corner of his eye, Siaka observed a man leaning against the bar reading a sports paper, who seemed to be checking him out. Maybe it was his imagination, but he'd caught the guy staring and then looking away when Siaka caught him—twice. He might have been one of Alcázar's thugs, someone on the Matryoshka's payroll, or just a man killing time, reading a paper and having his coffee. But Siaka wasn't willing to take his chances. Gonzalo was always punctual, and now he was fifteen minutes late. Siaka took a risk and phoned him. Out of range.

Run, Siaka, run, shouted the voice that had kept him alive on so many occasions. *Take that train to Paris.* What the fuck was he thinking, letting himself get caught up in this? Panicking, he couldn't even remember what Laura or Roberto looked like. But they were dead and he was alive. It was time to get out of there if he wanted to keep it that way.

Siaka took a few deep breaths in an attempt to bring down his heart rate, paid with the bill the tourist had given him (as if he was a common prostitute), and kept a furtive eye on the guy at the bar while waiting for his change. He relaxed a bit, the man looked harmless. But you never could tell. Zinoviev had once told him about a kind of spider that's almost invisible and yet injects you with a poison so deadly it can kill within hours.

He walked out and headed for the Metro, turning a few times, feeling he was being followed. But all he saw were passersby, caught up in their own lives.

Man, if you don't relax, your head's going to explode.

And in fact, that's exactly what happened. He felt the impact at the base of his skull while placing a foot on the top step leading down into the Metro station. Intense heat shot up and hit his brain like a fist. Siaka stumbled and fell down the stairs. He felt a crack and knew his tibia had just broken. Despite putting out his hands in an attempt to break the fall, his head hit the edge of the bottom step, which literally cracked his skull.

Reflected in the mirror was an unbearable image, but one that was impossible to erase, even by holding a hand up to cover half of its surface. It was too late. Carlos was still there, lying in bed, forearm under the pillow, looking at her like she was some kind of goddess.

A goddess? Lola closed her eyes so she wouldn't have to keep seeing her own face, lipstick smeared, mascara raccooning her eyes. She hated herself for what she'd done, wanted to rip off her skin to get rid of that smell. Reaching a hand out to the night table, she downed what remained of her whiskey. Nothing changes, she thought, full of self-loathing. The same emptiness, the same realization that it was impossible to become someone else by sleeping with someone else. Just like eighteen years ago, when she found out she was pregnant and knew Gonzalo wasn't the father.

"This didn't happen," she murmured, more to herself although she was looking at him when she said it.

Carlos reached out and stroked her spine. Lola shivered as though his fingers were made of ice.

"Oh, but it did, Lola. I love you. You have to understand. This isn't about sex; I really like you. We could do anything, go anywhere, you and me. Forget the past." He really believed what he was saying. Carlos was willing to erase the tape he'd made, and Lola would never even need to know how close she'd been to her own undoing. All she had to do was turn to him and say yes.

Lola stood, offering her whole body to the mirror: firm breasts, narrow hips, flat stomach, pubic hair still wet—a woman at her peak, fully mature. And yet she felt old and pathetic. She didn't know, and didn't want to know, how she'd let herself be talked into something so stupid. Screwing her son's friend in her own bed, in her own house.

She could try to come up with excuses, say she felt lonely and that the two bottles of wine had dampened her judgment, that that was why she'd let Carlos kiss her in the restaurant parking lot, let his hand reach into her blouse to touch her breast, given in to the fingers that sought their way inside her panties and touched her, an overexcited teenager. Yes, she could say she'd been swept up in the heat of the moment, overcome by the urge to live a little: it struck her every once in a while to remind her she was a hot-blooded woman. There was nothing wrong with it, Lola was an attractive woman and didn't want to miss out on what life had to offer. It was just sex with an attractive young stud who had muscles, a tight ass, and the thrust of a colt trying to prove its worth. A story like any other that she'd save for long winter nights, something to masturbate to when loneliness lay there on the other side of the mattress.

But the truth was quite different. She had been the one to set the whole thing in motion, the one to reach for Carlos's hand, fully aware of what she was doing and feeling no remorse until, when he penetrated her, Lola's glance fell on a photo of her husband and children, a photo from a time when they were happy, when she dreamed that they would be enough, that with her family, life would be complete. The sight of it had forced her to face up to her own failure, to her lies, to the fact that she was tired of all the pretending. Lola was filled with sadness on realizing that the reason it was impossible for her to be happy had nothing to do with a lack of sex, or falling out of love, or remorse over what had happened eighteen years ago. She herself was the problem.

And now Carlos's words, his naïve yet honest desire, made her feel even worse. Run away with a teenage boy? Throw her life overboard? For what? An affair that would last exactly as long as it took for desire to become routine, for the fact that their lives had nothing in common to become apparent, and then she'd grow old alone, embittered over the stupid decisions she'd made that were too late to change. All she wanted was for him to leave, to literally rip the sheets off the bed and stuff them into the washer, and scrub herself in the shower so hard she bled. And forget.

"You have to go. And this won't happen again, ever."

Carlos's face darkened ominously, all expression erased, as though he were a blank canvas to be painted. For a few seconds, he expected to see some tiny flicker of light in her face, a glimmer of hope, of gratitude at least. But all he saw was indifference, remorse, and scorn. Suddenly, looking around Lola's room, it all came clear: the unmade bed, the light filtering in through gauzy curtains, the pictures of her family, souvenirs and mementos of a life he played no part in and never would. The necklaces and bracelets in the jewelry box on the dresser, the rug on the floor where their underwear lay in a heap, the bottle of whiskey and expensive heavy-bottomed glasses. None of it belonged to him and none of it ever would. He was an accident in this picture, an unintentional brushstroke the artist would cover up the moment he walked out the door.

What an idiot he'd been, to think that things could be different with her. He belonged in the shadows, on dark streets, in diseased buildings with hookers and pimps. Anything else was just a dream. A stupid dream, a pipe dream. He saw that now, saw it clearly as he contemplated her body, which had been nothing but a vessel. And it made him tremble with rage. He thought of the small video camera hidden in his clothes; for a few minutes he'd forgotten why it was there. With Lola he had enjoyed the sex, never with her son. And he was glad not to have yielded to the temptation to tell her everything when she, in a fit of passion, had panted into his ear that she loved him.

"Really? Are you sure you want me to go?"

"I've never been more sure of anything in my life."

Carlos sat on the edge of the bed and looked down at the tips of his dirty boots. Love was fine as long as you didn't let it take shape, kept it within the manageable bounds of the abstract. Lola should never have been more than a name to him, one of many on a long and tedious list piling up on his table, a list that included her son Javier. They meant nothing to him, they were simply a means to an end, part of his plan. They meant money. Information, numbers, efficiency, economy. That was what mattered. He'd fallen into the trap of believing it could be different. Fortunately, Lola's expression had sent him crashing into a tangible reality, made him feel in his bones what had until now been a hazy notion, made him hear what had been the distant sound of cries he had ignored by closing the window. Now there was no way around the evidence: He meant nothing to her or those of her class, and he never would.

Carlos thought about showing her the tape, blackmailing her, asking for a serious amount of money in exchange for keeping her infidelity a secret, as he had with Javier. That was the original plan, but now—his mind was racing—it wasn't just a question of money.

Now it was personal. He was going to make this arrogant cow pay dearly for her scorn. He'd teach her a lesson she would never forget.

Carlos dressed slowly, with painstaking care, to make her uncomfortable. He took his time and hid the camera, repressing an urge to glance back at Lola as he walked out.

He knew where to find Javier.

Javier could tell there was something very wrong; he had a sick feeling that he didn't dare put a name to. Maybe it would have been undetectable to others, but he could see it in Carlos's eyes, hear it in his cocky tone, his words seeming to ooze contempt, something that had never been out in the open before, and yet now, for some reason, was on full display.

"What was so urgent? And what are we doing here?"

Carlos was pacing like a caged tiger. He'd told Javier to meet him in an old abandoned warehouse on the outskirts of Barcelona.

"You've never once asked me where I lived, never showed the slightest interest in my family or anything I do when I'm not with you." He sneered, looking down on Javier and the rest of the world, defiant, as though to prove that he'd been through hell and survived, nothing scared him. It was as if whatever inferno he'd lived through had burned away his humanity and transformed him into something else, something superior, and he wanted to show it.

"Welcome to my house."

Javier looked around. There was nothing but filth, trash and, in one corner, a small mattress and a few beat-up old suitcases.

"What's all this about?"

You poor fool, Carlos thought. Like his mother, Javier had made a grave mistake, disparaging him, thinking himself better simply because he'd been more fortunate.

"Surprised? Try not to look so disgusted. Do you ever stop navel-gazing long enough to look around and see what the world is actually like? Let me clue you in: One false step will seal your fate. You've got it all, and suddenly you look down and your hands are empty, you've got nothing. I could have been like you, but my luck ran dry: bad father, drugs, reform school, stupid shit. The thing is, you can do anything to people, put them through the worst hell imaginable, beat them like dogs, and it doesn't matter; they can take it, as long as they don't lose the hope that one day their suffering will come to an end. Without that hope, most people crumble and give up. But a few see the evidence and feel liberated. They've got nothing to lose, so they're not held back by fear."

Even the cruelest of torturers knows that at some point it is time to take pity. He lifted his gaze and swept his eyes across the abandoned warehouse, frighteningly detached.

"I'm one of those."

Carlos snapped his fingers as though having just divulged a secret that Javier had not grasped. Then suddenly he became courteous and self-assured although not overly friendly.

"Come, I want to show you something. Did you know I'm into film? I've always thought of myself as a talented cameraman. Especially when it comes to close-ups," he added, framing Javier's face by holding up thumbs and index fingers. "A world of appearances, it's all make-believe, that's what I like about movies."

"I thought you had something important to tell me," Javier said, starting to feel uneasy.

"I do, but we'll get to that, take it easy." Carlos smiled weirdly. "You know, there are two kinds of reality: the kind that just appears and the kind you create. The first kind is like in your dreams or, worse, your nightmares; it's all jumbled, disconnected, you can't find a way to explain it. That's why we produce it, like a script, we make an adaptation that's always incomplete and almost always a lie if you compare it to what you see. We each invent our own way to tell it, and all people expect is for the same things to be retold, over and over."

"I have no idea what you're talking about, Carlos. Why don't you just tell me what you want?"

Carlos pulled the video camera out of his pocket and held it up. He hit Play and handed it to Javier. The recording had been made right there, in the warehouse.

"What do you see?"

"A rat."

"A rat?"

Javier nodded slowly. "A disgusting, filthy black rat."

"I see something else. I see a little boy lying in bed, frightened at the sound of the rat running around in the drop ceiling above his bedroom. I think it must have been there for a long time, judging by the horrific sounds it made. You could hear it squeaking like a lunatic. I guess even rats lose their minds from loneliness. Then one day the boy's father grabbed a hook and ripped out the wood slats and climbed into the attic. He had a hard time catching that rat, the thing fought back—hissed, jumped, defended itself with teeth and claws. Finally, the boy's father speared it on his hook and slammed it against the floor, over and over... So, that's one kind of reality. A reality that can be replayed over and over, identical each time, it might even be true. But what that reality doesn't convey is the impression it made on that terrified boy, seeing the rat's guts spill out, its tail bang against his father's pants leg, the blood drip onto the tip of his shoe. And it also doesn't describe the drunken look on the father's face, a mix of pride and scorn, when he threw the dead rat into the boy's face, laughing as his son shrieked in terror."

What was Javier supposed to do with all this? What good would it do for him to tell Carlos that when he was a boy he'd been afraid of the rabbits in the hutch at his grandfather Agustín's estate in Cáceres. He was afraid of their eyes, the way they looked at him in hatred, as if they knew they were going to be killed with a karate chop to the neck, and that Javier could never do it on the first try, the way his grandfather had taught him. He was sure that was why they glared at him, gave him the same look that the tortured give the torturer.

Suddenly, with no transition, the film cut from that rat in the abandoned warehouse to a light-filled bedroom. A bedroom Javier recognized perfectly, though he had trouble recognizing the moans since he'd never heard his mother have an orgasm before.

As the images flashed by on the screen, Javier slowly shook his head. It was simply not possible that his mother had done this.

"Turn it off," he murmured as though in a trance. But Carlos didn't turn it off; in fact, he zoomed in. And when Javier tried to look away, Carlos grabbed his neck violently and forced him to watch.

"Here comes the best part, when she tells me she wants it up the ass. Is that some kind of obsession in your family? You all like it from behind? I bet it won't take long for your sister to get a taste for it, too."

Enraged, Javier thrashed away and tried to punch Carlos in the gut, but it was useless. Carlos was too big for him and almost without trying freed himself with a kick to Javier's stomach that sent him flying to the ground. With a look of disappointment, Carlos watched Javier writhe, as though he'd expected something more.

"It's not as easy as getting out of bed in the morning and wiping the mist off the frozen window so you can look at the scenery outside. It's not like that when you're on the inside, is it?" he asked, camera still rolling as he kicked Javier twice in the side, hard. "What a perfect family: the drug addict faggot son, watching his whore of a mother get screwed by her fucking angel. What are you going to do about it, Javier? Huh? What are you going to do?"

Carlos kicked him savagely, taking out all of the rage he'd been holding in for so long, filming all the while.

"Well, I'll tell you what *I'm* going to do: I'm going to send your mother this little gift, along with some lovely photos of you sucking my dick. What do you think? You think she'll like that? What's your boring lawyer father going to think about his ideal family then?"

"Why are you doing this to me?" Javier spluttered, slobber and blood dripping from his mouth.

The almost inaudible question seemed to affect Carlos, and he stopped as though surprised.

He thought back to one Christmas Eve. His father had come home drunk and dropped his sample case in the middle of the hall. He was a sales rep for a multinational: curtains, upholstery, that kind of thing. According to his father's theory, bars were a good place to find customers. And to play slot machines, watch soccer, and drink until you fell down; to stay up all night, meet hookers and hustlers, play illegal poker, and bet on the dog races at Meridiana. That Christmas Eve, his mother had dressed for midnight Mass and was sitting before the TV, hands pressed between her knees, paying no attention to the variety show on the screen.

Carlos had been helping her make traditional coconut cream pastries all evening. When he snuck a little of the dough, she pretended not to notice. His father stumbled into the living room, where the pastries were all arranged on little saucers on the table, decoratively displayed around the nativity scene. With a single smack, he knocked them off, scattering pastries all over the floor. Carlos saw his eyes full of rage, the way he grabbed his mother's shoulders and shook her, as though if he did it hard enough and beat her enough, a different person might emerge. Carlos stepped between them, screaming, asking his father why he was doing that.

His father simply met his gaze and flashed a cruel smile, impervious. He lit a Rex cigarette, blew smoke in Carlos's face, and spat: "'Because I can'...that's what he told me."

The recollection had momentarily distanced him from the present. When he returned, Carlos blinked in surprise.

"Where did you get that?"

Javier was aiming the old pistol at him. His hands shook so badly he had to grip it tightly. He wasn't sure what it was about Carlos's call that had made him decide to bring the gun and had no idea what he planned to do with it. Threaten Carlos, maybe, so that he'd stop trying to get money out of him. Or maybe something more dramatic, commit suicide, or at least pretend he was going to. The bottom line was, Javier was at his wit's end.

"This has to stop, it's got to stop," he whispered, his gaze absent. One eye had already swollen shut and blood was streaming from his nose and mouth, suffocating him.

Carlos narrowed his eyes and aimed the camera at the gun's barrel.

"You don't have the balls."

The shot took them both by surprise.

It was cold. Javier knew this not because he felt it physically but because he could see his own breath as he knelt before Carlos's disfigured face.

Patricia would to come to his bed, as she did every night; Javier would put his arm around her and say, drowsily, "You have to grow up, Patricia. I'm not always going to be here." And she'd fall asleep there, her arm heavy as a stone on his hip. This winter she was joining the school marching band as a majorette. Their mother had been restitching the shiny buttons on her blue jacket, with white embroidery matching her white skirt and patent leather boots. Her moment of glory! She'd spent days and weeks practicing in the mirror, twirling her batons, because Javier had told her that if she really did her best she would be chosen for the first line. The day of tryouts, she dropped the batons while trying to pass them from one hand to the other, but that was the least of it. From the start, Javier had known she'd never make it to the first line and yet didn't have the guts to tell her. Some lies and betrayals still sting, years later.

Javier contemplated Carlos's body, slumped to one side. Innocence can be dreadful; it makes you feel dirty.

He put the gun to his chest and pulled the trigger.

PART THREE

SILENCE

21

Although it hadn't yet started to rain, the sky was ash gray and the rough seas had the same bleak, wintry hue. Waves crashed onto the beach.

The French officer had ordered all of the newly arrived prisoners to gather. The foppish captain in the Mobile Guard was imbued with the vital import of his mission and delivered a fifteen-minute sermon more befitting a parish priest than an army man. Accompanied by a small squadron, the captain advised them to be prudent and show restraint as well as warned them what would happen if they disrupted order or tried to escape. He was, he claimed, open to dialogue but inflexible on matters of discipline inside the camp: Rules were sacred and had to prevail over all circumstances in order to guarantee order. After all, he added, they were civilized, and he hoped that they'd behave as such during their stay in the camp, which he assured them was temporary.

Elías listened to this Robespierre stand-in, exhausted. No prison camp was ever temporary. This camp would remain with the thousands of refugees arriving every day for the rest of their lives. They would never forget it. He and Esperanza had reached

Cerbère with the first waves of exiles in early February, when Franco's troops occupied Catalonia and the Republican Army dissolved like a sugar cube. Thousands of civilians—women, old people, children—along with soldiers who, in many cases, gave up both their uniforms and their weapons, huddled together on the border for weeks, awaiting authorization to cross onto French soil, where they assumed they would be safe.

The Algerian soldiers separated the men from the women and children, which had led to scenes of total desperation and terrible altercations that the *spahis* resolved with their rifle butts. The men—or those tall enough to look like them, even if only twelve or fourteen years old—were to be sent to a provisional camp on the beach. The women and children would be dispersed among various humanitarian centers in the eastern Pyrenees and other nearby camps separated by riverbeds and barbed wire extending miles down the coast.

Elías and Esperanza hardly had time to say goodbye. They saved their words and tried to put all of their feelings into looks that expressed their anguish and uncertainty. He smiled, trying to appear calm. They'd be together again soon. He wasn't going to let the same thing happen twice, there was no way he was going to lose her.

It wasn't far from the border to the fisherman's beach in Argelès. And yet their march had begun far earlier, in December 1938, when evidence of their impending defeat could no longer be ignored. Each of those men and women walked the last few miles coming to terms with the evidence that life as they knew it was over. Random images of their retreat had been etched in their minds: houses abandoned, the furniture all left behind, sheets on the bed, sometimes even breakfast on the table. Land left untilled, tools frantically thrown down in panic, schoolbooks left on desks, chalkboards still bearing the last lesson: "First declension: *rosa, rosae...*"

And the long column of refugees loaded down with chairs, blankets, mattresses—things that would sooner or later be abandoned because they slowed them down and proved useless—walked to the sound of church bells ringing, to the sight of nationalist flags flying, graffiti on walls and banners on occupied town halls: *¡Arriba España! ¡Arriba Fascism!* Images of Franco, of Hitler, of Mussolini accompanied them, mocking, and day and night the Luftwaffe's planes droned overhead, sometimes firing on them or doing low flyovers just for fun, to terrify them and watch them scatter, like a giant stepping on an anthill for sheer amusement. And they, the ants, would pick their way back to the road and slowly resume the horrific procession to the border.

Defeat was this: a conscious, collective, deathly silence, a silence that would remain with them forever more. On the way to France, people abandoned all forms of identification and the roads filled with shredded membership cards and IDs—Communist, Socialist, Catalan, workers, but also birth certificates, national identification, military ID. No longer were they Spanish or Basque or Catalan or Republican. They became instead a superstitious mob, exhausted and frantic, panicked by rumors that were sometimes true but more often sheer nonsense, tales of massacres in the occupied zone, warnings of the proximity of Italian or North African expeditionary forces. And, propelled by their fear, the silent mass grew furious and desperate and quickened their steps to the border, clashing violently with gendarmes. Many—too many—were killed by a foreign bullet or bayonet after believing they were safe.

Elías would have preferred to stay in Spain, to cross the lines and enter Madrid while the city was still an island of resistance inspiring the epic compassion of Europeans and the indifference of their governments. But he could already hear gunfire in the outskirts of Barcelona while organizing the transfer or destruction of thousands of MIS documents, and a brief and bureaucratic telegram arrived from Moscow, leaving no room for debate:

> *You are hereby ordered to travel to the border, acting as one of the people. You are to organize comrades in the Argelès camp, oversee the morale and principles of the Party, and await new orders.*
> *Signed:*
> *Colonel Orlov*

The so-called camp that Elías was transferred to was in fact nothing but several miles of empty coastland, fenced in by barbed wire. During the day, the north winds blew so hard that the flying sand bit into his skin like a plague of mosquitoes. There was nothing but fleas, lice, hunger, scarcity—and the misery they'd brought with them in lieu of luggage. The fence's inside perimeter was patrolled by the 24th Regiment of Senegalese Riflemen, but these soldiers in their red berets, armed with ancient rifles and World War I bayonets, were in no way prepared for the human avalanche that descended upon them. Elías observed them and, as with the guards on Nazino, realized that behind their violence lay fear, dread, and exasperation. They worried about what would happen if these thousands of refugees were to rebel. Who would stop them from spreading across the south of France like a plague of hungry locusts? As he suspected, the Senegalese applied themselves with rage, arrogance, and disgust in an attempt to maintain order.

This being the case, reality did not live up to the prisoners' expectations. They had hoped to be received warmly, like heroes, united with France's Popular Front against the imminent threat of Nazism; instead they'd come to a pigsty and been met with suspicious looks, mistrust, abuse, and hardship. The only thing to partly allay their misery was the solidarity shown by nearby residents in Argelès and surrounding areas, but soon even these well-intentioned locals felt overwhelmed by the unending human tide of exiles rushing in.

In spite of the chaos and the terrible facilities, people quickly began to organize, and something resembling life started to take shape. Initiatives were set up by international aid organizations, and even the French authorities—daunted by the size of the catastrophe—had asked the Red Cross for help. They tried to assist small children, some of whom had been separated from their parents in the mayhem and were reunited with their families. They set up dispensaries, recruiting medical staff from among the prisoners. Those who had been rural elementary school teachers joined forces with university professors and started something resembling a school, where they attempted to teach basic French to peasants who barely spoke Spanish, having used nothing but their native Catalan until that point. They tried to get back to normal, following—to the degree possible—a regular school calendar for the littlest ones. Soon the exiles created associations by affiliation, family, or neighborhood; they organized laborers to build their camp, as they had in Nazino, although here they had tools with which to dig latrines and erect columns and fences, and there were entire drums full of powdered disinfectant whose smell, at certain times of the day, was so overpowering that it became intolerable.

Although political meetings were prohibited, Elías had reached an agreement with other groups, especially those controlled by the CNT, allowing him to hold meetings and organize sit-ins and strikes in order to demand better conditions, and they had a few small victories. The Mobile Guard trucks, for instance, had established the practice of hurling bread at the hungry masses as though they were animals, laughing at the desperate who fought tooth and nail for a moldy loaf. One day, when the trucks rolled in, the people, although famished, turned their backs. No one responded to the guards' imprecations, nor were there crowds pushing or fighting. Amid tense silence, surrounded by thousands of quiet, angry faces, Elías's men—with the help of some well-disciplined Austrian and Yugoslav brigades—demanded that *they*, and not the gendarmes, be put in charge of distribution. Miraculously, the prisoners formed long orderly lines and all calmly received their share. From then on, trucks brought in the bread already cut into hunks, and the distribution was dignified. In addition, they organized a mail system, with friendly residents of Argelès supplying paper and stamps and picking their letters up from the camp.

Within a few weeks, long rows of triangular wooden barracks— the locals referred to them as "Spanish-style"—were visible from the road. Someone with a typically Spanish sense of humor had even tacked up a sign: WELCOME TO ARGELÈS, THE FRENCH COAST'S MOST LUXURIOUS HOTEL, COMPLETE WITH OCEAN VIEWS.

At the same time, however, the fissures that were partially responsible for the defeat of Catalonia quickly emerged there too: As they had in 1937, anarchists clashed with Communists, and POUM Trotskyists with PSUC Stalinists, only now not with gunfire but with subterfuge. They created miniborders within the camp itself, organized exclusionary committees, and launched initiatives that splintered—sometimes torpedoed—their adversaries. These internal struggles exasperated the civilians, who wanted only to be reunited with their families, heal their wounds, regain their strength, and try to forget about the past and future.

The French had just acknowledged the legitimacy of the Burgos government, with General Franco as chief of state. There was no longer a Republic, even if some in the camp continued to defend the government in exile and the Republican tricolor flag outside their barracks. Once a symbol of hope, the tattered flag was now simply an ideal that had been lost forever in the vast majority of people's hearts. So many dreams had been shattered, so many people's eyes opened to the cruel reality, that it was no longer possible to deny the obvious truth—and yet some still tried.

But none of this deterred Elías in the slightest. His orders were clear. He was to defeat their pessimism, round up all the comrades he could find, regroup, and organize them. Needless to say, it all had to be done behind the backs of the military and police forces who were in charge of everything—food, supplies, medicine, and education. He was to salvage what he could, foster the idea that any moment now Europe would be at war, and France would begin taking back Spanish soil with the help of the defeated Republican soldiers. They had to keep their spirits high because their experience would be critical when the time came. This was his primary role and he threw himself into it with renewed vigor, giving talks, circulating from group to group, listening to people, learning, and trying to remain informed about absolutely everything. Within a short time, Elías was in charge of something very similar to the MIS, monitoring the lives and activities of a good percentage of those living in the camp, and doing it with the same detached efficiency he'd shown in Barcelona.

One of his most pressing problems was informers. Rumor had it that there were spies in the camp, Francoist agents pretending to be prisoners, men who went from hut to hut carrying a secret list of key names. If they found a man of interest, a Senegalese guard would appear and lead him from the camp, probably to the border, where he'd be handed over to the Guardia Civil. Elías resolved to put a stop to these undercover agents. Whenever he suspected someone, a group of men found a way to silently drag the man off in the night to one of the hutches on the beach—miniature bunkers that had been dug in the sand and covered with tarps to protect people from the vicious north winds. There, much like in the old clandestine prisons, the subject would be interrogated. It was not uncommon for a body to appear the following morning, washed up with the debris that the tides brought in.

Also requiring Elías's attention was a disgraceful predicament, as problematic as that of the informants. There were men, even among the vanquished, determined to prosper at the expense of others. Thieves, blackmailers, and hustlers of all sorts came out of the woodwork like rats to gnaw at any scrap they could find. In a transit area parallel to the beach they set up a sort of bartering zone, a place where anything could be bought or sold. People called it the Barrio Chino, after the Barcelona neighborhood where similar things went on. They even set up a shop that doubled as a brothel, which the authorities essentially turned a blind eye to. Almost all stolen goods ended up there, and if anyone recognized a watch or piece of jewelry belonging to them, the most they could hope for in exchange for protesting was a black eye. Elías couldn't combat the black marketers, because the gendarmes and Senegalese were the ones who most benefited from their existence—often a single pack of French cigarettes could go for a gold ring—but he did know how to command respect. Every once in a while, he would confiscate something from the Barrio Chino, and anyone who objected too strenuously or tried to confront him would end up with a broken hand or a few amputated fingers. And when that happened, people knew who was responsible and kept quiet, occasionally complicit but more often simply terrified. If anyone affiliated with the Communist Party or the PSUC was robbed, all they had to do was let Elías know.

Within a few months, he had an efficient internal police force of enthusiastic young men who knew of his reputation and admired him with blind enthusiasm; although this made him cringe, it also came in handy. These men were his eyes, his ears, and his enforcers. At times he couldn't help but see the parallels between himself and Igor and his pack, and it made him feel he'd actually become all that he most detested.

· · ·

"**It's not the same**," Esperanza said one night. "Your intentions are completely different."

All along the fence separating the men's camp from the women's were areas patrolled by sympathizers; they cut through the wire, allowing families to spend a few hours together at night. Elías came to these buffer zones to see Esperanza. Paradoxically, their physical separation made him feel closer to her than ever. After spending all day surrounded by nothing but men and filth, he found being with her at night—touching her, making love to her in silence, or simply talking about what they'd do when they got out—the only truly human part of his life.

"My intentions? I was ordered to come here to organize our men, but it's like trying to empty the sea with a pail full of holes. At the end of the day, intentions translate into actions, and mine aren't much different from Stern's: I'm using violence to impose my will."

"The *Party's* will," Esperanza stressed.

Elías sighed in frustration. "The Party, the cause... It's all a form of power, of control. That's what it always comes down to, no matter where you are."

"We're fighting for our dignity, Elías. This is not Nazino, you are not Stern... And I am not Irina."

"How can you be so sure? You weren't there. It makes no difference what language we speak, or where we are, or why we treat one another like dogs. It's the same thing, Esperanza. Beneath it all lies the same hatred, the same disdain for human life, for our equals."

He hadn't forgotten about Irina and Anna, Esperanza knew that. In his pants pocket she'd found the locket containing their photo, now badly damaged by the salt and humidity. Irina's face was fading, and in that Esperanza saw a sign of hope. Fighting the memory of a ghost was exhausting, but Esperanza had an advantage: She had a body, hands, and a heart with which to love and touch Elías, desperate to wipe out that shadow. She embraced her husband, in his military coat, and gazed at his profile in the moonlight. Elías was only twenty-eight, but he looked old and tired. He'd seen so much horror in that time that he had nothing left inside. What had become of his dreams of a better, more just society? Where were the ideals his father had instilled in him from the time he was a boy?

Death, suffering, conspiracies, and power struggles; half of his time spent running away or locked up; fighting like a dog for every ounce of life—all of it had taken its toll. He had nothing left. She had only to look at him to know he was suffering one of his attacks, the terrible headaches and searing pain in his eye that drove him to distraction. Elías had nightmares about Anna and Irina, was plagued by horrific memories of Nazino, of the things he'd done there to survive and the atrocities he'd seen, and all of that blurred with what he was living through now, in Argelès. He couldn't relax, was unable to get the opiates that it took to kill the pain, nor could he lay his hands on enough alcohol to dull it. The only thing that curbed his fits of rage was to head to the sea, find some secluded spot and stay there, hoping his head would not explode. So Esperanza led him by the hand to the shore. There they sat and she held him like a little boy, stroking his hair and rocking him until she felt his breath deepen, his heart slowly return to its normal rhythm.

Elías kissed her fingers. Without her, he would have lost his mind long ago, would have done something stupid just to get himself shot by the guards patrolling the perimeter.

A baker in town who went by the name of Pierre was Elías's contact with Party authorities outside the camp. Pierre—Elías never knew the man's real name—was a member of the French Communist Party and passed Elías all of his orders and instructions. Despite his jovial appearance, typical of Catalans from the north, Elías had no doubt that he was an NKVD agent.

From time to time, Pierre would slip him a piece of paper with a name and date written on it. If the paper was red, the man in question—perhaps a Trotskyist with the POUM, a follower of Andreu Nin, or someone suspected of being a Francoist agent—was to disappear. The war was still being fought, only now in the form of targeted assassination. If the paper was blue, the man was lucky: Elías was to organize his escape. His success rate was astonishing. The camp had become increasingly difficult to get out of: barbed-wire fences two and three layers thick, and internal camp guards as well as outside guards who were much-hated Moors. But Elías always managed to "deliver his package" on the specified date. Sometimes he was rash and other times discreet, biding his time and slowly laying the groundwork, retreating when he feared being caught, advancing when the time was right. But he nearly always managed. Before winter descended on the camp, he had broken out over forty people.

That morning, the slip of paper Pierre handed him was red. When Elías saw the name, he couldn't believe his eyes. Pierre simply shrugged and offered him a Galoises cigarette.

"You know as much as me."

Tristán was a young man full of life. Elías had taken the kid under his wing when he was transferred from the camp at Saint-Cyprien. He still wore his bomber jacket proudly, and had explained to Elías that he'd survived a suicide mission against Franco's air force, over Vilajuïga airstrip. He'd been charged with protecting a convoy transporting works of art from Figueres to Geneva. Tristán's plane was hit in the wing just a few miles from the border, and he'd managed to crash onto French soil. The plane caught fire, and he'd lost his right hand.

"But I'll always be able to say I saved Velásquez's *Las Meninas*," he said proudly, holding up his infected stump. The kid was only seventeen years old.

Tristán was not a liar or a charlatan. There were hundreds of stories like his. Many of them were true, the displays of heroism were countless; but there were also fabrications told by cowards in search of favorable treatment, fantasists, bullshitters, and pathological liars. Not Tristán. He was a good-looking young man, proud and brave, who often snuck past the *spahi* guards and never got caught when areas surrounding the camp were raided in search of fugitives.

Tristán had no intention of escaping. He slipped out at night and returned every morning, smelling of wine and women and often bearing cigarettes and food, gifts from his many girlfriends in exchange for his promise to return. Elías had warned him that it was dangerous, but Tristán shook it off with the lightheartedness of a man who had almost died and now wanted to live life as though each day was his last.

"The only thing I'm sorry about is that I can't perform all my best moves with just one hand." He'd laugh at himself, holding up the stump, and sometimes amid their joking, Elías darkened. Tristán reminded him too much of Claude, which is probably why he was so fond of him.

Elías worried about Tristán, but with all of the other things on his mind and too much on his plate, he hadn't realized what was really going on until one night when one of his men appeared in the hutch as Elías sat staring at the red slip of paper Pierre had given him. Elías knew what it meant, so he put on his old military cape and walked out.

Lighting in the camp was practically nonexistent, and very few people ventured out into the impenetrable northern darkness of the beach. The water pumps broke down regularly, mixing groundwater and salt water with the fresh and causing mass

diarrhea. The sight of men running into the sea with their shorts
pulled down to relieve themselves on this side of the beach was
common and in other circumstances would have been comical.
But no one was in the mood for this. Dysentery, dehydration, and
diarrhea were decimating the camp. At dawn, when the tide came
in, lumps of excrement were returned to the sand as though even
the ocean rejected it. On this particular night, the smell of shit was
slightly attenuated by the sea breeze.

As he approached, Elías saw a semicircle of legs, viciously
kicking a lump on the ground between them. Judging by its stifled cries, muffled by the sound of crashing waves, the lump was
a man.

"Why have you brought him here?"

"He's a pansy. He was taking it up the ass; the other guy
got away."

"For that, you beat him like this?"

His assistant spat, full of scorn. "The guy on top was a guard,
one of the Senegalese bastards that patrols the camp."

Elías involuntarily scowled.

"And it wasn't rape, it was consensual."

He might have felt some sympathy, even compassion, if the
man being beaten had been forced. But the Senegalese were pigs,
and this wasn't the first time. They did it at the women's camp as
well, raping women and men both, although people elected not to
talk about it. But one of his men voluntarily having sex with the
scum that humiliated and abused them daily? This could not be
tolerated. Even from Tristán.

The kid was balled up, naked, covered in blood and sand; he
looked half dead. Elías wanted to scream and kick as well, but he
contained himself. All of them—himself included—had too much
pent-up rage and anger; they had to let it out somehow or they'd
lose their minds.

"Get him up!"

Tristán's head lolled to one side. Elías grabbed his chin and lifted his face to get a better look. The kid looked deranged, mouth open, drool hanging, sand and blood all over. His eyes were vacant, he seemed not to be there. There was not a trace of his once beautiful, carefree face.

"Why?" the young man managed to murmur.

Elías paled and showed him the red paper.

He carried Tristán back to his tent and didn't leave his side for the rest of the night. The boy shivered, refused to turn his face—now a pulpy mass—to Elías, hiding beneath a lice-ridden blanket. Before dawn, his breathing became labored and his wheezing loud, then he started to vomit thick clots of blood. This went on for several hours, and Elías spent the whole time wiping away the blood and pressing a damp towel to Tristán's lips. It took some time for him to realize that Tristán had died in his arms.

Elías held the red slip of paper to the candle flame and watched it burn down to nothing. And then he kept staring for quite some time.

The following morning, the Senegalese guards appeared, among them the sodomite. The man had a superficial knife mark on his neck, which he craned around in search of those who had attacked him the night before. Seeing Tristán's body, the guard looked at it like a piece of trash, something he didn't even recognize. Then he glanced up at Elías and smiled contemptuously.

"Now you'll be my whore."

Elías had not slept, was trembling from weakness, and was distraught. He glanced out of the corner of his eye at Tristán's body now being wrapped in the bloodstained blanket. Elías had been ordered to kill this young man and had no idea why. Maybe for being a snitch, maybe for something else that he'd never find out. But he had carried out his order.

That was the way it was supposed to end, in silence. But slowly he took off his filthy eye patch, exposing the dried-out socket, and glared at the Senegalese guard.

"I am going to cut you into little pieces and scatter your body all over this camp, you fucking piece of shit."

The guard didn't speak Spanish, or perhaps found it convenient not to, as did his companions, who despite being armed were at a disadvantage. Just one false move, no matter how small, and not one of them would get out of that hutch alive. He held Elías's gaze and something in the lieutenant's withered socket made him shiver. There wasn't a battalion of bayonets that could stop this Cyclops from carrying out his threat.

"They could have killed you then and there!" Esperanza reprimanded him in a whisper. Racked by sobs, Elías had told her what happened. It was the first time she had seen him cry like this and her heart clenched, frightened and confused.

"I killed that boy."

"This damned *war* killed him."

But that wasn't true. Elías was the one responsible, as he was for each of the deaths at his hands in Barcelona, as he was for Irina's. There was an excuse for every one of them: the need to survive, the war, his obligation to maintain order and discipline. But the only truth that mattered was that each of those deaths had been his personal decision.

It was a dark night, but slowly the wind pushed the clouds aside and there appeared a pale moon that gave shape to the jumbled shadows. A group of women crouched together furtively, defecating by the sea; they had aged and withered at the camps, robbed of their lives and their dignity. Why? What for? For tomorrow, people said, unshakable in their belief that everything they'd been through meant something. A better future for their children and grandchildren. Maybe so. Maybe he was just one drop in a million, a single drop in the dark sea that hemmed them in; maybe there were millions more all over the world, right now. But at that precise moment, the night was a wretched today and there was no tomorrow.

Two months later, a group of men found a black hand floating in the jetsam. The following day they found a black leg several miles away, in the women's camp, and for the next several days, body parts appeared all over, including at the town church. But no one found the head. Until one morning, when dawn broke blue and luminous with the promise of a beautiful day, and the head appeared on a stake in front of the Senegalese barracks, a sign on his forehead: ALLEZ, ALLEZ, SALOPE!

Like dust settling after a footstep, life and death became routine. With the help of aid organizations in Perpignan, they were able to establish regular—to a point—delivery of basic necessities: food, clothing, toiletries and, what was equally essential to many, mail from Spain and other parts of France. Some received money orders, and they set up a table where Republican money could be exchanged, at exorbitant rates, for French francs. For the first time, the prisoners stopped feeling isolated; they got news of the vehement discussions about their plight, taking place in both the press and public opinion, and this forced the camp authorities to make certain improvements. In several places they opened reception centers, which were run by the Swiss Red Cross, one of which had a maternity ward where women were allowed to remain with their newborns until they were deemed strong enough to return to their regular camp. They installed woefully basic lighting, sturdier barracks, and plumbing and latrines, and although none of it was sufficient for the ninety thousand people living there, all of it made life more bearable.

Little by little, resilience and the ability to adapt to anything replaced the despondency of the first few months. And part of that resilience was silence—a strategy against the evidence of the inevitable. Women walked around deranged, dead babies in their arms, and people looked away; a truck arrived to take the critically ill to the old barracks in Perpignan being used as a hospital, and no one wanted to go, knowing that this was nothing more than a morgue, a place people went to die. What happened to all of those anonymous bodies? They would never know. Some were buried close to their loved ones, others tossed into the sea with weights around their necks, many were put on Port-Vendres hospital boats. The majority, however, simply disappeared, like the clouds of dust that blew over their bonfires.

At the same time, though, babies were being born and thriving; couples were reunited after months of separation, their misfortune forging a stronger bond between them; people fell in love; friendships that would last a lifetime were made. The writers, actors, and musicians did what they could to put on recitals, plays, and concerts, keeping the maddening monotony at bay for hours. And all of it was happening at the same time, mixing together like the sand and sea.

Paradoxically, the better the camp's infrastructure became, the more their hopes of a temporary stay were dashed.

"They're starting to transfer people to other camps. The prefect is an open Fascist and has ordered forced repatriation, especially for women and children, and there are some who are willing to return, accepting Franco's offer of clemency."

"Who can blame them?"

Pierre shrugged. They were each on opposite sides of the fence, being watched by an Algerian guard on horseback who had been bribed with a few francs. Pierre passed Elías a few cigarettes, which he had no place to hide. In late August the heat was insufferable, and men walked around shirtless, in their shorts or underwear.

"I heard they're sending a new one, a police officer coming from Madrid expressly to return half a dozen men to Spain. Your name is on the list," Pierre told him.

"Who is he?"

"I don't know, but he seems more efficient than those they've sent before. You should lie low for a few days."

Elías smiled. Sure, he could hide at the bottom of the sea for a couple of days.

"I'm glad you're taking this so well, but it's not a joke. If you get deported, you know what will await you: a very summary trial and the firing squad. There are people here who would do anything they could to let that Fascist hunt you down. They haven't forgotten about the Senegalese guard."

"I don't know what you're talking about."

On August 23, the world awoke to staggering news, so unsettling it shook the very foundations of Europe. Germany and the Soviet Union had signed a nonaggression pact. A few days later, Germany invaded Poland from the west and the Soviet army from the east. This could mean only one thing: On September 3, France and Great Britain declared war on Germany.

In the camps, the news triggered a large-scale manhunt, an attempt to root out Communist elements and those considered extremists. The French Communist Party was declared illegal. Spanish Communists, tired of fighting the Fascist troops in Spain, were disconcerted by Stalin's signing an alliance with their greatest enemy. Despondent, resigned, they tried to find some sort of logic to what other Republican factions saw only as an act of treason. Elías too was confused but saw Stalin's move as logical. After all, the European powers weren't going to come to the Soviet Union's aid in case of Nazi aggression, so the *vozhd* was simply buying time in order to prepare the country for war, simultaneously creating a buffer zone between the USSR and Germany at the expense of the Poles. Right or wrong, this put no one's soul at rest, not even his comrades'.

Two days after a general mobilization was announced in France, a cadre of gendarmes turned up at Elías's hutch and arrested him. He and several other Communists were taken, heavily escorted, to the camp commander.

Elías was made to wait in the vestibule. Every five minutes the commander's door opened and a gendarme shouted someone else's name. Minutes later, the man in question would emerge, hands cuffed behind his back, face livid. No one said a word. They had orders to remain silent and under no circumstances betray their comrades. Elías, like most of his comrades with military or political responsibilities, was using a false identity, thanks to Pierre. When he heard them call the name Aurelio Gallart, born in Getafe, he looked up in resignation.

The commander was a hardened officer utterly unlike the humdrum captain who had greeted them upon arrival in February. To the right of his table was a stack of files, each with names and fingerprints. They were in Spanish and had been compiled by Franco's police. An officer checked them against those of the gendarmerie, which were less sophisticated.

"Name and date of birth."

"Aurelio Gallart, born in Getafe to Manuela and Ricardo, November 6, 1911."

The commander picked up one of the files on his right.

"According to the Spanish police, your name is Elías Gil Villa, born in Mieres, to Martín and Rocío, May 12, 1912."

The commander scrutinized the photo and compared it to Elías's expressionless face. He had changed—a lot—since the picture was taken, but he had no idea how the Spanish police had

gotten it. The photo was from long ago, when he was an engineering student at the university in Madrid, in 1930 or thereabouts.

"Your rank was lieutenant with the MIS, overseeing operations in Barcelona in 1937."

"I have no idea what the MIS is. I'm a mining engineer, and
that's what I did until I was forced to cross the border."

The commander dropped the file onto his desk and interlaced
his pudgy fingers. "We shall see about that."

He jerked his chin at a gendarme, who took Elías to an adjoining office. There he was greeted by dim light and the smell of
mildewed papers and files slowly decomposing.

A man in civilian clothes sat behind a table writing something. The first thing Elías saw was the hat, well made, by his right
elbow. The man looked up, eyes hidden behind thick glasses, and
exchanged glances with the French commander. Then he took in
Elías's rigid features. They stared at each other for a minute.

Elías Gil felt his strength give way. The Francoist officer
before him was Ramón Alcázar Suñer.

He, too, had changed a lot since that night in Sant Celoni.
There was no longer any fear in his expression; it had been replaced
by the cold calculation and grace of a man who has survived and
become powerful. He sported a pencil mustache, very popular at
the time, and wore an elegant gold pin in his silk tie. He'd gained
weight, too, and despite looking older and more tired, he also
looked more robust.

Ramón leaned back in his chair and ran a hand along his carefully slicked-back hair, revealing a large broad forehead. Elías saw
that he'd recognized him right away and knew that images of his
time at the clandestine prison in Barcelona—and his terror thinking he was going to be shot that night in 1938—were flashing
though his mind. Ramón turned his index finger into a gun aimed
it at Elías. He gave the hint of a delicate smile, which neither the
gendarme escorting Elías nor the commander in the other room

could see. A smile just for his childhood friend. Then he stood and strode past Elías without looking at him.

For a few minutes he spoke in hushed tones to the commander. Elías didn't turn, but he could hear the commander's words of shock and surprise, his dissent, and his fist banging on the table. Ramón Alcázar Suñer did not lose his cool.

"I repeat, Commander, that this man is not Elías Gil. I'm sure his identity is as false as that of the others, but he is not the man I came for. What you decide to do with him is of no concern to the government of Spain."

Elías's knees trembled. A knot of tangled emotions rose in his throat, forcing him to breathe through his mouth. Ramón Alcázar returned to his office and shot Elías a quick look of disdain. He took his place behind the desk and began concentrating on what he'd been writing.

"Get this trash out of here," he said, not looking up.

Although disconcerted by the Spanish officer's attitude, the commander refused to cave. He ordered the transfer of Elías to the castle at Colliure, now being used as a jail. While waiting to board the bus, Pierre approached. He'd finagled his way into being the only one allowed to serve bread to the guards, which meant he could come and go without raising suspicions.

Pierre passed Elías, pretending that he was going to talk to one of the guards escorting him.

From the window of the bus, Elías looked out for the last time over the triple fence of Argelès and felt a stab of anguish, thinking of Esperanza. Would she know that he'd been arrested and was being taken to Colliure? Esperanza had agreed to join a women's company of volunteers sent to work in factories and fields to make up for the workforce displaced by the draft. For the past two weeks she had been working at a factory in Le Boulou, under strict surveillance. Would they see each other again? he wondered. How, when, where?

The bus started slowly down a road filled with potholes that a brigade of exiles was covering with gravel. As the bus passed, many stopped working to raise a fist in solidarity. An Algerian mounted guard flashed a cruel smile, revealing his lack of teeth, and drew a finger across his neck, as though slitting a throat. Cold had returned to Argelès, and the north winds buffeted the camp, violently whipping the clothes hanging between refugees' barracks. Children dressed in rags scrabbled in the sand, digging for old cigarette butts. The sea, now off-limits to prisoners, was calm as a funeral shroud.

Elías felt in his jacket pocket for the familiar touch of his locket, the soothing presence of Irina and Anna. And then he felt a tiny piece of paper, folded in half.

It was blue.

22

"Why won't you say anything?"

Gonzalo gazed at Javier through the window. His fingers, pressed to the glass, longed to touch his son but couldn't. Nor could he hear his voice. Javier might never wake up. That was what the doctors who operated on him for six long hours had said. *Never.* The word fell heavy as a tombstone.

"Gonzalo, please, say something, anything. Shout at me, insult me, but don't shut me out."

He could see Lola's hand on his arm but felt nothing—not rage, not pity, not sorrow, not love. Nothing. Never. It was all too definitive. A few hours earlier he'd been sitting before Anna Akhmatova, listening to the old woman's voice in the gloom of the bookstore, a strange voice and a face he couldn't see, leaving him in the dark as to what emotions accompanied them.

"I don't want you seeing my daughter again."

And then a heavy silence, her intentions made clear.

"Excuse me for asking, but why should I listen to you?"

The old woman gestured casually, as though brushing something away as she rose from her chair and came toward the light with an innocent smile.

"Oh, I can think of lots of reasons, though I'm sure some of yours are more convincing. We've all suffered enough already, Gonzalo. No need to break the camel's back, don't you agree?"

She spoke with a forced offhandedness that betrayed a secret hidden in her words, something she apparently thought did not need to be named, something Gonzalo had once known but had chosen to forget.

"I don't understand."

"Of course you do. You understand perfectly."

The easy smile was still there, she looked friendly, and yet when her daughter walked in, Anna's determination hardened. Tania had heard them talking and come downstairs in bare feet, wearing only a shirt that barely covered her. She approached Gonzalo so silently that he didn't realize she was there until Anna looked up and fell silent. Tania stroked the back of his neck in passing, a gesture intended to make her presence known and reassure him.

"It's getting light, you should go."

Gonzalo picked up on the silent battle being waged between mother and daughter, each challenging the other to a fight, measuring the other's strength, uncertain who would win. He knew that he was the cause of this tension but didn't understand why. Yet it was clear that he was somehow infringing, violating something private that belonged to them alone, and so he left, with an awkward goodbye, unsure how to behave.

He was walking down the street, just passing by the lowered shutters of Flight, when his phone rang. It was Lola, her number flashing on the screen like an accusation. Gonzalo felt slightly dirty, and slightly petty, and slightly vile. Enough that he let the phone ring without picking up.

He should have picked up. Maybe he could have done something. It was a pathetic, illusory thought, but it later struck him. The desperate message Lola had left on the machine at his apartment left no room for deliberation. She was in the emergency room at Valle de Hebrón hospital. Javier had shot himself in the chest.

The details came out in the hours that followed, as his son was being operated on. It was life and death. His son. Suddenly that was the one certainty in his life: Javier was his son. He realized this as Lola confessed the truth, before the police arrived. Gonzalo listened without a sound, without moving a muscle on his stony face, but inside he felt he was being hacksawed to pieces, muscles torn from bone. As Lola's tears fell onto the hospital cafeteria table, he contemplated her painted fingernails, her hand still wearing the wedding ring, her fine gold bracelets, her pale knobby knuckles, and all he could think was that she was responsible for this, that it was her hands that had held the gun and pulled the trigger, firing at his son's heart. The bullet had been unpredictable, chosen not to find the way to its target, or perhaps Javier had wavered at the last second and that momentary hesitation had caused the bullet to lodge slightly to the right of his heart, leaving a minuscule chance for survival that the surgeons were now fighting for.

Patricia was the one who clued him in on the rest. Gonzalo told her that Javier had had an accident but that he'd get better. He clung to that belief so hard, willing it to be true, but Patricia sensed something. She'd always been too clever for her age, so much so that it scared people. Her eyes shot wide open, as wide as her mouth, it was as though she was screaming silently. When Gonzalo tried to hold her, she scrambled away and ran upstairs. Five minutes later, she came down with some photos. She wasn't crying, but her whole body shook.

"This is why, isn't it?"

Gonzalo glanced through the pictures of his naked son, kissing Lola's young lover and smiling. Naïve, reckless, he'd agreed to a painfully explicit photo session. Patricia told her father she'd known about the pictures for months, that she'd seen Javier look at them and "do that thing," and then cry inconsolably afterward.

Lola refused to look at them; she was hysterical, in a complete frenzy. Some of the photos had been torn up and then taped back together, testimony to the conflicting emotions Javier had been wrestling with in silence all that time. Gonzalo remembered being in the hospital after Atxaga's attack, what his son had said, and it all made sense. The way his sentences trailed off, his expression, his general mistrust—they were all cries for help, silent voices begging for some understanding. And Gonzalo had not heard them.

It was he, and not Lola, who had bought the revolver; he was the one who'd treated his son with undeserved scorn, the one who refused to see the signs, the one who hadn't realized that the wall of silence erected was becoming insurmountable. What right did he have to blame his wife? Hadn't he just done the same thing with Tania a few hours earlier? Did their individual reasons really matter? Did their excuses make any difference at all?

"I didn't know. My God, if only I had known!" Lola sobbed, curled into a ball on the bedroom floor, stifling her cries in a pillow so that Patricia wouldn't hear. Shattered, her eyes implored Gonzalo to believe her, and Gonzalo looked without seeing, without hearing, like when he took off his glasses and the world of appearances disappeared, leaving only hazy, indistinct outlines.

He sat next to her on the floor and mechanically encircled her in his arms. Slowly, Lola's stomach seized again and again, over and over, desperation catching in her throat, but no tears soothed her. Only the nausea that precedes a sense of total emptiness.

The old wolf at Ciutadella Zoo studied Gonzalo with indifference. He prowled his enclosure and at least once got close enough to the moat to show his decaying yellow fangs. The animal seemed to be wondering why this man kept coming, week after week, to sit behind the dirty partition and watch him with such focused attention. *Can't you see? This is what I am. Just go, leave me alone.*

But Gonzalo was still there, smoking one cigarette after another, wanting to confide things only this soulless old beast could understand.

"If I jumped over this partition, you wouldn't even attack, would you? You'd just sniff me and decide I wasn't worth wasting your energy. I bet you wouldn't even try to escape if I opened the gate. You don't care about anything outside your enclosure, not anymore. And you know what's funny? I wanted to be like you until I saw you like this. It wasn't actually you I was seeing, it was me. A wild wolf, not tied down. So stupid. This is what we become: broken, tamed, domesticated; we accept our lot in life. I wish I'd realized in time. This is insane. I'm not a wolf, I'm not Laura, I'm not my father. I'm not even the man my mother wants to believe I am."

The wolf shook his head, slowly circled his enclosure, sniffed his own shit, and then hid from Gonzalo behind some bushes. Through the branches, Gonzalo could see his honey-colored eyes and pink tongue, panting.

"This is what we do—hide, try to become invisible. We step lightly; it's called emotional economy. I have to accept it, and you seem to have managed. How? How do you learn to be so resigned?"

"It's called pragmatism, though some call it brains or adaptability."

Gonzalo would have liked to think it was the bored wolf that had finally spoken, in an attempt to rid himself of this annoying human and his depressing observations. But it wasn't the wolf. Or at least not the one in the cage, Gonzalo thought, turning to the right to see Alcázar.

"Strange place for us to meet," said the ex-inspector.

Strange? Why? Weren't they both caged monsters? They were in their element here. This was as fitting as meeting in a prison cell, which is what his son was looking at if—as the doctors said after a week in observation—he fully recovered from the coma and his postop continued to progress.

Alcázar sat beside him and looked around glumly.

"This place has changed a lot since the days my father used to bring me, when I was a kid. I remember the second you came in through the gate, the whole zoo smelled like animals. I loved that smell."

Gonzalo had to admire how effortlessly hypocrisy came to Alcázar. Luisa had put together a file on the ex-inspector; Gonzalo had read it.

"Your father used to bring you here?"

"He sure did."

Sitting there evoking memories, eating lupine beans from a paper cone like a nostalgic old man—charming, the world of appearances. It was amazing. No one would have guessed that this mild-mannered grandfatherly man with a mustache that wriggled like a caterpillar was a killer who'd threatened to harm Patricia if Gonzalo went against his wishes.

"So was that before or after throwing detainees from the police station window? How did it work? Did he sign police reports sentencing men to death first and then, to unwind, turn into a normal father?"

Alcázar took the blow without batting an eyelid. He was used to the uncomfortable way half-truths sat with half-lies, the midpoint between what people knew and what they thought they knew. It had taken him years to understand why his father insisted on protecting Elías to the end but was merciless with others just like him. Nor did Alcázar understand why, that night in 1967 when he called his father to ask what he should do with Gil's body, his father told him not to move and showed up at the lake an hour later—in the middle of the night—to say he'd take care of everything. Elías was still breathing despite the open wound on his back, and Ramón sat beside him and stroked his face, already starting to pale. Elías whispered something, and Ramón had to put his ear so close that it got covered in blood.

And then Ramón looked up at his son and asked where the Russian was. Alcázar had made her wait in the car. *Get her*, his father ordered. And to Anna Akhmatova, *He wants to talk to you.* Ramón moved off to give them some privacy after asking his son for a handkerchief to wipe the blood from Elías's face. *You need to leave*, Alcázar's father told him, *and don't tell anyone about this. I'll deal with it.*

It wasn't until his father was on his deathbed, a few years later, that Alcázar found out the truth. Ramón Alcázar Suñer had saved Elías's life in Argelès, and then several more times in subsequent years. He did it because Elías was his friend, but also because it was thanks to Elías that he—Alberto Alcázar—had grown up with a father. If Elías had not made the decision to be a man and not a Party member, on that night in 1938, everything about their lives would have been radically different. Gonzalo didn't know this. But Laura did. She knew the truth. And the truth would die when the last person who'd lived it did.

This was something he accepted with forbearance; he had to put aside his reticence and be the keeper of these shades of gray. Because the truth is never straightforward. In his personal opinion, Elías Gil was a bastard. But history, and his own father, had decided to make him into a hero.

"You shouldn't be so quick to pass judgment on what you don't know," was all he said in reply.

"I know what I know."

Alcázar spread his hands in resignation. "In that case, you know nothing."

"I don't want my family suffering anymore."

"I understand, and I know what you think. It's not like I enjoyed having to get your daughter involved in this."

He seemed sincere. Gonzalo wondered what Alcázar was capable of, how far he would be willing to go.

"Would you actually hurt her? A girl not yet ten years old?"

Alcázar gave him a look that said, *Blow out this candle before you start a huge fire.* It was hard to gauge his true feelings.

"You lied to my sister all these years. She trusted you, put herself at your mercy, and you betrayed her."

The ex-inspector examined the inside of his little cone, spat out a desiccated lupine, and tossed the paper cone into the trash. His mustache wormed along as he ran his tongue across his top teeth. Alcázar didn't want to get into this. Gonzalo was both right and wrong. But he really didn't care what the man thought about his relationship with Laura or his involvement in what happened to Roberto. There were already too many judges. And at least Gonzalo's low opinion of him gave him the freedom to act in a way that would live up to expectations.

"Look, you called me and here I am. Are you going to tell me who Laura's informer was or not?"

Gonzalo still acted as uncertain as the day Alcázar first met him. Still had the same evasive look, the timid way of avoiding dealing with things head-on, even now. Alcázar decided to give him an incentive.

"Atxaga is still out there, Gonzalo. I can call my men off, have them stop guarding your house, stop looking for him myself. And if I do, whatever happens will not be my responsibility."

Gonzalo gave Alcázar a sideways look that said this hesitation was not due to cowardice and that he found blackmail as repugnant as the ex-inspector's very presence. His eyes told Alcázar not to underestimate him or mistake prudence for something else. He might be like that old wolf, but he still had teeth and knew how to use them.

"I'll forget about the Matryoshka, I'll forget about Laura. I'll sell the house, do whatever it takes, let the old man fuck me over for the rest of my life if that's what he wants. But you have to get my family out of this."

"A man is dead, Gonzalo. It's not that easy."

"My son cannot go to jail, and Lola can't be implicated in any way. I don't want anyone pointing their fingers at Patricia when she walks down the street. You were chief inspector, there must be plenty of people who owe you favors. Call them in."

"Your father-in-law is on his way back. He'll be here in a couple of days and he's been apprised of the situation. He knows how to handle these kinds of things."

Gonzalo laughed disparagingly, teeth clenched.

"My father-in-law is the one who got me into this mess. The best I can hope for is that his plane crashes."

"Maybe, but he's one of the best criminal attorneys in the country. Your son killed a man, the evidence is irrefutable. The way I see it, the old man is the only one who could possibly save him. He'll get a lesser sentence, maybe three years in a juvenile detention center."

Gonzalo was prepared to give everything up, as long as in return he got the one assurance that Alcázar could give him. Agustín might be the finest scammer in the land, his influence might be enough to get a not-guilty verdict for Javier. But that wasn't what Gonzalo was talking about. He wanted none of it to come out in public, and there was only one way to ensure that.

"You misunderstand me, Inspector." When had he gotten the nerve to talk down to Alcázar, to give him threatening looks? "Change the proof or make it disappear. My son is not going to jail, not for a single day. Understood?"

"You're a lawyer, you know what you're asking is impossible. It's gone too far."

"I'll give you the name of Laura's informer, I'll refuse to testify against you and Agustín. I'll leave you in peace. In exchange for my son's freedom. And if you say no, then nothing will stop me—not your threats and not those of your Russian buddies."

"What about the laptop?"

"I don't know who has it, but that doesn't matter. If I don't give the prosecutor the information, it's as though it never existed. Besides, it wouldn't be valid without Siaka's testimony anyway."

Gonzalo realized he'd slipped up the second he spoke. And the dark glimmer in Alcázar's eyes told him how critical an error it was.

"The fucking African kid? Zinoviev's lapdog is Deep Throat?" Alcázar shook his head, almost amused, and smacked his forehead. He should have known from the start. It made sense.

"What are you going to do? Are you going to kill him?"

Alcázar didn't rule out the idea; in fact, it would be the most convenient solution. And if he didn't do it himself, someone in the organization would. Anna had warned him. It had all gone too far, perhaps past the point of no return. But Alcázar had his own plans.

"I told you once already, Gonzalo. I've done things any man would regret, but I'm not a killer. Where is he?"

"I haven't heard from him in days. We were supposed to meet at a café, but the waiter told me he left ten minutes before I got there. By now he's probably gone forever."

Neither of them believed that. Siaka was not the type to be scared of taking the next step.

The ex-inspector stood and observed the wolf's enclosure. There was no sign of the animal, but he was there, crouching in the bushes, waiting.

"I'll see what can be done about Javier. Meanwhile, I'm afraid I have to ask you something else. I can't force you, and the truth is it shouldn't even matter to me, but you should stop seeing Tania Akhmatova. It's none of my business who you cheat on your wife with, but it's good advice—especially if you want to leave all this behind."

Gonzalo stared at him in shock. "How do you even know about Tania?"

Alcázar shook out a cigarette and buried the filter under his furry upper lip.

"Why don't you ask her that, the next time you see her. Or better yet, ask her mother."

Whoever lived in this house gave no attention to detail. That was the first thing that occurred to Siaka. Over time he'd developed a taste for the flamboyant style of the rich, whose parties he'd attended on Zinoviev's arm. He liked ornate furniture, heavy curtains, gold-leaf crown molding, and fine china. The more garish, the more luxurious—in his mind that was the aesthetics of power. Despite Siaka's situation, displeasure at his surroundings was the first thing that registered.

The room had high, pitched ceilings, swanky exposed concrete beams, and sweeping curtainless windows that overlooked the sea. Approaching the window, he found it conveniently locked from the outside. An iroko wood deck jutted out several meters over the cliff. On the right was a large sunshade, its canvas down, and wicker furniture with thick colorful cushions. Siaka retraced his steps and tried to open to door. It was locked, too.

"What a lovely cell."

The smooth walls were entirely bare; the only furniture, minimalist. A glass table with steel legs on which sat a bowl of fruit and a tray of food. Perspex chairs matched the seeming transparency of the whole room: blindingly white, almost evanescent. A beautiful cell indeed.

His head still hurt. He touched the swollen nape of his neck and felt two tiny marks, hardly bigger than mosquito bites. A stun gun, that must have been what took him out. He had a thick bandage on his head and put a hand to it, remembering that before losing consciousness he had cracked it on a step at the entrance to the Metro. Aside from that, he seemed in fairly good shape.

But they haven't even started, Siaka thought.

He had little doubt as to why he was there but still felt upset at the décor—it was too modern for the likes of the Matryoshka. Those Eastern European thugs with their dirty wars weren't so considerate. They chose dank cellars and dungeons or abandoned warehouses for their interrogations. Sleaze and squalor were their modus operandi, a backdrop befitting the terror they inflicted. And it would definitely never have occurred to them to leave a tray with poached eggs, multigrain toast, and fresh fruit. They'd have forced him to eat his own shit.

The guy with the newspaper. It must have been him. So his instinct had warned him after all; Siaka simply hadn't listened in time.

He sat on one of the chairs and wondered what would happen now, looking around for a camera. He found it in a high corner, hidden between the joists. Siaka waved.

"I'm ready. We can start whenever you want. And by the way, the eggs need salt."

Two minutes later he heard the door being unlocked. It was him, the guy with the newspaper.

"Who the fuck are you?" Siaka asked, standing, eyes glued to the thick iron rod the man was wielding in his right hand as he approached.

The guy slipped his left hand into a pocket and pulled something out. A salt shaker. "I got your salt."

Siaka's eyes darted back and forth from one hand to the other but didn't manage to dodge the first blow; the iron bar slammed into his side full force.

"You should treat your guests a little better," he said, gasping for breath. He'd doubled over with the blow and was now staring at the tips of the stranger's shiny expensive shoes.

"And you should be less demanding of your host."

The second blow struck him right in the mouth, scattering his teeth like dice across the marble floor. So much for the perfect snake-charmer smile he used on unsuspecting tourists.

Siaka's mind flashed back to the Scotland Yard officer with great tits. He should have taken her .22. It would have come in really handy right now.

Over the next several days, Gonzalo hardly left the hospital. He spent hours behind the glass, gazing at the jumble of tubes and cables and machines keeping his son alive. Javier had regained consciousness, and that meant that beneath those closed eyelids, his mind was working; he was analyzing his surroundings, thinking about what had happened and about the consequences. But he still wasn't ready to deal with it.

"It's best not to upset him," the doctors had said.

Gonzalo respected his privacy, understood better than anyone that Javier needed to be alone for now, but he wasn't going anywhere. He wanted his son to know he was right there by his side, wanted the first thing Javier saw when he finally opened his eyes to be his father's arms, embracing him.

Lola came early in the mornings and sat with Gonzalo, saying nothing. She had an expectant, devoted demeanor. Over the course of those weeks she'd lost the last vestiges of her youth and become an empty shell, someone with no soul and no inner light; it was as though she'd given up. Her hair hung limp, her sunken eyes made her cheekbones jut out sharply, and her nose was permanently red. Despite the sleeping pills the doctor had prescribed, she got almost no rest and hardly ate at all. It was as though she'd shut her body down in order to devote all of her energy to the wait.

Ironically, Gonzalo and Lola seemed almost to bond over the cigarettes they shared, by the door of the hospital cafeteria.

"I sent Patricia to my father's estate in Cáceres until this is all over. I don't want her living through it."

Gonzalo nodded. It was better that way. Lola hadn't asked his opinion. Nor had Agustín. The second his father-in-law landed at the airport, he took charge of the situation. Suddenly nothing was more important than dealing with the murder his grandson had committed. The Matryoshka, the merger between their law firms, the sale of the property, and the whole ACASA project disappeared from his list of priorities in a single stroke.

"We'll take care of it later," he'd said to Gonzalo when he walked into the ICU, after embracing Lola, holding her tighter than Gonzalo had ever seen him do. He didn't want to see Javier, though; he was too shaken. Immediately he began pulling strings, running the game as only he knew how. But this would be the toughest round he'd ever played, the one that required all of his influence, forced him to make threats and beg and persuade and use up all the credit he'd accumulated over the course of forty years in the business.

Gonzalo and his father-in-law detested each other and nothing would ever mend that rift. But right then Gonzalo was grateful to him; it was all in his hands.

Her father's presence and the knowledge that he was taking care of things calmed Lola to a degree, allowing her to focus on her own guilt, which slowly consumed her.

"I didn't even know you smoked."

Lola twisted her lips, folds of loose flesh forming wrinkles at the corner of her mouth. "I quit before I met you. Filthy habit, I thought I'd beaten it."

He was no longer surprised by anything Lola did; she had so many faces. Their lives together had been like a masquerade. At this point, she could have shown him any facet of herself and he'd have accepted it with a shrug.

Her silence and the way she was gazing at the lipstick-stained cigarette filter—so out of character with the woman he thought he knew—were devastating.

"How could you have kept silent about something like that all these years?" she asked him. "You should have told me you'd seen me that day. We'd either have split up or gotten over it, and we wouldn't have wasted all these years, living without really living."

"What about you, Lola? How could you do it?" Maybe he was hoping to hear some kind of confession, glimpse even a smidgen of remorse, or see some impossible contradiction that he would have known how to deal with. But she fell silent and he stopped waiting for her to speak. Back then, he told himself, he'd loved her too much to concede the possibility of splitting up over pride or jealousy or cheating or loyalty. He told himself none of that mattered to him more than she herself did. The truth was, he'd taken on Agustín and he'd won, wresting away the man's own daughter, walking into a Falangist house and flying the Gil family's red flag, a supreme victory that he could not and would not give up. Wasn't that the real reason he pretended not to see what he'd seen? Arrogance, more than love. And when Javier was born and Gonzalo knew deep down that the boy wasn't his, the vague and ill-defined seeds of vengeance were planted in his heart. A desire to use silence as payback for Lola's sin, one that his son had paid the consequences for. It was despicable, *he* was despicable. But there was no sense salting the wound now.

"I suppose it would do no good to tell you that it was a mistake, that I'm sorry—you have no idea how sorry. It's over between us, isn't it?" Lola asked.

"Things are usually over well before the epilogue. It was between you and me a long time ago, but we both refused to see it. Your father will be happy; this is what he's wanted from the start."

"This isn't the end of the story, Gonzalo."

He'd betrayed Siaka and Laura; he'd betrayed himself. He'd
hit rock bottom. Perhaps Javier would recover, maybe the whole
Matryoshka mess would miraculously turn out okay, there was
even a chance Atxaga was out of their lives forever. But nothing
could change the things that had already happened. What was
broken could never be repaired—ever. A shattered vase is never
whole again, even if it's carefully glued and you can't see the cracks.

Gonzalo thought of Tania. Could she be his anchor? No. He
knew that, even before knowing it, even while they were still in bed.

"What are you going to do now?"

"Go back to being the son of Elías Gil. What else can I do?"

Lola crushed out her cigarette, blew smoke out one side of her
mouth, and swore to herself she was going to quit before getting
hooked again. She looked at Gonzalo and felt an incredible surge
of tenderness for him. It wasn't love, though, not anymore.

"You could try being yourself. That would be good."

Tania showed no signs of feeling trapped when Gonzalo asked
how she knew Alcázar and what her mother had been talking
about when she ambushed him on his way out of the bookstore.

They'd made love on the sofa in her studio, but she could tell
right away that Gonzalo wasn't really there, despite the effort he
made to prove that he was. In fact, it was precisely the effort that
gave him away.

She told him the truth. And she did so with detachment, in
an attempt to keep the events, facts, and dates as far as possible
from the sofa where they lay naked, to put a concrete border
between now and the past. She told him about the first time
she'd seen him, with his mother at the exhibit about the Argelès
internment camp, when they were much younger; about the way
the image of Elías Gil always loomed in her mother's silences and
how she'd become obsessed with him; about seeing the news of

Laura's death on TV and that it had been like a fuse, reigniting her interest in that one-eyed man she'd forgotten about for years. She told Gonzalo how she'd found him and begun to follow him, study him, try to understand him, wondering if he too was obsessed with the past that everyone else seemed so determined to bury. It was no coincidence that she was in the parking garage the day Atxaga attacked him, nor was it a coincidence that she'd been out on the balcony with a book of Mayakovsky poems the first time they spoke.

"I knew your story, I knew everything about you, but I felt the need to get closer, to smell you, to hear you. At first it was like a game, a jigsaw puzzle I had to finish, like the photos I take: They have to be perfect down to the last detail before I'm satisfied. You were the focal point in the image that was starting to develop. But I got too close, I slipped into your world without asking permission...And now here you are, with me, naked, on my sofa. And we're talking about this after making love and I know you're thinking I'm full of it. I didn't want this to happen, Gonzalo. But it is what it is."

Gonzalo was completely disconcerted. He couldn't take in the torrent of words streaming out of Tania's mouth, couldn't comprehend the detailed analysis she was giving him as she sat there, cross-legged, pubic hair on display, breasts inches from his face. It was too incongruous.

"Why didn't you tell me from the start? You could have just asked me. You didn't have to invent all this stuff."

"This is not an invention," Tania replied, pointing to their clothes strewn across the floor. "I am not an invention. But it shouldn't have happened. You don't understand, but my mother is right: You and me getting involved is no good for either of us. I was trying to get closer without your noticing, without putting you in danger, but I went too far."

"What kind of danger?"

Tania's head dropped between her shoulders. The wings of her tattoo looked different in the lamplight. They fluttered. She went to find the box of clippings that her mother kept about Elías to show Gonzalo. As he was searching for his glasses, she pulled a sheet up over herself.

"The first time my mother saw your father was in 1941, in Moscow, during the Nazi invasion. She was eleven and your father was almost thirty. Well, that wasn't actually the first time she saw him but it was the first time she has a concrete memory of it. Your father escaped from the military castle in the south of France where he was jailed after the war. He crossed all of Europe to join a platoon of Spanish soldiers, as political commissar."

Gonzalo slowly turned the pages of the album in which Anna had carefully noted all the dates and places the photos were taken: Colliure, 1939 (he recalled having seen that Robert Capa photo at the exhibit near Argelès, with his mother); Warsaw, 1940; Moscow, 1941; Leningrad and Stalingrad, 1942, 1943, 1945... And then suddenly he saw one that predated all the rest. It was from a local Russian paper, some sort of political newsletter from February 1933. Gonzalo's basic Russian was enough for him to read the caption beneath the photo of his smiling father, fist raised, with three other young men all posing before the Kremlin with identical enthusiasm.

The future talent of all of Europe, helping to build the Soviet dream.

"The redhead on the right, between your father and the short bowlegged guy, is my father, Martin. He was British. I never met him. He was almost sixty when I was born. My mother got pregnant the one and only time they were together. Then he disappeared without a word. Martin and your father are the only ones who survived Nazino... well, them and my mother."

Tania told Gonzalo to keep going, to the end of the album.

She pointed to a photo. "That's my grandmother, Irina. The girl in her arms is my mother."

It was the same image as the miniaturized one Gonzalo had in his pocket. Finally, he could reconstruct the cut-off portion of the mysterious woman in the photo, see who the worn name engraved on the back of the locket belonged to. She was a beautiful woman, no doubt, with a proud air that seemed to come not from wealth or ancestry but from some inner quality, a natural force emanating from within. Her eyes (so like Tania's!) and straight nose with a delicate bridge softened her beauty. Dark fleshy lips slightly parted in a tentative half smile that showed just a bit of her teeth. Firm, assured hands with long fingers and blunt nails held, between the folds of her dark skirt, a very young girl with the same defiant stance, strong and self-confident. Though it couldn't compare, the image of that little girl—like a miniature czarina—reminded him of Patricia. An inquisitive look, an uncanny wisdom. He imagined her as a curious, prying, dogmatic child.

"They met on the island of Nazino, in the winter of 1933. I think your father and my grandmother fell in love, but my mother isn't sure. Terrible things happened there, Gonzalo. Things that have nothing to do with you or me."

"What kind of things?"

"I already told you, it's not a good idea for us to stir all this up. It's dangerous for both of us."

"A little late for that."

Tania took the album from him and flipped back to the pages covering the time from the war against the Nazis. At one of them, she stopped.

"See that colonel in the NKVD uniform standing with your father? That's Beria, he became Stalin's right-hand man and the head of the secret police. For years he was your father's direct boss. Now look at this other man, the one behind them dressed like a 1940s American industrialist."

"Who is he?"

Tania closed the album and inhaled deeply.

"*He* is the reason Laura's dead, the source of all your pain, and your family's and mine. For years I was forced to call him 'Grandfather.' Isn't that funny? I never met my real grandfather, but if things had turned out differently on Nazino, it might have been your father. But this is the man who played the role. His name is Igor Stern."

23

Elías turned to the first page and read: *"All happy families are alike; each unhappy family is unhappy in its own way."* What did that mean? At the time, nothing more than words. He closed the book and stroked the green cover: *Anna Karenina*, Tolstoy, stamped in gold letters on the spine. He slid the novel back onto the shelf, between *The Idiot* and *The Mother*. Maybe these books were just part of the décor, like the enormous cubist mural on one wall. If you looked at it from a distance, there appeared to be a medieval warrior on a white battle stallion—the pride of the Polish cavalry, saber drawn; but from up close all you could see were large geometric shapes and splotches of bright paint.

In order to stop the German tanks in 1939, those valiant lancers had charged to their deaths. It must have been a horrific, spine-chilling sight to behold—thousands of steeds snorting, hooves thundering down the battlefield, the horsemen's battle cries ringing out as they charged the thunderous machinery. It was as poignant and dramatic as it was useless. A senseless massacre, thousands of men and animals, their blood spilled, corpses littering the battlefield, and after the onslaught, the Germans had not a scratch. But that wasn't what the painting was about.

On a woven chair lay several official military school bulletins and an issue of *Pravda*. Foreign Ministers Ribbentrop and Molotov exchanged a friendly handshake, but relations between the Germans and the Soviets were no longer as friendly as they had been the previous summer. For the first time, the Soviet press was criticizing German troop mobilization—specifically on the Eastern Front, the invasions of Yugoslavia and Greece. The Treaty of Friendship still prevailed: *If Stalin did it, then the Bolshevik Party did it, so it's all right.* It was certainly surreptitious. While the rest of Europe looked on in shock as France fell in just five weeks, the Soviet Union was annexing the territories in its sphere of influence as per the treaty. But when Elías crossed the Polish border, the air was one of imminent war.

On June 22, 1940, France had signed the armistice. Elías found out about it on a freight train, hidden among piles of cardboard as he was crossing the Low Countries, which had put up no resistance to occupation by the German troops. A Dutchman had shown him a paper with the news story. The Maginot Line—France's impressive defensive fortifications—had proved useless. The Germans simply skirted it, invading through the Ardennes and then cutting north toward the channel, where they'd forced the English and French into a humiliating retreat at Dunkirk. France was lost. Hitler, so fond of dramatic gestures, forced the French to sign the armistice in a rail carriage in Compiègne, the exact place the Germans had signed the armistice in 1918 after losing the Great War. He then ordered the carriage to be blown up.

Occupied France comprised the north and west of the country. Esperanza was still in so-called Free France whose capital was Vichy, in the south, but this did little to calm Elías's fears. Marshal Pétain, the new head of state, was subordinate to the occupation forces, and the French gendarmerie were collaborating openly with the Gestapo. There were rumors of deportations, executions, and mass detentions. And Elías still had no word of his wife. His orders were categorical: He was to report to Moscow without delay—alone. He'd hardly even had time to send her a message via Pierre, in defiance of the order not to disclose to anyone his escape from Colliure. He trusted that she had received it.

Without delay was both an ill-defined and euphemistic measure of time. Although after the fall of France, they'd theoretically entered the *drôle de guerre,* a so-called Phony War, the truth was that troop movements and conflicts were continuous, from the Arctic to Africa, west to east: the Nazi army and air force were spreading like a stain. Elías had been forced to employ endless forms of transportation and changes in both documentation and itinerary, as well as confront unforeseen circumstances and danger in order to reach the Polish border. It had taken him six long months to get to the grandiose building housing provincial headquarters of the NKVD, the new secret police. He'd reported immediately, but was sent to the living quarters occupied by Red Army officers, where he was made to wait three more months with absolutely no explanation. Finally, on a cold January morning in 1941, a driver from the Ministry of the Interior turned up with the order to escort him to NKVD offices.

He'd been waiting in an elegant room for an hour and a half. By the window was a large Italian ceramic vase with floral motif, a portrait of Stalin hanging above it. Why had he been summoned to a place like this? It didn't bode well.

Finally, the officer on duty appeared. He was a commander in the artillery, the Soviet army's preferred wing, and he observed Elías with undisguised mistrust. After looking left and right, finally he seemed satisfied. The man was tall and skinny as an unsteady tree; his arms and fingers waving like branches hatched with tiny blue veins.

Two minutes later a tiny man arrived, dressed in civilian clothing: an elegant, tailored Western-style dark suit. He was balding, with short curly hair only at the crown of his round head; his blue eyes looked kindly and he gazed over the top of his round glasses. The man watched Elías for a few seconds, giving him a friendly, protective look far different from that of the artillery officer. Despite not knowing who he was, Elías had no doubt that he held significant power; it was enough to see the stiffness with which the officer saluted him before exiting the room.

"All in order, Comrade Commissar."

This little man, although he resembled an innocuous midlevel manager, was Lavrenti Pavlovich Beria, commissar general of State Security, better known as commander of the NKVD—the new incarnation of the OGPU. A Georgian, like his idol Stalin, they called him "the peacemaker of Tbilisi" because that was where he rose to fame, purging and murdering those elements hostile to Stalin's ideas. Under his command were the military, state security, customs and border control, prison administration, and forced-labor camps. Additionally, in this current prewar climate, he had an army corps of ground, air, and artillery units. Not only that, but he presided over—and this was the reason Elías was there—all of the espionage and secret police agencies. With the exception of Stalin himself, he was, de facto, the most powerful man in the USSR. And none of this seemed to weigh on him or affect his calm demeanor.

He asked Elías to sit and inquired, in faultless French, about his trip. Beria spoke perfect German as well as English, too. Unfortunately, he apologized, his Spanish left much to be desired. He asked after Elías's wife, and knew not only her real name but everything about her, details that not even Elías himself knew. Additionally, he promised to ensure her safety and assured Elías that they would be reunited at the earliest opportunity. Elías understood that he was being lied to. It would be a long time, perhaps years, before he saw her again.

"I presume you understand the situation."

Elías nodded, adding nothing. This is what he was expected to do. Beria scrutinized him. He was the sort of man adept at finding invisible cracks in the smooth surface of a stone.

"Things have changed a lot since 1934. My predecessors had a different way of seeing things."

This was an indirect apology for what he'd been through on Nazino. In the three months he'd spent in Moscow waiting, Elías had already gotten an idea of the kinds of changes Beria was referring to. The first thing that this new Georgian commissar had done on taking power was to purge the NKVD itself. Yagoda, Berman, and their GULAG thugs were now victims of their own methods. Beria tried to make Elías see it was necessary to change the mind-set of those in the security services. It was no longer about summary executions and indiscriminate arrests like those Elías and thousands of others had suffered in 1933.

"New times require new behavior. We must be pragmatic, observe and understand before we act. Naturally, this does not preclude taking forceful action when necessary."

Naturally. The word was like a knife, slicing open the veil of innocence. Elías had already found Beria's police to be a formidable force, ever-present and striking hard where it hurt their enemies the most. Information and counterespionage were the two areas in the greatest need of restructuring in light of these new times they were living in.

"War with Hitler is now a certainty, no longer a matter for debate," declared this man who could have passed for a librarian or stamp collector. "They will lose, of course." He smiled. "The vastness of our land has always been the ace up our sleeve; the weather, too, has proved to be on our side ever since the Swedish and Napoleonic invasions, but we have to do our part. My guess is that the Germans will attack in spring or early summer. We must delay their advance as long as possible, until winter. Then will come the thaw, and in those conditions their style of war, this so-called blitzkrieg that has shocked the world, will prove useless. We need people well versed in modern warfare and intelligence services. And this is where men like you come in, comrade. Few agents have your experience, and your superiors have enthusiastically praised your work at the MIS and in Argelès. You are disciplined, cold, and efficient. And this is what I'm looking for in men for new service."

Beria stood, thereby concluding their meeting. Elías did the same, waiting for his new boss's final words.

"All men have a heart—an inconvenience, no doubt, but it's inevitable. Perhaps we place our ideals above our emotions, and this is as it must be, but there is no doubt that our sentiments remain, eating away at our determination."

This was a bona fide threat. No clear gestures or ominous expressions, but Beria was warning him.

"I know that you will never forget what happened on Nazino, and I can understand your frustration."

"With all due respect, Comrade Commissar, I believe I have thoroughly demonstrated that my loyalty is beyond reproach."

Beria nodded, unshakable.

"I was told that a Spanish police officer came to see you in Argelès but did not arrest you. Why?"

"He didn't recognize me."

Beria frowned and stroked the arm of the sofa.

"He didn't recognize you … but you recognized him. Ramón Alcázar Suñer is a childhood friend, and he was under your care in Barcelona. Mysteriously, he managed to escape with his wife and child."

Elías paled, which made Beria smile. He liked people to see from the first moment that nothing escaped him. He knew every-thing; this was his secret weapon.

"You organized quite a system in Argelès and many comrades are grateful to you for it; you saved many lives. But I have also heard stories of dismembered Senegalese, of beatings and killings not ordered by the Party. The Tristán business was a grave error, Elías. He worked for us. You knew this, yes?"

Elías's mouth fell open in shock. "I was given a red paper with his name on it. He was collaborating with the guards and—"

"Yes, sleeping with one of them, I know. Pierre and his little red papers...Don't worry, we'll take care of the baker when the time comes. The point is that you made decisions on your own. And this cannot be tolerated under current circumstances. Not anymore."

Elías wondered what would happen next. Maybe they'd forced him to come to Moscow simply to be executed. Maybe that was what Beria had in mind and for some reason couldn't do it.

"What does loyalty mean to you, comrade?" the commissar asked. This was a trick question, one of those dangerous games they liked so much, a chess match in which checkmate equaled a shot to the back of the head.

"It means subordinating personal emotions to the overall cause," Elías said without a pause.

Beria liked his reply, because it was honest. He knew when men were lying; that was his job. But he still had his doubts. That's why he'd come up with a test for this MIS lieutenant whom everyone raved about while overlooking his lack of discipline and contradictory actions. The man would be put to the test before Beria decided what to do with him.

"To the ultimate consequences?"

"To the ultimate consequences."

Beria strode to the telephone on the desk, issued a brief order, and hung up, observing Elías with an innocent smile.

Two minutes later, an elegant young man appeared in the door. He looked like a California industrialist, deeply tanned and smiling from ear to ear, in a bespoke pin-striped suit and ankle boots. His gold cuff links matched both his tie pin and watch. He had the air of a mafia boss on top of his game. And he was.

"Hello there, Elías. That eye patch looks good on you."

Igor Stern hadn't lost one ounce of his arrogance. In fact, it had multiplied exponentially, as had his wealth, by all appearances.

"Looks like we're going to be playing on the same team."

He looked to Beria for some explanation, but the commissar gauged Elías's reaction to this sudden shock before offering any information.

"Comrade Stern is an enthusiastic collaborator with our war effort. His services are very useful to the Red Army, providing us with much-needed supplies that must reach our borders inconspicuously. Comrade Molotov holds him in high regard. Does this in any way affect your loyalty?"

It had been a long time. Igor hadn't realized how quickly life had changed since the night his cell door opened in 1935 and he saw a pair of muddy boots and a military cape dripping rain onto the concrete floor. Someone shone a flashlight directly into his face.

"On your feet."

He was sure he was going to be executed; this time it was really going to happen. It had been over a year since he fled Nazino, and eight months since he finally found Elías and his gang on the run. Igor regretted the favor he'd done Elías by letting him live. It was a sign of weakness he came to lament, like not making certain that Martin, along with his lover boy Michael, was definitely dead. He'd been too cocky, too euphoric about having won: Elías's coat lay smoldering in the fire, and Anna, the little girl, was in his possession.

He should have carried out his threat, should have let his men rape her and then dismember her body. But he hadn't, and that, too, he would come to regret. Because when the patrol stopped him near the Urals, there was evidence against him. The redhead had testified against him after recovering; he told them everything that had happened—the cannibalism, the reign of terror that Igor had commanded. The only thing to be said in Martin's favor was that he'd neither exaggerated nor glossed over anything. Igor was convicted in court and sentenced to death, and they took Anna from him.

So there he was on that night in 1935 yet again, prepared to laugh in the face of death, when the door to his cell opened and a small man in military uniform appeared. He was led through the domed foyer and through an open side door onto the prison yard. The man in the cape pointed to a series of walkways and sheds to the west. The prison gates were open.

"We'll be in touch, comrade," he said, shouting to be heard above the roaring deluge that had flooded the clay yard, rain pinging off the metallic roof with such force it sounded like an army of tin drums. Igor looked up at the perimeter wall and guard post on the far side of the prison yard. Either intentionally or by coincidence, the guard was staring off in the opposite direction.

"What does this mean?" Igor asked mistrustfully.

"It means that, from now on, you will be the perfect Soviet. And you'd better be quick. Doors that open are also prone to close."

Igor knew all sorts of men and none of them frightened him. But something about this man's smile, his glasses drenched in rain, made him shudder.

He crossed the prison yard and walked out onto the road, boots getting soaked in the puddles, heart pounding as he wondered if the guard would shoot him.

He didn't.

Igor was free for almost an entire year. He could go wherever he wanted, steal, rape, and kill. Every time he was almost caught, someone loosened the rope around his neck. And he knew who it was, and knew that sooner or later he'd be called in to pay off his debt. It happened one night at a police station near Leningrad. This time he'd done nothing to be arrested for; the police came in search of him and presented him to the same man, Beria.

"You've had your fun. Now it's time to work."

Igor started out as part of a small network of informers and whistle-blowers under Beria's command. Normally he dealt with Beria's assistant—Vladimir Dekanozov, a man with a sinister sense of humor who disliked the sort of lowlifes with whom Igor felt right at home—but occasionally it was Beria himself.

Over time, Igor was given more responsibilities, and two years later his moment arrived. The deal was simple: Igor would be given carte blanche to organize a smuggling ring; they could bring in whatever illegal imports they wanted provided that a substantial portion of profits went to the NKVD coffers (that is, to Dekanozov and Beria's coffers). Whenever it was required of him, he was to bring in other types of merchandise, hidden in with his regular contraband: heavy weaponry, prototypes of German airplane engines, minerals like wolfram, experimental explosives. Sometimes he was to provide cover for NKVD agents, passing them off as members of his mafia crew, transporting them to Poland, Finland, France, England, or Germany. Other times he was ordered to act as an operative himself, infiltrating autonomous criminal networks in order to obtain information about people's vices—politicians, influential military officers, or other VIPs in foreign countries. Beria's men then used this to blackmail them for much more valuable information.

Igor enjoyed playing these games of chance; they made him feel alive, intense, always on the edge of a precipice. He was fully aware of the fact that Beria would get rid of him the moment he was no longer useful. So his job during those years was to ensure, at all costs, that he was necessary. After the Great Terror that did away with Yagoda and Berman, Beria was promoted to head of the NKVD and the doors to the future were flung wide open.

Now Igor was a wealthy, renowned entrepreneur tolerated by the Party, which turned a blind eye to his excessive vanity. His business dealings, in part, were legal: He provided equipment to the army, earned cash in dollars and German marks that he kept in Swiss banks. He had high-level contacts both inside and outside the country, access to most government ministries and important cultural icons as well as those in the world of intelligence. He'd become refined, his taste for music, theater, and grand salons had turned him into a sort of celebrity that almost made people forget his Jewish cartwright's background. Fate was finally smiling on him, and all he had to do was remain vital to Beria. He was twenty-seven years old and on top of the world.

And it was from this vantage point that he now observed Elías Gil. He, too, had changed over the course of those six years, and in a way his presence in Beria's office was evidence of the direction it had taken. Elías had become an officer in the service of those who had sentenced him to Nazino. What had he gotten in return? This was what Igor Stern wanted to know.

Beria had asked Elías a question and was awaiting a reply. So was Stern. Perhaps deep down both of them were expecting the same answer: that Elías couldn't work with the man who had caused all his misfortune. But they were wrong.

"My loyalty to the Party and the Soviet people remains intact, comrade. I can work with Stern if it is to the benefit of our cause."

"Oh, it will be, I'm quite sure of that," replied the NKVD commissar, thereby bringing to a close their meeting.

Two days later a car pulled up outside the modest apartment building where Elías was living. Two people stepped out, a man and a girl of about ten. Witnesses—slack jawed at the sight of this elegantly dressed pair in their poor neighborhood—would later say the girl looked like an angel, in a thick fur coat and matching hat, beautiful golden curls peeking out from beneath it. Her expression and demeanor were nearly as arrogant as those of the man holding her hand. The girl was Anna Akhmatova and the man holding her hand, Igor Stern.

"I wanted you to see her."

Elías remained standing in the middle of the room, staring at the little girl who no longer resembled in any way the one he had abandoned when he left her in Igor's hands six years earlier. Stern wanted Elías to admire his work of art, to see what he'd done with her, the way he was slowly shaping her in his own image and likeness.

"Who is this man, Papa?" Anna asked Igor, clinging to his leg. Hearing her call Stern *Papa* cut Elías to the quick and pleased Stern. Anna was taking on Stern's decisive air but would not yet let herself be loved by the man stroking her blond little head.

"Take a good look at him, Anna; don't forget his face. This is the man who killed your mother. He let her drown in Nazino River to save his own pathetic life. And he would no doubt have killed you, too."

The girl had no way of comprehending Igor's words, no way of processing what they meant, but she understood, the way animals do, that she was expected to glare at the stranger in hatred and disgust. And she did so quite convincingly.

"Go on back to the car and wait for me there. I'll be right out."

Anna cast one last sidelong glance at Elías, who caught a glimpse of something that had come from her mother, some learned behavior in the girl's expression. And something told him that one day the spirit she'd inherited would rebel against this shroud Igor was smothering her in. A faint hope in which to take comfort.

"So. I didn't eat her, after all."

He was trying to be caustic, but his comment was much more than that.

"Does Beria know who she is?"

Igor opened a silver cigarette case, took out an American cigarette, and tapped it several times against the cover. Everything about him had become more civilized, but beneath his affected sophistication lurked a hungry wolf, perhaps still longing for nomadic nights spent roaming the land.

"Beria knows how often every last peasant in this country takes a shit. And as long as his trucks and his cash keep coming in, he doesn't care. That little man might look like a hick, but he'd eat you and me alive in the same bite and not bat an eye. He's the one with the real power."

And that was what Igor was aspiring to; he'd become ambitious, much more than he used to be. Having seen the sparkle of that intangible good, he was unwilling to let it slip away. Elías could see it in his face. Some men succumb to misfortune, others are fortified by it. Igor was one of those. He'd negotiate with the Russians, the Germans, the English, or the devil himself if it was in his interest.

"What do you want, Igor?"

Stern lit his cigarette and shook his head.

"Everything?"

I want you, is what his furious look said. *I want what can't be bought with money. I want your respect and if I can't get that I want your fear and your submission.*

They were still, after six long years, engaged in the same battle; it was simply being waged on different territory.

"Any chance we could be friends? I'm not asking for your devotion, just a sign that the past has been forgotten."

"You just told that girl I killed her mother."

"Isn't it true? It sounds terrible because it is. We did what we had to do to survive. Like now. And when all this is over, we will be judged harshly, I assure you of that. Your children and grandchildren will point fingers, call you a savage and a murderer. They'll say worse about me, I'm sure. And they'll be right, but none of them will have been here, or on Nazino. Judges always cast judgment from up in their ivory towers. With a little luck, the coin might land heads up and you'll be remembered as a hero of the revolution, a brave and committed idealist. Personally, I don't give a shit about posterity, although maybe it means something to you."

Elías said nothing. Igor had always talked too much, trying to invent himself through words, using them to recant the evidence of his acts. He was a lowlife. That's all he was.

"You and I will be friends when heaven and earth become one. I don't care what kind of agreement you've made with Beria, or what you've done to get ahead, or how far you've come. There's one thing you need to know: You might have ripped out my eye, but it's going to follow you no matter how far you get. And one day, whether it's now or in a hundred years, I'm going to rip your head off with my bare hands."

Igor's composure melted away too quickly, making clear that his newly learned habits were but a shiny varnish, easily scratched off. He clenched his fists and tilted his head sinisterly toward the door Anna had walked out after calling him *Papa*.

"I'm still hungry, and I've still got my prey. Don't forget it."

Early the following month, Elías was given a military rank and sent to Moscow's School of Information Services, popularly known as the Academy. Students from various police academies who were considered to have the necessary aptitude were trained in general politics by commissars who, in addition to indoctrinating, taught classes on the history of the Communist Party. But the bulk of their training consisted of recruiting agents, handling information, learning espionage and counterespionage techniques, writing encoded reports, and doing fieldwork. After graduating, they were named NKVD captains or lieutenants.

One of the instructors was Vasili Velichko. He had been promoted since his days at the Tushino flight school and there was no longer any trace of the callow young man who in 1934 had presented a report on Nazino to Lenin's widow and head of the

Spanish Communist Party, José Díaz. He was now a colonel in the air force, his hair and thick goatee already gray. He'd aged a lot, despite being only twenty-seven. Those were the years of men growing old before their time, men for whom private lives didn't matter or exist.

Velichko had become skilled at avoiding the various purges of the security services, although he'd earned himself many enemies after his report made it all the way to Stalin's hands. People said that his uncle was head of the Fourth Department of the NKVD's Main Directorate—the military intelligence services unit created by Nikolai Yezhov—and this kept him safe. And so it was that this young civil defense academy instructor became a shrewd man, with unique insights, endowed with a sincere belief in the virtue of his mission and infallible patriotism. Together, these qualities made him both very efficient and highly regarded at the Academy, although his dream was to be posted to a combat fighter squadron.

He was genuinely happy to see Elías again. They talked about the past, and even more about the future. Velichko was up to date on the situation with Stern and his proximity to power.

"Hard times are coming, my friend, and we need horrible scavengers like him. People like Stern ignore the rules that the rest of us abide by, and unfortunately this makes them useful. Did you hear about General Kutepov?" Elías nodded, having been told about the old White Army general who was kidnapped by the OGPU in Paris and died before they had a chance to kill him. "Well, nine years later, the same thing happened with his successor, General Miller. The day they killed him, a Soviet merchant ship, the *Maria Ulyanova*, was docked at the port of Le Havre. One of our embassy vehicles unloaded an enormous container, which was immediately loaded onto the ship. It pulled up anchor minutes before the French police arrived. And do you know what was in the container?"

Elías had a guess: General Miller.

"Exactly. The ship, the crew, the men who transported the container—all Stern's. If the French police had caught them, they could never have formally accused our intelligence services. Stern would have been the one to go down. He charges quite a high price, but it's well worth paying. This is the reality we live in, Elías. While you were at war in Spain and France, Igor Stern didn't sit still for a minute. He's become a very important man."

"I saw Anna. Igor brought her to my house just so I could see her and hear her call him 'Papa' with my own ears."

Velichko narrowed his eyes and clenched his jaw, mulling something over.

"For the first four years, she was in an orphanage on the outskirts of Kiev. It wasn't a nice place, but I managed to find her and make sure she had everything she needed. She's a wonderful little girl." Vasili's eyes lit up. "Cheerful, intelligent, alert, and communicative. When I used to go visit, I pretended to be her older brother. Sometimes I was able to rent an apartment nearby and get her out of that awful place for a few days; we'd take walks in the forest, go ice skating on the lake...Even my hardheaded mother fell in love with her. Then one day I found out that Igor had declared paternity. He forged the papers, and I have no doubt that it was with the consent of Beria, a little bonus for having kidnapped Miller. I've managed to keep seeing her every once in a while. She's growing up quickly, and she realizes what kind of man Stern is but knows that all she can do is pretend to love him. A year ago, I got a call from a military patrol. They'd found her in Moscow and she gave them my name. She'd run away from the dacha where Igor keeps her locked up. Can you believe it? Nine years old and she came to Moscow alone! The authorities refused to listen to me: Igor demanded she be returned, and I was forced to give her up. I know what you think you saw, Elías. But Anna is Irina Akhmatova's daughter. I visit her whenever I can, especially when Igor is away. We talk a lot and I try not to let her lose hope.

But war is on the horizon and there's no time for sentimentality or personal concerns. Everything is on hold, *sine die*. You have to understand that."

And inevitably the war arrived right on schedule. That Sunday, Elías was reading *Izvestia*—the cover story was about public school education—when Vasili Velichko burst into his room looking fevered and troubled.

"The Germans have crossed the border. *Voina*, Elías, *voina!*" The cry of war shot through the nation like a surge of electricity. It was June 22, 1941.

Two days later, a general mobilization was ordered. Velichko and other pilot officers were sent to the airfields of Belorussia. The day he left, Vasili was not euphoric but did appear gravely resolute. He'd been preparing for this moment for the past two years and the time had come.

They embraced, promised they would meet again soon, and Vasili said goodbye with one final piece of advice.

"Be careful with Stern. He'll be more dangerous than the Nazis now. Filth is his natural environment."

In just a few short weeks, the Russian defense was decimated by three German armies, which managed to occupy a front almost two thousand miles long. Army Group North headed for Leningrad, Group Center went to Moscow, and Group South advanced at an alarming pace through Ukraine toward Kiev and Kharkov. Over three million men, more than six hundred thousand vehicles, nearly three thousand tanks, and two thousand planes attacked the Soviet units at full throttle. In the first week of the invasion alone, the Luftwaffe destroyed twelve hundred Soviet aircraft—among them Vasili's squadron, taken down over the Polish border. Elías read about it in the operational command dispatch on the Western Front, where he was stationed. Brave Velichko hadn't even had a chance to prove his skills as a pilot.

The news coming in to NKVD military headquarters on the Leningrad Front was devastating: On the first day of attack, German troops from Group Center had penetrated twenty-five miles along the Minsk–Smolensk–Moscow axis. On the Ukraine Front, Soviet prisoners captured in the Kiev pocket numbered over 650,000; hundreds of thousands more fell in Bialystok, Smolensk, and Bryansk. An officer gave Elías an issue of *Signal*, the Nazi propaganda magazine distributed to Axis soldiers. Its pages showed an illustrious prisoner who had surrendered on July 16 to the troops surrounding his artillery unit. The message was clear: If 7th Artillery lieutenant Yakov Dzhugashvili had fallen to the Germans, no Red Army soldier was safe. The man was Stalin's son.

Elías had lived through the war in Spain, the civil violence in Barcelona in 1937, the retreat, and French concentration camps. He thought that after all that, and Nazino, nothing could surprise him. But he was wrong. When, in October, the NKVD learned that a division of Spanish volunteers was going to enter combat in the Siege of Leningrad as part of the German army's Group North, he was immediately sent there.

What he found made his blood run cold. This was not a war whose objective was to conquer or defend territory; it was an extermination. It wasn't about defeating the enemy but literally wiping him off the map. They fought relentlessly, viciously, with merciless cruelty and unimaginable hatred. Perhaps Beria's prediction would prove true and the Germans would eventually be worn down by the endless expanse of Soviet land, but in the meantime, there might be not a single man left standing on either side.

The Soviets employed a scorched-earth policy, leveling entire towns and villages in their retreat, destroying means of communication, burning crops, and killing all of the farm animals and cattle they were unable to cart off. Dead soldiers were stripped of everything they had, abandoned in a shroud of ice. On his way to the Leningrad Front, Elías saw surreal, nightmarish scenes of destruction.

In the middle of an endless frozen expanse, a forest of bare hands emerged from the ice as though the dead were seeking the warmth of the winter sun. A dog had frozen after falling into the water, half of its body above the surface, front paws on the shore it had so nearly reached. And in the immense expanse of nothingness, here and there, a smoldering black dot—a scorched country house, its stone fireplace still smoking as though to warm the hearth. Crows perched on the icy heads of fallen soldiers, pecking at their frozen eyeballs, beaks bouncing off the ice.

The dead from the Spanish Volunteer Division were recognizable by their blue shirts. Although they wore German infantry uniforms, the men had refused to take off their Falangist shirts and became referred to as the Blue Division. Not all of them were in fact volunteers, but Elías was surprised at the number of those taken prisoner who were: university students from Franco's Spanish Students' Union, local politicians, teachers and doctors, and many men in midlevel and senior positions. According to the NKVD's information, there were eighteen thousand of them split into three regiments, in addition to sappers, artillerymen, and pilots.

"Why are you here, fighting a war that isn't yours?" Elías asked one of them.

The prisoner was an infantry sergeant. His platoon had been wiped out an hour earlier by a machine gun belonging to Elías's NKVD company. Elías had been astonished that even after being wounded, many Blue Division soldiers continued to drag themselves toward their defensive positions, leaving a literal trail of blood and guts behind them. The vast majority had been killed in the first attack, and yet they'd fought on, exposed in open country, until there were no troops left.

"It's cold in the trenches. Better to keep warm with a good fight," the sergeant responded, gravely injured, shot in the side. Two other prisoners laughed at his joke, harsh animal-like cackles.

Not one of them talked. They withstood torture, cursing Stalin and his mother, and when Elías aimed his revolver at the sergeant's skull, the man called his bluff by pressing his forehead to the barrel.

"*Arriba España*, you Red bastard!"

Elías pulled the trigger.

Why all this hatred?

He wrote to Esperanza that night.

> *Today I shot a Falangist in the head. And that's what I kept wondering, as I saw his body at my feet, a shapeless mass, an enemy. But the truth is that I killed a thirty-two-year-old chemical engineer named Rogelio Miranda from Medellín, according to his military ID. A miner from Mieres shoots a chemical engineer from Medellín in the head, in a land that means nothing to either one of them, before an orthodox church that we defend and they attack, thousands and thousands of miles from home, from our lives. He had a family, I saw a photo in his wallet. Two beautiful children, six or seven years old. His wife was pretty. Looking at her in this cold brings warmth.*
>
> *Who will tell her he's been killed? Will his children find out I was the one to murder him? Will they ever understand why their father died here? Will we ever understand it ourselves, Esperanza? The Nazis are surprised at how ferociously the Blue Division attacks our positions, having thought Spaniards rebellious and undisciplined. Red Army commissars are astonished at how valiantly the Spanish*

volunteers among our ranks fight, citing us as examples of
brave and battle-hardened soldiers. None of them understand,
not the Germans or the Soviets. They think we're fighting
for them, but we're simply fighting against each other. They
can't see that all it takes is a single man calling out the name
of a Spanish battle—Belchite or Badajoz or Toledo—for the
other side to pounce like rabid dogs. Seeing the Blue Division
banner riles our men up more than the swastika does; raising
the Republican flag on our side incites them to launch a brutal
attack. How much damage did the war do to Spain? Too
much. I wonder if we'll ever manage to leave it behind, and
I'm terrified of the answer.

Be careful, Esperanza, and take care, as I do. This
will end, one way or another, and we'll be together again, I
promise you.

In Leningrad, December 23, 1941
Your Husband

Elías reread his letter in his refuge by flickering candlelight. Amid the still-smoking ruins of the church, men lay dozing, tired of killing and of trying to keep from being killed. The wounded were lined up in what remained of the presbytery, not shouting, simply stirring uneasily and, from time to time, moaning or weeping softly, imploring their mothers, their girlfriends, their children not to abandon them on that cold dark night. They didn't want to die alone.

Through the shot-out church windows, Elías could see the field outside strewn with corpses, most of them from the Blue Division. Small mounds, slowly being covered in snow. From time to time he heard gunfire, saw the flash of a shot. A patrol circulated, finishing off those near death. They couldn't be taken prisoner; there was no medicine to treat them, no food or enough water. In the distance, beyond the lake, the glare of bombs falling on the city of Leningrad was like a beautiful fireworks display, the thunderous explosions sounding like a distant storm that was, perhaps, moving off. No one heard the cries of the wounded, the mutilated, and the dead.

Someone said that in the Blue Division trenches, men were singing Christmas carols. Elías smiled. His father was an atheist and had never allowed religious celebrations at home, and so Elías had always been jealous of friends like Ramón when he saw them on their way to midnight Mass, carrying drums and tambourines.

He would have liked to get up, leave his revolver and cartridge belt, and walk the quarter of a mile to enemy lines to sit with them and perhaps share some Christmas *turrón* and have them teach him the carols he never learned to sing as a boy. But he had to make do with the dark night, no stars to herald glad tidings or epiphanies.

Peace on earth to men of goodwill, someone had written in the snow. Maybe somewhere, but not on this earth. The only men of goodwill lay buried in the snow.

24

The first stone sailed over their heads and crashed against an excavator, shattering its cabin window. The fifty or so protesters momentarily stopped their chants against politicians and the Gil family and cried out in celebration. Gonzalo's property had, over the past several months, become a sort of stronghold, the final obstacle keeping construction on the lakeside development from continuing. But according to the protesters' signs, Gonzalo Gil and his mother had caved to the "interests of capital." An embarrassment to the memory of Communist hero Elías Gil. Gonzalo's name had gone from being hailed to hated the moment his signature dried on the bill of sale. Police were called in, their services exhaustively employed in order to clear a path to the machinery surrounding the lake. There were skirmishes and confrontations, and they even came to blows.

Agustín González and Alcázar watched the action from a hilltop, a Roman general with his centurion, following the unfolding of a battle from a strategic yet safe position.

"Why do they insist on defending something they don't care about? Half of these people aren't even from the region."

The man sounded genuinely astonished, unable to see the source of their strife. To him, it was all a question of numbers, a price per square foot, a matter to be resolved in offices by attorneys, notaries, urban-planning officials, and local authorities. The protesters were simply a nuisance, something incomprehensible that was interfering with the perfect mechanics of the plan as drawn up.

Alcázar saw it in a less pragmatic way. This landscape, vaguely similar to that of his own childhood, was going to disappear. He didn't feel nostalgic or have any romantic notions about it, but he understood that the protesters felt as though something that belonged to them was being taken away, something that had been appropriated by a band of speculators. And they were right.

"People pick their battles," he said laconically.

"Well, they've picked one they're not going to win."

That wasn't what it was about, Alcázar thought. It wasn't a question of winning but of standing up, defending what they thought was just and thereby soothing their conscience. In a few years, if the lake and its environs no longer existed, some of these protesters would visit the new golf course, walk around the luxury homes and tell their kids what used to be there, and with great self-regard they would recount the tale of being hit by a police baton in their attempt to preserve the land. And their children, if they were lucky, would be proud, and maybe deep in their hearts the desire to emulate their parents' rebellion would take root.

That's the way things advance: slowly, with small and futile heroic gestures. Generation after generation.

"Well, it seems that finally everything is going to go according to plan after all," Agustín concluded, brushing dust off of his coat. November had brought a significant drop in temperature. It wouldn't be long before snow returned to the mountains. With a little luck, the lawyer thought, blowing on his fingers to warm them, the complex could open in a couple of summers.

Alcázar was less optimistic. He still hadn't found Siaka, and although he knew Gonzalo had kept his part of the bargain—withdrawing his name from the Matryoshka proceedings—the prosecutor's office was forging ahead. Information obtained from Laura's computer was still being sent to the prosecutor, but that didn't seem to concern Agustín González.

"Without witness testimony at the oral hearing, they've got nothing. Their documentary evidence is circumstantial; it hasn't been cross-checked and there's no way for them to do it. The originals no longer exist; I made sure of that. So it comes down to the word of a depressed, unstable, drug-addicted murderer against ours."

Alcázar felt a wave of nausea on hearing Laura's memory trampled that way. And he himself had helped discredit her, so thoroughly that she'd turned into a different person.

"They have a lot of particulars, though, including lists of payments—and you and I are both on them. Whoever has that laptop is clearly coming after us."

Agustín hunched his head into the turned-up collar of his coat, gazing scornfully at what was taking place just a few yards away. Police had cleared a path, and the diggers advanced relentlessly.

"Don't let that worry you; they're firing blanks. I'll navigate these waters. You just worry about the witness. Find him and make sure he doesn't show up to testify."

"What's going to happen with Gonzalo?"

Agustín's expression shifted slightly. The whole Javier business had been unfortunate, something that required all of his skills and the cashing in of a considerable part of the favors owed him. But in the end, with Alcázar's help, things could be fixed. Carlos had turned out to be a professional blackmailer with more than twenty priors—all kinds of bribery and other misdemeanors. He was well known to both police and judges, who had no sympathy for leeches like him. It wasn't hard to find an empathetic judge who, aided by the evidence supplied by Alcázar's cronies, accepted the theory of legitimate defense: Carlos had been blackmailing Javier, as the photos proved (the few in which Javier wasn't openly obliging); Javier refused to keep paying and threatened to go to the police; Carlos tried to scare him by pulling a gun and there was a struggle; Carlos ended up dead and Javier gravely injured.

This was the line of defense they would have to present, although it still needed some finessing; there were loose ends to tie up. As soon as Javier was in a position to testify, Agustín would bring him up to speed and make sure he stuck to this version of events. He would have to deal with ridicule after coming out publicly as a homosexual, but that was no crime—although Agustín found it quite distasteful. Nothing at all would be said about Lola. Regardless of what Agustín thought about *that* side of things, the sense that he'd failed as a father didn't matter right now. She was his daughter and he'd do whatever was necessary to protect her.

And the truth was, the whole business, no matter how dramatic, had ended up benefiting him in a sense. Gonzalo turned out not to be as much of a milquetoast as he'd thought. All of his do-gooder lawyer scruples had gone right out the window the moment he realized that his son could go to jail, that his family could be torn apart. Agustín's son-in-law hadn't thought twice about lying, swearing that he had a feeling that someone was extorting his son, and that Carlos had even asked Gonzalo himself for money, thereby proving his suspicions. He also hid Lola's role in the whole thing from the police. The man bent to Agustín's will without a word, like an obedient little lamb, and had proved he was up to the task. Gonzalo had nerves of steel. If he divorced Lola in the end, under the circumstances, it would be a bittersweet victory. After all, his son-in-law had proved far more dignified than his daughter.

Agustín and Gonzalo had avoided each other while Javier was in the hospital, but they did so courteously, each giving the other space, putting their personal issues on the back burner for weeks while the boy recovered. And then one day, Gonzalo showed up at his office.

"How soon do you think we can go through with the merger?" he asked, as though picking up the thread of a conversation they'd left off the day before. In his hand was the bill of sale for the lake house, already signed.

Agustín would have preferred to win another way, this was what he thought as he drove off, with the demolition crew getting to work despite the protesters' opposition. But a victory was a victory, that was what counted.

Alcázar had parked beside Agustín's car. They shook hands and said goodbye. The ex-inspector had something he wanted to check.

He hardly remembered the house at all, having been there on only two occasions before the night at the lake. Both times, Elías had refused to let him through the front gate. It looked more or less the same as he remembered it. Maybe a little more welcoming. Laura, he recalled, had been at the far end of the yard, by the well. She was thirteen or fourteen years old, and at the time Alcázar hardly paid any attention to her. He remembered Gonzalo running around, too, barefoot and shirtless, a bag of bones with protruding ears and a crew cut—which kids wore back then to avoid lice.

"It must have been right here. This is where it happened."

The well was dry, covered with a large stone he could barely move. The bottom had grown over with whitish weeds that were tangled up with roots sticking out from between the mossy bricks. Alcázar tossed in a small stone and watched it bounce off the walls. Gonzalo's little body must have felt that fragile when his sister hid him in there, sliding him down on the pulley. How many hours did he spend down there, scared to death, water up to his waist? The night of San Juan in 1967, when he finally got Laura to tell him the truth, she'd said she didn't know. She was terrified.

The day had started like any other day. Laura had slept in her narrow room, holding Gonzalo, who'd had one of his nightmares and come running to the safety of her arms. On the other side of the wall she could hear her father's rasping breath. She couldn't hear her mother but knew that her eyes were open before the first light of dawn came in through the window. From her room, Laura must have seen her mother float past like a breeze, making no useless gestures, not opening her mouth, going downstairs to the fireplace to fan the embers. Laura dressed silently so as not to wake Gonzalo. Esperanza cocked her head on seeing her daughter, giving her the sad complicit smile of their shared fate. As if she didn't know what was going on. Her mother pretended not to see that Laura's eyes were swollen, after having cried all night. She hardly ever sang songs in Russian anymore, was no longer quick to laugh.

Esperanza pulled Laura to her, sat the girl on her lap and, as she fixed her hair with bobby pins, told her daughter about how she first met Elías and the things they'd had to go through before she was born. It was an attempt to convince her that her father was, despite it all, a good man. She told Laura about the years they'd had to spend apart because of the war in Europe, where her father had fought the Fascists in the Battle of Leningrad, first to defend the city and then to retake it. She proudly showed her the box of medals and awards he'd earned in that brutal war, the photos taken in Leningrad, and then Stalingrad, and in Berlin on Victory Day when Hitler was defeated. And she told Laura how, finally, after five long years, Elías had come and found her, simply turned up at the door of the Toulouse workshop where she worked.

"And what did you do all those years?"

Esperanza smiled wistfully. "I waited. I could have had a different life. One day a famous agent for performing artists saw me and said he wanted to take me to Paris and make me a star." Esperanza vividly evoked the enormous buildings and convertibles, recounted the hustle and bustle of the trams, the actresses' dresses and hairstyles and makeup, their long legs and narrow waists, the elegant way they moved and smoked. Talking about it, she was momentarily transformed; it was as if she was another person, the woman she could have been. But then suddenly Esperanza fell silent and looked around, eyes full of reproach. It smelled of manure, of damp straw. It smelled of everything she hated—the dry leather of harnesses, the sweat of animals, her own sweat.

"You mustn't hold on to anything that makes you sad, like memories. I chose my own destiny, and that's more than a lot of people can say. And my destiny was always your father."

"And why do you let this happen?"

Esperanza had half closed the door so that no one could hear them. She took a deep breath. "I don't know what you're talking about."

"Yes, you do."

Her mother's eyes grew distant, faraway, darkening as though a storm cloud had crossed through them. She had never hit either of her children. But her hand lashed out in fury at the truth her daughter spat at her, and she slapped Laura's mouth as though to seal it, so she wouldn't have to hear.

"Go fetch the water from the well," she said very quietly, gazing down at her fingers, wondering what she'd just done. She stepped back into the doorway and hugged herself with her arms, an icy chill running through her body, a pained and exhausted expression on her face.

That morning, the morning of the night of San Juan, Laura probably picked her way quickly along the low stone wall covered in dry vines and damp moss, made it to the well, and filled the pails with water. And when she returned, Elías was there, staring at her with his one eye. And what she saw in his face terrified her.

Alcázar gazed down into the bottom of the well. It was impossible for anything good to come from under the peat moss, where the clay was packed so tight not even water or air could penetrate it. He looked up at the house, decaying more each day, surrounded by barren fields, as though having given up. The only mercy it could hope for was that the weeds would hide its ruins, erasing it from the earth. That was the future awaiting the past. That and silence.

At eleven o'clock at night there were very few people out on the street. On the ground floor of his building was a trattoria that stayed open late, and customers' voices filtered up through the windows. When he got back from the hospital, Gonzalo took off his shoes and fell into bed, still fully clothed. He listened to conversations slowly dying down. A drunk with a beautiful voice was singing a Portuguese fado by Dulce Pontes that Gonzalo knew. He joined in as the drunk's voice trailed off in the distance.

> *Mãe adeus. Adeus, Maria*
> *Guarda bem no teu sentido*
> *Que aqui te faço uma jura:*
> *Que ou te levo à sacristia*
> *Ou foi Deus que foi servido*
> *Dar-me no mar sepultura*

The room was dark, but light came in from the streetlamps in the plaza below. It was raining and the raindrops shone in the yellow haze of the streetlamps. His balcony doors were wide open, and water ricocheted off the chipped railing. Thousands of tiny, fragmented drops bounced into the bedroom, wetting the back of an armchair and the floor tiles. It was lovely when it rained like that—musical. Rather than hide, it made you want to walk out in the downpour without an umbrella, to dissolve right along with those drops and become just one more of them.

Gonzalo's answering machine was flashing beside the phone. Since selling the lake house, he had received endless insulting messages calling him a traitor, a sell-out, a money-grabber, a scumbag. Not one of the people calling him those names had a kid in the hospital with his chest blown open, not one of them worried day and night about having their ten-year-old daughter kidnapped by murderers.

"You did what you had to do." Tania had been trying to comfort him. "No one can judge you for that."

And yet she had, that very afternoon when the two of them were sitting at a table at Flight and he told her that he needed some time to be alone and decide what to do. She'd given him a look, her eyes like two gray stones pushing him under.

"Wiping the slate clean, is that it?"

Gonzalo had nodded vaguely, as though somehow expecting this reaction. And although he had the urge to move closer to her, he didn't do it. Gonzalo didn't know what he expected of Tania; he hardly knew her, and from what he'd found out, she had lied to him from the start.

"The whole business with my father and your mother...I feel trapped by so many lies, Tania. I'm shaken up, I don't know what to do, what to believe," he explained, his face that of a man who has decided to stop fighting—even though whatever he's fighting will never go away, even though he'll never beat it.

Tania's jaw had clenched, and her pursed lips formed a thin line. But she'd been the one to take the first step. She did it slowly, giving him the chance to reject her, to listen to the skittish voice in his head screaming that this was not right. But the voice petered out like a death rattle when he felt the touch of her cracked lips, inhaled her faint smell of lipstick and cigarettes.

"You can believe in this. Because this is true."

Was it? He wasn't certain. But Tania made him feel good, didn't ask him to be someone he wasn't or push him in any one direction, Gonzalo thought as he erased the messages on his machine one by one after listening to them. A series of insults that he hardly even registered. The last one, though, was different.

> *So you threw in the towel, bent over for your father-in-law and the police. And you think that's the end of it? You think Laura would forgive you? You're not out of the game until the last round, Gonzalo. Not as long as Aldo Rossi has your sister's computer.*

It was Siaka's voice. But he was parroting someone else's words. Gonzalo knew the kid enough to be able to tell that beneath his defiant tone lay a tinge of fear.

Hearing some sort of disturbance down on the street, voices shouting, Gonzalo poked his head out to see three shapes in the dumpsters on the corner—beggars fighting over trash, most likely. He closed the window and listened to the message again. It had come in that very night.

Floren Atxaga never read much before going to prison, but now he couldn't stop. For that, if nothing else, he was thankful to that Cuban whore and her lawyer. Before, he'd seen books as nothing but two covers filled with dusty yellow pages. The only ones he'd even leafed through were the Bible and the book of psalms at church. Now he devoured books even if he didn't always understand what they said. He'd started off with one that seemed appropriate:

The Hive, by Camilo José Cela. It turned out to have too many characters and confused him. Another one, *My Artificial Paradises*, by Francisco Umbral, was complicated and had tons of words he didn't understand, which made him mad. It was like the author was making fun of him. Now he was reading *The Plague*, by Camus, but it was so sad. Life wasn't as bad as the guy made it out to be.

Maybe he'd go back to the Bible. He felt safe there, he thought, anxiously flipping through half a dozen books that had been tossed into a dumpster without finding any that interested him.

"What are you doing, man? Digging for food in the trash, like a rat?"

Atxaga turned and saw a couple of teenagers. One was swinging a stick like a bat. The other gave him an insolent look, though Atxaga could have been the kid's father. His pupils were dilated and his body twitched edgily. His mouth felt like it was full of bees, buzzing around. The kid was wearing a T-shirt that said something in English Axtaga couldn't read.

"I want everything you've got."

"Excuse me?"

"You're looking at my shirt, right? That's what it says: 'I want everything you've got.'"

Atxaga was pretty sure that wasn't actually what it said, but this was the least of his worries. He was being held up. These little shits were holding him up.

He observed them with a mix of rage and apprehension, two rivers that always ran parallel beneath the surface of his feelings. He thought they could be his sons, who would inevitably turn out the same way and end up robbing people if they stayed with their whore of a mother in a sleazy neighborhood like this.

There was no way he was going to stand for it.

He wasn't excessively vicious. Atxaga detested violence, but sometimes it overtook him, like Jehovah when he tired of giving the chosen people opportunities. Then he would send them plagues, slaughter them, and hope they'd learn their lesson. But they didn't learn; they never learned. And this forced him to be more and more exacting.

By the time he stopped beating the kid with the stick, he was covered in blood. The kid dragged himself away like a dying rat, which was appropriate given that he'd called Atxaga one. He'd slammed the head of the kid in the T-shirt against a car fender. He didn't kill either of them, just hoped they'd learned their lesson.

"You force me to be a plague, and this one is just the first."

He picked a book up off the ground, the pages wrinkled and spattered with blood.

Two households both alike in dignity (in fair Verona, where we lay our scene). From ancient grudge break to new mutiny, where civil blood makes civil hands unclean.

He glanced at the title: *Romeo and Juliet.* Atxaga smiled; he liked love stories.

That night, having parked himself in a doorway, as he watched the light in attorney Gonzalo Gil's window, Atxaga discovered that he and Shakespeare had a similar view of things.

Old Lukas gave a grumbling sort of growl, demanding to be taken for his walk.

"All right, you old grouch."

Alcázar needed to clear his head anyway. He was no longer young and couldn't sit at a computer and concentrate for as long as he used to. But he knew one thing: Siaka hadn't left the country, at least not on any sort of ticket in his own name. What did that mean? Nothing. He could have crossed the border any number of other ways or used a fake ID. But something told him the kid was still in Barcelona.

That afternoon he'd returned to the café-bar where Siaka was supposed to have met Gonzalo. It was the last place he'd been seen, as far as Alcázar knew. The waiter who had served him told Alcázar the same thing he'd told Gonzalo: good-looking, well-dressed black guy; he'd been in before, usually accompanied by an attractive tourist who looked like she had money, generally American or British and staying at an expensive hotel.

"The women always paid, but when he came alone, he left unbelievable tips. He was a good kid, if a little eccentric."

"Eccentric how?"

"He liked being called 'sir.' Pretty unusual for someone so young. I think all the five-star hotels he stayed in must have gone to his head."

"Was there anyone with him?"

The waiter was sure he was alone. He mentioned an elegant man who'd been having coffee at the bar.

"Seemed interested in him, if you know what I mean."

"I don't."

"Well, like I said, he's a good-looking young man, and the guy at the bar, I don't know, I just got the feeling he was gay. Took off right after the kid left."

The waiter provided him with a rough sketch: tall, dark, in good shape, polite, and well dressed. Like a hundred thousand other executives walking around Barcelona every day.

Lukas let out an insistent, whimpering bark. Alcázar rubbed his eyes and stretched. It was almost midnight. He hadn't eaten at all, but the ashtray was full. After putting on the dog's leash, he took Lukas down to the street. It was raining, but Alcázar had never minded walking in the rain. It felt like he breathed better that way. Cecilia's voice came to him, calling out from the bed: *Don't forget the umbrella.* Alcázar didn't like umbrellas but he used to take one with him so she'd rest easy, sticking it under his arm and circling the block without raising it. He still did; it was like having her company: two old boys and a ghost, out for a walk in the rain.

Alcázar thought about Siaka again as Lukas sniffed a fresh pile of shit. He didn't know much about the kid, and his file stated only that he'd been arrested a few times for minor offenses: prostitution, robbing tourists at luxury hotels...Suddenly the rain cleared his mind.

He jerked the dog all the way home and rushed to search the Internet for all luxury hotels close to the center. There weren't that many, maybe half a dozen.

The following morning, he got out a photo of Siaka and did the rounds. They recognized him at most of the hotels, either because a tourist had lodged a complaint or because he'd stayed in one of their suites, always one with a balcony facing the sea. But the dates on which he'd been there were all prior to his appearance at the café-bar. Until he got to Hotel Majestic, across from where the international cruise ships docked. The head of security remembered him perfectly.

"He tried to rob a British woman. Coincidentally, she turned out to be with Scotland Yard."

"Did she file a complaint?"

"No, she said it wasn't worth it. The truth is, I think she wanted to avoid calling attention to the matter. She rented the room by the hour, you get me? She did recommend, very coolly, that we do a better job monitoring the people at our hotel."

"Did she pay?"

The head of security searched their computer records and showed Alcázar a copy of the receipt. The date coincided with the day Siaka was at the café-bar. A few hours earlier he'd been at this hotel. It didn't necessarily mean anything, but it was an important detail nonetheless. The kid knew that the Matryoshka was after him, and rather than hide or run, he was going about his everyday life. This might indicate that he had no intention of bolting, and that either he was reckless or feeling very sure of Gonzalo's safety net. The idea that he'd been snatched began turning in his mind. But by whom?

The fact was, Alcázar knew no more than he had to begin with. He phoned Gonzalo.

"Any news from our friend Deep Throat?"

"No, and at this rate I don't think there will be. Everyone and their mother knows I caved to Agustín González's wishes. You should hear the lovely messages I'm getting on my answering machine."

Gonzalo seemed chattier than usual. Maybe the fact that his kid's condition was improving had perked him up, or maybe it was Anna's daughter who was doing it. The idiot hadn't listened to Alcázar and was still seeing her. But that wasn't his problem— Anna and her old friend Velichko could deal with it.

"I'm sure he's taken off by now," Gonzalo added.

Alcázar knew it was a possibility he had to consider, but his instincts told him otherwise.

When Gonzalo hung up, he wondered if he'd done the right thing in hiding Siaka's message from the ex-inspector. Maybe in some way, he told himself, he still had a chance to do the right thing.

The street was blocked off. Apparently the fight between beggars the night before had been a big deal. There was blood everywhere, and a patrol car had come, the officer asking neighbors what they'd seen. An ambulance was taking one of the men away, his face a bloody pulp. The other was trying to give a muddled description of the attacker. Gonzalo paid no attention; he had other things on his mind.

The second he got to the office, he took Luisa by the elbow and pulled her to one side.

"The tape from the day Atxaga attacked me—did you put it in the safe?"

"With the rest of my gore collection," she said facetiously. "Why? You want to get all hot and bothered again?"

Even the idea of seeing those images again made Gonzalo wince; he was still recovering from the injuries. Every night, as he lay there breathing, he thought about the stab wounds and how close they were to his lung. He steeled his nerves and began going over the tape, frame by frame, concentrating on any details he might have missed. There was Tania, leaning over him, distraught. Gonzalo thought about the times they'd made love, about her kiss at the bar and what she'd said: *You can believe in this. Because it's true.* Seeing that image, he had no doubt. Tania had saved his life.

He watched her get up, hands bloody, and search frantically for the cell phone in her purse; he watched her call emergency services. Not until the flashing lights of the ambulance were visible on the parking garage ramp did she leave his side, darting to the elevator. Then the paramedics appeared, and shortly thereafter, the police. Gonzalo focused all of his attention on the SUV and its back door, where he'd left the laptop. He'd already gone over this scene dozens of times, searching for something without knowing what he was looking for, sure he wouldn't find it.

This time, though, he did see something. It had been there all along, so obvious that he hadn't realized. There it was in the background, in the camera's gray area, hardly distinguishable from the dark wall. Almost a ghost. Tania and Atxaga had not been the only ones waiting for him in the garage. There was someone else, someone who knew where the security camera was, where it focused, and where to stand so as not to be seen. The figure crouched motionless for a long time, until the paramedics and police were entirely focused on Gonzalo and placing him gently into the ambulance. It was just a minute, but enough time for the shadow behind the SUV to creep up to the side door and take the briefcase with Laura's computer. Then the figure slipped away between the cars, hugging the wall until he got to the elevator.

And for a fraction of a second, an instant, it was almost possible to see a face.

Gonzalo had no trouble confirming the hunch he'd had since hearing Siaka's message. The man was Luis.

"On your feet."

He'd appeared suddenly, making a stealthy approach. Siaka shrank from the kick. It was getting harder and harder to stay alert. He sat up, leaning on one elbow. It took all of his effort not to collapse back down. His bones felt like broken glass.

"You want another dance?" Siaka asked, gazing at his jailer, his eyelid still swollen, dried blood crusted on his face. How long had it been since the last beating? An hour? A day? He'd lost all sense of time, and soon, he knew, he would lose what little sarcasm he had left.

Luis pulled a chair over to the middle of the room.

"Sit."

Siaka obeyed reluctantly.

"You seem like an educated guy. Didn't anyone teach you to say please?"

Luis took a step back and examined the kid carefully. He was younger than he looked, and more frightened than his bravado let on. But he was hard, too, no doubt about that.

"Do you know where we are?"

Luis walked over to the enormous window overlooking the sea and gazed out distractedly. The water was an infinite expanse of gray. This would have been the master suite, with the bed by the window so that every morning when they woke up, the first thing they saw was the beautiful sunrise.

"This was where we were going to build our dream, the dream you and Zinoviev stole from me."

"I told you already," Siaka said for the nth time, his stomach lurching, "I had nothing to do with Roberto's death. I really liked your son."

Luis came away from the window and inspected the cathedral ceiling carefully. He'd planned to finish it with hardwood. Laura liked the more reddish tones of chestnut and oak, but Luis preferred beech, so light and airy. It didn't matter anymore. After he was done here, he'd set fire to the house and the insurance would take care of it. Then he'd go back to London and never return. Ever.

"You *liked* him? How much did you *like* him? Enough to earn his confidence in addition to Laura's? Enough for the teachers at his school to know your face so that nobody would be surprised when you came to pick him up five minutes before his mother arrived? Did you *like* my son enough for him to trust you when you asked him to get into Zinoviev's car? Was *liking* him what made you drive to the lake and help Zinoviev kill him?"

Luis had stationed himself behind the chair so that Siaka couldn't see him. He'd cuffed Siaka's hands and feet so tightly to the chair that it was cutting off his circulation.

"I called Laura to tell her, I swear I did. But I couldn't risk it, I had to go with Zinoviev. He thought I'd earned Roberto's trust because I offered to follow him and keep my eye on him. I thought..."

"What did you think?"

"I thought that if I was with him, I could do something, help him somehow."

He really did, he believed it right to the end. He pictured himself tackling Zinoviev, snatching Roberto from him as they walked toward the lake. Siaka tried to gather the courage to do it, to confront the man who had owned him for the past eleven years, the man who held crippling power over him. But by the time he gathered the courage and ran toward them, Roberto was already floating in the lake.

He craned his neck, trying to see Luis. He could hear something, a small motor. An electric drill.

What good is regret? he wondered. None at all. Luis wasn't going to believe him, no matter what he said; he'd already made up his mind. Luis was going to carve him up, but first he wanted to humiliate him, make Siaka fall to his knees and beg for his life.

"Did Zinoviev beg? Did he? You're the one who killed him, aren't you? It wasn't the Matryoshka, or Laura. It was you."

Luis grabbed Siaka's scalp and tugged backward, hard. "Yes, he begged, of course he begged. But it didn't do him any good. He didn't answer my question—the same one I'm going to ask you, just once: Why there? Why did you kill my son at the lake where Laura grew up?"

25

"Commander, a photo for posterity."

Elías Gil and the commander of the 4th Company posed in their Internal Security Forces battle uniforms. Elías had just been promoted to commander of the NKVD and awarded the Order of the Red Star for the taking of Berlin; the Communist Party officially recognized him as a hero. Prominent Party members and politicians like Enrique Líster and even Dolores Ibárruri, who'd lost her son Rubén Ruiz in Stalingrad, had sent telegrams of congratulation; and Beria let drop that Elías's new title—very unusual for a non-Soviet—had been suggested by Stalin himself, who had followed Gil's exploits in Leningrad, Moscow, Stalingrad, Warsaw, and finally Berlin. Lies, falsehoods, and propaganda most likely. What did it matter? All he wanted was to end this charade. So he put on a brave face for the army journalists, smiled, and held up the scorched and bloodstained Nazi flag that a propagandist handed him.

"A great victory for all Spanish Communists, comrade!"

Celestino Alonso was political commissar of the 4th Company, composed originally of Spanish combatants led by Commander Pérez Galarza. Since the start of the conflict, they had lost over three-quarters of the company, so this "victory" that the commander so euphorically alluded to could be shared by very few. The last of his comrades had fallen only four hundred yards from the Reichstag, and their bodies were still floating in the River Spree, shot down by the only SS sharpshooters still defending the center of Berlin. To honor them, a young officer had climbed up to the Stephanstrasse plaque with a bucket of paint and renamed it José Díaz Street. A Spanish Communist's name, tattooed in the heart of Prussia. Despite the air of glory, Elías wasn't letting any of it go to his head. He especially could not forget the cowardly, incomprehensible decisions he'd been forced to preside over during the four long years of war.

What stung the most was that Soviet troops had called off the seemingly unstoppable Warsaw offensive, after the Polish— knowing that the Red Army vanguard was near—had risen up against the Nazis. Stalin stood by unperturbed as the Germans crushed the uprising, viciously attacking the insurgents. Over 250,000 died in Warsaw, and the city was literally razed. The Nazis, therefore, effectively saved Stalin the trouble of purging a people who would never forget that in 1939 the USSR had invaded them with their allies, the Nazis. War and politics had no time for ideals or heroic gestures. It was all death and suffering, adminis- tered at the pleasure of those who massacred because it made sense on paper—the kind of sense that soldiers in the trenches and peo- ple on the streets of ravaged cities could not grasp.

Still, Commander Gil posed with his men for the Red Army magazine, made patriotic declarations, and strolled among the smoldering ruins looking proud, trailed after by a camera crew from the NKVD Documentation Service. Pure theater, in which everyone had a part to play. Someone had written on a wall a famous line by the poet and journalist Ilya Ehrenburg:

German cities burn and I feel joy.

Elías trembled in rage. No doubt the ever-present, sensational-istic journalist had averted his eyes from the German soldiers piled up—hands tied behind their back, a shot to the head—beneath his ominous verse. They were just kids, young men who hadn't had the chance to fire a single shot from their obsolete rifles.

"Make sure to record that," he ordered the cameraman accompanying him.

"But, Comrade Commander, that would go against directives. No acts of cruelty."

Elías Gil spat on the fire-blackened ground his hero's boots walked.

"I said, film it. It might give that idiot Ehrenburg heartburn, but I'm sure he'll write an epic poem to get over it."

It drove Elías insane. He couldn't care less if the Nazis had done much the same in the territories they occupied. Their men carried the red flag, paraded and sang songs commemorating Leningrad and Stalingrad, and then sullied their names by literally raping girls to death, stealing, plundering, and giving free rein to the basest of instincts. Over the course of those first few days, Elías didn't hesitate to have soldiers as well as officers in his own army shot, executed; other force commanders did the same.

"We are not barbarians; we're Soviets."

He no longer knew what he was. All he wanted was to go home. And where was that? Wherever Esperanza was.

Not everything was sheer horror, though. In Tegel, Elías had seen soldiers freely give their rations to hungry local children, unprompted by camera crews or propaganda. Field hospitals and medics treated injured civilians and German soldiers with the same professional care they gave to their own troops. There were even cases of Soviet soldiers and German girls falling in love, starting families who would one day face mistrust from both sides.

Slowly, military units returned to a state of discipline and, after the initial days of chaos, Berlin went from being a death trap for its citizens to an occupied city. On April 25, Soviet and American troops met on the River Elbe, near Torgau. Five days later, Adolf Hitler committed suicide, leaving Admiral Karl Dönitz to sue for peace, after pointlessly attempting to convince the Allies to join forces against the Soviet Union. On May 2, Marshal Zhukov informed Stalin that Berlin had been conquered. The red flag flew above the Reichstag, over the bodies of 150,000 Soviet soldiers killed in combat. Germany officially surrendered unconditionally on May 7, 1945.

He should have been out celebrating with the rest of the officers and soldiers occupying the German capital, yet that night Elías was drinking alone in a seedy bar on the shores of the River Spree. Yes, it was true that artillery no longer boomed and bombs no longer fell, that the tanks would soon be decommissioned and the soldiers sent home in endless convoys, but for Elías and the NKVD, the war was not over, simply shifting fronts.

The man he was awaiting appeared five minutes later, glanced around cautiously and, judging himself to be safe, approached one of the girls. German women now sold their bodies for almost nothing—a scrap of food, a few cigarettes, some clothing. Had they fallen on the American side, they'd have been far luckier, but this was the Soviet side and men like the one who had just walked in didn't pay in chocolates and silk stockings. Elías watched him follow a redhead with hard features up the stairs. He waited five more minutes, smoking a cigarette and finishing his drink, and then headed up himself.

The door was unlocked; the redhead had kept her word. Elías turned the handle and walked in. The woman was washing her crotch at a small chamber pot; the man had taken off his shirt.

"What's going on here? Who are you?"

Elías gave the woman a meaningful glance, and she pulled up her panties and rushed out, pausing briefly to take the money Elías had promised her.

"You've got a poor memory, Pierre. Or is that no longer the name you go by? Should I call you the baker?"

The Argelès baker's jaw dropped. He should have recognized Elías immediately. War changed people, no doubt, but the patch over his right eye and the green intensity of his left were unmistakable.

"*Quelle surprise!* Look at you. I hear you're a commander now, a real war hero," Pierre fumbled. He stuck out a friendly hand, but it was trembling.

"What are you doing in Berlin?"

Pierre shrugged, rummaging in his shirt for a pack of cigarettes to buy time. Elías saw the outline of a German gun beneath the clothes piled on a chair.

"You know I'm not going to answer that question, right? We're little fish, each in their own pond, but it's all the same sea. I, however, can guess what you're doing in my room and why you paid the girl to leave the door open. This is how it works, I know that. Just a little unexpected, caught me off guard."

Elías quickly glanced around the room, assessing his options. The window opened onto an alley running parallel to the river. That would be a good place.

He pulled out a slip of red paper and placed it on the bed. "It's got your name on it."

Pierre weighed the chances of snatching his gun before Elías had time to react. Dismally low.

"So you know."

Yes, Elías knew. During the time he'd been in Argelès, Elías had been spending much of his time doing things for Pierre that the Party knew nothing about. The red and blue papers, it turned out, were often edicts made out of self-interest.

"Why the boy, why Tristán? What did he ever do to you?"

It had been personal. Pierre sat down on the bed and looked at the paper, as though to ensure there was no mistake.

"Too happy-go-lucky, too good-looking, too seductive. I've never liked men who look like they walked out of an American movie. But it seems my wife did."

Elías swallowed. People always thought they'd been called to a higher mission, something greater than themselves. But time after time, they succumbed to their own self-interest.

"I could have spoken to him, convinced him to stop seeing her if that's what was bothering you."

Pierre laughed bitterly. "You don't get it, do you? It was him, his existence, that bothered me. Women like my wife are easy to come by. But men like that kid…I just couldn't stand it."

The next morning, the military police found Pierre's body in the alley, his throat slit, no documentation on him. By the time they figured out who he was, Elías Gil would be in Paris on his new posting with papers proving that he was a harmless civil engineer. He was finally going to be reunited with Esperanza.

He'd forgotten how much he loved her dark nipples. And the smell of her sex, the touch of her fingers. It was like starting over, slowly reconquering a lost territory. Speaking without embarrassment, without the unpleasant sensation of having interrupted a life that no longer needed another presence by its side. Esperanza was the same, but different. Like the set of matryoshka dolls he'd brought her as a souvenir. Hiding, secret, but more and more real the deeper he went. Sometimes from the window ledge where she often perched like a gargoyle, watching rain fall over Paris, she observed him walking around the apartment naked with what might have been a look of astonishment. The first few days she didn't even dare to take off his eye patch, and it was like making love fully clothed, or with the lights turned out.

They recounted their lives to each other, what had happened over the course of those years, although really Esperanza was the one who spoke. Elías listened absently, wearing an innocent smile, as she told him of the casting calls she'd gone on for a film producer. They made no mention of what had happened in Argelès; it was as though one horror simply replaced another, like a child's game.

"Would you like to go back to Spain?" he asked out of the blue one morning, walking in with his feet soaking wet, the newspaper drenched.

Esperanza gazed sadly at him. He hadn't even considered the fact that if she went with him, her future as an actress was over. It was true that from 1946 to 1947 she'd made only a couple of movies with very minor roles, but she hadn't lost hope. People said that Esperanza had talent and all she needed to do was to be patient and determined. Elías wasn't concerned in the slightest. He was on a mission and was going to carry it out, whether Esperanza followed him or not.

"It would be dangerous to return."

"If things were too calm, we'd be bored to tears," he said playfully, and they both smiled. And that smile put the seal on it.

But Elías hadn't asked to be sent to Spain because he was bored in France.

Two weeks earlier he'd had a shocking encounter in front of the Church of Saint-Germain-des-Prés. A beggar taking shelter from the rain beneath the portico had attracted his attention, banging on a tin pot. Elías looked away and continued down the road, but then something about the man made him retrace his steps. The shadowy light of the arcade distorted the beggar's face when he stood, as though in a trance, contemplating a gargoyle spouting dirty water from its mouth. The man's head jerked spasmodically, as if he'd lost control of his body. He was wrapped in a filthy military cape, his nose and reddish eyebrows sticking out, dripping rain onto his pointy chin.

"Martin?" The beggar turned sideways and squinted, then wordlessly rushed off through the plaza, turning in alarm every few steps to see that Elías was still following him.

"Martin, wait! It's me, Elías Gil."

The beggar stopped. For a second, the sun going down behind the bell tower cast a surreal reddish glow on his face. It had been so long since anyone called Martin by his name that he dropped his bundle, trembling with emotion.

Two hours later, after showering at an old pension on Rue du Dragon, Martin stared at the filthy clothes he'd been wearing continuously for the past several months. The contrast between the tattered rags and his now clean, soap-smelling skin made him feel smaller and more insignificant than he had in a long time.

"You should have just left me alone, pretended you didn't recognize me," he said reproachfully.

Elías stared at Martin's wounds, both the old scars Igor Stern's torture had left on his body and the clear marks and bruises of more recent fights and beatings. Life on the streets must have been so hard, and Martin obviously had paid the consequences. For an hour, the Englishman recounted his travails since the two of them had parted ways in 1934. The tale of those thirteen years was horrifying, and in truth Elías got a better picture of how bad it had been from Martin's telling silences than from the words he spoke. Elías asked only a few questions about things he could make no sense of.

"Didn't you enlist in the British army at the start of the war?"

Martin flashed a bitter smile. There was little left of the sweet, naïve seventeen-year-old Elías had met on that train to Moscow in 1933.

"After the Soviets deported me, the embassy treated me like a leper. I don't know what they found most troubling—that I was a Communist, that I'd escaped the gulag, or my sexual tendencies. I'm inclined to think, though, that the latter is what made them declare me unfit for armed service."

He was choked by fear and sorrow, trying to explain the things he'd been forced to endure for being homosexual. Describing the scenes filled his eyes with panic and he looked half crazed, reliving the horror and momentarily forgetting where he was, his mind focused on nothing but the nightmare he'd been through.

"They played with me like a toy, passed me around from hand to hand, I suffered things no man could endure. And then I suppose at some point I had a change of heart: I went from feeling tormented to feeling like a tormenter. I worked for some really shady characters in London, earned some money, broke a few bones, and made dangerous enemies. So I had to run, and this is the only place I felt safe."

"In occupied France?"

"The Nazis weren't as scrupulous as SS officers liked to make out. When it came to recruiting informers, they cared very little about one's race, religion, or sex life. I had a lover who was a lieutenant, and I can't say I'm sorry about it. I collaborated with the Gestapo, turned in a few spies planted in the German rear guard...I guess you could say I got by."

Martin stopped talking to gauge Elías's reaction. His old friend seemed to be making judgments, deeming his crimes voluntary, when the truth was there had been no other way to keep his head above water. No one had called him back to Moscow, decorated him, given him the chance to erase his past on Nazino with a Tommy gun in one hand and his ideals in the other. Unlike Elías, Martin had been spat out by the sea, washed up on the shore like detritus.

"After '45 came the hour of vengeance—executions, reprisals against the collaborators. It's funny: When the Germans were marching down the Champs-Élysées, the heroes were nowhere to be found, hiding under the brims of their hats; but the moment liberation came, the arbiters of justice crawled out from under their rocks. You had to point fast and furious at all the guilty before they pointed at you. In the end, you could say I was lucky: I was jailed in Bordeaux for eight months, raped, humiliated, treated like scum in a cell with eight other men who'd lost all measure of humanity except for their cruelty. No one ever imagines how twisted people become when put in the role of executioner, how cruel and sadistic they are, what pleasure they take in torturing their victims. How proud they are, how wild their cries. I experienced every facet of the disease that turns men into monsters—but they didn't hang me. I made it out alive, if breathing counts as life. And now here you are. You've found me and judged me and are here to treat me with the victor's hypocritical mercy. Isn't that right?"

Elías looked away, unable to hold Martin's gaze. It was true that he didn't know what his old friend had been through, nor did he want to imagine it. Martin no longer bore any resemblance to the young man he used to know. This one was lost in his own bizarre, obsessive world as he buttoned the clean shirt Elías had bought him. He was a stranger.

"I'm not the victor, Martin. Since Nazino, there are no failures and no victories."

Martin stiffened and gazed warily at Elías, as though in his paranoia he'd somehow imagined that Elías was trying to wheedle information out of him.

"I've seen him. He's here, in Paris."

"Who?"

"Igor Stern. I can show you the hotel where he stays, the restaurant where he has breakfast every day with his two bodyguards."

Martin smiled broadly, noting that he'd captured Elías's attention. He tucked in his shirttail and realized, self-consciously, that there weren't enough holes on the belt to fit his waist, so emaciated had he become.

"Anna is with him, you know."

The bistro was deserted, rain pooling on chairs at the outdoor tables and forming puddles on the ground. From a window, Elías sat observing the hotel's gray façade.

"Here he comes." Martin pointed to a hunched figure making its way wearily up the hill toward the steps of Sacré-Coeur. One man protected him from the rain with an outsized umbrella, while the other walked a few steps behind, turning constantly to make sure no one was following them. The three of them walked up to the hotel but only one entered. The other two stayed outside beneath the marquee.

"I know his room number. We could do it now, his goons wouldn't even realize."

Elías wondered how Martin had managed to find out what room Igor was in but decided not to ask. Beneath that shock of red hair, his glassy eyes looked feverish, insane. He really was out of his mind if he thought they could simply walk up to Igor Stern's room and bump him off, just like that. It wasn't that easy. Stern today was a thousand times more dangerous than he had been on Nazino. He was rich now, and far more powerful and sadistic. He was backed by the Politburo, and half of the diplomats in Europe owed him favors that he knew how to call in. Besides, there was a chance that Anna was in the room with him.

"I assumed you'd hate him as much as I do," Martin said contemptuously, after hearing what sounded like clumsy excuses.

Oh, Elías hated him. Of course he did. But not for the reasons that Martin or anyone else who knew what had happened on

Nazino might imagine. And part of him—a part that he refused to recognize or listen to—admired Igor Stern. He was the only truly free man Elías had ever met in his life.

Over the course of years, Elías had been forced to work with him on various operations devised by Beria, and this had provided the opportunity to study him up close, to come to understand him. Despite never for an instant forgetting his compulsive urge for vengeance, he realized that Stern was different from any other man he'd ever come across. Different not only in his way of being and thinking but also in his way of feeling. Igor's thoughts, desires, and emotions were never hindered by any sort of morality whatsoever.

Killing, stealing, lying, manipulating—they were all means to an end he pursued with cold and relentless calculation, never veering in the slightest from his meticulous plan. He derived neither pleasure nor displeasure from the crimes he committed, nor did he boast about what he was or blame the world for having made him that way. He looked down on his fellow men for being bound by ties that he couldn't feel. And that made him a better opponent than Elías, who was incapable of letting go of the festering memories that weakened and undermined him more each day.

"You're no better than me," Igor had said to him after they'd murdered a Gestapo informer in Kursk. Igor had killed the man with his bare hands, and then they'd both watched his body execute a tragic pirouette after being hurled from the balcony and crashing against the cobblestones below. Observing the unnatural position he'd landed in, Igor smiled sadly. "I bet you're responsible for more death, abuse, beatings, and torture than I am, Commander Gil. The difference resides in the fact that you serve a cause, whereas I serve only myself. But we both know it's a false distinction. I don't feel the need to throw myself into the trenches to defy death, because I'm not ashamed of what I am. I'm not proud either—both are useless emotions. We are what we are and should simply accept it. We fight for our place, seize it, defend it tooth and nail, and then, one day, age and exhaustion make us weak and we're defeated by others who have become more powerful. That's the way it goes, always has and always will. No point making a big deal of it. But you insist on fooling yourself, refusing to accept that your true nature is actually identical to mine. You could be me, and you'd enjoy it. What a terrible paradox it must be, Commander—to admire your tormenter."

Igor's words were as true as they were horrific. Elías's moral superiority, his silence and loyalty, left some sort of evil aftertaste. Something about the way he accepted orders and carried them out that made it clear that one day he was going to explode. He wasn't capricious or anarchic like Stern; he knew that the fear he inspired was in fact based on the opposite: the conviction that the punishment he meted out was never arbitrary. But deep down he often longed to be given a valid reason to behave as cruelly as Igor himself. And when he did, Elías became merciless. And therein lay his weakness. Igor had nothing to prove, nothing he yearned to be forgiven for. He had no regrets, no memories, no guilt. When it was required of him, Igor both obeyed and demanded obedience. It was something he'd long grown accustomed to, like a trained dog. For Elías, on the other hand, lurking beneath the cruelty were anguish and remorse.

He blamed his weakness on Irina. It was an irresolute feeling, one that was tearing him apart. His memory of her had become a maddening obsession, the embodiment of all that was odious and despicable about Elías, a monster he had to keep under wraps at any cost. Each time he was awarded a medal, given a pat on the back or any form of congratulations, each time his comrades in arms praised his performance in battle, the image of Irina drowning in that river defiled the moment, reminding him of what he truly was—a coward who hadn't hesitated to consider eating her daughter, just as he hadn't hesitated to kill Irina and hand over Anna to Igor in order to save his own miserable life.

One day he'd seen a girl on the outskirts of Warsaw. She wasn't very tall, but she looked like Irina—the same open defiant expression, same long face and tantalizing mouth and a mop of hair that hung halfway down her back. Elías paid her for sex and spent hours covering part of her face with her hair so that he could see only one mysterious eye. He realized, then, that he'd looked for Irina in all women, to an almost depraved extreme. He was turning her ghost into flesh and blood, surrendering to an obsessive ritual of possession that frightened his lovers, who in the end always fled, refusing the role he'd assigned them. And then would come a period of self-loathing, the shame over the absurd extremes of his game, and he would try to free himself of Irina, disavow her, hate her for making him feel weak. Elías would then throw himself into his work to show the world—and himself—that he was free of her memory. And that was when he became more unpredictable, more violent, more taciturn.

Igor Stern knew all of this and delighted in using it against Elías. He often turned up accompanied by Anna, who was slowly becoming a young lady as attractive as her mother. She looked so much like Irina that Elías had to turn away, offended, when Igor grabbed her by the waist and kissed her neck obscenely, despite still forcing her to call him *Papa*.

"I know what you feel, Gil. It scares you so much that you don't dare name it, but I can see it in your eye when you look at her, thinking no one can see you. She reminds you so much of Irina that you can't help wanting her, even if only to destroy her, to erase her from your mind. Isn't that so? I could give her to you, you know. Would you sleep with her? With Irina's daughter? I'm sure you would, and then like a hypocrite you'd jump off a bridge into the river or stick a gun in your mouth. Because you're weak and phony. You're nothing but a clay hero... Commander."

. . .

"We could go right now. We could kill him, Elías."

Elías Gil parted the lace curtain and looked through the enormous window at the front of the hotel. It was raining even harder, torrents of water flowing down the gutters. Igor's henchmen stood smoking irritably, squeezed tightly into their coats.

She was probably in the room with him. Perhaps naked, kneeling before him. She was just a girl, aware of her fate but not beaten by it, her expression resolute but not defeated. Anna was like her mother, born to be free, and she'd hold on to that freedom at all costs, even if it meant subjecting herself to Igor's depraved humiliations. She would never be broken, Elías was sure of that.

"We can't touch him, Martin."

Those were the last words they exchanged. Martin stormed out of the glass-fronted bistro and, outside, turned to look back at Elías, one hand on something that was sticking out of his waistband. Elías realized that it was a dagger. They looked at each other through the misty glass for a second, and then the Englishman seemed to realize that he'd never make it past even one of the bodyguards. Suddenly, Martin's head began to twitch convulsively; he burst into tears, placed both hands against the window, then rushed off down the street. He disappeared into the Paris rain, withered and distraught, hunched in his beggar's stance, crestfallen, nursing a sorrow no one would ever understand.

It's better this way, Elías thought despondently. He wanted no witnesses to what he'd decided to do the moment he saw Igor Stern.

"I have to think about it."

Ramón Alcázar Suñer had become a stern, arrogant official at the Spanish embassy in Paris. In theory, his mission was to oversee the economic interests of Spanish corporations, but the truth was he was there to keep tabs on Spanish Communists who had settled in France and to round up those sentenced by military tribunals in Spain. Elías knew this, and since returning to France, the two had studiously avoided contact so as not to be undone by a friendship that had benefited both of them more than once. It seemed their relationship had not turned into bitterness or mistrust, despite the harrowing violence each of them had suffered at the hands of the other's party. From a distance, they sincerely appreciated each other and had somehow managed to preserve the best of their childhood memories. But friendship was something warm and gray in an age of Manichaean black and white: If anyone found out about this meeting, they would both be in a terrible bind.

"Think about *what?*" Elías protested vehemently. "I'm handing you one of the NKVD's most important agents on a platter."

Ramón Alcázar gazed pensively out at the street from the window of his car, feebly raising a hand as though his friend was asking something entirely out of reach.

"What you're handing me is the opportunity to take revenge for you rather than doing it yourself."

It was true, there was no denying it. Elías stared at his friend, trying to make him see how much he hated Igor Stern and the lengths he was willing to go for that hatred.

"What do you care? You have no idea what Stern is like, how he torments people, toys with them until he's bored, like a cat, not killing them."

Ramón exhaled cigarette smoke, violently.

"I'm not your whipping boy, Elías! Don't think for a minute you can manipulate me or use me at will. Soviet agents are not my concern. Killing Igor Stern could have serious repercussions." Ramón's harsh look softened slightly before he continued. "Is this about the girl? What happened on Nazino is still eating you alive, isn't it? You did what you could to help them, Elías. No one can blame you or say otherwise. Forget about that girl, about the past, about Stern. Go home to your pretty wife, make love, have kids, and sink into a comfortable, anonymous life."

It was a lovely idea, no doubt. But they both knew that Elías wouldn't even consider it.

"Every time I see a girl who reminds me of Anna, I'm afraid. I start following her down the street, watch her for days, clock her routines, find out who her friends and family are. I make a move, talk to them, and in their naïveté they have no idea what's going on in my head."

Ramón leaned back impatiently against the car seat. "I don't need to hear this."

"But I need to tell you. You have to understand, Ramón. When I see those girls, I feel sick, it's as if their innocence tarnished me with guilt over what I did to Irina, and what I would have done to Anna if necessary. And I hate them, hate their purity and their blond hair and their angelic expressions. I hate them because they're like an accusation and I want them to be gone, I want to beat them to death, to disfigure the faces that make me see Irina sinking to the bottom of the river. It's driving me insane...And Igor Stern is behind it all. He knows how I feel, he understands my weakness and uses it to torture me; that's the only reason he keeps Anna by his side. She's the reminder of the day I handed over my coat, and with it what remained of my dignity as a man."

Elías closed his eyes, spent. His breath was shallow, and he opened his mouth as though struggling for air in the car.

"I want him dead, Ramón. I'm prepared to pay the price."

"It will be a very high price indeed."

"I don't care."

"You don't understand, Elías. If you start this, you won't be able to stop. They'll keep asking for more and more. You'll have jumped out of the frying pan and into the fire."

Since the day he'd seen Martin, Elías had had a lot of time to think. His memory of Irina was now so distorted that sometimes he saw her in Esperanza. He would watch his wife, buzzing around their tiny apartment like a bee, and wonder again and again why he hadn't wanted her to become pregnant. Why he kept coming up with excuses not to bring children into the world. And the truth was that he was afraid, terribly afraid, when he imagined what they'd turn out like—if they would be like him instead of her, if they'd inherit his character, his brooding silences, and the violence that seethed quietly within him, day after day. Sometimes he took off his patch and found himself staring into the mirror, trying to gauge the darkness in his empty socket, searching for a light that was not there. And then he'd wonder if his horrific deformity, the irreparable damage that Igor had done and was symbolized by his empty eye, was hereditary.

"I understand perfectly," Elías replied.

When his damaged side came out, he had to accept it, accept that the endless suffering he'd seen had destroyed part of his soul. Elías was not the man his father dreamed he would become but the man others had turned him into. Well, then: It was time for others to pay.

Elías pulled out a folded piece of paper, handed it to Ramón. On it was a detailed list of names and addresses where the French gendarmerie could find and arrest Spanish Communist Party members wanted by Spain for violent crimes. Six names, sentenced to death for an act of revenge in which their only involvement was having come between Elías Gil and Igor Stern.

"When they discover there's an inside leak, I'll make sure the Party puts me in charge of the investigation. I'll find someone responsible," he said coldly, and then added that he'd need compensation.

"What kind of compensation?"

Elías passed Ramón another note. "This man is a professional torturer. He's killed several of ours, and he lives here under embassy protection. To avoid suspicion and keep from being a suspect, I need to earn some points. Then I'll find a way to get posted to Spain. Once I'm there, you make sure Igor Stern disappears forever."

Ramón nodded wordlessly and remained silent for quite some time, gazing at his friend as though he didn't recognize him, in a mix of shock, disgust, and sorrow.

"I'd almost prefer you didn't do this, didn't sink this low."

Elías's eye flashed in anger. How could Ramón ask him to remain dignified when he'd been in the depths of depravity? What did he expect, for Elías to be an honest enemy? Had he disappointed his friend? Well, what a shame, but the rest of humanity had disappointed Elías as well.

They weren't heroes; they were simply wretched, confused, frightened men.

"I want the torturer. It's nothing to you, you've got a lot of young blood, and it will make a good alibi for me."

Ramón Alcázar glanced at the note. He hardly knew the man, perhaps had seen him a couple of times and, needless to say, didn't like him. And that, it seemed, was enough to sign his death sentence. Though he didn't know it, the man was as good as dead. Maybe at the moment he was strolling around Paris, admiring Notre-Dame or gazing out over the melancholy banks of the Seine. But he was already dead, and Ramón reddened at how easily he'd just disposed of a life.

"I'll tell you where he lives and how to ambush him."

Five minutes later, Elías stepped out of the car and put on his coat. The cold was returning, and with it the sense that all Paris was still, quiet, practically dead.

"One more thing," he said to Ramón. "When Stern dies, I want you to make sure he knows that I'm the one who sent him to hell."

Ramón nodded again, glancing at the list of names that Elías was willing to sacrifice for the sake of revenge.

"Don't you care about what will happen to your comrades, their families? There's still time to turn back, Elías. I can burn this list and forget we ever saw each other."

Elías clenched his teeth and stared directly at his friend. "What about me, Ramón? Can I burn my memories and pretend all of these things never happened to me?"

"You're going to hate yourself for this. You know that, don't you?"

Elías muffled himself up in his coat and said goodbye to his friend. Yes, he'd hate himself forever, but that was nothing new. Self-loathing had been with him since the day he struck Irina to keep from drowning in the river off Nazino Island.

26

The newly inaugurated building was blindingly white, in sharp contrast to the earth tones of those wedged around it. Its open-plan architecture afforded magnificent views of the rooms inside, which were bathed in sunlight; sparse, neutral furnishings seemed to induce well-being. Gonzalo had to admit that his ex-brother-in-law was one stylish architect. He designed light, airy spaces that were perfectly suited to his discreet, elegant personality.

Guests had gathered on one of the sprawling upper balconies, created by eliminating the bay of the façade overlooking the plaza below. From that lovely wide-open space they could see most of the city's historic quarter, the cathedral towers as well as the rooftops of old buildings in the Raval. A small cadre of impeccable waiters stood lining the wall, awaiting the host's signal to begin parading around with trays held aloft, plying guests with canapés and glasses of cava. Pleasant music played in the background; Gonzalo listened closely and decided it was Bach, one of his sacred pieces. Very fitting.

That morning, Luis had picked out a neutral-colored suit and skipped the tie, a reflection of his decorous character—unpretentious despite the glowing tributes—and proportionate to the visual impact of both building and creator. The fact that it had been dubbed "the Aldo Rossi," after the Italian master architect, was a display of pride that couldn't be blamed on Luis.

"Gonzalo, what a surprise!"

Gonzalo saw nothing out of the ordinary in Luis's sincere exclamation, nor in the friendly, self-assured way he shook his hand.

"I saw in the paper that your building was being inaugurated and thought it would be a good time to stop by and see you."

Luis nodded slowly, though a slight hint of doubt flashed in his eyes; his expression had become almost imperceptibly more questioning, mistrustful.

"We just landed. I'll be here in the morning but we go back to London tomorrow night." The plural included a slim-waisted blonde almost six feet tall, poured into an elegant pearl-gray dress with matching shoes. Luis gently guided her over to introduce her to Gonzalo: Erika, the English fiancée. "We're getting married in a month," he said, and it sounded strangely like an alibi.

Gonzalo exchanged a few polite words with her in English, they had a toast, and she made a discreet exit.

"I was hoping we could have a little talk, just the two of us," Gonzalo ventured, angling them to a corner of the enormous balcony.

Luis smiled politely and handed him a glass of cava, plucked off a passing tray. He seemed to need people to see his display of affability.

"This really isn't the time or place for that kind of conversation, as I'm sure you can see. And the truth is, my schedule is a little tight."

Gonzalo downed his cava and pulled out a cigarette. These were the most disturbing, agonizing days of his life, but he was trying to keep calm. Sometimes he pretended it was all simply a long, suffocating nightmare, and that helped a little, made things slightly more bearable.

"I think we both know that you'd better find an opening in your schedule, Luis. Otherwise you'll be making time for the police."

Luis had the good sense and dignity not to feign incredulity or babble idiotically. He simply clenched his right fist slightly, more unconscious gesture than open threat. A nice, elegant warning. That was Luis.

"I guess I'm supposed to tell you what I think or feel now."

Gonzalo finished his cigarette.

"I really don't care what you feel or think right now. I'll be waiting for you in ten minutes, in the plaza across the street. If you don't show, I'm going to the police."

Shortly thereafter, they sat face-to-face at a greasy hole-in-the-wall, slot machines pinging in the background. Both men were out of place, too extravagant among the small-time neighborhood thugs who were regulars at this foul-smelling dive bar.

"I don't understand you," Luis said finally, still staring at Gonzalo. His once friendly expression was now dark, deep, and mysterious.

"That's what I should be saying. I saw the tape, Luis. You were there the day Atxaga attacked me; you stole Laura's computer. It was right there in front of me the whole time, so obvious that I didn't see it. And it didn't click until I heard Siaka's message."

Luis smiled. "Pretty clever, my using Aldo Rossi's name. He's quick, a smart kid, but it would never have occurred to him if I hadn't written down what to say. I was hoping that by having him call you and mention the architect's name, you'd put two and two together."

"You wanted me to catch you?"

Luis shrugged, indifferent. He'd been wondering for some time how and when his desperation to escape would end, how long it would take for the men who killed his son and destroyed his marriage to figure out that it was him and not Laura who had tortured and killed Zinoviev.

"Turns out I'm not a good killer. I don't have what it takes, the coolness, the mettle. It's not worth the suffering I've caused or the suffering I feel. I guess I'm looking for a way to put an end to the whole thing."

Gonzalo tried to imagine what the man must have gone through after the death of his son. Still mourning when he decided to move to London, Luis fell into the arms of a beautiful girl in an attempt to forget the woman he loved. Here was the evidence: Behind the successful and triumphant façade lay a man consumed by sorrow, perhaps shame—alone, unable to repair the damage done.

"When Alcázar went to Laura's apartment and accused her of Zinoviev's murder, she knew it was you. And yet she protected you."

"I told her myself. I wanted her to see what her selfishness, her determination had done to me. I wanted to accuse her of turning me into a monster. I waited for hours on the old sofa, my hands bloody, the nail gun on the table. When she walked in, I didn't even have to tell her what I'd done."

There, in the dimly lit bar, Luis recounted the scenes of horror and what he'd said to Laura.

"I told her I was going to turn myself in, but she convinced me not to. She thought fast and decided I should leave the country, go back to London, pretend I had nothing to do with it. It would look like the mafia settling a score, that kind of thing was common. Laura knew how investigators' minds work, how judges think. Later, I realized she knew that, sooner or later, I'd be caught. If not by the police, then by the Matryoshka. She knew I wouldn't survive prison and that I could never stand up to those people. So she gave me the perfect alibi...When I found out about her suicide, I realized no one was going to hold me accountable. She took all the blame. Until you turned up with your suspicions, found her laptop, and asked for the case to be reopened."

Gonzalo squinted slightly and gave Luis a look, as though trying to hypnotize him, but was met stubbornly with Luis's implacably calm expression, exquisite manners, self-restraint, and alluring smile. He'd hardly narrowed his eyes, but his expression had become a delicate line nailed to the bar's filthy yellow wall, had taken on a helplessness that not even he was aware of. The affable, polite, sensitive man sitting before him was also that other one—the one acting like he had nothing to do with Zinoviev's torture and death. Luis himself probably didn't even understand why he'd done what he'd done; it had all been so fast, and by the time the insane impulse that had overtaken him subsided, Zinoviev was a mass of flesh in his trembling hands. His mind took refuge, cloaked in a dark veil that was impervious to pity or reason. All he could think of was hurting his son's murderer, ripping apart every inch of his life in the most painful way possible. He couldn't, or wouldn't, or didn't know how to stop the orgy of violence that went on for hours. Each time Zinoviev's voice begged hoarsely for mercy, something ordered Luis to be even more vicious.

"Why did you steal Laura's computer from my car? Were you afraid I'd find something to incriminate you?"

Luis calmly smoothed back his hair, as though discipline and self-control were the most important things at that critical moment.

"When I found out you were asking for the case to be reopened, I guessed that you had Laura's laptop. So I simply followed you and waited. I had no intention of hindering the investigation, even though I was pretty sure you'd find out Laura didn't kill Zinoviev. But I decided to take the risk because I had to learn who his accomplice was, the person who was with him at the lake the day my son died. I had to know, I needed closure. And that information was on the computer. At first I thought that if I kept sending you files, you'd keep your word and carry the investigation through to the end, but then I realized that Alcázar and your father-in-law had convinced you to back out. So I decided to take action."

"What are you going to do with Siaka?"

"I haven't decided yet. I need your help; that's why I made him leave that message on your machine...What do you think I should do?"

Gonzalo was unequivocal. "You've killed one man and kidnapped another. If you kill Siaka, they will have won, Luis. Without his testimony, all the evidence Laura gathered will be circumstantial. It will be our word against theirs, justice will never be served. You have to let him go. Give me the computer and turn yourself in."

Luis stroked the back of one hand with the other, tracing the outline of his knuckles and veins. He saw that everything had gone past the point of no return. There was little chance of returning to London with beautiful Erika, getting married and starting over, living a happy, well-ordered life. One way or another, it would all go wrong, as it had with Laura. His years with Roberto were a lovely fiction. Lovely and unrepeatable.

He was destined never to feel anything again. Luis realized this as he was torturing Siaka. It had been different with Zinoviev— brutal, visceral, impulsive. The second time was more refined; he'd gotten a taste for it, the bluffing and the feints, the waiting game, terrifying his victim one second and showing compassion the next. Still, what had made him see his true nature was the lack of justification. Finally, his true self had been set free: He wasn't doing it to avenge Roberto and Laura's deaths, at least not after the first initial instinct, which was just a flimsy excuse. He was doing it for himself, and even if he didn't actively enjoy inflicting pain on Siaka, he did not feel remorse either. Rather, he simply needed to impose justice and some sort of universal order, to find a place where things were in balance.

He shook his head. "If I do what you're asking, one of my son's killers will go free. He'll bargain with the judge, be given a new identity, get off scot-free. And I'll go to jail, because it will come out that I killed Zinoviev."

"That's possible," Gonzalo admitted.

"And for what? Do you really think it will have been worth it? Do you think your sister's wish will come true and the Matryoshka will be disbanded? That Alcázar and your father-in-law will pay for their scheming all these years? Or will they all go unpunished?"

"With the proof on Laura's laptop and Siaka's testimony, neither of them will go unpunished, I can guarantee it."

"Even if they pay, won't there be a thousand other Matryoshkas waiting in the wings? Wasn't Laura fighting evil, writ large? And hoping, absurdly, to win? What she never understood is that you can't defeat something that lives in every one of us. And the fact is that evil resides in the deepest part of human nature, don't you think? She died for nothing, just like my son, and here you are asking me to throw myself at the altar of sacrifice, for nothing. Because nothing will ever change."

What was it that his father used to say? That silent line in Gonzalo's dream, the one he had to remember in order to save Laura, the line that always came to him too late?

"The first drop to fall starts breaking down the stone."

Luis shot him a sideways look. "A bit trite, don't you think? That might be the case for those who are patient, but you and I don't have a lifetime to watch the edifice be worn down."

"It was something my father used to say. Every man chooses the battles he's going to fight and win."

Luis cleared his throat, stood, and asked for the check.

"Yeah? And which battle did you choose?"

Gonzalo remained pensive. The recurring dream he'd had all his life—it was so vivid.

"The same one as my sister."

"Well, then?"

"I can help you, Luis. You need a good lawyer. We can come up with plenty of mitigating circumstances, but you have to stop.

Now. I'm here to accompany you to the police. If you don't go voluntarily, I'll report you and they'll come after you."

Luis told the waiter to keep the generous tip. He smiled imperturbably, as always—sure of himself, not a threat to anyone.

"A real shame to hear you say that, Gonzalo. See, I have a different way of looking at things. I hear what you're saying, and though I understand your reasoning, it's got nothing to do with mine. Plus, I think you've made a pretty serious miscalculation: You hardly know me, yet you come here and threaten me. That's something I can't tolerate. The truth is, there's another reason why I let Siaka leave you that message."

Most of the time, Siaka remained in a sort of semiconscious dream state, like a fetus floating in formaldehyde, unaware of the physical reality of his surroundings. The immense room could go from torture chamber to beautiful salon from which to contemplate the sea, lost in melancholy. When he awoke, Siaka saw that Luis had ripped off his clothes and then soaked his body. He was freezing and shivering, cold to the bone. He slid down the wall to the floor, head tilted back.

His nose must have been broken—holding his head like that made it easier to breathe. Siaka put a hand to his cheekbones, swollen large as tennis balls, and bit his lip to keep from crying out in pain. Feeling sorry for himself was a waste of time, not to mention energy, and he was going to need every bit of it he had to survive. It was clear, since the first blow, that there was no turning back. The way Siaka saw it, he had two choices: either he killed Luis, or that lunatic killed him. So he obsessed over the prospect of catching him with his guard down, working away at a plan with chisel and hammer. He dreamed up wild scenarios, discarded them, reworked the details. He would have only one opportunity.

In the meantime, Siaka had to tough it out, and that meant submission was not an option. He knew the way Luis thought and acted, and knew that the second he begged for his life it was all over. That was what Luis had done with the Russian: tortured him until finally Zinoviev begged for an end to the torment. And then he let him die, and felt magnanimous about it. Luis forgave him and then executed him. But Siaka had no intention of dying and therefore no intention of begging. All he had to do was force his mind to go blank, numb the pain. He couldn't give in to Luis and his mind games, appealing to Siaka's emotions by telling stories about holidays with Laura, recounting tales of Roberto, saying things to try to make Siaka cry and get him to pronounce the words *Forgive me.*

He had to blunt the pain, wear it like a shroud the way he'd done as a boy when he was kidnapped and trained by the militia, the way he'd done to endure being raped by Zinoviev and taking part in macabre spectacles for rich degenerate clients. It was the only way he'd make it, by not thinking. It was the only way out.

He heard a key turn in the lock and his body tensed, preparing for another session.

Luis appeared in the doorway, glancing around quickly. Then he focused on Siaka and smiled amiably.

"There's someone here who wants to say hello." He turned to the door and pushed in Gonzalo.

Gonzalo stepped cautiously into the room. His heart clenched on seeing the swollen mass that Siaka had become. He turned to Luis, disdainful.

"How could you do this to a person?"

Luis observed Siaka attentively, as though seeing him for the first time, then nodded.

"I don't have a lot of time, Gonzalo. And I need to be sure of your loyalty."

He walked over to Siaka, took out a gun, and aimed it at his head.

"This bastard betrayed your sister; she trusted him and he used her trust to kidnap my son and hand him over to his killer. And you're worried about him. What kind of a brother are you?"

Gonzalo became distressed. "What are you going to do?"

Siaka stood slowly, his gaze steadily fixed on the barrel of the gun. Unfathomably, he looked into Luis's face and challenged him.

"Listen to the lawyer. If you kill me, the Matryoshka wins, but I don't think you care about that, despite your song and dance about loving Laura and your son. So if you're going to kill me, do it, but don't expect me to get down on my knees."

Luis's finger gripped the trigger, and he slowly cocked the hammer.

"Luis, don't do it," Gonzalo said.

"I won't, unless you tell me to."

"Are you insane? I'm not going to tell you to kill a man."

The hammer clicked, making a disappointed sound. Empty chamber, no bullet. Luis slammed the butt of the gun into Siaka's head and wheeled to face Gonzalo, enraged.

"Next time it won't be empty. And I'll give you the same choice. If you say no, I'll ask him and aim at you. And I'll go back and forth until one of you decides that the other one dies."

Gonzalo stared in wonder at this complete stranger, an expression of utter horror on his face. "Why are you doing this?"

Luis gave a malevolent smile and shrugged.

"Your sister once told me the story of a woman and her daughter your father met when he was young—I'm sure you know who I'm talking about. Someone forced your father to make an impossible choice: the hero and his virtue or the man and his needs. The monster won. Your father made his choice—he chose to live. I've picked my battle, and I'm fighting it my way, Gonzalo. You think I didn't see how you looked at me in the bar? You, the virtuous lawyer, Elías Gil's perfect son, and me, the cruel sadist. Your cause is right; mine is wrong. Your view of the world makes me sick! And

I'm going to prove that you're no better than me or your father. In forty-eight hours or less, either you ask me to shoot Siaka or he'll ask me to shoot you."

Miranda loved dancing to Compay Segundo y Sus Muchachos. There was something about Cuban *son* that went straight to her core, made all her worries float away. As long as the lights in the club were down, she could dance away her cares and dream she was still a little girl, holding on to her mother as they twirled through the laundry lines at their house in Havana, faded cotton sheets hanging out to dry, the smell of soap and yucca filling the air.

This was the fragile state of euphoria Miranda was in as she walked out of the dance hall, sweaty and tired but still light on her feet, tingling. She leaned against the hood of a car to wriggle her toes. She was no longer twenty years old, and wearing tight high-heeled shoes was torture. Miranda rummaged in her sequined bag for a pack of cigarettes.

"You need a light?"

The voice caressed the hairs on the back of her neck and she wanted to burst into tears. Slowly, her eyes scanned the parking lot for help. She was alone, the lights of the dance hall like an unreachable beacon for a shipwrecked sailor. Miranda knew that even if she shouted, no one would get there in time.

Floren Atxaga knew it, too, but he wasn't taking any chances. He didn't want any meddlers ruining his plans. With his right hand he grabbed Miranda's scalp and jerked her head back. With his left, he poured a bottle of acid onto her face.

The guy was tall and good-looking, like an ad agency creation. Alcázar remembered him well.

"Luis, what a coincidence."

They'd just bumped into each other in the waiting area of Gonzalo's office. For a second, Laura's ex-husband didn't recognize him, or that's what he made out. But then he seemed to remember and held out his hand sincerely, with a big open smile.

"Hey there, Inspector."

Alcázar felt a stab of envy at his tanned athletic body. Luis was one of those guys who seemed inhuman. Not an ounce of fat, flawless skin, every hair in place. It was enough to depress mere mortals. In a tiny display of self-pity, the ex-inspector decided not to tell him that in fact he'd retired. This, at least, made him feel slightly superior.

"What brings you here?"

Luis's reply was so quick as to be suspicious: He was just passing through Barcelona and had decided to say hello to Gonzalo but, he was sad to say, Luisa had told him that he wasn't in.

That was unfortunate, thought Alcázar. He said goodbye to Luis as he left and approached Luisa's desk. There was no need to introduce himself; he and Gil's assistant knew each other and neither one liked the other.

"What did he want?"

Luisa watched Luis walk down the hall.

"Who? Hot stuff? He was trying to get me into bed but I gave him the brush-off."

"Very funny. What did he want?"

Luisa shot him a wry look, perhaps comparing Alcázar's wrinkled skin, thickset body, and buffalolike wheeze to the almost feline perfection that had just slunk down the corridor leaving a trail of cologne in his wake.

"I'm afraid that's attorney-client privilege."

Alcázar slammed his hands onto Luisa's desk as though slapping down a dead fish. "I don't have time for nonsense, lady. Where's your boss?"

"He's not here."

Alcázar raised a lip and his mustache lifted, displaying a dirty eyetooth.

"How long since he was last in?"

"A couple of days."

"Has he called? Have you heard from him?"

Alcázar's somber expression was beginning to alarm Luisa, so she stopped kidding around.

"No, and to be honest he doesn't usually disappear without letting me know. Generally, he at least calls to tell me he won't be in, or that he's going to be late. Is something wrong?"

More brusquely than necessary, Alcázar strode past Luisa's desk and into Gonzalo's office, ignoring her protestations.

"I told you he's not here."

Indeed, the office was empty. But there was something in the air that made Alcázar's mustache tingle, coarse whiskers trembling.

"*He* was in here," he said, emphasizing the pronoun.

"Dream boy, you mean?"

Alcázar nodded. The scent of Luis's cologne was everywhere.

"I was only away for a minute," Luisa said in panic. "I went to the bathroom and when I came back he was sitting there, in Gonzalo's chair. He apologized, really politely, said the door was open and that he was hoping to talk to Gonzalo... It gave me a funny feeling."

"What kind of feeling?"

Luisa did a little wave with her hand, as though brushing away an absurd thought. "Nothing, really. It's just that I got the impression he'd been snooping around. Gonzalo has a very particular way he keeps his files, and it seemed like they'd been moved."

Alcázar made a mental note to possibly have a chat with Laura's ex, but that wasn't why he was there.

"Gonzalo's not in his apartment, hasn't been by the hospital to see his son. Lola says she hasn't seen him in two days."

Luisa nodded, twisted her lips pensively. "It's none of my business, but he's got a...friend. Tania."

Alcázar clenched his jaw. He'd already checked: Gonzalo hadn't been at Flight, Anna's bookstore, or Tania's studio.

"I think it's important for you to know: Floren Atxaga attacked his ex-wife last night, threw acid in her face when she was leaving a club." Luisa looked appalled, but Alcázar didn't let her speak. "She'll recover, although her face will be permanently scarred. Before he took off, Atxaga left a message for Gonzalo. He said he wasn't going to disfigure him, he was going to finish what he'd started in the parking garage. It's not likely, but he could come here. Just in case, I put an armed man in the lobby, and you need to be on the lookout...Stop shaking. Are you listening to me?"

"Do you think that son of a bitch has Gonzalo?"

Alcazar rejected the possibility, at least for the time being.

"He made that threat last night, and it sounds like Gonzalo's been missing for a couple of days. Do you think you'd recognize Atxaga if he appeared? I can get a photo faxed over to you."

Luisa nodded her head vehemently. "I'd recognize him in a second, I've seen that tape so many times." Stunned at how quickly she'd spoken, Luisa suddenly felt apprehensive and was sorry the words had slipped out of her mouth.

Alcázar gave her a penetrating stare. "Why have you seen the tape so many times?"

Luisa tried to avoid the trap his expression seemed to lay for her, but Alcázar wouldn't let up. He amped up the pressure until she told him the truth.

"Gonzalo asked me to get him a copy on the sly. He was obsessed with his sister's laptop and thought the key to what happened to it was on the tape."

"There's nothing on the tape. I've gone over it thoroughly myself."

"Well, that may be, but I think Gonzalo found something...The last time he watched it was exactly two days ago, here, in his office."

"Where does he keep it?"

"In the safe."

"Do you have the combination?"

Luisa nodded. Gonzalo had no memory for numbers and could barely remember his own phone number or national identification number, so he'd used a date he couldn't forget.

"23-06-1967."

Alcázar shook his head in resignation: the date Elías Gil disappeared at the lake.

He typed the code into the digital keypad, swung open the door, and saw a few documents and contracts but no tape.

"It was here, I watched him put it in with my own eyes."

"Who else has been in here since then?"

Luisa remained pensive. The scent of Luis's cologne was beginning to fade, blending in with the smoky stench of the ex-inspector's clothes.

The doorman tried to protest and very politely requested that Alcázar come back and show him the police credentials he'd flashed too quickly.

"Give me the damn key or I'm going to come down on you like a ton of bricks," Alcázar replied with affected severity, designed to overcome reservations.

The doorman was clearly daunted and handed over the spare apartment key.

Everything was silent, and the place gave off the impression that it always would be. Things said and done in those rooms, between those four walls, were invisible to strangers' eyes, inaudible to their ears.

Gonzalo was a methodical man, some might say clinical: everything in its place, nothing superfluous. But the apartment's orderliness seemed precarious, half done. There were very few personal effects—just a couple of books and photos—and the furniture looked out of place, as though awaiting more cozy environs. This could have been a criminal's hideout, a safe house, a rarely used office—any one of a number of places used temporarily, for folks just passing through. There was unfinished painting, really just a few brushstrokes...was Gonzalo after a new life? Was he planning on moving in? Alone, or with Tania? It had been almost six months since Laura's death, long enough for Alcázar to be able to see how similar Gonzalo was to his sister, despite their apparent differences.

It struck him that, in other circumstances, he would have gotten along well with Gonzalo, better than he had with Laura, whose character was so combative and rage fueled. And yet they were both Elías Gil's kids, there was no doubt about it. Gonzalo might be more even-keeled, more balanced, like his mother, but beneath the surface you could see the Gil in him. The old Cyclops would have been proud of his offspring; he was just as hardheaded. If there was one thing Gonzalo hated, it was people trying to manipulate or trap him, and Alcázar and Agustín González had made the mistake of underestimating him.

Given what the ex-inspector had just discovered by watching the security tape yet again, that miscalculation could turn out to be quite costly. There was no doubt it was Luis who had taken the computer. Why? The answer was there, blinking on Gonzalo's answering machine: He wanted Siaka. Gonzalo must have discovered Luis on the tape after hearing the message. And if Luis had stolen the tape from his office that very morning, almost right out from under Alcázar's nose—which infuriated him—that meant he had the safe's combination. How he'd gotten it seemed obvious: Gonzalo had given it to him, and unless Alcázar was mistaken, it hadn't been voluntarily. They had an agreement and Alcázar was convinced that Gonzalo wouldn't break it unless he was forced to: protection and immunity for Javier in exchange for Siaka, the computer, and forgetting about the Matryoshka.

But Luis was a new variable, and that changed the whole equation. His behavior was disconcerting. On the one hand, he'd stolen the laptop and kidnapped Siaka, thereby scotching the Matryoshka investigation; on the other, he seemed to have no qualms about sending the prosecutor files and telling Gonzalo that he had Laura's witness in his clutches.

Gonzalo had been right: Laura hadn't killed Zinoviev, and there was now proof of that. Gonzalo was so headstrong that Alcázar worried he might have tried to convince Luis to turn himself in. Picturing it almost made him laugh. The man lived in a world of his own, a complete idealist. He would have made appeals to Luis's sense of loyalty, to Laura's memory, tried to find any heartstrings he could tug.

But Luis's son had been murdered, and no wheedling or smooth talking could counter that. Mr. Elegant was going to blow it all sky-high, but how exactly?

Alcázar could sit and wait. After all, events seemed to be playing out in his favor and there was no doubt that's what Agustín would have recommended. Let them destroy each other, and all they'd need to do is come by with a dustpan to sweep up the mess. Who cared if Luis killed both Siaka and Gonzalo? In fact, that would serve their own interests as well as those of the Matryoshka. All they'd have to do is wait, and then in a few months send someone to quietly take care of Luis, after things had calmed down—a fatal accident that no one would be able to connect to the deaths of Siaka and Gonzalo.

So why was he picking up the phone and calling Anna Akhmatova to tell her they needed to talk?

"Thirty minutes, at the bookstore," was her terse reply.

Alcázar stood there for a few seconds, phone in hand, shaking his head. He was thinking about Cecilia, the days he'd spent wiping her after she'd gone to the bathroom because she could no longer do it herself. *Sometimes it amazes me, what a softie you are inside*, she'd told him. Alcázar recalled his shit-covered hands, the stench of his wife's guts slowly dissolving, the disgust he had to choke back each time he carried her to the toilet, the love he felt for her as he watched her struggle to move her corroding bowels. So many different men, inside the same one. He was like the dolls Laura liked so much. The thing was, you had to have patience to get to the last one. Alcázar thought of the Florida Keys on the travel brochure he always kept with him and smiled: The truth was, a humid seaside bothered his joints. And he'd never really liked Yanks anyway.

Anna Akhmatova listened to Alcázar's account without batting an eye, a requiem playing in the background, the volume down low. She'd hung the *Closed* sign on the door before taking him to the back of the shop.

Alcázar had never been there before. The back was split into a living area and a storage space where boxes of books were piled up. Anna took a seat in a rocking chair with a lace shawl over the back, an embroidered cushion beneath her. The image of the mild-mannered old lady would have been entirely credible had it not been for the Davidoff she'd taken out and lit with a match, like a truck driver. The cigarette had a strong, sweetish smell.

"Why are you telling me all this?"

Anna felt a tender sort of fondness for Alcázar. Thirty-four years ago, when it was still possible to believe she'd escaped Igor forever, the inspector had helped her. But over the years, he had called in that favor and then some. He was one of countless men whose excessive ambition ended up destroying their lives, whose high opinion of their own limitations—which they exhibited like battle scars—left them twisted. But beneath his outward cynicism and undisguised avarice, beneath his supposed lack of scruples lay the distant glimmer of the man he could have been. Today, the man before her was engaged in one last showdown between two irreconcilable sides of himself, and for some reason unfathomable to Anna, he'd chosen her as his battlefield.

"I think I know where Siaka is and who has Laura's computer."

She lifted her chin and eyed him haughtily. "Then you know what you have to do."

Alcázar nodded, not really listening, still wrestling with his own thoughts. "It's not that easy. I have a feeling Elías's son found out first. The idiot tried to act on his own and I'm pretty sure he's with the kid."

"Well, then, you can take care of him at the same time," Anna replied without a moment's hesitation.

"What about your daughter? Don't you care about her feelings for him?"

Anna smoothed the sleeve of her crimson blouse. A near-invisible thread hung from one of the buttons on the cuff. She quickly circled it around her pinkie and snapped it off.

"My daughter's feelings are none of your business. You should worry about your own position. If that kid ends up testifying in court, you and Agustín González are the two with the most skin to lose in this game, the ones who most benefit by his disappearance."

Alcázar walked over to a shelf and absently stroked the spine of a book.

"How old is he, Anna? Eighty? Ninety?"

"I have no idea what you're talking about."

"It's him, isn't it? Igor still controls your destiny. You're afraid of him, you loathe him, and yet you've turned out just like him. He decides who lives and who dies. He was the one who decided to kidnap Roberto, who ordered his execution and wanted his body thrown in the same lake where it all went down in 1967. He took revenge on Laura, and now it's Gonzalo's turn. I suppose next it will be his wife and kids. In fact, the whole ACASA project is just a form of vengeance when it comes down to it, a way of taking from Elías Gil the only thing he had left—his old house and empty grave—burying it beneath newly laid ground on which Igor Stern will take his last triumphant march and spit on the ghost of Elías, who is actually the one who won. Igor's still alive, isn't he? He's the Matryoshka."

"Watch what you say, Alcázar."

But the ex-inspector refused to hold back. He'd spent too long figuring it out.

"You used me that night, but I was too young and big-headed to realize. When I found you at the lake, shirt soaked in Elías's blood, I didn't understand that the both of you were caught in the same quandary. You and Elías shared a credo: Rules don't matter, right and wrong don't matter, truth and lies don't matter, morality doesn't matter—they're just dogmas to be overcome in the search for some sort of peace. You knew from the start that he was a double agent, that he was collaborating with my father. And that Igor Stern was still alive because my father hadn't kept his side of the bargain, which meant Elías had betrayed his comrades for nothing. You went to the lake to tell him, Igor Stern used you to confront Elías with the terrible truth. You were there to turn him in, take him down, destroy the myth of the hero once and for all. Stern wanted to watch him crumble. But you had no idea the effect your revelation would have.

"I always suspected that there was something between Gil and my father that I didn't know about, a friendship I never understood, because despite how risky it was for him to be friends with a Communist, he always maintained their friendship. I never found out why my father protected him. Maybe it's just that friendship means more than allegiance—but that would be too poetic, and my father was never one for poetry.

"You couldn't have guessed that thirty-four years later, your words would echo in your daughter's ears, that the shock waves would affect us all. The shrewdest man never imposes his will; he makes others believe that they're acting of their own volition. The most loyal slave is the one who feels free. I've thought about it a lot and I can't believe I didn't realize it sooner: Igor is behind all of this, controlling us like puppets, making us believe we're in control of our decisions. It's been so many years that it's hard to believe he's still fighting Elías, and in his war we're all just pawns, expendable chess pieces."

"Are you out of your mind?"

"There's not a single person he respects...except you. You're living proof of his victory. But now you're afraid of him, too. Not for your sake but for Tania's. He never loved her, he feels she doesn't belong. And it's through her that he controls you, isn't it? The sword of Damocles hanging over her head—that's what makes you his puppet. You know it's true, you know he'd take her away from you without giving it a thought if that could hurt the Gil family."

"I have no idea what you're talking about," Anna said once again.

"You know *exactly* what I'm talking about, Anna. And it's absurd—old rancor, played out by old men and women like you, Esperanza, me, Velichko...and Igor Stern. Our time is over, but we refuse to let go of the hatred, we hold on to it like a life preserver because without it we'd drown, even though staying afloat means drowning those whose only crime was to inherit our venom."

He sat close to Anna and stroked her cheek.

"It's time to weigh anchor, Anna. You need to speak to him. This has got to end."

Anna gazed at Alcázar, an unhinged gleam in her eye.

"You have no idea what you're asking. Honestly, you don't have a clue."

27

A summer storm rolled through the valley like a ship with a black flag, searching for a place to discharge its fury. The first drops came down like buckshot on the jetty by the lake, and although the boy kept looking up in alarm at the darkening sky, his father made no move nor did he divert his attention from the fishing rod.

"Concentrate on those things you can control and forget about the rest," he said to his son, elbowing the boy lightly to keep him from letting the line go slack.

The boy tried to remember the sentence so that he could decipher it later, but like almost everything, in time he'd forget the words and all that would be left was the vague sense that his father often tried to tell him important things while they were fishing.

By the time Elías Gil decided that it was pointless to keep standing there in the hopes that a fish might bite, father and son were soaked to the bone and the storm was lashing down on the valley with rage, making it impossible to see more than a few feet ahead. Unfazed, Elías gathered up their tackle and the pair headed home, letting the rain soak them through. Gonzalo looked up from time to time at his father's dripping face, staring straight ahead, brow slightly furrowed, raindrops falling from the tip of his smashed nose onto the front of his unbuttoned shirt. *Now, that's a real man,* Gonzalo had heard a woman in town say after she passed one day, which made him wonder if the others were not. But to Gonzalo, Elías seemed less like a man and more like a one-eyed giant, the Cyclops Ulysses fought in the illustrated books his teacher showed them at school while talking about a place called Ithaca.

Despite the storm and the fact that their fishing expedition had been a failure, the boy was relieved. He could feel, in the way his father held his hand, that Elías was in a good mood today. Strength flowed from his hand protectively, not threateningly. Gonzalo crossed his fingers that it would last.

"Why are you looking at me like that?" Elías asked without slowing his pace or looking down.

Gonzalo looked away, embarrassed. He didn't know what way he was looking at his father and wondered if it was the wrong one. He knew that sometimes his heart felt warm, like it was going to explode, and other times it felt cold and shrank in fear. On this morning, as the storm hammered the birch trees and the trail turned into a muddy river, his heart felt warm. It didn't happen often, but when it did it was the most extraordinary feeling ever.

"Are you scared about what happened last night?"

Ears sticking out, hair plastered to his brow, Gonzalo shook his head. He didn't know if he was still afraid or not, but he hoped Laura wouldn't hide him in the well again while there was so much shouting and the sound of things being broken in the shed. And he hoped he wouldn't wet the bed again, too. Suddenly, Elías stopped and sighed deeply. Rain bounced off his dark eye patch and Gonzalo pictured water penetrating the cloth, filling his father's eye

socket and running out. Then it would be like his father was crying, even though he was really only overflowing.

"You didn't see what you saw; you didn't hear what you heard.
You have to forget some things quickly so there's room to remember others. Do you understand?"

Gonzalo said yes, although of course he had no idea what his
father was talking about. He'd add this to the other sentence and
think about them both later, before he forgot.

Elías glanced skeptically at his son and then let out a quick
flash of laughter, like lightning.

"I can't fill your little head with these things yet. I'm a fool."

The only thing Gonzalo remembered from the previous night
was that he'd sobbed, in the darkness of the well, and felt terribly
alone and panicked, thinking his sister might forget to come for
him, that he'd never see her appear at the top of the shaft, never
feel her arms pull him up as she had on other occasions.

But Laura always came in the end. His loved his big sister
more than anything, more than his favorite toys, more than his
father, and much more than his mother. More than swimming
naked in the lake every morning, and more than making snow
angels in the winter. Maybe the only thing that came close to his
love for Laura was the joy that flowed through him some mornings when he opened his eyes in fear, felt the sheets, and realized
that he had not wet the bed.

She was protecting him, although Gonzalo didn't exactly
understand from what. But when the shouting began, and his
father began moving quickly and jerkily, or started feverishly
pounding on his typewriter in the shed, she would come and carry
him to the well, kiss him on the lips, and whisper soothing words,
promising that she'd come back for him.

That morning, Laura hadn't come downstairs. She stayed in
her room until lunchtime, and when Gonzalo's mother told him

to go up and get her, he found her on the floor in the narrow gap between the bed and the window, curled into a ball. The noonday sun flooded one side of her face; the other, hidden by her tangled hair, was in darkness.

"Don't look at me like that," she ordered, and he wondered anxiously why everyone criticized his way of looking and what was wrong with trying to see.

"You have a bump on your cheek. And scratches on your neck."

Laura instinctively hid her face. She was thirteen years old but sometimes seemed much older, as old as their mother—at least that's what Gonzalo thought. Especially when she touched her hair nervously or avoided his eyes.

"I went hunting for blackberries and I fell."

On days like this, Gonzalo felt as though his sister was a completely different person, someone he didn't know, and everyone behaved differently. His mother was especially nice to Laura, but nice in the way she was when one of their father's friends came to visit and she offered coffee and cakes, and Laura was almost rude in response. Under normal circumstances that would have gotten her in trouble with their father, but he didn't even look at her, and in fact seemed to be trying to avoid her.

And something told him that these were scenes he should erase from his memory.

The good thing about storms was the calm that followed. That's what Vasili Velichko was thinking as he got out of the car and observed the green mountains and the lake in the distance, reflecting the cloudless sky. The earth's gentle, quiet dripping was like the slow thaw that always came to Siberia, simply arriving one morning as the icicles hanging from the ceiling of the barracks began to melt, wetting their wooden cots. The unrivaled feeling of having survived one more winter in the gulag.

"Are you sure you want to do this?" He turned to the car door. Anna had stuck her head out and was resting her chin on one forearm smoking calmly. Her eyes drank in the landscape greedily.

"It will be a lovely surprise," she said, turning to stroke her daughter's face. Tania was asleep on her lap; the curvy mountain roads had upset her stomach, and she was pale.

Velichko got back behind the wheel.

"We haven't seen him in over twenty years. I'm not sure it's worth it, Anna," he said, adjusting the rearview mirror. "He probably won't even remember us."

Anna frowned her pretty lips and leaned back against the seat, gazing at her daughter's red hair. Tania was the spitting image of Martin, who she was sure would have given anything to witness this moment.

"What matters, Vasili, is that we remember him."

News spread like wildfire that a beautiful Russian writer had rented a house on the north shore of the lake for the summer. Deputy Inspector Alcázar was the first to hear about it and pay her a visit.

"It's not often that we get visitors from the Soviet Union," he told her.

He had to force himself to keep from ogling her ample bosom and staring at her pearl-gray eyes, which seemed to be either mocking or scorning him, he couldn't tell which. No doubt Alcázar was not used to women like her: Anna Akhmatova was thirty-five years old, a native of Western Siberia, a professional writer and cultural attaché with the Soviet consul. She had been civilly wed to the Englishman Martin Balery, and then divorced, and now here she was with a daughter, Tania Balery Akhmatova, three years old.

"Your picture doesn't do you justice," Alcázar said, handing back her passport. "You're much more beautiful in person."

It was true, she was. Any man in his right mind would relish the hope of seducing her or winning her heart. And this was a fact that soon incited the virtuous rage of certain local parishioners. Things had moved on since the forties, but Spain was still partial to witch hunts. And here was a woman who was beautiful to the point of distraction, a divorced Soviet, and with a child; it was as though someone had sent Alcázar a bomb, wrapped in pretty paper and tied with a bow.

"And you are...?" he asked, turning to the man who until now had remained discreetly in the background. He could have been Anna's father, or her lover.

Vasili Velichko detested weasels in the service of power and conveniently overlooked—for his sanity's sake—the fact that he himself had been one for a large portion of his life. Even during his years in the gulag, after being freed from the internment camp in Poland, he had forced himself to be disciplined and uphold Party orthodoxy among the prisoners. But Velichko was a man of conviction and believed firmly in his cause—not in *men* but in *ideas*—and that set him apart from men like this police officer in his ridiculous toupee, questioning him from behind a walruslike mustache. Vasili had met plenty of men like him before, mercenaries serving no one but themselves. He held out his passport and stood stiffly, waiting for it to be handed back.

"This is my brother, he doesn't speak Spanish very well," Anna said by way of excuse.

"You don't have the same surname."

"But we have the same heart; that's what counts," Velichko shot back drily.

Alcázar could tell this guy was trouble. Luckily, he said he wasn't planning to stay at the house. He had a business to run in Barcelona and had come only to ensure that his "sister" and "niece" got settled in.

"Enjoy your summer, miss. I hope you'll write kind things about us," the deputy inspector said, thereby concluding formalities and promising to return soon in a less official capacity.

Before leaving, Vasili tried once more—though without much conviction, given how many times he'd failed already—to convince Anna that what she was doing was senseless.

"We came here to make a fresh start, Anna. And all you're doing is digging yourself a hole. Come with me to Barcelona. We can raise Tania there and leave the past in the past. Please."

Anna gave sweet old Vasili the sort of weary look someone might give a once-fresh bouquet of flowers that had wilted. The man who throughout her childhood had looked out for her was still in the gulag—or at least his spirit was—and he didn't realize she was no longer a girl who, far from needing his protection, now took care of him. She had been the one who managed to do the impossible: obtain three passports, the chance for a new life, and get Velichko out of the USSR where he would no doubt have been arrested yet again and executed for his refusal to keep quiet about Khrushchev and the new post-Stalin leaders. And now she had to pay the price she'd agreed to.

"I can't go. I have to hold up my end of the bargain, Vasili."

He gazed at Anna in resignation. "It's not just because you promised Igor Stern that you're here. This is personal. No matter what you say, this is something you want to do, isn't it?"

Anna poked her head out the window of the lake house, which had yet to sense that she was in control. The place was still vague and uninhabited; she needed to settle in and make her mark.

"I owe it to my mother. And I owe it to myself."

"Think of Tania, Anna. Your mother is the past, Nazino is the past, Elías is the past. Your daughter is the future, the hope of a new life."

Anna smiled. Men like Vasili were so naïve. No matter how many times life knocked them down, they always thought that things could be different, better.

.   .   .

Laura let out a whimper as she touched her side. Gonzalo realized and stopped chasing her around the patio with his arms spread like airplane wings.

"Does it hurt?"

She made a face. "Inside."

She'd thought it was never going to happen again. After the last time, Elías had gotten down on his knees and wrapped his arms around her legs, leaving them wet with his tears. He'd begged forgiveness so many times that Laura had lost count, and almost unwillingly she'd ended up stroking his gray hair and crying along with him. She loved him, despite it all, and the older she got, the more she realized that she couldn't stop her love from growing even though it kept happening. That was why she wanted to believe him. And for a few years, two at least, he had kept his word and Laura believed it was all over, squirreled away in the back of her mind, someplace she'd never let anyone see. But now it had happened again, and this time it was so violent she'd been unable to react.

This time, Elías hadn't begged for forgiveness or told terrible stories about the past. It was as though he'd realized that it had gone too far and that Laura would never forget. Now he spent his nights locked in the shed, and when her mother tried coax him out, they fought viciously, hitting and insulting each other; they were destroying themselves. The one thing Laura was determined to do was keep Gonzalo away from it all. Lately she'd sensed a change in the way Elías behaved with him. Gonzalo was so innocent and pure, and he admired his father so much that Elías felt guilty and undeserving; he fought the temptation to prove to his son how wrong he was about his father. It was as though he hated Gonzalo's respect, could not stand his innocence and admiration.

"Get him out of my sight," Elías had warned Laura more than once, tongue thick with alcohol, his green eye darkening.

Laura had no intention of allowing her brother to get hurt in any way. She could take it herself, could endure terrible things, because she was like her father. They had the same horrific knack for indifference to their own suffering and contempt for the idea of ever achieving happiness. At the age of thirteen, Laura already knew the ways of the world and the rules she would have to play by. But Gonzalo was like Esperanza—selfless, timid, silent, obedient; he was unable to accept that even if you turn your back, life won't go away and often reminds you of its existence in the cruelest ways. He wasn't ready to fight for his own survival and never would be. Gonzalo idolized his father, and that was as it should be. Ignorance was his best defense.

Laura was the first to see the woman at the gate, catching sight of her before Gonzalo raced after his sister, before the dogs began to bark. The woman stared fixedly at her, with a somber look. Then she raised her eyes to the house, saw something that made her smile, and ambled off down the path to the road. A minute later, Laura heard the sound of a car driving away. She retraced her steps to the house and looked up at where the woman had been gazing. Her mother stood at one of the upstairs windows, tightly gripping the sill and staring at the path the woman had walked down. Laura had never before seen such rage in Esperanza's eyes.

Two minutes later, her father's old Renault appeared, rattling at the barn door. Before Laura could stop Gonzalo, he raced after Elías's car like a little dog. He chased after his father clumsily for as long as he could, finally stopping to catch his breath, the tailpipe leaving a thick trail of exhaust in its wake.

The old are humbled by youth only if they haven't lived enough. And yet all the sorrows of age came crashing down upon Elías the moment Anna stood there before him. Not a trace remained of the girl he'd carried, day after endless day, across the steppe, and this meant that not a trace was left of the young man who had cared for her, either. Elías was losing more ground each day.

"So, you're a writer," he said, glancing around the small library Anna was setting up on the first floor, next to the living room. "What kind of writer are you?"

Anna pondered this for a moment and then gave him a somber look. "The kind who writes."

"And you expect me to believe you came here just to write a book?"

"I don't expect you to believe anything."

Elías was standing at the back door. Outside, in the garden, the grass was shimmering and Anna watched Tania pass by quickly, chasing butterflies.

"What do you want? Why are you here?" Elías asked aggressively, after a prolonged silence.

Anna felt rage surge through her, but it was discernible only by the slight flash in her eye.

"You're not very happy to see me, are you?"

Elías stood stiffly in the doorway. "What I see is not what I remember. I'm no fool; I know you detest me. I suppose after all those years with Stern you were infected by his poison. Nothing I could say in my defense would change your mind, so I may as well save my breath."

"I'd like to hear your version of the story. Something that differs from the one I know: that a coward killed my mother and handed me over to a bunch of cutthroats to save his own life."

The house must have been sealed for quite some time before she rented it. The old pine furniture was covered in dust, and thick cobwebs hung in the corners and between the ceiling beams. As he moved to one side, Elías felt a sticky web catch in his hair. He reached into a pocket and felt the familiar touch of Irina's locket, then weighed the idea of showing it to Anna. After all, it belonged to her.

"I'm sure you've read the report Vasili wrote in 1934."

"I have. But I haven't heard it from your mouth."

Memories are not classical paintings in ornate frames, or snap-shots on shelves in people's homes. Memories are wide-open spaces often visited in silence. What good would it do to evoke them? Nothing he could say about the past would ring any more true to her than anything Stern might have said. People are inclined to believe whatever best fits their character. And Anna's was cold and aloof.

"I have nothing to say to you."

She lit one of her sweetish cigarettes and tossed the lighter carelessly onto a desk, then exhaled in exasperation and flashed Elías an irritated look.

"I'd heard you weren't very talkative, but I thought a trip this long might merit a bit more consideration on your part. As you wish. I, on the other hand, do have something to say to you."

She pulled open a drawer and tossed him an envelope.

"What's this?"

"Friends sending their regards. Open it."

Anna walked out into the garden and left him alone. The envelope contained photographs of a dozen or more men and women, each with a date on the back—the date of their death—and place of execution: A.S., Paris 1947; S.M., Lyon 1947; W.B., Toulouse 1948; G.T., Arles 1948...Madrid...London...Marseilles...Berlin...1949, 1950, 1952, 1958, 1962, 1963, 1965...Each of them denounced by Elías, who had handed them over to Ramón Alcázar personally. Nothing was said of the dozens of men and women whose lives he had saved with the tip-offs his friend gave him about raids and ambushes planned for leaders of the Party, trade unions, and student associations. Or those he'd smuggled out of Spain with false identification in the past decade. None of that balanced things out, and he knew it—the idea of like curing like was a bunch of hogwash. The deaths of each of the comrades, NKVD agents, anti-Franco activists in Spain and France, anarchists, and CNT supporters were all on his back. And so were

those of the Spanish police and spies whom the NKVD had eliminated thanks to Ramón's information, which they believed came
from Elías. They were all simply pawns, whether black or white.
It didn't matter which side they were on; they were dispensable. It
was the important chess pieces that had to be safeguarded.

He took a few minutes before going out to the garden, the
photos of the dead clutched in his hand. They burned him,
insulted him, shouted at him, bit his fingers. Anna was innocently
chasing her daughter through the field. Finally the summer sun
had come out, and the air was filled with color. A beautiful scene
on a bucolic June day.

Seeing Elías, Anna told her daughter to go play in the house.
Tania whined for a bit, but she obeyed.

"What is this supposed to mean?" Elías asked, pointing at her
with the crumpled photos in his hand.

Anna chose her words carefully. "I think you know what it
means. You've been collaborating with the Franco police since
1947, even though you still have contacts in the Party and still,
unofficially, work for them. But you don't need to fret; they don't
know...yet."

She let the threat sink slowly into Elías's consciousness. He
sat on a tree stump a few feet away and, for a long time, remained
silent, head bowed. Elías showed no sign of feeling defeated and
instead reclassified the situation, modifying his next steps. If Anna
had expected his nerves to be shot, she was now realizing what a
miscalculation that had been. But she had an ace up her sleeve,
something that would certainly bring him to his knees.

"Your friend Ramón lied to you all these years. You betrayed
all those people for nothing. Igor Stern is still alive; in fact, he
sends his regards."

Elías observed Irina's daughter attentively, exhaustively, trying to discern what it was he saw in her face: scorn, indifference,
hatred, or simply exhaustion. There was certainly no trace of

gratitude, affection, or doubt. She had already judged him and found him guilty. Her announcement had clenched his stomach and made him want to vomit, but he'd controlled it, with effort. He needed a minute to stop sweating and recover, to regain control of his body, which seemed suddenly to have lolled, as though he had no bones.

"What is this, some kind of blackmail?"

Anna slowly shook her head. "I'm afraid it's not that easy. He wants to see you, tomorrow."

"Igor. You're telling me he's here? In Barcelona?"

"He's never been far from you, the man followed you wherever you went." Anna considered what she was about to say as if she herself couldn't make sense of it. "He's obsessed with you. He says you're the only man he's never been able to defeat."

Elías emitted a broken laugh, almost a howl, and flew to his feet.

"He got my coat, and he got you. What else does that son of a bitch want?!"

Anna was unimpressed by the outburst.

"He wants you."

Elías struggled to calm down when the redheaded girl approached, her large eyes open wide. She vaguely reminded him of someone.

"He's using you against me, Anna, because he knows that will hurt me more than anything. And you happily lend yourself to his game."

Anna gazed tenderly at her daughter and recalled the night she was conceived, over three years ago. She could never thank the frail, unstable redhead enough for what he'd done—risk his life to help her escape the hotel where Igor had been keeping her, in Paris. Anna was a teenager at the time, and he—a raving beggar—had managed to get her to Gare du Nord and put her on a train to Le Havre. But it didn't take Igor long to find her. Years later, she ran into Martin again, in Frankfurt. He'd rebuilt his life and was having an affair with a Canadian diplomat. He looked happy, and helped her yet again, obtaining—through his lover—a visa so that she could travel to Canada. That time she managed to escape for a couple of years and actually believed Martin's help was going to allow her to have a normal existence.

She got a job in a clothing store in Ontario, met a French Canadian, and they began a relationship that ended abruptly one night when he didn't turn up for a date to go to the movies. In his place, Igor Stern arrived at her door. It was during her two years in Canada that Martin told her about Elías and her mother, Irina. He also spoke affectionately of Claude, and especially of Michael, who'd been the love of his life. Martin detested Igor and Anna realized that this was the main reason he was determined to help her. He wanted to destroy Igor, and taking something that he considered his property was one way to do that.

Perhaps that was why, when they met yet again in Moscow three years ago, he was willing—for the first and only time in his life—to make love to a woman who was almost twenty years his junior. Martin had arranged to meet her at the grand Lenin Hotel; he was traveling with his diplomat lover on a tour of a dozen or more countries. He'd aged a lot and looked exhausted, she thought, and Martin admitted dispassionately that he was dying. They drank too much, and when he walked her back to her apartment on Bolshoi Street and Anna kissed him on the lips, he didn't seem surprised or protest, letting himself be swept along—albeit with no curiosity or passion. He spilled his seed inside her with restrained tenderness. Martin died two months later, in the first-class carriage of a train on the Trans-Siberian Railway somewhere near Turkmenistan, traveling the same snow-covered landscape that had shattered all of his youthful dreams and aspirations thirty years earlier. He never knew that he'd left behind a daughter, and was thus the only man who'd managed to beat Igor Stern.

There was no doubt that Anna owed the best thing in her life to Martin, just as she owed her love and loyalty to Vasili. What she felt for Elías Gil, though, was exactly the same as what she felt for Igor Stern—deep, sharp hatred. They were two rabid dogs who longed for nothing but the other's obliteration and didn't hesitate to use everyone around them in an attempt to achieve their goal. There was nothing inside them but death and destruction.

"I wish I could kill both of you with the same bullet," she replied.

Igor looked so full of vim and vigor it was staggering. At fifty-three, he still dressed fashionably young: flared trousers, tight wide-collared shirts, and bushy sideburns. His skin had taken on a honeyed tone, and his manners were so refined that the elegance he exhibited on lifting a fork or dabbing his lips with a napkin seemed innate rather than learned. Aware of his effect on Elías, Igor steepled his fingers and bowed his head slightly. The man looked so sure of himself and the personality he'd created that he was willing to adopt a fatherly demeanor with his old enemy.

"I see the years have not treated you as you deserve, Elías," he said with a benevolent smile.

"Things have gone all right, until now."

They were not alone in the hotel lobby. At some distance, three of Igor's men sat with their eyes glued on him. Stern had become respectable, the most coveted victory for an outcast. Real triumph lay not in riches or the influence he had over politicians, army officers, and police but in respectability: a box seat at the Liceo, rooms booked at luxurious hotels in every capital all year long, a social life with the upper crust and those in the world of official culture. He collected photos of actors, musicians, writers, scientists, aristocrats, and clergy as if they were the heads of animals he'd shot on safari. Only occasionally did he visit the dungeons of his empire—the world of contraband, drugs, prostitution, and illegal gambling—and when he did, it was out of nostalgia for his beginnings.

"Did you actually think I wouldn't find out that you sold yourself to Ramón Alcázar for the price of my head?" Elías sensed Igor's rage despite the unaltered Buddha-like expression he wore, the one that said he was above worldly concerns.

Igor was a born survivor, and that was something Elías had never appreciated, he said. He negotiated with whomever he had to, made and broke promises with equal effortlessness, and showed no loyalty to anyone if it didn't benefit him. He never gave an inch but knew how to make others believe that he had, and this kept them happy. Igor also worked for certain higher-ups in the Franco dictatorship, important entrepreneurs whom he made very rich, and had been doing it since long before Elías made his deal with Ramón Alcázar.

"Don't hold it against him. He didn't know, and he tried to uphold his end of the bargain, I can assure you of that. If his superiors in Paris hadn't tipped me off, your friend would have blown my brains out." Suddenly his manner changed, and he became imperious. "If you were so set on seeing me dead, you should have done it yourself."

"Those photos—what do you want for them?"

Elías felt the burden of Igor's expression bore into him, coercing him.

"I remember when you used to be harder to convince."

Igor enjoyed this game, it was like opening a closet full of costumes and trying them on, one by one. This was what power and money had taught him—to become any man that circumstances required, and he wondered which one to be now. His instincts told him that it was time to take off the mask and crush Elías once and for all. With just one call to Moscow, in under twenty-four hours Gil would be stuffed in a trunk on his way to the Kremlin. But he had to consider his own position, play his cards right. He, too, had been a double agent for years and was sure both sides knew it. They tolerated Igor because he could be used as an enforcer or a Trojan horse, depending on the circumstances. And they were starting to fear him, and that was no good.

For years, Igor Stern had been very careful, followed the rules, made everyone believe he was one of the nouveau riche, a brainless idiot who dreamed of nothing but spending money on girlfriends and high-class whores, like some two-bit actor on the Côte d'Azur. He'd played his role so well that by the time they realized it was all a charade, he was too far out of their grasp, too influential, too rich, and knew too many secrets. Checkmate? Not in this never-ending chess match.

He hadn't waited all these years just to hand over Elías, and with him the reason they were keeping him alive. No, he'd thought of something better, something worthy of the battle the pair of them had been waging for so long.

"I presume I don't need to explain what would happen to you and your family if this news came out, do I?"

"Since when do you like rhetorical questions?"

Igor let out a hissing little laugh and fastidiously adjusted his gold watch chain.

"Since I became a discriminating sophisticate. I've read a few books and met a few people over the years. And they've all taught me that there exists a sublime pleasure in the elegance of our violence when we express our feelings. An aria, when it comes down to it, is not so different from a battle cry; it gives voice to the same fury and power, expresses the same things: fear, courage, heroism. But what's seen as bel canto on stage is considered savagery on a field full of mud, dead bodies, and explosions. That's what it means to be civilized, and I've come to see that it has many advantages. For example, I've learned that true pain is inflicted not with an ax but a needle."

"I have no idea where you're going with this."

"Nowhere but here, the exact point where you and I are now. This is what I've wanted since the day I saw you on that filthy train and you forced me to take your eye out over a stupid coat. I wanted to be your friend, Elías. I respected you as much as I despised you, and I know you felt something similar. Attraction and repulsion; virtue and dishonor. You want what I am, and in a way you are what I want. We could have been brothers and none of this would have been necessary, but nature separates twosomes, forces them into confrontation like pups in a litter of wolves. They end up tearing one another apart and that's inevitable. And once again, here we are."

Igor Stern stood. His bodyguards pricked up their ears like Dobermans, but he gave a subtle gesture to put them at ease; he felt no threat.

"Given that we can't be enemies or friends, you're going to work for me. You'll be my subordinate—my slave, in fact. You'll give me your virtue, the recognition you receive from your family and others, your medals. You'll give me everything, drag yourself through the mud, and not for your ideals but simply because I require it, to make me richer, more powerful. And you'll do it so that I don't take from you the one thing you care about: the respect you'll be accorded by history, the idiotic immortality that fools like you aspire to. I hear you have a very pretty daughter. How old is she? Thirteen? And a five-year-old boy. What will he think of his hero when he grows up and learns the truth?"

Elías had been slowly edging toward the door. He calculated that the two bodyguards were in range before pulling out the Colt .45 automatic and shooting each man twice.

It was all so fast that when he turned to aim the cocked gun at Igor, the Russian's mouth was still hanging open.

"Martin was right. I should have killed you with my bare hands in Paris when I had the chance."

He stuck the barrel in Igor's mouth and thought of Irina, of the nights they'd made love in silence, surrounded by strangers. He thought of the endless stifling walks, carrying Anna; of Claude's death; of Martin's cries as he was tortured while Michael bled out at his feet. But more than anything, he relived the pain of that wooden stick that had made his eyeball burst, the pain that been imprinted in his mind forever, tormenting him, a wave whose intensity ebbed and flowed but never disappeared. The pain that sometimes made him inhuman, a crazed beast who tortured those he loved most, a degenerate whose only limits were inside him.

He pulled the trigger and blew Igor's brains out.

And then finally Elías cried out in victory.

28

According to the airline's passenger list, Luis should have been on a flight to London, on his way to marry the beautiful woman who'd waited for him until his arrival disappeared from the list of those displayed on the console. But instead of relaxing in a first-class seat and thanking his lucky stars, Luis left the stunning beauty waiting and was instead driving a rented Mercedes along the coastal highway. Alcázar followed at a prudent distance, shaking his head disapprovingly at the news on the radio. Clashes at the lake between police and environmental groups were heating up. Two officers had been wounded and a Molotov cocktail had blown up a digger. Construction, for the time being, was still on course. He knew that the news would not be well received by Agustín González. The companies invested in ACASA didn't need this kind of noise; the rich liked the politics of fait accompli, wanted their plans to go smooth as silk, and the lake project had been nothing but one problem after another. One of those problems, and not the smallest, was the one he was now being sent to take care of.

Agustín González was of the same opinion as Anna: He had to stop the leaks that were coming from Siaka and Laura's laptop.

Alcázar warned Agustín that his son-in-law would probably be there as well, but the man's response was categorical.

"Dead dogs don't bite."

This made him think of the previous evening with Anna, when she'd refused to discuss Igor Stern. Alcázar had kept insisting until she sealed his mouth with an affectionate kiss on the lips. They were in a dark alley and her face seemed to float above him in the hazy light of the streetlamps.

"After all this time, you're still just a poor boy who never lived up to his father. You could have been such a magnificent man, Alberto, the man Cecilia wanted you to be." She never called him by his first name. "But it's too late for that kind of nostalgia."

Rather than bitterness, her words were spoken with genuine affection, but they made him feel terribly alone and vulnerable. And it was then, at that instant, as the venerable old woman leaned on his arm to light one of her Davidoffs with a long match, that he understood what her kiss meant.

There was no Igor Stern.

Outside of business hours, Flight was quiet as a tomb, with just one light on in the back where Vasili Velichko had made his favorite dish for Tania: roast pork with dumplings and sauerkraut, served with a good red wine. It was too rich for his delicate stomach, but he loved watching Tania eat it, seeing the enjoyment on her face and in her eyes.

"Would you like seconds?"

Tania was stuffed, though, and to Velichko's exasperation she pushed her chair back from the table and patted her thighs, satisfied.

"I'd love a strong coffee."

Vasili poured her coffee and brought out a bottle of vodka and two shot glasses. Tania was surprised.

"No liquor. Doctor's orders, in case you'd forgotten."

Velichko flared his nostrils and snapped his teeth in the air with a grumble.

"This morning I shat blood again. I can see the signs. A little vodka isn't going to keep me out of the grave, but it's not going to send me there any faster either."

Tania reached a hand across the flowered tablecloth to squeeze Velichko's wrinkled fingers. Suddenly, she realized that he was an old man who had seen more over the course of his life than she ever would.

"How old are you, Uncle Vasili?"

Velichko scratched a white eyebrow with his knuckle.

"I don't know. I've been born so many times." He let out a cackle, which quickly led to a cough and a nip of vodka.

Tania wiped a drop of liquor from his lips with her thumb. She felt safe in the halo of light cast by the candles around them. The rest of the bar was in darkness and the shadows allowed her to escape her uncle's inquisitive gaze. Although not completely.

"You've eaten my food and drunk my coffee and vodka, so I think the least you can do is tell me what's wrong."

"We both know what's wrong, Vasili."

The old man stood very slowly and began clearing dishes. Tania took hold of his arm, to keep him from leaving.

"You have to help me. She'll listen to you."

Velichko freed himself of Tania's hand and shuffled to the sink.

"Anna Akhmatova listens only to classical writers, especially if they're dead. She doesn't like the living because they talk back. Patience was never her forte. You should know that by now."

"But you're like her brother."

Velichko placed his palms on the marble countertop and shook his head crossly.

"The woman lives a hundred yards away and hasn't deigned to visit me in a year."

"I still don't understand the ridiculous grudge between the two of you. Neither of you will tell me what happened."

"I just did. Your mother doesn't like it when people disagree with her or tell her the truth."

"And what truth did you tell her, to offend her so deeply?"

Vasili had begun to turn the glasses upside down on the counter. As though unhappy with the way they were now arranged, he realigned them all.

"When that poor boy, Roberto, was killed, I said what I had to say, and she hasn't forgiven me for it, nor will she. Your mother is no different from *him*, you know that? Just like Stern. If she weren't convinced of my loyalty, and of the fact that I'm already on death's door, she'd have taken me out herself by now."

"Don't say that."

Velichko banged the marble with his fist.

"I will say it, and why shouldn't I? If you're not willing to accept it, you can simply walk out the door this minute. Nobody, listen to me, nobody knows your mother better than I do. I know her virtues and her faults and I've seen plenty of both of them over the course of more than sixty years. I saw her as a filthy child living in an orphanage and I saw her take Igor Stern's throne and become the Matryoshka. Your mother won't listen to me, Tania. And I don't know if I want to help you."

"She swore that what happened to that boy was an accident, that she never ordered Zinoviev to kidnap him and certainly didn't say to kill him."

Vasili Velichko raised his head and wished it would explode. He returned to the table, filled his glass with vodka, and cursed his heartburn and his doctor. The glass trembled in his hands, spilling a bit of the liquid.

"And you believed her, because it was the easiest thing to do. You're but a pure, clean soul. Is that it?"

Tania didn't want to hear any more. She'd never wanted to know anything about her mother's transactions; that was why she'd left home so young, and that was why they were always engaged in some sort of secret battle, a clash of wills. Tania had nothing to do with Laura's or Roberto's deaths and knew nothing of the Matryoshka or Igor.

"You're drinking too much, Vasili."

The old man snatched up the bottle and hurled it against the wall with all his might.

"I could drink this whole damned bar and it wouldn't change what I know, or what you know. Where do you think the money for this bar came from? Or the money for your mother's bookstore, for your university fees and all your travel when you were off being such a rebel? The Matryoshka supports us—their dirty dealings, which we cloak in honor and memories and nostalgia. And we know it, and we accept it. We made a decision on the night of San Juan in 1967 and we've never backed down from it. But you broke the rule."

"That rule had nothing to do with me!"

"You lied to Gonzalo from the start, Tania. Why didn't you tell him who you were, who your mother was, what she did?"

Tania shook her head obstinately. "I am not my mother. I don't care about her obsessive hatred for Elías Gil. For the love of God, I was just a kid when all that happened! I can't even picture my grandmother Irina's face! Plus, you wrote in the report yourself that Elías tried to save both of them for as long as he could."

Vasili Velichko regained his composure and gazed at the broken glass, small pools of vodka forming on the floor. A single ant struggled, dying in a sea of liquor.

"You don't understand; you've never understood. The resentment that turned your mother into what she is today isn't about Nazino. That might be where it began, but it grew under the shadow of Igor. I admit that she resisted for years before being devoured by a hatred that was never hers. Through me, and then Martin, she escaped, endured, fought back. And I'm sure that your mother could have beaten Stern, that she didn't have to become someone shaped by his every whim. When you were born, it gave her the strength to run away one more time. But that night in 1967, the real Anna died and the Matryoshka took her place. And Elías Gil is entirely to blame for that. It's an interesting paradox, don't you think? Elías and Igor always hated each other and took the battle with them everywhere they went. And then, bizarrely, after he shot Igor in the face and killed him, Elías conceded his victory just a few hours later at the lake.

"With the old Anna, I could have intervened on your behalf, on Gonzalo's behalf, and could have done more to save Laura and her son, but the woman your mother has become is hard as stone. Believe me, words are like smoke that she just blows away. I warned you, I told you this would happen sooner or later. Your mother will never allow it, will never consent to you being with Elías's son. You thought you could fool around with him innocently, snoop into his life with no consequences. You flirted recklessly, knowing you were safe, still spoiled despite it all. And you kept going, ignoring the danger you put him in. I mean, you took the man to your bed. Did you honestly think Anna would simply stand back, fold her arms, and do nothing?"

"You have to speak to her. Please," Tania begged. "She knows where he is, she can bring him back. He won't pose a threat, he'll be no danger to her. We'll leave Barcelona, go someplace far away and never come back."

Vasili crouched down and began picking up the broken shards of glass.

"It's a little late for that. Your mother already has everything all planned out."

.   .   .

Luis's midnight blue Mercedes exited the national highway and took a minor road that wound its way tortuously along the jagged coastline, passing through small summer towns that, this being November, were curled up like little animals hibernating for the winter. When he stopped in front of a house still under construction, high on a cliff surrounded by pine trees, it was already dark.

For the final stretch, Alcázar had had to follow at a distance with his lights off so as not to be seen. But the road led only to this house, whose foundation had been built into the rock for even more space. The outside looked more or less completed and resembled a cathedral made of steel, glass, and stone, with three terraced stories jutting out of the rock face at right angles, like a giant staircase. Enormous picture windows afforded dizzying ocean views. It was an extravagant dream, albeit unfinished, perhaps due to the dreamer's fatigue. Luis was an architect with boundless imagination and too much money for his own good. Alcázar let out a low whistle of admiration. He'd never understood how Laura could reconcile a cop's life with this kind of lavishness.

The Mercedes was parked in a carport. Alcázar saw no lights on in the house, nor could he detect any movement inside. There was no reason for things to get complicated. He opened the glove compartment and took out an unregistered Glock. He'd never killed anyone in his life, and certainly not in cold blood, but that didn't mean he was incapable of doing it if the situation so required. He wrapped his hand firmly around the butt of the gun and noted that he was not trembling. His heart was not racing, he didn't feel rushed. For the first time in ages, his thinking was cold and clear. He knew this feeling—the tense focus, muscles primed, breath held, ears pricked, eyes alert. The ritual of the hunter, calm before erupting with devastating force.

He had to admit, he was made for this.

Alcázar got out of the car with the weapon in his jacket pocket. His finger was not on the trigger, but there was a bullet in the chamber and the safety catch was off.

"Do it fast, do it well," he said to himself, searching the rubble and construction for a way to slip inside.

The moon cast a half-circle glow through the ground-floor windows. Alcázar watched from outside for a while before finding an open slat he could slip through, which put him in what seemed to be a guest bathroom. The tile had been laid but the tub was filled with construction dust and a dead bird. Shame, he thought, noticing the high quality of the abandoned materials.

The first floor was open-plan, and Alcázar estimated it at about sixteen thousand square feet. Although the floor was parquet in some places, in others the concrete slab was still visible. The walls were half painted, and loose wires stuck out where light fixtures and electrical outlets would go. He saw a quivering light coming from behind a column. Approaching slowly, Alcázar avoided the rubble so as not to make any noise. He saw a gray basalt wall with a built-in wrought-iron fireplace that was lit, the dry wood crackling. To the right was a large armchair, a bottle of liquor on the floor beside it. Luis was leaning against the chair back, contemplating the fire, his back to Alcázar.

"What kind of cop are you, Inspector? Certainly not a very subtle one," he said, turning, his expression downcast, disheveled hair falling across his scowling face. The house was in ruins—the house where he, Laura, and Roberto should have shared their lives—and the sea roared in the background, the storm a sound track to their encounter.

"Were you expecting me?"

Luis smiled, though Alcázar couldn't see it in the shadows. "I've been expecting you since the day I killed Zinoviev. Not only are you indiscreet, Inspector, you're also very slow."

Luis moved away from the fire to stand defiantly facing Alcázar. He held up his hands to show that he posed no threat. But he did, and the danger came from his crazed expression, almost like a centrifuge.

Alcázar refused to be trapped by the eyes pulling him in like quicksand. He moved cautiously around Luis, observing him carefully.

"Well, I'm here now," he said deviously. "Are you going to tell me where Siaka and Gonzalo are, or will we have to fight?"

Luis hesitated before replying. His glance flew instinctively to the staircase, a detail that Alcázar noted immediately.

"They're off pondering a game I proposed. They'll make a decision soon." It was clear he wasn't trying to deny anything. In fact, he seemed eager to discuss it. "She doesn't think you're capable of doing it," he added.

"Doing what? And who's 'she'?"

"Killing Siaka and Gonzalo. That's why she called me, to tell me you'd be following me here."

Alcázar realized he was talking about Anna. That affectionate kiss, the irony of her tender goodbye. He'd been so stupid, voicing his theory that Igor was the Matryoshka. Anna must have been laughing at him for years, fooling him into believing that there was a man at the head of the organization she worked for. Why a man? Because Alcázar was old-school and thought, absurdly, that some things could be done only by men.

Luis glanced at his watch. How long was it going to take them to decide?

"How do you think I even got close to Zinoviev? I'd never have managed if she hadn't put me on to him. And I would never have found out that you were double-crossing Laura, accepting bribes from the very people she was intent on destroying."

Alcázar gazed at him at length, wondering what was going on in his head, which was twitching in a strange, anxious way.

"Did Laura know?"

"That you were corrupt?" Luis nodded. "She found out just before she killed herself."

"She could have reported me."

Luis shook his head. "With you being protected by the most important lawyer in the country?" How far would a report like that go? Besides, Siaka told Laura that you saved her from the Matryoshka's wrath several times. The truth is, you were protecting her from Anna, even though you didn't know it. No, she wanted to keep you out of it, despite your betrayal."

Alcázar recalled their breakfast at the beachside shack the day he went to tell her that Zinoviev was dead and she was going to be accused of his murder. He remembered her look. Laura had known everything—that Luis had killed Zinoviev and Alcázar was tied up with the Matryoshka. Did she know who Anna really was? Did she suspect who fronted the organization? Maybe.

Luis intuited the question in Alcázar's mind.

"She felt like she owed you something, after that night at the lake in 1967. What exactly she owed you, or why, was something she always refused to tell me, but it was important enough that she wouldn't betray you even after Roberto died. I've always wondered what could make someone like Laura feel beholden to someone like you."

Alcázar walked over to one of the enormous windows jutting out over the sea. In the distance, the lights of Barcelona formed a wide band; on the horizon, the positioning lights of cargo ships approaching the shore blinked off and on. Laura had told him that her father loved going fishing at the lake and often took Gonzalo with him. Gonzalo would run after him without a word. She, on the other hand, found all the waiting around boring and never enjoyed those excursions.

"Why would Anna have called to say I was following you? When it comes down to it, she's the one responsible for your son's death."

Luis shook his head energetically. "Anna didn't tell Zinoviev to kill Roberto, or even kidnap him. He acted on his own. I already told you, she's the one who put me on to him, and she did nothing to stop me from killing him."

Alcázar gave Luis a contemptuous look.

"She used you; that's what she does. She ordered the kidnapping, and now I can see why. She convinced you to kill Zinoviev by making you think he was responsible for your son's death. And that killed two birds with one stone: She got rid of Zinoviev, who had become dangerous and indiscreet, and got Laura out of the way, because she'd been getting too close to the Matryoshka. Anna would have been content to have Laura accused of Zinoviev's murder and put in jail, but then you showed up, and it was a bonus for Anna that Laura killed herself. And now she's brought us both to this mousetrap, to finish it all off."

"That's very melodramatic of you, almost like a Russian opera."

"You don't believe me? She wants us to kill each other, then she can just wipe up the blood—that's what Agustín is for."

"It doesn't matter what I believe, Inspector. What matters is what happens now."

"And what's going to happen?"

"She told me she sent you here to kill me."

He was insane, completely out of his mind. Alcázar realized this when he saw the twisted, mocking expression on his face just as he was about to pounce. But Alcázar pulled out his Glock and aimed at Luis's chest.

"Don't be an idiot, man. You've committed enough crimes as it stands."

Luis leaped at Alcázar and threw a punch, hitting him in the face, although not hard enough to knock him down. Alcázar was shocked; he stumbled but didn't lose his balance.

"Stop!" he shouted, wielding his gun. But Luis didn't stop. He was smiling maniacally, as though urging Alcázar to shoot him.

Wasn't that what he wanted? Alcázar aimed at his knee and fired as Luis prepared to attack again. He collapsed, shrieking in pain, holding his bloody leg.

Alcázar pulled out his handcuffs and dragged Luis to a heavy concrete-and-rebar block, cuffing him to it.

"Now. Are you going to tell me where Siaka and Gonzalo are?"

"Fuck you," Luis mumbled, holding back the urge to sob like a little boy. "Call an ambulance, you crippled me."

"You'll get over it—not much need to run in jail; the prison yard is pretty small."

Just then a shot was fired upstairs.

"What the fuck was that?"

Siaka and Gonzalo stared at each other, perplexed at the fact that they were both still alive. Neither man had a scratch, and the gun that had been on the table now lay on the floor. The time set by Luis, a lunatic playing at avenger, for his "game" had nearly come to an end.

"Time's almost up," Gonzalo said, consulting his watch. Luis had been very explicit: In ten minutes he'd come back, by which time one of them had to have fired a shot, leaving the other dead on the ground. Otherwise, he'd kill them both.

"We should have saved the bullet. At least that way we'd be able to defend ourselves when he comes back."

Siaka was the one who'd fired the gun, a bullet hole clearly visible in the wall a few inches from Gonzalo.

"I thought you were going to shoot me," he murmured.

"I was, but I missed," Siaka replied.

Gonzalo couldn't tell if he'd missed by accident or on purpose. A few moments earlier they'd each been staring at the pistol, hypnotized, refusing to say a word or look at each other for fear of what they might see. And when Siaka finally grabbed the gun and gazed blankly at Gonzalo, the lawyer thought he'd made a deadly mistake by refusing to take part in Luis's sick coercion. It struck him that convictions served only to let people die feeling smug.

But intentionally or not, Siaka had missed, and they were both alive.

"What do we do now?" he asked.

Siaka crept over to the door to listen. Gonzalo saw him tense his muscles, primed for a fight. Siaka was a soldier, a man accustomed to pain—both causing it and suffering it. Fighting and violence were everyday modes for him. He'd withstood Luis's torture, beatings and blows, for days and was so physically broken that he had no chance of defeating Luis, yet his expression was fierce and determined. Gonzalo wasn't like that. He'd never have been able to endure even a tenth of the torment that this kid had gone through and was petrified, rooted to his spot as though his feet were nailed down.

"I can't do it. I can't face him."

Siaka shot him a furious look. "All men can do anything they have to; I've seen it. If you're desperate enough, fear turns to rage, I assure you. Think of your kids, or the redhead you told me about. Think of something you want to live for and fight for it. Fight, Gonzalo."

Approaching footsteps became louder, and a few seconds later the door handle turned. The door barely opened, casting in a sliver of light from the hallway.

The first thing Alcázar's gaze took in was the pathetic sight of Gonzalo, standing in the middle of the room, a gun at his feet, eyes flicking to the right just in time to warn the inspector of a figure leaping at him with a table leg in one hand. Alcázar had no trouble ducking the blow and came back with a forceful punch to the man's ribs.

Before Siaka could react, Alcázar kicked, hard, forcing him to double over with a sharp whimper.

"Freeze!" Gonzalo shouted.

Alcázar turned to him. "What do you think you're doing with that, Gonzalo?"

He'd picked the gun up off the floor and was aiming it at Alcázar, hoping he wouldn't guess that it wasn't loaded.

"Step away from him!"

Alcázar glanced indifferently at Siaka as the kid dragged himself out of reach like a squashed worm.

"I'm not going to hurt you, Gonzalo. I'm here to help you. Put down the weapon."

"I said, step away!"

Alcázar was beginning to lose patience. He snorted in annoyance, touching the barrel of the Glock to his temple.

"Or…what? You'll spit at me? I'm perfectly aware that the gun had only one bullet, and it seems you wasted it. I, on the other hand, have six left, and I'll use them if you don't stop pissing me off. I'm beginning to get sick of all of you."

Gonzalo had no choice but to relent. Alcázar approached and took the gun from his hands, examining it to ensure that there were, in fact, no more bullets, and then tucked it into his waistband. He sat on a chair and watched Siaka struggle to stand, maneuvering awkwardly with Gonzalo's help.

"Did they send you to finish us off?"

The plural made him laugh.

"There is no 'they.' There never was. There's only 'she.' The charming Anna Akhmatova is not a mother-in-law I would recommend," he retorted. "Tania's mother is the Matryoshka, Gonzalo. And yes, she's the one who sent me here to finish you off—you, him," he said, pointing to Siaka with the gun, "and your lunatic ex-brother-in-law, who's bleeding out downstairs."

"You don't have to do this, Alcázar. Luis has the laptop."

"I know that. I watched the security tape of you being attacked after I saw him at your office. And I heard the message Siaka left on your answering machine. You should have come to me rather than try to play the hero." Alcázar gave him a look of sympathy and clucked his tongue. "You always wanted to be like your father and sister, didn't you? It's in the Gil blood, you're like a bunch of suicidal moths crashing into the lightbulb because you can't stand the darkness. You'd rather die than accept how dark the real world is."

No, thought Gonzalo, not moths, more like butterflies. That's what Gonzalo and Laura had been like as kids running after each other playing at the lake house, the afternoon sun setting fire to their laughter and shining through their hair. Brave children who didn't want to accept the real world, the one beyond their games.

"Don't go, let's keep flying," Gonzalo begged when their father appeared in the doorway, one enraged eye beckoning to Laura.

Had he forgotten? No, he hadn't. It was all still there, in the back of his mind, a petrified footprint from another life that many layers of earth had not entirely buried. Like Laura's courageous look as she stroked his cheeks.

"Go to the well, don't let him catch you."

"No, not the well. Not the dark."

He wanted to keep playing, keep flying with his sister, follow her blond ponytail, roll down the hill with her in his mother's Republican bomber jacket, skinning his knees and elbows on dry pine needles and then having his mother make it better. He wanted to run to Laura's arms after the nightmare in which he couldn't remember the word until it was too late, the thing he had to say to save her. And feel the relief of finding her in her bed, asleep, opening her arms without opening her eyes, to hold him as she slept. The two of them, together, forming a single thing. Fireflies who kept their fire till the end of their days. He'd always thought he wanted to be a lean wolf like Elías, like his father, a rebel in search of who knows what absurd idea of liberty. But now he saw that he was always one of those fireflies—that was why he'd been taken with Tania from the start, her wings on fire like a phoenix, reborn of herself, reinventing herself so she could be anything she wanted to. Because that's what Laura was like.

And now, facing the barrel of Alcázar's gun, he could see that night laid bare, unveiled; his mind let the wall come down brick by brick, no more lying: the shed, the image of Laura on the ground, crying, her skirt up above her hips. And Gonzalo there, at the barn door.

"I told you to stay in the well."

But he was afraid, afraid of the dark. And then he saw his father, hunched over the typewriter. What was that verse, how did it go? And Gonzalo whispered, almost to himself, "The first drop to fall starts breaking down the stone." And Elías's eye turned, searching for him in the darkness. And then finding him in the corner doorway.

"You were there, at the police station," Gonzalo remembered. "You talked to my mother, you told her what happened. And she tried to scratch your face but you held her wrists. And then you threatened her, told her that if she laid a hand on Laura you'd take care of her and make sure everyone knew what kind of hero Elías Gil really was."

Alcázar swallowed. His tiny eyes glimmered, like hard kernels beneath his bushy brows, far from a universe expanding, their center filled with profound sadness. He recalled the hard candies he used to give Laura, the way they laughed together and the times he was almost convinced by her enthusiasm and her faith, almost stood up to the Matryoshka. She believed in human kindness, believed that evil could be defeated, and nearly got him to join her ranks. After Cecilia died, Laura was the only decent thing in his life. And he betrayed her.

"Too late to open that door, Gonzalo."

He walked over to Siaka and aimed at his temple.

Gonzalo tried to stop him. "Let him go. He won't say a word, and I won't either. I swear."

Siaka leaned his head against the wall and dragged his shoulders up. He swallowed and faced Alcázar's eyes.

Siaka had seen too many men like this. Cowards who were brave only when they had a weapon in their hands. Weak men who became strong when others were afraid. Throughout his life, his flesh had suffered at their hands. He was tired. Laura was right, she was always right: He could win, and in order to win he didn't have to beat them, just had to stare them in the face. Again and again, over and over, one after the other, until they were laid bare, until they were forced to face their own shortcomings—sick, incomplete beings. It was enough to start, to be the first. Others would come later. She'd already done it. Now it was his turn.

"Don't listen to this guy, Inspector. If you don't pull that trigger and blow my brains out right now, I promise you I'll drag myself down to the prosecutor's office and tell him absolutely everything I know about the Matryoshka. And you'll be the first one they come after. So you'd better get it over with, here and now."

Alcázar listened to him and noted not a trace of fear or doubt.

"You're right, son. It's too late to change anything."

The shot echoed through the room and then throughout the house, and so did Gonzalo's desperate cry as Siaka slid to the floor, staring at him all the while, eyes wide open.

29

Elías didn't know how long he'd spent hiding like a swamp creature before deciding to approach the house, trampling the poppies that grew between the paving stones along the path. The night air was soft and peaceful, yet he was sweating profusely, his heart pounding so hard he feared it would give him away.

Through the window he heard the joyous sound of Tchaikovsky's *1812 Overture* being played on the record player and saw Anna dancing in circles in the candlelight, holding her daughter's hands. Tania was shrieking with laughter, flying through the air, and her laughter took forever to reach Elías. In the brief moment during which he observed them unseen, he wondered, dazed, if the blood on his shirt and hands was real or he'd only dreamed that he just shot Igor Stern in front of a dozen witnesses as well as two bodyguards.

He gazed at his trembling fingers. The police were probably already looking for him, Ramón's son leading the pack. And this time his childhood friend could do nothing to help him.

The music stopped, and when he looked back through the window, Elías was confronted with Anna's flushed face, staring fixedly at him. She bent down and said something to Tania, and the girl scurried upstairs. For a moment, Anna seemed undecided but then marched straight to the door and stood before Elías, arms crossed, blocking his entry. Elías saw the face she made after noticing his bloodstained shirt and hands, and he bluntly answered the question in her eyes.

"I killed him," he said, no trace of pride or of guilt.

Anna looked at him with something resembling nausea, touching a hand lightly to her stomach before quickly recovering. Her eyes took him in, inquisitive.

"And what do you expect from me?"

Right at that instant, firecrackers exploded in the distance. It was the night of San Juan, a night of witches and magic, the moon and bonfires purifying everything. Simultaneously, they raised their heads to a star-filled sky and watched the first colorful explosion extend like a wave and then disintegrate into a thousand bright particles of light, illuminating the surface of the placid lake. When the glow died out, they gazed back at each other. The candles backlit Anna's silhouette in the doorframe but her face remained in shadow. Elías's form was partially lit by the moon. They both looked like ghosts. But they were real. Elías reached out and tried to touch Anna's face, but she jerked away in disgust.

"Don't you dare touch me."

Shocked, he rubbed his brow. "You're free now."

Anna gaped, eyes open wide as if he were insane. She let out a cackle that rose up from deep within her and seemed to struggle to the surface, then shook her head in genuine shock.

"You can't be serious. Do you actually want me to believe you killed him for my sake?"

"For you, for Irina, for Claude, for Michael, for Martin, for me."

Anna's laughter grew agitated, almost rabid. She hated him, God how she hated him. Almost as much as she'd hated Igor Stern.

"Were you expecting me to leap into your arms, Elías? To revere you? Kiss your feet like my savior? You're a little late—thirty-four years, in fact," she spat, unable to keep these last words from escalating into a sorrowful sob, which she fought back, rubbing the back of her hand furiously over her red eyes.

So-called honorable people think that not doing anything ill judged—sometimes, not doing anything at all—is enough. They're swept along by inertia, openly accepting their venial sins and extolling their own virtues with much chest-thumping. They all judge from the safety of their winged chariots, dripping decency and honor. But the rules of civilized society were useless in the barbaric land of Igor Stern, and Anna had long ago crossed the Rubicon. Indeed, Igor had bequeathed her the dubious legacy of his empire, and with it the worst of himself. If only she hadn't bitten the apple of knowledge, if only she'd held out a little longer before bending to his will; but it was too late now. She'd tasted power and control, and the absurdly fine line separating what the naïve refer to as good and evil.

"Where were you when I was three, five, eight, ten, twelve years old? Where were you when I was screaming, crying in fear every time Igor passed me to his men so they could rape me, force me to endure every humiliation under the sun? Where were you when I was hiding under the bed, freezing and trembling, in the hopes he wouldn't find me when he was drunk? You never came to my aid when I tried to escape, never protected me from the world. I learned to do that on my own, and I had to learn fast. And then it finally came to me: I was his creation, and only when I accepted it would I stop suffering."

And with that realization, she stopped resisting the hands that shaped her and allowed herself to fall; nothing mattered anymore, and she discovered it wasn't so bad in the dark. Anna became an obliging and adaptable young woman, proved herself to be quite cunning and with a talent for manipulating men. And she had the patience to keep her mouth shut, to listen and learn.

"What did I learn? More than I wanted to and much more than I needed to know about human nature."

As the years went by she became more and more distant, isolated from anything outside the bounds of Igor's world of brothels, dirty dealings, drugs, and weapons. She grew up under his strict rules and then adopted them as her own, earning the respect of Igor and his men. Did he ever once behave like a father, ever love her, even in his own twisted brutal way? No. Never. But at times he managed to pretend, creating a fairy tale existence in which she sat among princesses in a box seat at the opera, in which Paris looked like a postcard view from the windows of a limousine driving along the Seine in the wee hours of the night, in which the water lapped calmly to the song of a gondolier in Venice.

Anna came to admire the fear and respect Igor inspired, one always inseparable from the other and so close to the admiration that even his enemies professed. He molded himself into a dandy who never raised his voice or argued over the details of his operations. But when Igor made a decision, he expected it to be carried out to the letter, without delay, and everyone knew it. Nothing and no one moved him. And was that not, after all, a virtue of the gods?

"I was never the little girl you think you remember or, if so, it certainly wasn't for long."

Her voice was blunt, but she was weakening, showing a touch of anxiety. *Look at me now*, said her tearstained eyes, *because neither you nor anyone will ever see me waver again.* The night of San Juan was unfolding before them, the bonfires in town already burning, although from the house their ghost lights were only faint glimmers. It was supposed to be a beautiful night, a night when people fell in love, when the heavens and the earth almost touched. Families in all their finery gathered jovially around the plaza, grandparents brought out chairs to sit in, people played

guitar and tambourine and *dulzaina*, they laughed and drank and
forgot their cares. But their joy was infected with evil as it spread
across the valley and made its way up to the lake and house, enveloping Elías and Anna.

There was a moment of silence, and then Anna raised her head
and straightened her shoulders. She'd regained control.

"Do you think killing Igor somehow cancels out your debts?
Don't be a fool. Deep in your hearts, you and Stern are the same.
You have the same desires: power, pride, vanity. You dress yours up
in virtue, but he was more honest. Control over others became his
obsession, the activity he found most captivating. He prided himself on knowing every corner of the human soul, but you eluded
him over and over. Like that stupid story about the coat that you
lost your eye over; he never stopped talking about it. He told that
story over and over, and he admired you for it, as if it was worthy
of him, something his own son had done, or his brother. That's
the paradox: The more he admired you, the more he hated you;
and the more your reputation as a hero grew, the more detestable
he became, because he wanted to be like you, to have the recognition you got from your equals. It's a symbiotic relationship: You
pretend to care about principles but don't hesitate to betray them if
it's in your interest. You did it with my mother, you let her drown
to save your own life. You gave me to Igor to save your life and
didn't hesitate to sell out your comrades to the Spanish police to
take revenge on Igor. He never condemned you for that, because
he'd have done exactly the same thing if he was in your position.

"What offended him was your cowardice, the way you refused
to accept your true nature. You tortured and killed pretending it
was in the name of ethics, whereas he simply called it pragmatism.
He was convinced that human nature is inherently corrupt, but
you hid behind your nauseating theoretical idealism.

"You're no better than him, Elías; in fact, you might be worse.
You come here to my house, show me clothes stained with Igor's

blood, and think I'm going to absolve you, going to uphold your honesty."

Anna Akhmatova was now gazing at Elías, calm and watchful.

"It's tempting, isn't it? The idea that we could just hug, pretend we're not what we are, forgive each other for the sake of a past that's not the same for either of us. But don't fool yourself: You're a coward. You killed Igor in broad daylight in front of all those witnesses because you want to be remembered as the killer of a Soviet mafioso and not as a traitor or a man with feet of clay. You thought he was going to denounce you, thought that Velichko's report would become public and prove that you were a collaborator, that it would show your ties to the murders Beria ordered and to Igor's dirty dealings throughout the war. But even more than that, what scared you was the possibility of people knowing that you collaborated with Ramón Alcázar, finding out you were dealing directly with the commissioner of Franco's secret police. All of those dead comrades jailed or disappeared because of you—that was something your vanity could never accept. You still want your place in history and a place in your son's memory. You expect to be admired when you're dead. And deep down, that's all it is: narcissism."

She fell silent and then cautiously weighed her next words, aiming them with care before she fired, attempting to destroy Elías.

"Igor Stern is dead. But I'm not, and I know all the same things."

Elías struggled to breathe and felt the stabbing pain in his eye socket, the worms were gnawing their way into his brain again, making him feel insane. He held his head as though it was about to explode.

"Don't threaten me, Anna. I don't deserve it; this isn't fair. You can't possibly remember what it was like."

Shockingly, Anna allowed herself to reach out and stroke Elías's eye patch.

"I've been there, many times, after what happened. It's funny how the grass has grown back over everything; people no longer recall, it's as if it never happened. You're right, I can't remember. But I do know everything that happened afterward."

Instinctively, Elías grabbed Anna's wrist and yanked her fingers away. He'd fought his whole life against Igor Stern and had never been able to beat him. By finally killing him, Elías thought he would be able to take Anna—Stern's most prized creation—from him, but even from the grave, Igor was mocking him. Anna was slipping from his grasp like the stranger she was, and he could feel hatred on his fingertips, scalding him.

"What do you want? What do you want from me?"

It was an absurdly naïve question, one that forced her to come up with something. Her fingers undulated like the tentacles of a jellyfish, trapped in Elías's fist.

"You disappoint me. What do you expect? What do you think I'm going to do? Why do you think I've come, after all these years? Out of nostalgia? Curiosity? Don't be ridiculous."

"You're going to report me."

Anna gazed at him curiously.

"Maybe I'll wait until your son grows up to tell him the truth. Or maybe I'll follow your daughter everywhere she goes, waiting for the moment to pounce. Or maybe I won't do any of that, maybe I'll just carry on my way and forget about the Gils altogether...if you do something for me."

Anna's face was like the surface of the lake, tranquil, no dark waters, no danger.

"What do you want?"

"Two things, both of which are mine by right."

"Don't be coy; tell me what they are, damn it!"

"First, I want my mother's locket back. It never belonged to you and nor did she."

Elías Gil gazed at her, perplexed. A cold gust blew through him, one that seemed to come from the Siberia within him, from his empty eye.

"What's the second thing?"

Anna took a step toward the light streaming out from the doorway. Beyond it, the moon was reflected on the lake's surface.

"Your life. The life you should have lost in the river. I want you to kill yourself at the lake where you take your son fishing."

Elías stared in shock and sorrow. "Anna, I saved your life in that river."

"And then gave it away not long after," she retorted, unyielding.

Elías was suddenly overcome by infinite exhaustion. He closed his eyes and remained still, frustration coursing through him.

"No!" he replied categorically.

She smiled. She'd been expecting this.

"Do you know what this means for you and your family, as long as I'm alive?"

Elías clenched his fists and caught a dark glimpse of another way out.

"As long as you're alive..."

He pounced, lifting her off the ground, one hand wrapped around her neck, and then hurled her down, attempting to restrain her with his knees and other hand. But Anna was not a submissive woman. She fought back, writhed and clawed, kicked and bit ferociously. He had to hit her with all his strength to stop her from fighting and then wrapped both hands around her trachea. Elías was in a frenzy, out of control, and all of the rage he'd felt over the course of his entire life flowed through his hands in desperate waves, screaming, *Kill her! Save yourself!*

"Mamá?"

The little girl's voice rose over his shoulder. Elías lifted his head and saw her standing brightly in the doorway, long red hair falling loosely over her bony, freckled shoulders. The girl's eyes were like copper, wide with fear. And Elías saw himself reflected in those eyes, saw himself as what he most hated, saw himself on the train tracks, vanquished and at death's door, witness to the death of a majestic elk felled just yards away, blood streaming from its mouth and forming a tiny river in the snow. He saw Irina, her hand outstretched, holding out her fingers and asking him to stand up.

His memory became manic, fighting him as hard as Anna was, and Elías released the pressure on her neck and stared at his hands in shock, not recognizing his own fingers. He was like a tree that's been axed and needs only one final push before it falls; all it took was Anna's knee for Elías to collapse, sobs racking his entire body. She struggled to stand and dragged herself over to Tania, taking her daughter desperately in her arms and then locking herself and her daughter in the house, closing all doors and windows.

Elías lay on the ground, faceup. The sky looked down on him, an outpouring of stars and sparkling lights. And in the radiance, Elías glimpsed the opportunities lost.

"Coward," he spat. "Goddamned coward!"

If he'd been hoping for a reply from the million stars up there twinkling, it was not to come.

Gonzalo tried to disguise his fear of fireworks with a nervous smile. With each explosion he pressed closer to his sister, and Laura, who was mindful of the panic he felt, decided it was not the time to tease him. So without saying anything that might embarrass him, she put an arm around his shoulders and suggested they head home. This way, Gonzalo could bow out gracefully from the celebration, at which the local kids would spend a good part of the night jumping over bonfires, throwing firecrackers, and running in and out between tables where the adults would sit until daybreak, laughing, gossiping, and listening to music.

The hill sloped gently downward, so before their descent they had a full view of the valley below and the houses bordering the lake. There weren't many of them, just a handful within a two-mile radius, and Laura asked Gonzalo if he could tell which one was theirs. He pointed to the southernmost house, set a little farther back from the lake than the others. The lights were on, and from where they stood it looked like a gas lamp, floating in the darkness. Laura nodded, but her attention had refocused on the road hugging the lakeshore. She could see a car's headlights heading for their house and hear the engine purring in the distance. It was the sound of her father's old Renault, and she could tell that it was coming from the summerhouse that had been rented by the Russian woman and her daughter, the lady everyone in town talked about.

Laura had seen her only from a distance and thought she was very pretty, or at least very different from the sort of woman Laura was used to being around. The woman often strolled through town with her daughter, and the town kids followed at a distance like she was a fairground attraction. Everyone was captivated by her flaming red hair and the gleam in her intensely gray eyes. A few days earlier, Laura had come upon mother and daughter near the jetty, watching Elías and Gonzalo fish. She wondered what they were doing there and got the feeling that the woman's stance— partially hidden behind the black pines—showed that she was up to no good.

Laura made a sound to announce her presence, and the woman turned and saw her in the distance. She smiled timidly, took her daughter by the hand, and went off in the opposite direction down the path. When Laura reached the place where they'd been spying from, she saw that the girl had been drawing in the dirt, that she'd cleared a spot of pine needles. Laura gazed out from between the branches at the tranquil silhouettes of her father and brother, who hadn't realized she was there, and for some reason decided to keep the whole event a secret. She had noticed that, since the woman and her daughter came to the valley, her father had become as anxious and unpredictable as he'd ever been, even in his worst periods. And now, in addition to that, her mother, too, seemed upset every time anyone mentioned the woman.

For her father to be coming from the woman's house could mean nothing good for Laura. She tugged doubtfully at her faded wool shirt. There was no choice but to climb down the hill, which got steeper toward the bottom, and cross her fingers that he wouldn't be there waiting for her.

Laura took Gonzalo by the arm and began the descent, digging in her heels and skipping a bit to keep from losing her balance. Gonzalo imitated her, natural as a mountain goat, laughing, but she put a finger to her lips to tell him to be quiet. Disconcerted by the sudden change in his sister's demeanor, he complied.

Before raising the slats on the fence, Laura gave her brother an inspection to make sure there was nothing that might provoke their father's wrath. Of course, Elías needed no provocation, any excuse would set him off, but she always tried to minimize the opportunities to enrage him. She pulled up her socks, straightened the waistband on her skirt, and used the inside of her sleeve to shine her shoes as well as Gonzalo's.

"Listen to me: If I look at you and give you a signal, you go to the well without a word. Got it?"

Gonzalo flat-out refused. He was scared of the well, and tonight was worse, with all the firecrackers going off, putting his nerves on edge. But Laura wouldn't relent. She grabbed him by the shoulders and shook him urgently.

"I mean it, Gonzalo. Without a word!"

Laura squeezed his hand so tightly that he yelped. She was so frightened that she didn't realize she was holding her brother not to protect him but to be anchored to something herself, something that wouldn't make her feel as alone as they walked slowly toward the front door. At least the shed light wasn't on, Laura thought, grasping for any detail that might counter her intuition. To the right of the house she saw her mother's shadow among the clothes hung out to dry and called out. But it wasn't her mother who appeared, stumbling and bringing down a sheet as he fell. When her father stood, absurdly tangled in the sheet like a ghost, he cursed. It would have been comical had it not been for the bottle in his right hand, and the bloodstained shirt he wore. The moon was behind him, and it made Elías glow like shimmering liquid.

"A giant firefly," Gonzalo said. Laura covered his mouth, but her father had already seen them and stumbled in their direction, swaying precariously.

"Go to the well," Laura whispered.

"I don't want to."

She dug her nails into Gonzalo's skin to get him to obey, but when he disappeared around the back of the house, her sense of relief was minimal. Turning back to the clothesline, all she saw was her father's enormous hand, grabbing her by the hair.

"Shhhh, don't scream. We don't want to wake your mother up, do we?"

Laura shook her head back and forth mechanically.

"Tonight I feel like writing while you recite Mayakovsky. Let's review what you've learned." Elías's breath was sharp and he stumbled over his words, leaving them unfinished.

Laura knew that if she cried, it would be far worse. Her father could not tolerate weakness; if she begged, he only got angrier. The best thing to do was keep quiet, turn to stone, and wait for the storm to pass. It usually worked: He would simply shout, drink, and write, sometimes hurl himself against the wall or insult her. That was what usually happened, but sometimes keeping still as a statue was not enough. And by the look in her father's green eye, she saw that this would be one of those nights when nothing could prevent whatever was going to happen from happening.

She couldn't remember the first time. Sometimes Laura thought she'd been born with a stigma, believing for years that it was normal for her father to hurt her, until she started to pick up on the silent guilt in her mother's evasive eyes, and the tortured regret her father showed the next day, when he was cruel and distant with both of them. Once—the only time she'd ever told her mother what happened in the shed—Esperanza had smacked her so hard that drops of blood flew from her nose. Her mother had insulted her, called her a whore, dragged her by the hair. Laura thought she was going to kill her until finally she calmed down and then remained very still, gazing at the handful of hair she'd ripped from Laura's head. She straightened her shoulders and clenched her jaw.

"You're lying. And if I ever hear you repeat that lie to anyone, I will kick you out of this house."

Laura was eleven at the time and thought that it was all her fault—because that's what her parents made her believe. She lived in such fear of the idea that they might not love her, and that her mother would kick her out, that she never again mentioned what went on in the shed.

But it did keep happening, not every time, and not in the same way, but the nightmare never went away. Months would go by, sometimes even years, but the monster who seized control of her father would always come back looking for her.

Gonzalo knew that his sister would be furious if she discovered he hadn't obeyed. But that night he was so scared and anxious that he simply couldn't brave waiting alone in the damp, dark well. Instead, he pushed the front door open and walked into the house, trying not to make any noise. His mother got terrible headaches— migraines—and he had to move cautiously, quietly, like a ghost in an abandoned monastery, in the dark.

"Did you wipe off your shoes?"

Esperanza's voice made Gonzalo freeze, halfway down the hall. He tilted his head and saw her sitting before the cold, dark fireplace, contemplating the dried wood and blackened chimney. On her lap was the beautiful Republican bomber jacket, which she was stroking, and in her hand was the locket. She'd been crying;

her red nose and puffy eyes gave her away. A lock of hair had escaped her clip and hung like a gray waterfall.

"Yes, Mother," Gonzalo said, holding up his two shoes in his hands like a pair of rabbits he'd just shot. Esperanza smiled vacantly and stretched out her arm to beckon him closer. Gonzalo went to her with no fear and let her stroke his shaved head and protruding ears. He loved his mother—though not as much as Laura, of course.

"Where is your sister?"

"In the shed, with Father."

Esperanza's glance was like a crack in the ice, the one caused by the weight of someone's foot that comes just before the frozen surface gives way. Gonzalo didn't understand why, but she pulled him to her tightly and then leaned over him, slid his arm through one jacket sleeve, then the other, zipped it up, and smiled.

She recited something in Russian, but Gonzalo understood only a few words. His mother rarely spoke to him in Russian.

"Что ета значит?" he asked her.

"It means, once the first drop falls, water will pour from the stone. It's from an old poem your father and I used to recite."

Gonzalo had no idea what his mother was trying to tell him, and she, seeming suddenly to realize that her son was only a boy, stroked the patch on the jacket and gave him a kiss.

"It's late. Go up to your room."

"Can I sleep in the jacket?"

Esperanza nodded.

That night, the moths hurled themselves in a suicidal frenzy against the small lightbulb by the shed. From his bedroom window, Gonzalo could almost hear their wings catch fire. He wasn't tired, and though the weight and lining of his mother's jacket made him sweat, he had no intention of taking it off. For a while he sat on the window ledge, gazing at the locket with the faded image of a woman holding a girl in her arms. His mother had left it in the inside pocket. Gonzalo thought it must be important to her and put it back.

Watching the last lights from the celebrations in town, he began to recite the long verse his mother had taught him. Gonzalo struggled to memorize anything in the difficult language that she and his father sometimes spoke, mostly when they were angry. Laura had no problem, she learned quickly, and Gonzalo was hoping to surprise her. Yet after just a few minutes he'd forgotten almost all the words.

He was afraid of what Laura would say when she left the shed, went to the well to find him, and discovered that he wasn't there. Gonzalo didn't like being at home alone when Elías locked himself up with Laura. He could hear his father shouting and throwing things against the wall, but in the house it was the opposite: Everything was perfectly still, as if his mother and even the furniture were trying to make themselves invisible, to take up as little space as possible, press up against the walls so that he wouldn't find them.

But now Gonzalo had his mother's jacket, and he was sure that his sister would forget her anger if she saw him wearing it. And his father would stop being angry if he could recite this verse in Russian before forgetting it. His childish heart suddenly told him that it was imperative that he climb out the window and down the big birch tree, then run to the shed. It didn't matter that his mother had strictly forbidden him to go there when his father was locked inside. Something told him that his sister needed him.

His hand got tangled in the lowest branch, scratching him badly, but Gonzalo was more concerned that the jacket might have ripped. Seeing that it had not, he was flooded with relief. He walked barefoot to the shed, impervious to the pine needles pricking the soles of his feet. Gonzalo could navigate their entire property with his eyes closed—the house, barn, shed, the land out beyond the well, the creek, and the wooden bridge over the hollow that led to the pine forest. He approached the shed window on tiptoes in order to look inside. Above his head, frantic moths darted back and forth, unable to make up their minds.

Inside the shed his father was hunched over his typewriter. Gonzalo could hear the clacking of keys and the ping of the carriage return. His eyes sought Laura and found her standing a few feet behind Elías, stiff as a board, hands clasped tightly together. In the dim light, Gonzalo saw part of her face and was petrified, stepping back so quickly that he nearly fell. Laura's face was bruised and covered in blood.

The shed door was ajar, the light cast at such an angle that his father's elongated shadow looked enormous. Gonzalo heard his gruff, drunken voice speaking to Laura in Russian. He asked something, and she responded in a voice that sounded nothing like hers. It was as though she had become a different person, so softly did she speak. Gonzalo got down on all fours, crawled in, and hid in a dark corner of the shed. Suddenly, his father hurled the typewriter against the wall so hard that several ivory keys popped off. A chip of the $ñ$ key bounced and impaled his knee. Then his father turned to Laura, challenging her, an inch from her face, shouting and then ripping her blouse so that the buttons popped off, exposing her small breasts. He lifted her two feet in the air and threw her to the floor.

"How does the rest of the poem go? I've taught it to you a thousand times!"

She couldn't remember. Laura couldn't remember and she was trying desperately but it was no use. Elías was berating her, and fear clouded her brain. Her face was on fire and she could see the blood dripping from it, forming a pattern on the floor. She tried not to hear her father, not to think about what would happen next, when he forced her to sit as though riding a horse, legs apart. Focusing on the sound of her own blood dripping onto the stone floor, she caught sight of Gonzalo. And the blood that had not yet spilled from her body suddenly froze.

He watched her panic, not understanding what was happening. Laura tried to reach out a hand to calm him, but her father dragged her off by the feet and forced her to turn over.

"Once the first drop falls..."

Elías stared into the darkness from which the voice had just emerged. His demented, manic eye narrowed and he caught sight of the trembling shadow of his young son. Letting go of Laura, he approached the dark corner.

"Leave him be, don't touch him!" Laura begged, but Elías paid no attention. He snatched Gonzalo's hand and yanked him into the light.

The boy began crying disconsolately, eyes darting back and forth between his father and sister without recognizing either one. He wanted to break free of his father, but Elías held him tighter and tighter.

"What did you say? Repeat yourself!"

But he was terrified now and couldn't get out a single word, and the harder he cried, the sharper the pain searing through Elías's head, making everything boil like an oven.

"Where did you learn that? That verse?"

Elías tried to calm down but couldn't. His empty eye was throbbing like the heart of a Venus flytrap, blinded by rage, engorged with fury.

"Stop crying, damn it. I can't stand tears!"

But Gonzalo couldn't stop. He couldn't stop, and Elías's head was going to explode. Gonzalo shouldn't be there, shouldn't see him like this. Neither of them should. He turned to Laura, who had stood up and was now fighting to wrest away Gonzalo's hand. Why would she do that? Gonzalo was his son, he wouldn't hurt him, he wasn't going to...

For a moment he gazed at his son like the last glimmer of light before his green eye closed forever. Then his hand reached behind him to touch his back, and his fingers hit the handle of a wooden knife. Fuck, a knife in his back. He turned slowly and saw Laura standing there frozen, saw the way she looked at him with hatred as cold and unequivocal as Anna's. They were so alike, the two of them, without even knowing each other, and both reminded him so much of Irina. They could both have been his and Irina's daughters.

He struggled to breathe. He wasn't dying, not yet. The knife was not sharp and his daughter hadn't been strong enough to plunge it in to the hilt. But if he didn't get to a hospital, he'd bleed out.

"Don't touch him. Not Gonzalo."

Elías blinked, let out a wheeze, and fell to his knees between his son and daughter. Laura skirted him nervously, as though he was an injured bear that might reach out and swipe at her. She clasped Gonzalo tightly against her, attempting to calm him.

How does a man start out human and become an abomination? When did he lose his bearings, his way, and finally himself? It must have been on Nazino, on the train taking him from Moscow to Tomsk; or it could have been in Spain during the Civil War; or in France; or maybe on the battlefield, fighting the Germans. Or perhaps the monster had always been there, lurking inside him, waiting patiently for the moment to cast off the disguise that hid him from the rest of the world. Because only an abomination, a monster, could so brutally hurt those he loved most.

If only he'd had a compass, something to guide him so he could stay on course and not rely on the whims of destiny, which had taken its rage out on him and left him disfigured. But he hadn't, and his thinking had become blinded by obfuscation and guilt. He could no longer recall the faces and voices of his friends, almost never dreamed anymore of making love to Irina, of her voice and the touch of her skin. He could hardly even recognize the deranged, bitter man looking out at him in the mirror year after year. And so this seemed a fine way to end things. He would

A MILLION DROPS

erase himself from his son's memory, so that the boy remembered him not like this but as he wanted to be.

Elías smiled, head lolling forward and back. He said something in Russian and then remained there, kneeling, head bowed forward, the back of his hands on the ground. He wasn't going to die. He wasn't going to die until the pain began to fade, to ebb like a wave that had passed over. A tranquil sea in which he could finally relax, and float. And that wasn't too bad, not too bad at all.

After Laura drove the knife into her father's back, Gonzalo ran to find their mother and explain incoherently what had happened. When they reached the shed, Laura was sitting with her back against the wall, legs stretched out on the floor. Elías lay on his side at her feet. He was still breathing, although his face was turning the color of olives in September.

"Help me get him up," Esperanza ordered, but Laura didn't move. She was in shock, absently scratching the ground with a broken fingernail and banging her head against the wall. Esperanza slapped her hard and shook her shoulders.

"Help me move him!"

Laura blinked, frightened, as though awakening from a bad dream. She saw her father's body before her, looked at the blood in dismay, glanced back and forth between her mother and brother, and—without a word—obeyed.

Elías was heavy as a ton of bricks, and it was quite a task for mother and daughter to get him into the back of the old Renault. Esperanza got behind the steering wheel and started the engine.

"Go home and put Gonzalo to bed; I'll be right back. And if anyone comes by asking for your father, not a word. Do you understand me?" She had to repeat her question firmly to startle Laura into doubtful assent.

Gonzalo watched the taillights as the car made its way down the road, finally disappearing around a curve on the way to the lake. The moon slipped behind the trees' leaves, and what returned was the image of Laura, frozen on the porch, by the door. Now that his father's body had disappeared and the sound of the car's engine was fading, she looked like his sister again. As long as he didn't look her in the eye, he could believe that.

"Nothing happened here, Gonzalo. Do you understand?"

Gonzalo nodded. At that moment, only five years old, when his mind was just beginning to form memories, he decided that indeed, this night had never existed.

30

From the balcony of Luis's unfinished house, he could see the dense woodlands that extended almost to the sea. Alcázar imagined that Siaka had made it to the road on the other side by now. He tried not to think about it, to keep from regretting his decision. By letting him escape, he'd also let escape the only chance he had of things ending remotely well for him. Alcázar felt around in his jacket pocket for his cigarettes and offered one to Gonzalo, who almost refused out of habit. Then something inside him gave a wry smile. What absurd gestures we go through, he thought, to fool ourselves into thinking we haven't thrown in the towel. He accepted the cigarette, lit it, and inhaled deeply.

"I thought you were going to kill Siaka," Gonzalo said, staring in the same direction. The sea was calm, the sound of the surf gradually making its way over the cliffs to them. The sky was beginning to take on the dusky tones it did every afternoon, bathing their faces in violent colors—oranges, reds, yellows, violets.

Alcázar smoked slowly, savoring the tobacco like a man on death row.

"I thought so, too," he admitted, "but I told you once: I'm not a murderer. I've never killed anyone in my life and I'm not about to start now."

In spite of that fact, he didn't tell Gonzalo that when he'd fired the gun it was only in the last fraction of a second that he'd decided to misfire slightly so as to graze Siaka's cheek and dust his face with plaster. Only at that moment did something tell him that there had been enough senseless death already.

"I hope he got the message: Run and don't look back."

Gonzalo turned to glance inside the house. Luis was still hand-cuffed by the fireplace downstairs, but his cries had died down to a soft whimper, as if he was dreaming. His pant leg had taken on the brownish tone of dried blood and urine.

"What are you going to do with Luis?"

Alcázar shrugged. Maybe Gonzalo should take him to a hospital and leave him there, at the door of the emergency room. Anything he might possibly say or do would be irrelevant within a few hours.

"This is all I need," Alcázar said, stroking the smooth surface of Laura's laptop with his thumb. His hostility seemed to have morphed into sad resignation, and this disturbed Gonzalo, who recognized it as the feeling that overtakes those who are about to abandon the fight. It was something commonly seen in soldiers who decided to desert or switch sides, and in those who decided to place themselves—unprotected—in the line of enemy fire at the next opportunity, because they no longer had the strength to keep fighting.

"So, what happens now?"

The ex-inspector finished his cigarette and contemplated the hot ash as it slowly died out. He looked strangely placid. "Whatever is meant to happen. Isn't that the way it's always been? Every step we've taken, believing it was done of our own free will, was nothing but a dance choreographed by Anna." Alcázar smiled ruefully on recollecting that he'd talked to her about Igor as though the man was still alive, the high priest of the Matryoshka. He thought of all the years he'd known Anna, how intransigent she was despite her friendly words, the way she left no room for doubt, no loopholes. He thought of the way her unbending will was always made clear in those gray eyes. She'd been the one there the whole time, behind every decision, behind every death.

He turned to Gonzalo and gave him a look approaching admiration, though it was too somber to be affection. One of the things he'd admired about Laura in the beginning, when they met again all those years after the night at the lake, was her happiness. Her smile made everything seem possible. And it made him feel like a better person than he was. Cecilia had been the same way.

"Good people, if you think about it, tend to laugh more than others. I don't know why, but you end up remembering them by their laughter, their joy. But you're like your father, Gonzalo. You never laugh, you're too sensitive, too aware of everything."

Alcázar glanced at his watch.

"Give me a couple of hours. That will be long enough to visit Laura's prosecutor friend. Then take Luis to the hospital and go see your father-in-law. Tell him what happened and make sure he understands that you had nothing to do with Siaka getting away or me ending up with the laptop. Lie. Tell him I threatened you, tell him whatever you want."

"But without Siaka, the evidence on the laptop is useless."

Alcázar exhaled deeply. Night fell so quickly in November, he noted. Cecilia preferred the summer, sitting at the window watching dusk go on forever. He did, too, he liked standing close behind her, his arms wrapped around her, absently stroking her head as she leaned back into him to trap his hand. Cecilia would close her eyes and say that it was beautiful to be alive. Yes, it was. Or it had been.

"It doesn't matter if he doesn't testify. In fact, I think the prosecutor will prefer my testimony."

Gonzalo blinked. "You'll be sent to prison. Or worse."

"Worse. The good thing about fear, Gonzalo, is that once you're free of it, it suddenly stops crippling you. I'm old, and tired, and sick of being used and manipulated. One way or another, my fate is sealed, but you have something you still need to do and that's what you should focus on: Keep your family safe. Take care of your son and daughter, and don't let the Matryoshka hurt them."

With that, Alcázar and his bushy gray mustache, shaved head, and droopy shoulders walked away.

"Would you have done it?"

Alcázar turned and gazed back at him, one eyebrow arched. "Done what?"

"At the breakwater that day, you threatened to kidnap my daughter if I didn't get out of your and Agustín's way. Would you have hurt her?"

The ex-inspector's look was so cold it hurt.

Two hours later, Luis was nearly unconsciousness. Gonzalo examined the wound on his ex-brother-in-law's knee. It didn't look good. Rock climbing, skiing, horseback riding, and riding a motorcycle could all be crossed off the list: His Roman centurion body was going to be on crutches for life. Gonzalo unlocked the handcuffs with the keys Alcázar had given him and lifted Luis by the armpits, helping him stand. Luis swore under his breath, cursing the pain.

"I need your car keys."

"Are you turning me in to the police?"

Gonzalo still didn't know what he was going to do.

"For now, I'm taking you to a hospital, though what I should do is let you lie here and bleed out. You're a sick, evil son of a bitch."

Luis tucked a lock of hair behind his ear in an absurd attempt to maintain style. He glared at Gonzalo in restrained rage. "You shouldn't have let Siaka go. And you shouldn't have let the inspector walk out like that. They betrayed her."

Gonzalo squeezed the cuffs in his hand like brass knuckles and fought the urge to smash them into Luis's pretty-boy face to destroy his flawless features.

"What about you? Didn't you betray her? Weren't you the one who pushed her to take her own life?"

He grabbed Luis by the lapels and kicked his wounded knee. His ex-brother-in-law howled in pain and fell like a rotted tree. Gonzalo watched him squirm without an ounce of compassion, lips trembling, body shaking with rage, dried up old rage that was now gushing forth, coming back to life.

"When Roberto died, what did you do? You accused her, destroyed her, simply because you could, because deep down you're the kind of vulture who feeds off of those weaker than yourself. And then what did you do? You took off to London, got a divorce, and left her to spiral into self-destruction as you watched from the distance, reveling in what you saw because you thought she deserved it. Who the fuck do you think you are—God? You're a piece of shit, a coward and a scumbag! Don't you dare talk to me about justice, because all I can think of right now is bashing your skull in with an iron rod. So shut the fuck up before I regret my decision."

Luis squirmed like a worm that's been cut in two, but he kept his mouth shut. He'd never seen Gonzalo with such fury in his eyes and realized the man would carry out his threat without thinking twice.

They struggled the last few yards to Luis's car, moving carefully. Luis weighed too much for Gonzalo, who huffed and snorted like an exhausted horse. After stopping countless times, he managed to get his ex-brother-in-law into the passenger seat. As soon as he stuck the key in the ignition, music began to play: one of Chopin's nocturnes.

How appropriate, Gonzalo thought, pulling out.

It took no more than fifteen minutes to reach the city. Driving along Ronda de Dalt, Gonzalo quickly made it to Valle de Hebrón hospital and drove straight into the emergency parking lot—the one reserved for ambulances. When a security guard came to tell him off, Gonzalo said he that he had a gravely injured man who'd been shot. The guard immediately radioed in and asked him not to move until the police arrived.

Gonzalo had no intention of going anywhere. He was going to tell the truth, all of it, regardless of how bizarre and far-fetched it sounded. Perhaps Alcázar was signing his confession with Laura's prosecutor and the examining judge at the same time, telling the same version that Gonzalo had decided to tell the police. Alcázar had given him good advice: Take care of his family, his kids. That's what he was going to do. He had no intention of letting Anna Akhmatova manipulate him at will.

The paramedics and on-call doctor rushed over, tending to Luis as Gonzalo stood to one side.

"She told me, once, what your father used to do to her when she was a girl," Luis said, grabbing hold of Gonzalo's wrist. Gonzalo could hardly make out the words, with so many voices speaking at once and Luis moaning in pain. Or perhaps he simply didn't want to.

The sun shone directly into his eyes as he walked out of the police station. The empty streets smelled damp; it had just rained and a dawn chill was in the air. Gonzalo wished he had a cigarette. His eyelids were heavy, drooping after hours spent giving testimony. In his jacket pocket was a summons to appear before the judge in a few days' time, in theory as a witness. There were officers with Luis in the hospital room where he was recovering after an emergency operation, agents who would wait for him to wake from the anesthesia before officially informing him that he was under arrest for murder, attempted murder, torture, and unlawful detention. Was Gonzalo satisfied with that? Not in the slightest. Discovering that his sister was innocent only to find that it was her husband who'd been the murderer was not what he'd expected.

Nothing was what he'd expected.

Eyes were watching him from a car window across the street, waiting for him. Gonzalo couldn't deny that he was happy to see Tania. Perhaps after what he and Alcázar had just set in motion, Anna Akhmatova's daughter was not the best person for him to be seen with in front of a police station, but he was exhausted and needed to take refuge—even if for only a few minutes—in her smile, the smile of the woman he now knew he was falling in love with.

Tania couldn't conceal her nervousness when Gonzalo got into her car. She stroked his stubbly, pale, flaccid jaw.

"How did you know I'd be here?" he asked.

She kissed his chapped lips and had the urge to linger over them, to soothe him, but Gonzalo swiftly closed the door on that possibility, at least for the moment. It was inevitable, she thought sadly, for mistrust to have risen between them like a shadow. It was up to her to make sure it didn't turn into a wall, and the best way to do that was to be blunt and not beat around the bush.

"Alcázar called my mother to tell her what happened and what he was planning to do. If I'm not mistaken, by now he's given his statement and the police will have a warrant to search your father-in-law's office. And quite probably yours as well."

Gonzalo thought about calling Luisa but realized it was unnecessary. If Tania was right, no doubt his assistant was in the loop, and as soon as it happened she'd be the one to phone him.

"And what about your mother?"

Tania took off his glasses and began cleaning the lenses. He hadn't realized until that moment how dirty they were. For a minute, Tania's face went blurry but her voice remained clear.

"They have nothing on her. My mother would never risk being caught by a signature or compromising document. Stern trained her too well for that. Officially, she's just an old woman who runs a neighborhood bookstore. Of course, there will still be consequences. The corporations in the ACASA consortium will be investigated and the ones your father-in-law represents will pull out of the lake development immediately."

"Which means..."

"...that they'll halt all construction. There's been too much commotion already—environmental organizations, police raids, neighborhood protests. With Agustín González being charged, that will be the final blow. My mother's associates don't like attention; they'll go back into hiding and wait for another opportunity. In Spain there's always another opportunity."

But that wasn't what Gonzalo was thinking about, and although the idea of his arrogant father-in-law's downfall was appealing, he worried about the position it would put Lola and the kids in. Lola might have found out by now—if not, she'd hear about it this morning—and she would need Gonzalo by her side, to comfort her. And here he was letting Tania fuss over him, longing to go to her apartment and make love to her to the point of exhaustion and then fall into a deep sleep in her arms, the smell of her hair tickling his nose.

But what he was thinking about was Laura, and his mother, and the empty grave where only shrubs seemed to survive, only weeds seemed to bury their roots. If they didn't end up dredging the lake, perhaps they'd never find out what happened to his father's body that night—whether it was dumped in the lake as his mother maintained, or taken someplace else as Alcázar had always claimed. Maybe it was better this way, he thought, better to let still waters lie, not to make waves, to allow the secrets to remain hidden. And maybe it was also better for him to get out of the car right now, say goodbye to Tania forever, forget about the beautiful butterfly on her neck fluttering like a promise. Maybe he should go back to Lola and the kids, promise to take care of everything, do what was expected, take over Agustín's firm, and fight Anna Akhmatova head-on until he could finally pull off the mask, as Laura had.

Perhaps it was better to forget some offenses and tackle others, pick a side and remain loyal to it.

He took his glasses from Tania's hands and put them back on. The contours of her face came clear, and he examined her with poorly disguised concern and then shook his head.

"I don't know if I can trust you, Tania. I don't know which parts of you are true. You're her daughter."

Tania said simply, "And you're Elías Gil's son, and Esperanza's son. But here we are, and it's time that we live our own history."

Tania spent the next twenty minutes telling him everything she knew about the Matryoshka—what she knew for certain, what she intuited, and what she suspected. She also tried to convince him that Anna had never hated Gonzalo or Laura, that she'd always set them apart from her fights with Elías and her resentment, and that Anna had had nothing to do with Roberto's death.

"She would never have allowed anything like that. Zinoviev acted on his own, he got spooked by how close Laura was getting and lost his nerve."

"You certainly seem convinced of this."

"To you and Laura, or to Alcázar and Agustín, Anna Akhmatova is the Matryoshka. But to me, she's my mother, and I know her better than anyone. She would never do anything that barbaric."

"It was an atrocity not very different from the ones Laura was investigating, from the evidence she'd gathered on her laptop proving that your mother—venerable old woman that she is—is responsible for all sorts of dealings involving drugs, weapons, child prostitution, extortion, bribery..."

Tania's face darkened. "You're judging me by her. Or maybe it's her you're judging by me. Couldn't I just as easily say that your father was a murderer, a torturer, and a traitor—and the rapist of his own daughter?"

Gonzalo took some time to order his thoughts. Until that moment, no one had articulated it so bluntly, so brutally—not Alcázar while the two of them were at Luis's house after he let Siaka go, not Luis at the hospital.

So his dreams about his sister in the shed weren't, in fact, dreams. For years he'd refused to accept what his mind knew, deep down: the kind of man his father was, what happened that night and many others. The whole story about Franco's police that his mother talked him into believing, the idea he'd formed based on invented or borrowed memories—all of it was but a sandcastle washed away with one word from Tania's mouth. She'd spoken with no animosity, but without glossing anything over either. Perhaps the mythos that had been constructed by his own and others' notions really did exist in part, but the man who was in the shed that night existed too, and Gonzalo's attempt to pretend otherwise for so many years was now pointless. He hadn't dreamed it. He'd lived it. And Laura, his sister, had never forgotten it.

The pain had accumulated in her body, the body of a frightened girl who screamed every time the woman she became saw other children suffering the same fate. She'd been begging him to do something, to keep it from happening again. And he—blind, stupid, foolish—never understood that she'd protected him, that she'd taken sole responsibility for his safety, that she'd killed their father that night because she refused to let Elías lay a finger on him. All those years of bitter silence just so that he could live a life free of blame, of sin, sitting in judgment of her, writing Laura off because of the article in which, at least in part, she'd told the truth.

The evidence of his injustice and the impossibility of redressing it made him recoil, there in Tania's car. No matter how many Matryoshkas fell, how many people like Anna, Alcázar, and Agustín ended up rotting behind bars, nothing would ever put to rights the damage he had done, the terrible injustice of his love. He thought of Javier, whom he'd almost lost; of Lola and the way they had wasted their best years by not knowing how to forgive; of little Patricia, always so close to the edge of the pool, like one of those glowing fireflies waiting for tomorrow. And he wept.

He wept like the little boy he'd carried with him for so long, hiding in his sister's skirts, hands over his ears so as not to hear his father screaming, not to hear the beatings Laura received, not to hear his mother crying in the dark of her bedroom, hiding like a coward. He wept disconsolately for Laura, and for her son, and for all the children who had turned into versions of Siaka, and for those who would never make it that far, those who fell along the way.

He wept because he would never again wear Esperanza's jacket and fly, chasing his sister's shiny hair, never again hear her laugh, or tease him, or get angry, or sing.

Tania pulled him into her lap and stroked his graying hair, the hair of a man who'd grown up in fits and starts, naïve. And she loved him as she'd never loved anyone else in her life. And promised herself that she would do whatever it took to protect him. Whatever it took.

The trees surrounding the residence were bare, a layer of gold on the paths and benches and the gazebo in the plaza. The weekend storm had been intense, stripping off the remaining leaves that had been holding out since fall. The weather had turned harsh, but Esperanza refused to give up her morning walks to the stone bench along the waterfront promenade, from where she looked out over the ocean. The wind was fierce, and it whipped through her gray hair, hiding her face. Cocooned in her jacket, diminutive, motionless, she blended in with the mist.

Sometimes she thought about things, important things as well as frivolous things, and her thoughts came unbidden, with

no warning, and then drifted off the same way. Other times, like
that morning, she thought of nothing at all, her mind blank, and
for this she was thankful. She could sit for an hour, hardly even
blinking, gazing out at the gray occasionally interrupted by the
outline of a boat or rock in the distance, the lighthouse beacons
at the entrance to the port revolving continuously. And although
she couldn't see them, Esperanza heard the seagulls and the sound
of the waves at high tide that almost kissed her toes. She felt the
damp and cold penetrate her jacket, and beneath a thick black
sweater her skin was icy. She didn't worry about the tingling in her
hands and feet that preceded her limbs going numb. It would take
a long time to warm up again but she didn't mind.

She was old, and old people had ailments, and one of them
would be the one to take her. That was her reasoning as well
as her secret desire: that one day, as she sat there, far from her
thoughts and memories, alone, her heart would say *enough*, and
thus her long and eventful, disturbing, and blame-ridden life
would end without fanfare. She'd done everything she had to do:
Her things—if not her conscience—were all in order, her notebooks well organized, the letters to Elías tucked in the bottom
of a drawer that Gonzalo would find when the time came. The
night before, as the storm battered her bedroom window and
thunder boomed and cracked in the silence, she'd even tried to
make peace with what some people called God. She felt strange,
trying to address something or someone she'd never taken seriously. It was hard to find the words, and she was self-conscious,
imagining Elías laughing at her as she spoke those words, sitting
in the chair at the foot of her bed.

She'd seen him as though in a dream, sitting with his legs
crossed, his one eye watchful and slightly mocking, his smile
twisted, a cigarette dangling from the corner of his mouth. But she
ignored the vision and kept trying to find a way to communicate
with the supposed creator who made sense of everything everyone

did in this life and the next—if there was such a thing as the after-life. She spoke of her fear, of the things people do for love until they discover that love and enslavement are two different things though they sometimes feel the same.

Should she ask forgiveness for having loved Elías more than what seemed humanly possible? Could that love justify her many complicit silences? Did Laura ever understand? Would Gonzalo understand now? Could her children ever forgive her?

God had no answers to these questions, and Esperanza was thankful for his understanding silence. She tried to remember one of the prayers she'd been taught as a girl, an old lullaby about the baby Jesus playing with other children and sending them chubby little angels to protect the four corners of their dreams at night. And then, for hours, almost until dawn, she lay there in bed with her eyes open staring at the vision of Elías at the foot of the bed until—at first light—he stood, came over to give her a kiss and, before disappearing, said, "There is no heaven or hell, Esperanza. There's only the ocean."

And now here she was, waiting for it to be her turn to become one with the ocean. She was convinced it would be today. She knew because that's what she had decided. Today she would stop fighting and submit to death. A synergistic system.

"Hello, Caterina. It's been a long time."

Esperanza had no need to turn. She pursed her lips and shook her head in disapproval.

"It certainly took you long enough," she said in Russian.

Anna Akhmatova gave her a defiant smile and a shrewd look. It had been thirty-four years since the night Esperanza showed up at her house with Elías's body in the back of the car, but in essence she was the same woman, the same arrogant woman she had been back then. Not even when she'd come to ask a favor like the one she asked that night would she beg. Esperanza had hated Anna even before she met her, since the first time Elías showed her the locket with the photo of mother and child, Irina and Anna. And her hatred, like deadwood, was still getting in the way.

"You're still not thinking clearly," Anna scolded, like a kindly sister.

Esperanza adopted an abrupt manner, straightened her spine and held up a hand in sign of warning.

"Save your sermons; we both know why you're here, and if you're expecting me to give you more than I can, then you still don't understand after all these years."

Anna smiled, ignoring Esperanza's admonition, delighted to have upset her. They were no longer living in heroic times, and Esperanza was no longer the woman who'd arrived that night with her inflammatory rhetoric, inveigling Anna, going on and on about the need to preserve the political and historical memory of Elías and the damage it would do if people found out what kind of man the hero they'd believed in all these years had turned into. Politics were nothing but a power play, and history showed no compassion, it just bulldozed over the indisputable deeds. And Esperanza needed to preserve both of them.

That night Anna decided to help her, convinced by Esperanza's rousing speech, but over time, when she found out what Elías was doing to Laura and what Esperanza was hiding, she realized that what the woman had really been trying to save that night was not the memory of her husband but the image of a perfect life that she'd constructed for herself. She was unwilling to accept anything but the fantasy of total faith, undying love, and absolute admiration. And the idea of not deserving any of those things was eating her alive.

"You knew all along, or at least you suspected. You knew what was going on in the shed when Elías was drunk and enraged, but you refused to admit it because it would have forced you to act." She paused before continuing hesitantly. "That night when you said it had all been a terrible accident, that Elías didn't mean to do what he'd done, that your daughter had gotten scared and you couldn't let her take the blame, you lied. You didn't care about Laura, or what had happened. You were concerned only about your own prestige, about what people would say if they found out that a mother had allowed her daughter to be raped and abused by her father for so long."

It was easier, she continued, for Esperanza to pretend that it had been the police settling a score, or Stern's henchmen. By that time everyone in the valley had heard about the shooting at the hotel and knew the police were looking for Elías. It wouldn't be long before they found out about Igor's record, and if Elías had murdered a mafioso or died at the hands of Franco's police, the great man's reputation would remain intact, his honor established. And Esperanza would be the guardian of his legacy, the Russian who came with him to Spain for love, the selfless mother, a modern-day Dolores Ibárruri, heroine of the cause who would nurture his legend year after year. And so Gonzalo had grown up believing all the things she'd carefully selected for him; in fact, everyone had—everyone but Laura.

For some time, Esperanza's daughter went along with the silence, horrified, perhaps paralyzed by what Esperanza caller her: murderer of her father. Caught in the web of silence tacitly woven by Esperanza and Anna, Laura felt trapped, suffocated by a lie that over time took on the weight of the only truth possible. On the rare occasion when she brought it up with her mother or tried to open her brother's eyes, Esperanza called her crazy, a fabricator— Had she seen him die? Did she know where his body was?—and defended the line that his followers wanted to hear: The great man was killed by Franco's police, who then got rid of the body.

And Laura was the only obstacle in the way of this truth.

"In the classic drama, the pendulum swings between forgetting, revenge, and the need for reparations. It's clear you chose forgetting. Which is why you never forgave your daughter for writing that article about Elías years later, proving his ties to the Spanish police that started in 1947. But that wasn't what concerned you most, was it?"

"You're not one to judge me."

"Are you kidding? I have every right to do just that. With her article, Laura was giving you one last chance to admit the truth. She wanted—she needed—to forgive you, and all you had to do in exchange was publicly admit the truth, tell the world, and especially Gonzalo, what had really happened. But you dug your heels in like the hardheaded, shriveled-up old woman you are. You chose to turn your back on your daughter. You made sure that all of her hatred and rage and pain focused instead on my business, on Igor's legacy. I tried to help her, believe me, I wanted to protect her because I knew what she'd been through, knew where her self-destructive, messianic volatility came from. But she took things too far, and when Zinoviev felt cornered, he turned, like one of his attack dogs, and destroyed her..."

Anna turned red, looking ashamed. Her own words had led her to a conclusion she would have preferred to avoid: that she was as guilty as Esperanza. There was no point denying it.

"I want to atone for the damage we've done, to the degree possible."

"Very laudable," Esperanza said tersely, "if a bit late."

Anna stood up and tucked her hair behind one ear. She gazed indifferently out at the gray sea and then looked uneasily at Esperanza. The woman was over eighty years old and had one foot in the grave but still clung obstinately to her absurd idea of dignity.

"I'll leave Gonzalo and his family in peace. I don't care about whatever testimony he might give about the Matryoshka. They won't find anything on me; I'm just a poor old bookseller. The wolves will come hounding me for revenge, of course, but I'll give them Alcázar and Agustín. I think that's just."

Esperanza shot her a mocking look. "Since when have we cared about justice?"

Anna pretended not to have heard. The cold had seeped into her bones; it was as though she'd caught Esperanza's chill, been infected by her agony. She was in a hurry to leave.

"But I have one condition. And you're the one who must fulfill it. It's up to you whether or not your son and his family live."

It had been three weeks since Alcázar gave his testimony against the Matryoshka, three weeks since he was sentenced to prison without bail. Agustín had been charged, too, but had managed to stay out of jail for now by posting outrageously high bail, playing his last card with several friends, and calling in all favors. His father-in-law was alone now, Gonzalo knew this, and it was only a matter of time until he fell. Aware of how delicate the situation was, Lola had taken Patricia to the country house in Extremadura where her father was waiting it out.

Gonzalo was more worried about Alcázar. He had little sympathy for the man, of course, but at the end of the day he'd saved Gonzalo's life. Alcázar could have killed Siaka, too, gotten rid of the laptop and fled the country, run off to one of the Florida Keys he talked about every time Gonzalo visited him in jail. But instead he'd decided on what amounted to suicide, for there was no doubt that his testimony had been like signing his own death sentence. Alcázar was aware of that, of course, and he looked more anxious, exhausted, and drawn each time Gonzalo saw him.

"Any day now, out on the yard, someone will appear out of nowhere and slit my throat. They won't let me get far."

"Then why did you do it?"

Alcázar didn't reply. A man's reasons for doing something were none of anyone else's concern.

The last time he saw him through the glass partition in the visiting room, he noticed Alcázar had lost weight. To Gonzalo's surprise, he had also shaved off his mustache and looked like a different man, almost innocuous, with a harelip he'd apparently been hiding all these years. When Gonzalo was ready to leave, Alcázar called him back.

"To answer your question: no. I would never have hurt your daughter, or let anyone else hurt her. I want you to know that."

Two days later, a prison guard found his body in the corner of his cell. He'd been beaten to a pulp and was curled up like a rat between his cot and the wall.

In the days following, Gonzalo was given a police bodyguard, but the cop at Javier's room wasn't there for protection.

"I think I'll have a heart of glass for the rest of my life. Every time I breathe, I'm afraid it might break," Javier said by way of greeting. He'd just been given conditional discharge. Gonzalo carefully helped him dress and then picked up his suitcase.

Javier glanced over at the woman waiting in the hallway, visible through the half-open door. "She's pretty," he conceded.

Gonzalo nodded. "I thought it was time you met. Tania is an amazing woman, in so many ways. I think you two will hit it off."

Javier frowned, eyeing the officer stationed outside the door.

"Tell her to come visit me on Sundays at the detention center. We'll have nine long years to get to know each other."

Gonzalo's eyes enveloped his son in a protective mantle. Seventeen years couldn't be undone in a few short weeks and he knew that bridging the distance between them would take a long time, but he wanted to show Javier that he was a new man, prepared to act like a father.

"That won't be necessary. Your grandfather and I have taken care of everything. You just stick to the story, okay? Carlos tried to extort you, you refused, and he pulled out a gun. You were defending yourself and accidentally shot him, and before he died he shot you. Alcázar has taken care of the evidence; it will corroborate everything. You won't be held accountable."

Javier gave him a grave and steady look, one Gonzalo couldn't read, and then sat back down on the bed and shook his head. "It's not that simple."

Gonzalo was tempted to reply, *No, of course it's not.* After all, he himself had sacrificed quite a lot just to get things to this point, but it didn't matter. He was starting to intuit that something in Javier had changed, that he'd become a different young man, more subdued and sure of himself, more restrained. The experience he'd been through had definitely cracked his shell. He was no longer an arrogant, anguished boy but a man calmly attempting to face things head-on.

"This has got to stop," Javier said. "At some point, the chain has to be broken. I killed Carlos, and I did it out of hatred and jealousy— hatred and jealousy of my own mother. That's what happened and that's what I'll tell the police when we walk out that door."

Gonzalo sat down beside him, lowered his voice considerably, and squeezed his son's forearm.

"You don't have to do that, Javier. If you're trying to punish your mother and me, we accept our portion of the blame. But you don't have to go through this; there's got to be another way."

Javier shrugged and looked his father in the eye. He had his mother's inborn pride and his grandfather's mistrust, but he was certainly Gonzalo's son even if he wasn't fruit of his loins. Deep down he was a Gil to the core, a dreamer who willed himself to believe that if you tried hard enough, you could alter destiny.

"There is no other way, Papá. We both know that."

"That bastard deceived you; the son of a bitch took advantage of you, used you, and seduced your mother just to hurt you. You owe him nothing, Javier. Nothing."

"So, it's better for us to be malicious than for others to be virtuous—is that what you're trying to tell me?"

Gonzalo looked at his son long and hard, and then said selflessly, "It was my fault. I should have paid more attention. You were crying out for help, but I was too angry with your mother, your grandfather, you. I was in a daze and didn't even realize it. None of this would have happened if I'd done what I should have. But I can fix it now, son. I don't want you to go to jail; I could never forgive myself."

Javier gazed sadly at his father. Sometimes you couldn't keep the lid on things; silence and lies could be the norm for only so long. Javier wasn't a pawn and didn't want what had happened to his parents to happen to him. He was unwilling to pay the price of silence for the rest of his life, to be indebted to someone, always waiting for them to show up and call in the favor.

"I don't want to owe anyone anything—not my grandfather, not the inspector or my mother or even you."

Gonzalo appreciated his son's honestly but couldn't applaud this folly.

"We always owe someone, Javier. Our lives are bound to others. We make decisions thinking of ourselves, but what we do affects so many other people, and we rarely keep that in mind."

Javier shook his head resolutely. "I don't want to be like you or Mamá. I don't want silence to eat away at me. It's my decision and you have to accept it."

"What do you think is going to happen when they lock you up? Your life will be over; it will be as if all those years never existed. When you get out you'll be incomplete, feel like something is missing, and what's missing will be all of that time. Think about it."

Javier shrugged again. He didn't want to think about it. It scared him too much. He fell silent for a second and saw that Tania was watching him from the hallway. They smiled at each other and she waved timidly.

"When I get out, I'll start over, far from you and Mamá."

"Son, let me help you—please!"

Javier smiled. He felt no bitterness. Goodbye to the elite university his grandfather was hoping he'd attend; goodbye to the gossiping friends whose sharp tongues would cut him to ribbons. His parents would have to deal with the shame and ridicule of a public trial. The whole world would see the dirty laundry of a perfect family aired, would judge them mercilessly, hypocritically. Then if they were lucky, time would pass and people would forget about them, and maybe over the course of years, Javier would forgive his parents and his parents would forgive him.

Two months later, taking into consideration that he was a minor when the events occurred and making allowances for some extenuating circumstances, the judge sentenced him to eight years in a juvenile detention center for homicide.

When the sentence was read out, Gonzalo collapsed. He paid no attention to Lola, who sat sobbing on a bench farther back. Agustín had decided not to appear, to avoid additional media attention that might make things worse for his grandson. Gonzalo was able only to hug him and exchange awkward words for a minute before the police led him off in handcuffs. Seeing his son's wrists shackled was more than he could bear.

"We both know it could have gone far worse," he said an hour later, trying to console Lola as they sat in a café across the street from the courthouse. They smoked openly now, and although their fingers intertwined on the table for a moment, it was simply by chance, like mountains of memories that collide with no intention of joining and then pull apart once more.

"What are we going to do now?" Lola asked mechanically, toying with a sugar packet that ruptured, spilling the contents onto her saucer. She looked older and had large bags under her pretty eyes. The corners of her mouth drooped in exhaustion and a deep wrinkle furrowed her brow.

"Take care of Patricia, see to your father's affairs with regard to the indictment. Keep working at the travel agency and visiting your son on Sundays, look for the silver lining and prove to him that you're out here fighting to save the world so that when he gets out he'll find it just as it was."

Lola pushed her coffee cup away and traced a curve in the sugar crystals.

"I mean us, Gonzalo. What's going to happen with you and me?"

Nothing, he thought. What needed to happen had already occurred. The only thing left was the sad and humiliating epilogue: paperwork, agreements, signatures on a divorce settlement. Then would come the struggle to get along and act civilized, marked by the need to stay in contact through Patricia. Detached discussions about her education, practical questions that would allow them to slowly drift apart.

Lola saw what was on Gonzalo's mind and a sense of failure consumed her.

"Would we stand a chance, if it weren't for Tania?"

The two women had seen each other only once, exchanging a strained greeting, but neither had forgotten the encounter.

"We don't need excuses, Lola. Not us."

Gonzalo was hoping to leave as quickly as possible and get back home. His rented apartment was starting to resemble a home. Tania had moved in, against her mother's wishes. She seemed destined to fight with her mother about those she picked as lovers, but he wasn't concerned. Anna and Gonzalo had reached an agreement that Tania knew nothing about.

And as soon as he walked out of the café with Lola he was going to fulfill his end of the bargain.

"I have a message from my father," Lola said, seeing that Gonzalo was ready to stand up.

"What message is that?"

"They've stopped construction on the lakeside development. In fact, the whole project is being abandoned. ACASA's investors have pulled out."

Although he didn't know the details, Gonzalo was not surprised. "And what does that mean?"

"My father is willing to sell you the land; he no longer needs it. He'll give it up for a purely symbolic price, in exchange for your testimony—if this goes trial—not being too aggressive." She'd emphasized that trial was only a possibility.

Gonzalo burst out laughing. "That's a charming way to put it. But the truth is, now that my mother's dead, I no longer have any interest in the house."

That wasn't entirely true. Esperanza had died of a heart attack in early December. "Death by giving up" was how the doctor at the nursing home had put it. She had simply told her heart to stop beating. She had left no last will and testament, but had left a motley pile of papers that they'd handed Gonzalo in a cardboard box that now sat in the back of a closet with her books and journals. He hadn't been able to bring himself to go through it all yet.

"As far as not being 'aggressive' goes, I don't know what your father is talking about. After all, what do I know that the prosecutor and judge—and by this time, the press—don't already know? Unless I'm sorely mistaken, your father is going to worm his way out of this just fine. He knows the ins and outs of the system; this is his game, and I bet he's enjoying his last battle. It's going to be a tough one, up to his standards, which is something I never was."

"But that woman is still around, isn't she? The old lady in charge of the organization? She could hurt any of us, not just my father but the kids and me, too."

Gonzalo took no joy in watching Lola humiliate herself this way. He didn't want her to beg, to act desperate. Nervous, he glanced down at his watch. It was getting late, and Tania had arranged for him to meet Anna at Flight. She'd warned him that her mother would not tolerate being made to wait.

"She won't bother anyone but your father. You have my word."

"How can you be so sure?"

Because I'm one of hers now, like it or not. Tania is pregnant with my child, and Anna, in spite of herself, is a traditional old woman who dreams of a house full of kids running around, saying good night before bed. She wants grandchildren and great-grandchildren to spoil, and big Christmas dinners, and a son-in-law to pass the throne to when the time comes. And even though she might not be happy about it, that's going to be me.

That's what he was tempted to reply, because it was essentially true. But it was a truth that Gonzalo still wasn't prepared to accept, even to himself. He slipped a hand into his pocket and felt the metallic touch of Irina's locket and then glanced up at a television perched on a stand high up in one corner. It was January, and on the news they were talking about an area of low pressure that would bring cold temperatures and heavy snowstorms to lower altitudes. Winter was hitting hard.

"Because I have something that cancels our debt."

Gonzalo never made it to that date, never got to close one door on the past and open another to an uncertain but possible future.

When he stepped out of the café, he saw Tania on the other side of the street, standing by her car. He didn't like seeing her smoke; their child was now growing in her smooth taut belly. Squeezing the locket between his fingers, he began to cross, determined to leave the past where it belonged.

"Hey, Mr. Lawyer. You didn't think I'd forgotten about you, did you?"

Gonzalo felt a chill. No. Not now, he thought, recognizing Atxaga's voice.

But the present is always more dogged than the future.

For a fraction of a second, Gonzalo thought it was all connected: Atxaga's voice, the sound of his saliva as he swallowed in fear, Tania's scream, the sudden flash, the blast in his temple, and everything slowly fading to black.

And then lying on the ground, slipping away, the confirmation of the weatherman's prediction.

It was starting to snow.

EPILOGUE

The woman I'd arranged to meet over the phone had a pleasant voice, but I was still nervous. That morning I shaved carefully, searched my armoire for a decent shirt, and dug out a tie from back when I was in high school. I looked reasonably presentable but couldn't help feeling ridiculous. Standing in the rain in front of the shuttered shop where we'd agreed to meet, ducking to avoid deadly umbrellas, I wondered what I was doing there, what I was playing at. I've always been more like Fitzgerald than Hemingway, the sort who prefers battling my own soul to actual battlefields.

I had just begun to consider the possibility of beating a hasty retreat—after all, I'd held up my end of the bargain—I'd shown up. And then I saw her. I knew it was her even before she pulled off the red hood of her raincoat and stared at me with eyes so gray and captivating that I've never forgotten them, though I doubt I'll ever see them again.

"Are you the writer?" she asked dubiously, wondering if she'd made a mistake. When I replied in the affirmative, she couldn't seem to hide a certain disappointment, as though suspecting I wasn't up to the task.

She looked me up and down shamelessly. "How old are you?"

I hesitated before replying, which made me sound like a liar. I remember her eyebrows—so sharp they looked sculpted—and a raindrop sliding down her nose. She must have been close to fifty but was one of those timeless women whom you dream of your whole life.

"You seemed older on the phone," she said, and it sounded like a reproach, as though I'd somehow faked my low voice.

She hunted around in her purse for a key and crouched down to unbolt the metal shutters, and as she did I glimpsed a tattoo beneath her dyed-black hair. It looked like faded butterfly wings, but I didn't dare ask. Instead I bent down to help her raise the shutters, screeching like a rusty drawbridge on a medieval castle.

"So this used to be Flight?"

It smelled musty, with a lingering stench of excrement. There was hardly any furniture, only a few dust-covered tables and broken chairs. The bar had been destroyed and the floor was covered in boards, broken glass, and garbage.

"I'm going to sell the place," she said by way of excuse. "Since Vasili died there's no one to take care of it, and I can't do it."

"When did Velichko die?"

She'd undone her raincoat, which was now dripping onto the dusty floor and leaving little drop marks in the dirt. Her slender figure and bright red coat contrasted vividly with the grayness of the place.

"In March 2003. A few months after his report was published, alongside the study put out by the Institute of Russian History and the Nazino Memorial. That was his great success. I think he lived to see it published and then decided that it was okay to let go."

I had recently read both reports and knew what had happened on Nazino in 1933. Alfonso, a bookseller friend of mine, had passed on to me the documentation he'd gotten hold of. It had been released after glasnost, thanks to political commissar Vasili Velichko's report. Immediately, it struck me as something that deserved to be studied in detail, and I thought of turning it into a novel. But I soon lost heart. There were almost no written documents about it, much less testimonials. So I put an ad up on the Internet, soliciting information.

Two weeks later, she called.

For more than two hours, she told me most of what I've written here. Although, as I now understand, it wasn't actually me she was telling it to.

As she paced up and down Flight, sadly melancholic, she put a glass in its place here, picked a photo off the floor there, dusted off a sketch, and talked and talked and talked. Sometimes she seemed not to realize she was mixing in Russian, and although I didn't fully understand I also didn't want to interrupt her train of thought or the stories that left me stunned, convinced that her accounts were unique and also concerned that my lack of Russian would keep me from doing the stories justice.

So I sat there and listened and observed her. At times she seemed irritated and furious, as though it had all happened just days or months ago and was still fresh in her mind's eye. At other moments she seemed to wilt, become overwrought, almost cry. But she never quite did...

I asked almost no questions, even though there were plenty in my head. I articulated only one, and it was a silly one.

"If Gonzalo knew what kind of things Anna did, how could he be willing to become part of it? Those were the same things his sister had fought against."

Or maybe it wasn't a silly question after all. For a moment I saw a glimmer of complicity in her eyes.

"We'll never know."

"That's not a very fair answer."

She smiled, honestly amused at my naïveté. I think it was at that moment that she decided to put her faith in me, if not my talent. She opened her purse and handed me an envelope containing a letter.

"Read this and then decide if you want to tell the story. I won't object, but I do have one condition: If you write this story, I want you to include the letter, word for word."

I don't like it when people impose conditions on me, but I think if she'd asked me, at that moment, to throw myself under the next bus, I would have, so strong was her power of attraction. I promised I'd read it carefully. She nodded and gave one last nostalgic look around Vasili Velichko's place.

"I brought you here because I wanted you to see how characters turn into stories." And before I knew what she was doing, she took out a little camera and snapped my photo. "For my personal gallery," she said, with what struck me as a touch of malice.

When I got home I read the letter, which was accompanied by an article that had been published in 1992 in a magazine whose name I won't mention. The article was signed Laura G. M. and called "A Million Drops." I read it attentively and found a condemnation, full of passion and sadness, of the mythos surrounding Elías Gil. She laid his public life bare, and although nowhere did she refer to his private life, it was obvious that something shadowy lurked beneath the tale. It was impossible to believe that anyone who knew Elías Gil's life story—his and Esperanza's—couldn't read between the lines. Last, Laura denounced Gil as a double agent for over three decades; this was why those who admired Elías had repudiated her. Even Esperanza, her own mother.

The letter that this woman gave me was from Esperanza and had been written in 2002, shortly before her death. It was addressed to the ghost of Elías. Several paragraphs of tiny scrawl that took me hours to decipher:

My Beloved.
Dear Ghost.

We both know that this is my last letter. And I do not write it
of my own free will but because Anna Akhmatova has made it
a condition for leaving our son in peace.

I was always trying to ask you if you loved me, if you
ever truly loved me during the more than thirty years I spent
with you. I never got a clear answer, and that in itself was
your answer, although I refused to take it as such. Those whose
love is unrequited are terribly vulnerable; it's like only being
able to breathe, live, or feel through the other person, through
the beloved, fearing at every second and with every step that
the one you love might suddenly, selfishly decide to take off,
leaving you a pile of ashes. That's how I felt with you my whole
life: a mound of ashes swept this way and that by a changeable
wind. Indigent, begging for your touch, your glance, a kind
word that rarely came.

I don't condemn you for it, I've never condemned you.
I was the one who agreed to wither so that you could shine.
I chose my fate, which was to be your shadow, stuck to your
side. And in my own way, almost without your permission, I
was sometimes immensely happy, caught up in a heady mix of
desire and anxiety, the bittersweet triumph of jealousy. I was
never at peace: you never granted me peace, and I never asked
for it. I accepted the fact that I would always have to fight the
invisible enemy sleeping between us each night: Irina. And
then her daughter, Anna. I thought I would eventually beat
them, because time was on my side. So many times I longed
to see you grow old and tired so that I could come to you, my
arms outstretched to protect you... You did me as much harm
as good, and you were completely unaware of both.

Love is a decision that you make. And it hurts. There's

nothing new about that. If I'd accepted the fact that you would never be entirely mine until you wanted to, if—when the first shadow of doubt was cast—I'd said goodbye and left you while there was still time, my life could have been completely different. I might have found success on the stage in Paris. Or even before then—maybe one of those Spanish pilots might have come back for me. Why was I never able to be unfaithful to you, during the war years, the years we were apart? Why did I not let myself dream a single dream that didn't revolve around you, no matter how small? I simply didn't. I suppose, as they say in my country, I had hammered the nail all the way in.

And by that time, it was already too late, that first night when I saw the shed door ajar, when our daughter was barely eight years old. She was sprawled in a corner, face and arms terribly bruised, wearing a look that could bore through walls. I couldn't break through her stubborn silence. And suddenly it was as though you had reached inside me and ripped my heart out, though I was somehow standing there breathing as you watched it throbbing in your hand. I remember running from the shed and vomiting.

Why did I not leave you then and there? Why did I not take my children and run from that house, that life? I've often tried to tell myself that Gonzalo was still a baby, that I was a foreigner in a strange country where I could hardly make myself understood, that there was nowhere for me to go. I looked for any excuse, but the truth was that I couldn't believe it had happened. My mind refused to accept the evidence. Had I actually given my life, my loyalty, my love to a stranger, a monster? Absolutely not.

And then I fell into the most twisted behavior a mother can resort to: I took your side. And although I tried to protect Laura, something inside me began to hate her, and I blamed

*her for awakening the evil in you, saw her as living proof of my
failure.*

*I destroyed my life and as well as my daughter's because
I was unwilling to admit that mine had been a charade, a
terrible mistake.*

*That night, when I put you in the car to take you to the
hospital, I begged God not to let you die, not to leave me alone
with such a burden on my soul. I was so frantic that I almost
drove off the road, blinded by my tears.*

*And then you—the man I'd given my life to, surrendered
my daughter's innocence to—mumbled words that were etched
in my soul forever, Elías. Forever.*

*"Take me to her. Take me to Anna." That's what you
said.*

*No one can possibly know how much pain that caused me.
You were dying, bleeding to death right beside me as I held
your hand, and you asked me to take you back to the place
you'd never wanted to leave to begin with. To that river, the
steppe, that barge.*

*And I did. I pulled the car to the side of the road as the
last of the San Juan bonfires died down with the coming
dawn. I gazed at you for a long time, and then I put my hand
over your mouth and nose, and I squeezed. I squeezed until
the light in your beautiful, intense green eye went out, and you
put up no resistance.*

I'll take you to her, I said. To Irina. Forever.

*I don't know where the line between good and evil lies,
Elías. I do know that future generations will judge us, and
they will show no mercy. Why should they? Do we deserve their
forgiveness, their compassion? Do we actually need it?*

*Yes. Or at least I do. I lost my daughter, renounced her for
you, for a memory concocted to keep your reputation safe. You
could have been a good man, Elías. And perhaps I could have*

been a good woman. We gave it our best effort; we strived, didn't we? We withstood more than our children will ever understand. We suffered beyond all comprehension and we endured. But then at some point we lost our way, we strayed from the path and couldn't find the way back.

The time for scorn, justice, and anger is approaching. Your son, the boy I tried so hard to protect from you, will hate us, like our daughter. Our comrades-in-arms will hate us, as will our victims. Time and History will hate us.

But who knows, maybe in time our names will be covered in dust, our son will grow old and speak of us to our grandchildren without rancor. The world will forget us. One drop in a million, we'll simply dissolve into the vastness of humanity.

Because that's what we always were: human. Not heroes, not villains. Just men and women. And we lived.

God knows we lived, when so many died.

Two years later, in March 2012, my version of this story came out. It was published without much fanfare, making it onto the shelves of a few friendly bookstores. It got a lukewarm reception, a little mild criticism, and some praise that was more benevolent than ardent.

I never heard from Tania Akhmatova, and so didn't learn her opinion of what I'd done with her tale. I tried to track her down, to no avail. The one person I did manage to find was Luis, Gonzalo's ex-brother-in-law. He'd spent ten years in a penitentiary center, and although he'd served only part of his sentence, it was impossible to have any sort of coherent conversation with the man. He spent the entire interview rubbing the knee Alcázar had shot and making erratic comments entirely unrelated to the reason for my visit. The only thing about him that moved me was this: On the wall by the headboard of his bed hung a dog-eared photo of his son, Roberto.

As far as I know, Agustín González never went to jail. He got the trial postponed repeatedly with multiple recusals and ended up being absolved of the charges of money laundering and conspiring with organized crime bosses. From what I understand, he died in Bangkok, in bed with a high-class prostitute forty years his junior, in 2008. Neither his daughter Lola nor either of her children agreed to speak to me. Javier served out his sentence without complaint and moved to the United States when he got out. Patricia is in her first year of law school, which would have pleased her father; she's planning to train at the firm that Luisa, Gonzalo's old assistant, now runs in the same building. Lola remarried a wealthy young Australian, and they live on the estate her father left her in Extremadura.

I met Atxaga's ex-wife. She'd become a depressive alcoholic who sold her body on street corners for a few euros. Her face was completely disfigured and I didn't dare to bring up the past that, for her, was present every time she looked in the mirror. I took her out to lunch and gave her fifty euros, and left feeling like a miserable wretch. Floren Atxaga was killed in jail—oddly enough the same one where Alcázar died, although a different cellblock. It's more than likely that the two never met. According to the warden I interviewed, who remembered Atxaga, he was found hanging from the bars of his cell. No one shed too many tears.

I visited Gonzalo's grave, as well as his mother's and the columbarium where Roberto and Laura's ashes lay. But there is no emotion in the dead, only silence.

Also silent were the ruins of the lake house, by that time overrun by weeds and roots that had broken through walls and roof. The dam that people call "the lake" is still there, and I wonder if Elías's body is still at the bottom of it. Or if it was ever there to begin with. I would have liked to meet Alcázar and his father;

they may be the only two people who ever knew what actually happened to his body at the end of that night.

I never heard anything from Anna Akhmatova. I visited the place where Karamazov Bookstore used to be, but today it's a drugstore and the current owners had never heard of her. Oddly, when I asked a friend on the *mossos d'esquadra*, the Catalan police force, about anything like the Matryoshka, he looked at me and said blithely there were dozens of mafias operating in Barcelona that he knew of, but none with that name, and certainly none headed by a woman.

I assumed that was the end of this story. Esperanza was right when she said in her letter that everything turns to dust and oblivion if you have the patience to wait.

But then one day in 2014, two years later, when the story had faded from my mind almost as much as it had from the protagonists' memories, I got a package in the mail. It was certified, sent from somewhere in eastern Russia.

It contained a photo of a good-looking boy, about twelve years old. He was standing with Tania, posing in front of a rusted cross in the ground, in the middle of a high meadow. At the cement base was written:

NAZINO 1933–1934.
IN MEMORY OF THE INCREDULOUS, WHO WERE VICTIMS OF THE INCONCEIVABLE.

Also in the package was a silver locket. My heart skipped a beat. Irina's name was engraved on the back. I touched it, stroked it with my own fingers, and it was like touching Elías, and Esperanza, and Anna, and even Irina herself, and I was filled with a strange emotion.

I opened the locket. Inside was a photo of Gonzalo and Laura as children: two smiling kids, the boy with gaps between his teeth, the girl in braces. Innocent, pure, still full of love.

Tania had had two lines of verse engraved inside:

The first drop to fall starts breaking down the stone.
The first drop to fall begins to form the ocean.

ACKNOWLEDGMENTS

A story like the one told here could never come exclusively from a writer's imagination. Many people have helped me make sense of things, and I am grateful to them all. Many thanks to Memorial, the Russian NGO; to Robert de Torcatis in Perpignan for putting me in touch with so many people who lived through Spanish Republicans' retreat and exile; thanks to Gildas Girodeau for giving me new perspective on the beaches of Argelès and for our trip back in time at the castle at Colliure; thanks to Carlos Pujol for sharing family memories with events in my narration, and for locating them so precisely in the Barcelona of the day; my gratitude goes to Alfons Cervera for his lucid discussion on the importance of memory and our talks about dignity and utopia; thanks to Alfonso at Maite Bookstore for putting me on the trail of the Nazino tragedy.

And my most immense gratitude goes to all of those anonymous people who in one way or another lived through what has been told here; thank you for breaking your silence and sharing it with me. Words may not always do justice, but this small victory is for all of them, in the hopes of meeting their expectations.

And on a very personal level, infinite thanks to my father.

Barcelona, February 2014